STUCK RUBBER BABY

BY HOWARD CRUSE

OTHER BOOKS BY HOWARD CRUSE

WENDEL

WENDEL ON THE REBOUND

DANCIN' NEKKID WITH THE ANGELS

EARLY BAREFOOTZ

STUCK RUBBER BABY

BY HOWARD CRUSE

DC Comics

Jenette Kahn
president & editor-in-chief

Paul Levitz
executive vp & publisher

Andrew Helfer
group editor

Bronwyn Carlton Taggart
editor

Jim Higgins
assistant editor

Robbin Brosterman
art director

Joe Orlando
vp-creative director

Bruce Bristow
vp-sales & marketing

Patrick Caldon
vp-finance & operations

Terri Cunningham
managing editor

Chantal d'Aulnis
vp-business affairs

Lillian Laserson
vp & general counsel

Seymour Miles
vp - associate publisher

Bob Rozakis
executive director - production

DEDICATION

FOR KIM,
FOR PAM,
AND
(AS ALWAYS)
FOR EDDIE

INTRODUCTION
by TONY KUSHNER

I first encountered book-length comic book art when I was ten or eleven years old, browsing the shelves of my synagogue library: a history of the Soviet Union, told in black and white drawings and word balloons. I remember neither its title nor its author, only that its pages teemed with burly, gap-toothed, Mongol-faced, furhatted greatcoated or butcher-aproned Ivans. This was a cold war history produced entirely from a right perspective, so the Ivans were invariably drawn steeped to their swollen upper biceps in blood — the blood rendered simply, and appropriately, in smears and swaths of black ink, slathered generously in practically every panel.

The effect was thrilling, alarming, faintly nauseating: in addition to the dark pools of gore it was meant to evoke, the flat black called to mind mud, excrement, and the burnt bones that are the source of a carbon soot pure enough for India ink. The technique more than successfully intimated sensational levels of depravity and bestiality. As I read the book I imagined its author in the grim ecstasy of graphically depicting the uncountable crimes of the Stalin era; with his oversoaked, ink-logged brushes dripping midnight, murder, and despair, the righteously aroused and enflamed cartoonist-historian-ideologue winds up as smudged and stained as the sadistically grinning commissars he is depicting, indicting. In this image there is a suggestion of some sort of disquieting complicity between the accuser and the accused: the accuser as creative artist, through the act of representing, having created the accused. I remember feeling extremely uncomfortable and impressed. The image of the inkstained artist, muddied up to his elbows with the grime he's busily, inexactly but passionately slinging about, will to this day flash through my mind on any occasion when I encounter a troubling, stirring example of the exuberant, complicitous outrage of the writers and the artists of the political right.

The cartoon history of the USSR, with its ardent, serious, political intentions, its screaming for justice and the world's attention, was similar to but also different from the super-hero comics I devoured monthly the instant they appeared on the local 7-Eleven magazine racks. Comic books were an important part of my transition to adulthood. My childhood, like most, was preoccupied with magic and enchantment, with day-dream versions of the world, in which the Terrors with which one would eventually come to terms were expressed in a guise sufficiently metaphorical to countenance unflinchingly. Comic books paved the path up to the portals of adulthood, offering sexy and dangerous fantasies in which the sex was present but still subliminal (muscular men in BVDs), the danger grand and improbable enough to be intensely gratifying and yet manageable for a neurotic, rather cowardly gay boy entering early adolescence. The super-heros were, like me, full of anxieties of being unmasked, rendered powerless, and destroyed. Unlike me they were beautiful and irresistibly strong, able to participate fearlessly in the violence that seemed increasingly to be the true language of the world.

My parents worried about the growing stacks of comic books in my room, believing that my addiction to pictures would keep me from becoming the adult reader I ought to become. I pointed out that the comic books I read were strewn with literary references, mostly unattributed quotes from the Bible, Shakespeare, Milton, and Coleridge; and the villains especially possessed an ambitious vocabulary — I remember learning "meretricious" and "invidious," among other useful words. My parents, unimpressed, continued to worry. Perhaps it was my unmistakable fascination for the muscular men in their BVDs.

I no longer remember when or even why I stopped reading comic books. I completed the transition they had helped me through, I suppose. Having found the nerve and the necessity, I turned to a literature that addressed sex and danger costumed as I was encountering them in real life, the drab drag of the quotidian.

But I never stopped adoring the drawing and word-balloon form. An adult now, free enough to indulge in all manner of parentally banned activities, I read the daily comic strips in the newspaper. I find that when the news is awful, as it almost always is, it's only the promise of the comic strips that keeps me wading through the pages of holocaust, catastrophe, psychosis, abuse, and chicanery that are, they tell me, the proper business of an adult.

Playwrights work within many of the same drastic economies of dialogue and image as comic book artists; both have to grapple, albeit in differ-ent ways, with severe limitations and pressures of time and space. So my admiration for the artists who produce good comic strips is unbounded, and yet I still detect in myself a certain furtiveness when I'm reading these strips out in the open, on the subway. Shame, an unavoidable residue of any successful transformation, attaches itself to the comics, as if reading them were age-inappropriate. The generic name, "comics" (or its earlier version, "funnies"), is no help in this regard.

My appetite for longer narratives in comic book form was left largely unsatisfied, and guiltily repressed, till the day I first purchased *The Advocate*. In the Pink Pages section at the back of the magazine, I discovered (along with many other forbidden delights) a picaresque novel, meted out in one-page installments in every issue. It was complicated, politically-minded, gently humorous and psychologically sophisticated. It was called *Wendel*, and for the next several years I followed its recountings of the lives of lesbians and gay men, while at the same time becoming acquainted with the previous work of its author, Howard Cruse, and with the author himself.

Howard Cruse is a pioneer in the field of lesbian and gay comics, an important participant in the underground comics movement, and in my opinion one of the most talented artists ever to work in the form. His short pieces are wonderful examples of narrative compression, politically and emotionally complex, provocative and moving. In short and longer works, like *Wendel*, Howard demonstrates a quicksilver intelligence and imagination that can shift, with lightning speed, from the hallucinatory and visionary to the gnarly and grotty, from the sexy and sublime to the downright revolting, from the comic to the tragic, and from one side of a political argument to the other. One part of this ability he owes to his region; such graceful, wry, apparently effortless chameleoning is a Southern virtue. The other part is attributable to sheer talent and a serious commitment to art that is unafraid of its usefulness in a political fight.

Howard was a body-and-soul participant in the '60s revolution, which made him an anarchist, or left-libertarian. His politics are the antithesis of doctrinaire; I find his opinions, as expressed in his work, irresistibly attractive, even when I disagree.

Howard told his friends a few years ago that he was stopping work on *Wendel* to devote himself to writing and drawing a graphic novel: the result of that labor you are holding in your hands.

It is ever the conundrum of the introducer of something really good that the thing itself needs no introduction, it needs only to be read. Its readers will surely find in *Stuck Rubber Baby* all manner of richness and depth and value, only one aspect of which is political. But as political art this book is timely. It articulates a crying need for solidarity, it performs the crucial function of remembering, for the queer community, how essential to the birth of our politics of liberation the civil rights movement was. The point, it seems to me, is not that one movement co-opts the energy or the nobility or the history of another; not that one people, rising to an angry knowledge of how it has been abused, competes for status of "most abused" with any other; but rather that we need to know the genealogies of our movements, and with that knowledge come to understand the interdependence of all liberation struggles. We must finally accept and practice what we've been saying for decades, for centuries: Freedom is only possible when it's everyone's freedom, and slavery anywhere means slavery everywhere.

To overcome the perils of the present moment will require all the human force and power and collective will we can bring to bear. Our political leaders these days seem more and more like the caricatures political cartoonists draw. Even a supremely gifted political cartoonist will have trouble exaggerating the malevolence of Gingrich, the manifest instability of Dole, the dithering and waffling of Clinton, the satanic flatulent eructations of Limbaugh. They're all bespattered with the inky muck of extremism, heartlessness, and criminality.

Here is a book drawn in a finer, more scrupled and scrupulous, more rigorous style. In the beauty of its details, in the subtlety of its narrative, its heart is manifest: Its author addresses his work to the labyrinthine internal politics one encounters in trying to be a good person in the world. This book is quiet, elegiac, and turned toward the past. In reconstructing a memory of a time when one struggle lit up the path for another, and an oppressed people gave instruction, through example, in the ways of resistance to the entire watching world, Howard Cruse offers us something deeply important and fortifying, something we need.

"The antonym of *forgetting*," says the Jewish historian Yosef Hayim Yerushalmi, "is not *remembering*, but *justice*."

*Tony Kushner is the author of **Angels in America: A Gay Fantasia on National Themes**, among other plays.*

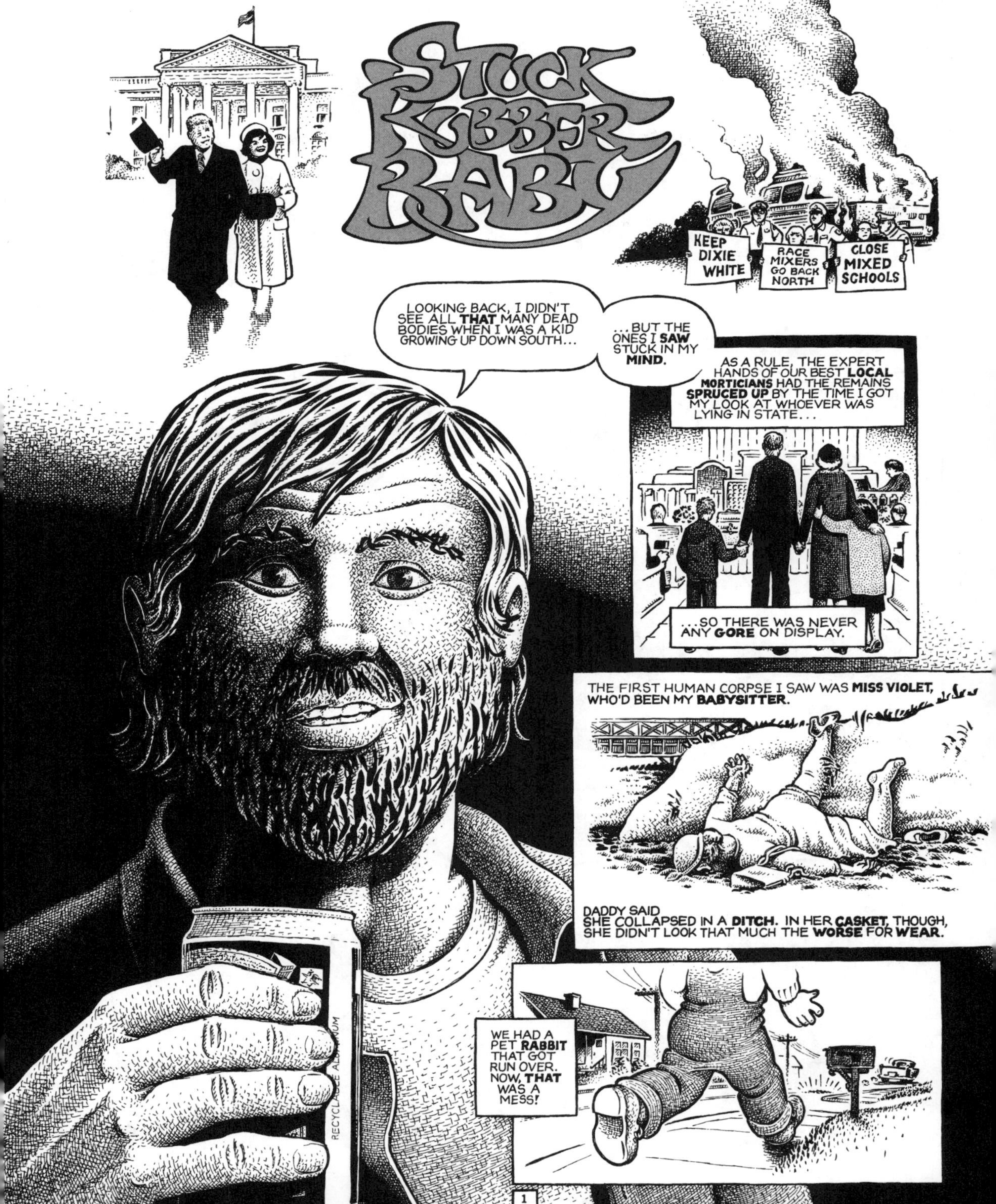

STUCK RUBBER BABY
KEEP DIXIE WHITE
RACE MIXERS GO BACK NORTH
CLOSE MIXED SCHOOLS
LOOKING BACK, I DIDN'T SEE ALL THAT MANY DEAD BODIES WHEN I WAS A KID GROWING UP DOWN SOUTH...
...BUT THE ONES I SAW STUCK IN MY MIND.
AS A RULE, THE EXPERT HANDS OF OUR BEST LOCAL MORTICIANS HAD THE REMAINS SPRUCED UP BY THE TIME I GOT MY LOOK AT WHOEVER WAS LYING IN STATE...
...SO THERE WAS NEVER ANY GORE ON DISPLAY.
THE FIRST HUMAN CORPSE I SAW WAS MISS VIOLET, WHO'D BEEN MY BABYSITTER.
DADDY SAID SHE COLLAPSED IN A DITCH. IN HER CASKET, THOUGH, SHE DIDN'T LOOK THAT MUCH THE WORSE FOR WEAR.
WE HAD A PET RABBIT THAT GOT RUN OVER. NOW, THAT WAS A MESS!
RECYCLABLE ALUMINUM

AS A DUMB **KID**, THOUGH, I CONVINCED MYSELF THAT HUMAN BEINGS WERE **DIFFERENT** FROM ANIMALS.

THE **FUNERALS** I ATTENDED LEFT ME REASSURED THAT, WHATEVER TOLL GOT TAKEN ON MY **OTHER** BODY PARTS, MY **HEAD** WOULD SURVIVE DEATH **INTACT**.

THEN MY FRIEND BO WISED ME UP.

WANNA SEE SOMETHIN' **GROSS**, TOLAND?

SURE.

I FOUND A NIGGER MAGAZINE IN A TRASH CAN DOWNTOWN. LOOK AT THIS **PICTURE**....

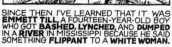

IT WAS A CLOSE-UP PHOTOGRAPH OF A **DEAD BLACK PERSON** WHOSE **SKULL** WAS ALL CAVED IN.

SINCE THEN I'VE LEARNED THAT IT WAS **EMMETT TILL**, A FOURTEEN-YEAR-OLD BOY WHO GOT **BASHED, LYNCHED,** AND **DUMPED** IN A **RIVER** IN MISSISSIPPI BECAUSE HE SAID SOMETHING **FLIPPANT** TO A **WHITE WOMAN**.

SOMETHING IN MY BRAIN PERMANENTLY BLEW A **FUSE** WHEN I SAW THAT PICTURE.

I HAD **NIGHTMARES**.

I WAS WORRIED ABOUT MY **SKULL**.

DADDY, IS THERE ANY **DIFFERENCE** BETWEEN **NEGRO SKULLS** AND **WHITE PEOPLE'S SKULLS?**

HOW D'YA **MEAN**, SON?

ARE WHITE PEOPLE'S SKULLS **HARDER** THAN NEGRO SKULLS?

OH, I **DOUBT** IT, TOLAND, I DOUBT IT **SERIOUSLY**.

IF **ANYTHING**, NEGRO BONES ARE PROBABLY **TOUGHER**, SINCE COLORED FOLKS ARE CLOSER TO THE **ANIMAL STATE** THAN WE ARE AND HAVE GOTTEN **STRONGER** FROM HAVIN' TO GET BY IN THE **WILD**.

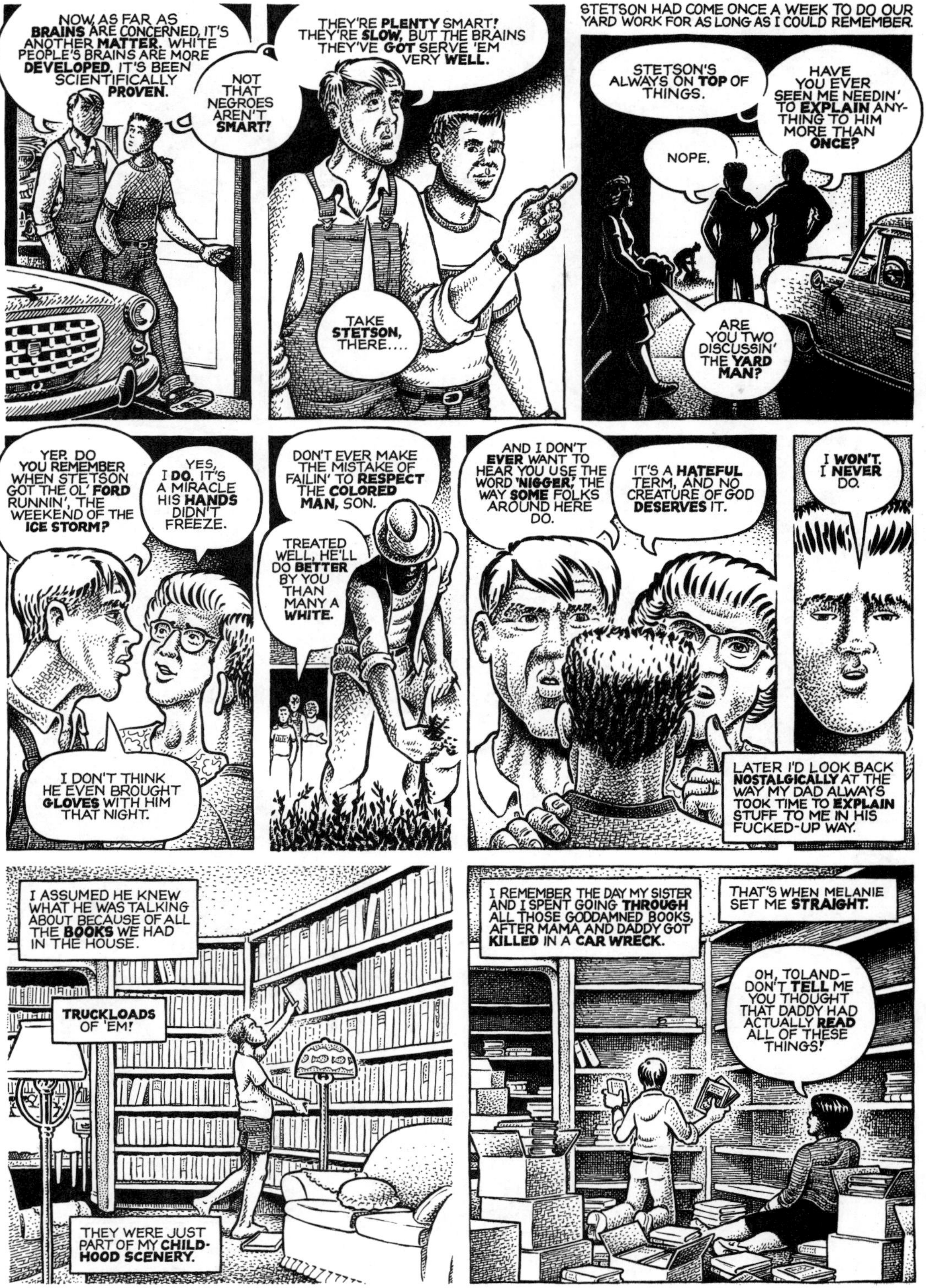
NOW, AS FAR AS BRAINS ARE CONCERNED, IT'S ANOTHER MATTER. WHITE PEOPLE'S BRAINS ARE MORE DEVELOPED. IT'S BEEN SCIENTIFICALLY PROVEN.
NOT THAT NEGROES AREN'T SMART!
THEY'RE PLENTY SMART! THEY'RE SLOW, BUT THE BRAINS THEY'VE GOT SERVE 'EM VERY WELL.
TAKE STETSON, THERE....
STETSON HAD COME ONCE A WEEK TO DO OUR YARD WORK FOR AS LONG AS I COULD REMEMBER.
STETSON'S ALWAYS ON TOP OF THINGS.
HAVE YOU EVER SEEN ME NEEDIN' TO EXPLAIN ANY-THING TO HIM MORE THAN ONCE?
NOPE.
ARE YOU TWO DISCUSSIN' THE YARD MAN?
YEP. DO YOU REMEMBER WHEN STETSON GOT THE OL' FORD RUNNIN', THE WEEKEND OF THE ICE STORM?
YES, I DO. IT'S A MIRACLE HIS HANDS DIDN'T FREEZE.
I DON'T THINK HE EVEN BROUGHT GLOVES WITH HIM THAT NIGHT.
DON'T EVER MAKE THE MISTAKE OF FAILIN' TO RESPECT THE COLORED MAN, SON.
TREATED WELL, HE'LL DO BETTER BY YOU THAN MANY A WHITE.
AND I DON'T EVER WANT TO HEAR YOU USE THE WORD 'NIGGER,' THE WAY SOME FOLKS AROUND HERE DO.
IT'S A HATEFUL TERM, AND NO CREATURE OF GOD DESERVES IT.
LATER I'D LOOK BACK NOSTALGICALLY AT THE WAY MY DAD ALWAYS TOOK TIME TO EXPLAIN STUFF TO ME IN HIS FUCKED-UP WAY.
I WON'T. I NEVER DO.
I ASSUMED HE KNEW WHAT HE WAS TALKING ABOUT BECAUSE OF ALL THE BOOKS WE HAD IN THE HOUSE.
TRUCKLOADS OF 'EM!
THEY WERE JUST PART OF MY CHILD-HOOD SCENERY.
I REMEMBER THE DAY MY SISTER AND I SPENT GOING THROUGH ALL THOSE GODDAMNED BOOKS, AFTER MAMA AND DADDY GOT KILLED IN A CAR WRECK.
THAT'S WHEN MELANIE SET ME STRAIGHT.
OH, TOLAND— DON'T TELL ME YOU THOUGHT THAT DADDY HAD ACTUALLY READ ALL OF THESE THINGS!

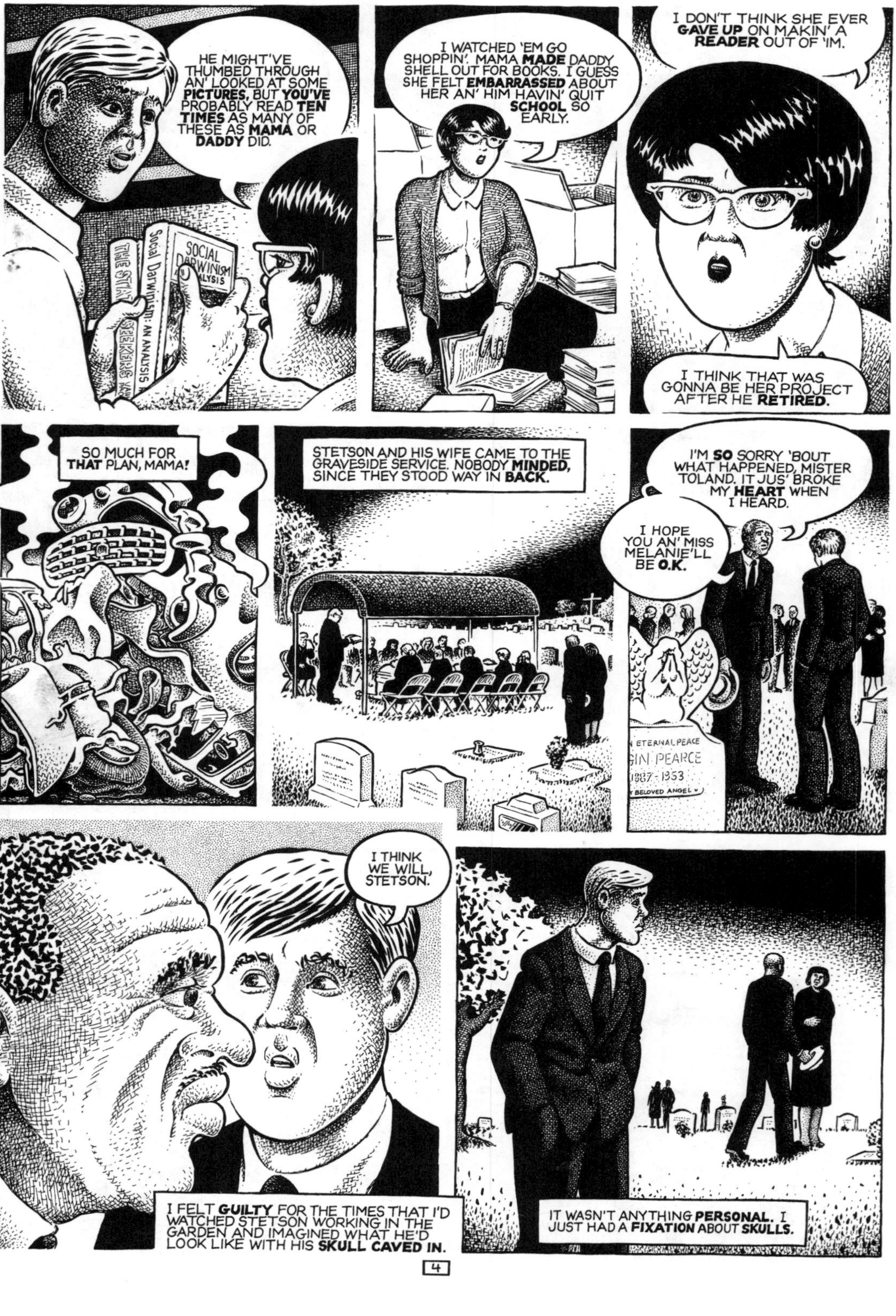
HE MIGHT'VE THUMBED THROUGH AN' LOOKED AT SOME **PICTURES**, BUT **YOU'VE** PROBABLY READ **TEN TIMES** AS MANY OF THESE AS **MAMA** OR **DADDY** DID.
SOCIAL DARWINISM
Social Darwinism: AN ANALYSIS
THE STAT
SEEKERS
I WATCHED 'EM GO SHOPPIN'. MAMA **MADE** DADDY SHELL OUT FOR BOOKS. I GUESS SHE FELT **EMBARRASSED** ABOUT HER AN' HIM HAVIN' QUIT **SCHOOL** SO EARLY.
I DON'T THINK SHE EVER **GAVE UP** ON MAKIN' A **READER** OUT OF 'IM.
I THINK THAT WAS GONNA BE HER PROJECT AFTER HE **RETIRED.**
SO MUCH FOR **THAT** PLAN, MAMA!
STETSON AND HIS WIFE CAME TO THE GRAVESIDE SERVICE. NOBODY **MINDED**, SINCE THEY STOOD WAY IN **BACK.**
I'M **SO** SORRY 'BOUT WHAT HAPPENED, MISTER TOLAND. IT JUS' BROKE MY **HEART** WHEN I HEARD.
I HOPE YOU AN' MISS MELANIE'LL BE **O.K.**
ETERNAL PEACE
GIN PEARCE
1887-1953
BELOVED ANGEL
I THINK WE WILL, STETSON.
I FELT **GUILTY** FOR THE TIMES THAT I'D WATCHED STETSON WORKING IN THE GARDEN AND IMAGINED WHAT HE'D LOOK LIKE WITH HIS **SKULL CAVED IN.**
IT WASN'T ANYTHING **PERSONAL.** I JUST HAD A **FIXATION** ABOUT **SKULLS.**

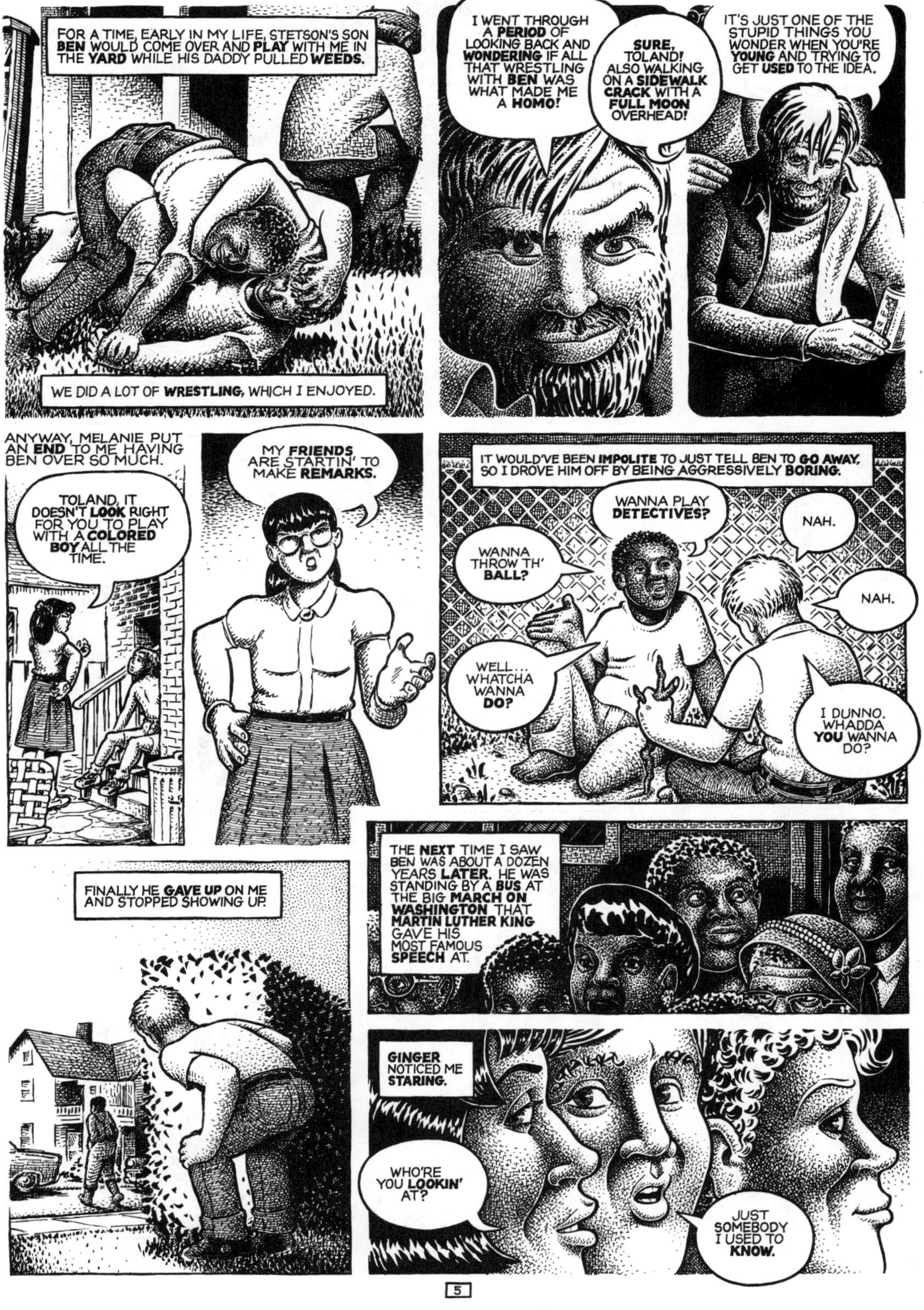
FOR A TIME, EARLY IN MY LIFE, STETSON'S SON BEN WOULD COME OVER AND PLAY WITH ME IN THE YARD WHILE HIS DADDY PULLED WEEDS.
WE DID A LOT OF WRESTLING, WHICH I ENJOYED.
I WENT THROUGH A PERIOD OF LOOKING BACK AND WONDERING IF ALL THAT WRESTLING WITH BEN WAS WHAT MADE ME A HOMO!
SURE, TOLAND! ALSO WALKING ON A SIDEWALK CRACK WITH A FULL MOON OVERHEAD!
IT'S JUST ONE OF THE STUPID THINGS YOU WONDER WHEN YOU'RE YOUNG AND TRYING TO GET USED TO THE IDEA.
ANYWAY, MELANIE PUT AN END TO ME HAVING BEN OVER SO MUCH.
TOLAND, IT DOESN'T LOOK RIGHT FOR YOU TO PLAY WITH A COLORED BOY ALL THE TIME.
MY FRIENDS ARE STARTIN' TO MAKE REMARKS.
IT WOULD'VE BEEN IMPOLITE TO JUST TELL BEN TO GO AWAY, SO I DROVE HIM OFF BY BEING AGGRESSIVELY BORING.
WANNA PLAY DETECTIVES?
NAH.
WANNA THROW TH' BALL?
NAH.
WELL... WHATCHA WANNA DO?
I DUNNO. WHADDA YOU WANNA DO?
FINALLY HE GAVE UP ON ME AND STOPPED SHOWING UP.
THE NEXT TIME I SAW BEN WAS ABOUT A DOZEN YEARS LATER. HE WAS STANDING BY A BUS AT THE BIG MARCH ON WASHINGTON THAT MARTIN LUTHER KING GAVE HIS MOST FAMOUS SPEECH AT.
GINGER NOTICED ME STARING.
WHO'RE YOU LOOKIN' AT?
JUST SOMEBODY I USED TO KNOW.

I TOLD GINGER **WHO** BEN **WAS**. **SAMMY NOONE** OVERHEARD AND SAID I SHOULD GO OVER AND GIVE THE DUDE A BIG **HELLO**.

WHO **KNOWS?** THOSE MOMENTS HE SPENT **WRITHING** WITH YOU IN THE **DUST** MAY BE AMONG BEN'S MOST **CHERISHED** MEMORIES!

NOT TOO **LIKELY**, SAMMY!

I'D FEEL MORE **PLEASED** WITH MYSELF IF I COULD CLAIM THAT IT WAS PURE **SOCIAL CONSCIENCE** THAT GOT MY ASS OUT TO THE LINCOLN MEMORIAL THAT SUMMER, OR **THE MEMORY** OF HOW I HAD FELT ABOUT **EMMETT TILL**...

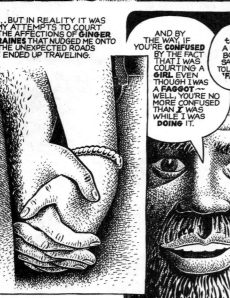

...BUT IN REALITY IT WAS MY ATTEMPTS TO COURT THE AFFECTIONS OF **GINGER RAINES** THAT NUDGED ME ONTO THE UNEXPECTED ROADS I ENDED UP TRAVELING.

AND BY THE WAY, IF YOU'RE **CONFUSED** BY THE FACT THAT I WAS COURTING A **GIRL** EVEN THOUGH I WAS A **FAGGOT**~~ WELL, YOU'RE NO MORE CONFUSED THAN **I** WAS WHILE I WAS **DOING** IT.

Tsk, tsk! BE A **GOOD** BOY AND SAY '**GAY**', TOLAND. NOT '**FAGGOT**.'

I DIDN'T **FEEL** 'GAY' BACK THEN. I FELT LIKE A **FAGGOT**!

YOU'VE GOTTA BE AT LEAST A **LITTLE** BIT **UN-SCREWED-UP** TO BE 'GAY'!

ANYWAY, MY **INTENTION** FOR QUITE SOME TIME WAS TO TURN MYSELF AROUND AND **NOT** BE GAY...

...WHICH I **KIDDED** MYSELF INTO VIEWING AS AN **OPTION**.

I SUBSCRIBED TO **PLAYBOY** AND HAD AN ABSOLUTE **RULE** THAT I WOULDN'T LET MYSELF **MASTURBATE** UNLESS I WAS LOOKING AT ONE OF THE **CENTERFOLD PLAYMATES** AT THE TIME.

Red Masque

Red Masque

I HELD TO THAT RULE FOR OVER **THREE** YEARS, WITH ONLY A **COUPLE** OF LAPSES.

WET DREAMS DIDN'T COUNT.

UNH-H-H-H...

IT WAS PLAYBOY THAT LED TO ME BEING FRIENDS WITH **RILEY WHEELER,** WHO I GOT TO KNOW AT CLAYFIELD'S MAIN **BOWLING ALLEY** SHORTLY BEFORE HE GOT **DRAFTED.**

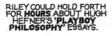

RILEY COULD HOLD FORTH FOR **HOURS** ABOUT HUGH HEFNER'S **'PLAYBOY PHILOSOPHY'** ESSAYS.

HE HAD A **POINT.** THERE WAS DEFINITELY SOMETHING TO HEF'S **SOCIOLOGICAL VIEWS,** AND IT WAS OBVIOUS FROM THE **PHOTO SPREADS** THAT THEY WERE GETTING THE PUBLISHER A HELLUVA LOT OF **SEX!**

IRONICALLY, DESPITE RILEY'S ENTHUSIASM FOR THE WILD PLAYBOY LIFESTYLE, HE AND HIS GIRLFRIEND **MAVIS** SEEMED ABOUT AS **MONOGAMOUS** AS ANYBODY COULD **ASK.** I ONLY KNEW RILEY **ONCE** TO STRAY.

WHICH ISN'T TO SAY THEY LIVED BY STANDARD SOUTHERN **MORES.** THEY'D ALREADY BEGUN SHACKING UP WHILE THEY WERE IN **HIGH SCHOOL**—AND THEY HAD NO **APOLOGIES** FOR IT.

HEF WOULD'VE **LIKED** THAT.

AROUND A YEAR AFTER MY FOLKS DIED, RILEY INVITED ME TO MOVE INTO THE OLD **HOUSE** HE SHARED WITH MAVIS.

The Wheelery

SINCE RILEY'S NAME WAS **WHEELER,** WE CALLED THAT HOUSE **'THE WHEELERY.'**

UNTIL THEN I HAD LIVED WITH MY SISTER AND HER HUSBAND **ORLEY** IN THE HOUSE MELANIE AND I HAD BEEN **REARED** IN — WHICH WAS **ROOMIER** NOW, WITH ALL THE **BOOKCASES** TAKEN OUT.

Marshal Dillon! Marshal Dillon!

I HAD AN UNGLAMOROUS JOB AS A GAS STATION **PUMP JOCKEY.** MAMA WENT TO HER GRAVE ROYALLY **PISSED** THAT I WAS SPENDING MY TIME PUMPING **GAS** WHILE I WAS OF **COLLEGE AGE.**

BUT THAT'S JUST THE WAY IT WAS—AND THE WAY **I** WAS!

THERE WAS A LOT ABOUT THAT TIME THAT WAS **FUN,** ESPECIALLY **EARLY ON** — BEFORE THE **SHIT** HIT THE FAN.

NOT HAVING A GOOD HEAD FOR **DATES,** I JUST REMEMBER THE YEARS WHEN THIS STORY HAPPENED TO ME AS **'KENNEDY TIME.'**

33⁹/₁₀ GAL.

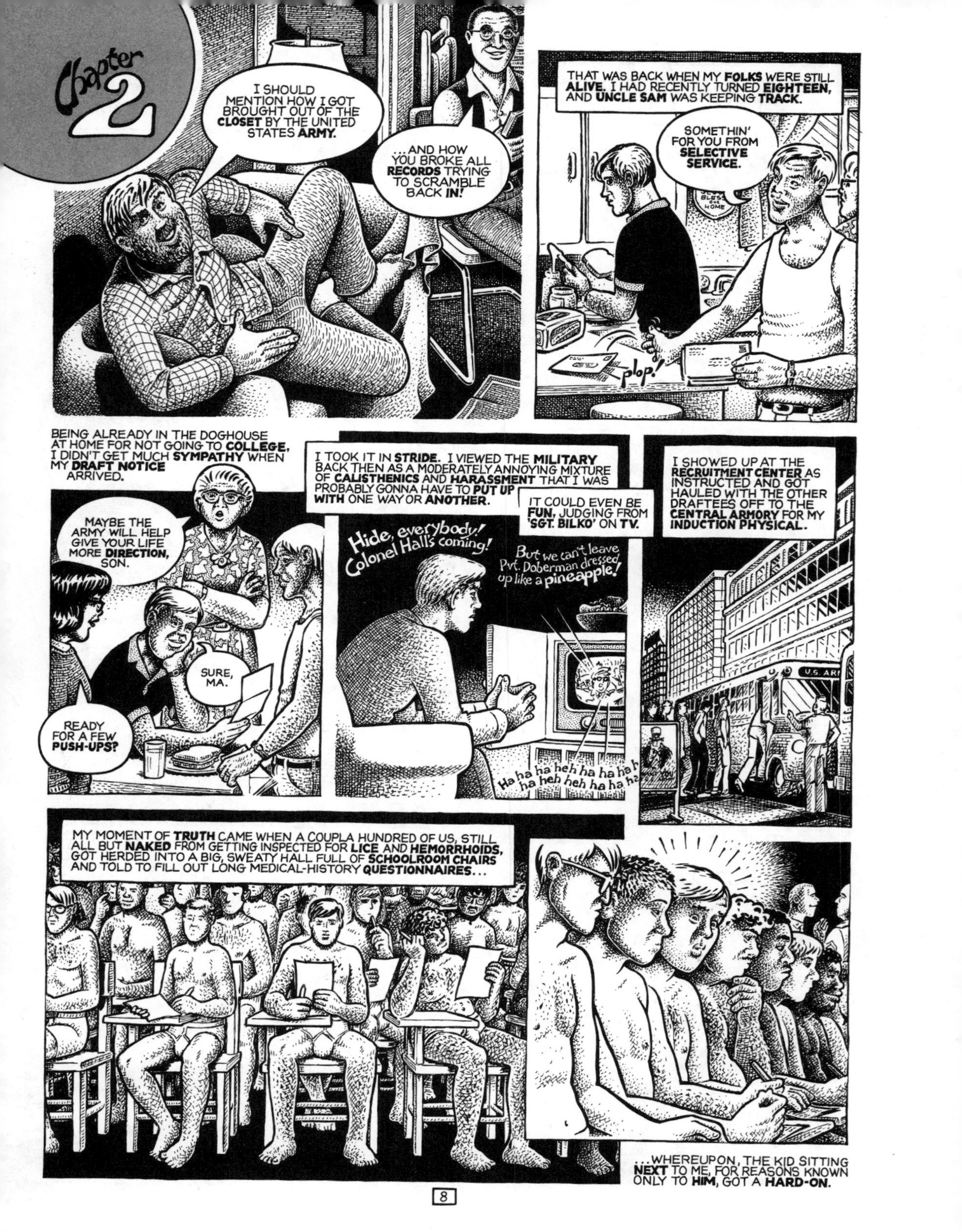
Chapter 2
I SHOULD MENTION HOW I GOT BROUGHT OUT OF THE CLOSET BY THE UNITED STATES ARMY.
...AND HOW YOU BROKE ALL RECORDS TRYING TO SCRAMBLE BACK IN!
THAT WAS BACK WHEN MY FOLKS WERE STILL ALIVE. I HAD RECENTLY TURNED EIGHTEEN, AND UNCLE SAM WAS KEEPING TRACK.
SOMETHIN' FOR YOU FROM SELECTIVE SERVICE.
plop!
BEING ALREADY IN THE DOGHOUSE AT HOME FOR NOT GOING TO COLLEGE, I DIDN'T GET MUCH SYMPATHY WHEN MY DRAFT NOTICE ARRIVED.
MAYBE THE ARMY WILL HELP GIVE YOUR LIFE MORE DIRECTION, SON.
SURE, MA.
READY FOR A FEW PUSH-UPS?
I TOOK IT IN STRIDE. I VIEWED THE MILITARY BACK THEN AS A MODERATELY ANNOYING MIXTURE OF CALISTHENICS AND HARASSMENT THAT I WAS PROBABLY GONNA HAVE TO PUT UP WITH ONE WAY OR ANOTHER.
IT COULD EVEN BE FUN, JUDGING FROM 'SGT. BILKO' ON TV.
Hide, everybody! Colonel Hall's coming!
But we can't leave Pvt. Doberman dressed up like a pineapple!
Ha ha ha heh ha ha ha ha ha heh heh ha ha ha
I SHOWED UP AT THE RECRUITMENT CENTER AS INSTRUCTED AND GOT HAULED WITH THE OTHER DRAFTEES OFF TO THE CENTRAL ARMORY FOR MY INDUCTION PHYSICAL.
MY MOMENT OF TRUTH CAME WHEN A COUPLA HUNDRED OF US, STILL ALL BUT NAKED FROM GETTING INSPECTED FOR LICE AND HEMORRHOIDS, GOT HERDED INTO A BIG, SWEATY HALL FULL OF SCHOOLROOM CHAIRS AND TOLD TO FILL OUT LONG MEDICAL-HISTORY QUESTIONNAIRES...
...WHEREUPON, THE KID SITTING NEXT TO ME, FOR REASONS KNOWN ONLY TO HIM, GOT A HARD-ON.

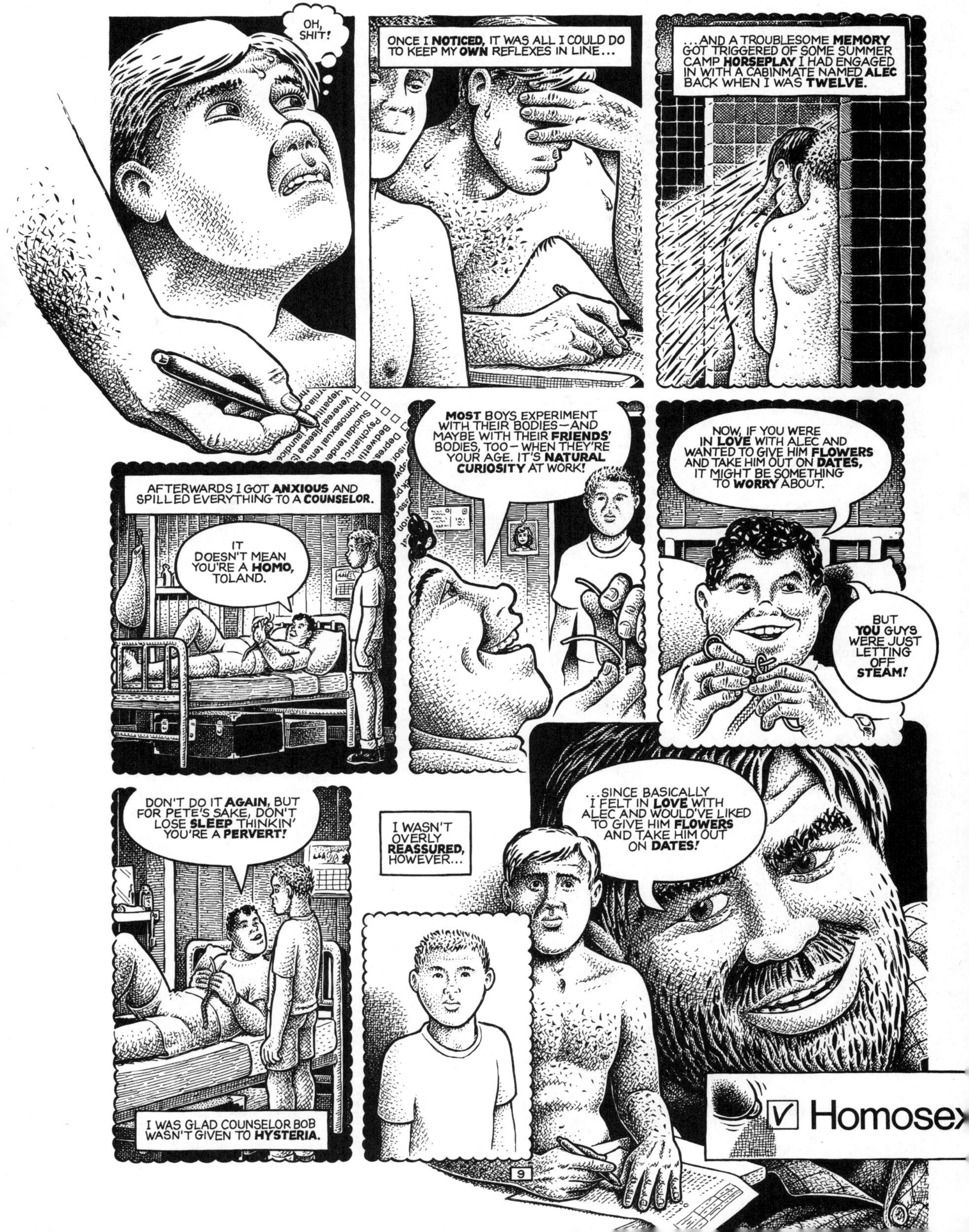

OH, SHIT!
ONCE I NOTICED, IT WAS ALL I COULD DO TO KEEP MY OWN REFLEXES IN LINE...
...AND A TROUBLESOME MEMORY GOT TRIGGERED OF SOME SUMMER CAMP HORSEPLAY I HAD ENGAGED IN WITH A CABINMATE NAMED ALEC BACK WHEN I WAS TWELVE.
AFTERWARDS I GOT ANXIOUS AND SPILLED EVERYTHING TO A COUNSELOR.
IT DOESN'T MEAN YOU'RE A HOMO, TOLAND.
MOST BOYS EXPERIMENT WITH THEIR BODIES—AND MAYBE WITH THEIR FRIENDS' BODIES, TOO—WHEN THEY'RE YOUR AGE. IT'S NATURAL CURIOSITY AT WORK!
NOW, IF YOU WERE IN LOVE WITH ALEC AND WANTED TO GIVE HIM FLOWERS AND TAKE HIM OUT ON DATES, IT MIGHT BE SOMETHING TO WORRY ABOUT.
BUT YOU GUYS WERE JUST LETTING OFF STEAM!
DON'T DO IT AGAIN, BUT FOR PETE'S SAKE, DON'T LOSE SLEEP THINKIN' YOU'RE A PERVERT!
I WAS GLAD COUNSELOR BOB WASN'T GIVEN TO HYSTERIA.
I WASN'T OVERLY REASSURED, HOWEVER...
...SINCE BASICALLY I FELT IN LOVE WITH ALEC AND WOULD'VE LIKED TO GIVE HIM FLOWERS AND TAKE HIM OUT ON DATES!
Homosex

HEY, SARGE! WE'VE GOT A **HOMO** HERE!!!

I HAD LOTS OF QUIET TIME TO **MULL** THINGS **OVER** DURING THE RIDE BACK **HOME,** SINCE NOBODY ELSE ON THE BUS WOULD SIT **NEXT** TO ME.

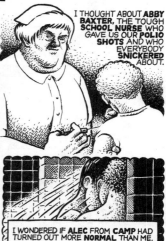

I KEPT THINKING DEPRESSING THOUGHTS ABOUT THE **DRAWBACKS** OF BEING A HOMO.

Bzz bzz-bzz bz.

zz faggot bzz.

THE **ZEST** THAT THE GUYS IN CHARGE BROUGHT TO MAKING SURE EVERYONE KNEW EXACTLY **WHO** AMONG US HAD 'CHECKED THE BOX' CAUGHT ME A LITTLE BY **SURPRISE.**

I THOUGHT ABOUT **EZRA GABLE,** WHO WAS PRESIDENT OF THE BIGGEST **BANK** IN CLAYFIELD FOR NEARLY **TWENTY YEARS...**

...UNTIL HE GOT **MURDERED** IN BACK OF THE **SAWMILL.**

SOME TEENAGERS ADMITTED **BLUDGEONING** HIM TO DEATH. THEY SAID THEY'D BEEN **TRAUMATIZED** BECAUSE HE'D **LOOKED** AT THEM 'IN A NASTY WAY.'

THE DISTRICT ATTORNEY SAID THEY WERE **GOOD BOYS** AT **HEART,** SO HE LET THE PROSECUTION **SLIDE.**

I THOUGHT ABOUT **ABBY BAXTER,** THE TOUGH **SCHOOL NURSE** WHO GAVE US OUR **POLIO SHOTS** AND WHO EVERYBODY **SNICKERED** ABOUT.

I WONDERED IF **ALEC** FROM **CAMP** HAD TURNED OUT MORE **NORMAL** THAN ME.

BY THE TIME **CLAYFIELD STADIUM** CAME INTO VIEW, I'D DECIDED THAT THIS **HOMO** STUFF HAD TO GET NIPPED **RIGHT** IN THE **BUD!**

SO I SET ABOUT DOING JUST **THAT.**

AND PRETTY **SUCCESSFULLY,** TOO, AS BEST I COULD **JUDGE.**

WHICH SHOWS WHAT A **LOUSY** JUDGE OF SUCH THINGS I COULD BE!

BUT HINDSIGHT **ASIDE,** NOBODY'S EVER **SWEATED** MORE THAN **I** DID TO PERFECT ALL THE **MOVES** THAT COMMONLY PASS FOR **HETERO-SEXUAL** BEHAVIOR.

MAVIS, I FEEL **AWFUL** ABOUT THE WAY I ACTED LAST NIGHT.

DON'T **DWELL** ON IT, HON.

RILEY'S TOLD ME HOW YOU MEN GET ALL **FRUSTRATED** WHEN YOUR **CUM** GETS BACKED UP IN YOUR **BALLS.**

I **LIKE** YOU, TOLAND...

...BUT **RILEY'S** THE ONE I **LOVE.**

I HAD BEHAVED LIKE A **RAT** WITH MY **BEST FRIEND'S** GIRL THE NIGHT BEFORE — AND WITH HIM AWAY SERVING HIS **COUNTRY,** YET!

JUST BECAUSE HE'S OUT OF **SIGHT** FOR A WHILE DOESN'T MEAN HE'S 'OUT OF **MIND.'**

WHAT **YOU** NEED IS A GIRLFRIEND OF YOUR **OWN.**

IMPEACH EARL WARREN
THE JOHN BIRCH SOCIETY

TICKET INFORMATION

UNLIKE **ME,** RILEY HAD GOTTEN CLASSIFIED **1-A** BY THE DRAFT BOARD WHEN HIS CALL CAME, WHICH WAS EIGHT MONTHS AFTER **MINE.**

SO BEFORE WE **KNEW** IT, HE WAS OFF GETTING A TOUR OF THE WORLD **OUTSIDE** CLAYFIELD, COURTESY OF THE **U.S. ARMY.**

AND EACH TIME HE CAME BACK ON **LEAVE...**

...RILEY HAD MORE THINGS STORED UP TO MAKE **FUN** OF ABOUT OUR HOMETOWN.

IS CLAYFIELD **FAMOUS?**

HOW D'YA LIKE LIVIN' IN A TOWN THAT'S GETTIN' **FAMOUS?**

DIDN'T YOU **SEE,** TOLAND? WE GOT WRITTEN UP IN **TIME** THIS WEEK.

'LOOKS LIKE 'THE **CHOPPER'** PLANS TO RUN FOR **GOVERNOR** ON THE **NUMBSKULL** TICKET!

SUTTON CHOPPER WAS CLAYFIELD'S LONGTIME **POLICE COMMISSIONER,** WHO SEEMED TO DRIFT FURTHER AROUND THE **BEND** EVERY DAY.

THE CHOPPER TOLD A REPORTER HE'D KEEP CLAYFIELD'S SCHOOLS **SEGREGATED** IF HE HAD TO **DEPUTIZE** THE **KU KLUX KLAN** TO **DO** IT!

BUT DONCHA THINK EVERYBODY **KNOWS** THE CHOPPER IS A PURE **FOOL?** THE ONLY REASON PEOPLE KEEP **ELECTIN'** HIM IS SO THEY CAN KEEP AN **EYE** ON HIS **WHEREABOUTS!**

THE CHOPPER'S BOUND TO WIN IN THE **END,** THOUGH.

GETTIN' **CLAYFIELD** TO **INTEGRATE** IS LIKE GETTIN' A **TURTLE** TO WALK ON ITS **HIND** LEGS...

IT'S A NOBLE **THOUGHT,** BUT AN EVOLUTIONARY **UNLIKELIHOOD.**

POP!

SPLASH!

KNOCKING BACK A FEW **SIX-PACKS** BESIDE **BLUERABBIT LAKE** WAS STANDARD **PRACTICE** FOR THE THREE OF US WHEN RILEY CAME HOME ON **FURLOUGH.**

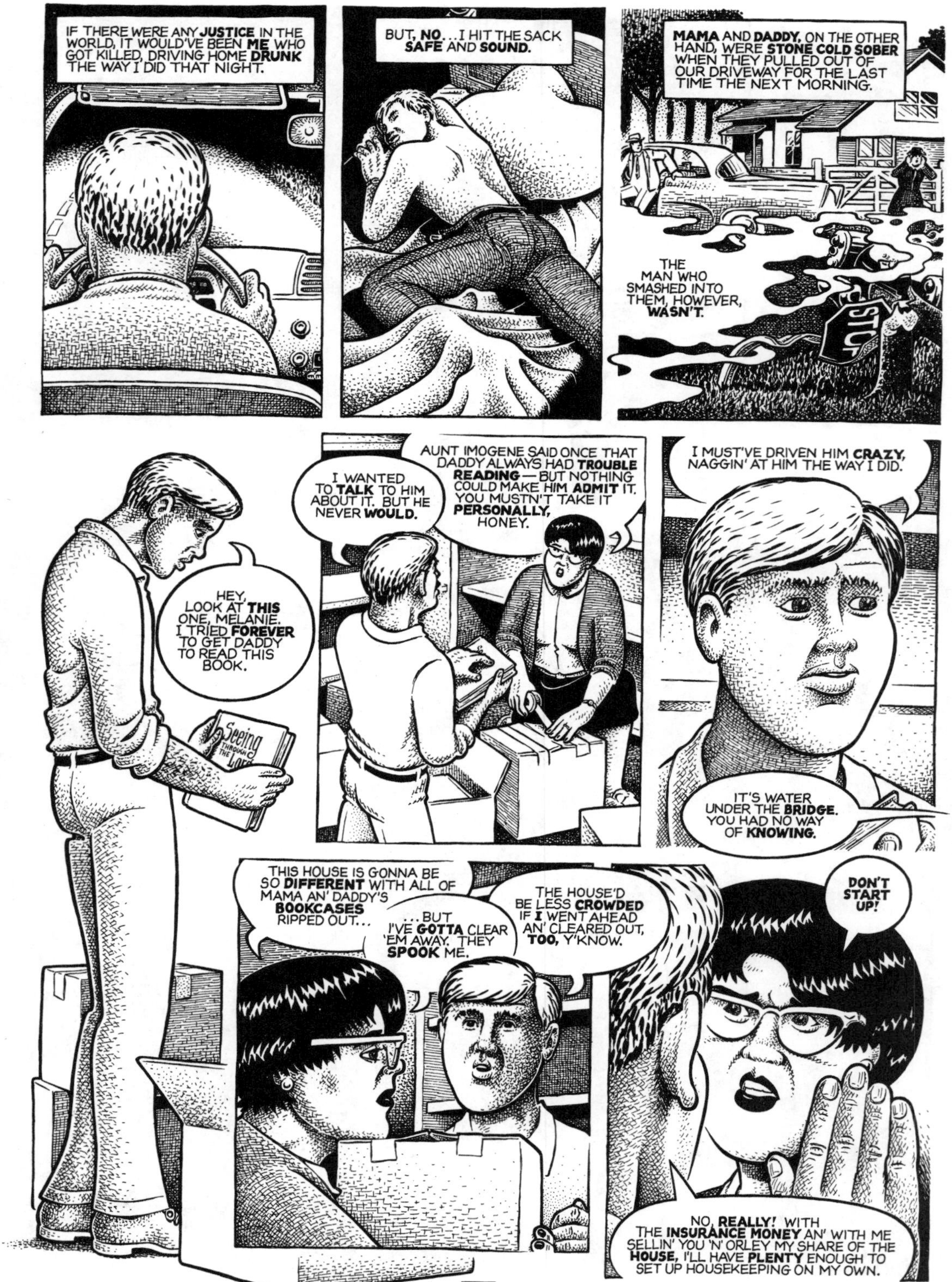
IF THERE WERE ANY JUSTICE IN THE WORLD, IT WOULD'VE BEEN ME WHO GOT KILLED, DRIVING HOME DRUNK THE WAY I DID THAT NIGHT.
BUT, NO...I HIT THE SACK SAFE AND SOUND.
MAMA AND DADDY, ON THE OTHER HAND, WERE STONE COLD SOBER WHEN THEY PULLED OUT OF OUR DRIVEWAY FOR THE LAST TIME THE NEXT MORNING.
THE MAN WHO SMASHED INTO THEM, HOWEVER, WASN'T.
STOP
HEY, LOOK AT THIS ONE, MELANIE. I TRIED FOREVER TO GET DADDY TO READ THIS BOOK.
Seeing THROUGH THE
I WANTED TO TALK TO HIM ABOUT IT. BUT HE NEVER WOULD.
AUNT IMOGENE SAID ONCE THAT DADDY ALWAYS HAD TROUBLE READING — BUT NOTHING COULD MAKE HIM ADMIT IT. YOU MUSTN'T TAKE IT PERSONALLY, HONEY.
I MUST'VE DRIVEN HIM CRAZY, NAGGIN' AT HIM THE WAY I DID.
IT'S WATER UNDER THE BRIDGE. YOU HAD NO WAY OF KNOWING.
THIS HOUSE IS GONNA BE SO DIFFERENT WITH ALL OF MAMA AN' DADDY'S BOOKCASES RIPPED OUT...
...BUT I'VE GOTTA CLEAR 'EM AWAY. THEY SPOOK ME.
THE HOUSE'D BE LESS CROWDED IF I WENT AHEAD AN' CLEARED OUT, TOO, Y'KNOW.
DON'T START UP!
NO, REALLY! WITH THE INSURANCE MONEY AN' WITH ME SELLIN' YOU 'N' ORLEY MY SHARE OF THE HOUSE, I'LL HAVE PLENTY ENOUGH TO SET UP HOUSEKEEPING ON MY OWN.

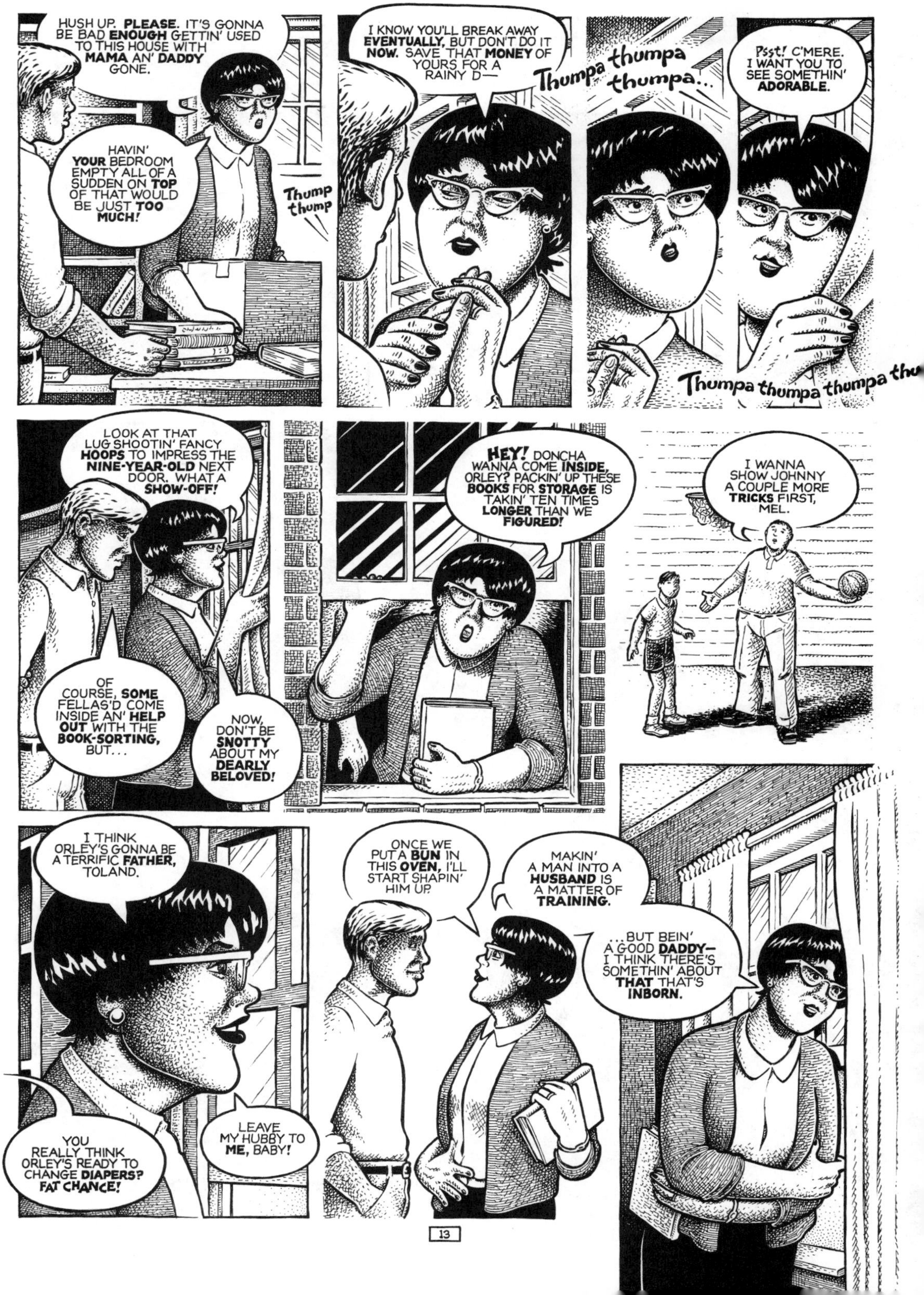
HUSH UP. PLEASE. IT'S GONNA BE BAD ENOUGH GETTIN' USED TO THIS HOUSE WITH MAMA AN' DADDY GONE.
HAVIN' YOUR BEDROOM EMPTY ALL OF A SUDDEN ON TOP OF THAT WOULD BE JUST TOO MUCH!
Thump thump
I KNOW YOU'LL BREAK AWAY EVENTUALLY, BUT DON'T DO IT NOW. SAVE THAT MONEY OF YOURS FOR A RAINY D—
Thumpa thumpa thumpa...
Psst! C'MERE. I WANT YOU TO SEE SOMETHIN' ADORABLE.
Thumpa thumpa thumpa thu
LOOK AT THAT LUG SHOOTIN' FANCY HOOPS TO IMPRESS THE NINE-YEAR-OLD NEXT DOOR. WHAT A SHOW-OFF!
OF COURSE, SOME FELLAS'D COME INSIDE AN' HELP OUT WITH THE BOOK-SORTING, BUT...
NOW, DON'T BE SNOTTY ABOUT MY DEARLY BELOVED!
HEY! DONCHA WANNA COME INSIDE, ORLEY? PACKIN' UP THESE BOOKS FOR STORAGE IS TAKIN' TEN TIMES LONGER THAN WE FIGURED!
I WANNA SHOW JOHNNY A COUPLE MORE TRICKS FIRST, MEL.
I THINK ORLEY'S GONNA BE A TERRIFIC FATHER, TOLAND.
YOU REALLY THINK ORLEY'S READY TO CHANGE DIAPERS? FAT CHANCE!
LEAVE MY HUBBY TO ME, BABY!
ONCE WE PUT A BUN IN THIS OVEN, I'LL START SHAPIN' HIM UP.
MAKIN' A MAN INTO A HUSBAND IS A MATTER OF TRAINING.
...BUT BEIN' A GOOD DADDY— I THINK THERE'S SOMETHIN' ABOUT THAT THAT'S INBORN.

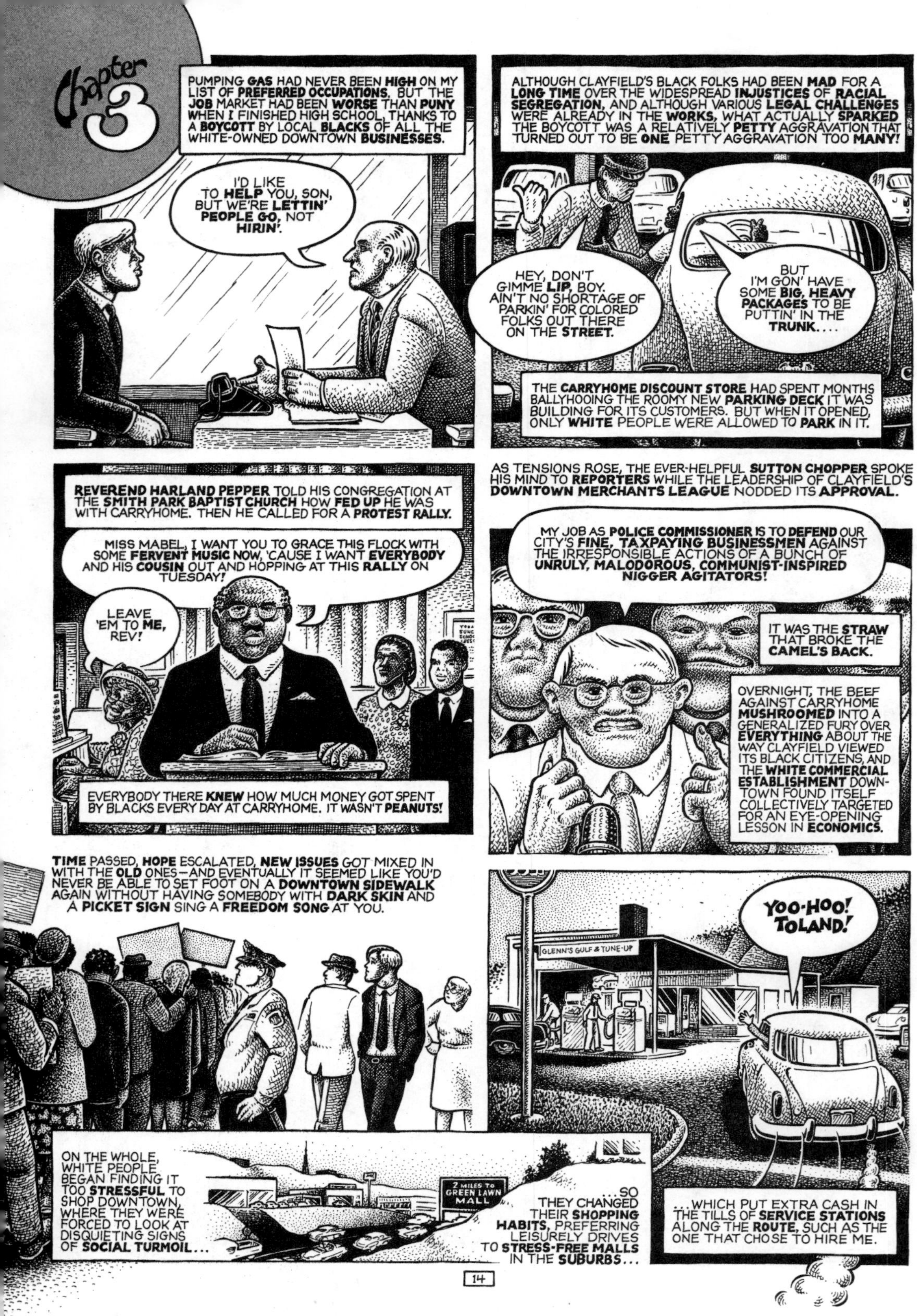
Chapter 3
PUMPING GAS HAD NEVER BEEN HIGH ON MY LIST OF PREFERRED OCCUPATIONS. BUT THE JOB MARKET HAD BEEN WORSE THAN PUNY WHEN I FINISHED HIGH SCHOOL, THANKS TO A BOYCOTT BY LOCAL BLACKS OF ALL THE WHITE-OWNED DOWNTOWN BUSINESSES.
I'D LIKE TO HELP YOU, SON, BUT WE'RE LETTIN' PEOPLE GO, NOT HIRIN'.
ALTHOUGH CLAYFIELD'S BLACK FOLKS HAD BEEN MAD FOR A LONG TIME OVER THE WIDESPREAD INJUSTICES OF RACIAL SEGREGATION, AND ALTHOUGH VARIOUS LEGAL CHALLENGES WERE ALREADY IN THE WORKS, WHAT ACTUALLY SPARKED THE BOYCOTT WAS A RELATIVELY PETTY AGGRAVATION THAT TURNED OUT TO BE ONE PETTY AGGRAVATION TOO MANY!
BUT I'M GON' HAVE SOME BIG, HEAVY PACKAGES TO BE PUTTIN' IN THE TRUNK....
HEY, DON'T GIMME LIP, BOY. AIN'T NO SHORTAGE OF PARKIN' FOR COLORED FOLKS OUT THERE ON THE STREET.
THE CARRYHOME DISCOUNT STORE HAD SPENT MONTHS BALLYHOOING THE ROOMY NEW PARKING DECK IT WAS BUILDING FOR ITS CUSTOMERS. BUT WHEN IT OPENED, ONLY WHITE PEOPLE WERE ALLOWED TO PARK IN IT.
REVEREND HARLAND PEPPER TOLD HIS CONGREGATION AT THE SMITH PARK BAPTIST CHURCH HOW FED UP HE WAS WITH CARRYHOME. THEN HE CALLED FOR A PROTEST RALLY.
MISS MABEL, I WANT YOU TO GRACE THIS FLOCK WITH SOME FERVENT MUSIC NOW, 'CAUSE I WANT EVERYBODY AND HIS COUSIN OUT AND HOPPING AT THIS RALLY ON TUESDAY!
LEAVE 'EM TO ME, REV!
EVERYBODY THERE KNEW HOW MUCH MONEY GOT SPENT BY BLACKS EVERY DAY AT CARRYHOME. IT WASN'T PEANUTS!
AS TENSIONS ROSE, THE EVER-HELPFUL SUTTON CHOPPER SPOKE HIS MIND TO REPORTERS WHILE THE LEADERSHIP OF CLAYFIELD'S DOWNTOWN MERCHANTS LEAGUE NODDED ITS APPROVAL.
MY JOB AS POLICE COMMISSIONER IS TO DEFEND OUR CITY'S FINE, TAXPAYING BUSINESSMEN AGAINST THE IRRESPONSIBLE ACTIONS OF A BUNCH OF UNRULY, MALODOROUS, COMMUNIST-INSPIRED NIGGER AGITATORS!
IT WAS THE STRAW THAT BROKE THE CAMEL'S BACK.
OVERNIGHT, THE BEEF AGAINST CARRYHOME MUSHROOMED INTO A GENERALIZED FURY OVER EVERYTHING ABOUT THE WAY CLAYFIELD VIEWED ITS BLACK CITIZENS, AND THE WHITE COMMERCIAL ESTABLISHMENT DOWNTOWN FOUND ITSELF COLLECTIVELY TARGETED FOR AN EYE-OPENING LESSON IN ECONOMICS.
TIME PASSED, HOPE ESCALATED, NEW ISSUES GOT MIXED IN WITH THE OLD ONES—AND EVENTUALLY IT SEEMED LIKE YOU'D NEVER BE ABLE TO SET FOOT ON A DOWNTOWN SIDEWALK AGAIN WITHOUT HAVING SOMEBODY WITH DARK SKIN AND A PICKET SIGN SING A FREEDOM SONG AT YOU.
GLENN'S GULF & TUNE-UP
YOO-HOO! TOLAND!
ON THE WHOLE, WHITE PEOPLE BEGAN FINDING IT TOO STRESSFUL TO SHOP DOWNTOWN, WHERE THEY WERE FORCED TO LOOK AT DISQUIETING SIGNS OF SOCIAL TURMOIL...
2 MILES TO GREEN LAWN MALL
...SO THEY CHANGED THEIR SHOPPING HABITS, PREFERRING LEISURELY DRIVES TO STRESS-FREE MALLS IN THE SUBURBS...
...WHICH PUT EXTRA CASH IN THE TILLS OF SERVICE STATIONS ALONG THE ROUTE, SUCH AS THE ONE THAT CHOSE TO HIRE ME.

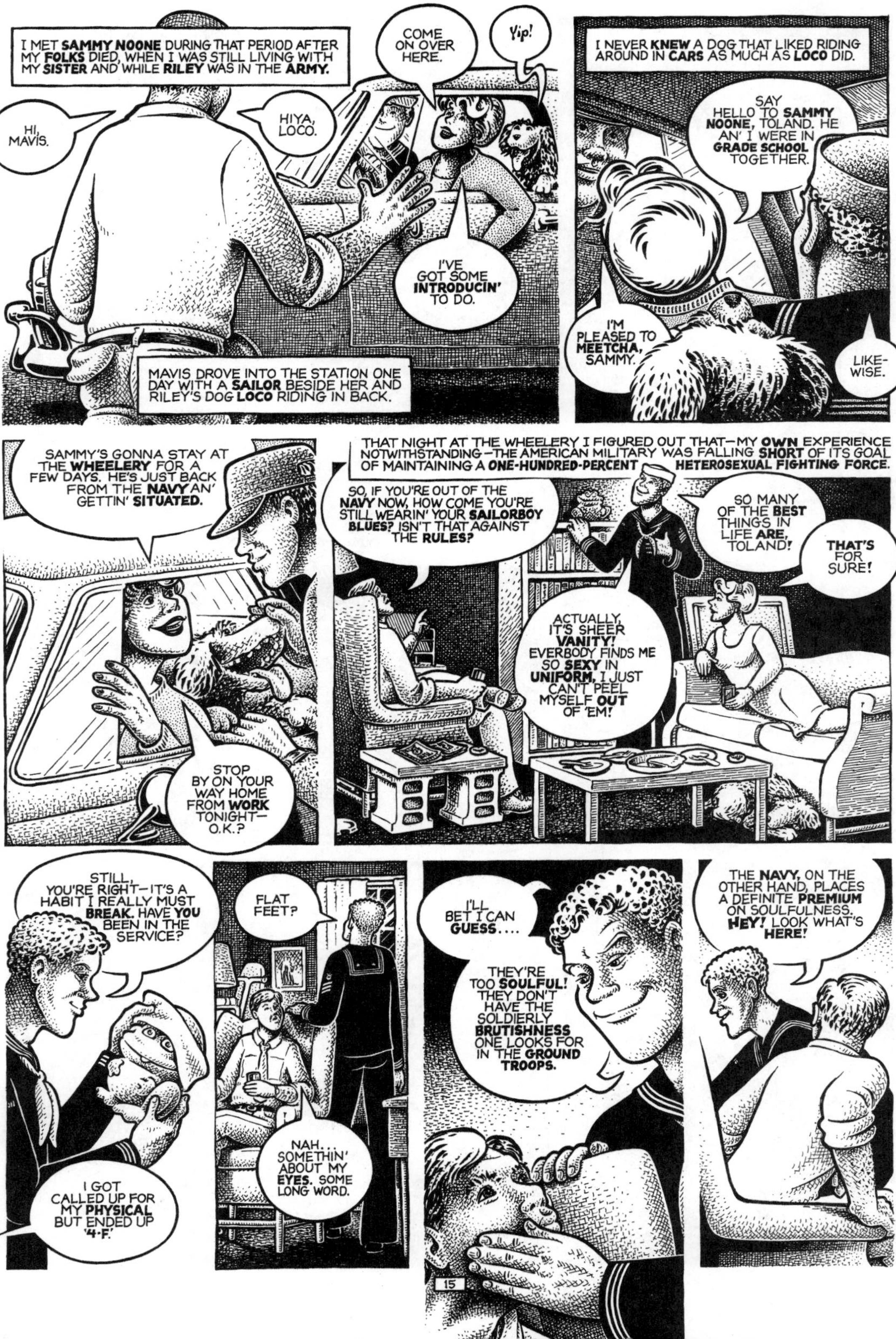
I MET SAMMY NOONE DURING THAT PERIOD AFTER MY FOLKS DIED, WHEN I WAS STILL LIVING WITH MY SISTER AND WHILE RILEY WAS IN THE ARMY.
COME ON OVER HERE.
Yip!
HI, MAVIS.
HIYA, LOCO.
I'VE GOT SOME INTRODUCIN' TO DO.
MAVIS DROVE INTO THE STATION ONE DAY WITH A SAILOR BESIDE HER AND RILEY'S DOG LOCO RIDING IN BACK.
I NEVER KNEW A DOG THAT LIKED RIDING AROUND IN CARS AS MUCH AS LOCO DID.
SAY HELLO TO SAMMY NOONE, TOLAND. HE AN' I WERE IN GRADE SCHOOL TOGETHER.
I'M PLEASED TO MEETCHA, SAMMY.
LIKE-WISE.
SAMMY'S GONNA STAY AT THE WHEELERY FOR A FEW DAYS. HE'S JUST BACK FROM THE NAVY AN' GETTIN' SITUATED.
STOP BY ON YOUR WAY HOME FROM WORK TONIGHT—O.K.?
THAT NIGHT AT THE WHEELERY I FIGURED OUT THAT—MY OWN EXPERIENCE NOTWITHSTANDING—THE AMERICAN MILITARY WAS FALLING SHORT OF ITS GOAL OF MAINTAINING A ONE-HUNDRED-PERCENT HETEROSEXUAL FIGHTING FORCE.
SO, IF YOU'RE OUT OF THE NAVY NOW, HOW COME YOU'RE STILL WEARIN' YOUR SAILORBOY BLUES? ISN'T THAT AGAINST THE RULES?
ACTUALLY, IT'S SHEER VANITY! EVERBODY FINDS ME SO SEXY IN UNIFORM, I JUST CAN'T PEEL MYSELF OUT OF 'EM!
SO MANY OF THE BEST THINGS IN LIFE ARE, TOLAND!
THAT'S FOR SURE!
STILL, YOU'RE RIGHT—IT'S A HABIT I REALLY MUST BREAK. HAVE YOU BEEN IN THE SERVICE?
I GOT CALLED UP FOR MY PHYSICAL BUT ENDED UP '4-F.'
FLAT FEET?
NAH... SOMETHIN' ABOUT MY EYES. SOME LONG WORD.
I'LL BET I CAN GUESS....
THEY'RE TOO SOULFUL! THEY DON'T HAVE THE SOLDIERLY BRUTISHNESS ONE LOOKS FOR IN THE GROUND TROOPS.
THE NAVY, ON THE OTHER HAND, PLACES A DEFINITE PREMIUM ON SOULFULNESS. HEY! LOOK WHAT'S HERE!

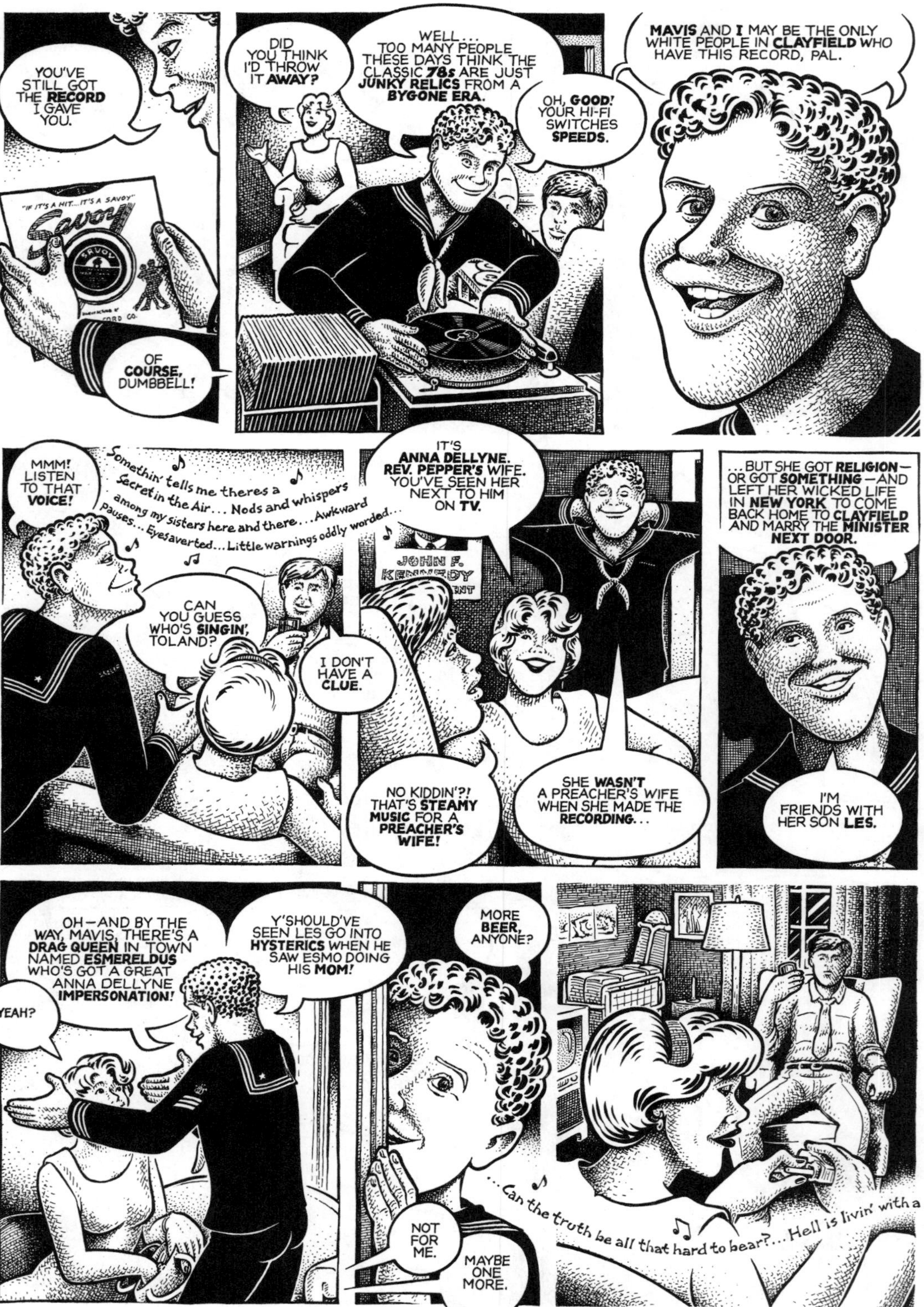
YOU'VE STILL GOT THE RECORD I GAVE YOU.
"IF IT'S A HIT... IT'S A SAVOY"
Savoy
OF COURSE, DUMBBELL!
DID YOU THINK I'D THROW IT AWAY?
WELL... TOO MANY PEOPLE THESE DAYS THINK THE CLASSIC 78s ARE JUST JUNKY RELICS FROM A BYGONE ERA.
OH, GOOD! YOUR HI-FI SWITCHES SPEEDS.
MAVIS AND I MAY BE THE ONLY WHITE PEOPLE IN CLAYFIELD WHO HAVE THIS RECORD, PAL.
MMM! LISTEN TO THAT VOICE!
Somethin' tells me theres a Secret in the Air... Nods and whispers among my sisters here and there... Awkward pauses... Eyes averted... Little warnings oddly worded...
CAN YOU GUESS WHO'S SINGIN', TOLAND?
I DON'T HAVE A CLUE.
IT'S ANNA DELLYNE. REV. PEPPER'S WIFE. YOU'VE SEEN HER NEXT TO HIM ON TV.
NO KIDDIN'?! THAT'S STEAMY MUSIC FOR A PREACHER'S WIFE!
SHE WASN'T A PREACHER'S WIFE WHEN SHE MADE THE RECORDING...
...BUT SHE GOT RELIGION— OR GOT SOMETHING—AND LEFT HER WICKED LIFE IN NEW YORK TO COME BACK HOME TO CLAYFIELD AND MARRY THE MINISTER NEXT DOOR.
I'M FRIENDS WITH HER SON LES.
OH—AND BY THE WAY, MAVIS, THERE'S A DRAG QUEEN IN TOWN NAMED ESMERELDUS WHO'S GOT A GREAT ANNA DELLYNE IMPERSONATION!
YEAH?
Y'SHOULD'VE SEEN LES GO INTO HYSTERICS WHEN HE SAW ESMO DOING HIS MOM!
MORE BEER, ANYONE?
NOT FOR ME.
MAYBE ONE MORE.
...Can the truth be all that hard to bear?... Hell is livin' with a Secret in the

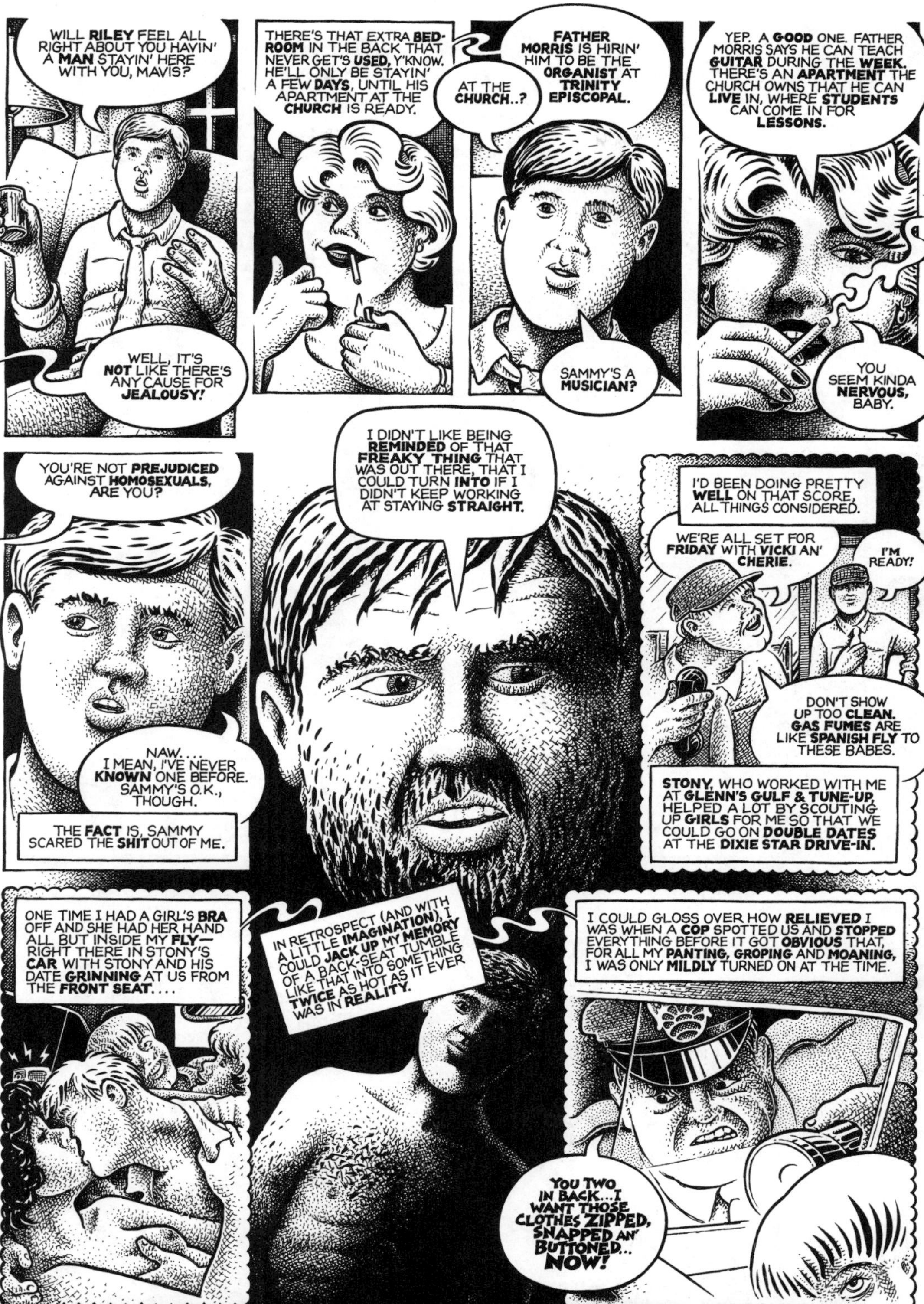

WILL RILEY FEEL ALL RIGHT ABOUT YOU HAVIN' A MAN STAYIN' HERE WITH YOU, MAVIS?
WELL, IT'S NOT LIKE THERE'S ANY CAUSE FOR JEALOUSY!
THERE'S THAT EXTRA BEDROOM IN THE BACK THAT NEVER GET'S USED, Y'KNOW. HE'LL ONLY BE STAYIN' A FEW DAYS, UNTIL HIS APARTMENT AT THE CHURCH IS READY.
AT THE CHURCH..?
FATHER MORRIS IS HIRIN' HIM TO BE THE ORGANIST AT TRINITY EPISCOPAL.
SAMMY'S A MUSICIAN?
YEP. A GOOD ONE. FATHER MORRIS SAYS HE CAN TEACH GUITAR DURING THE WEEK. THERE'S AN APARTMENT THE CHURCH OWNS THAT HE CAN LIVE IN, WHERE STUDENTS CAN COME IN FOR LESSONS.
YOU SEEM KINDA NERVOUS, BABY.
YOU'RE NOT PREJUDICED AGAINST HOMOSEXUALS, ARE YOU?
NAW. . . I MEAN, I'VE NEVER KNOWN ONE BEFORE. SAMMY'S O.K., THOUGH.
THE FACT IS, SAMMY SCARED THE SHIT OUT OF ME.
I DIDN'T LIKE BEING REMINDED OF THAT FREAKY THING THAT WAS OUT THERE, THAT I COULD TURN INTO IF I DIDN'T KEEP WORKING AT STAYING STRAIGHT.
I'D BEEN DOING PRETTY WELL ON THAT SCORE, ALL THINGS CONSIDERED.
WE'RE ALL SET FOR FRIDAY WITH VICKI AN' CHERIE.
I'M READY!
DON'T SHOW UP TOO CLEAN. GAS FUMES ARE LIKE SPANISH FLY TO THESE BABES.
STONY, WHO WORKED WITH ME AT GLENN'S GULF & TUNE-UP, HELPED A LOT BY SCOUTING UP GIRLS FOR ME SO THAT WE COULD GO ON DOUBLE DATES AT THE DIXIE STAR DRIVE-IN.
ONE TIME I HAD A GIRL'S BRA OFF AND SHE HAD HER HAND ALL BUT INSIDE MY FLY— RIGHT THERE IN STONY'S CAR WITH STONY AND HIS DATE GRINNING AT US FROM THE FRONT SEAT. . . .
IN RETROSPECT (AND WITH A LITTLE IMAGINATION), I COULD JACK UP MY MEMORY OF A BACK-SEAT TUMBLE LIKE THAT INTO SOMETHING TWICE AS HOT AS IT EVER WAS IN REALITY.
I COULD GLOSS OVER HOW RELIEVED I WAS WHEN A COP SPOTTED US AND STOPPED EVERYTHING BEFORE IT GOT OBVIOUS THAT, FOR ALL MY PANTING, GROPING AND MOANING, I WAS ONLY MILDLY TURNED ON AT THE TIME.
YOU TWO IN BACK... I WANT THOSE CLOTHES ZIPPED, SNAPPED AN' BUTTONED... NOW!

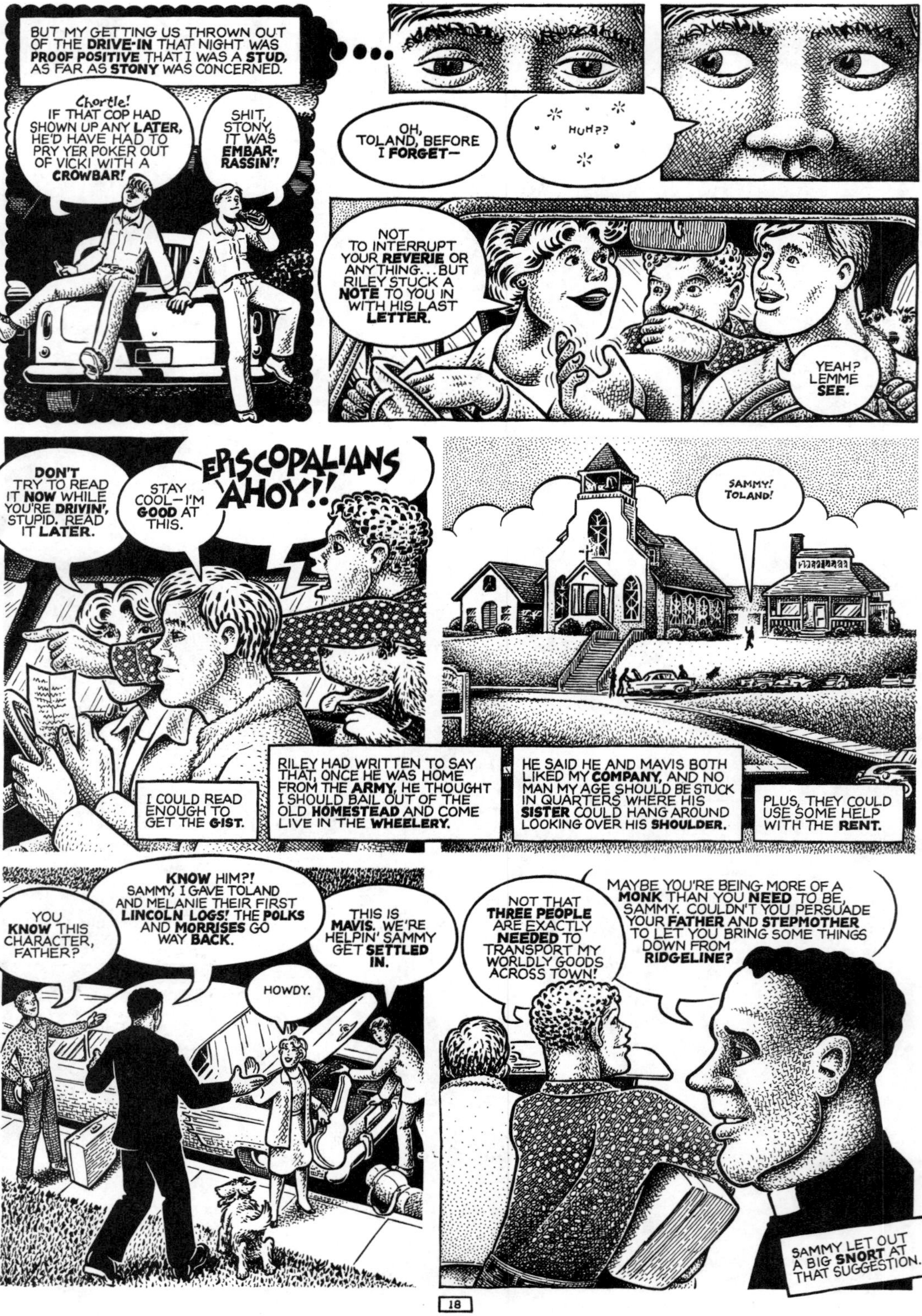
BUT MY GETTING US THROWN OUT OF THE DRIVE-IN THAT NIGHT WAS PROOF POSITIVE THAT I WAS A STUD, AS FAR AS STONY WAS CONCERNED.
Chortle! IF THAT COP HAD SHOWN UP ANY LATER, HE'D HAVE HAD TO PRY YER POKER OUT OF VICKI WITH A CROWBAR!
SHIT, STONY, IT WAS EMBARRASSIN'!
OH, TOLAND, BEFORE I FORGET—
HUH??
NOT TO INTERRUPT YOUR REVERIE OR ANYTHING... BUT RILEY STUCK A NOTE TO YOU IN WITH HIS LAST LETTER.
YEAH? LEMME SEE.
DON'T TRY TO READ IT NOW WHILE YOU'RE DRIVIN', STUPID. READ IT LATER.
STAY COOL—I'M GOOD AT THIS.
EPISCOPALIANS AHOY!!
SAMMY! TOLAND!
I COULD READ ENOUGH TO GET THE GIST.
RILEY HAD WRITTEN TO SAY THAT, ONCE HE WAS HOME FROM THE ARMY, HE THOUGHT I SHOULD BAIL OUT OF THE OLD HOMESTEAD AND COME LIVE IN THE WHEELERY.
HE SAID HE AND MAVIS BOTH LIKED MY COMPANY, AND NO MAN MY AGE SHOULD BE STUCK IN QUARTERS WHERE HIS SISTER COULD HANG AROUND LOOKING OVER HIS SHOULDER.
PLUS, THEY COULD USE SOME HELP WITH THE RENT.
YOU KNOW THIS CHARACTER, FATHER?
KNOW HIM?! SAMMY, I GAVE TOLAND AND MELANIE THEIR FIRST LINCOLN LOGS! THE POLKS AND MORRISES GO WAY BACK.
THIS IS MAVIS. WE'RE HELPIN' SAMMY GET SETTLED IN.
HOWDY.
NOT THAT THREE PEOPLE ARE EXACTLY NEEDED TO TRANSPORT MY WORLDLY GOODS ACROSS TOWN!
MAYBE YOU'RE BEING MORE OF A MONK THAN YOU NEED TO BE, SAMMY. COULDN'T YOU PERSUADE YOUR FATHER AND STEPMOTHER TO LET YOU BRING SOME THINGS DOWN FROM RIDGELINE?
SAMMY LET OUT A BIG SNORT AT THAT SUGGESTION.

MAVIS HAD ALREADY **TOLD** ME THAT SAMMY'S FOLKS HAD BIG **BUCKS,** BUT THAT HE AND THEY DIDN'T HAVE MUCH **USE** FOR EACH OTHER.

WELL... PERHAPS **NOT.** —Cough!—

I HAVEN'T SEEN **YOU** SINCE THE **FUNERAL,** TOLAND.

YOU'RE LOOKING **WELL.**

WHY DON'T YOU EVER COME BY FOR ONE OF OUR **SERVICES?**

YOU AN' I HAVE **TALKED** ABOUT THAT, FATHER.

YOU **KNOW** I GOT **JESUS-ED** OUT AT AN **EARLY** AGE.

PEOPLE HAVE BEEN KNOWN TO **RECOVER** FROM THAT AFFLICTION. YOU DON'T MIND THAT I **CHECK** PERIODICALLY, DO YOU?

WATCH OUT HE DOESN'T **SNAG** YOUR **JACKET** AN' DRAG YOU DOWN TO PERDITION **WITH** HIM, FATHER.

SAMMY'S AN INCREDIBLE **ORGANIST.** WHY DON'T YOU JUST COME **WARM** A **PEW** AND LISTEN TO HIS **MUSIC** SOME SUNDAY?

SLAM!

YOU CAN DAYDREAM ABOUT **BASEBALL** DURING THE **HOMILY** IF YOU LIKE.

YOU'RE A SUCKER FOR **LOST CAUSES,** FATHER.

I'LL COME AN' HEAR SAMMY PLAY SOME-TIME, FATHER MORRIS.

I'M NOT AS **COMMITTED** TO MY HEATHENISM AS TOLAND.

I KEPT THINKING ABOUT RILEY'S **INVITATION** WHILE I WAS AT WORK LATER IN THE DAY.

FOR A SISTER AND BROTHER, MELANIE AND I DID BETTER THAN **AVERAGE** AT TOLERATING **FAMILY TOGETHERNESS.** BUT **ORLEY** COULD BE HARD TO **TAKE.** AND EVEN **SIS** GOT **INTENSE** SOMETIMES.

LIKE WHEN SHE'D GET ME ALONE AND START TALKING ABOUT THE **GHOSTS** IN HER BEDROOM.

IT'S **MAMA** AN' **DADDY,** I'M SURE.

THEY FLOAT NEAR THE **CEILING** AN' WATCH TO SEE IF ORLEY AN' I ARE **DOIN' IT** RIGHT.

MAMA'S GHOST IS ALWAYS PEEKIN' INSIDE MY HEAD TO SEE IF I **LOVE ORLEY** AS MUCH AS I'M **SUPPOSED** TO.

WELL... YOU **DO** LOVE HIM, DON'T YOU?

OF **COURSE** I DO.

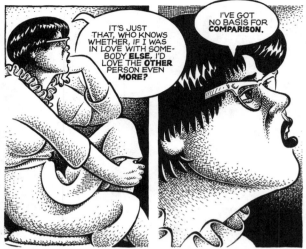

IT'S JUST THAT, WHO KNOWS WHETHER, IF I WAS IN LOVE WITH SOME-BODY **ELSE**, I'D LOVE THE **OTHER** PERSON EVEN **MORE?**

I'VE GOT NO BASIS FOR **COMPARISON.**

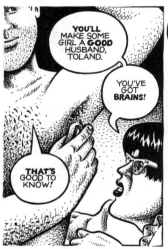

YOU'LL MAKE SOME GIRL A **GOOD** HUSBAND, TOLAND.

YOU'VE GOT **BRAINS!**

THAT'S GOOD TO KNOW!

MOST OF THE BOYS I HAD TO PICK FROM IN **HIGH SCHOOL**— WELL, YOU COULDN'T GET A GOOD **BRAIN** OUT OF 'EM IF YOU BOILED ALL THEIR **HEADS** TOGETHER IN ONE **POT!**

NO REFLECTION ON **ORLEY.** ORLEY CAN BE A **LIVELY TALKER.** BUT YOU'VE GOTTA PICK THE RIGHT **SUBJECT.**

ALSO, YOU HAD TO KNOW WHICH SUBJECTS TO STAY **AWAY** FROM.

DID YOU SEE WHERE THEY'VE DUG UP AN ACTUAL **PHOTO** OF MARTIN LUTHER KING ATTENDIN' A **SCHOOL** FOR **COMMUNISTS?**

UH... IS THAT **SO**, ORLEY?

ALL I CAN SAY IS, I'M GLAD I'VE GOT PLENTY OF **BOOKS** TO READ!

YOU DIDN'T THROW AWAY NEARLY AS MANY OF THOSE OLD BOOKS AS YOU **THOUGHT** YOU WERE GOING TO, DID YOU?

NO. I HELD ON TO MORE THAN A **FEW.**

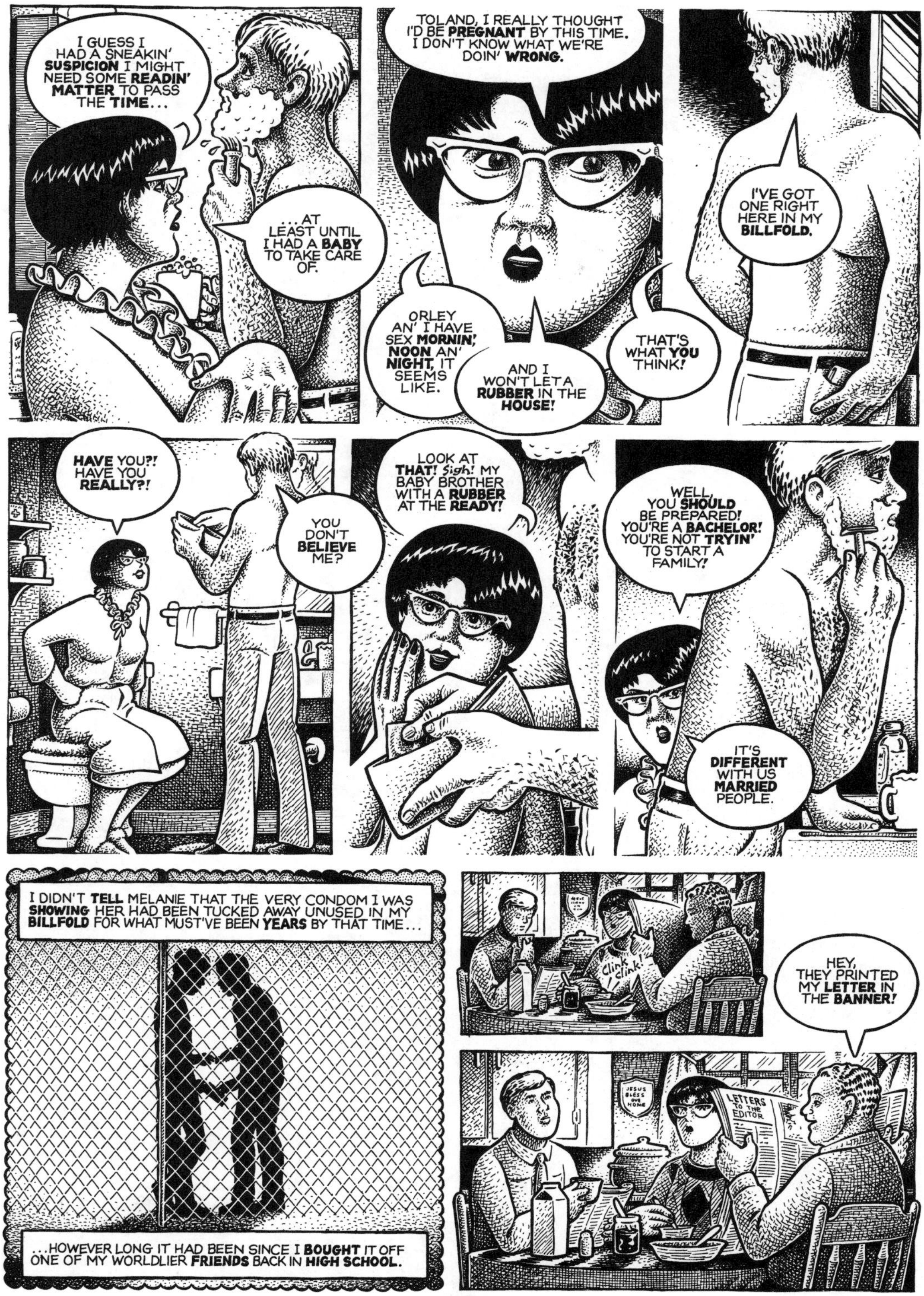
I GUESS I HAD A SNEAKIN' SUSPICION I MIGHT NEED SOME READIN' MATTER TO PASS THE TIME...
...AT LEAST UNTIL I HAD A BABY TO TAKE CARE OF.
TOLAND, I REALLY THOUGHT I'D BE PREGNANT BY THIS TIME. I DON'T KNOW WHAT WE'RE DOIN' WRONG.
ORLEY AN' I HAVE SEX MORNIN', NOON AN' NIGHT, IT SEEMS LIKE.
AND I WON'T LET A RUBBER IN THE HOUSE!
THAT'S WHAT YOU THINK!
I'VE GOT ONE RIGHT HERE IN MY BILLFOLD.
HAVE YOU?! HAVE YOU REALLY?!
YOU DON'T BELIEVE ME?
LOOK AT THAT! Sigh! MY BABY BROTHER WITH A RUBBER AT THE READY!
WELL, YOU SHOULD BE PREPARED! YOU'RE A BACHELOR! YOU'RE NOT TRYIN' TO START A FAMILY!
IT'S DIFFERENT WITH US MARRIED PEOPLE.
I DIDN'T TELL MELANIE THAT THE VERY CONDOM I WAS SHOWING HER HAD BEEN TUCKED AWAY UNUSED IN MY BILLFOLD FOR WHAT MUST'VE BEEN YEARS BY THAT TIME...
...HOWEVER LONG IT HAD BEEN SINCE I BOUGHT IT OFF ONE OF MY WORLDLIER FRIENDS BACK IN HIGH SCHOOL.
Clink clink!
HEY, THEY PRINTED MY LETTER IN THE BANNER!
LETTERS TO THE EDITOR

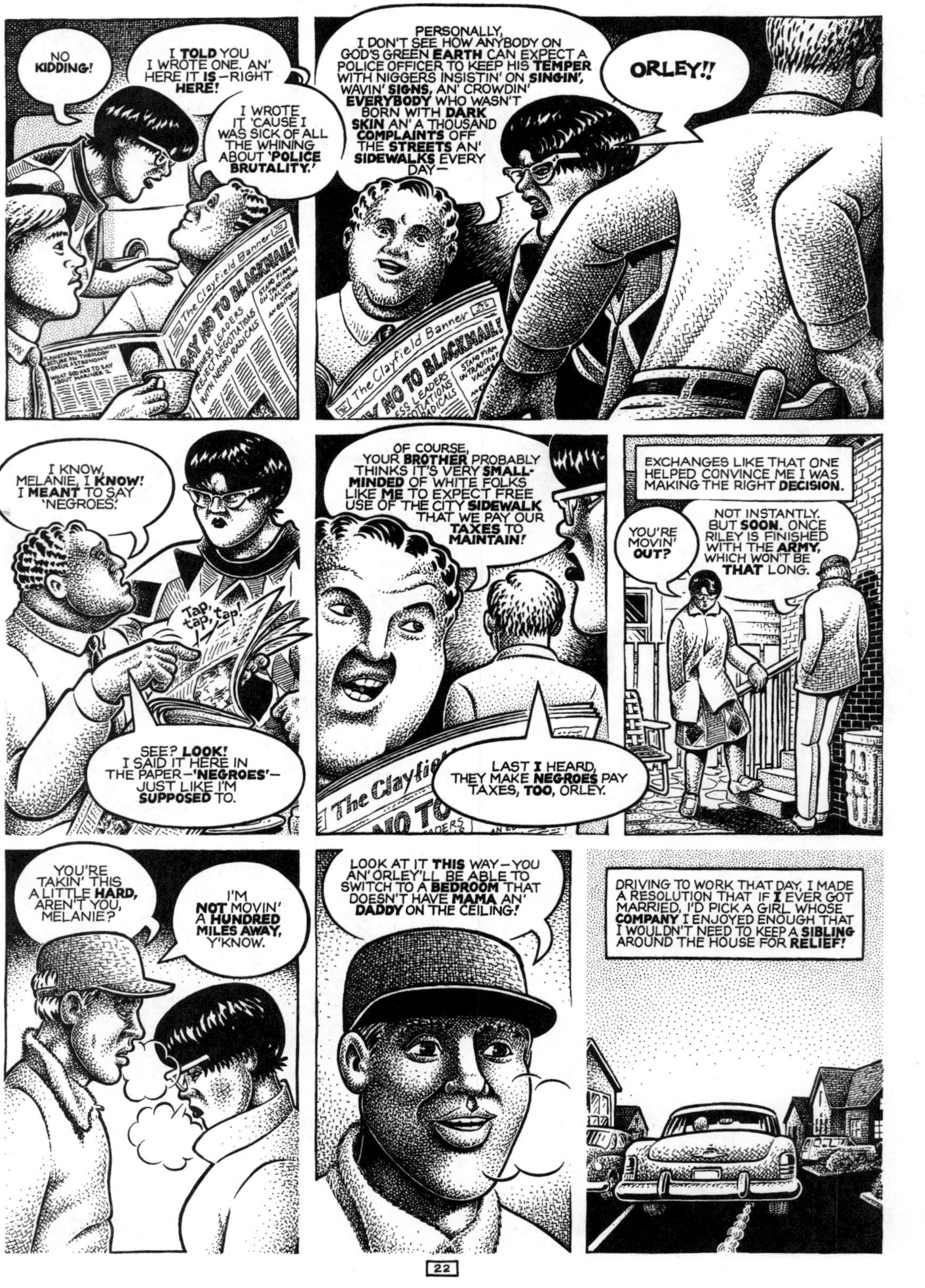

NO KIDDING!
I TOLD YOU I WROTE ONE. AN' HERE IT IS—RIGHT HERE!
I WROTE IT 'CAUSE I WAS SICK OF ALL THE WHINING ABOUT 'POLICE BRUTALITY.'
The Clayfield Banner
SAY NO TO BLACKMAIL!
PERSONALLY, I DON'T SEE HOW ANYBODY ON GOD'S GREEN EARTH CAN EXPECT A POLICE OFFICER TO KEEP HIS TEMPER WITH NIGGERS INSISTIN' ON SINGIN', WAVIN' SIGNS, AN' CROWDIN' EVERYBODY WHO WASN'T BORN WITH DARK SKIN AN' A THOUSAND COMPLAINTS OFF THE STREETS AN' SIDEWALKS EVERY DAY—
ORLEY!!
I KNOW, MELANIE, I KNOW! I MEANT TO SAY 'NEGROES.'
Tap, tap, tap!
SEE? LOOK! I SAID IT HERE IN THE PAPER—'NEGROES'—JUST LIKE I'M SUPPOSED TO.
OF COURSE, YOUR BROTHER PROBABLY THINKS IT'S VERY SMALL-MINDED OF WHITE FOLKS LIKE ME TO EXPECT FREE USE OF THE CITY SIDEWALK THAT WE PAY OUR TAXES TO MAINTAIN!
LAST I HEARD, THEY MAKE NEGROES PAY TAXES, TOO, ORLEY.
EXCHANGES LIKE THAT ONE HELPED CONVINCE ME I WAS MAKING THE RIGHT DECISION.
YOU'RE MOVIN' OUT?
NOT INSTANTLY. BUT SOON. ONCE RILEY IS FINISHED WITH THE ARMY, WHICH WON'T BE THAT LONG.
YOU'RE TAKIN' THIS A LITTLE HARD, AREN'T YOU, MELANIE?
I'M NOT MOVIN' A HUNDRED MILES AWAY, Y'KNOW.
LOOK AT IT THIS WAY—YOU AN' ORLEY'LL BE ABLE TO SWITCH TO A BEDROOM THAT DOESN'T HAVE MAMA AN' DADDY ON THE CEILING!
DRIVING TO WORK THAT DAY, I MADE A RESOLUTION THAT IF I EVER GOT MARRIED, I'D PICK A GIRL WHOSE COMPANY I ENJOYED ENOUGH THAT I WOULDN'T NEED TO KEEP A SIBLING AROUND THE HOUSE FOR RELIEF!

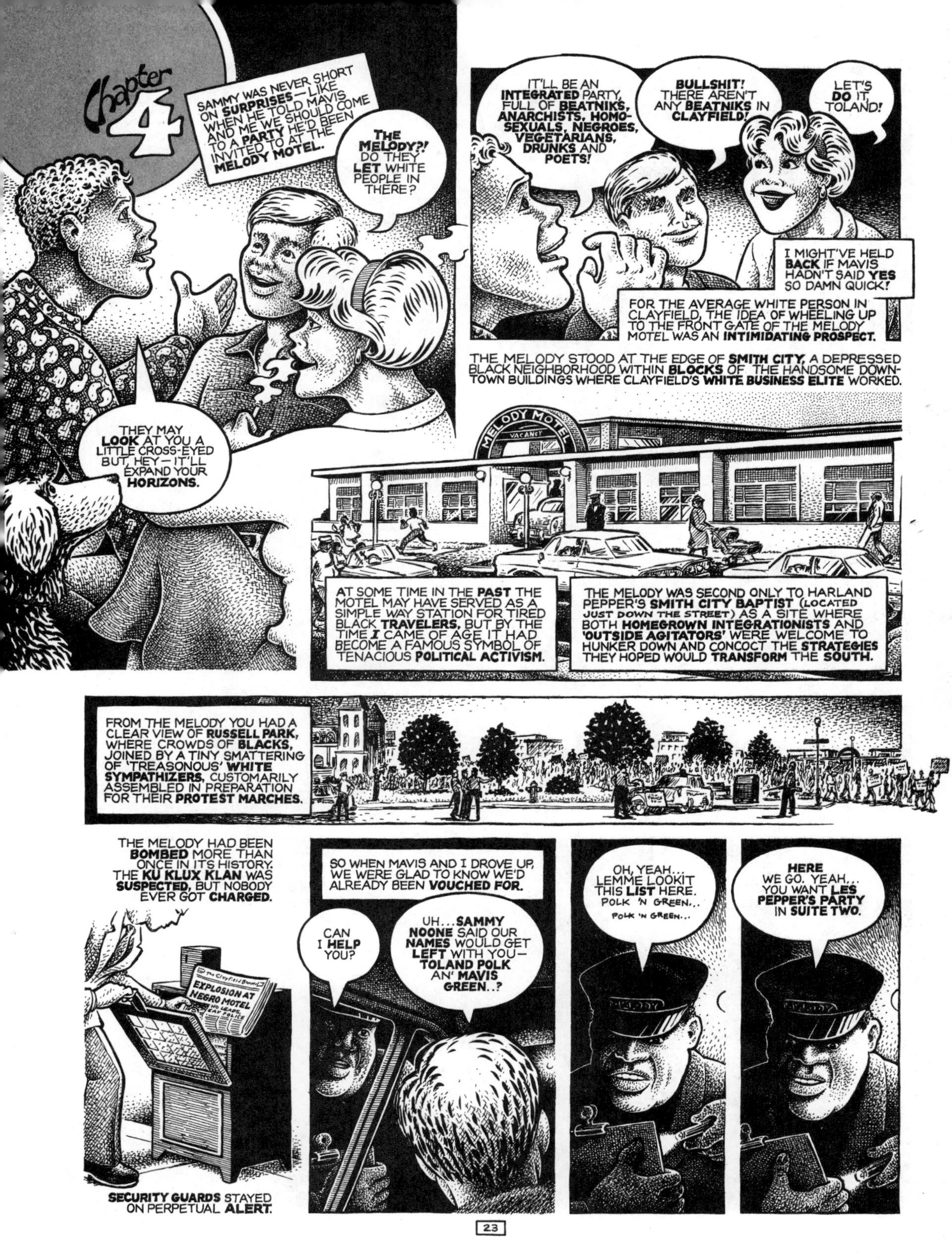
Chapter 4
SAMMY WAS NEVER SHORT ON SURPRISES—LIKE WHEN HE TOLD MAVIS AND ME WE SHOULD COME TO A PARTY HE'D BEEN INVITED TO AT THE MELODY MOTEL.
THE MELODY?! DO THEY LET WHITE PEOPLE IN THERE?
THEY MAY LOOK AT YOU A LITTLE CROSS-EYED BUT, HEY—IT'LL EXPAND YOUR HORIZONS.
IT'LL BE AN INTEGRATED PARTY, FULL OF BEATNIKS, ANARCHISTS, HOMOSEXUALS, NEGROES, VEGETARIANS, DRUNKS AND POETS!
BULLSHIT! THERE AREN'T ANY BEATNIKS IN CLAYFIELD!
LET'S DO IT, TOLAND!
I MIGHT'VE HELD BACK IF MAVIS HADN'T SAID YES SO DAMN QUICK!
FOR THE AVERAGE WHITE PERSON IN CLAYFIELD, THE IDEA OF WHEELING UP TO THE FRONT GATE OF THE MELODY MOTEL WAS AN INTIMIDATING PROSPECT.
THE MELODY STOOD AT THE EDGE OF SMITH CITY, A DEPRESSED BLACK NEIGHBORHOOD WITHIN BLOCKS OF THE HANDSOME DOWNTOWN BUILDINGS WHERE CLAYFIELD'S WHITE BUSINESS ELITE WORKED.
MELODY MOTEL
VACANCY
AT SOME TIME IN THE PAST THE MOTEL MAY HAVE SERVED AS A SIMPLE WAY STATION FOR TIRED BLACK TRAVELERS, BUT BY THE TIME I CAME OF AGE IT HAD BECOME A FAMOUS SYMBOL OF TENACIOUS POLITICAL ACTIVISM.
THE MELODY WAS SECOND ONLY TO HARLAND PEPPER'S SMITH CITY BAPTIST (LOCATED JUST DOWN THE STREET) AS A SITE WHERE BOTH HOMEGROWN INTEGRATIONISTS AND 'OUTSIDE AGITATORS' WERE WELCOME TO HUNKER DOWN AND CONCOCT THE STRATEGIES THEY HOPED WOULD TRANSFORM THE SOUTH.
FROM THE MELODY YOU HAD A CLEAR VIEW OF RUSSELL PARK, WHERE CROWDS OF BLACKS, JOINED BY A TINY SMATTERING OF 'TREASONOUS' WHITE SYMPATHIZERS, CUSTOMARILY ASSEMBLED IN PREPARATION FOR THEIR PROTEST MARCHES.
THE MELODY HAD BEEN BOMBED MORE THAN ONCE IN ITS HISTORY. THE KU KLUX KLAN WAS SUSPECTED, BUT NOBODY EVER GOT CHARGED.
The Clayfield Banner
EXPLOSION AT NEGRO MOTEL
NO LEADS, SAY POLICE
SECURITY GUARDS STAYED ON PERPETUAL ALERT.
SO WHEN MAVIS AND I DROVE UP, WE WERE GLAD TO KNOW WE'D ALREADY BEEN VOUCHED FOR.
CAN I HELP YOU?
UH... SAMMY NOONE SAID OUR NAMES WOULD GET LEFT WITH YOU—TOLAND POLK AN' MAVIS GREEN..?
OH, YEAH... LEMME LOOKIT THIS LIST HERE. POLK 'N GREEN... POLK 'N GREEN...
MELODY
HERE WE GO. YEAH... YOU WANT LES PEPPER'S PARTY IN SUITE TWO.
MELODY

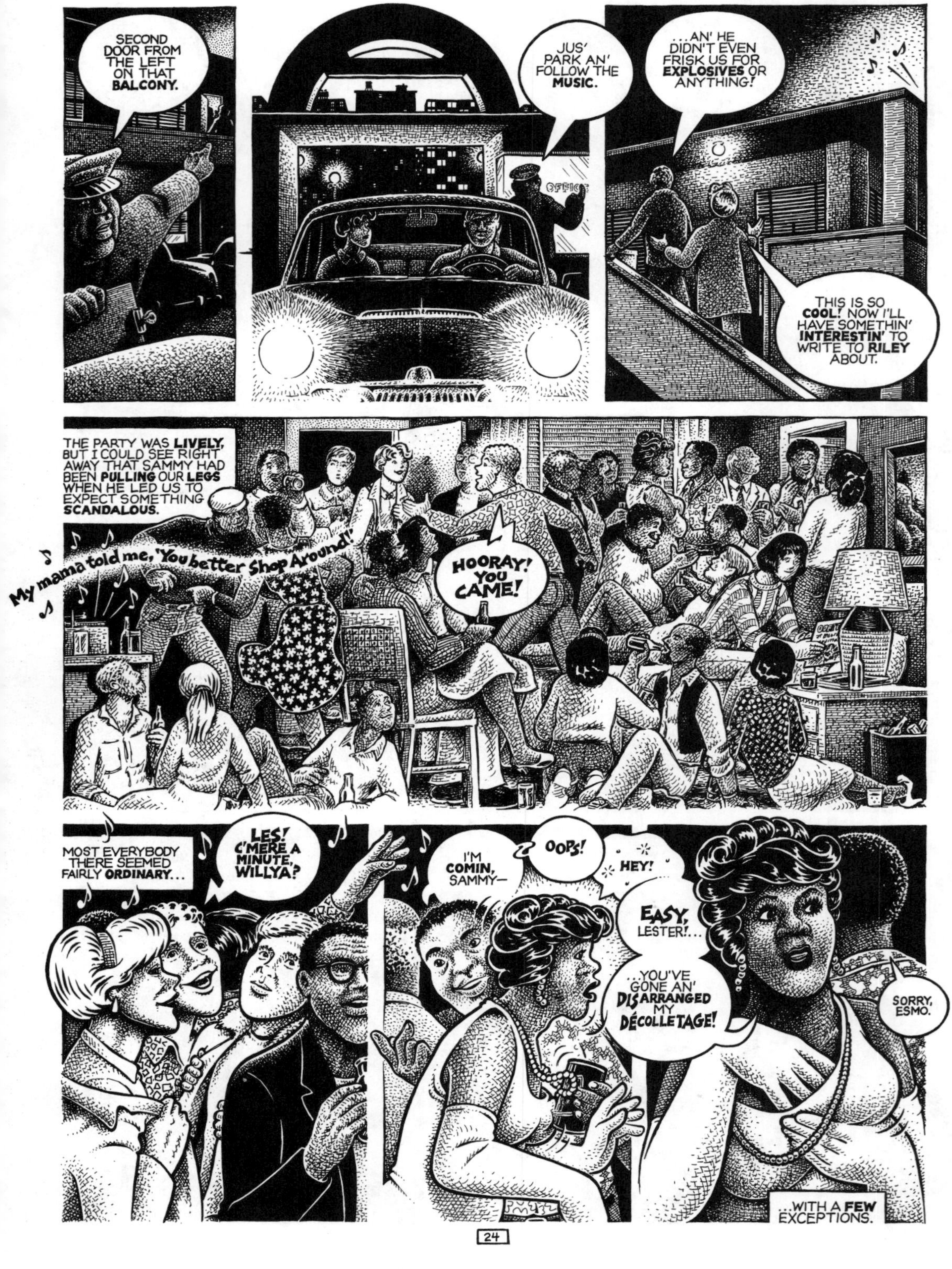
SECOND DOOR FROM THE LEFT ON THAT BALCONY.
JUS' PARK AN' FOLLOW THE MUSIC.
OFFICE
...AN' HE DIDN'T EVEN FRISK US FOR EXPLOSIVES OR ANYTHING!
THIS IS SO COOL! NOW I'LL HAVE SOMETHIN' INTERESTIN' TO WRITE TO RILEY ABOUT.
THE PARTY WAS LIVELY, BUT I COULD SEE RIGHT AWAY THAT SAMMY HAD BEEN PULLING OUR LEGS WHEN HE LED US TO EXPECT SOMETHING SCANDALOUS.
My mama told me, 'You better Shop Around!'
HOORAY! YOU CAME!
MOST EVERYBODY THERE SEEMED FAIRLY ORDINARY...
LES! C'MERE A MINUTE, WILLYA?
I'M COMIN, SAMMY—
OOPS!
HEY!
EASY, LESTER!...
...YOU'VE GONE AN' DISARRANGED MY DÉCOLLETAGE!
SORRY, ESMO.
...WITH A FEW EXCEPTIONS.

LES, MEET **MAVIS**, AN OLD **FRIEND** OF MINE, AND **TOLAND**, A **NEW** FRIEND WHO'S PROBABLY AGING **RAPIDLY!**

LOOKS LIKE A **NICE PARTY** YOU'VE GOT GOIN', LES.

SHIT! IS IT STILL 'NICE'?!

DON'T BE **DISCOURAGED**, LES—THE EVENING IS **YOUNG.**

BY THE TIME I HAD ADDED OUR **BEER** TO THE **COOLER** AND OPENED A CAN FOR **MYSELF**, MAVIS WAS TOO BUSY DANCING WITH **SAMMY** TO NEED MY ATTENTION.

I DECIDED TO **DRIFT AROUND** FOR A WHILE ON MY **OWN.**

TOLAND, HOW ABOUT STOWIN' THE **COATS** AND PUTTIN' OUR **SIX-PACKS** IN THE **ICE CHEST** OVER THERE?

MY FIRST GLIMPSE OF **GINGER** CAME WHEN SHE POPPED OUT OF **NOWHERE**, NUDGED MY **ARM**, AND ASKED ME A **QUESTION.**

HAVE YOU SEEN **SHILOH?**

UH...

OH, NEVER MIND. **THERE** HE IS.

SHILOH, THE GUY SHE WAS **LOOKING** FOR, HAD ALREADY CAUGHT MY **EYE.** IT WAS **OBVIOUS** FROM A **DISTANCE** THAT HE HAD ONE OF THOSE 'MAGNETIC PERSONALITIES' THEY TALK ABOUT.

IT SEEMED LIKE EVERYBODY IN THE ROOM HAD TO **DRIFT OVER** TO HIM PERIODICALLY TO GET THEIR **PARTY BATTERIES** RECHARGED BY THAT **LAUGH** OF HIS.

HI, SWEETIE. HAVIN' **FUN?**

I'M **SWIMMIN'** RIGHT **ALONG!**

TAKE A LOOK AT **LES** AN' **SAMMY** OVER THERE.

I'D NEVER **SEEN** TWO **MEN** DOIN' A **SLOW DANCE** TOGETHER BEFORE...

...MUCH **LESS** ONE OF 'EM **WHITE** AND ONE OF 'EM **BLACK.**

HOW CAN LES BE A **HOMO** WHEN HIS DADDY'S A PROMINENT **PREACHER** AND ALL?

SAMMY SAYS LES JUST ACTS LIKE WHO HE **IS.** THE PEOPLE HE'S **GAY** AROUND ARE CONTENT TO KEEP THE **SECRET.**

IN THE COURSE OF THE EVENING I MET **MARGE** AND **EFFIE**, A LESBIAN COUPLE WHO TOLD ME THEY RAN A **NIGHTCLUB** LOCATED ON THE CITY'S OUTSKIRTS. IT WAS MAINLY FOR **BLACKS**, BUT ANY-BODY FRIENDLY WAS WELCOME.

YOU'LL HAFTA COME AN' **VISIT**, HONEY. WE **COOK** OUT THERE!

THERE AIN'T A **COLORED JAZZMAN** IN THE **WORLD** WHO'D **DARE** COME TO CLAYFIELD WITHOUT STOPPIN' OVER TO JAM AT **ALLEYSAX**.

ALL THE **DYKES** AN' **QUEENS** FROM THE RHOMBUS HAUL ASS OUT TO ALLEYSAX MOST SATURDAYS AFTER **CLOSIN' TIME**. I'M ASSUMIN' YOU'RE FAMILIAR WITH THE **RHOMBUS..?**

ACTUALLY, I'M **NOT**.

ACTUALLY, I DAMN WELL WAS!

EVEN US **HICK** TEENAGERS HAD BEEN HIP ENOUGH TO FIGURE OUT THAT THE RHOMBUS WAS A BAR THAT **'FAIRIES'** LIKED TO GO TO.

I HAD NEVER BEEN INSIDE OF IT **MYSELF**, THOUGH.

WHAT?!-ARE YOU **STRAIGHT??** I THOUGHT YOU CAME HERE WITH SAMMY NOONE!

NO, NO, MARGE! YOU GOT IT ALL **WRONG**! HE CAME WITH THAT SKINNY **REDHEADED GIRL** NAMED **MAVIS**.

WELL, HELL—EVEN **SO**, YOU OUGHTA CHECK OUT THE RHOMBUS AT LEAST **ONCE**!

IT AIN'T **ALLEYSAX**, BUT IT'S THE **ONLY** DOWNTOWN NIGHTSPOT THAT'S GOT ANY **LOOSENESS** TO IT.

EFFIE'S SISTER **MABEL** PLAYS THE **PIANO** THERE ON SATURDAY NIGHTS.

MABEL'S **STRAIGHT**, BUT THEY DECLARED HER AN **HONORARY DYKE**! THE QUEENS ALL **LOVE** HER 'CAUSE SHE **MOTHER-HENS** 'EM TO DEATH.

ANOTHER CONVERSATION FROM THAT PARTY THAT STICKS IN MY MIND WAS WITH A COUPLE NAMED **MACON** AND **ROSE** –PLUS A DUDE NAMED **RAEBURN**, WHO MADE ME **NERVOUS**.

NAW-w-w, I DON'T **HATE** THE CHOPPER. I **LOVE** THE CHOPPER!

SUTTON CHOPPER'S DONE **BETTER** BY US THAN THE MANGY CUSS'LL EVER **KNOW**!

AIN'T **SO**, ROSE?

YOU **KNOW** IT IS, MACON!

IF THE CHOPPER'S **BULB** WASN'T SO FUCKIN' **DIM**, HE WOULDN'T GET US NEARLY AS MUCH GOOD **PRESS** AS HE DOES.

THE **TOUGHER** THAT OL' **BUZZARD** TRIES TO BE, THE BETTER HE MAKES **US** LOOK.

WHEN WE WANNA PLAN A **DEMONSTRATION**, WE JUS' SIT AROUN' AN' SAY, 'NOW WHAT CAN WE DO **THIS** WEEK TO MAKE THE CHOPPER PUT ON HIS **KLAN DANCE** FOR THE TV NEWS?'

Y'DON'T HAFTA DO MUCH MORE'N SLIDE YOUR **FEET** OUTA BED IN THE MORNIN' TO GET **THAT** CRACKER TO PLAY THE FOOL!

MACON, JUS' HOW MANY OF OUR **TRADE SECRETS**'RE YOU **TWO GIVIN' AWAY** TO THIS **STRANGER** HERE?

AN' HOW MANY OF J. EDGAR HOOVER'S **BUGS** D'YA THINK HE'S WEARIN' UNDER THAT **SHIRT**?

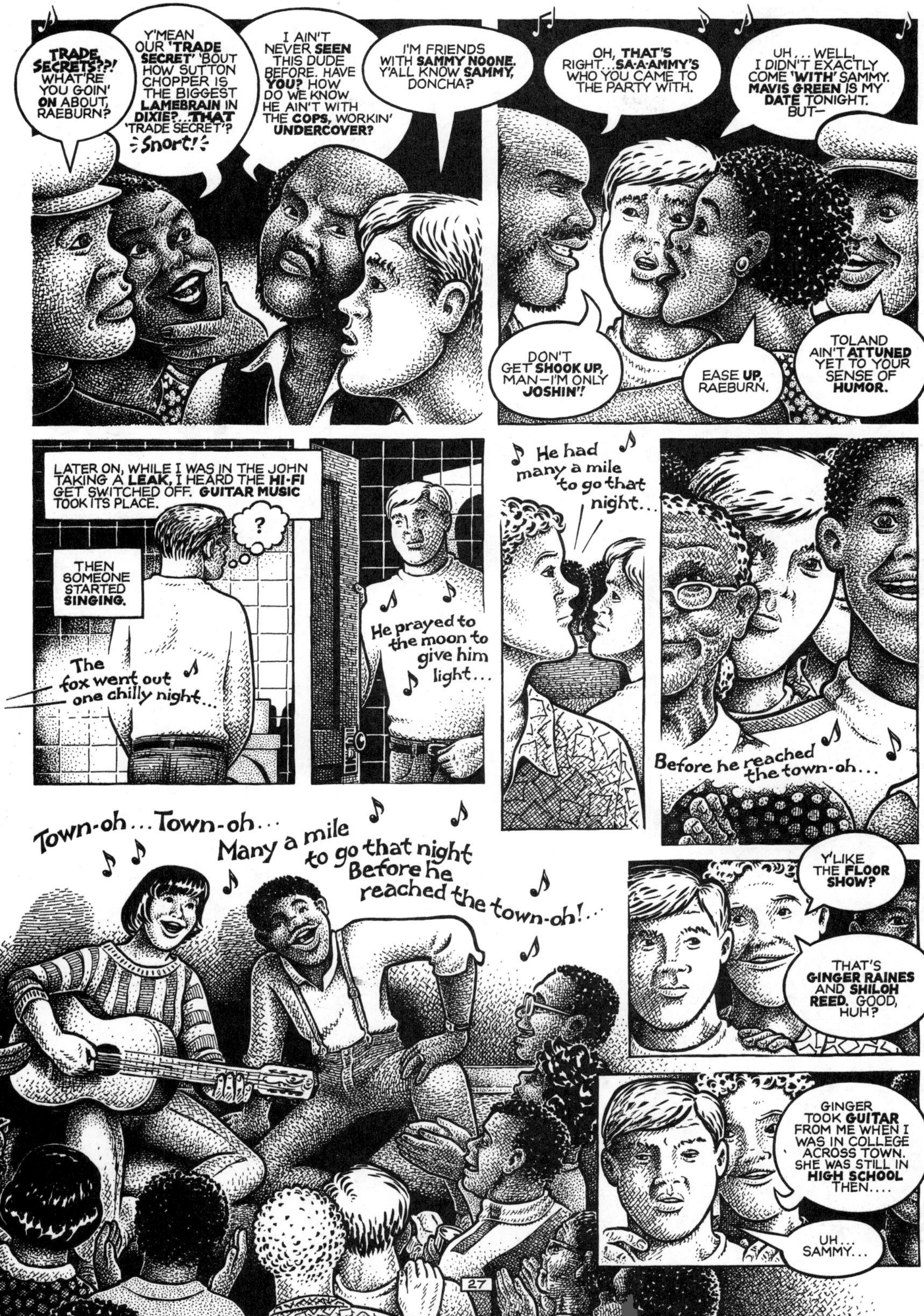
TRADE SECRETS??! WHAT'RE YOU GOIN' ON ABOUT, RAEBURN?
Y'MEAN OUR 'TRADE SECRET' 'BOUT HOW SUTTON CHOPPER IS THE BIGGEST LAMEBRAIN IN DIXIE?...THAT 'TRADE SECRET'?
Snort!
I AIN'T NEVER SEEN THIS DUDE BEFORE. HAVE YOU? HOW DO WE KNOW HE AIN'T WITH THE COPS, WORKIN' UNDERCOVER?
I'M FRIENDS WITH SAMMY NOONE. Y'ALL KNOW SAMMY, DONCHA?
OH, THAT'S RIGHT...SA-A-AMMY'S WHO YOU CAME TO THE PARTY WITH.
UH... WELL, I DIDN'T EXACTLY COME 'WITH' SAMMY. MAVIS GREEN IS MY DATE TONIGHT. BUT—
DON'T GET SHOOK UP, MAN—I'M ONLY JOSHIN'!
EASE UP, RAEBURN.
TOLAND AIN'T ATTUNED YET TO YOUR SENSE OF HUMOR.
LATER ON, WHILE I WAS IN THE JOHN TAKING A LEAK, I HEARD THE HI-FI GET SWITCHED OFF. GUITAR MUSIC TOOK ITS PLACE.
?
THEN SOMEONE STARTED SINGING.
The fox went out one chilly night...
He prayed to the moon to give him light...
He had many a mile to go that night...
Before he reached the town-oh...
Town-oh... Town-oh...
Many a mile to go that night
Before he reached the town-oh!...
Y'LIKE THE FLOOR SHOW?
THAT'S GINGER RAINES AND SHILOH REED. GOOD, HUH?
GINGER TOOK GUITAR FROM ME WHEN I WAS IN COLLEGE ACROSS TOWN. SHE WAS STILL IN HIGH SCHOOL THEN....
UH... SAMMY...

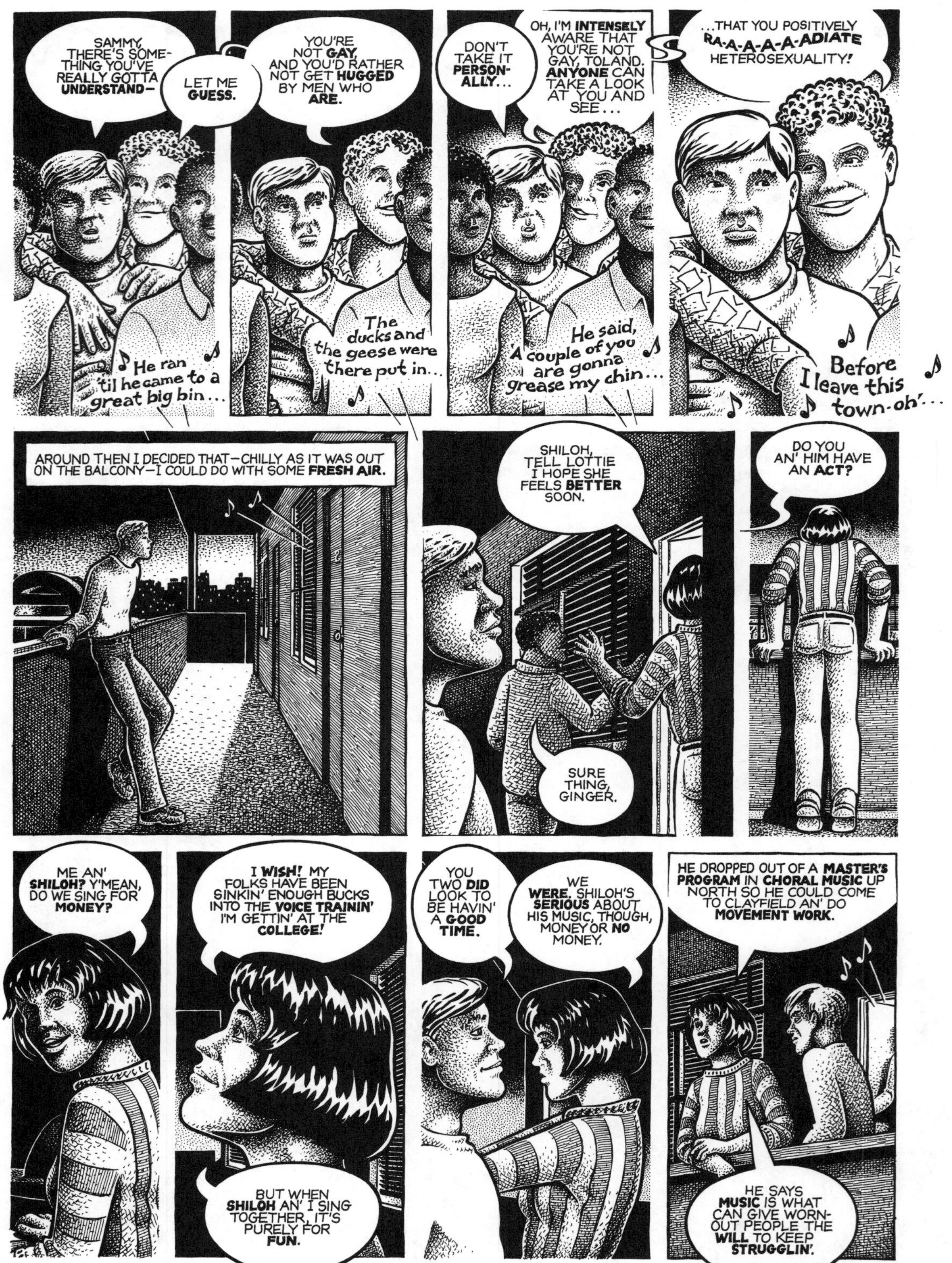
SAMMY, THERE'S SOME-THING YOU'VE REALLY GOTTA UNDERSTAND—
LET ME GUESS.
YOU'RE NOT GAY, AND YOU'D RATHER NOT GET HUGGED BY MEN WHO ARE.
DON'T TAKE IT PERSON-ALLY...
OH, I'M INTENSELY AWARE THAT YOU'RE NOT GAY, TOLAND. ANYONE CAN TAKE A LOOK AT YOU AND SEE...
...THAT YOU POSITIVELY RA-A-A-A-A-ADIATE HETEROSEXUALITY!
He ran 'til he came to a great big bin...
The ducks and the geese were there put in...
He said, A couple of you are gonna grease my chin...
Before I leave this town-oh'...
AROUND THEN I DECIDED THAT—CHILLY AS IT WAS OUT ON THE BALCONY—I COULD DO WITH SOME FRESH AIR.
SHILOH, TELL LOTTIE I HOPE SHE FEELS BETTER SOON.
SURE THING, GINGER.
DO YOU AN' HIM HAVE AN ACT?
ME AN' SHILOH? Y'MEAN, DO WE SING FOR MONEY?
I WISH! MY FOLKS HAVE BEEN SINKIN' ENOUGH BUCKS INTO THE VOICE TRAININ' I'M GETTIN' AT THE COLLEGE!
BUT WHEN SHILOH AN' I SING TOGETHER, IT'S PURELY FOR FUN.
YOU TWO DID LOOK TO BE HAVIN' A GOOD TIME.
WE WERE. SHILOH'S SERIOUS ABOUT HIS MUSIC, THOUGH, MONEY OR NO MONEY.
HE DROPPED OUT OF A MASTER'S PROGRAM IN CHORAL MUSIC UP NORTH SO HE COULD COME TO CLAYFIELD AN' DO MOVEMENT WORK.
HE SAYS MUSIC IS WHAT CAN GIVE WORN-OUT PEOPLE THE WILL TO KEEP STRUGGLIN'.

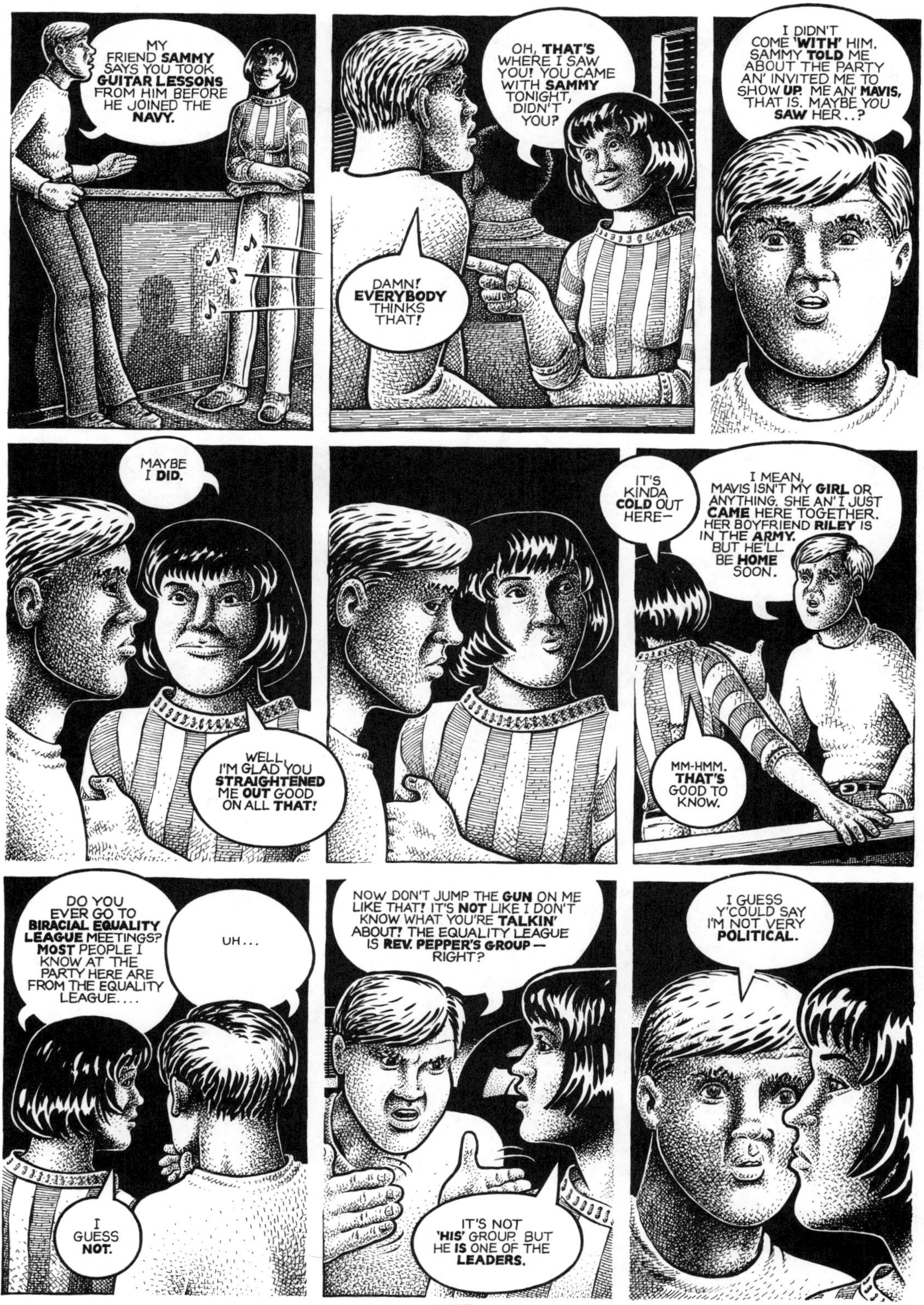
MY FRIEND SAMMY SAYS YOU TOOK GUITAR LESSONS FROM HIM BEFORE HE JOINED THE NAVY.
OH, THAT'S WHERE I SAW YOU! YOU CAME WITH SAMMY TONIGHT, DIDN'T YOU?
DAMN! EVERYBODY THINKS THAT!
I DIDN'T COME 'WITH' HIM. SAMMY TOLD ME ABOUT THE PARTY AN' INVITED ME TO SHOW UP. ME AN' MAVIS, THAT IS. MAYBE YOU SAW HER..?
MAYBE I DID.
WELL, I'M GLAD YOU STRAIGHTENED ME OUT GOOD ON ALL THAT!
IT'S KINDA COLD OUT HERE–
I MEAN, MAVIS ISN'T MY GIRL OR ANYTHING. SHE AN' I JUST CAME HERE TOGETHER. HER BOYFRIEND RILEY IS IN THE ARMY. BUT HE'LL BE HOME SOON.
MM-HMM. THAT'S GOOD TO KNOW.
DO YOU EVER GO TO BIRACIAL EQUALITY LEAGUE MEETINGS? MOST PEOPLE I KNOW AT THE PARTY HERE ARE FROM THE EQUALITY LEAGUE....
UH...
I GUESS NOT.
NOW DON'T JUMP THE GUN ON ME LIKE THAT! IT'S NOT LIKE I DON'T KNOW WHAT YOU'RE TALKIN' ABOUT! THE EQUALITY LEAGUE IS REV. PEPPER'S GROUP — RIGHT?
IT'S NOT 'HIS' GROUP. BUT HE IS ONE OF THE LEADERS.
I GUESS Y'COULD SAY I'M NOT VERY POLITICAL.

NOT TO **PUT DOWN** THE EQUALITY LEAGUE OR ANYTHING...

...BUT THESE **MARCHES** AN' **DEMONSTRATIONS** COME **ONE** ON TOP OF THE **OTHER** FOR MONTHS ON END —AND WHAT REALLY GETS **ACCOMPLISHED?**

PEOPLE ARE JUST AS **SCREWED UP** AN' **HATEFUL** TO EACH OTHER AS THEY'VE **EVER** BEEN, AS FAR AS I CAN TELL.

OH. WELL, MAYBE WE OUGHT TO STOP **DOIN'** IT, THEN.

WE CAN LEAVE THINGS THE WAY THEY **ARE** AN' PUT OUR ENERGIES INTO SOME- THIN' **USEFUL.**

I'LL BRING THAT UP AT THE NEXT **MEETING.**

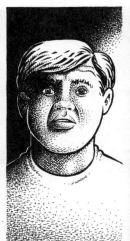

I'M **SLEEPY,** TOLAND, CAN YOU TAKE ME **HOME?**

I'LL BE READY IN JUST A **MINUTE,** MAVIS.

EXCUSE ME. I DON'T MEAN TO BE A **NUISANCE—**

—BUT IF YOU'RE NOT EVEN GONNA **ARGUE** WITH ME, WHAT'S THE POINT IN MY BOTHERIN' TO SAY SOMETHIN' **ASININE?**

Chapter **5**

When you wake, you will find...

...All the pretty little horses...

MAYBE YOU'D HAVE TO HAVE SEEN GINGER FOR THE FIRST TIME THE WAY **I** DID — MAKING **MUSIC** FOR THAT CROWD AT THE **MELODY MOTEL** — TO UNDERSTAND WHAT LED ME TO **SEIZE** ON HER THE WAY I DID, AND WHAT LED **HER** TO GET TANGLED UP IN MY **DREAMS** OF **STRAIGHTNESS.**

SHE STRUCK ME **RIGHT OFF** AS BEING IN A WHOLE DIFFERENT **CATEGORY** FROM THE GIRLS STONY AND I HAD BEEN PARTYING WITH AT THE **DIXIE STAR.**

IT'S TRUE I'D FUCKED UP OUR FIRST ENCOUNTER, BUT I STARTED **MENDING FENCES** A DAY OR TWO LATER BY OFFERING TO DRIVE HER TO SOME **AUDITIONS** THAT SAMMY TOLD ME WERE COMING UP SOON IN **ATLANTA.**

THAT'S REAL **NICE,** SWEET-HEART!

SOME HOTSHOT HAD DECIDED THERE WAS A **FORTUNE** TO BE MADE BY SETTING UP A CHAIN OF SOUTHERN **COFFEE-HOUSES.** HE FIGURED HE COULD ORDER **ESPRESSO** IN **BULK** AND HIRE SOME **FOLK-SINGERS** FOR **ATMOSPHERE.**

HE SAID HIS **FIRST** IDEA HAD BEEN TO SCARE UP SOME **BEATNIK** POETS, BUT HIS WIFE INSISTED **BOHEMIANS** WERE **NEVER** GONNA CATCH ON BELOW THE **MASON-DIXON LINE.**

GINGER DIDN'T GET **HIRED,** BUT THE GUY TOLD HER SHE WAS GOOD AND SHOULD GET BACK IN **TOUCH** ONCE THE CHAIN HAD GOTTEN **LAUNCHED.**

CALL IT A PREMONITION, BUT I THINK I'M GONNA BE KNOWN SOMEDAY AS THE MAN THAT **DISCOVERED** GINGER RAINES!

THAT WAS THE LAST WE EVER HEARD ABOUT **HIM** OR HIS **COFFEEHOUSES.**

DRIVING HOME AFTERWARDS, GINGER WAS SO **HYPER** THERE WAS NO **DEALING** WITH HER.

WHAT DO YOU **MEAN,** I SANG WELL?! I WAS **AWFUL!**

DIDN'T YOU HEAR ME GO **FLAT** IN '**DEEP RIVER**'?

YOU **WEREN'T** AWFUL! YOU SOUNDED **GREAT!** YOU COULD PASS FOR **PROFESSIONAL** ALREADY!

IT REALLY ISN'T **HELPFUL** TO HAVE PEOPLE PATRONIZE ME. BE **HONEST.**

HOW COME YOU'RE ASSUMIN' I'M **DISHONEST?** MAYBE I'M JUST **TIN-EARED!** CAN'T YOU MAKE **ALLOWANCES** FOR THE **AFFLICTED?**

SHE GOT **CALMER** ALONG THE WAY, THANK GOD, AND WE WERE FINDING THINGS TO **LAUGH** ABOUT BY THE TIME I GOT HER BACK TO **WESTHILLS COLLEGE**, WHERE SHE WAS A **MUSIC** MAJOR.

...AN' ONCE I NOTICED THAT HIS **LIPS** LOOKED LIKE A **FRIED PIE**, I COULDN'T LOOK AT 'IM WITHOUT **CRACKIN' UP!**

YEAH, IT'S **HARD** TO **TALK POLITELY** TO A GUY WHILE YOU'RE TRYIN' TO STOP YOUR **EYES** FROM DRIFTIN' DOWN TO THE **BOTTOM** OF HIS **FACE!**

ALTHOUGH I'D BEEN THROUGH THE **GATES** ONLY A COUPLE OF TIMES IN MY LIFE, THE **WESTHILLS CAMPUS** WAS A FAMILIAR **SIGHT** TO ME, SINCE I DROVE PAST IT EVERY MORNING ON MY WAY TO **WORK.**

PARK FURTHER UP THE **STREET.** WE NEED TO SLIP IN BY A **BACK PATH.**

A **CAMPUS COP!** DUCK **DOWN!**

WE HAD TO SKULK AROUND LIKE **SNEAK THIEVES** ONCE WE GOT NEAR HER **DORM,** IT BEING AGAINST THE COLLEGE'S **RULES** FOR HER TO BE COMING IN SO **LATE.**

IT WAS ONLY THE **GIRLS** WHO HAD A CURFEW, OF COURSE. **BOYS** COULD ROAM FREE AT ALL **HOURS.**

THE GIRLS HAD SYSTEMS FOR BEATING THE CURFEW WHEN THEY **NEEDED** TO, THOUGH.

ALL CLEAR. LET'S GO.

UH... RIGHT.

Y'SEE THAT **WINDOW?** THAT'S MY **DORM ROOM.**

I JUST GRAB A **PEBBLE** AND...

PING!

I FELT PRETTY **CHEERY,** WALKING BACK TO THE CAR.

THAT'S THE SIGNAL FOR **SHARON** TO COME DOWN AN' LET ME IN THE **BACK DOOR.**

SHARON'S MY **ROOMMATE.**

GOTCHA.

THANKS FOR TAKIN' ME TO THE **AUDITION.** IT WAS ALMOST **FUN.**

THANKS FOR THE DORM **PHONE NUMBER.** I'LL **CALL.**

32

GINGER WASN'T A HUNDRED PERCENT **EASY** TO GET **ALONG** WITH, BUT THE DAY HAD LEFT ME OPTIMISTIC THAT I HAD A **FAIR CHANCE** OF GETTING SOMETHING **GOING** WITH HER.

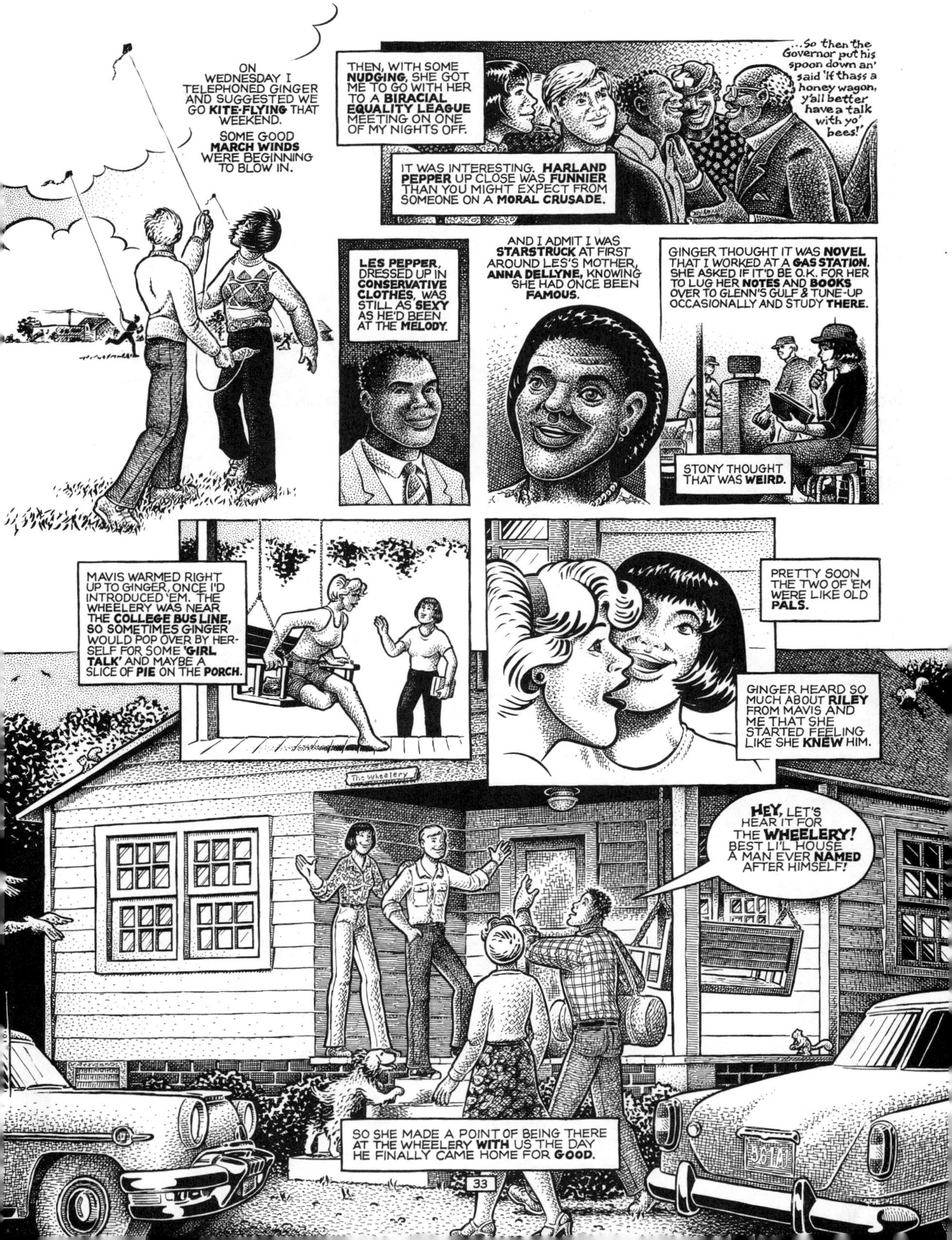

ON WEDNESDAY I TELEPHONED GINGER AND SUGGESTED WE GO KITE-FLYING THAT WEEKEND.
SOME GOOD MARCH WINDS WERE BEGINNING TO BLOW IN.
THEN, WITH SOME NUDGING, SHE GOT ME TO GO WITH HER TO A BIRACIAL EQUALITY LEAGUE MEETING ON ONE OF MY NIGHTS OFF.
...So then the Governor put his spoon down an' said 'If thass a honey wagon, y'all better have a talk with yo' bees!'
IT WAS INTERESTING. HARLAND PEPPER UP CLOSE WAS FUNNIER THAN YOU MIGHT EXPECT FROM SOMEONE ON A MORAL CRUSADE.
LES PEPPER, DRESSED UP IN CONSERVATIVE CLOTHES, WAS STILL AS SEXY AS HE'D BEEN AT THE MELODY.
AND I ADMIT I WAS STARSTRUCK AT FIRST AROUND LES'S MOTHER, ANNA DELLYNE, KNOWING SHE HAD ONCE BEEN FAMOUS.
GINGER THOUGHT IT WAS NOVEL THAT I WORKED AT A GAS STATION. SHE ASKED IF IT'D BE O.K. FOR HER TO LUG HER NOTES AND BOOKS OVER TO GLENN'S GULF & TUNE-UP OCCASIONALLY AND STUDY THERE.
STONY THOUGHT THAT WAS WEIRD.
MAVIS WARMED RIGHT UP TO GINGER, ONCE I'D INTRODUCED 'EM. THE WHEELERY WAS NEAR THE COLLEGE BUS LINE, SO SOMETIMES GINGER WOULD POP OVER BY HER-SELF FOR SOME 'GIRL TALK' AND MAYBE A SLICE OF PIE ON THE PORCH.
PRETTY SOON THE TWO OF 'EM WERE LIKE OLD PALS.
GINGER HEARD SO MUCH ABOUT RILEY FROM MAVIS AND ME THAT SHE STARTED FEELING LIKE SHE KNEW HIM.
The Wheelery
HEY, LET'S HEAR IT FOR THE WHEELERY! BEST LI'L HOUSE A MAN EVER NAMED AFTER HIMSELF!
SO SHE MADE A POINT OF BEING THERE AT THE WHEELERY WITH US THE DAY HE FINALLY CAME HOME FOR GOOD.

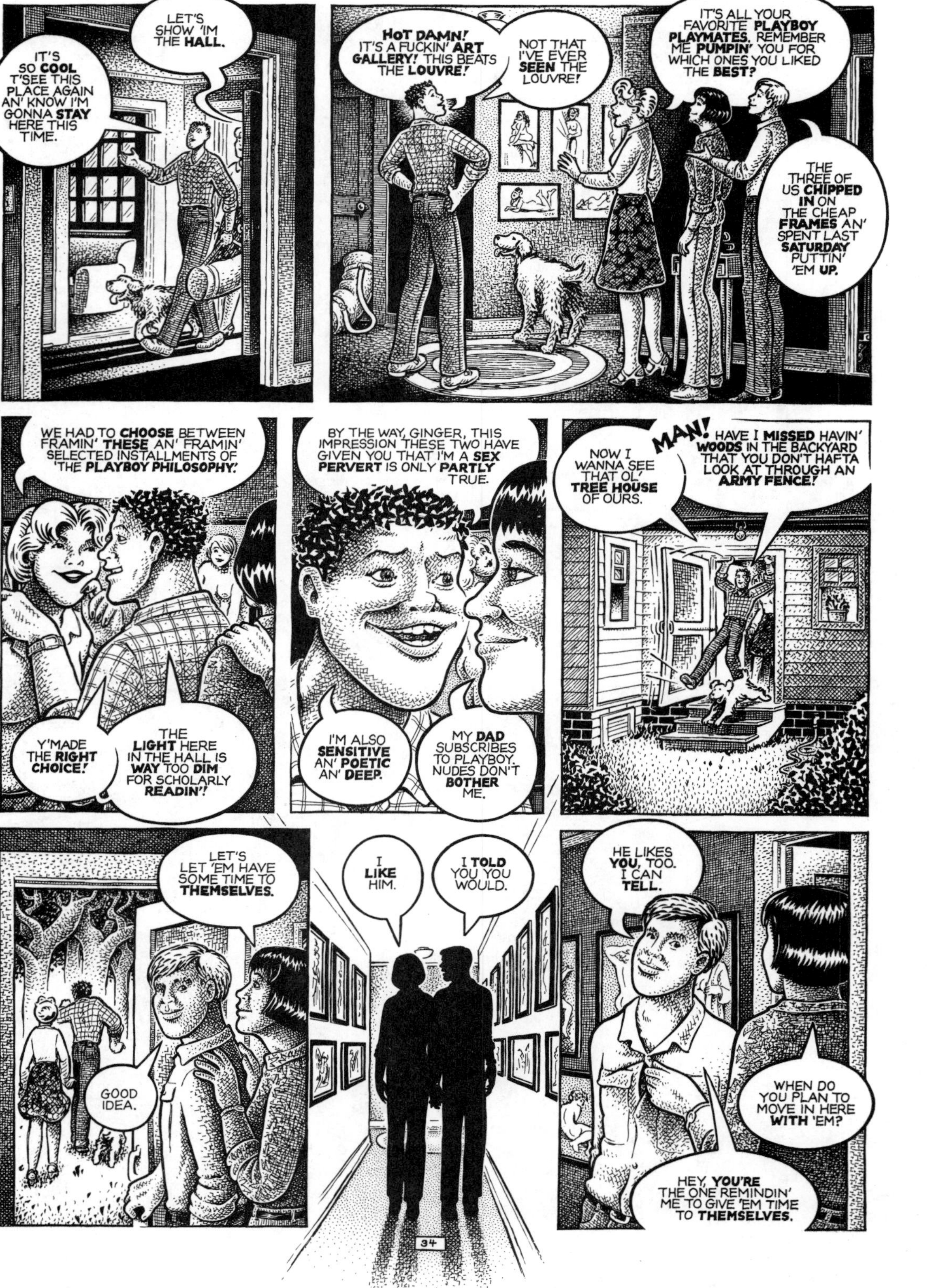
IT'S SO COOL T'SEE THIS PLACE AGAIN AN' KNOW I'M GONNA STAY HERE THIS TIME.
LET'S SHOW 'IM THE HALL.
HOT DAMN! IT'S A FUCKIN' ART GALLERY! THIS BEATS THE LOUVRE!
NOT THAT I'VE EVER SEEN THE LOUVRE!
IT'S ALL YOUR FAVORITE PLAYBOY PLAYMATES. REMEMBER ME PUMPIN' YOU FOR WHICH ONES YOU LIKED THE BEST?
THE THREE OF US CHIPPED IN ON THE CHEAP FRAMES AN' SPENT LAST SATURDAY PUTTIN' 'EM UP.
WE HAD TO CHOOSE BETWEEN FRAMIN' THESE AN' FRAMIN' SELECTED INSTALLMENTS OF 'THE PLAYBOY PHILOSOPHY.'
Y'MADE THE RIGHT CHOICE!
THE LIGHT HERE IN THE HALL IS WAY TOO DIM FOR SCHOLARLY READIN'!
BY THE WAY, GINGER, THIS IMPRESSION THESE TWO HAVE GIVEN YOU THAT I'M A SEX PERVERT IS ONLY PARTLY TRUE.
I'M ALSO SENSITIVE AN' POETIC AN' DEEP.
MY DAD SUBSCRIBES TO PLAYBOY. NUDES DON'T BOTHER ME.
NOW I WANNA SEE THAT OL' TREE HOUSE OF OURS.
MAN! HAVE I MISSED HAVIN' WOODS IN THE BACKYARD THAT YOU DON'T HAFTA LOOK AT THROUGH AN ARMY FENCE!
LET'S LET 'EM HAVE SOME TIME TO THEMSELVES.
GOOD IDEA.
I LIKE HIM.
I TOLD YOU YOU WOULD.
HE LIKES YOU, TOO. I CAN TELL.
WHEN DO YOU PLAN TO MOVE IN HERE WITH 'EM?
HEY, YOU'RE THE ONE REMINDIN' ME TO GIVE 'EM TIME TO THEMSELVES.

SOON. I **HOPE**.

DO YOU THINK YOU'LL **ENJOY** SLEEPIN' IN A BEDROOM THAT DOESN'T COME WITH A **SISTER** AN' **BROTHER-IN-LAW** NEXT DOOR?

DEFINITELY.

I JUST NEED AN **ALL-CLEAR** FROM RILEY.

'**SPECIALLY** IF RILEY AN' GINGER'LL LET ME INVITE A CERTAIN **FRIEND** TO SLEEP OVER. . . .

A KISS **HERE**. AN INNUENDO **THERE**.

LOVE **BLOOMS**.

IF **INNUENDOES** COULD MAKE YOU **PREGNANT**, GINGER AND I WOULD'VE HAD A **HEFTY BROOD** BY THE TIME **SPRING** AND **RILEY** CAME BACK TO CLAYFIELD.

FORTUNATELY, INNUENDO IS A **LOW-RISK ACTIVITY** IN A **LOT** OF WAYS.

MY KISSES WEREN'T **INSINCERE**. BY THEN I HAD WORKED UP A **BONA FIDE**, AUTHENTIC **CRUSH** ON GINGER.

I TOOK ITS MEASURE EVERY MORNING AND WATERED IT LIKE A **BEGONIA**.

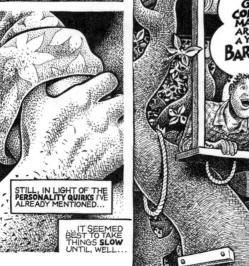

STILL, IN LIGHT OF THE **PERSONALITY QUIRKS** I'VE ALREADY MENTIONED . . .

. . . IT SEEMED **BEST** TO TAKE THINGS **SLOW** UNTIL, WELL . . .

TOLAND! GINGER! COME ON **OUT**! **MAVIS** AN' ME ARE GETTIN' A YEN FOR **BARBEQUE**!

IT'S GREAT TO **SEE** YA AGAIN, OL' BUDDY. AN' GINGER— HEY, **WELCOME** TO THE **GANG**!

IT'S GREAT TO SEE **YOU**, TOO, RILEY. WELCOME **HOME**!

. . . JUST **UNTIL**!

35

SAMMY HAD NEVER **MET** RILEY BUT HE WORKED UP A **WELCOME-HOME TREAT** FOR HIM **ANYWAY.**

HE PROMISED THAT, IF WE'D JUST GO TO THE MORNING SERVICE AT TRINITY AND LISTEN TO HIM **PLAY**, WE WOULDN'T BE **SORRY.**

I **RESISTED**, BUT GINGER AND MAVIS WERE SO **TAKEN** WITH THE IDEA THAT I **GAVE IN.**

THEN — **SURPRISE!** MY **SISTER**, WHO HAD GOTTEN WIND FROM MAVIS THAT HER WAYWARD **BROTHER** HAD BEEN ROPED INTO SITTING STILL FOR A **CHURCH SERVICE**, DECIDED THAT SHE AND ORLEY SHOULD **CRASH** THE **PARTY.**

WELL, LOOK WHO'S **HERE!**

SAMMY PLAYED **BEAUTIFULLY**—EVEN MY 'TIN EARS' COULD TELL **THAT!** MEANWHILE, HIS PRIVATE JOKE TO **US** WAS THROWING IN FRAGMENTS OF **BOB DYLAN SONGS** DURING SUCH MUSICAL INTERLUDES AS ALLOWED FOR **IMPROVISATION.**

IT WASN'T AS **WICKED** AS IT SOUNDS IN THE **TELLING**, SINCE SAMMY WAS A MASTER AT **CHURCHING UP** HIS **ARRANGEMENTS.**

IS IT MY **IMAGINATION** OR AM I HEARIN' 'DON'T THINK TWICE'...?

AS FAR AS **MOST** OF THE WORSHIPERS WERE CONCERNED HE COULD JUST AS WELL HAVE BEEN PLAYING SOME **BACH GOLDEN OLDIE!**

ORLEY **NEVER** CAUGHT ON.

WHAT TH' **DINGDONG** ARE ALL YOU PEOPLE **GIGGLIN'** ABOUT?

I'LL TELL YOU **LATER.**

I GUESS YOU'D HAVE TO CLASSIFY IT ALL AS **BAD BEHAVIOR.** STILL, THE CHURCH CAME OUT **AHEAD** ON THE DEAL, SINCE I ENDED UP PUTTING MORE IN THE **COLLECTION PLATE** THAN I PROBABLY WOULD HAVE IF I HADN'T FELT **GUILTY.**

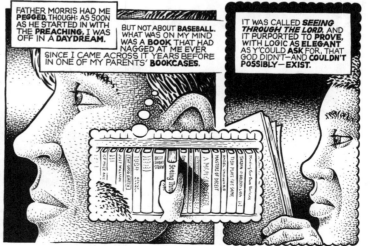

FATHER MORRIS HAD ME **PEGGED**, THOUGH: AS SOON AS HE STARTED IN WITH THE **PREACHING**, I WAS OFF IN A **DAYDREAM.**

BUT NOT ABOUT **BASEBALL.** WHAT WAS ON MY MIND WAS A **BOOK** THAT HAD NAGGED AT ME EVER SINCE I CAME ACROSS IT YEARS BEFORE IN ONE OF MY PARENTS' **BOOKCASES.**

IT WAS CALLED **SEEING THROUGH THE LORD**, AND IT PURPORTED TO **PROVE**, WITH LOGIC AS **ELEGANT** AS Y'COULD **ASK** FOR, THAT GOD DIDN'T—AND **COULDN'T** POSSIBLY—EXIST.

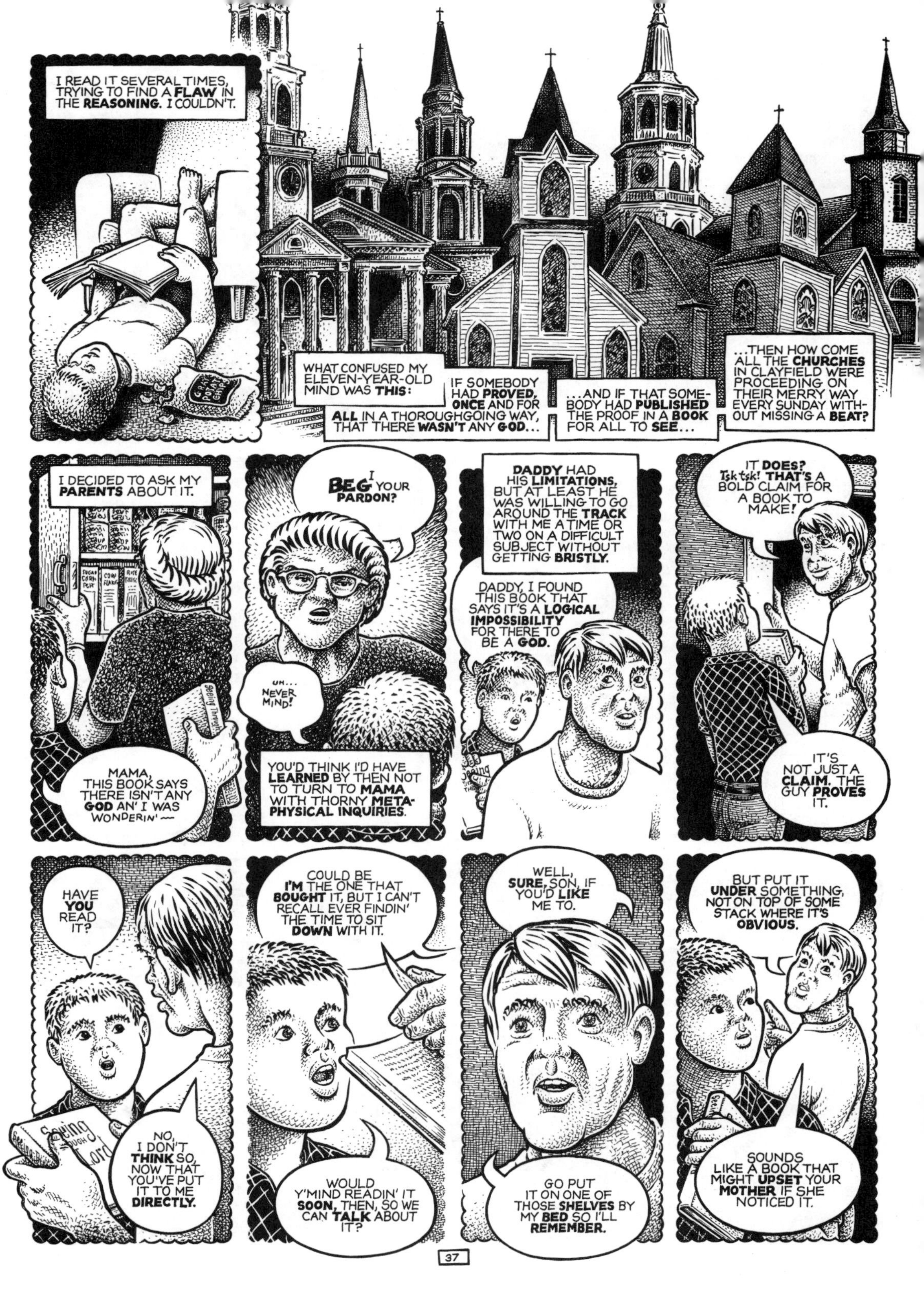

I READ IT SEVERAL TIMES, TRYING TO FIND A **FLAW** IN THE **REASONING**. I COULDN'T.
WHAT CONFUSED MY ELEVEN-YEAR-OLD MIND WAS **THIS**:
IF SOMEBODY HAD **PROVED, ONCE** AND FOR **ALL** IN A THOROUGHGOING WAY, THAT THERE **WASN'T** ANY **GOD**...
...AND IF THAT SOMEBODY HAD **PUBLISHED** THE PROOF IN A **BOOK** FOR ALL TO **SEE**...
...THEN HOW COME ALL THE **CHURCHES** IN CLAYFIELD WERE PROCEEDING ON THEIR MERRY WAY EVERY SUNDAY WITHOUT MISSING A **BEAT**?
I DECIDED TO ASK MY **PARENTS** ABOUT IT.
MAMA, THIS BOOK SAYS THERE ISN'T ANY **GOD** AN' I WAS WONDERIN' —
BEG I YOUR **PARDON?**
UH... NEVER MIND!
YOU'D THINK I'D HAVE **LEARNED** BY THEN NOT TO TURN TO **MAMA** WITH THORNY **META-PHYSICAL INQUIRIES**.
DADDY HAD HIS **LIMITATIONS**, BUT AT LEAST HE WAS WILLING TO GO AROUND THE **TRACK** WITH ME A TIME OR TWO ON A DIFFICULT SUBJECT WITHOUT GETTING **BRISTLY**.
DADDY, I FOUND THIS BOOK THAT SAYS IT'S A **LOGICAL IMPOSSIBILITY** FOR THERE TO BE A **GOD**.
IT **DOES?** Tsk tsk! **THAT'S** A BOLD CLAIM FOR A BOOK TO MAKE!
IT'S NOT JUST A **CLAIM**. THE GUY **PROVES** IT.
HAVE **YOU** READ IT?
NO, I DON'T **THINK** SO, NOW THAT YOU'VE PUT IT TO ME **DIRECTLY**.
COULD BE **I'M** THE ONE THAT **BOUGHT** IT, BUT I CAN'T RECALL EVER FINDIN' THE TIME TO SIT **DOWN** WITH IT.
WOULD Y'MIND READIN' IT **SOON**, THEN, SO WE CAN **TALK** ABOUT IT?
WELL, **SURE**, SON, IF YOU'D **LIKE** ME TO.
GO PUT IT ON ONE OF THOSE **SHELVES** BY MY **BED** SO I'LL **REMEMBER**.
BUT PUT IT **UNDER** SOMETHING, NOT ON TOP OF SOME STACK WHERE IT'S **OBVIOUS**.
SOUNDS LIKE A BOOK THAT MIGHT **UPSET** YOUR **MOTHER** IF SHE NOTICED IT.

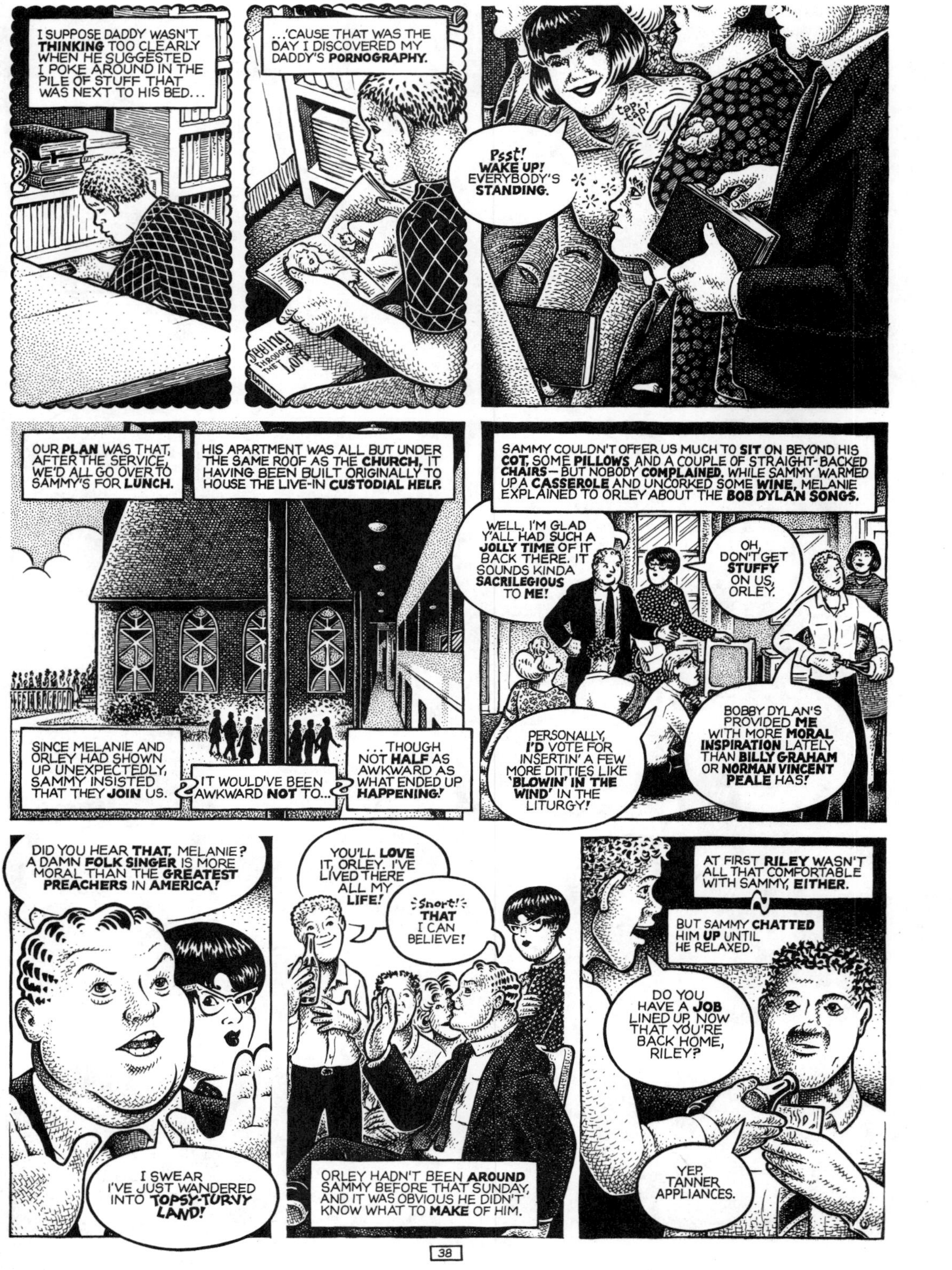

I SUPPOSE DADDY WASN'T THINKING TOO CLEARLY WHEN HE SUGGESTED I POKE AROUND IN THE PILE OF STUFF THAT WAS NEXT TO HIS BED...
...'CAUSE THAT WAS THE DAY I DISCOVERED MY DADDY'S PORNOGRAPHY.
Psst! WAKE UP! EVERYBODY'S STANDING.
tap tap
OUR PLAN WAS THAT, AFTER THE SERVICE, WE'D ALL GO OVER TO SAMMY'S FOR LUNCH.
HIS APARTMENT WAS ALL BUT UNDER THE SAME ROOF AS THE CHURCH, IT HAVING BEEN BUILT ORIGINALLY TO HOUSE THE LIVE-IN CUSTODIAL HELP.
SINCE MELANIE AND ORLEY HAD SHOWN UP UNEXPECTEDLY, SAMMY INSISTED THAT THEY JOIN US.
IT WOULD'VE BEEN AWKWARD NOT TO...
...THOUGH NOT HALF AS AWKWARD AS WHAT ENDED UP HAPPENING!
SAMMY COULDN'T OFFER US MUCH TO SIT ON BEYOND HIS COT, SOME PILLOWS AND A COUPLE OF STRAIGHT-BACKED CHAIRS—BUT NOBODY COMPLAINED. WHILE SAMMY WARMED UP A CASSEROLE AND UNCORKED SOME WINE, MELANIE EXPLAINED TO ORLEY ABOUT THE BOB DYLAN SONGS.
WELL, I'M GLAD Y'ALL HAD SUCH A JOLLY TIME OF IT BACK THERE. IT SOUNDS KINDA SACRILEGIOUS TO ME!
OH, DON'T GET STUFFY ON US, ORLEY.
PERSONALLY, I'D VOTE FOR INSERTIN' A FEW MORE DITTIES LIKE 'BLOWIN' IN THE WIND' IN THE LITURGY!
BOBBY DYLAN'S PROVIDED ME WITH MORE MORAL INSPIRATION LATELY THAN BILLY GRAHAM OR NORMAN VINCENT PEALE HAS!
DID YOU HEAR THAT, MELANIE? A DAMN FOLK SINGER IS MORE MORAL THAN THE GREATEST PREACHERS IN AMERICA!
I SWEAR I'VE JUST WANDERED INTO TOPSY-TURVY LAND!
YOU'LL LOVE IT, ORLEY. I'VE LIVED THERE ALL MY LIFE!
Snort! THAT I CAN BELIEVE!
ORLEY HADN'T BEEN AROUND SAMMY BEFORE THAT SUNDAY, AND IT WAS OBVIOUS HE DIDN'T KNOW WHAT TO MAKE OF HIM.
AT FIRST RILEY WASN'T ALL THAT COMFORTABLE WITH SAMMY, EITHER.
BUT SAMMY CHATTED HIM UP UNTIL HE RELAXED.
DO YOU HAVE A JOB LINED UP NOW THAT YOU'RE BACK HOME, RILEY?
YEP. TANNER APPLIANCES.

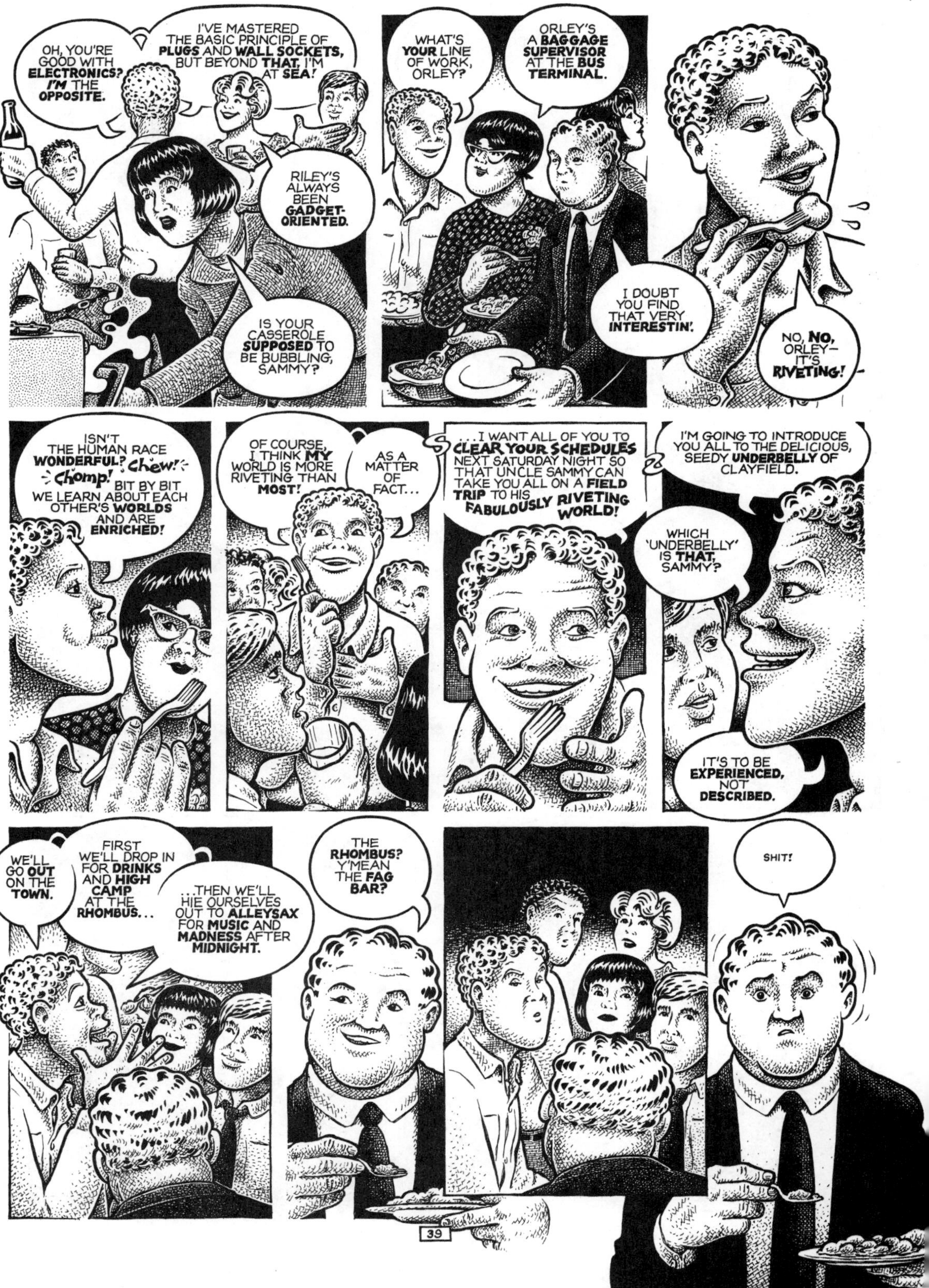

OH, YOU'RE GOOD WITH ELECTRONICS? I'M THE OPPOSITE.
I'VE MASTERED THE BASIC PRINCIPLE OF PLUGS AND WALL SOCKETS, BUT BEYOND THAT, I'M AT SEA!
RILEY'S ALWAYS BEEN GADGET-ORIENTED.
IS YOUR CASSEROLE SUPPOSED TO BE BUBBLING, SAMMY?
WHAT'S YOUR LINE OF WORK, ORLEY?
ORLEY'S A BAGGAGE SUPERVISOR AT THE BUS TERMINAL.
I DOUBT YOU FIND THAT VERY INTERESTIN'.
NO, NO, ORLEY— IT'S RIVETING!
ISN'T THE HUMAN RACE WONDERFUL? Chew! Chomp! BIT BY BIT WE LEARN ABOUT EACH OTHER'S WORLDS AND ARE ENRICHED!
OF COURSE, I THINK MY WORLD IS MORE RIVETING THAN MOST!
AS A MATTER OF FACT...
...I WANT ALL OF YOU TO CLEAR YOUR SCHEDULES NEXT SATURDAY NIGHT SO THAT UNCLE SAMMY CAN TAKE YOU ALL ON A FIELD TRIP TO HIS FABULOUSLY RIVETING WORLD!
I'M GOING TO INTRODUCE YOU ALL TO THE DELICIOUS, SEEDY UNDERBELLY OF CLAYFIELD.
WHICH 'UNDERBELLY' IS THAT, SAMMY?
IT'S TO BE EXPERIENCED, NOT DESCRIBED.
WE'LL GO OUT ON THE TOWN.
FIRST WE'LL DROP IN FOR DRINKS AND HIGH CAMP AT THE RHOMBUS...
...THEN WE'LL HIE OURSELVES OUT TO ALLEYSAX FOR MUSIC AND MADNESS AFTER MIDNIGHT.
THE RHOMBUS? Y'MEAN THE FAG BAR?
SHIT!

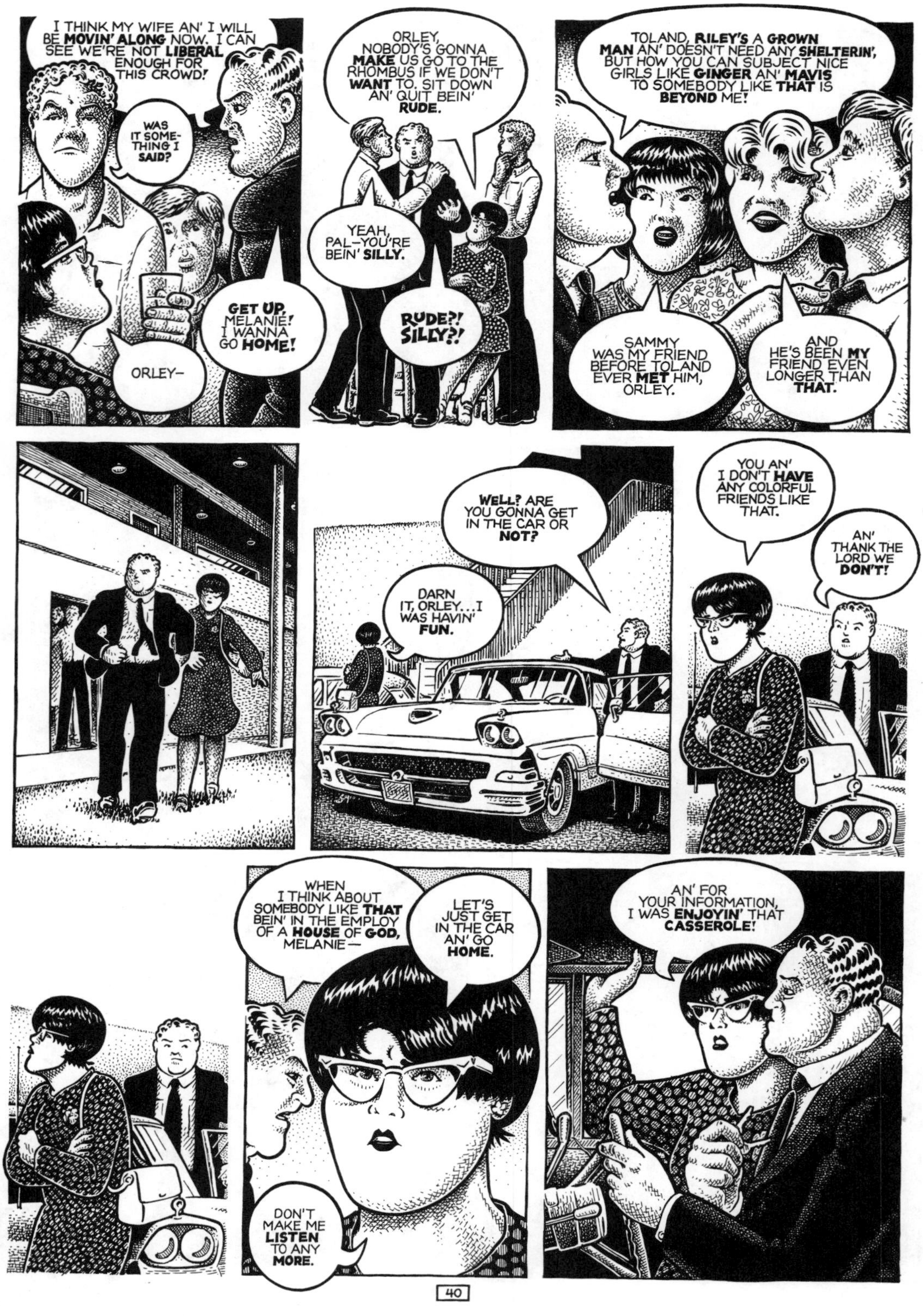

I THINK MY WIFE AN' I WILL BE MOVIN' ALONG NOW. I CAN SEE WE'RE NOT LIBERAL ENOUGH FOR THIS CROWD!
WAS IT SOMETHING I SAID?
GET UP, MELANIE! I WANNA GO HOME!
ORLEY—
ORLEY, NOBODY'S GONNA MAKE US GO TO THE RHOMBUS IF WE DON'T WANT TO. SIT DOWN AN' QUIT BEIN' RUDE.
YEAH, PAL—YOU'RE BEIN' SILLY.
RUDE?! SILLY?!
TOLAND, RILEY'S A GROWN MAN AN' DOESN'T NEED ANY SHELTERIN', BUT HOW YOU CAN SUBJECT NICE GIRLS LIKE GINGER AN' MAVIS TO SOMEBODY LIKE THAT IS BEYOND ME!
SAMMY WAS MY FRIEND BEFORE TOLAND EVER MET HIM, ORLEY.
AND HE'S BEEN MY FRIEND EVEN LONGER THAN THAT.
WELL? ARE YOU GONNA GET IN THE CAR OR NOT?
DARN IT, ORLEY...I WAS HAVIN' FUN.
YOU AN' I DON'T HAVE ANY COLORFUL FRIENDS LIKE THAT.
AN' THANK THE LORD WE DON'T!
WHEN I THINK ABOUT SOMEBODY LIKE THAT BEIN' IN THE EMPLOY OF A HOUSE OF GOD, MELANIE—
LET'S JUST GET IN THE CAR AN' GO HOME.
DON'T MAKE ME LISTEN TO ANY MORE.
AN' FOR YOUR INFORMATION, I WAS ENJOYIN' THAT CASSEROLE!

Chapter 6

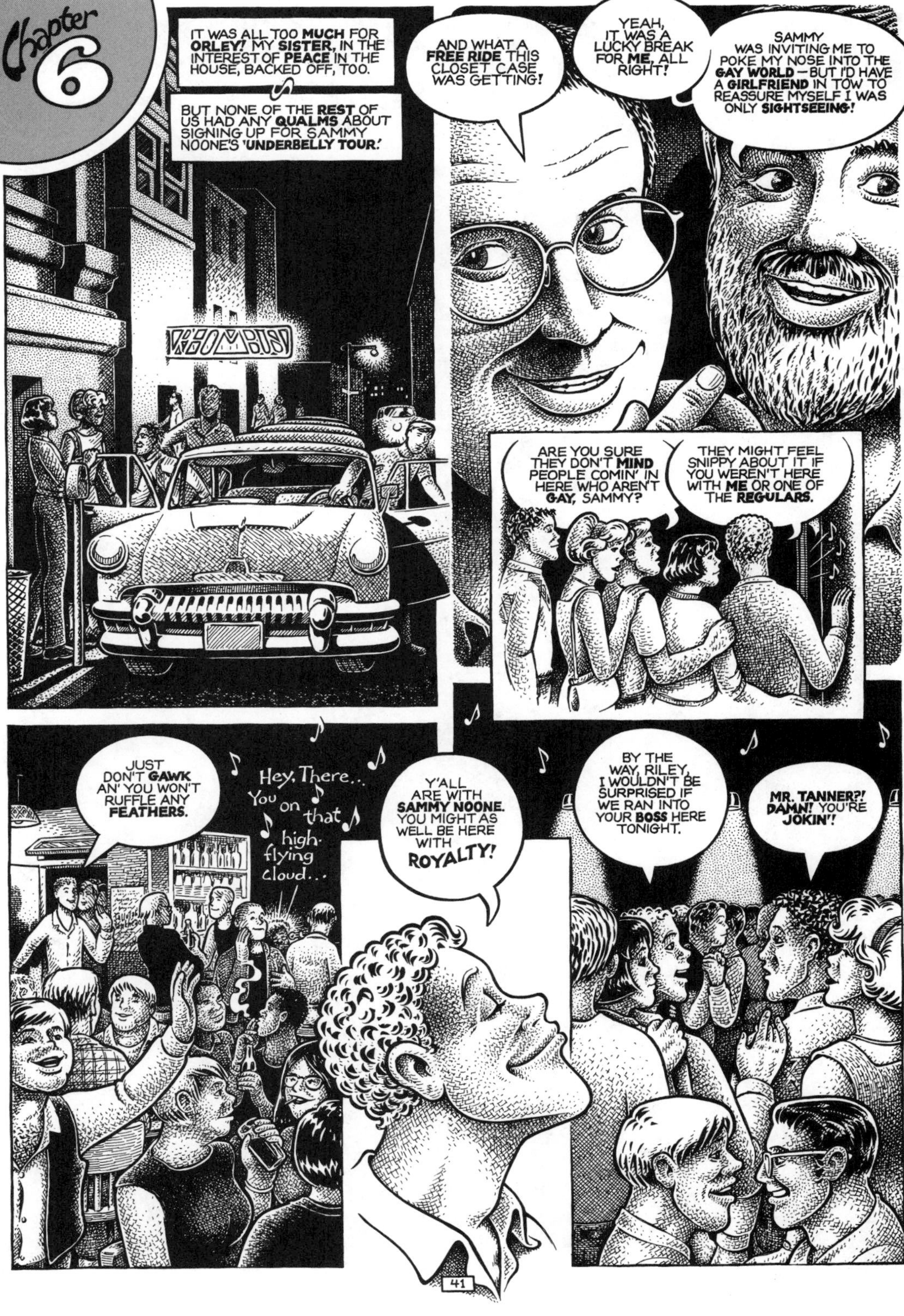

IT WAS ALL TOO MUCH FOR ORLEY! MY SISTER, IN THE INTEREST OF PEACE IN THE HOUSE, BACKED OFF, TOO.
BUT NONE OF THE REST OF US HAD ANY QUALMS ABOUT SIGNING UP FOR SAMMY NOONE'S 'UNDERBELLY TOUR.'
AND WHAT A FREE RIDE THIS CLOSET CASE WAS GETTING!
YEAH, IT WAS A LUCKY BREAK FOR ME, ALL RIGHT!
SAMMY WAS INVITING ME TO POKE MY NOSE INTO THE GAY WORLD — BUT I'D HAVE A GIRLFRIEND IN TOW TO REASSURE MYSELF I WAS ONLY SIGHTSEEING!
ARE YOU SURE THEY DON'T MIND PEOPLE COMIN' IN HERE WHO AREN'T GAY, SAMMY?
THEY MIGHT FEEL SNIPPY ABOUT IT IF YOU WEREN'T HERE WITH ME OR ONE OF THE REGULARS.
JUST DON'T GAWK AN' YOU WON'T RUFFLE ANY FEATHERS.
Hey, There.. You on that high-flying cloud...
Y'ALL ARE WITH SAMMY NOONE. YOU MIGHT AS WELL BE HERE WITH ROYALTY!
BY THE WAY, RILEY, I WOULDN'T BE SURPRISED IF WE RAN INTO YOUR BOSS HERE TONIGHT.
MR. TANNER?! DAMN! YOU'RE JOKIN'!

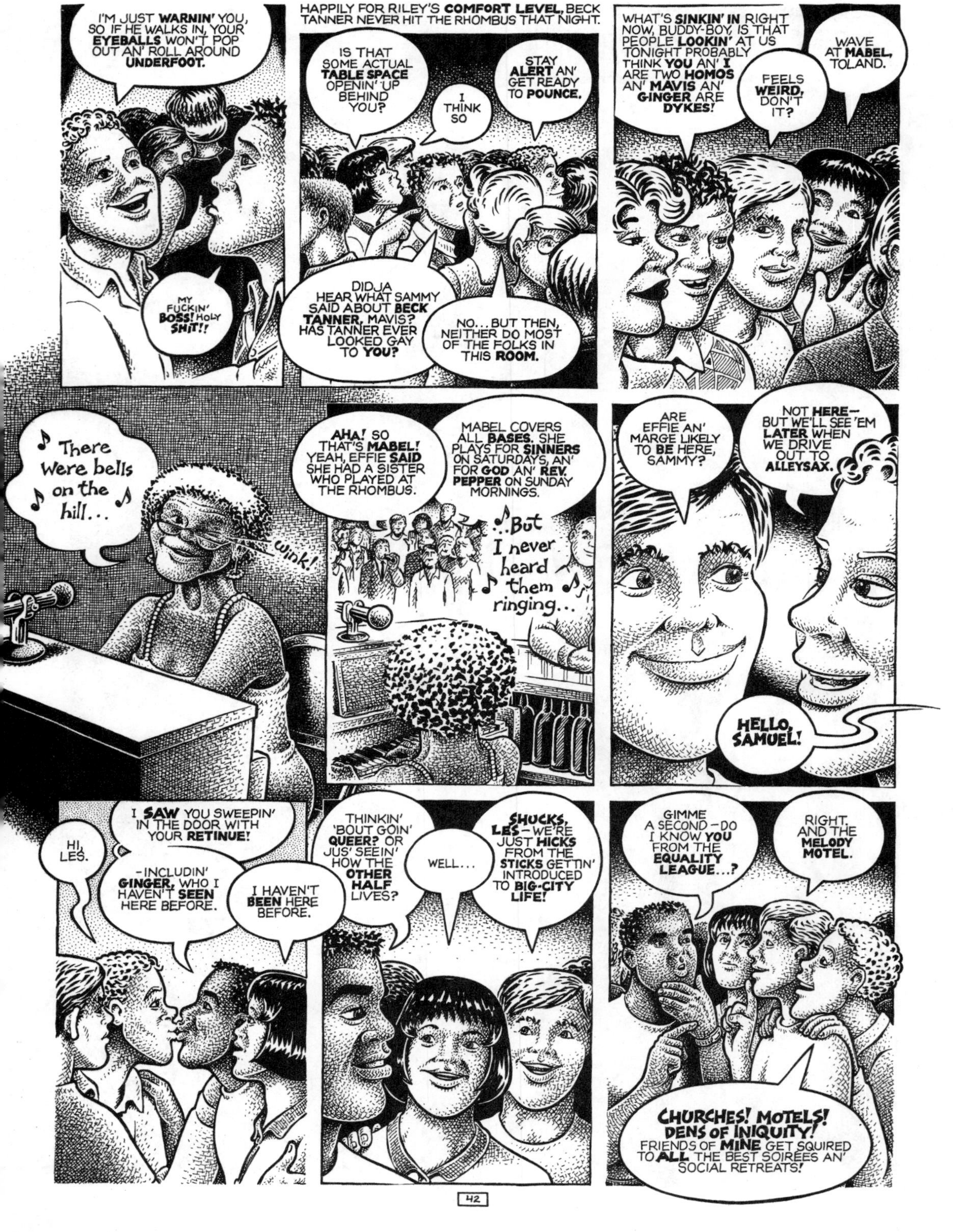

I'M JUST WARNIN' YOU, SO IF HE WALKS IN, YOUR EYEBALLS WON'T POP OUT AN' ROLL AROUND UNDERFOOT.
MY FUCKIN' BOSS! HOLY SHIT!!
HAPPILY FOR RILEY'S COMFORT LEVEL, BECK TANNER NEVER HIT THE RHOMBUS THAT NIGHT.
IS THAT SOME ACTUAL TABLE SPACE OPENIN' UP BEHIND YOU?
I THINK SO
STAY ALERT AN' GET READY TO POUNCE.
DIDJA HEAR WHAT SAMMY SAID ABOUT BECK TANNER, MAVIS? HAS TANNER EVER LOOKED GAY TO YOU?
NO... BUT THEN, NEITHER DO MOST OF THE FOLKS IN THIS ROOM.
WHAT'S SINKIN' IN RIGHT NOW, BUDDY-BOY, IS THAT PEOPLE LOOKIN' AT US TONIGHT PROBABLY THINK YOU AN' I ARE TWO HOMOS AN' MAVIS AN' GINGER ARE DYKES!
FEELS WEIRD, DON'T IT?
WAVE AT MABEL, TOLAND.
There were bells on the hill...
wink!
AHA! SO THAT'S MABEL! YEAH, EFFIE SAID SHE HAD A SISTER WHO PLAYED AT THE RHOMBUS.
MABEL COVERS ALL BASES. SHE PLAYS FOR SINNERS ON SATURDAYS, AN' FOR GOD AN' REV. PEPPER ON SUNDAY MORNINGS.
But I never heard them ringing...
ARE EFFIE AN' MARGE LIKELY TO BE HERE, SAMMY?
NOT HERE— BUT WE'LL SEE 'EM LATER WHEN WE DRIVE OUT TO ALLEYSAX.
HELLO, SAMUEL!
HI, LES.
I SAW YOU SWEEPIN' IN THE DOOR WITH YOUR RETINUE!
-INCLUDIN' GINGER, WHO I HAVEN'T SEEN HERE BEFORE.
I HAVEN'T BEEN HERE BEFORE.
THINKIN' 'BOUT GOIN' QUEER? OR JUS' SEEIN' HOW THE OTHER HALF LIVES?
WELL...
SHUCKS, LES—WE'RE JUST HICKS FROM THE STICKS GETTIN' INTRODUCED TO BIG-CITY LIFE!
GIMME A SECOND—DO I KNOW YOU FROM THE EQUALITY LEAGUE...?
RIGHT, AND THE MELODY MOTEL.
CHURCHES! MOTELS! DENS OF INIQUITY! FRIENDS OF MINE GET SQUIRED TO ALL THE BEST SOIRÉES AN' SOCIAL RETREATS!

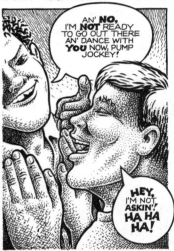

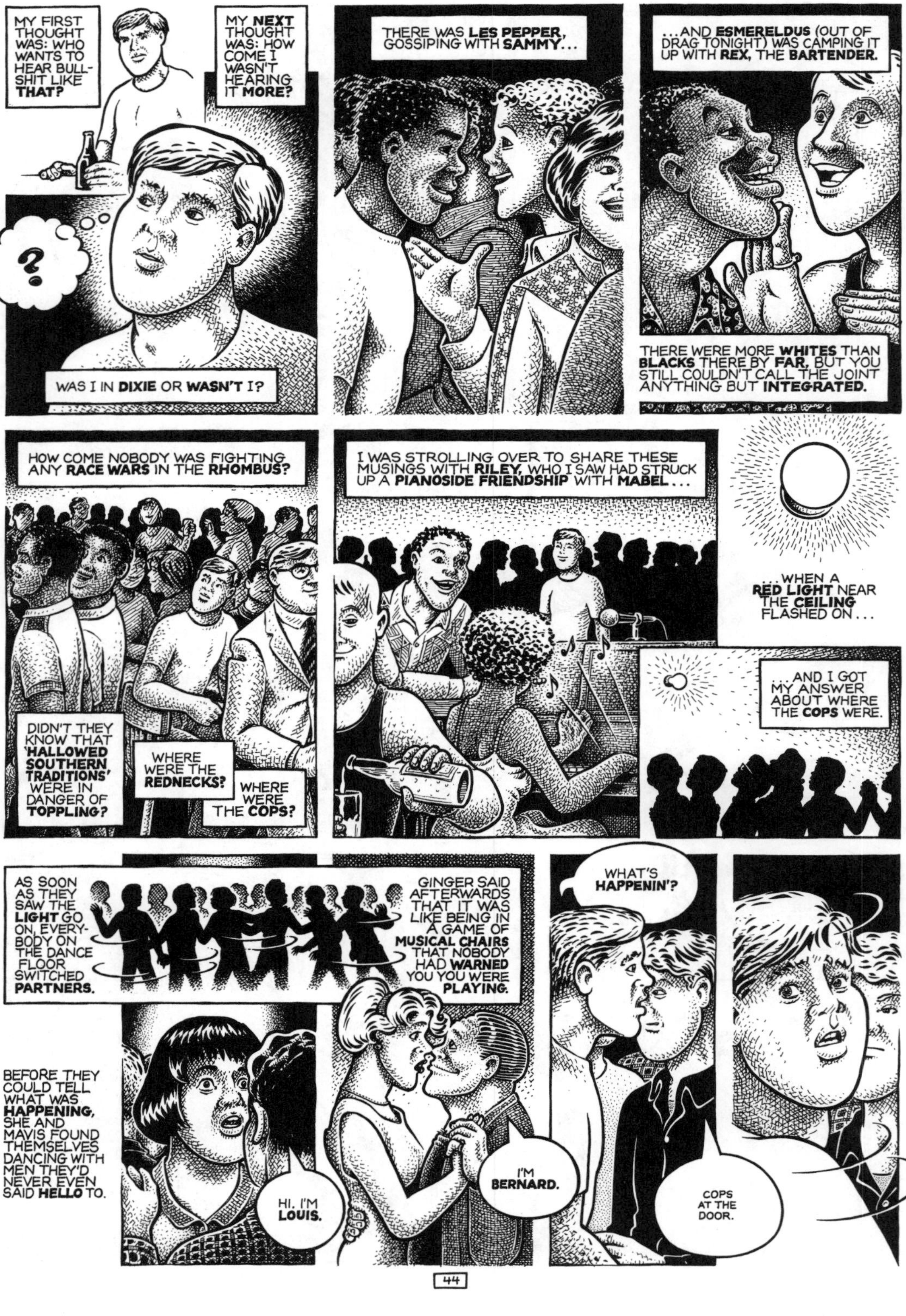

MY FIRST THOUGHT WAS: WHO WANTS TO HEAR BULL-SHIT LIKE THAT?
MY NEXT THOUGHT WAS: HOW COME I WASN'T HEARING IT MORE?
?
WAS I IN DIXIE OR WASN'T I?
THERE WAS LES PEPPER, GOSSIPING WITH SAMMY...
...AND ESMERELDUS (OUT OF DRAG TONIGHT) WAS CAMPING IT UP WITH REX, THE BARTENDER.
THERE WERE MORE WHITES THAN BLACKS THERE BY FAR, BUT YOU STILL COULDN'T CALL THE JOINT ANYTHING BUT INTEGRATED.
HOW COME NOBODY WAS FIGHTING ANY RACE WARS IN THE RHOMBUS?
DIDN'T THEY KNOW THAT 'HALLOWED SOUTHERN TRADITIONS' WERE IN DANGER OF TOPPLING?
WHERE WERE THE REDNECKS?
WHERE WERE THE COPS?
I WAS STROLLING OVER TO SHARE THESE MUSINGS WITH RILEY, WHO I SAW HAD STRUCK UP A PIANOSIDE FRIENDSHIP WITH MABEL...
...WHEN A RED LIGHT NEAR THE CEILING FLASHED ON...
...AND I GOT MY ANSWER ABOUT WHERE THE COPS WERE.
AS SOON AS THEY SAW THE LIGHT GO ON, EVERY-BODY ON THE DANCE FLOOR SWITCHED PARTNERS.
GINGER SAID AFTERWARDS THAT IT WAS LIKE BEING IN A GAME OF MUSICAL CHAIRS THAT NOBODY HAD WARNED YOU YOU WERE PLAYING.
BEFORE THEY COULD TELL WHAT WAS HAPPENING, SHE AND MAVIS FOUND THEMSELVES DANCING WITH MEN THEY'D NEVER EVEN SAID HELLO TO.
HI. I'M LOUIS.
I'M BERNARD.
WHAT'S HAPPENIN'?
COPS AT THE DOOR.

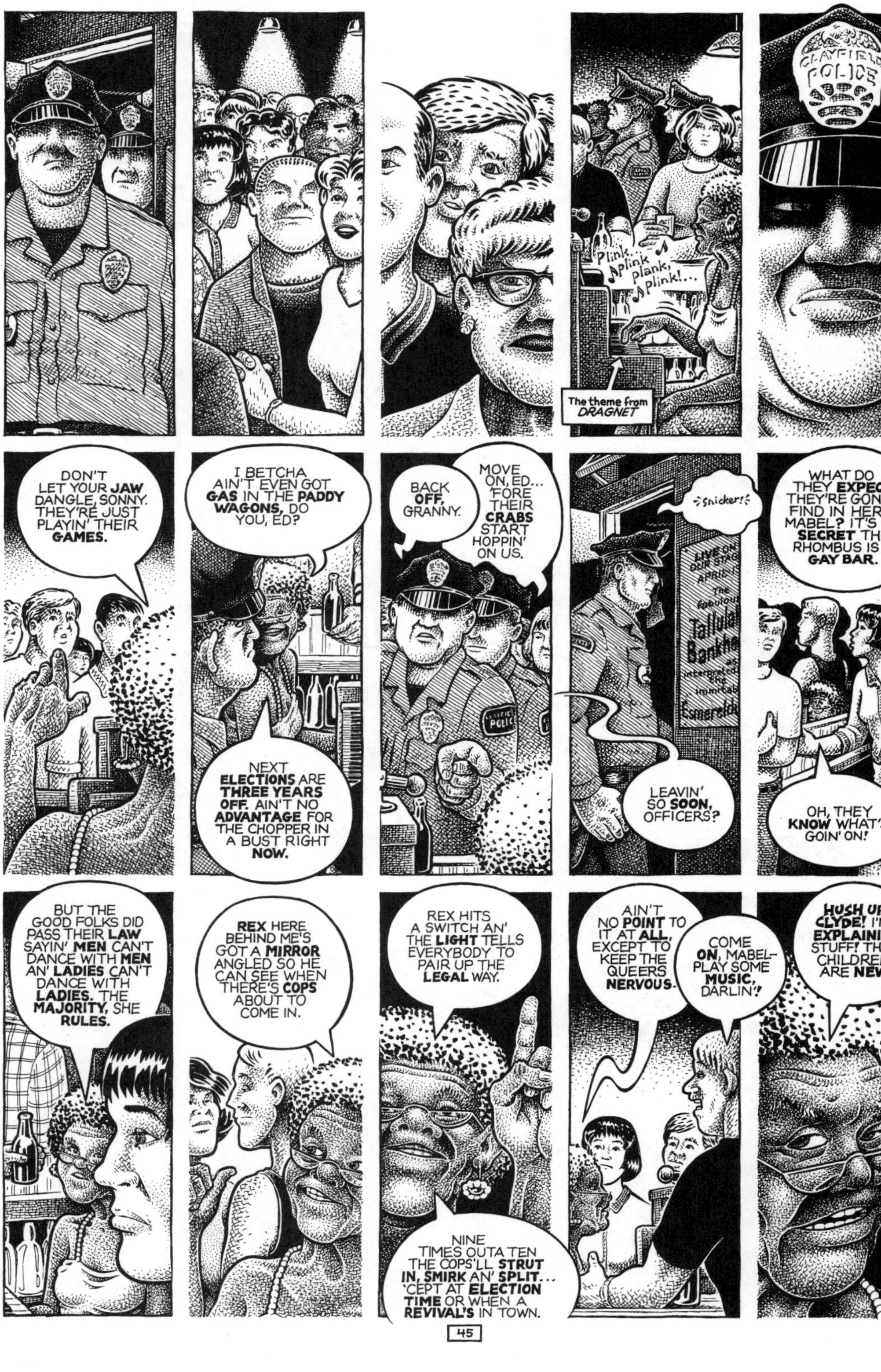
Plink, plink plank, plink!...
The theme from DRAGNET
DON'T LET YOUR JAW DANGLE, SONNY. THEY'RE JUST PLAYIN' THEIR GAMES.
I BETCHA AIN'T EVEN GOT GAS IN THE PADDY WAGONS, DO YOU, ED?
NEXT ELECTIONS ARE THREE YEARS OFF. AIN'T NO ADVANTAGE FOR THE CHOPPER IN A BUST RIGHT NOW.
MOVE ON, ED... 'FORE THEIR CRABS START HOPPIN' ON US.
BACK OFF, GRANNY.
Snicker!
LEAVIN' SO SOON, OFFICERS?
WHAT DO THEY EXPECT THEY'RE GONNA FIND IN HERE, MABEL? IT'S NO SECRET THE RHOMBUS IS A GAY BAR.
OH, THEY KNOW WHAT'S GOIN' ON!
BUT THE GOOD FOLKS DID PASS THEIR LAW SAYIN' MEN CAN'T DANCE WITH MEN AN' LADIES CAN'T DANCE WITH LADIES. THE MAJORITY, SHE RULES.
REX HERE BEHIND ME'S GOT A MIRROR ANGLED SO HE CAN SEE WHEN THERE'S COPS ABOUT TO COME IN.
REX HITS A SWITCH AN' THE LIGHT TELLS EVERYBODY TO PAIR UP THE LEGAL WAY.
NINE TIMES OUTA TEN THE COPS'LL STRUT IN, SMIRK AN' SPLIT... 'CEPT AT ELECTION TIME OR WHEN A REVIVAL'S IN TOWN.
AIN'T NO POINT TO IT AT ALL, EXCEPT TO KEEP THE QUEERS NERVOUS.
COME ON, MABEL-PLAY SOME MUSIC, DARLIN'!
HUSH UP, CLYDE! I'M EXPLAININ' STUFF! THESE CHILDREN ARE NEW!

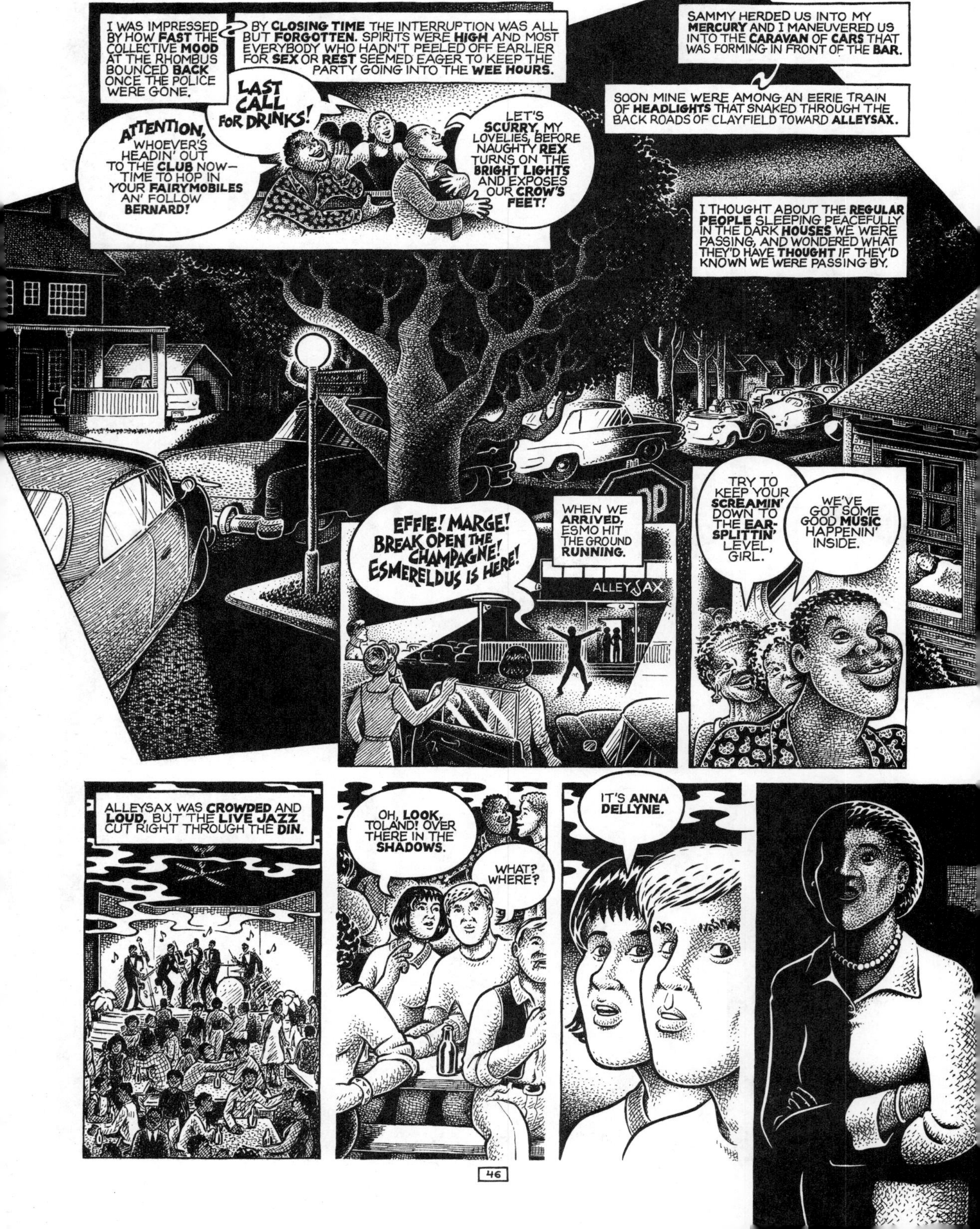
I WAS IMPRESSED BY HOW FAST THE COLLECTIVE MOOD AT THE RHOMBUS BOUNCED BACK ONCE THE POLICE WERE GONE.
BY CLOSING TIME THE INTERRUPTION WAS ALL BUT FORGOTTEN. SPIRITS WERE HIGH AND MOST EVERYBODY WHO HADN'T PEELED OFF EARLIER FOR SEX OR REST SEEMED EAGER TO KEEP THE PARTY GOING INTO THE WEE HOURS.
ATTENTION, WHOEVER'S HEADIN' OUT TO THE CLUB NOW— TIME TO HOP IN YOUR FAIRYMOBILES AN' FOLLOW BERNARD!
LAST CALL FOR DRINKS!
LET'S SCURRY, MY LOVELIES, BEFORE NAUGHTY REX TURNS ON THE BRIGHT LIGHTS AND EXPOSES OUR CROW'S FEET!
SAMMY HERDED US INTO MY MERCURY AND I MANEUVERED US INTO THE CARAVAN OF CARS THAT WAS FORMING IN FRONT OF THE BAR.
SOON MINE WERE AMONG AN EERIE TRAIN OF HEADLIGHTS THAT SNAKED THROUGH THE BACK ROADS OF CLAYFIELD TOWARD ALLEYSAX.
I THOUGHT ABOUT THE REGULAR PEOPLE SLEEPING PEACEFULLY IN THE DARK HOUSES WE WERE PASSING, AND WONDERED WHAT THEY'D HAVE THOUGHT IF THEY'D KNOWN WE WERE PASSING BY.
WHEN WE ARRIVED, ESMO HIT THE GROUND RUNNING.
EFFIE! MARGE! BREAK OPEN THE CHAMPAGNE! ESMERELDUS IS HERE!
ALLEYSAX
TRY TO KEEP YOUR SCREAMIN' DOWN TO THE EAR-SPLITTIN' LEVEL, GIRL.
WE'VE GOT SOME GOOD MUSIC HAPPENIN' INSIDE.
ALLEYSAX WAS CROWDED AND LOUD, BUT THE LIVE JAZZ CUT RIGHT THROUGH THE DIN.
OH, LOOK, TOLAND! OVER THERE IN THE SHADOWS.
WHAT? WHERE?
IT'S ANNA DELLYNE.

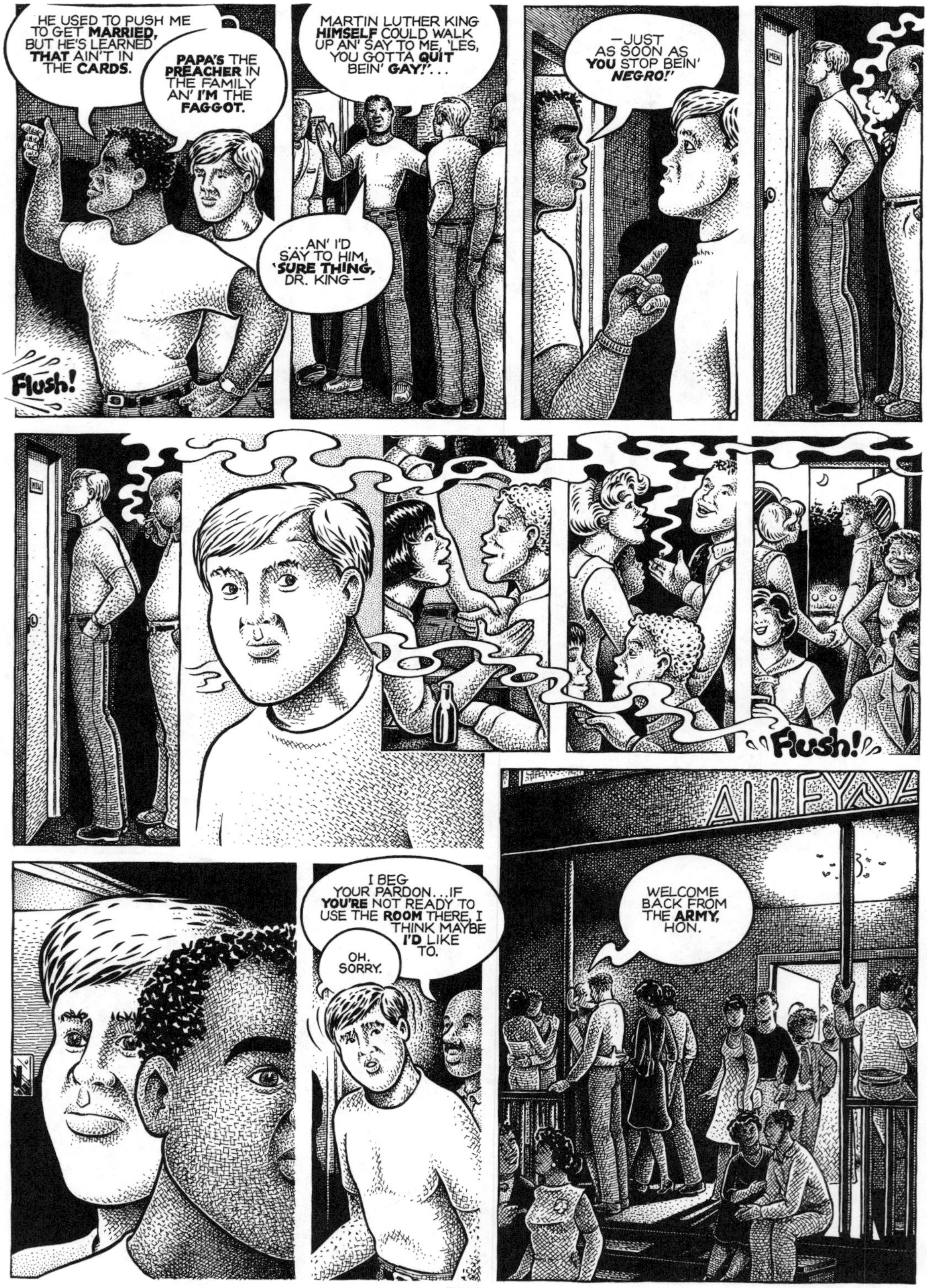

HE USED TO PUSH ME TO GET **MARRIED**, BUT HE'S LEARNED **THAT** AIN'T IN THE **CARDS**.
PAPA'S THE **PREACHER** IN THE FAMILY AN' **I'M** THE **FAGGOT**.
Flush!
MARTIN LUTHER KING **HIMSELF** COULD WALK UP AN' SAY TO ME, 'LES, YOU GOTTA **QUIT** BEIN' **GAY!**'...
...AN' I'D SAY TO HIM, '**SURE THING**, DR. KING—
—JUST AS SOON AS **YOU** STOP BEIN' ***NEGRO!***'
MEN
MEN
Flush!
I BEG YOUR PARDON...IF **YOU'RE** NOT READY TO USE THE **ROOM** THERE, I THINK MAYBE **I'D** LIKE TO.
OH. SORRY.
WELCOME BACK FROM THE **ARMY**, HON.

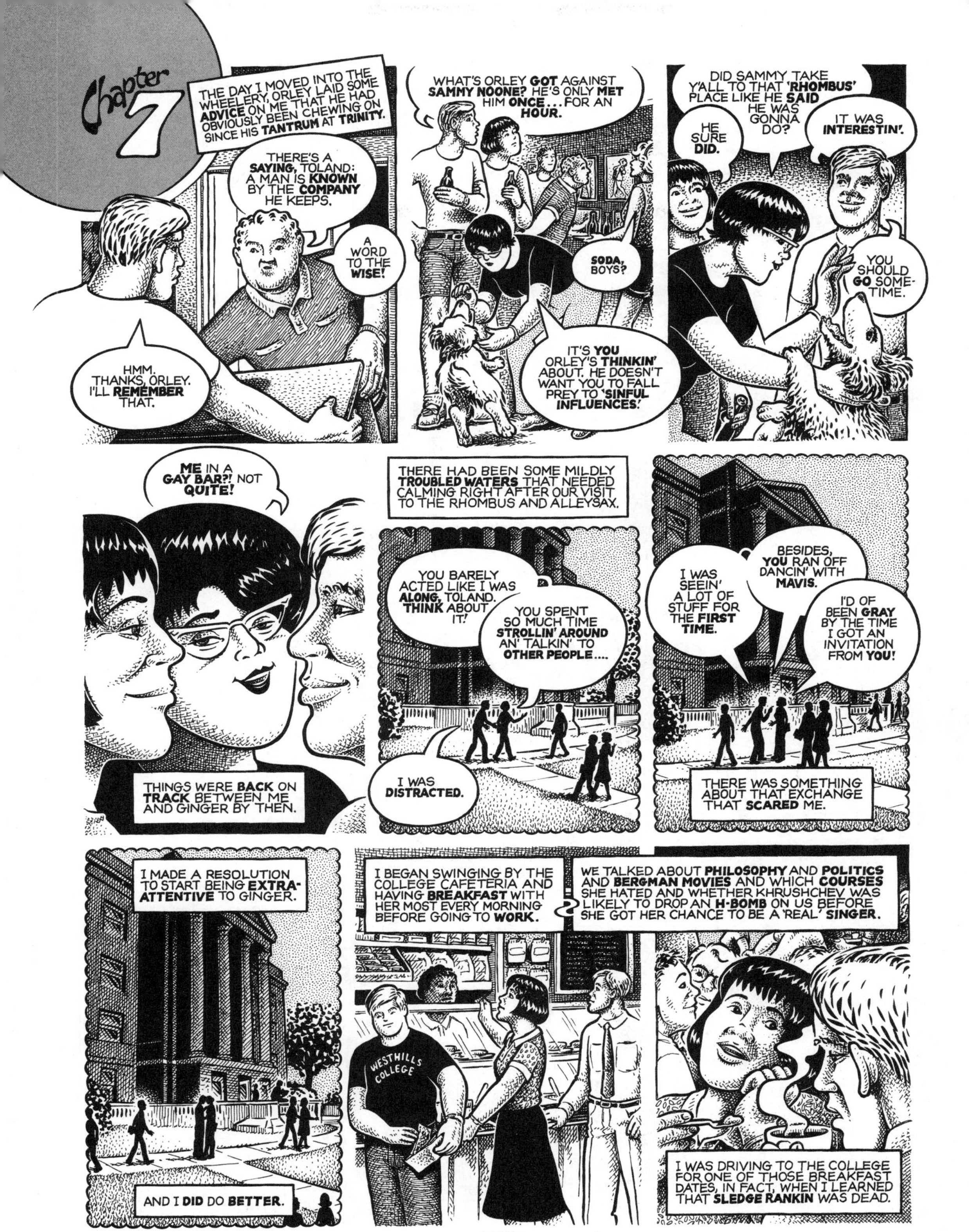
Chapter 7
THE DAY I MOVED INTO THE WHEELERY, ORLEY LAID SOME ADVICE ON ME THAT HE HAD OBVIOUSLY BEEN CHEWING ON SINCE HIS TANTRUM AT TRINITY.
THERE'S A SAYING, TOLAND: A MAN IS KNOWN BY THE COMPANY HE KEEPS.
A WORD TO THE WISE!
HMM. THANKS, ORLEY. I'LL REMEMBER THAT.
WHAT'S ORLEY GOT AGAINST SAMMY NOONE? HE'S ONLY MET HIM ONCE... FOR AN HOUR.
SODA, BOYS?
IT'S YOU ORLEY'S THINKIN' ABOUT. HE DOESN'T WANT YOU TO FALL PREY TO 'SINFUL INFLUENCES.'
DID SAMMY TAKE Y'ALL TO THAT 'RHOMBUS' PLACE LIKE HE SAID HE WAS GONNA DO?
HE SURE DID.
IT WAS INTERESTIN'.
YOU SHOULD GO SOME-TIME.
ME IN A GAY BAR?! NOT QUITE!
THINGS WERE BACK ON TRACK BETWEEN ME AND GINGER BY THEN.
THERE HAD BEEN SOME MILDLY TROUBLED WATERS THAT NEEDED CALMING RIGHT AFTER OUR VISIT TO THE RHOMBUS AND ALLEYSAX.
YOU BARELY ACTED LIKE I WAS ALONG, TOLAND. THINK ABOUT IT!
YOU SPENT SO MUCH TIME STROLLIN' AROUND AN' TALKIN' TO OTHER PEOPLE....
I WAS DISTRACTED.
I WAS SEEIN' A LOT OF STUFF FOR THE FIRST TIME.
BESIDES, YOU RAN OFF DANCIN' WITH MAVIS.
I'D OF BEEN GRAY BY THE TIME I GOT AN INVITATION FROM YOU!
THERE WAS SOMETHING ABOUT THAT EXCHANGE THAT SCARED ME.
I MADE A RESOLUTION TO START BEING EXTRA-ATTENTIVE TO GINGER.
AND I DID DO BETTER.
I BEGAN SWINGING BY THE COLLEGE CAFETERIA AND HAVING BREAKFAST WITH HER MOST EVERY MORNING BEFORE GOING TO WORK.
WE TALKED ABOUT PHILOSOPHY AND POLITICS AND BERGMAN MOVIES AND WHICH COURSES SHE HATED AND WHETHER KHRUSHCHEV WAS LIKELY TO DROP AN H-BOMB ON US BEFORE SHE GOT HER CHANCE TO BE A 'REAL' SINGER.
WESTHILLS COLLEGE
I WAS DRIVING TO THE COLLEGE FOR ONE OF THOSE BREAKFAST DATES, IN FACT, WHEN I LEARNED THAT SLEDGE RANKIN WAS DEAD.

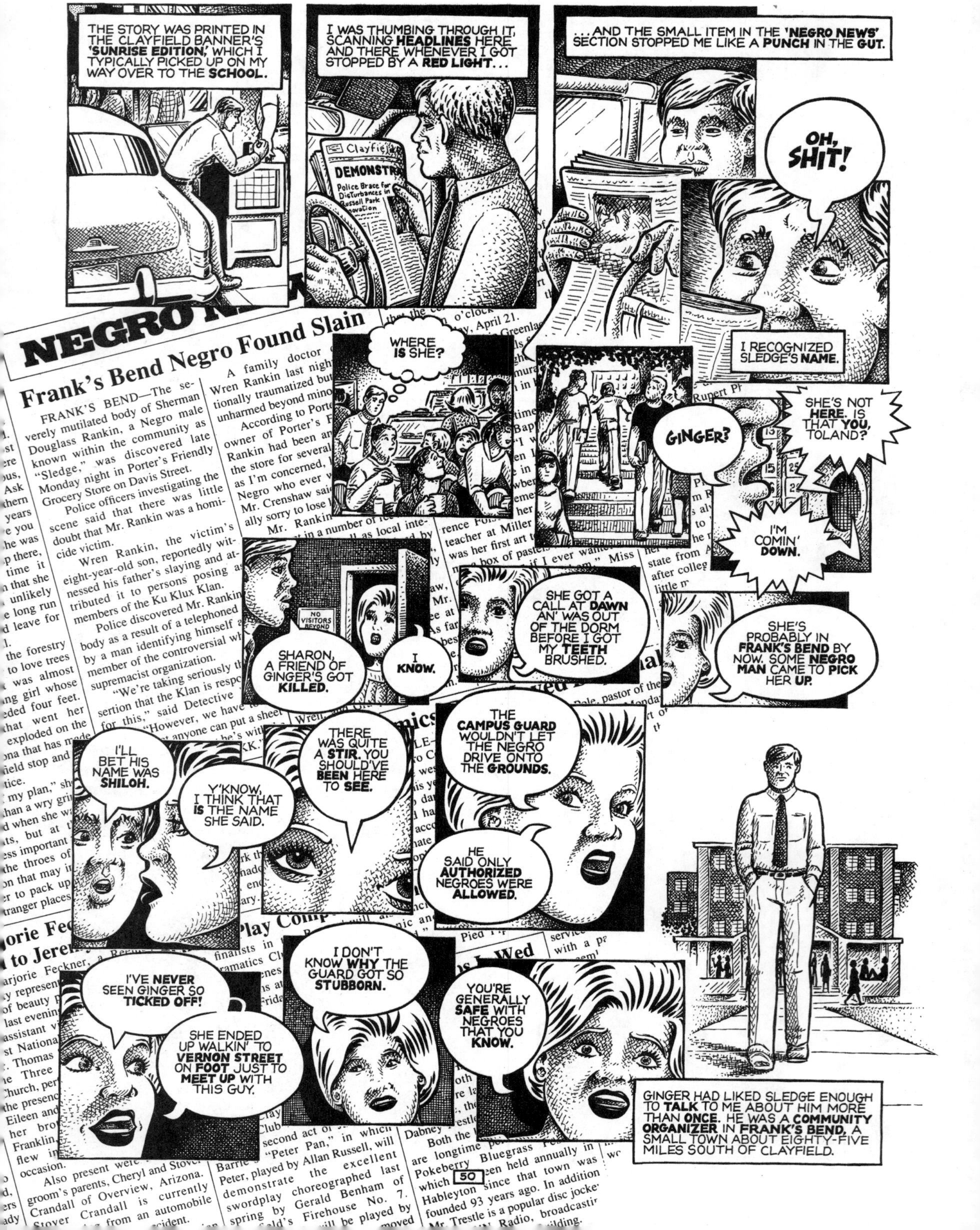

THE STORY WAS PRINTED IN THE CLAYFIELD BANNER'S 'SUNRISE EDITION,' WHICH I TYPICALLY PICKED UP ON MY WAY OVER TO THE SCHOOL.
I WAS THUMBING THROUGH IT, SCANNING HEADLINES HERE AND THERE WHENEVER I GOT STOPPED BY A RED LIGHT...
Police Brace for Disturbances in Russell Park
...AND THE SMALL ITEM IN THE 'NEGRO NEWS' SECTION STOPPED ME LIKE A PUNCH IN THE GUT.
OH, SHIT!
I RECOGNIZED SLEDGE'S NAME.
Frank's Bend Negro Found Slain
FRANK'S BEND—The severely mutilated body of Sherman Douglass Rankin, a Negro male known within the community as "Sledge," was discovered late Monday night in Porter's Friendly Grocery Store on Davis Street.
Police officers investigating the scene said that there was little doubt that Mr. Rankin was a homicide victim.
Wren Rankin, the victim's eight-year-old son, reportedly witnessed his father's slaying and attributed it to persons posing as members of the Ku Klux Klan.
WHERE IS SHE?
GINGER?
SHE'S NOT HERE. IS THAT YOU, TOLAND?
I'M COMIN' DOWN.
NO VISITORS BEYOND
SHARON, A FRIEND OF GINGER'S GOT KILLED.
I KNOW.
SHE GOT A CALL AT DAWN AN' WAS OUT OF THE DORM BEFORE I GOT MY TEETH BRUSHED.
SHE'S PROBABLY IN FRANK'S BEND BY NOW. SOME NEGRO MAN CAME TO PICK HER UP.
I'LL BET HIS NAME WAS SHILOH.
Y'KNOW, I THINK THAT IS THE NAME SHE SAID.
THERE WAS QUITE A STIR. YOU SHOULD'VE BEEN HERE TO SEE.
THE CAMPUS GUARD WOULDN'T LET THE NEGRO DRIVE ONTO THE GROUNDS.
HE SAID ONLY AUTHORIZED NEGROES WERE ALLOWED.
I'VE NEVER SEEN GINGER SO TICKED OFF!
SHE ENDED UP WALKIN' TO VERNON STREET ON FOOT JUST TO MEET UP WITH THIS GUY.
I DON'T KNOW WHY THE GUARD GOT SO STUBBORN.
YOU'RE GENERALLY SAFE WITH NEGROES THAT YOU KNOW.
GINGER HAD LIKED SLEDGE ENOUGH TO TALK TO ME ABOUT HIM MORE THAN ONCE. HE WAS A COMMUNITY ORGANIZER IN FRANK'S BEND, A SMALL TOWN ABOUT EIGHTY-FIVE MILES SOUTH OF CLAYFIELD.

THAT AREA WAS **KLAN COUNTRY**, FOR SURE!

OFFICIALS MADE **DISAPPROVING NOISES** ABOUT THE PERIODIC **LYNCHINGS**, BUT NO WHITE PERSON HAD **EVER** BEEN INDICTED FOR THE MURDER OF SOMEONE **BLACK**.

GINGER LIKED TO TELL HOW SLEDGE HAD DRIVEN TO CLAYFIELD AND PRACTICALLY **KIDNAPPED** SHILOH AND HER TO GET THEM TO PERFORM AT A **RALLY** FOR SOME **PAPER MILL WORKERS** WHO WERE ON **STRIKE**.

...OH, YOU CAN'T SCARE ME! I'M STICKIN' WITH THE UNION...

STRIKE FOR FAIR PAY

AFTERWARDS THEY'D GONE BACK TO SLEDGE'S **HOME** FOR A **CHICKEN DINNER** TOPPED OFF WITH **BLACKBERRY COBBLER**.

WREN, SHOW SHILOH AN' GINGER THAT **MAGIC TRICK** YOU DO WITH THE **PENNIES** AN' THE PEOPLE'S **EARS**....

IT WAS A VISIT THAT LEFT EVERYBODY FEELING LIKE THEY'D ALL BEEN **REARED** IN THE SAME **CRADLE**, ACCORDING TO GINGER.

I WAS **UPSET** ABOUT SLEDGE BEING KILLED, BUT THERE WASN'T ANYTHING I COULD FIGURE OUT TO **DO** BUT GO ON TO **WORK** AND HOPE TO HEAR FROM GINGER **EVENTUALLY**.

I WAS SLIGHTLY **BOTHERED**, TO BE HONEST, THAT IT WAS **SHILOH** SHE'D HOOKED UP WITH IN HER TIME OF GRIEF INSTEAD OF **ME**.

YOUR **GIRLFRIEND'S** ON THE HORN **LONG-DISTANCE**, POLK.

IN THE LATE AFTERNOON, SHE **CALLED**.

WILL YOU BE GOIN' STRAIGHT **HOME** FROM **WORK** TONIGHT? SHILOH AN' I WILL BE LEAVIN' **FRANK'S BEND** SOON, AN' WE WERE CONSIDERIN' STOPPIN' BY THE **WHEELERY**.

I'VE HAD TO BE **STRONG** ALL DAY FOR SLEDGE'S **FAMILY** AN' I'M GOIN' **CRAZY** FOR A **CRY**.

MY SHOULDER'LL BE **WAITIN'** FOR YOU.

NOW **SOME** FELLAS WOULD'VE HAD THE GOOD SENSE TO LEAVE IT **THERE**—BUT NOT **ME**!

I WISH YOU COULD'VE **PHONED** ME THIS MORNIN' BEFORE YOU LEFT. IT WAS **WEIRD** GETTIN' TO THE CAFETERIA AN' YOU NOT **BEIN'** THERE.

OPEN **MOUTH**; INSERT **FOOT**!

I **APOLOGIZE**, TOLAND. I'LL TRY TO BE MORE **CONSIDERATE** OF YOU THE NEXT TIME SOMEBODY I LOVE GETS **MURDERED**.

HONEY, I DIDN'T **MEAN** THAT THE WAY IT—

I'LL SEE YOU **LATER**. Click!

I **LOVE** YOU.

I SPENT A **LOVELY** COUPLE OF HOURS **KICKING** MYSELF UNTIL MY SHIFT WAS OVER AND I COULD **LEAVE**.

WHEN I GOT HOME TO THE WHEELERY, SHILOH'S **CAR** WAS ALREADY IN THE **DRIVEWAY**. RILEY AND LOCO WERE ON THE FRONT PORCH LOOKING **TENSE**.

WHAT'S WITH THE **GUN**?

SOME GODDAM **JERKS** FOLLOWED GINGER AN' HER FRIEND ALL THE WAY FROM **FRANK'S BEND.**

WHOEVER THEY WERE, THEY'RE **GONE** NOW— AN' I WANNA ENCOURAGE 'EM TO **STAY** GONE!

HI.

YOU'RE O.K.?

INSIDE THE **HOUSE,** AFTER GINGER AND I HAD HAD A CHANCE TO **HUG** FOR A MINUTE...

YEAH.

...I GOT TOLD MORE ABOUT THE **CAR** THAT HAD FOLLOWED THEM BACK TO **CLAYFIELD.**

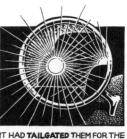

IT HAD **TAILGATED** THEM FOR THE WHOLE **EIGHTY-FIVE MILES,** ITS HEADLIGHTS ON **BRIGHT...**

...SO THAT SHILOH WAS HALF-**BLINDED** BY THE **REFLECTION** IN THE **REARVIEW MIRROR.**

ALL I COULD THINK OF WAS HOW **STUPID** WE WERE—A **'NIGGER AGITATOR'** FROM UP **NORTH** AN' A **WHITE SOUTHERN FEMALE,** DRIVIN' **MILE** AFTER MILE THROUGH DIXIE FARMLAND AT NIGHT WITH THE **KLAN** ON OUR TAILS!

YOU DIDN'T **THINK** ABOUT IT BEIN' **DANGEROUS** WHEN YOU **SET OUT?**

WE WEREN'T USIN' OUR **HEADS.**

SHEER FOOL RECKLESSNESS IS WHAT IT **WAS!** WE WERE SO LOST IN THOUGHTS ABOUT **SLEDGE,** WE IGNORED THE **OBVIOUS!**

THERE WAS A FAIR AMOUNT OF **TRAFFIC** ON THE ROAD. THAT MIGHT'VE DISCOURAGED 'EM FROM GETTIN' ANY **NASTIER** WITH THE TWO OF **US.**

GUNS! DAMN!

DID RILEY TELL YOU HOW THEY PARKED OUT IN FRONT OF THE **HOUSE** FOR A TIME, TOLAND? THAT'S WHY RILEY'S OUT ON THE **PORCH** WITH HIS **GUN.**

THEY STILL MIGHT HAVE A **TEACHIN' SPOT** FOR YOU BACK AT THAT **CONSERVATORY** IN BOSTON, SHILOH.

DON'T THINK LOTTIE AN' I DON'T **THINK** ABOUT THAT EVERY MORNIN' WHEN WE POUR OUR **CORN FLAKES,** MISS GINGER.

I KEPT WAITING FOR GINGER TO LET DOWN AND **CRY** ON MY **SHOULDER** LIKE SHE'D **SAID** SHE MIGHT. BUT HER FACE STAYED **NUMB** AND **DISTANT.**

OCCASIONALLY SHILOH WOULD REACH OVER AND SQUEEZE HER **FOOT.**

I DON'T KNOW HOW TO **TALK** ABOUT WHAT HAPPENED TO SLEDGE....

YOU DON'T HAVE TO TELL US **NOW,** GINGER, IF IT **HURTS** TOO MUCH.

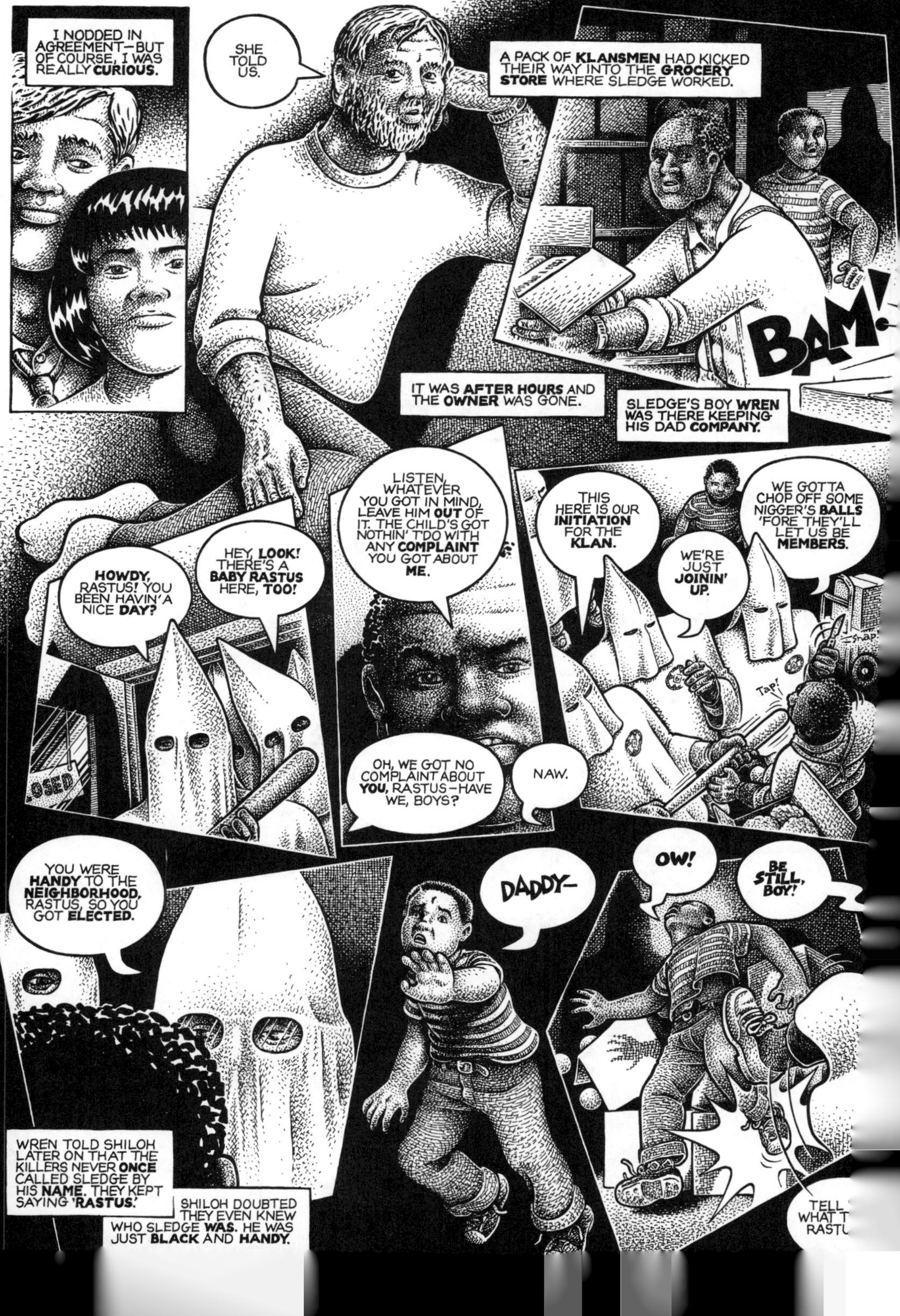
I NODDED IN AGREEMENT—BUT OF COURSE, I WAS REALLY **CURIOUS**.
SHE TOLD US.
A PACK OF **KLANSMEN** HAD KICKED THEIR WAY INTO THE **GROCERY STORE** WHERE SLEDGE WORKED.
IT WAS **AFTER HOURS** AND THE **OWNER** WAS GONE.
SLEDGE'S BOY **WREN** WAS THERE KEEPING HIS DAD **COMPANY**.
BAM!
HOWDY, RASTUS! YOU BEEN HAVIN' A NICE **DAY?**
HEY, **LOOK!** THERE'S A **BABY RASTUS** HERE, **TOO!**
LISTEN, WHATEVER YOU GOT IN MIND, LEAVE HIM **OUT** OF IT. THE CHILD'S GOT NOTHIN' T'DO WITH ANY **COMPLAINT** YOU GOT ABOUT **ME.**
OH, WE GOT NO COMPLAINT ABOUT **YOU,** RASTUS—HAVE WE, BOYS?
NAW.
THIS HERE IS OUR **INITIATION** FOR THE **KLAN.**
WE'RE JUST **JOININ'** UP.
WE GOTTA CHOP OFF SOME NIGGER'S **BALLS** 'FORE THEY'LL LET US BE **MEMBERS.**
TAP!
YOU WERE **HANDY** TO THE **NEIGHBORHOOD,** RASTUS, SO YOU GOT **ELECTED.**
DADDY—
OW!
BE STILL, BOY!
WREN TOLD SHILOH LATER ON THAT THE KILLERS NEVER **ONCE** CALLED SLEDGE BY HIS **NAME.** THEY KEPT SAYING **'RASTUS.'**
SHILOH DOUBTED THEY EVEN KNEW WHO SLEDGE **WAS.** HE WAS JUST **BLACK** AND **HANDY.**
TELL WHAT T RASTU

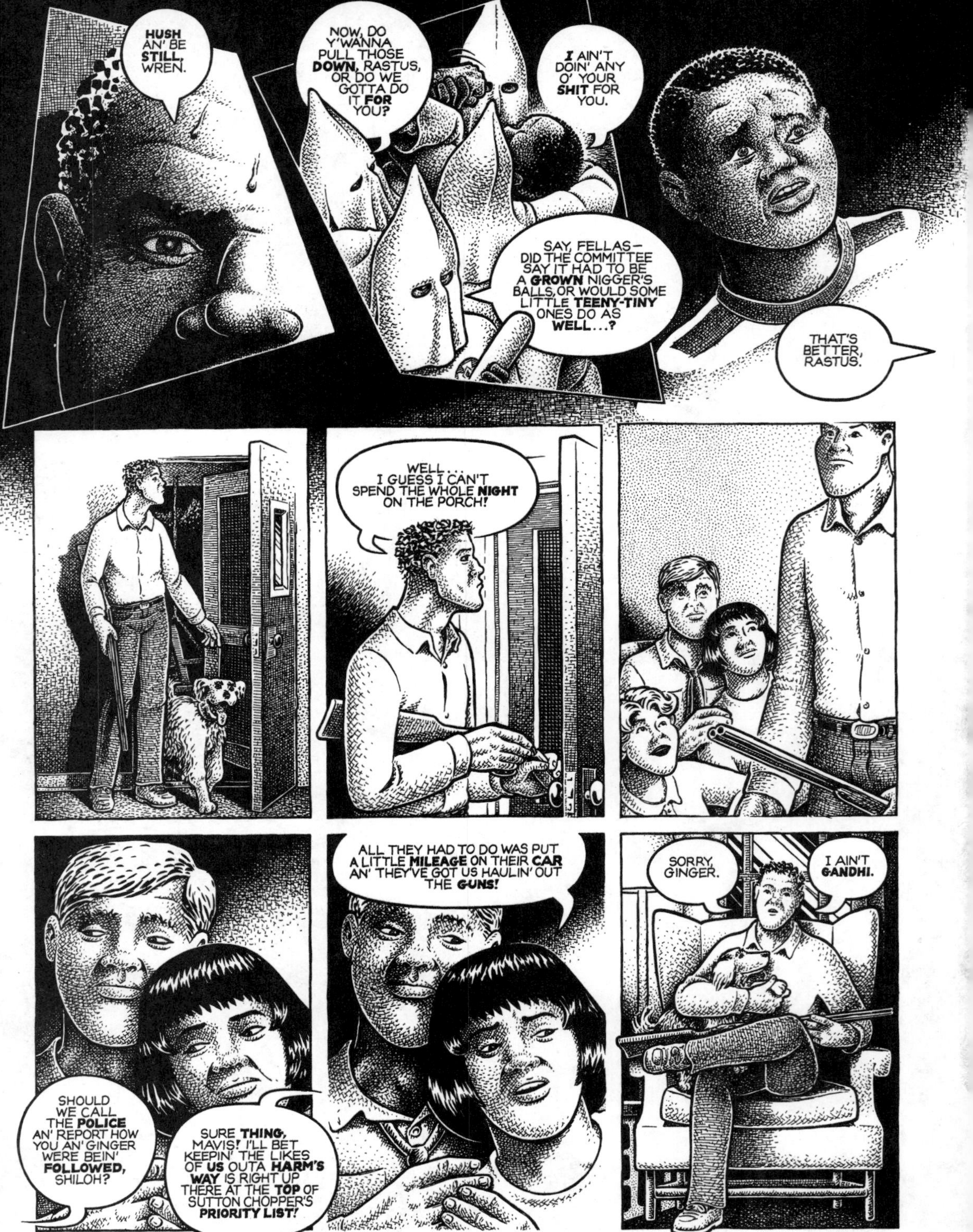
HUSH AN' BE STILL, WREN.
NOW, DO Y'WANNA PULL THOSE DOWN, RASTUS, OR DO WE GOTTA DO IT FOR YOU?
I AIN'T DOIN' ANY O' YOUR SHIT FOR YOU.
SAY, FELLAS— DID THE COMMITTEE SAY IT HAD TO BE A GROWN NIGGER'S BALLS, OR WOULD SOME LITTLE TEENY-TINY ONES DO AS WELL...?
THAT'S BETTER, RASTUS.
WELL... I GUESS I CAN'T SPEND THE WHOLE NIGHT ON THE PORCH!
SHOULD WE CALL THE POLICE AN' REPORT HOW YOU AN' GINGER WERE BEIN' FOLLOWED, SHILOH?
SURE THING, MAVIS! I'LL BET KEEPIN' THE LIKES OF US OUTA HARM'S WAY IS RIGHT UP THERE AT THE TOP OF SUTTON CHOPPER'S PRIORITY LIST!
ALL THEY HAD TO DO WAS PUT A LITTLE MILEAGE ON THEIR CAR AN' THEY'VE GOT US HAULIN' OUT THE GUNS!
SORRY, GINGER.
I AIN'T GANDHI.

Chapter 8

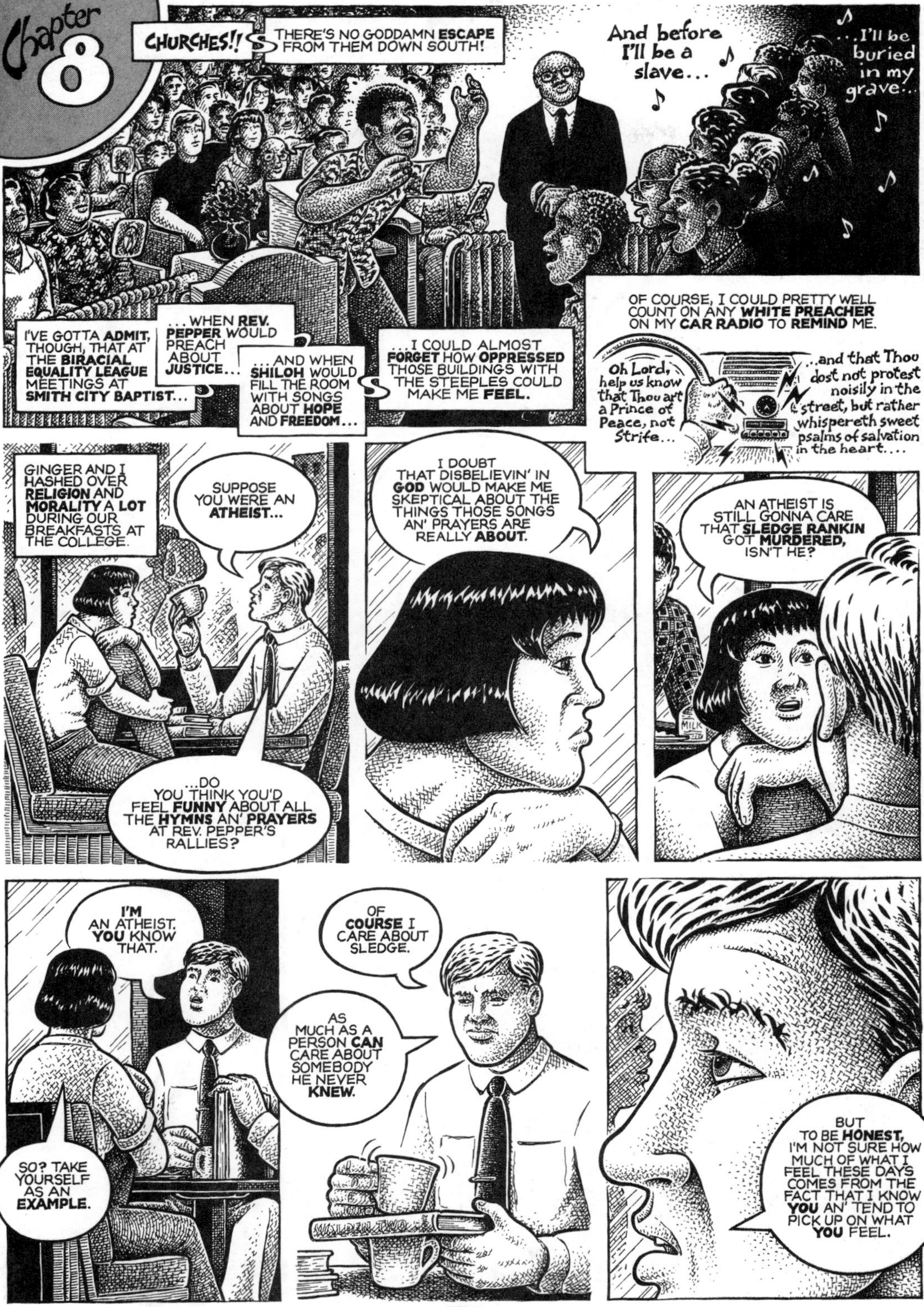
CHURCHES!!
THERE'S NO GODDAMN ESCAPE FROM THEM DOWN SOUTH!
And before I'll be a slave...
...I'll be buried in my grave...
I'VE GOTTA ADMIT, THOUGH, THAT AT THE BIRACIAL EQUALITY LEAGUE MEETINGS AT SMITH CITY BAPTIST...
...WHEN REV. PEPPER WOULD PREACH ABOUT JUSTICE...
...AND WHEN SHILOH WOULD FILL THE ROOM WITH SONGS ABOUT HOPE AND FREEDOM...
...I COULD ALMOST FORGET HOW OPPRESSED THOSE BUILDINGS WITH THE STEEPLES COULD MAKE ME FEEL.
OF COURSE, I COULD PRETTY WELL COUNT ON ANY WHITE PREACHER ON MY CAR RADIO TO REMIND ME.
Oh Lord, help us know that Thou art a Prince of Peace, not Strife...
...and that Thou dost not protest noisily in the street, but rather whispereth sweet psalms of salvation in the heart...
GINGER AND I HASHED OVER RELIGION AND MORALITY A LOT DURING OUR BREAKFASTS AT THE COLLEGE.
SUPPOSE YOU WERE AN ATHEIST...
...DO YOU THINK YOU'D FEEL FUNNY ABOUT ALL THE HYMNS AN' PRAYERS AT REV. PEPPER'S RALLIES?
I DOUBT THAT DISBELIEVIN' IN GOD WOULD MAKE ME SKEPTICAL ABOUT THE THINGS THOSE SONGS AN' PRAYERS ARE REALLY ABOUT.
AN ATHEIST IS STILL GONNA CARE THAT SLEDGE RANKIN GOT MURDERED, ISN'T HE?
MILK
I'M AN ATHEIST. YOU KNOW THAT.
SO? TAKE YOURSELF AS AN EXAMPLE.
OF COURSE I CARE ABOUT SLEDGE.
AS MUCH AS A PERSON CAN CARE ABOUT SOMEBODY HE NEVER KNEW.
WALDEN TWO
BUT TO BE HONEST, I'M NOT SURE HOW MUCH OF WHAT I FEEL THESE DAYS COMES FROM THE FACT THAT I KNOW YOU AN' TEND TO PICK UP ON WHAT YOU FEEL.

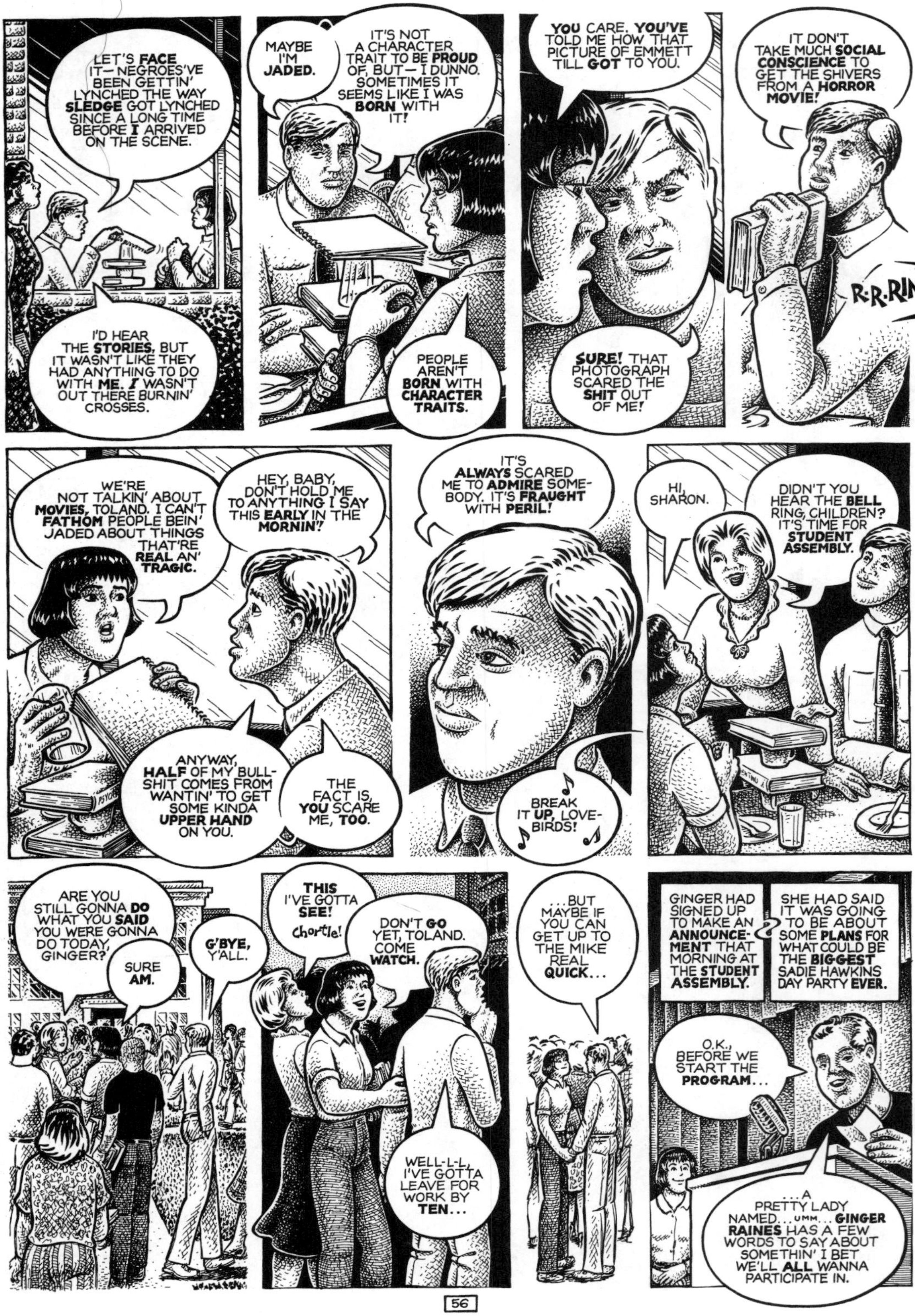
LET'S FACE IT—NEGROES'VE BEEN GETTIN' LYNCHED THE WAY SLEDGE GOT LYNCHED SINCE A LONG TIME BEFORE I ARRIVED ON THE SCENE.
I'D HEAR THE STORIES, BUT IT WASN'T LIKE THEY HAD ANYTHING TO DO WITH ME. I WASN'T OUT THERE BURNIN' CROSSES.
MAYBE I'M JADED.
IT'S NOT A CHARACTER TRAIT TO BE PROUD OF, BUT—I DUNNO. SOMETIMES IT SEEMS LIKE I WAS BORN WITH IT!
PEOPLE AREN'T BORN WITH CHARACTER TRAITS.
YOU CARE. YOU'VE TOLD ME HOW THAT PICTURE OF EMMETT TILL GOT TO YOU.
SURE! THAT PHOTOGRAPH SCARED THE SHIT OUT OF ME!
IT DON'T TAKE MUCH SOCIAL CONSCIENCE TO GET THE SHIVERS FROM A HORROR MOVIE!
R-R-RING!...
WE'RE NOT TALKIN' ABOUT MOVIES, TOLAND. I CAN'T FATHOM PEOPLE BEIN' JADED ABOUT THINGS THAT'RE REAL AN' TRAGIC.
HEY, BABY, DON'T HOLD ME TO ANYTHING I SAY THIS EARLY IN THE MORNIN'!
ANYWAY, HALF OF MY BULL-SHIT COMES FROM WANTIN' TO GET SOME KINDA UPPER HAND ON YOU.
THE FACT IS, YOU SCARE ME, TOO.
IT'S ALWAYS SCARED ME TO ADMIRE SOME-BODY. IT'S FRAUGHT WITH PERIL!
BREAK IT UP, LOVE-BIRDS!
HI, SHARON.
DIDN'T YOU HEAR THE BELL RING, CHILDREN? IT'S TIME FOR STUDENT ASSEMBLY.
ARE YOU STILL GONNA DO WHAT YOU SAID YOU WERE GONNA DO TODAY, GINGER?
SURE AM.
G'BYE, Y'ALL.
THIS I'VE GOTTA SEE! Chortle!
DON'T GO YET, TOLAND. COME WATCH.
WELL-L-L, I'VE GOTTA LEAVE FOR WORK BY TEN...
...BUT MAYBE IF YOU CAN GET UP TO THE MIKE REAL QUICK...
GINGER HAD SIGNED UP TO MAKE AN ANNOUNCE-MENT THAT MORNING AT THE STUDENT ASSEMBLY.
SHE HAD SAID IT WAS GOING TO BE ABOUT SOME PLANS FOR WHAT COULD BE THE BIGGEST SADIE HAWKINS DAY PARTY EVER.
O.K., BEFORE WE START THE PROGRAM...
...A PRETTY LADY NAMED...UMM...GINGER RAINES HAS A FEW WORDS TO SAY ABOUT SOMETHIN' I BET WE'LL ALL WANNA PARTICIPATE IN.

SHE HAD LIED.

IF YOU'VE BEEN READIN' THE **PAPERS**, YOU KNOW THAT OUR BELOVED **CITY FATHERS** VOTED THIS WEEK TO CLOSE DOWN **RUSSELL PARK**—SUPPOSEDLY 'FOR **RENOVATIONS.**'

AND IF YOU'VE PAID ATTENTION TO RECENT SOUTHERN **HISTORY**, YOU KNOW EXACTLY **WHY** THE MAYOR AND POLICE COMMISSIONER CHOPPER **WANT** THAT PARK CLOSED!

BARRY...?

THE GUY WHO HAD TURNED THE MIKE OVER TO GINGER LOOKED LIKE HE WAS ABOUT TO **PEE** IN HIS **CHINOS.**

IT'S BECAUSE RUSSELL PARK IS WHERE CLAYFIELD'S **NEGRO CITIZENS** HAVE ALWAYS GATHERED TO DEMONSTRATE AGAINST **RACIAL SEGREGATION!**

UH... 'SCUSE ME, GINGER...

WHICH THEY HAVE A **CONSTITUTIONAL RIGHT** TO **DO!**

WESTHILLS COLLEGE

NOW, FOR THE LAST **YEAR** I'VE BEEN A MEMBER OF THE **BIRACIAL EQUALITY LEAGUE** HERE IN CLAY-FIELD—

GINGER, YOU **KNOW** THE COLLEGE HAS **RULES** AGAINST GIVIN' **POLITICAL SPEECHES** THAT AREN'T ON THE **SCHEDULE.**

IT WAS **STARTLING** TO SEE GINGER TURN INTO SUCH A **LIVE WIRE** ONCE SHE WAS UP IN FRONT OF A **CROWD.**

IT BROUGHT BACK THE QUALITY ABOUT HER THAT HAD **FASCINATED** ME THE NIGHT I FIRST **SAW** HER SINGING WITH **SHILOH** AT THE **MELODY MOTEL.**

BARRY, I'LL BE DONE A LOT **QUICKER** IF YOU'LL STOP BREAKIN' MY TRAIN OF **THOUGHT.**

WHOA, GIRL!

I'D HAD SO MANY **QUIET** TIMES WITH HER SINCE THEN THAT I'D LET THE **OTHER** SIDE OF HER SLIP MY **MIND,** ALMOST.

IT WAS A REAL **SEXY** SIDE.

WE'D ALL LIKE TO ASK YA REAL **NICELY** TO **SIT DOWN** AN' LET US GET ON WITH THE **PROGRAM.**

DON'T YOU HAVE A **PLEDGE SWAP** OR SOMETHIN' Y'CAN GO TO? THIS IS **IMPORTANT!**

FROM MY OBSERVATION POST BESIDE THE DOOR I COULD VIEW A **FAIR PERCENTAGE** OF THE **FACES** IN THE ROOM.

GINGER—

MY **POINT,** IF BARRY'LL QUIT **INTERRUPTIN',** IS THAT IT'S TIME FOR US WESTHILLS COLLEGE STUDENTS TO DO OUR **PART** TO KEEP RUSSELL PARK **OPEN!**

GINGER... SERIOUSLY, NOW—

SOME **GRINNED** AND APPEARED TO THINK THE COMMOTION WAS **FUN.**

I **AM** SERIOUS! WE'VE GOTTA PROVE THAT **YOUNG WHITE PEOPLE** IN THE SOUTH CARE ABOUT **JUSTICE!**

GINGER!

IF Y'THINK SHE'S A SPITFIRE UP **THERE,** YOU SHOULD TAKE CONTEMPORARY SOCIOLOGY WITH 'ER.

OTHERS NARROWED THEIR EYES AND LOOKED **HOSTILE.**

I WANT US TO START A WESTHILLS COLLEGE **CHAPTER** OF THE **EQUALITY LEAGUE!**

I STARTED HEARING **HISSES...**

...AND I **BRACED** MYSELF FOR THE **HECKLERS.**

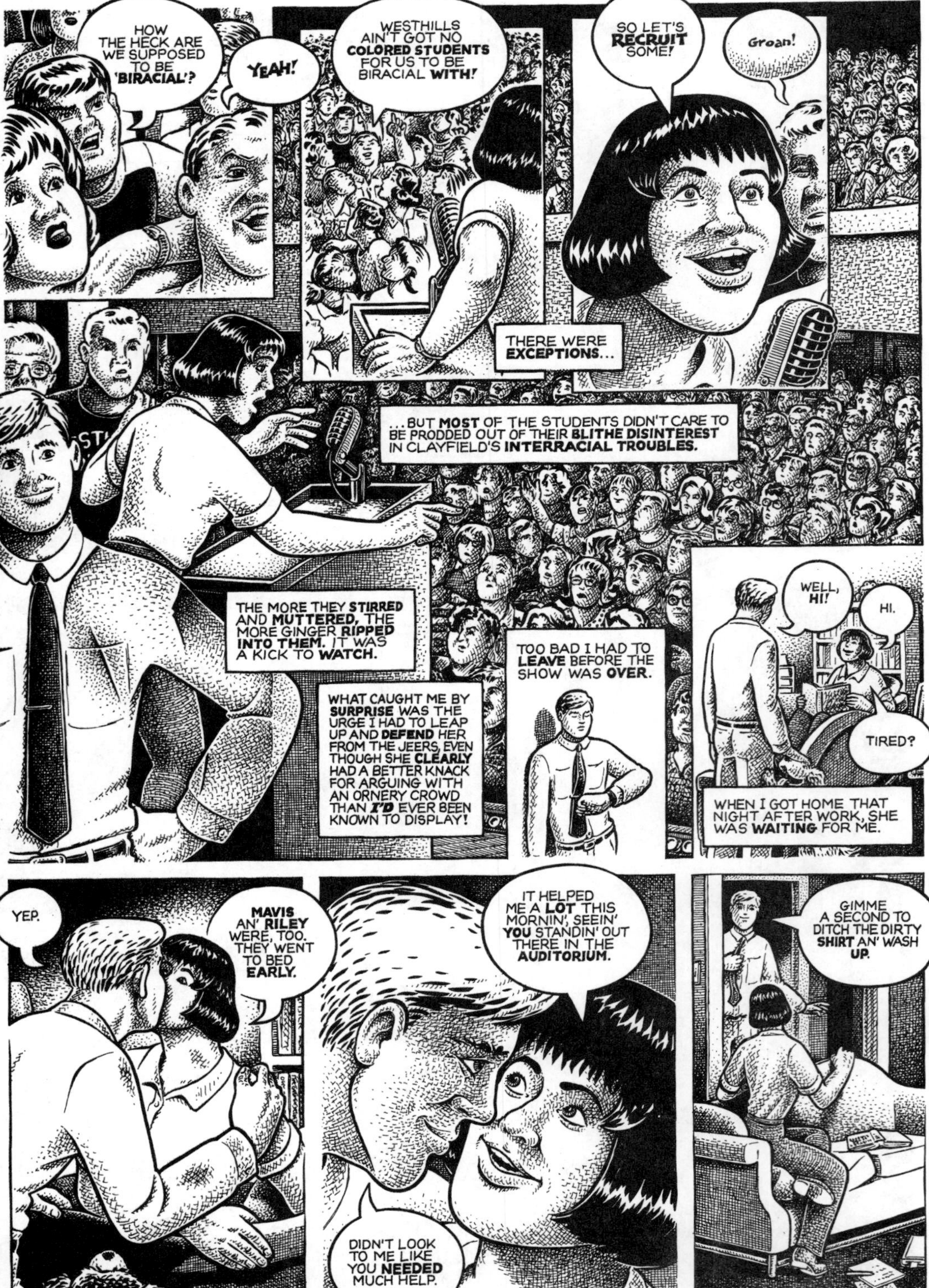

HOW THE HECK ARE WE SUPPOSED TO BE 'BIRACIAL'?
YEAH!
WESTHILLS AIN'T GOT NO COLORED STUDENTS FOR US TO BE BIRACIAL WITH!
SO LET'S RECRUIT SOME!
Groan!
THERE WERE EXCEPTIONS...
...BUT MOST OF THE STUDENTS DIDN'T CARE TO BE PRODDED OUT OF THEIR BLITHE DISINTEREST IN CLAYFIELD'S INTERRACIAL TROUBLES.
THE MORE THEY STIRRED AND MUTTERED, THE MORE GINGER RIPPED INTO THEM. IT WAS A KICK TO WATCH.
WHAT CAUGHT ME BY SURPRISE WAS THE URGE I HAD TO LEAP UP AND DEFEND HER FROM THE JEERS, EVEN THOUGH SHE CLEARLY HAD A BETTER KNACK FOR ARGUING WITH AN ORNERY CROWD THAN I'D EVER BEEN KNOWN TO DISPLAY!
TOO BAD I HAD TO LEAVE BEFORE THE SHOW WAS OVER.
WELL, HI!
HI.
TIRED?
WHEN I GOT HOME THAT NIGHT AFTER WORK, SHE WAS WAITING FOR ME.
YEP.
MAVIS AN' RILEY WERE, TOO. THEY WENT TO BED EARLY.
IT HELPED ME A LOT THIS MORNIN', SEEIN' YOU STANDIN' OUT THERE IN THE AUDITORIUM.
DIDN'T LOOK TO ME LIKE YOU NEEDED MUCH HELP.
GIMME A SECOND TO DITCH THE DIRTY SHIRT AN' WASH UP.

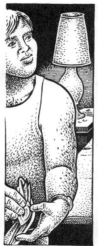

WINE?

ALL MY **INSTINCTS** WERE TELLING ME THAT GINGER FELT THE SAME WAY **I** DID.

TONIGHT WAS THE **NIGHT**.

YOU WERE PURE **DYNAMITE** AT THAT **ASSEMBLY** TODAY.

Wurf!

DID YOU GET ANY OF YOUR **FELLOW STUDENTS** SIGNED UP FOR THE **EQUALITY LEAGUE**?

A FEW SAID THEY **WISHED** THEY COULD **HELP**, BUT THEY'RE **SCARED**.

Whimper!

THERE'S PRESSURE ON THE SCHOOL TO **SUSPEND** ANYBODY WHO GETS INVOLVED IN **SOCIAL UNREST**!

I'D LIKELY BE LONG GONE **MYSELF** IF THE DEAN'S **COUSIN** WASN'T A **BUSINESS PARTNER** OF MY DAD'S UP IN **OHIO**.

AREN'T COLLEGE STUDENTS SUPPOSED TO HAVE FREEDOM OF **SPEECH** AN' FREEDOM OF **ASSEMBLY** AN'—

TOLAND, THIS IS THE **SOUTH**! WHERE DO YOU THINK YOU **ARE**, ANYWAY— IN **AMERICA**?!

POLITICAL TALK. NOT SO **EROTIC**.

IT CAN BE **TOUGH** TO SWITCH GEARS.

WINE HELPS.

BY THE WAY...

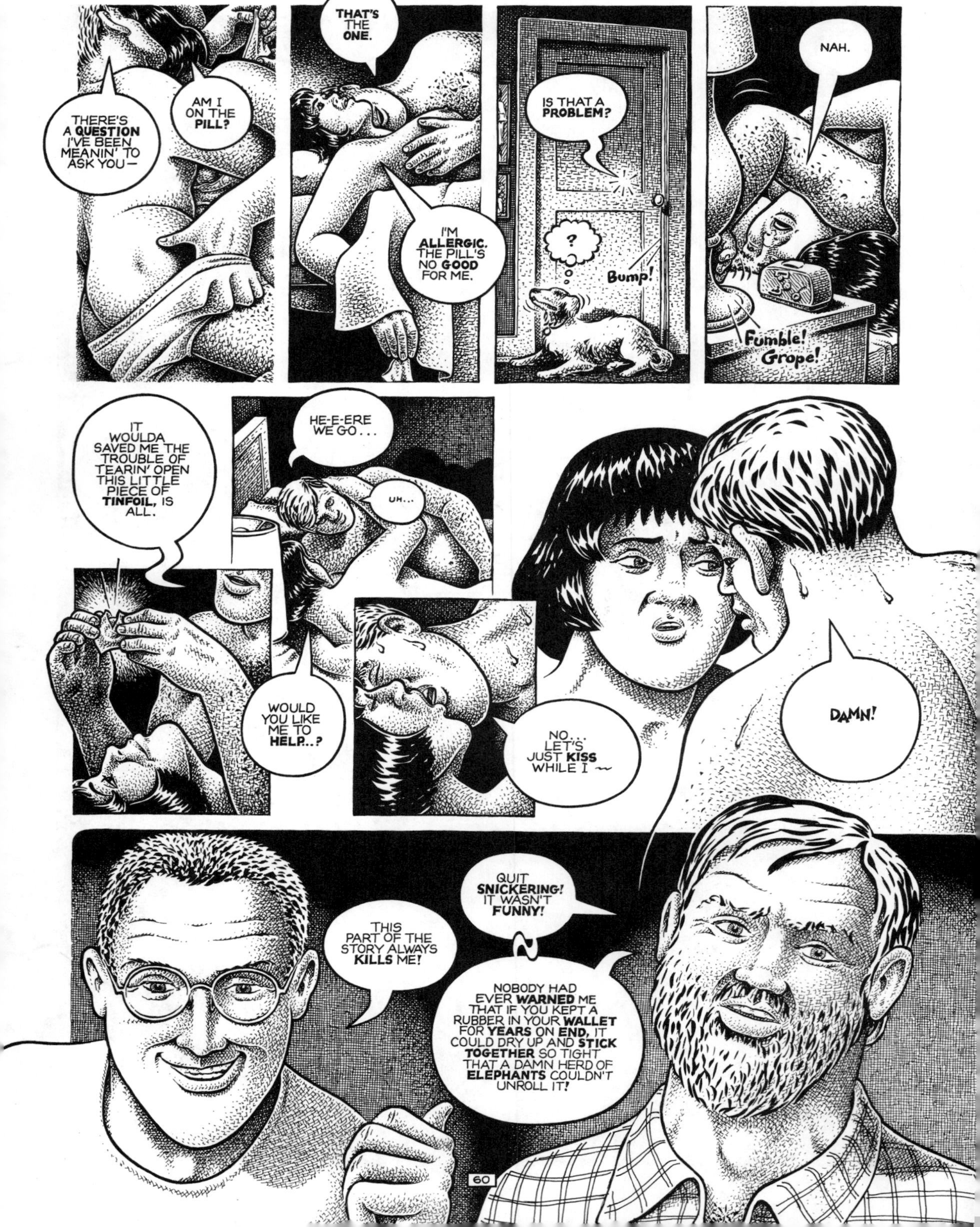

THERE'S A QUESTION I'VE BEEN MEANIN' TO ASK YOU—
AM I ON THE PILL?
THAT'S THE ONE.
I'M ALLERGIC. THE PILL'S NO GOOD FOR ME.
IS THAT A PROBLEM?
?
Bump!
NAH.
Fumble! Grope!
IT WOULDA SAVED ME THE TROUBLE OF TEARIN' OPEN THIS LITTLE PIECE OF TINFOIL, IS ALL.
HE-E-ERE WE GO...
UH...
WOULD YOU LIKE ME TO HELP...?
NO... LET'S JUST KISS WHILE I ~
DAMN!
THIS PART OF THE STORY ALWAYS KILLS ME!
QUIT SNICKERING! IT WASN'T FUNNY!
NOBODY HAD EVER WARNED ME THAT IF YOU KEPT A RUBBER IN YOUR WALLET FOR YEARS ON END, IT COULD DRY UP AND STICK TOGETHER SO TIGHT THAT A DAMN HERD OF ELEPHANTS COULDN'T UNROLL IT!

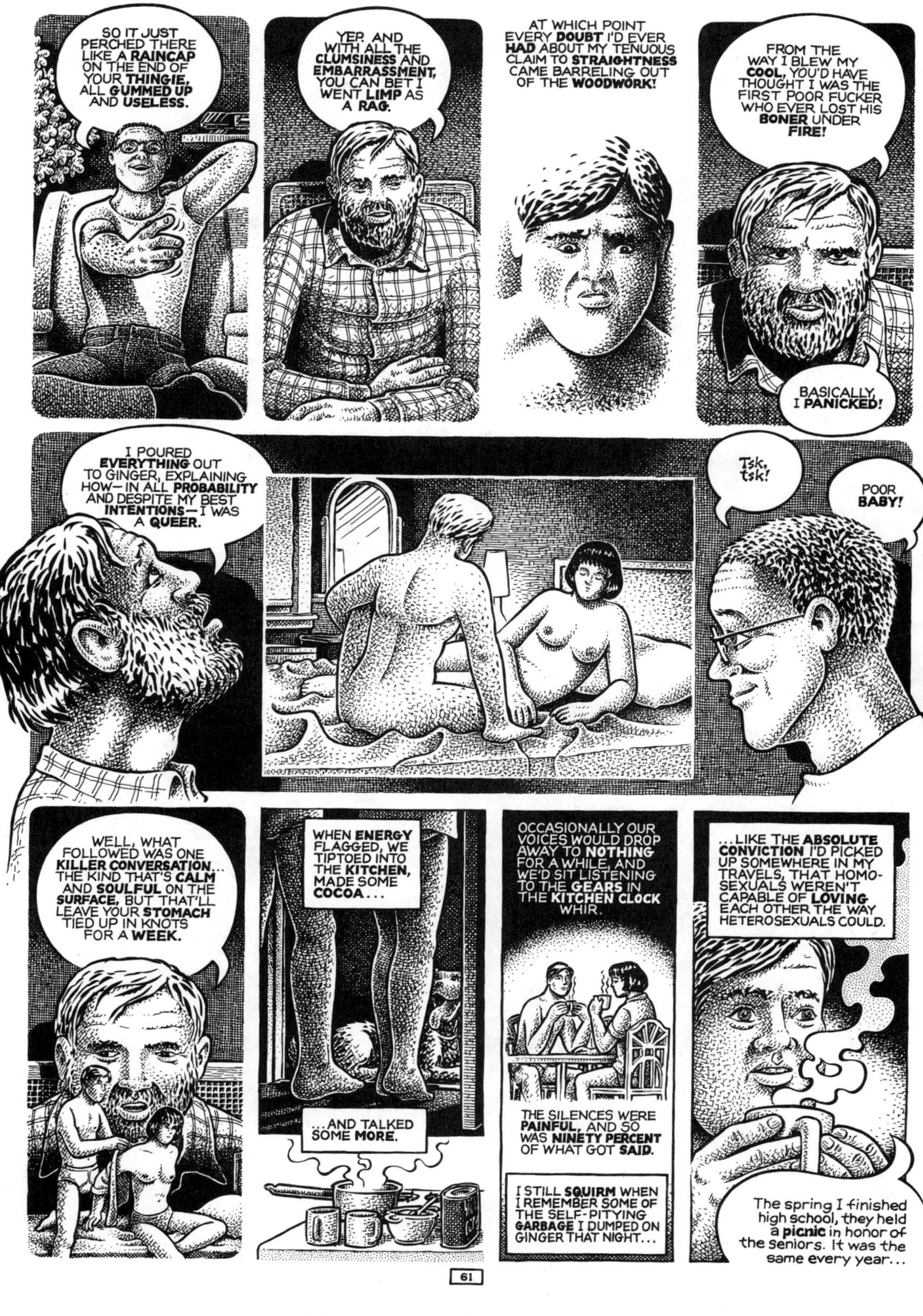

SO IT JUST PERCHED THERE LIKE A RAINCAP ON THE END OF YOUR THINGIE, ALL GUMMED UP AND USELESS.
YEP. AND WITH ALL THE CLUMSINESS AND EMBARRASSMENT, YOU CAN BET I WENT LIMP AS A RAG.
AT WHICH POINT EVERY DOUBT I'D EVER HAD ABOUT MY TENUOUS CLAIM TO STRAIGHTNESS CAME BARRELING OUT OF THE WOODWORK!
FROM THE WAY I BLEW MY COOL, YOU'D HAVE THOUGHT I WAS THE FIRST POOR FUCKER WHO EVER LOST HIS BONER UNDER FIRE!
BASICALLY, I PANICKED!
I POURED EVERYTHING OUT TO GINGER, EXPLAINING HOW—IN ALL PROBABILITY AND DESPITE MY BEST INTENTIONS—I WAS A QUEER.
Tsk, tsk!
POOR BABY!
WELL, WHAT FOLLOWED WAS ONE KILLER CONVERSATION... THE KIND THAT'S CALM AND SOULFUL ON THE SURFACE, BUT THAT'LL LEAVE YOUR STOMACH TIED UP IN KNOTS FOR A WEEK.
WHEN ENERGY FLAGGED, WE TIPTOED INTO THE KITCHEN, MADE SOME COCOA...
...AND TALKED SOME MORE.
OCCASIONALLY OUR VOICES WOULD DROP AWAY TO NOTHING FOR A WHILE, AND WE'D SIT LISTENING TO THE GEARS IN THE KITCHEN CLOCK WHIR.
THE SILENCES WERE PAINFUL, AND SO WAS NINETY PERCENT OF WHAT GOT SAID.
I STILL SQUIRM WHEN I REMEMBER SOME OF THE SELF-PITYING GARBAGE I DUMPED ON GINGER THAT NIGHT...
...LIKE THE ABSOLUTE CONVICTION I'D PICKED UP SOMEWHERE IN MY TRAVELS, THAT HOMOSEXUALS WEREN'T CAPABLE OF LOVING EACH OTHER THE WAY HETEROSEXUALS COULD.
The spring I finished high school, they held a picnic in honor of the seniors. It was the same every year...

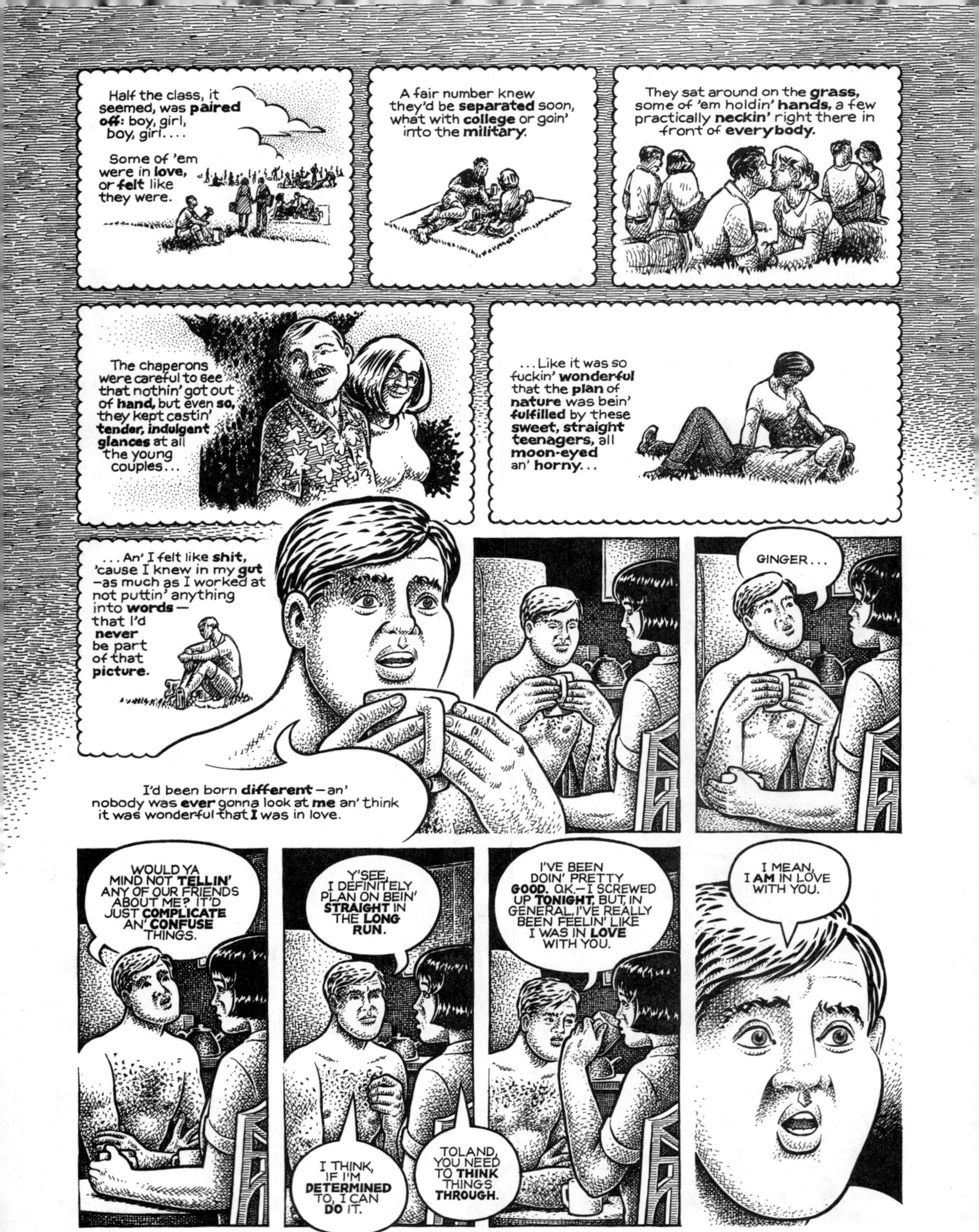

Half the class, it seemed, was **paired off**: boy, girl, boy, girl. . . .
Some of 'em were in **love**, or **felt** like they were.
A fair number knew they'd be **separated** soon, what with **college** or goin' into the **military**.
They sat around on the **grass**, some of 'em holdin' **hands**, a few practically **neckin'** right there in front of **everybody**.
The chaperons were careful to see that nothin' got out of **hand**, but even **so**, they kept castin' **tender, indulgent glances** at all the young couples...
...Like it was so fuckin' **wonderful** that the **plan** of **nature** was bein' **fulfilled** by these **sweet, straight teenagers**, all **moon-eyed** an' **horny**...
...An' I felt like **shit**, 'cause I knew in my **gut** —as much as I worked at not puttin' anything into **words**— that I'd **never** be part of that **picture**.
I'd been born **different** —an' nobody was **ever** gonna look at **me** an' think it was wonderful that **I** was in love.
GINGER...
WOULD YA MIND NOT **TELLIN'** ANY OF OUR FRIENDS ABOUT ME? IT'D JUST **COMPLICATE** AN' **CONFUSE** THINGS.
Y'SEE, I DEFINITELY PLAN ON BEIN' **STRAIGHT** IN THE **LONG RUN**.
I THINK, IF I'M **DETERMINED** TO, I CAN **DO** IT.
TOLAND, YOU NEED TO **THINK** THINGS **THROUGH**.
I'VE BEEN DOIN' PRETTY **GOOD**. O.K.—I SCREWED UP **TONIGHT**, BUT, IN GENERAL, I'VE REALLY BEEN FEELIN' LIKE I WAS IN **LOVE** WITH YOU.
I MEAN, I **AM** IN LOVE WITH YOU.

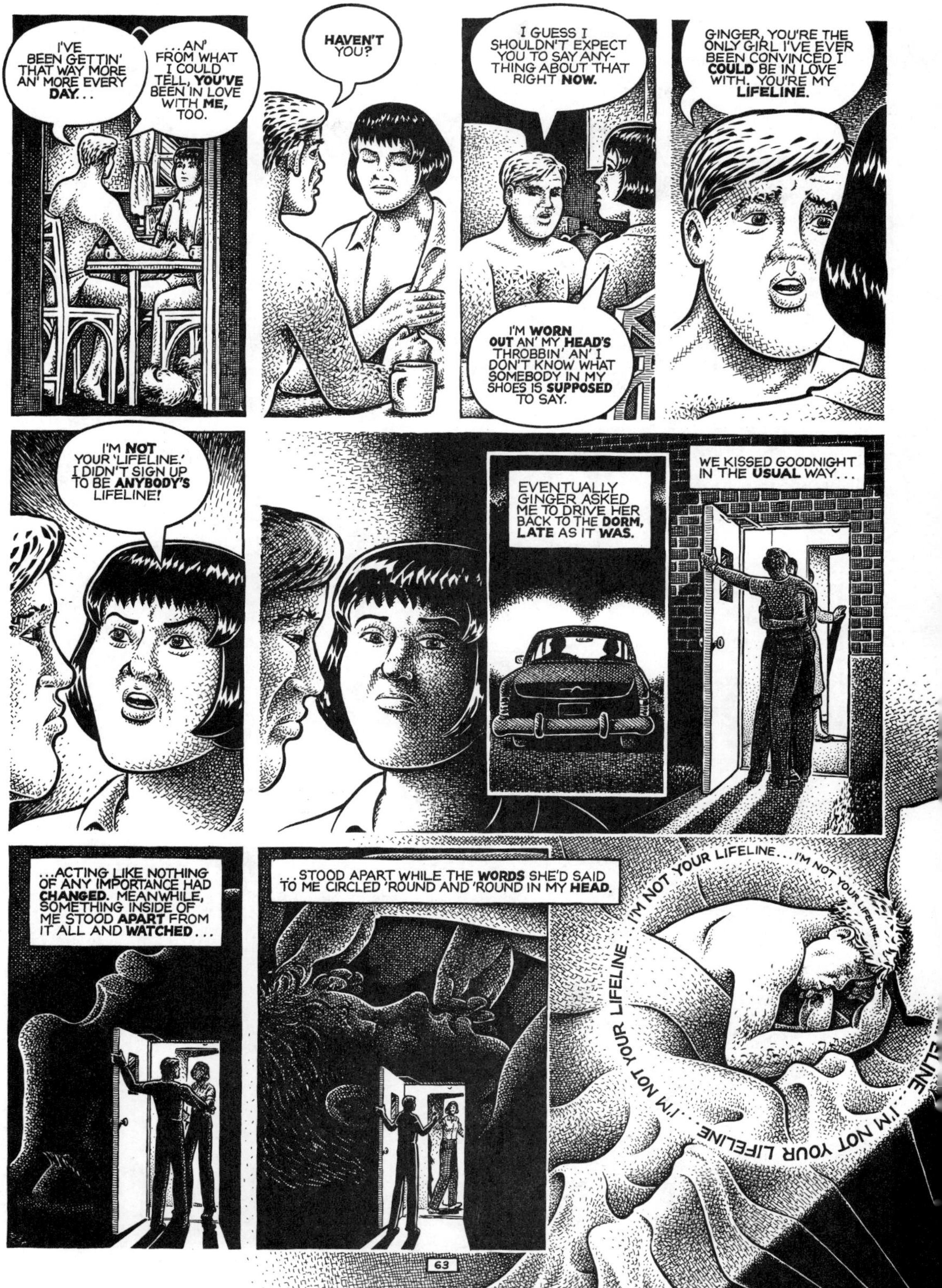
I'VE BEEN GETTIN' THAT WAY MORE AN' MORE EVERY DAY...
...AN' FROM WHAT I COULD TELL, YOU'VE BEEN IN LOVE WITH ME, TOO.
HAVEN'T YOU?
I GUESS I SHOULDN'T EXPECT YOU TO SAY ANYTHING ABOUT THAT RIGHT NOW.
I'M WORN OUT AN' MY HEAD'S THROBBIN' AN' I DON'T KNOW WHAT SOMEBODY IN MY SHOES IS SUPPOSED TO SAY.
GINGER, YOU'RE THE ONLY GIRL I'VE EVER BEEN CONVINCED I COULD BE IN LOVE WITH. YOU'RE MY LIFELINE.
I'M NOT YOUR 'LIFELINE.' I DIDN'T SIGN UP TO BE ANYBODY'S LIFELINE!
EVENTUALLY GINGER ASKED ME TO DRIVE HER BACK TO THE DORM, LATE AS IT WAS.
WE KISSED GOODNIGHT IN THE USUAL WAY...
...ACTING LIKE NOTHING OF ANY IMPORTANCE HAD CHANGED. MEANWHILE, SOMETHING INSIDE OF ME STOOD APART FROM IT ALL AND WATCHED...
...STOOD APART WHILE THE WORDS SHE'D SAID TO ME CIRCLED 'ROUND AND 'ROUND IN MY HEAD.
I'M NOT YOUR LIFELINE...I'M NOT YOUR LIFELINE...I'M NOT YOUR LIFELINE...I'M NOT YOUR LIFELINE...I'M NOT YOUR LIFELINE...I'M NOT YOUR LIFELINE

Chapter 9

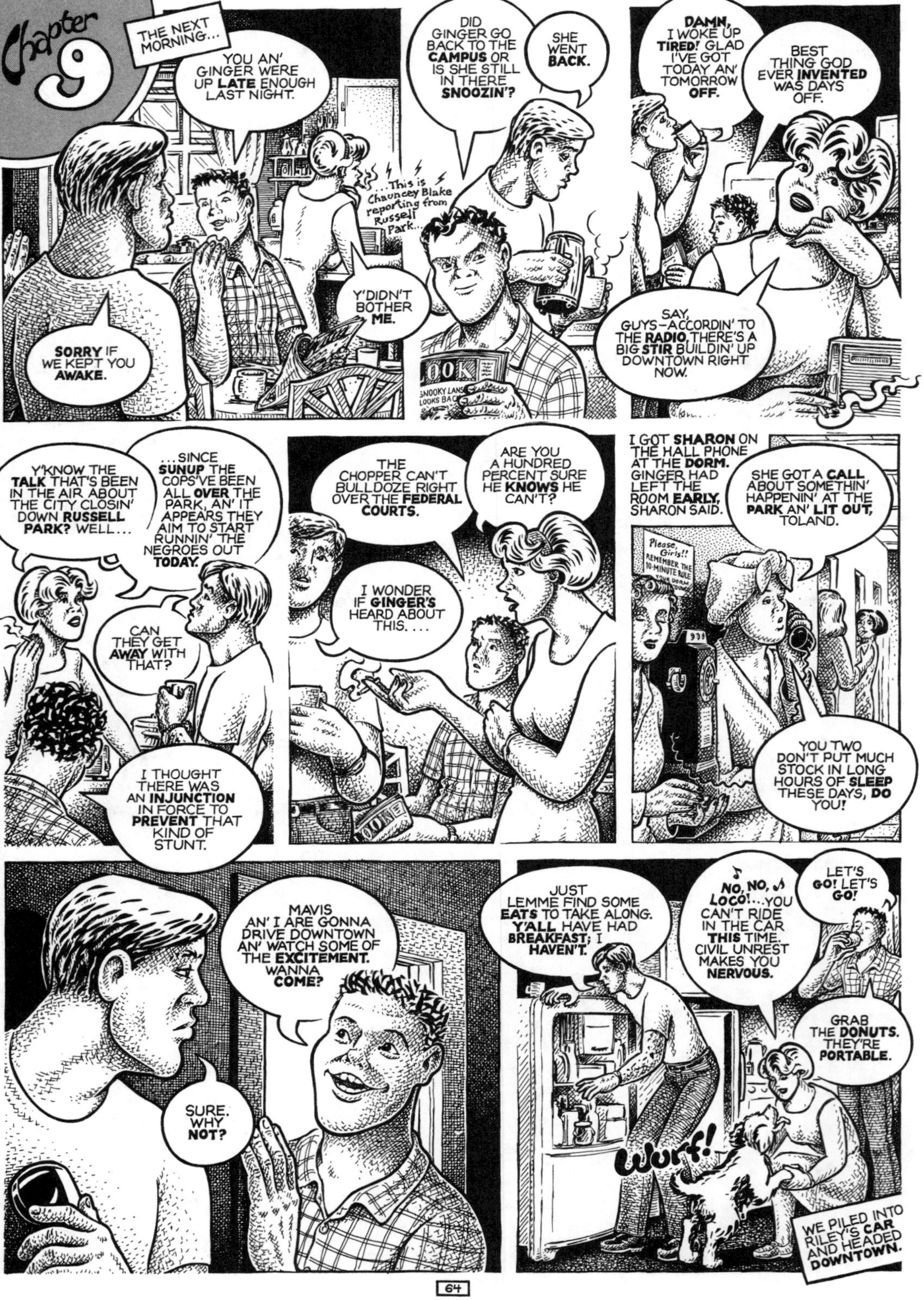

THE NEXT MORNING...
YOU AN' GINGER WERE UP LATE ENOUGH LAST NIGHT.
SORRY IF WE KEPT YOU AWAKE.
...This is Chauncey Blake reporting from Russell Park...
Y'DIDN'T BOTHER ME.
DID GINGER GO BACK TO THE CAMPUS OR IS SHE STILL IN THERE SNOOZIN'?
SHE WENT BACK.
LOOK
SNOOKY LANS LOOKS BACK
DAMN, I WOKE UP TIRED! GLAD I'VE GOT TODAY AN' TOMORROW OFF.
BEST THING GOD EVER INVENTED WAS DAYS OFF.
SAY, GUYS—ACCORDIN' TO THE RADIO, THERE'S A BIG STIR BUILDIN' UP DOWNTOWN RIGHT NOW.
Y'KNOW THE TALK THAT'S BEEN IN THE AIR ABOUT THE CITY CLOSIN' DOWN RUSSELL PARK? WELL...
...SINCE SUNUP THE COPS'VE BEEN ALL OVER THE PARK, AN' IT APPEARS THEY AIM TO START RUNNIN' THE NEGROES OUT TODAY.
CAN THEY GET AWAY WITH THAT?
I THOUGHT THERE WAS AN INJUNCTION IN FORCE TO PREVENT THAT KIND OF STUNT.
THE CHOPPER CAN'T BULLDOZE RIGHT OVER THE FEDERAL COURTS.
ARE YOU A HUNDRED PERCENT SURE HE KNOWS HE CAN'T?
I WONDER IF GINGER'S HEARD ABOUT THIS....
I GOT SHARON ON THE HALL PHONE AT THE DORM. GINGER HAD LEFT THE ROOM EARLY, SHARON SAID.
Please, Girls!! REMEMBER THE 10-MINUTE RULE
SHE GOT A CALL ABOUT SOMETHIN' HAPPENIN' AT THE PARK AN' LIT OUT, TOLAND.
YOU TWO DON'T PUT MUCH STOCK IN LONG HOURS OF SLEEP THESE DAYS, DO YOU!
MAVIS AN' I ARE GONNA DRIVE DOWNTOWN AN' WATCH SOME OF THE EXCITEMENT. WANNA COME?
SURE. WHY NOT?
JUST LEMME FIND SOME EATS TO TAKE ALONG. Y'ALL HAVE HAD BREAKFAST; I HAVEN'T.
♪ NO, NO, LOCO! ♪ ...YOU CAN'T RIDE IN THE CAR THIS TIME. CIVIL UNREST MAKES YOU NERVOUS.
LET'S GO! LET'S GO!
GRAB THE DONUTS. THEY'RE PORTABLE.
Wurf!
WE PILED INTO RILEY'S CAR AND HEADED DOWNTOWN.

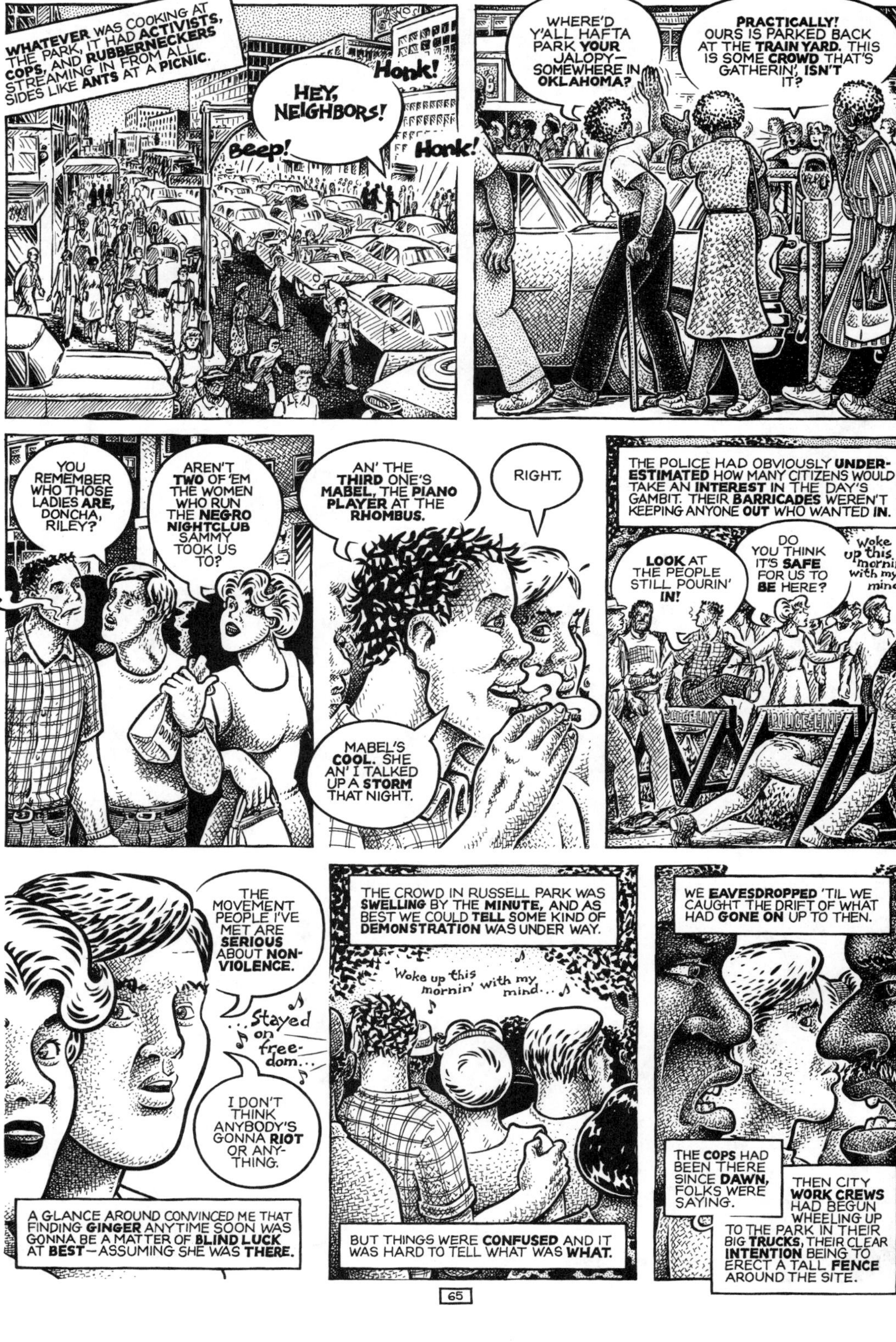
WHATEVER WAS COOKING AT THE PARK, IT HAD ACTIVISTS, COPS, AND RUBBERNECKERS STREAMING IN FROM ALL SIDES LIKE ANTS AT A PICNIC.
HEY, NEIGHBORS!
Honk!
Beep!
Honk!
WHERE'D Y'ALL HAFTA PARK YOUR JALOPY— SOMEWHERE IN OKLAHOMA?
PRACTICALLY! OURS IS PARKED BACK AT THE TRAIN YARD. THIS IS SOME CROWD THAT'S GATHERIN', ISN'T IT?
YOU REMEMBER WHO THOSE LADIES ARE, DONCHA, RILEY?
AREN'T TWO OF 'EM THE WOMEN WHO RUN THE NEGRO NIGHTCLUB SAMMY TOOK US TO?
AN' THE THIRD ONE'S MABEL, THE PIANO PLAYER AT THE RHOMBUS.
RIGHT.
MABEL'S COOL. SHE AN' I TALKED UP A STORM THAT NIGHT.
THE POLICE HAD OBVIOUSLY UNDERESTIMATED HOW MANY CITIZENS WOULD TAKE AN INTEREST IN THE DAY'S GAMBIT. THEIR BARRICADES WEREN'T KEEPING ANYONE OUT WHO WANTED IN.
LOOK AT THE PEOPLE STILL POURIN' IN!
DO YOU THINK IT'S SAFE FOR US TO BE HERE?
Woke up this mornin' with my mind...
POLICE LINE
POLICE LINE
THE MOVEMENT PEOPLE I'VE MET ARE SERIOUS ABOUT NON-VIOLENCE.
...Stayed on free-dom...
I DON'T THINK ANYBODY'S GONNA RIOT OR ANY-THING.
A GLANCE AROUND CONVINCED ME THAT FINDING GINGER ANYTIME SOON WAS GONNA BE A MATTER OF BLIND LUCK AT BEST—ASSUMING SHE WAS THERE.
THE CROWD IN RUSSELL PARK WAS SWELLING BY THE MINUTE, AND AS BEST WE COULD TELL SOME KIND OF DEMONSTRATION WAS UNDER WAY.
Woke up this mornin' with my mind...
BUT THINGS WERE CONFUSED AND IT WAS HARD TO TELL WHAT WAS WHAT.
WE EAVESDROPPED 'TIL WE CAUGHT THE DRIFT OF WHAT HAD GONE ON UP TO THEN.
THE COPS HAD BEEN THERE SINCE DAWN, FOLKS WERE SAYING.
THEN CITY WORK CREWS HAD BEGUN WHEELING UP TO THE PARK IN THEIR BIG TRUCKS, THEIR CLEAR INTENTION BEING TO ERECT A TALL FENCE AROUND THE SITE.

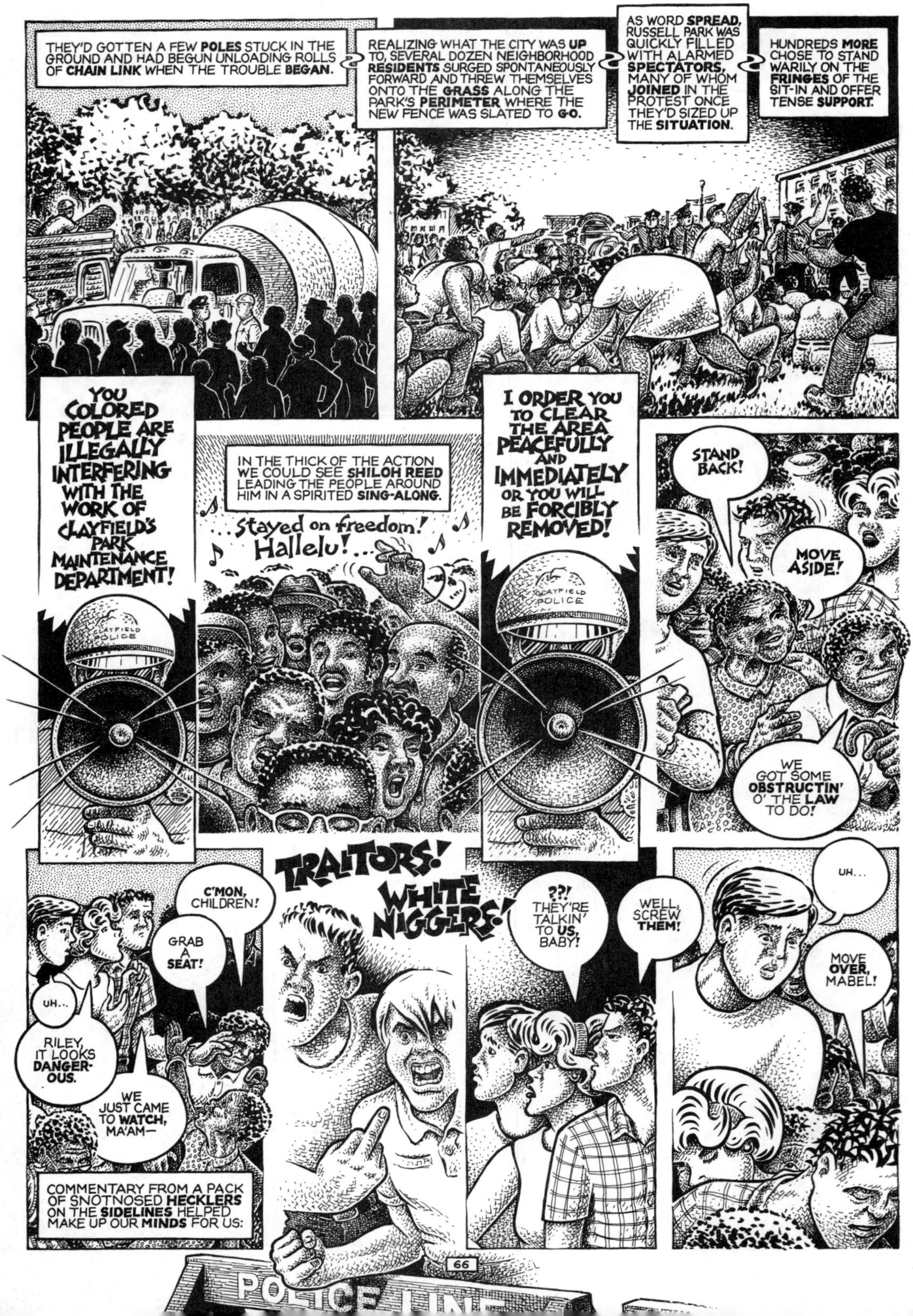

THEY'D GOTTEN A FEW POLES STUCK IN THE GROUND AND HAD BEGUN UNLOADING ROLLS OF CHAIN LINK WHEN THE TROUBLE BEGAN.
REALIZING WHAT THE CITY WAS UP TO, SEVERAL DOZEN NEIGHBORHOOD RESIDENTS SURGED SPONTANEOUSLY FORWARD AND THREW THEMSELVES ONTO THE GRASS ALONG THE PARK'S PERIMETER WHERE THE NEW FENCE WAS SLATED TO GO.
AS WORD SPREAD, RUSSELL PARK WAS QUICKLY FILLED WITH ALARMED SPECTATORS, MANY OF WHOM JOINED IN THE PROTEST ONCE THEY'D SIZED UP THE SITUATION.
HUNDREDS MORE CHOSE TO STAND WARILY ON THE FRINGES OF THE SIT-IN AND OFFER TENSE SUPPORT.
YOU COLORED PEOPLE ARE ILLEGALLY INTERFERING WITH THE WORK OF CLAYFIELD'S PARK MAINTENANCE DEPARTMENT!
CLAYFIELD POLICE
IN THE THICK OF THE ACTION WE COULD SEE SHILOH REED LEADING THE PEOPLE AROUND HIM IN A SPIRITED SING-ALONG.
...Stayed on freedom! Hallelu!...
I ORDER YOU TO CLEAR THE AREA PEACEFULLY AND IMMEDIATELY OR YOU WILL BE FORCIBLY REMOVED!
CLAYFIELD POLICE
STAND BACK!
MOVE ASIDE!
WE GOT SOME OBSTRUCTIN' O' THE LAW TO DO!
C'MON, CHILDREN!
GRAB A SEAT!
UH...
RILEY, IT LOOKS DANGER-OUS.
WE JUST CAME TO WATCH, MA'AM—
COMMENTARY FROM A PACK OF SNOTNOSED HECKLERS ON THE SIDELINES HELPED MAKE UP OUR MINDS FOR US:
TRAITORS!
WHITE NIGGERS!
??! THEY'RE TALKIN' TO US, BABY!
WELL, SCREW THEM!
UH...
MOVE OVER, MABEL!
POLICE LINE

BEFORE I KNEW IT I WAS ON THE GROUND GIVING THE **POLICE** AND **FENCE-BUILDING CREW** A HARD TIME LIKE EVERYBODY **ELSE.**

OF COURSE, AS SOON AS I WAS **DOWN** THERE AND **COMMITTED,** I STARTED WONDERING WHAT I HAD GOTTEN MYSELF **INTO.**

MARGE, **LOOK!** HERE COMES TH' **REVEREND.**

AN' THERE'S **LES** AN' **RAEBURN** HELPIN' OUT.

LISTEN **UP,** EVER'BODY— WHO HERE AIN'T HAD THE EQUALITY LEAGUE'S **CIVIL DISOBEDIENCE** TRAININ'? LEMME SEE **HANDS.**

LES!

'LO, **TOLAND.** SAY-Y-Y! LOOKS LIKE THE **GANG'S** ALL **HERE!**

WHADDAYA THINK'S GONNA **HAPPEN?**

O.K., IF YOU **AIN'T** BEEN TO THE WORKSHOPS, **FORGET** ANY NOTIONS Y'GOT ABOUT REFUSIN' TO **DO** WHAT THE MAN **SAYS** IF A COP LOOKS STRAIGHT AT YOU AN' TELLS YOU TO **MOVE.**

WELL, TOLE, THERE'S **ONE** THING OPERATIN' IN OUR FAVOR: THE **CHOPPER** AIN'T ON THE SCENE SO FAR.

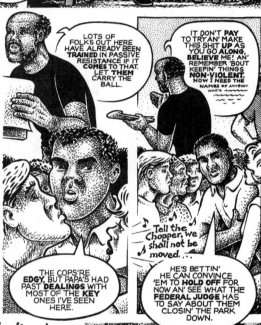

LOTS OF FOLKS OUT HERE HAVE ALREADY BEEN **TRAINED** IN PASSIVE RESISTANCE IF IT **COMES** TO THAT. LET **THEM** CARRY THE BALL.

IT DON'T **PAY** TO TRY AN' MAKE THIS SHIT **UP** AS YOU GO ALONG, BELIEVE ME! AN' REMEMBER 'BOUT KEEPIN' THINGS **NON-VIOLENT.** NOW I NEED THE NAMES OF ANYBODY WHO'S

THE COPS'RE **EDGY,** BUT PAPA'S HAD PAST **DEALINGS** WITH MOST OF THE **KEY** ONES I'VE SEEN HERE.

♪ Tell the Chopper, we shall not be moved... ♪

HE'S BETTIN' HE CAN CONVINCE 'EM TO **HOLD OFF** FOR NOW AN' SEE WHAT THE **FEDERAL JUDGE** HAS TO SAY ABOUT THEM CLOSIN' THE PARK DOWN.

♪ ..We shall not be moved... ♪ ♪

AROUND THEN WE NOTICED THAT THE **BACKGROUND MUSIC** WAS COMING FROM A **SMALLER** SET OF **VOICES.**

♪ Tell the... ♪

WHO'RE THE **KIDS** THAT'RE SINGIN'?

♪ ..Chop-per... ♪

THAT'S SHILOH'S **FREEDOM CHORUS.**

THEY ALL GREW UP HARMONIZIN' FOR **FUN.**

WHEN HE GOT TO **TOWN,** SHILOH MADE A **PROJECT** OF TEACHIN' 'EM ALL THE **FREEDOM SONGS** HE KNOWS.

HE'S ABOUT GOT 'EM READY TO DO **CONCERTS,** SHILOH SAYS.

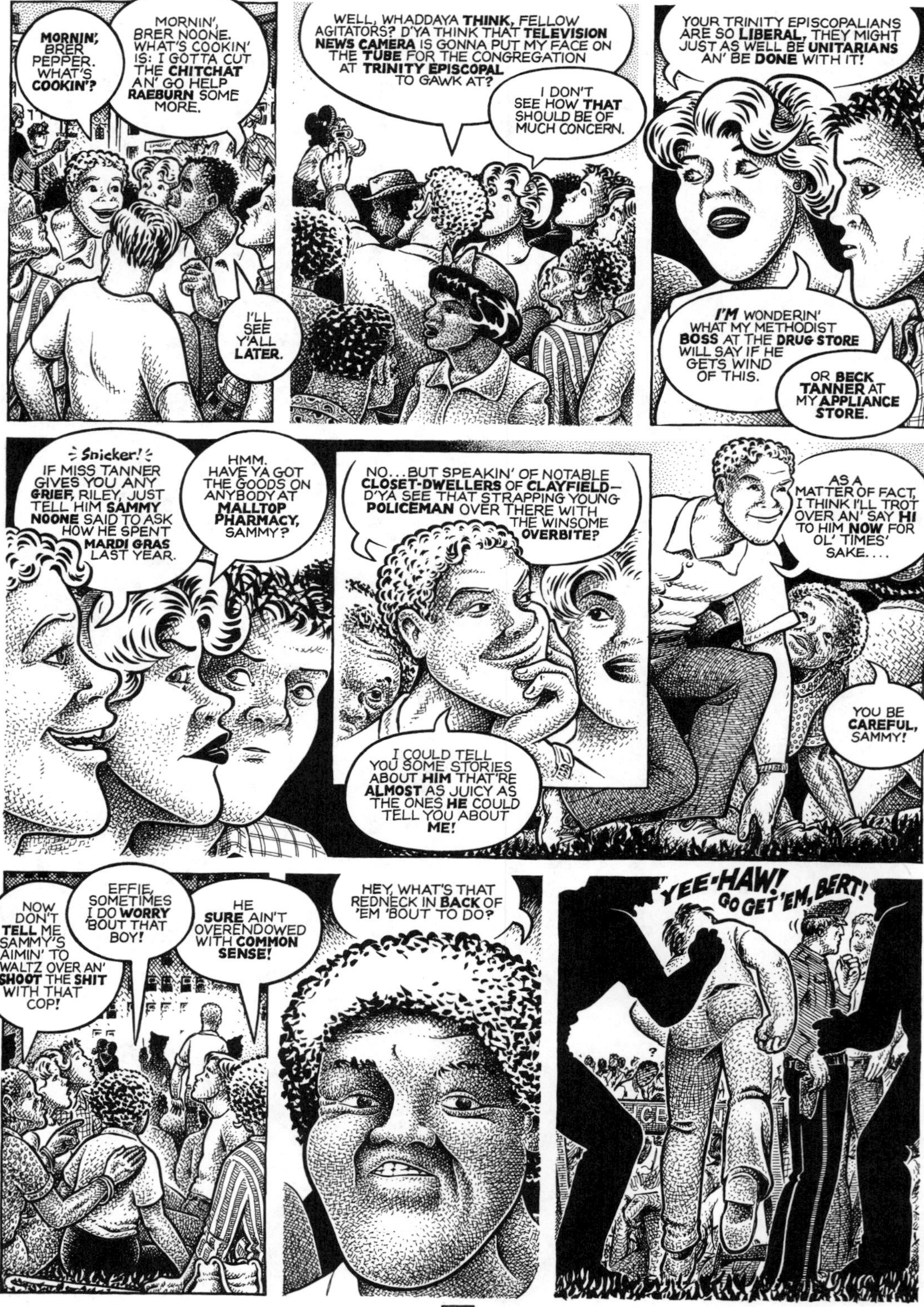
MORNIN', BRER PEPPER. WHAT'S COOKIN'?
MORNIN', BRER NOONE. WHAT'S COOKIN' IS: I GOTTA CUT THE CHITCHAT AN' GO HELP RAEBURN SOME MORE.
I'LL SEE Y'ALL LATER.
WELL, WHADDAYA THINK, FELLOW AGITATORS? D'YA THINK THAT TELEVISION NEWS CAMERA IS GONNA PUT MY FACE ON THE TUBE FOR THE CONGREGATION AT TRINITY EPISCOPAL TO GAWK AT?
I DON'T SEE HOW THAT SHOULD BE OF MUCH CONCERN.
YOUR TRINITY EPISCOPALIANS ARE SO LIBERAL, THEY MIGHT JUST AS WELL BE UNITARIANS AN' BE DONE WITH IT!
I'M WONDERIN' WHAT MY METHODIST BOSS AT THE DRUG STORE WILL SAY IF HE GETS WIND OF THIS.
OR BECK TANNER AT MY APPLIANCE STORE.
Snicker!
IF MISS TANNER GIVES YOU ANY GRIEF, RILEY, JUST TELL HIM SAMMY NOONE SAID TO ASK HOW HE SPENT MARDI GRAS LAST YEAR.
HMM. HAVE YA GOT THE GOODS ON ANYBODY AT MALLTOP PHARMACY, SAMMY?
NO...BUT SPEAKIN' OF NOTABLE CLOSET-DWELLERS OF CLAYFIELD— D'YA SEE THAT STRAPPING YOUNG POLICEMAN OVER THERE WITH THE WINSOME OVERBITE?
I COULD TELL YOU SOME STORIES ABOUT HIM THAT'RE ALMOST AS JUICY AS THE ONES HE COULD TELL YOU ABOUT ME!
AS A MATTER OF FACT, I THINK I'LL TROT OVER AN' SAY HI TO HIM NOW FOR OL' TIMES' SAKE....
YOU BE CAREFUL, SAMMY!
NOW DON'T TELL ME SAMMY'S AIMIN' TO WALTZ OVER AN' SHOOT THE SHIT WITH THAT COP!
EFFIE, SOMETIMES I DO WORRY 'BOUT THAT BOY!
HE SURE AIN'T OVERENDOWED WITH COMMON SENSE!
HEY, WHAT'S THAT REDNECK IN BACK OF 'EM 'BOUT TO DO?
YEE-HAW! GO GET 'EM, BERT!

Whoopee-e-e...!
GO! GO! GO
YAY-Y-Y!!
GO BACK TO AFRICA, NIGGAHS!
UNH!!
BEHIND Y— ?! WHAT'S HE—?? I DON'T—
NGGA
WHY AREN'T Y— ??!
KEEP Y'SHIRT ON.
flick!
EASY, FELLA! Y'BETTER COOL OFF SOME— Y'HEAR?
WHY'D YA WAIT SO LONG??
YOU SAW WHAT WAS GOING ON!
YOU JUST STOOD THERE WHILE HE GOT IN A FEW MORE KICKS!
SHADDUP!
OW!
WHACK!
AN' DON'T YOU GO SPREADIN' LIES ABOUT ME EITHER, FAGGOT!

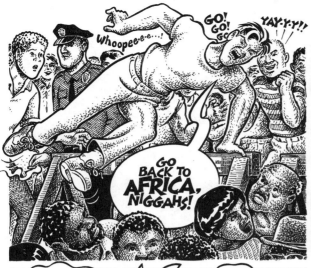

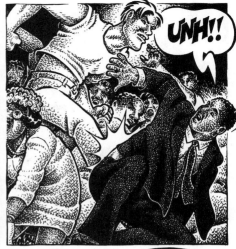

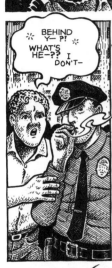

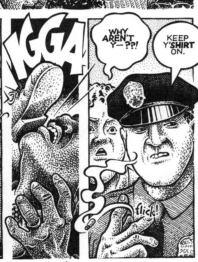

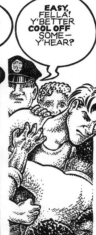

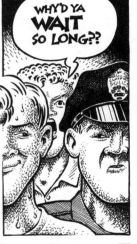

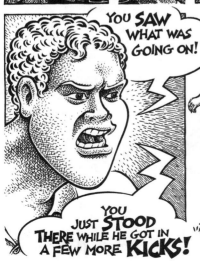

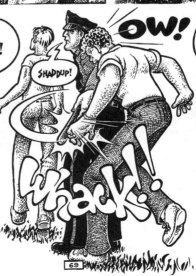

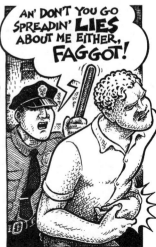

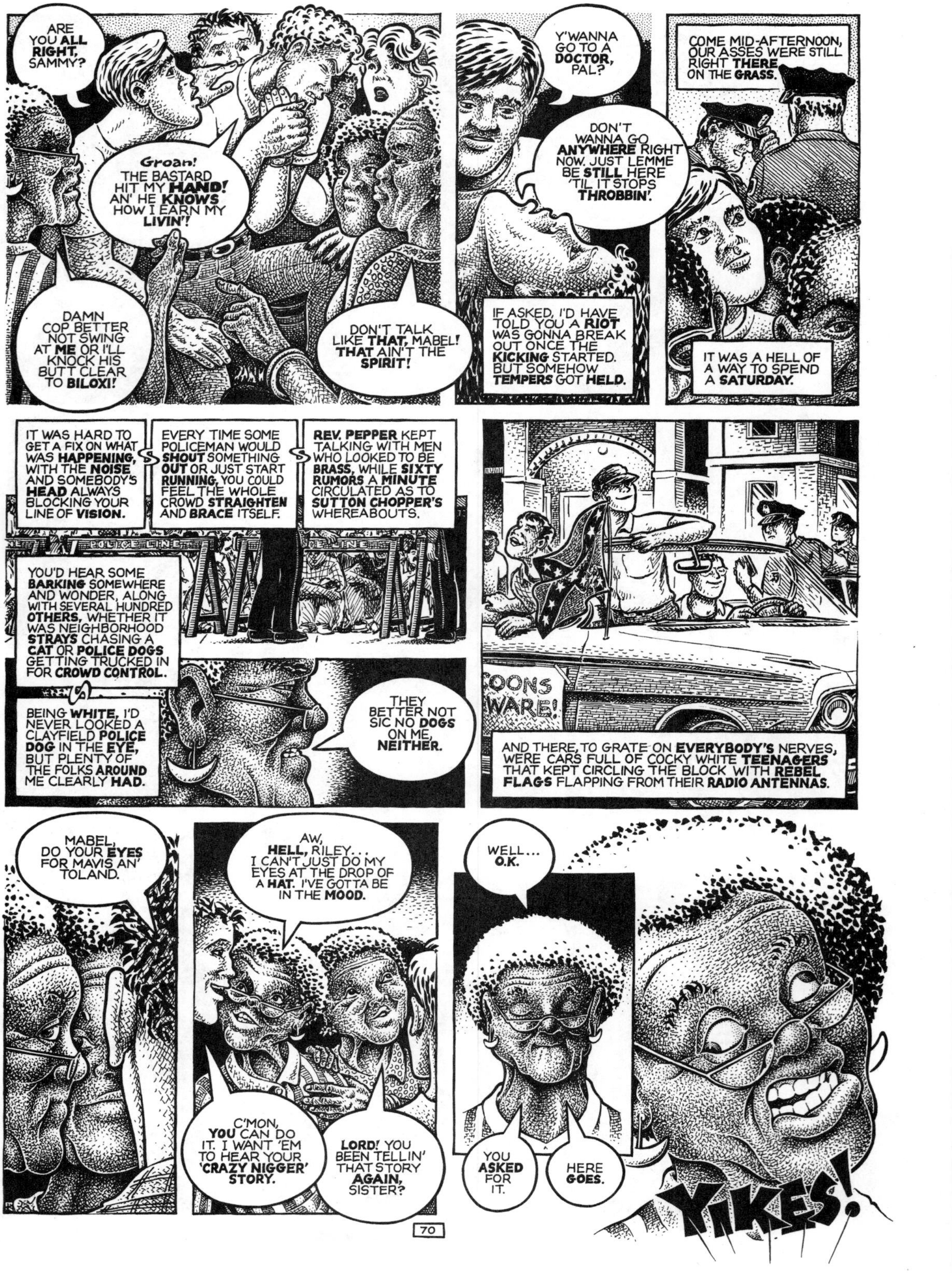

ARE YOU **ALL RIGHT,** SAMMY?
Groan! THE BASTARD HIT MY **HAND!** AN' HE **KNOWS** HOW I EARN MY **LIVIN'!**
DAMN COP BETTER NOT SWING AT **ME** OR I'LL KNOCK HIS BUTT CLEAR TO **BILOXI!**
DON'T TALK LIKE **THAT,** MABEL! **THAT** AIN'T THE **SPIRIT!**
Y'WANNA GO TO A **DOCTOR,** PAL?
DON'T WANNA GO **ANYWHERE** RIGHT NOW. JUST LEMME BE **STILL** HERE 'TIL IT STOPS **THROBBIN'.**
IF ASKED, I'D HAVE TOLD YOU A **RIOT** WAS GONNA BREAK OUT ONCE THE **KICKING** STARTED. BUT SOMEHOW **TEMPERS** GOT **HELD.**
COME MID-AFTERNOON, OUR ASSES WERE STILL RIGHT **THERE** ON THE **GRASS.**
IT WAS A HELL OF A WAY TO SPEND A **SATURDAY.**
IT WAS HARD TO GET A FIX ON WHAT WAS **HAPPENING,** WITH THE **NOISE** AND SOMEBODY'S **HEAD** ALWAYS BLOCKING YOUR LINE OF **VISION.**
EVERY TIME SOME POLICEMAN WOULD **SHOUT** SOMETHING **OUT** OR JUST START **RUNNING,** YOU COULD FEEL THE WHOLE CROWD **STRAIGHTEN** AND **BRACE** ITSELF.
REV. PEPPER KEPT TALKING WITH MEN WHO LOOKED TO BE **BRASS,** WHILE **SIXTY RUMORS** A **MINUTE** CIRCULATED AS TO **SUTTON CHOPPER'S** WHEREABOUTS.
POLICE LINE
YOU'D HEAR SOME **BARKING** SOMEWHERE AND WONDER, ALONG WITH SEVERAL HUNDRED **OTHERS,** WHETHER IT WAS NEIGHBORHOOD **STRAYS** CHASING A **CAT** OR **POLICE DOGS** GETTING TRUCKED IN FOR **CROWD CONTROL.**
BEING **WHITE,** I'D NEVER LOOKED A CLAYFIELD **POLICE DOG** IN THE **EYE,** BUT PLENTY OF THE FOLKS **AROUND** ME CLEARLY **HAD.**
THEY BETTER NOT SIC NO **DOGS** ON ME, **NEITHER.**
COONS WARE!
AND THERE, TO GRATE ON **EVERYBODY'S** NERVES, WERE CARS FULL OF COCKY WHITE **TEENAGERS** THAT KEPT CIRCLING THE BLOCK WITH **REBEL FLAGS** FLAPPING FROM THEIR **RADIO ANTENNAS.**
MABEL, DO YOUR **EYES** FOR MAVIS AN' TOLAND.
AW, **HELL,** RILEY... I CAN'T JUST DO MY EYES AT THE DROP OF A **HAT.** I'VE GOTTA BE IN THE **MOOD.**
C'MON, **YOU** CAN DO IT. I WANT 'EM TO HEAR YOUR **'CRAZY NIGGER' STORY.**
LORD! YOU BEEN TELLIN' THAT STORY **AGAIN,** SISTER?
WELL... **O.K.**
YOU **ASKED** FOR IT.
HERE **GOES.**
YIKES!

THERE! Y'SATISFIED, RILEY?

THE STORY I TOLD RILEY WHEN Y'ALL WAS AT THE **RHOMBUS** WAS 'BOUT HOW, BACK IN THE **'THIRTIES** WHEN I LIVED IN PARTS OF THE SOUTH MORE **BACKWARDS** EVEN THAN **CLAYFIELD**...

Nossir! In fact, I usually sat right up in **front** by the **driver.**

I **WILL** BE WHEN YOU TELL MAVIS AN' TOLAND THE **STORY**.

TELL US, MABEL.

HE'S GOT US **CURIOUS** NOW.

... I **never** used to let 'em put me in the **back** of a bus.

DIDN'T THEY HAVE THE **BUS LAWS** BACK THEN?

OH, INDEED THEY **DID!**

JIM CROW WAS **KING O' THE HILL!**

COLORED FOLKS GOT **BEAT UP** OR **TOSSED OFF** THE BUS **ALL** THE TIME FOR NOT STEPPIN' **FAST** ENOUGH WHEN A DRIVER TOLD 'EM TO MOVE ON **BACK**.

NOW ASK 'ER HOW SHE GOT **AWAY** WITH IT EVEN **SO.**

I had a job **housekeepin'** in the next **county**, an' most of the time I was ridin' the **same** bus at the **same** times of the **day**... ...So the drivers got to **know** me.

But even when I was on a **different** bus with a **different** driver from usual, I pulled the **same** stunt.

YOU BE THE **BUS DRIVER, EFFIE.**

SEE, THE DRIVER, HE'D SWING 'ROUND TO SISTER **THIS** AN' SAY:

'**YOU GOTTA MOVE—Y'HEAR?** LAW SAYS **COLORED PEOPLE** GOTTA BE BACK OF THAT THERE **MARKER!**'

NOW SHOW 'EM WHAT YOU'D **DO, MABEL.**

I'D GO:

WHUH-WHUH-WHUH-**WHUH'D** JOO SAY?

Well, he'd say it **again:**

YOU GOTTA MOVE BACK **THERE**... **Y'HEAR??**

WHUH-**WHUH'D** JOO SAY?

AN' AS MANY TIMES AS HE'D TELL 'ER TO **MOVE**, SHE'D GIVE 'IM BACK THAT **SPOOKY LOOK**, LIKE SHE DIDN'T HAVE A **CLUE** WHAT HE WAS **TALKIN'** 'BOUT.

AN' THEY'D GO **BACK** AN' **FORTH**, 'ROUND AN' 'ROUND.

I LEARNED I COULD DO THAT THING WITH MY **EYES** WHEN I WAS A **BABY.** cackle!

MOST PEOPLE CAN'T **DO** IT! I'M GONNA GET A **PATENT** ON IT, I THINK!

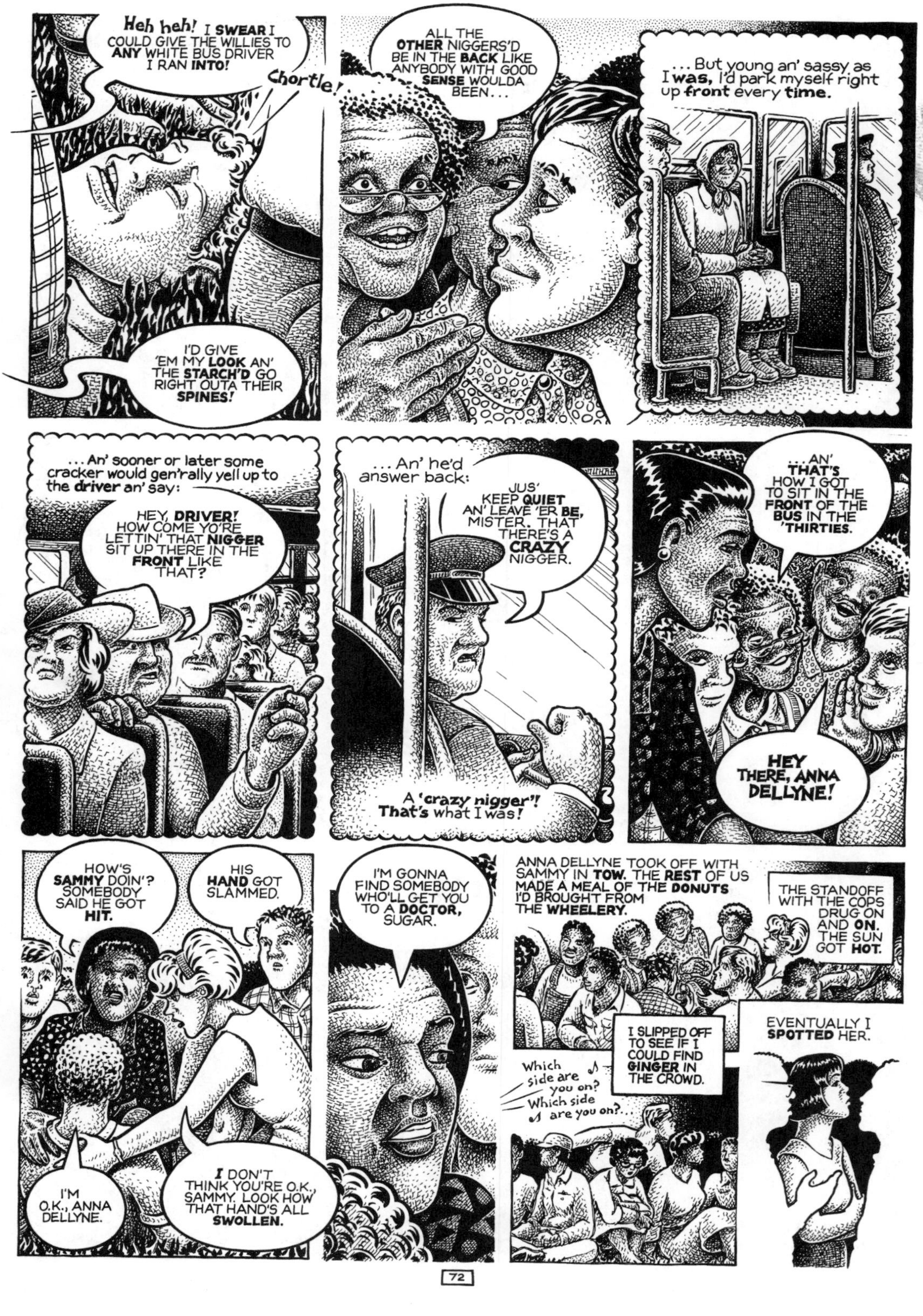

Heh heh! I SWEAR I COULD GIVE THE WILLIES TO ANY WHITE BUS DRIVER I RAN INTO!
Chortle!
I'D GIVE 'EM MY LOOK AN' THE STARCH'D GO RIGHT OUTA THEIR SPINES!
ALL THE OTHER NIGGERS'D BE IN THE BACK LIKE ANYBODY WITH GOOD SENSE WOULDA BEEN...
...But young an' sassy as I was, I'd park myself right up front every time.
...An' sooner or later some cracker would gen'rally yell up to the driver an' say:
HEY, DRIVER! HOW COME YO'RE LETTIN' THAT NIGGER SIT UP FRONT THERE IN THE FRONT LIKE THAT?
...An' he'd answer back:
JUS' KEEP QUIET AN' LEAVE 'ER BE, MISTER. THAT THERE'S A CRAZY NIGGER.
A 'crazy nigger'! That's what I was!
...AN' THAT'S HOW I GOT TO SIT IN THE FRONT OF THE BUS IN THE 'THIRTIES.
HEY THERE, ANNA DELLYNE!
HOW'S SAMMY DOIN'? SOMEBODY SAID HE GOT HIT.
HIS HAND GOT SLAMMED.
I'M O.K., ANNA DELLYNE.
I DON'T THINK YOU'RE O.K., SAMMY. LOOK HOW THAT HAND'S ALL SWOLLEN.
I'M GONNA FIND SOMEBODY WHO'LL GET YOU TO A DOCTOR, SUGAR.
ANNA DELLYNE TOOK OFF WITH SAMMY IN TOW. THE REST OF US MADE A MEAL OF THE DONUTS I'D BROUGHT FROM THE WHEELERY.
THE STANDOFF WITH THE COPS DRUG ON AND ON. THE SUN GOT HOT.
I SLIPPED OFF TO SEE IF I COULD FIND GINGER IN THE CROWD.
Which side are you on? Which side are you on?...
EVENTUALLY I SPOTTED HER.

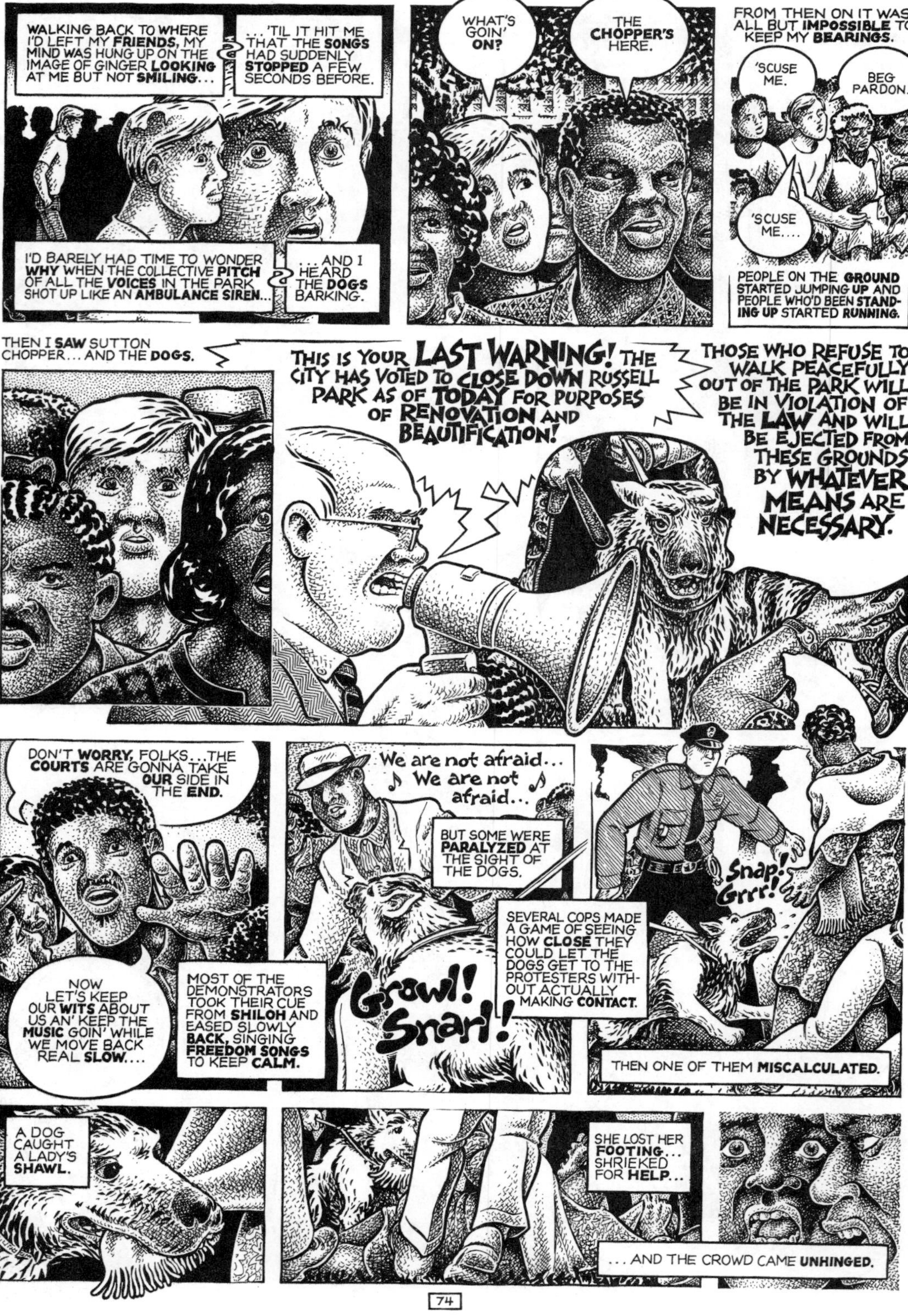
WALKING BACK TO WHERE I'D LEFT MY FRIENDS, MY MIND WAS HUNG UP ON THE IMAGE OF GINGER LOOKING AT ME BUT NOT SMILING...
... 'TIL IT HIT ME THAT THE SONGS HAD SUDDENLY STOPPED A FEW SECONDS BEFORE.
I'D BARELY HAD TIME TO WONDER WHY WHEN THE COLLECTIVE PITCH OF ALL THE VOICES IN THE PARK SHOT UP LIKE AN AMBULANCE SIREN...
... AND I HEARD THE DOGS BARKING.
WHAT'S GOIN' ON?
THE CHOPPER'S HERE.
FROM THEN ON IT WAS ALL BUT IMPOSSIBLE TO KEEP MY BEARINGS.
'SCUSE ME.
BEG PARDON.
'SCUSE ME....
PEOPLE ON THE GROUND STARTED JUMPING UP AND PEOPLE WHO'D BEEN STANDING UP STARTED RUNNING.
THEN I SAW SUTTON CHOPPER... AND THE DOGS.
THIS IS YOUR LAST WARNING! THE CITY HAS VOTED TO CLOSE DOWN RUSSELL PARK AS OF TODAY FOR PURPOSES OF RENOVATION AND BEAUTIFICATION!
THOSE WHO REFUSE TO WALK PEACEFULLY OUT OF THE PARK WILL BE IN VIOLATION OF THE LAW AND WILL BE EJECTED FROM THESE GROUNDS BY WHATEVER MEANS ARE NECESSARY.
DON'T WORRY, FOLKS... THE COURTS ARE GONNA TAKE OUR SIDE IN THE END.
NOW LET'S KEEP OUR WITS ABOUT US AN' KEEP THE MUSIC GOIN' WHILE WE MOVE BACK REAL SLOW....
MOST OF THE DEMONSTRATORS TOOK THEIR CUE FROM SHILOH AND EASED SLOWLY BACK, SINGING FREEDOM SONGS TO KEEP CALM.
We are not afraid... We are not afraid...
BUT SOME WERE PARALYZED AT THE SIGHT OF THE DOGS.
Growl! Snarl!
SEVERAL COPS MADE A GAME OF SEEING HOW CLOSE THEY COULD LET THE DOGS GET TO THE PROTESTERS WITHOUT ACTUALLY MAKING CONTACT.
Snap! Grrr!
THEN ONE OF THEM MISCALCULATED.
A DOG CAUGHT A LADY'S SHAWL.
SHE LOST HER FOOTING... SHRIEKED FOR HELP...
... AND THE CROWD CAME UNHINGED.

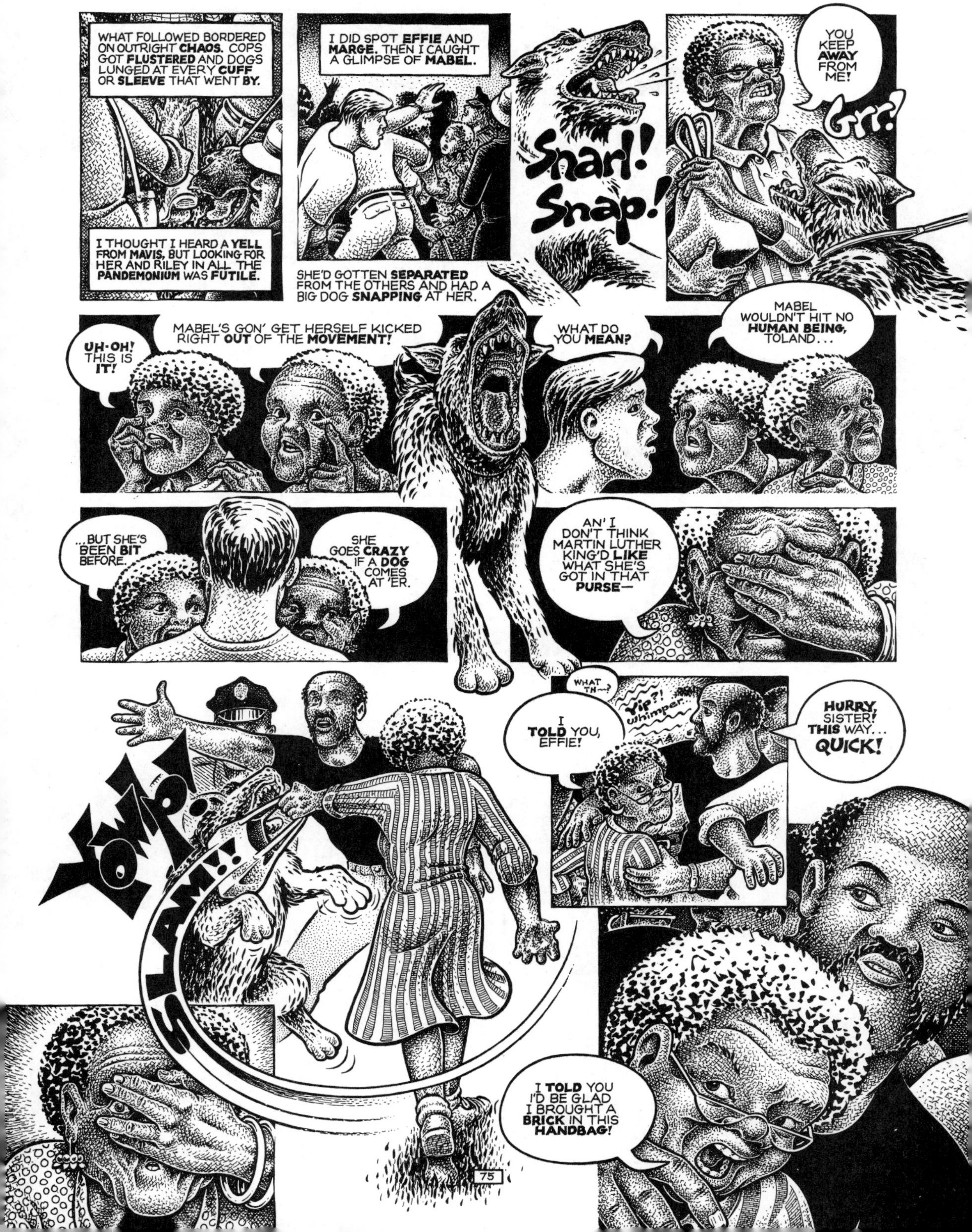

WHAT FOLLOWED BORDERED ON OUTRIGHT CHAOS. COPS GOT FLUSTERED AND DOGS LUNGED AT EVERY CUFF OR SLEEVE THAT WENT BY.
I THOUGHT I HEARD A YELL FROM MAVIS, BUT LOOKING FOR HER AND RILEY IN ALL THE PANDEMONIUM WAS FUTILE.
I DID SPOT EFFIE AND MARGE. THEN I CAUGHT A GLIMPSE OF MABEL.
SHE'D GOTTEN SEPARATED FROM THE OTHERS AND HAD A BIG DOG SNAPPING AT HER.
Snarl! Snap!
YOU KEEP AWAY FROM ME!
Grr?
UH-OH! THIS IS IT!
MABEL'S GON' GET HERSELF KICKED RIGHT OUT OF THE MOVEMENT!
WHAT DO YOU MEAN?
MABEL WOULDN'T HIT NO HUMAN BEING, TOLAND...
...BUT SHE'S BEEN BIT BEFORE.
SHE GOES CRAZY IF A DOG COMES AT 'ER.
AN' I DON'T THINK MARTIN LUTHER KING'D LIKE WHAT SHE'S GOT IN THAT PURSE—
YOWP!
SLAM!!
WHAT TH—?
Yip?! whimper
I TOLD YOU, EFFIE!
HURRY, SISTER! THIS WAY... QUICK!
I TOLD YOU I'D BE GLAD I BROUGHT A BRICK IN THIS HANDBAG!

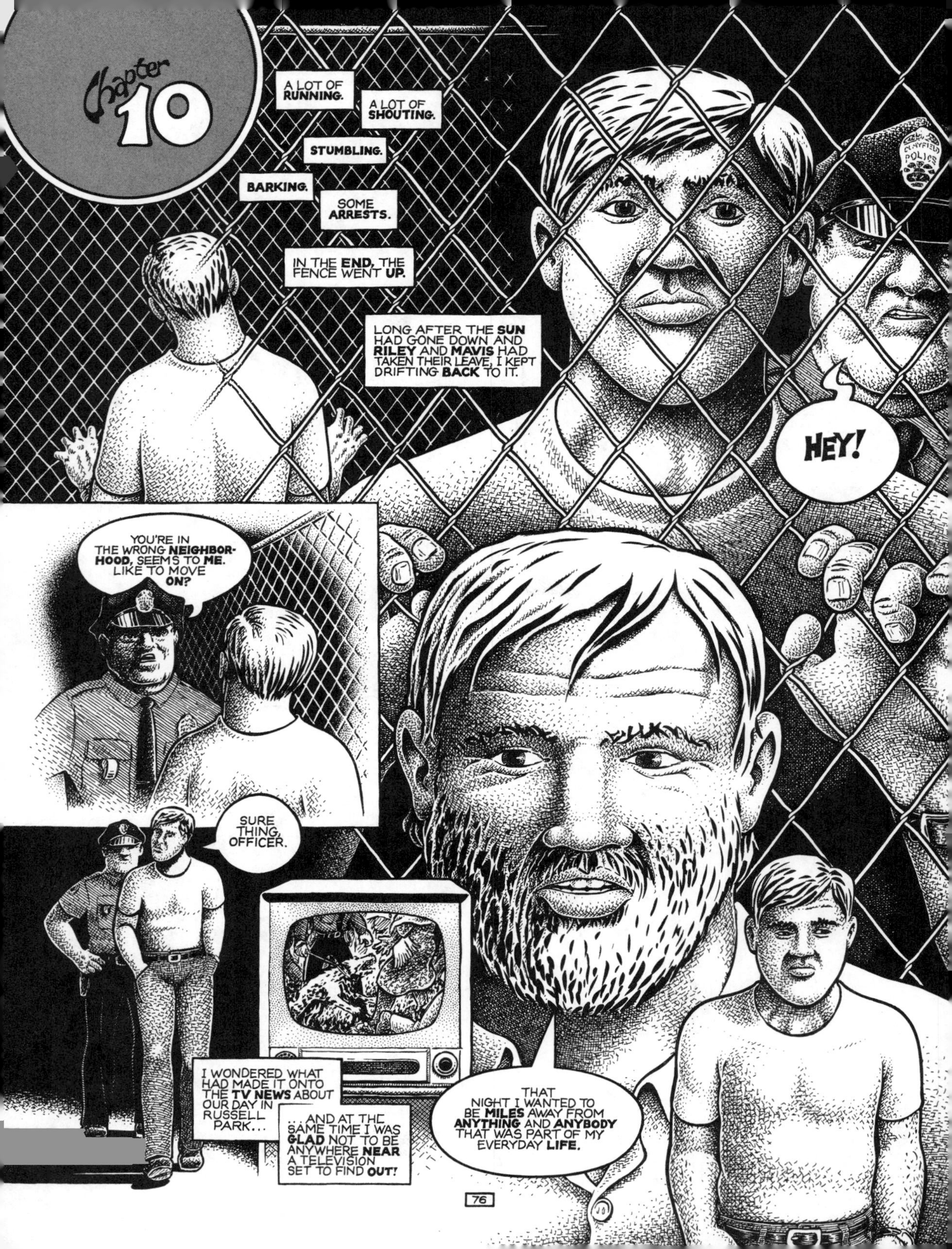
Chapter 10
A LOT OF RUNNING.
A LOT OF SHOUTING.
STUMBLING.
BARKING.
SOME ARRESTS.
IN THE END, THE FENCE WENT UP.
LONG AFTER THE SUN HAD GONE DOWN AND RILEY AND MAVIS HAD TAKEN THEIR LEAVE, I KEPT DRIFTING BACK TO IT.
HEY!
YOU'RE IN THE WRONG NEIGHBOR-HOOD, SEEMS TO ME. LIKE TO MOVE ON?
SURE THING, OFFICER.
I WONDERED WHAT HAD MADE IT ONTO THE TV NEWS ABOUT OUR DAY IN RUSSELL PARK...
...AND AT THE SAME TIME I WAS GLAD NOT TO BE ANYWHERE NEAR A TELEVISION SET TO FIND OUT!
THAT NIGHT I WANTED TO BE MILES AWAY FROM ANYTHING AND ANYBODY THAT WAS PART OF MY EVERYDAY LIFE.

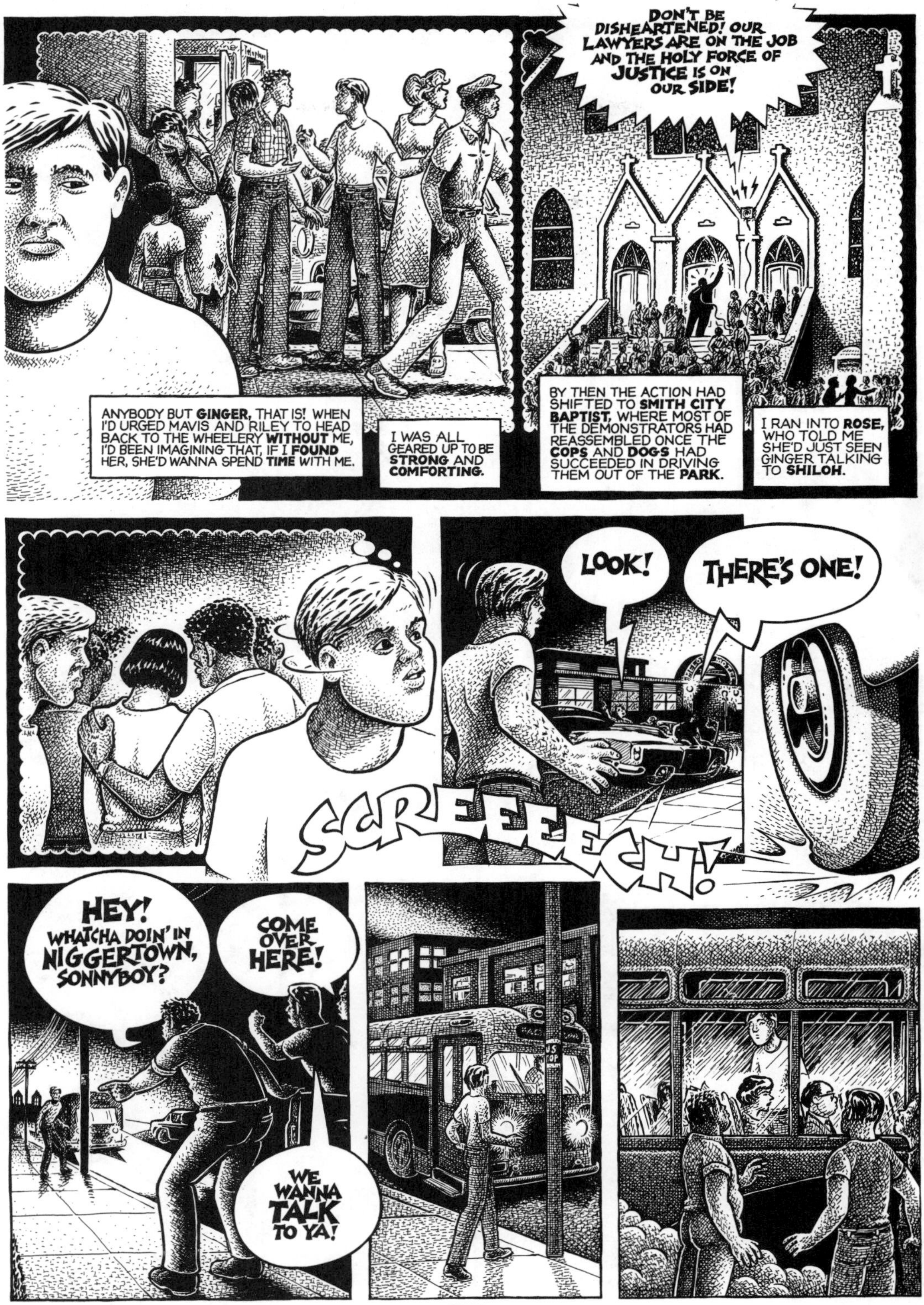

ANYBODY BUT GINGER, THAT IS! WHEN I'D URGED MAVIS AND RILEY TO HEAD BACK TO THE WHEELERY WITHOUT ME, I'D BEEN IMAGINING THAT, IF I FOUND HER, SHE'D WANNA SPEND TIME WITH ME.
I WAS ALL GEARED UP TO BE STRONG AND COMFORTING.
DON'T BE DISHEARTENED! OUR LAWYERS ARE ON THE JOB AND THE HOLY FORCE OF JUSTICE IS ON OUR SIDE!
BY THEN THE ACTION HAD SHIFTED TO SMITH CITY BAPTIST, WHERE MOST OF THE DEMONSTRATORS HAD REASSEMBLED ONCE THE COPS AND DOGS HAD SUCCEEDED IN DRIVING THEM OUT OF THE PARK.
I RAN INTO ROSE, WHO TOLD ME SHE'D JUST SEEN GINGER TALKING TO SHILOH.
LOOK!
THERE'S ONE!
SCREEEEECH!
HEY! WHATCHA DOIN' IN NIGGERTOWN, SONNYBOY?
COME OVER HERE!
WE WANNA TALK TO YA!

WHEN I GOT ON THE BUS, MY **INTENTION** WAS TO TRANSFER AT **EIGHTEENTH STREET** TO THE **COLLEGE LINE**, WHICH WOULD HAVE TAKEN ME DIRECTLY OUT TO THE **WHEELERY.**

BUT I NEVER **TRANSFERRED.**

INSTEAD I RODE ON TO **NINTH STREET.**

YOU HAVEN'T EATEN A **BURGER** UNTIL YOU'VE EATEN A **DONBURGER**

DON'S **BLACKBERRY COBBLER.** FAMOUS THROUGHOUT THE SOUTH

"WE RESERVE THE RIGHT TO REFUSE SERVICE TO ANYONE AT THE DISCRETION OF THE MANAGER"

COME AGAIN! YOU'RE ALWAYS **WELCOME** AT **DON'S DINER**

DID YOU KNOW ABOUT THESE **DIXIE PATRIOTS** BEIN' STACKED THERE BY THE DOOR?

OH, **THOSE** THINGS! AREN'T THEY **AWFUL?**

SOME MAN **INSISTS** ON COMIN' AN' PUTTIN' **PILES** OF THOSE PAPERS OUT FRONT. MY **BOSS** LETS HIM DO IT. NOBODY ASKS **ME!**

THE PEOPLE THAT PUT THAT OUT **SAY** THEY'RE **CHRISTIANS**, BUT I DON'T THINK THEY **ACT** VERY CHRISTIAN... DO **YOU?**

THEY **SAY** THINGS ABOUT PEOPLE THAT DON'T SEEM CHRISTIAN TO **ME** AT **ALL!**

OF COURSE, I **DO** THINK THEY HAVE A **POINT** WHEN THEY SAY IT'S PROBABLY THE **COMMUNISTS** WHO'RE CONVINCIN' THE NEGROES THAT THEY'RE SO **DISSATISFIED.**

BUT IT'S THE UGLY **WAY** THEY SAY IT!

UHN-UH!!

IT'S **WAY** TOO UNCHRISTIAN FOR **ME!**

AFTER MY **MEAL...**

I STOOD, THEN STOOD SOME **MORE.** THEN FINALLY I WENT **IN.**

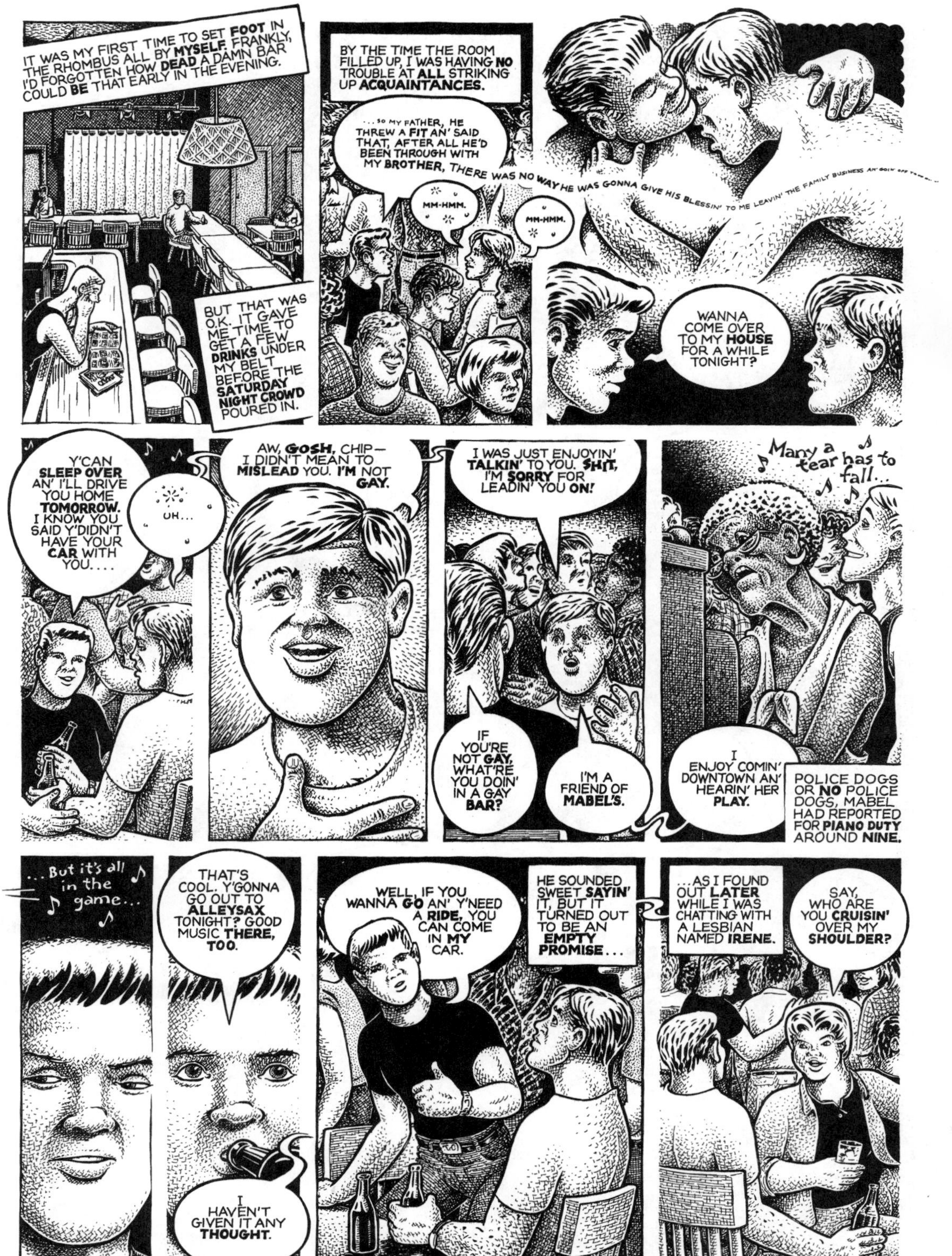
IT WAS MY FIRST TIME TO SET FOOT IN THE RHOMBUS ALL BY MYSELF. FRANKLY, I'D FORGOTTEN HOW DEAD A DAMN BAR COULD BE THAT EARLY IN THE EVENING.
BUT THAT WAS O.K. IT GAVE ME TIME TO GET A FEW DRINKS UNDER MY BELT BEFORE THE SATURDAY NIGHT CROWD POURED IN.
BY THE TIME THE ROOM FILLED UP, I WAS HAVING NO TROUBLE AT ALL STRIKING UP ACQUAINTANCES.
...SO MY FATHER, HE THREW A FIT AN' SAID THAT, AFTER ALL HE'D BEEN THROUGH WITH MY BROTHER, THERE WAS NO WAY HE WAS GONNA GIVE HIS BLESSIN' TO ME LEAVIN' THE FAMILY BUSINESS AN' GOIN' OFF
MM-HMM.
MM-HMM.
WANNA COME OVER TO MY HOUSE FOR A WHILE TONIGHT?
Y'CAN SLEEP OVER AN' I'LL DRIVE YOU HOME TOMORROW. I KNOW YOU SAID Y'DIDN'T HAVE YOUR CAR WITH YOU....
UH...
AW, GOSH, CHIP— I DIDN'T MEAN TO MISLEAD YOU. I'M NOT GAY.
I WAS JUST ENJOYIN' TALKIN' TO YOU. SHIT, I'M SORRY FOR LEADIN' YOU ON!
IF YOU'RE NOT GAY, WHAT'RE YOU DOIN' IN A GAY BAR?
I'M A FRIEND OF MABEL'S.
I ENJOY COMIN' DOWNTOWN AN' HEARIN' HER PLAY.
Many a tear has to fall...
POLICE DOGS OR NO POLICE DOGS, MABEL HAD REPORTED FOR PIANO DUTY AROUND NINE.
...But it's all in the game...
THAT'S COOL. Y'GONNA GO OUT TO ALLEYSAX TONIGHT? GOOD MUSIC THERE, TOO.
I HAVEN'T GIVEN IT ANY THOUGHT.
WELL, IF YOU WANNA GO AN' Y'NEED A RIDE, YOU CAN COME IN MY CAR.
HE SOUNDED SWEET SAYIN' IT, BUT IT TURNED OUT TO BE AN EMPTY PROMISE...
...AS I FOUND OUT LATER WHILE I WAS CHATTING WITH A LESBIAN NAMED IRENE.
SAY, WHO ARE YOU CRUISIN' OVER MY SHOULDER?

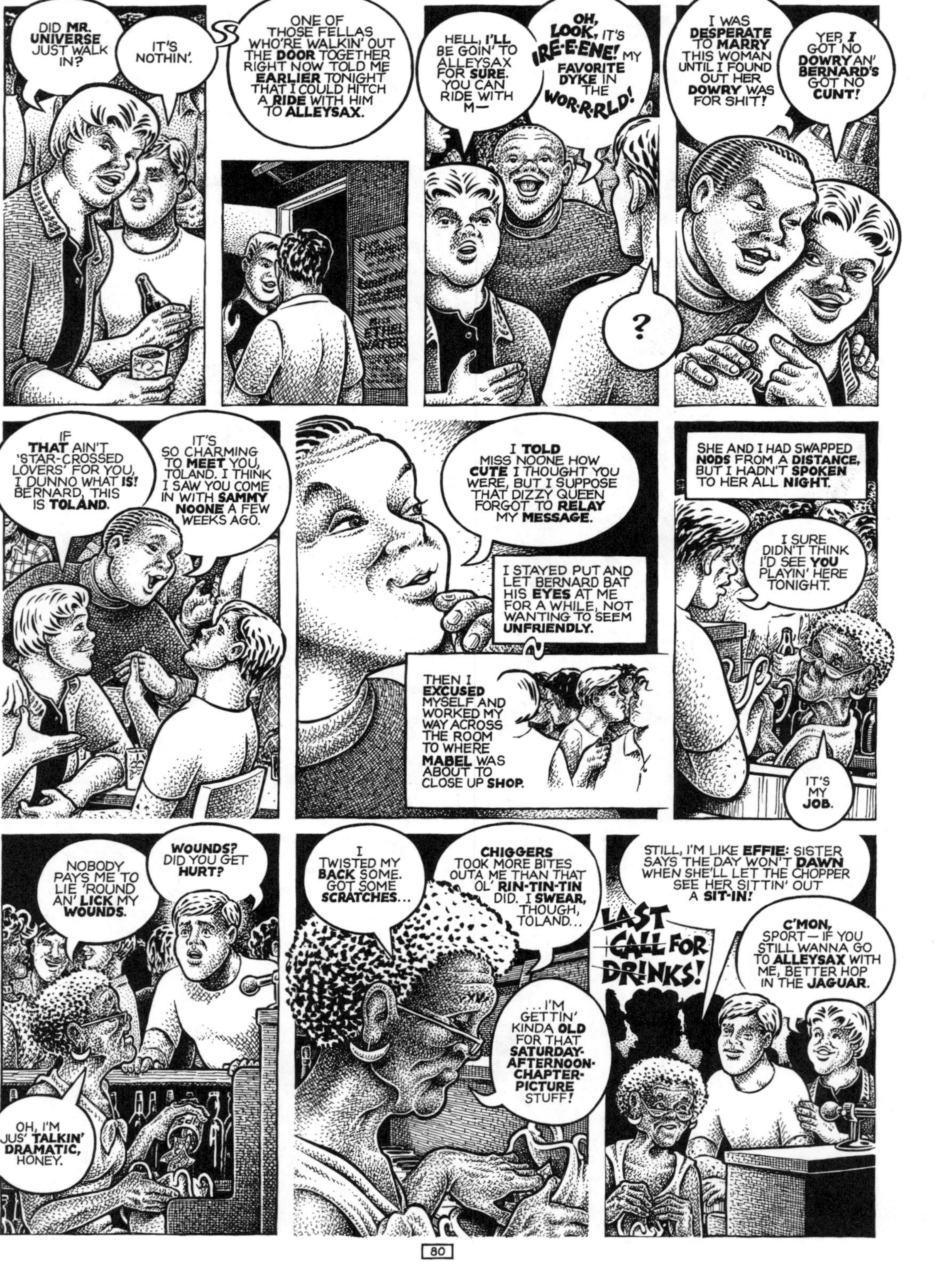

DID MR. UNIVERSE JUST WALK IN?
IT'S NOTHIN'.
ONE OF THOSE FELLAS WHO'RE WALKIN' OUT THE DOOR TOGETHER RIGHT NOW TOLD ME EARLIER TONIGHT THAT I COULD HITCH A RIDE WITH HIM TO ALLEYSAX.
HELL, I'LL BE GOIN' TO ALLEYSAX FOR SURE. YOU CAN RIDE WITH M—
OH, LOOK, IT'S IRE-E-ENE! MY FAVORITE DYKE IN THE WOR-R-RLD!
?
I WAS DESPERATE TO MARRY THIS WOMAN UNTIL I FOUND OUT HER DOWRY WAS FOR SHIT!
YEP, I GOT NO DOWRY AN' BERNARD'S GOT NO CUNT!
IF THAT AIN'T 'STAR-CROSSED LOVERS' FOR YOU, I DUNNO WHAT IS! BERNARD, THIS IS TOLAND.
IT'S SO CHARMING TO MEET YOU, TOLAND. I THINK I SAW YOU COME IN WITH SAMMY NOONE A FEW WEEKS AGO.
I TOLD MISS NOONE HOW CUTE I THOUGHT YOU WERE, BUT I SUPPOSE THAT DIZZY QUEEN FORGOT TO RELAY MY MESSAGE.
I STAYED PUT AND LET BERNARD BAT HIS EYES AT ME FOR A WHILE, NOT WANTING TO SEEM UNFRIENDLY.
THEN I EXCUSED MYSELF AND WORKED MY WAY ACROSS THE ROOM TO WHERE MABEL WAS ABOUT TO CLOSE UP SHOP.
SHE AND I HAD SWAPPED NODS FROM A DISTANCE, BUT I HADN'T SPOKEN TO HER ALL NIGHT.
I SURE DIDN'T THINK I'D SEE YOU PLAYIN' HERE TONIGHT.
IT'S MY JOB.
NOBODY PAYS ME TO LIE 'ROUND AN' LICK MY WOUNDS.
WOUNDS? DID YOU GET HURT?
OH, I'M JUS' TALKIN' DRAMATIC, HONEY.
I TWISTED MY BACK SOME. GOT SOME SCRATCHES...
CHIGGERS TOOK MORE BITES OUTA ME THAN THAT OL' RIN-TIN-TIN DID. I SWEAR, THOUGH, TOLAND...
...I'M GETTIN' KINDA OLD FOR THAT SATURDAY-AFTERNOON-CHAPTER-PICTURE STUFF!
STILL, I'M LIKE EFFIE: SISTER SAYS THE DAY WON'T DAWN WHEN SHE'LL LET THE CHOPPER SEE HER SITTIN' OUT A SIT-IN!
LAST CALL FOR DRINKS!
C'MON, SPORT — IF YOU STILL WANNA GO TO ALLEYSAX WITH ME, BETTER HOP IN THE JAGUAR.

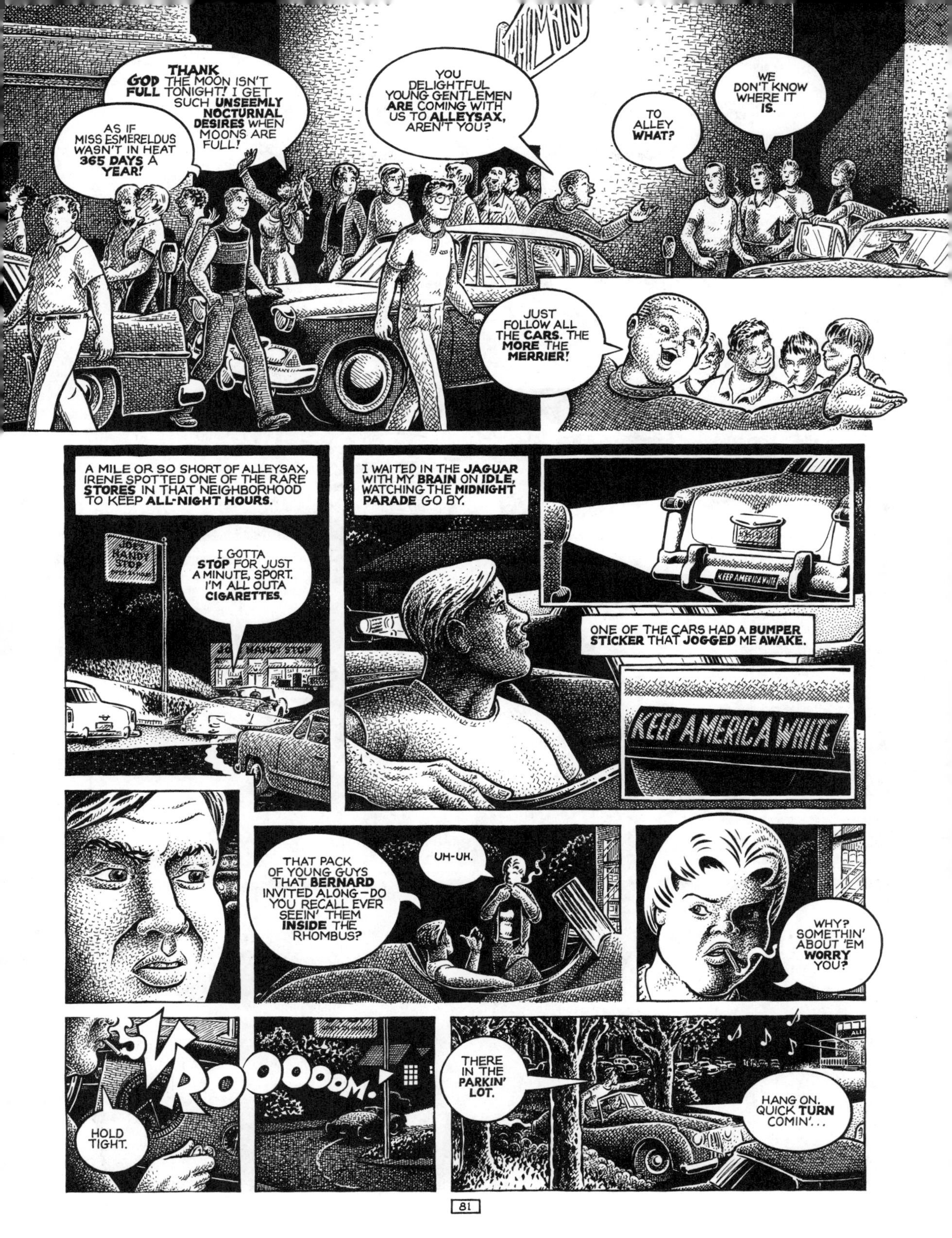
AS IF MISS ESMERELDUS WASN'T IN HEAT 365 DAYS A YEAR!
THANK GOD THE MOON ISN'T FULL TONIGHT! I GET SUCH UNSEEMLY NOCTURNAL DESIRES WHEN MOONS ARE FULL!
YOU DELIGHTFUL YOUNG GENTLEMEN ARE COMING WITH US TO ALLEYSAX, AREN'T YOU?
TO ALLEY WHAT?
WE DON'T KNOW WHERE IT IS.
JUST FOLLOW ALL THE CARS. THE MORE THE MERRIER!
A MILE OR SO SHORT OF ALLEYSAX, IRENE SPOTTED ONE OF THE RARE STORES IN THAT NEIGHBORHOOD TO KEEP ALL-NIGHT HOURS.
I GOTTA STOP FOR JUST A MINUTE, SPORT. I'M ALL OUTA CIGARETTES.
I WAITED IN THE JAGUAR WITH MY BRAIN ON IDLE, WATCHING THE MIDNIGHT PARADE GO BY.
ONE OF THE CARS HAD A BUMPER STICKER THAT JOGGED ME AWAKE.
KEEP AMERICA WHITE
THAT PACK OF YOUNG GUYS THAT BERNARD INVITED ALONG—DO YOU RECALL EVER SEEIN' THEM INSIDE THE RHOMBUS?
UH-UH.
WHY? SOMETHIN' ABOUT 'EM WORRY YOU?
SVROOOOOOM!
HOLD TIGHT.
THERE IN THE PARKIN' LOT.
HANG ON. QUICK TURN COMIN'...

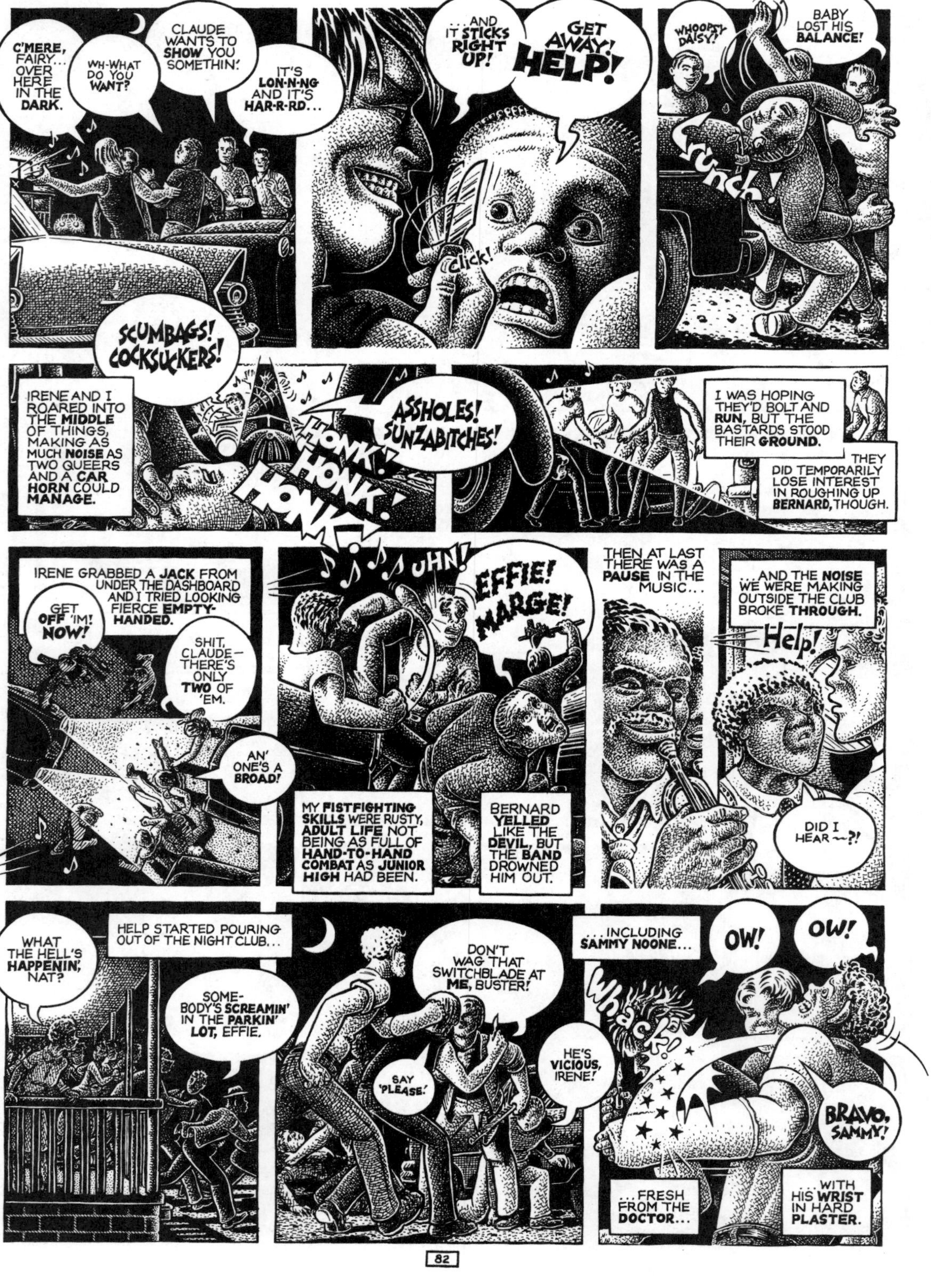

C'MERE, FAIRY... OVER HERE IN THE DARK.
WH-WHAT DO YOU WANT?
CLAUDE WANTS TO SHOW YOU SOMETHIN'.
IT'S LON-N-NG AND IT'S HAR-R-RD...
...AND IT STICKS RIGHT UP!
GET AWAY! HELP!
CLICK!
WHOOPSY DAISY!
BABY LOST HIS BALANCE!
CRUNCH!
SCUMBAGS! COCKSUCKERS!
IRENE AND I ROARED INTO THE MIDDLE OF THINGS, MAKING AS MUCH NOISE AS TWO QUEERS AND A CAR HORN COULD MANAGE.
ASSHOLES! SUNZABITCHES!
HONK! HONK! HONK!
I WAS HOPING THEY'D BOLT AND RUN, BUT THE BASTARDS STOOD THEIR GROUND.
THEY DID TEMPORARILY LOSE INTEREST IN ROUGHING UP BERNARD, THOUGH.
IRENE GRABBED A JACK FROM UNDER THE DASHBOARD AND I TRIED LOOKING FIERCE EMPTY-HANDED.
GET OFF 'IM! NOW!
SHIT, CLAUDE— THERE'S ONLY TWO OF 'EM.
AN' ONE'S A BROAD!
UHN!
EFFIE! MARGE!
MY FISTFIGHTING SKILLS WERE RUSTY, ADULT LIFE NOT BEING AS FULL OF HAND-TO-HAND COMBAT AS JUNIOR HIGH HAD BEEN.
BERNARD YELLED LIKE THE DEVIL, BUT THE BAND DROWNED HIM OUT.
THEN AT LAST THERE WAS A PAUSE IN THE MUSIC...
...AND THE NOISE WE WERE MAKING OUTSIDE THE CLUB BROKE THROUGH.
Help!
DID I HEAR ~~?!
WHAT THE HELL'S HAPPENIN', NAT?
HELP STARTED POURING OUT OF THE NIGHT CLUB...
SOME-BODY'S SCREAMIN' IN THE PARKIN' LOT, EFFIE.
DON'T WAG THAT SWITCHBLADE AT ME, BUSTER!
SAY 'PLEASE.'
HE'S VICIOUS, IRENE!
...INCLUDING SAMMY NOONE...
OW!
OW!
WHACK!
BRAVO, SAMMY!
...FRESH FROM THE DOCTOR...
...WITH HIS WRIST IN HARD PLASTER.

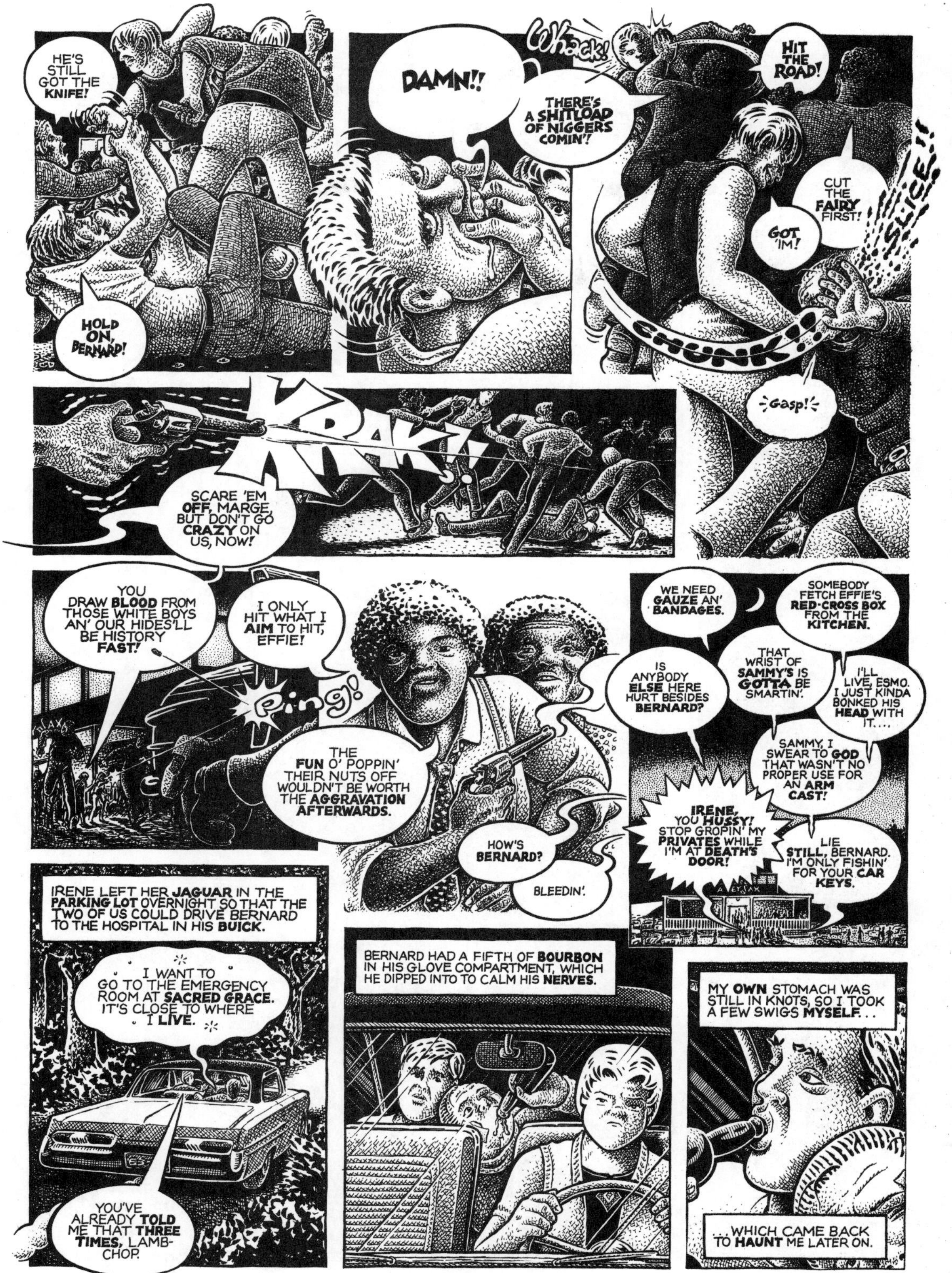
HE'S STILL GOT THE KNIFE!
HOLD ON, BERNARD!
DAMN!!
WHACK!
THERE'S A SHITLOAD OF NIGGERS COMIN'!
HIT THE ROAD!
CUT THE FAIRY FIRST!
GOT 'IM!
SLICE!!
CHUNK!!
Gasp!
KRAK!!
SCARE 'EM OFF, MARGE, BUT DON'T GO CRAZY ON US, NOW!
YOU DRAW BLOOD FROM THOSE WHITE BOYS AN' OUR HIDES'LL BE HISTORY FAST!
I ONLY HIT WHAT I AIM TO HIT, EFFIE!
Ping!
THE FUN O' POPPIN' THEIR NUTS OFF WOULDN'T BE WORTH THE AGGRAVATION AFTERWARDS.
HOW'S BERNARD?
BLEEDIN'.
WE NEED GAUZE AN' BANDAGES.
SOMEBODY FETCH EFFIE'S RED-CROSS BOX FROM THE KITCHEN.
IS ANYBODY ELSE HERE HURT BESIDES BERNARD?
THAT WRIST OF SAMMY'S IS GOTTA BE SMARTIN'.
I'LL LIVE, ESMO. I JUST KINDA BONKED HIS HEAD WITH IT....
SAMMY, I SWEAR TO GOD THAT WASN'T NO PROPER USE FOR AN ARM CAST!
IRENE, YOU HUSSY! STOP GROPIN' MY PRIVATES WHILE I'M AT DEATH'S DOOR!
LIE STILL, BERNARD. I'M ONLY FISHIN' FOR YOUR CAR KEYS.
IRENE LEFT HER JAGUAR IN THE PARKING LOT OVERNIGHT SO THAT THE TWO OF US COULD DRIVE BERNARD TO THE HOSPITAL IN HIS BUICK.
I WANT TO GO TO THE EMERGENCY ROOM AT SACRED GRACE. IT'S CLOSE TO WHERE I LIVE.
YOU'VE ALREADY TOLD ME THAT THREE TIMES, LAMB-CHOP.
BERNARD HAD A FIFTH OF BOURBON IN HIS GLOVE COMPARTMENT, WHICH HE DIPPED INTO TO CALM HIS NERVES.
MY OWN STOMACH WAS STILL IN KNOTS, SO I TOOK A FEW SWIGS MYSELF. . .
. . . WHICH CAME BACK TO HAUNT ME LATER ON.

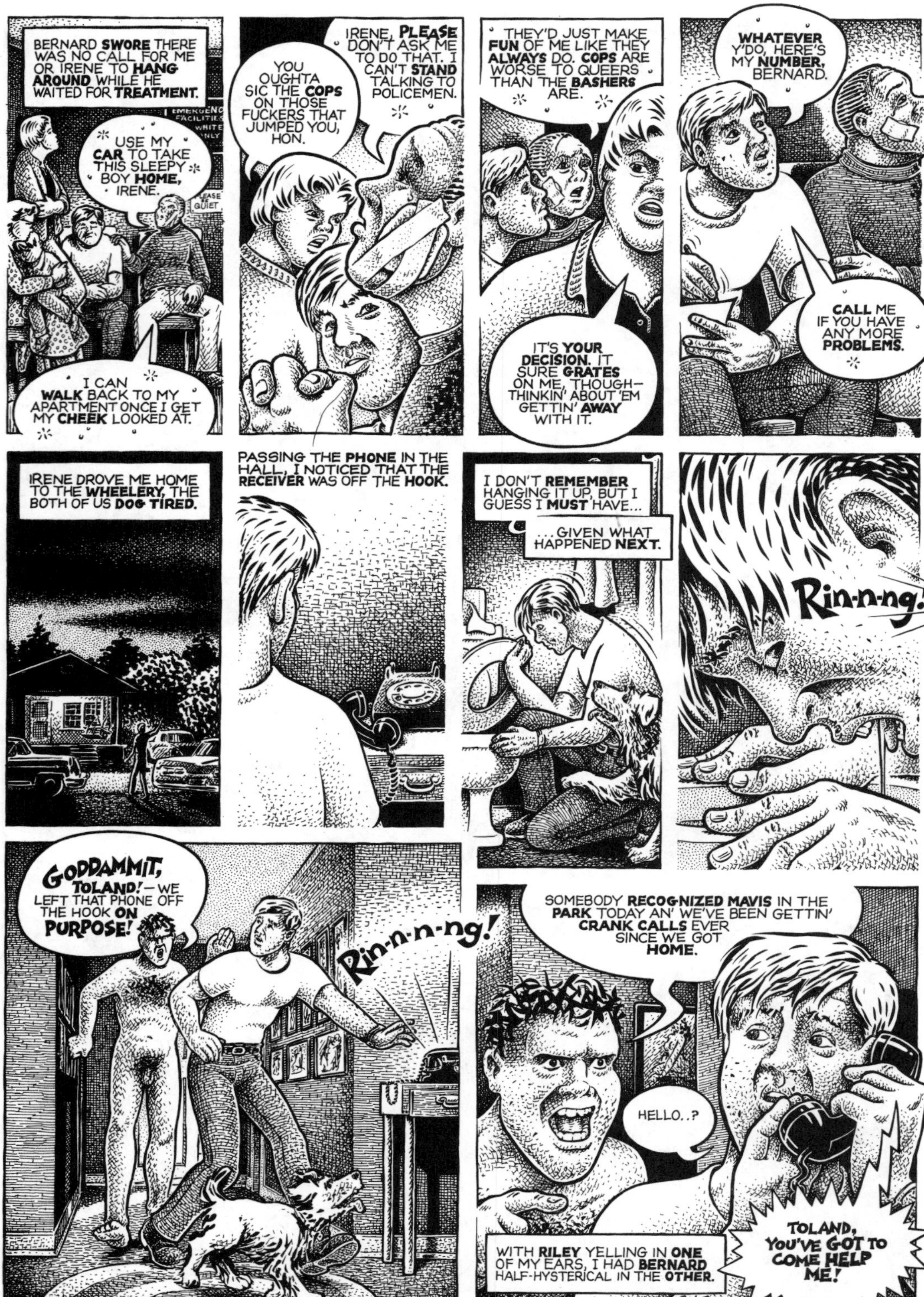
BERNARD SWORE THERE WAS NO CALL FOR ME OR IRENE TO HANG AROUND WHILE HE WAITED FOR TREATMENT.
EMERGENCY FACILITIES WHITE ONLY
USE MY CAR TO TAKE THIS SLEEPY BOY HOME, IRENE.
I CAN WALK BACK TO MY APARTMENT ONCE I GET MY CHEEK LOOKED AT.
YOU OUGHTA SIC THE COPS ON THOSE FUCKERS THAT JUMPED YOU, HON.
IRENE, PLEASE DON'T ASK ME TO DO THAT. I CAN'T STAND TALKING TO POLICEMEN.
THEY'D JUST MAKE FUN OF ME LIKE THEY ALWAYS DO. COPS ARE WORSE TO QUEERS THAN THE BASHERS ARE.
IT'S YOUR DECISION. IT SURE GRATES ON ME, THOUGH— THINKIN' ABOUT 'EM GETTIN' AWAY WITH IT.
WHATEVER Y'DO, HERE'S MY NUMBER, BERNARD.
CALL ME IF YOU HAVE ANY MORE PROBLEMS.
IRENE DROVE ME HOME TO THE WHEELERY, THE BOTH OF US DOG TIRED.
PASSING THE PHONE IN THE HALL, I NOTICED THAT THE RECEIVER WAS OFF THE HOOK.
I DON'T REMEMBER HANGING IT UP, BUT I GUESS I MUST HAVE...
...GIVEN WHAT HAPPENED NEXT.
Rin-n-ng!
GODDAMMIT, TOLAND!— WE LEFT THAT PHONE OFF THE HOOK ON PURPOSE!
Rin-n-n-ng!
SOMEBODY RECOGNIZED MAVIS IN THE PARK TODAY AN' WE'VE BEEN GETTIN' CRANK CALLS EVER SINCE WE GOT HOME.
HELLO..?
WITH RILEY YELLING IN ONE OF MY EARS, I HAD BERNARD HALF-HYSTERICAL IN THE OTHER.
TOLAND, YOU'VE GOT TO COME HELP ME!

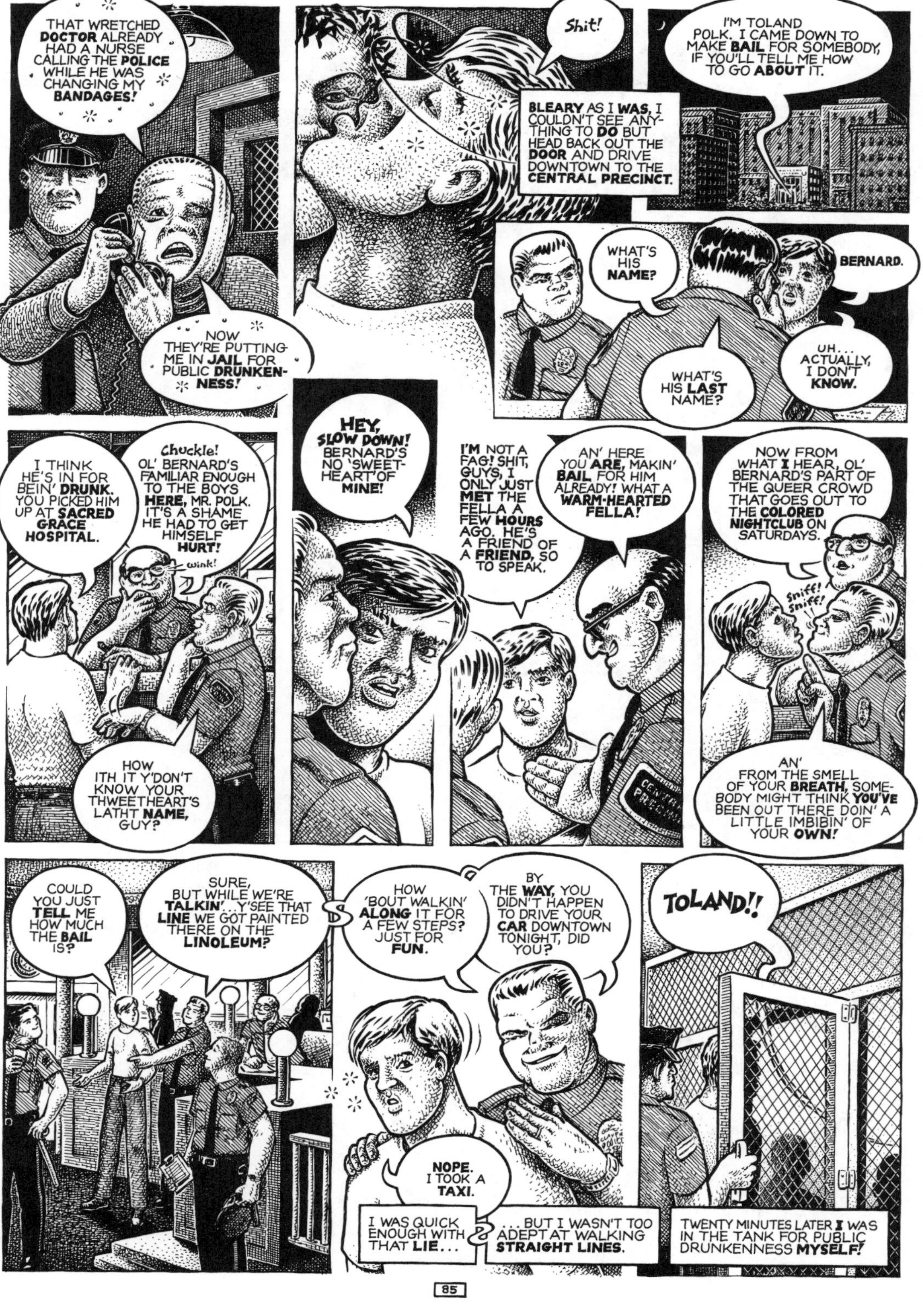

THAT WRETCHED DOCTOR ALREADY HAD A NURSE CALLING THE POLICE WHILE HE WAS CHANGING MY BANDAGES!
NOW THEY'RE PUTTING ME IN JAIL FOR PUBLIC DRUNKEN-NESS!
Shit!
BLEARY AS I WAS, I COULDN'T SEE ANYTHING TO DO BUT HEAD BACK OUT THE DOOR AND DRIVE DOWNTOWN TO THE CENTRAL PRECINCT.
I'M TOLAND POLK. I CAME DOWN TO MAKE BAIL FOR SOMEBODY, IF YOU'LL TELL ME HOW TO GO ABOUT IT.
WHAT'S HIS NAME?
BERNARD.
WHAT'S HIS LAST NAME?
UH... ACTUALLY, I DON'T KNOW.
I THINK HE'S IN FOR BEIN' DRUNK. YOU PICKED HIM UP AT SACRED GRACE HOSPITAL.
Chuckle! OL' BERNARD'S FAMILIAR ENOUGH TO THE BOYS HERE, MR. POLK. IT'S A SHAME HE HAD TO GET HIMSELF HURT!
wink!
HOW ITH IT Y'DON'T KNOW YOUR TWEETHEART'S LATHT NAME, GUY?
HEY, SLOW DOWN! BERNARD'S NO 'SWEETHEART' OF MINE!
I'M NOT A FAG! SHIT, GUYS, I ONLY JUST MET THE FELLA A FEW HOURS AGO. HE'S A FRIEND OF A FRIEND, SO TO SPEAK.
AN' HERE YOU ARE, MAKIN' BAIL FOR HIM ALREADY! WHAT A WARM-HEARTED FELLA!
NOW FROM WHAT I HEAR, OL' BERNARD'S PART OF THE QUEER CROWD THAT GOES OUT TO THE COLORED NIGHTCLUB ON SATURDAYS.
Sniff! Sniff!
AN' FROM THE SMELL OF YOUR BREATH, SOMEBODY MIGHT THINK YOU'VE BEEN OUT THERE DOIN' A LITTLE IMBIBIN' OF YOUR OWN!
COULD YOU JUST TELL ME HOW MUCH THE BAIL IS?
SURE, BUT WHILE WE'RE TALKIN'... Y'SEE THAT LINE WE GOT PAINTED THERE ON THE LINOLEUM?
HOW 'BOUT WALKIN' ALONG IT FOR A FEW STEPS? JUST FOR FUN.
BY THE WAY, YOU DIDN'T HAPPEN TO DRIVE YOUR CAR DOWNTOWN TONIGHT, DID YOU?
NOPE. I TOOK A TAXI.
I WAS QUICK ENOUGH WITH THAT LIE...
... BUT I WASN'T TOO ADEPT AT WALKING STRAIGHT LINES.
TOLAND!!
TWENTY MINUTES LATER I WAS IN THE TANK FOR PUBLIC DRUNKENNESS MYSELF!

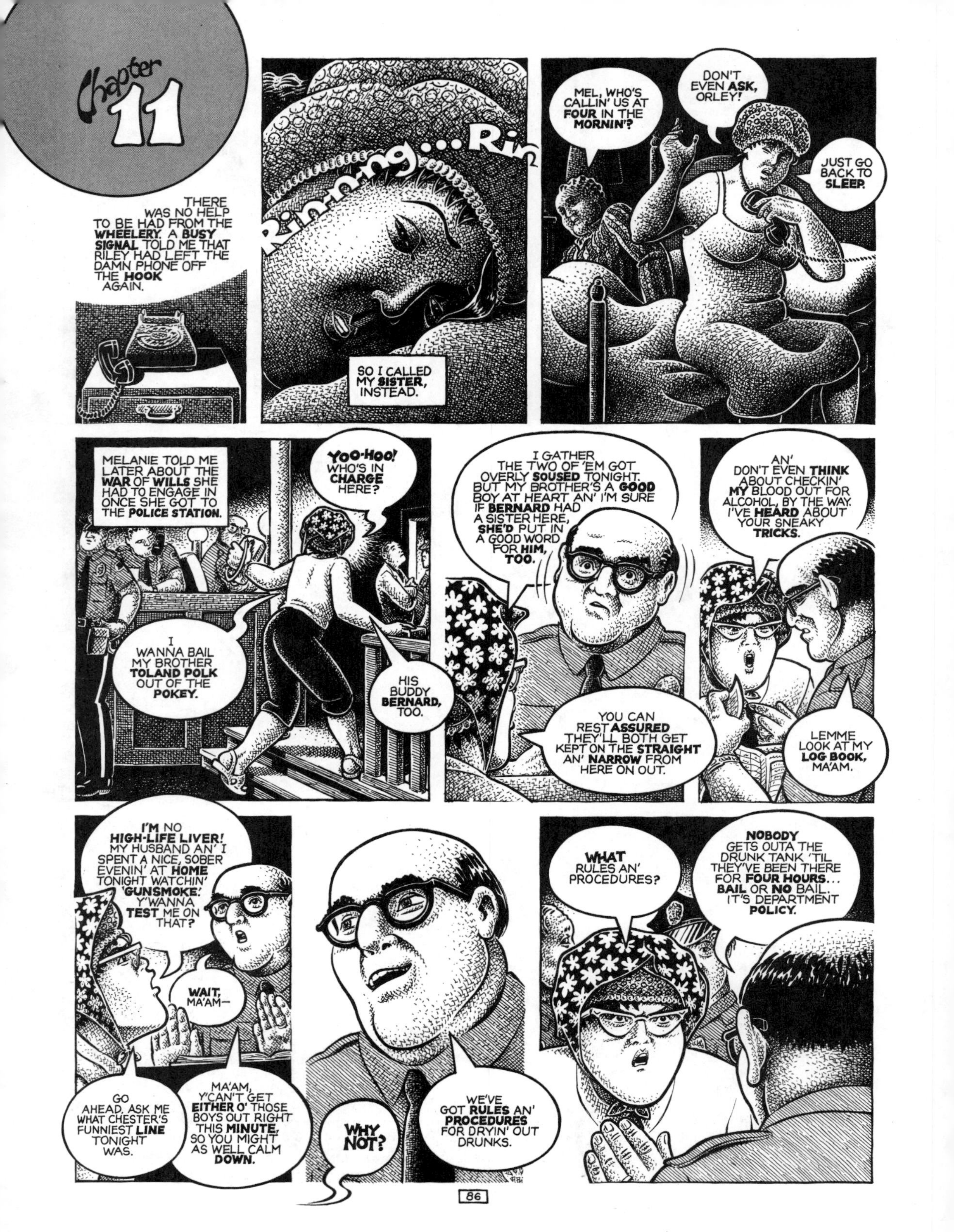
Chapter 11
THERE WAS NO HELP TO BE HAD FROM THE WHEELERY. A BUSY SIGNAL TOLD ME THAT RILEY HAD LEFT THE DAMN PHONE OFF THE HOOK AGAIN.
Rinnng...Rin
SO I CALLED MY SISTER, INSTEAD.
MEL, WHO'S CALLIN' US AT FOUR IN THE MORNIN'?
DON'T EVEN ASK, ORLEY!
JUST GO BACK TO SLEEP.
MELANIE TOLD ME LATER ABOUT THE WAR OF WILLS SHE HAD TO ENGAGE IN ONCE SHE GOT TO THE POLICE STATION.
YOO-HOO! WHO'S IN CHARGE HERE?
I WANNA BAIL MY BROTHER TOLAND POLK OUT OF THE POKEY.
HIS BUDDY BERNARD, TOO.
I GATHER THE TWO OF 'EM GOT OVERLY SOUSED TONIGHT. BUT MY BROTHER'S A GOOD BOY AT HEART AN' I'M SURE IF BERNARD HAD A SISTER HERE, SHE'D PUT IN A GOOD WORD FOR HIM, TOO.
YOU CAN REST ASSURED THEY'LL BOTH GET KEPT ON THE STRAIGHT AN' NARROW FROM HERE ON OUT.
AN' DON'T EVEN THINK ABOUT CHECKIN' MY BLOOD OUT FOR ALCOHOL, BY THE WAY. I'VE HEARD ABOUT YOUR SNEAKY TRICKS.
LEMME LOOK AT MY LOG BOOK, MA'AM.
I'M NO HIGH-LIFE LIVER! MY HUSBAND AN' I SPENT A NICE, SOBER EVENIN' AT HOME TONIGHT WATCHIN' 'GUNSMOKE.' Y'WANNA TEST ME ON THAT?
WAIT, MA'AM—
GO AHEAD, ASK ME WHAT CHESTER'S FUNNIEST LINE TONIGHT WAS.
MA'AM, Y'CAN'T GET EITHER O' THOSE BOYS OUT RIGHT THIS MINUTE, SO YOU MIGHT AS WELL CALM DOWN.
WHY NOT?
WE'VE GOT RULES AN' PROCEDURES FOR DRYIN' OUT DRUNKS.
WHAT RULES AN' PROCEDURES?
NOBODY GETS OUTA THE DRUNK TANK 'TIL THEY'VE BEEN THERE FOR FOUR HOURS... BAIL OR NO BAIL. IT'S DEPARTMENT POLICY.

FOUR HOURS?!

JUST HEAR ME OUT, MA'AM. **BERNARD'S** BEEN DRYIN' OUT FOR **THREE** HOURS ALREADY, SO Y'CAN WALK OUTA HERE WITH **HIM** AN **HOUR** FROM NOW.

BUT MY **LOG** SAYS YOUR **BROTHER'S** DUE TO PUT IN ANOTHER **THREE** HOURS. NO GETTIN' **AROUND** IT.

SO **MY** SUGGESTION WOULD BE THAT YOU WAIT THE ONE HOUR 'TIL **BERNARD** GETS FREE, TAKE **HIM** HOME, THEN COME BACK FOR YOUR **BROTHER** LATER IN THE **MORNIN'.**

YOUR... 'SUGGESTION'... WOULD... BE... THAT...

NOW AS '**PROCEDURES**' GO, THAT'S THE **DUMBEST** I'VE HEARD OF **YET!** I'M SUPPOSED TO SPEND MY TIME SHUTTLIN' **BACK** AN' **FORTH** TO THIS POLICE STATION **TWICE** WITH THE **MORNIN'** **SUN** ALREADY THINKIN' ABOUT COMIN' UP??!

FORGET **THAT!**

LOOK— TELL YOU WHAT I'LL **SETTLE** FOR... AN' DON'T MAKE ME COPE WITH ANY **HAGGLIN'** ABOUT THIS 'CAUSE IT'S THE MIDDLE OF THE **NIGHT** AN' EVERY MINUTE OF **SLEEP** I LOSE MAKES ME **CRANKIER.**

WELL, MA'AM...

DON'T **TALK**, JUST **LISTEN!**

WE'LL **SPLIT** THE **DIFFERENCE!** I'LL COOL MY HEELS HERE FOR **TWO HOURS** AN' **NOT** A **MINUTE MORE!** THEN I WANT 'EM BOTH **OUT!**

IT'S **FAIR**, **SQUARE**, AN' I DON'T WANT TO HEAR ANY **ARGUMENTS** OUT OF YOU!

GOT IT? **BERNARD'LL** STAY A LITTLE **LONGER** AN' MY **BROTHER'LL** STAY A LITTLE **LESS.** **THAT** WAY, Y'BREAK **EVEN.**

BELIEVE IT OR NOT, THE COP BOUGHT THE **DEAL.**

MELANIE WAS A FORCE TO BE **RECKONED** WITH WHEN HER **DANDER** WAS UP.

SOMETIME AFTER **SUNRISE** I DUMPED MYSELF LIKE A SACK OF **BRUISED PRODUCE** INTO MY OLD CHILDHOOD **BED** AT **MELANIE'S.**

SHE HAD TAKEN **BERNARD** HOME BUT SAID THAT TO DRIVE **ME** ALL THE WAY BACK TO THE WHEELERY AT THAT HOUR WOULD BE GOING **WAY** BEYOND THE CALL OF **DUTY.**

AND SHE HAD NO **INTENTION,** MELANIE SAID, OF LETTING ME GET BEHIND THE WHEEL OF MY **OWN** CAR IN MY EXHAUSTED CONDITION.

I DIDN'T **CARE.** I COULD'VE SLEPT ON A **ROLLER COASTER.**

IT WAS WELL INTO THE **AFTERNOON** WHEN I GOT JOGGED AWAKE BY WEIRD **NOISES** COMING FROM A HULKING **SHAPE** NEXT TO THE BED.

?

Choke!

Sob!

Sniff!

JESUS!

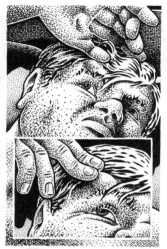

WELL, LOOK WHO'S BACK IN THE **LAND** OF THE **LIVING!**

Yawn! WHAT **DAY** IS IT?

IT'S STILL **SUNDAY.** I'VE ALREADY PUT SOME HOT **COFFEE** ON THE TABLE FOR YOU.

I HOPE THE **PHONE** DIDN'T WAKE YOU UP WHEN IT RANG A WHILE AGO.

NOPE.

MAVIS CALLED, TRYIN' TO TRACK YOU **DOWN.**

SHE AN' RILEY GOT **UNEASY,** NOT KNOWIN' WHY YOU NEVER CAME BACK **HOME** LAST NIGHT.

IF THEY WOULDN'T LEAVE THEIR **PHONE** OFF THE **HOOK** ALL NIGHT, I MIGHT KEEP IN BETTER **TOUCH.**

HMM... THAT'S QUITE A **GOOSE EGG** YOU'RE SPORTIN' ON YOUR FOREHEAD.

I **TOLD** YOU I GOT IN A **FIGHT** AT ALLEYSAX.

WELL, IF YOU'RE PLANNIN' ON TURNIN' INTO A **BRAWLER,** BUBBA, MAYBE I SHOULDN'T BE SO **QUICK** TO SPRING YOU OUT OF **JAIL.**

Poke!

HOW MUCH DOES IT **HURT?**

DON'T COME SO **CLOSE.** I SMELL BAD.

WELL... I WON'T EXACTLY **CONTRADICT** YOU....

I'VE GOTTA **CLEAN** UP BEFORE I GO HOME, ORLEY WON'T MIND IF I USE HIS **SHAVIN' GEAR,** WILL HE?

NEVER **ASK** HIM AN' HE CAN'T SAY **NO.**

Y'MIGHT WANNA AVAIL YOURSELF OF A LITTLE MOUTHWASH, TOO, WHILE YOU'RE **AT** IT....

AN' I'M **NOT** GONNA LET YOU **LEAVE** IN THOSE FILTHY **CLOTHES,** HONEY.

LET ME **HAVE** 'EM WHILE YOU'RE IN THE **SHOWER** SO I CAN PUT 'EM IN TO **WASH.**

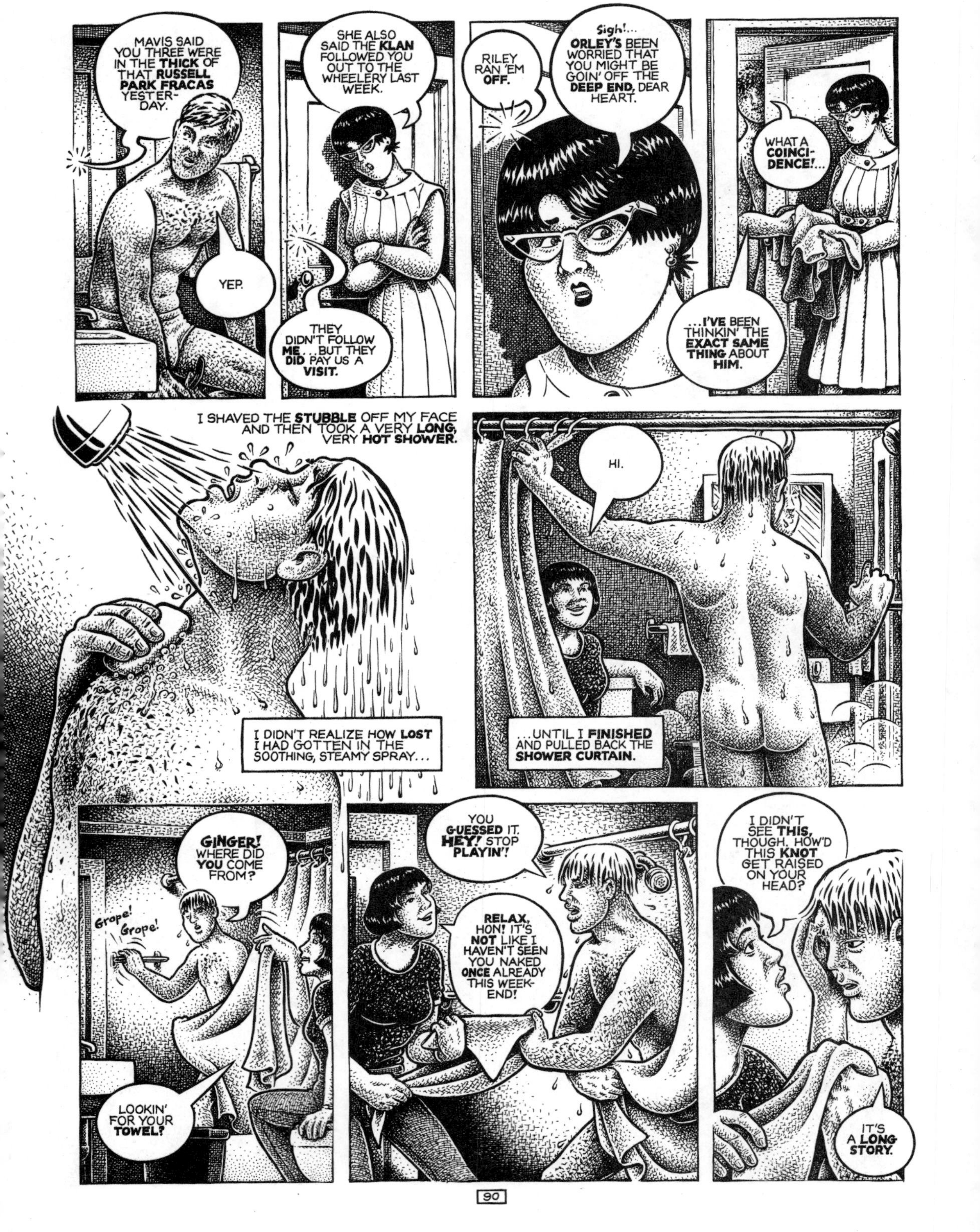

MAVIS SAID YOU THREE WERE IN THE THICK OF THAT RUSSELL PARK FRACAS YESTER-DAY.
YEP.
SHE ALSO SAID THE KLAN FOLLOWED YOU OUT TO THE WHEELERY LAST WEEK.
THEY DIDN'T FOLLOW ME... BUT THEY DID PAY US A VISIT.
RILEY RAN 'EM OFF.
Sigh!... ORLEY'S BEEN WORRIED THAT YOU MIGHT BE GOIN' OFF THE DEEP END, DEAR HEART.
WHAT A COINCI-DENCE!...
...I'VE BEEN THINKIN' THE EXACT SAME THING ABOUT HIM.
I SHAVED THE STUBBLE OFF MY FACE AND THEN TOOK A VERY LONG, VERY HOT SHOWER.
I DIDN'T REALIZE HOW LOST I HAD GOTTEN IN THE SOOTHING, STEAMY SPRAY...
HI.
...UNTIL I FINISHED AND PULLED BACK THE SHOWER CURTAIN.
GINGER! WHERE DID YOU COME FROM?
Grope! Grope!
LOOKIN' FOR YOUR TOWEL?
YOU GUESSED IT. HEY! STOP PLAYIN'!
RELAX, HON! IT'S NOT LIKE I HAVEN'T SEEN YOU NAKED ONCE ALREADY THIS WEEK-END!
I DIDN'T SEE THIS, THOUGH. HOW'D THIS KNOT GET RAISED ON YOUR HEAD?
IT'S A LONG STORY.

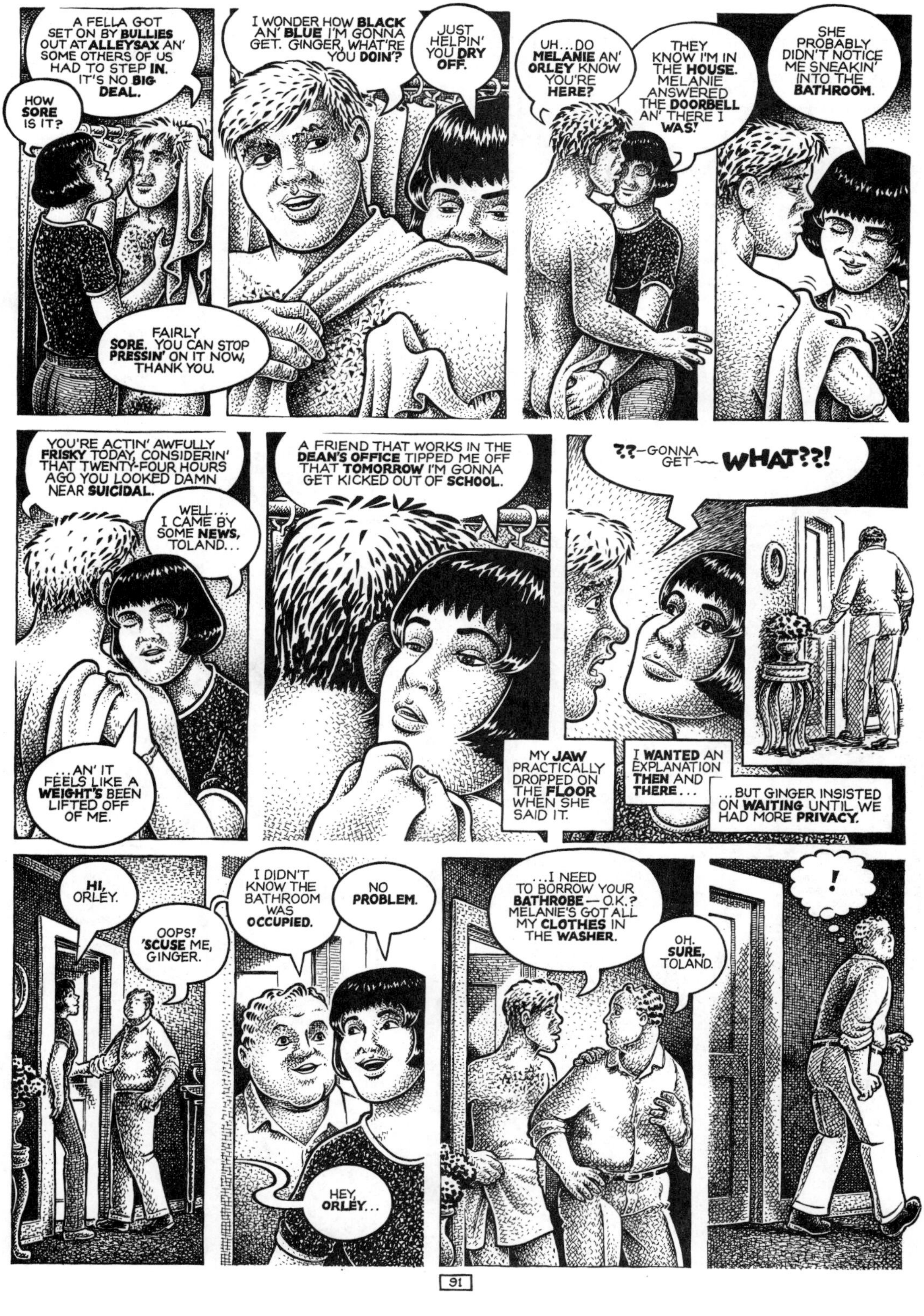
A FELLA GOT SET ON BY BULLIES OUT AT ALLEYSAX AN' SOME OTHERS OF US HAD TO STEP IN. IT'S NO BIG DEAL.
HOW SORE IS IT?
FAIRLY SORE. YOU CAN STOP PRESSIN' ON IT NOW, THANK YOU.
I WONDER HOW BLACK AN' BLUE I'M GONNA GET. GINGER, WHAT'RE YOU DOIN'?
JUST HELPIN' YOU DRY OFF.
UH... DO MELANIE AN' ORLEY KNOW YOU'RE HERE?
THEY KNOW I'M IN THE HOUSE. MELANIE ANSWERED THE DOORBELL AN' THERE I WAS!
SHE PROBABLY DIDN'T NOTICE ME SNEAKIN' INTO THE BATHROOM.
YOU'RE ACTIN' AWFULLY FRISKY TODAY, CONSIDERIN' THAT TWENTY-FOUR HOURS AGO YOU LOOKED DAMN NEAR SUICIDAL.
WELL... I CAME BY SOME NEWS, TOLAND...
...AN' IT FEELS LIKE A WEIGHT'S BEEN LIFTED OFF OF ME.
A FRIEND THAT WORKS IN THE DEAN'S OFFICE TIPPED ME OFF THAT TOMORROW I'M GONNA GET KICKED OUT OF SCHOOL.
MY JAW PRACTICALLY DROPPED ON THE FLOOR WHEN SHE SAID IT.
??–GONNA GET— WHAT??!
I WANTED AN EXPLANATION THEN AND THERE...
...BUT GINGER INSISTED ON WAITING UNTIL WE HAD MORE PRIVACY.
HI, ORLEY.
OOPS! 'SCUSE ME, GINGER.
I DIDN'T KNOW THE BATHROOM WAS OCCUPIED.
NO PROBLEM.
HEY, ORLEY...
...I NEED TO BORROW YOUR BATHROBE — O.K.? MELANIE'S GOT ALL MY CLOTHES IN THE WASHER.
OH. SURE, TOLAND.
!

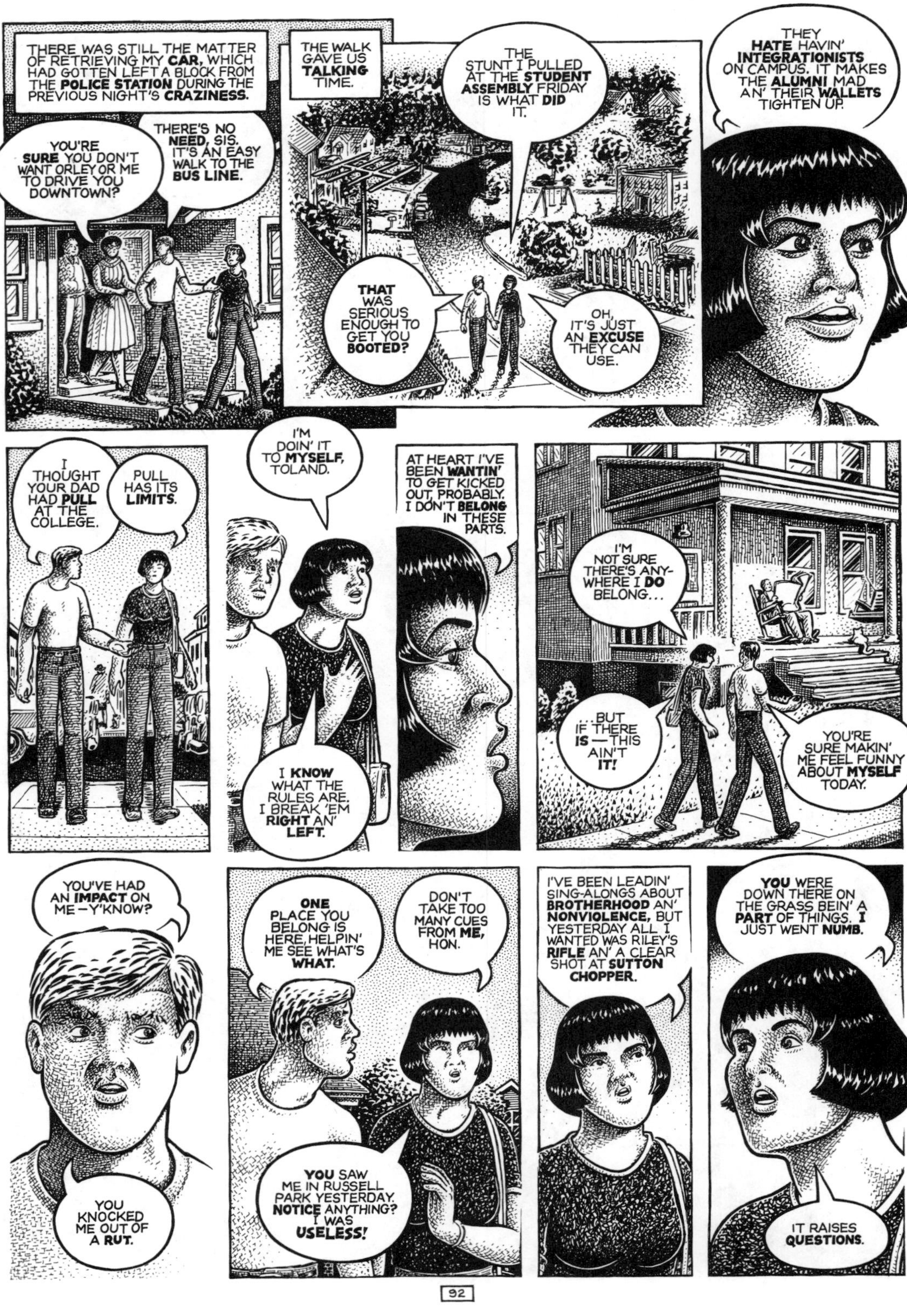
THERE WAS STILL THE MATTER OF RETRIEVING MY CAR, WHICH HAD GOTTEN LEFT A BLOCK FROM THE POLICE STATION DURING THE PREVIOUS NIGHT'S CRAZINESS.
YOU'RE SURE YOU DON'T WANT ORLEY OR ME TO DRIVE YOU DOWNTOWN?
THERE'S NO NEED, SIS. IT'S AN EASY WALK TO THE BUS LINE.
THE WALK GAVE US TALKING TIME.
THE STUNT I PULLED AT THE STUDENT ASSEMBLY FRIDAY IS WHAT DID IT.
THAT WAS SERIOUS ENOUGH TO GET YOU BOOTED?
OH, IT'S JUST AN EXCUSE THEY CAN USE.
THEY HATE HAVIN' INTEGRATIONISTS ON CAMPUS. IT MAKES THE ALUMNI MAD AN' THEIR WALLETS TIGHTEN UP.
I THOUGHT YOUR DAD HAD PULL AT THE COLLEGE.
PULL HAS ITS LIMITS.
I'M DOIN' IT TO MYSELF, TOLAND.
I KNOW WHAT THE RULES ARE. I BREAK 'EM RIGHT AN' LEFT.
AT HEART I'VE BEEN WANTIN' TO GET KICKED OUT, PROBABLY. I DON'T BELONG IN THESE PARTS.
I'M NOT SURE THERE'S ANY-WHERE I DO BELONG...
...BUT IF THERE IS — THIS AIN'T IT!
YOU'RE SURE MAKIN' ME FEEL FUNNY ABOUT MYSELF TODAY.
YOU'VE HAD AN IMPACT ON ME — Y'KNOW?
YOU KNOCKED ME OUT OF A RUT.
ONE PLACE YOU BELONG IS HERE, HELPIN' ME SEE WHAT'S WHAT.
DON'T TAKE TOO MANY CUES FROM ME, HON.
YOU SAW ME IN RUSSELL PARK YESTERDAY. NOTICE ANYTHING? I WAS USELESS!
I'VE BEEN LEADIN' SING-ALONGS ABOUT BROTHERHOOD AN' NONVIOLENCE, BUT YESTERDAY ALL I WANTED WAS RILEY'S RIFLE AN' A CLEAR SHOT AT SUTTON CHOPPER.
YOU WERE DOWN THERE ON THE GRASS BEIN' A PART OF THINGS. I JUST WENT NUMB.
IT RAISES QUESTIONS.

YOU DID SEEM **UPSET**. I SAW YOU LATER ON AT THE **CHURCH**, GETTIN' SOME COMFORT FROM **SHILOH**.

YOU **SAW** US? WE DIDN'T SEE **YOU**.

YOU SHOULD'VE COME **OVER**.

I DIDN'T WANNA **INTRUDE**.

ARE YOU **JEALOUS** OF SHILOH?

NO. NOT AT **ALL**.

BUT I WISH I COULD BUY A **BOTTLE** OF WHATEVER PEOPLE LIKE SHILOH HAVE.

LOOK HOW HE'S **CHEERED** YOU **UP!**

I'M NOT **CHEERFUL.** I'M **ADRIFT.**

THERE'S A CERTAIN **GIDDINESS** IN THAT.

WHAT'LL YOU **DO** WITH YOURSELF IF YOU DO GET KICKED OUT OF WESTHILLS?

GO BACK TO **AKRON**, I GUESS.

DO YOU **HAFTA** LEAVE **TOWN**...?

I'LL HAVE SOME **FENCES** TO MEND WITH MY **FOLKS.**

AT TIMES LIKE THAT, THEY TEND TO WANT ME AT **CLOSE RANGE.**

I'M **CONFUSED. I** THOUGHT THE LAST FEW MONTHS WERE WHAT YOU'D CALL **HAPPY** TIMES FOR THE TWO OF US.

BUT NOW YOU'RE ACTIN' PLEASED AS **PUNCH** AT THE THOUGHT OF LEAVIN' CLAYFIELD AN' ME **BEHIND.**

ANY CHANCE THE **RELIEF** YOU'RE FEELIN' COMES FROM SHEDDIN' A BOYFRIEND THAT'S GONE **QUEER** ON YOU?

GOD DAMN IT, TOLAND!

EVERYTHING THAT GOES ON INSIDE OF ME DOESN'T HAVE TO DO WITH **YOU!** QUITE A **LOT** GOES ON THAT DOESN'T HAVE **ANYTHING** TO DO WITH YOU AT **ALL!**

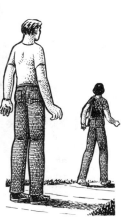

WELL... HERE'S THE **BUS STOP**. SHALL WE **WAIT?**

I **DUNNO.**

THERE'LL BE **MORE** OF 'EM DOWN THE **ROAD**, Y'KNOW.

THERE'S SOMETHIN' YOU SAID TO ME FRIDAY NIGHT THAT'S BEEN **BOTHERIN'** ME EVER **SINCE**, TOLAND.

YOU SAID THAT **HOMOSEXUALS** DON'T FEEL REAL **LOVE** FOR EACH OTHER.

I DON'T THINK THAT'S **TRUE.**

I woke up this mornin' rememberin' somethin' I haven't thought about in **years**. It happened when I was **six**...

...at a **party** my parents threw at our **home.**

Bein' a **kid**, I couldn't have **alcohol**, of course—but I could get **almost** drunk from soakin' up the **party noise** and **music.**

So I noticed **instantly** when somethin' made everything go **silent** out on the **patio.**

I went to see what was **up**. Everyone was watchin' two **men** who were standin' **facin'** each other. I'd seen 'em at various gatherings before...always **together.**

At first I thought it was an **argument** about to happen.

But they never **spoke**. They just looked with an awful **sadness** into each other's **eyes.**

When my aunt saw that I was about to whisper a **question**, she put a **finger** to her **lips** and looked **away.**

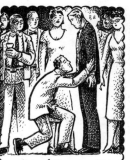

One of the men slid down on his **knees** ...

...And pressed his **cheek** against the **leg** of the one still **standing.**

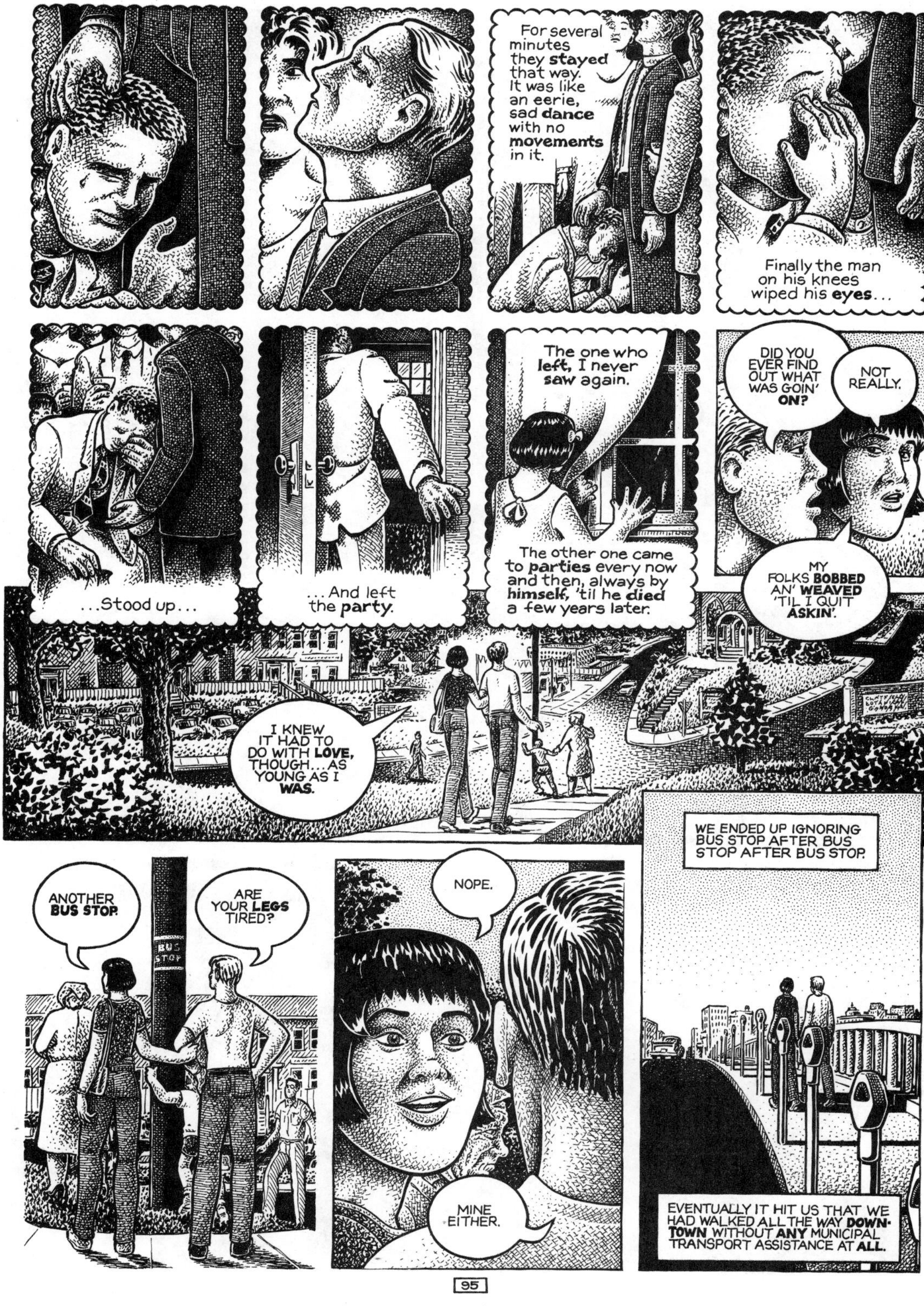
For several minutes they stayed that way. It was like an eerie, sad dance with no movements in it.
Finally the man on his knees wiped his eyes...
...Stood up...
...And left the party.
The one who left, I never saw again.
The other one came to parties every now and then, always by himself, 'til he died a few years later.
DID YOU EVER FIND OUT WHAT WAS GOIN' ON?
NOT REALLY.
MY FOLKS BOBBED AN' WEAVED 'TIL I QUIT ASKIN'.
I KNEW IT HAD TO DO WITH LOVE, THOUGH... AS YOUNG AS I WAS.
WE ENDED UP IGNORING BUS STOP AFTER BUS STOP.
ANOTHER BUS STOP.
ARE YOUR LEGS TIRED?
BUS STOP
NOPE.
MINE EITHER.
EVENTUALLY IT HIT US THAT WE HAD WALKED ALL THE WAY DOWNTOWN WITHOUT ANY MUNICIPAL TRANSPORT ASSISTANCE AT ALL.

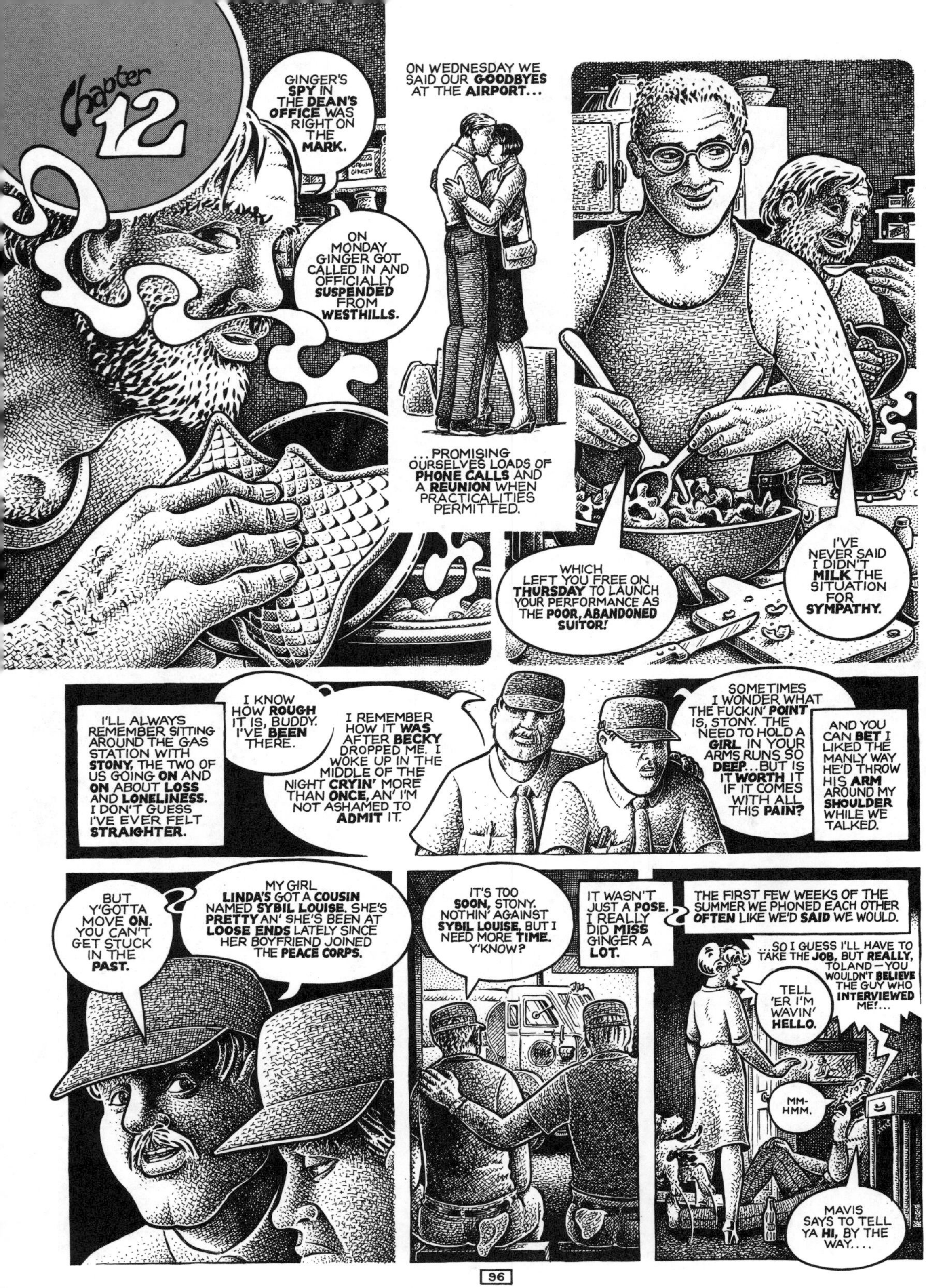

Chapter 12
GINGER'S SPY IN THE DEAN'S OFFICE WAS RIGHT ON THE MARK.
ON MONDAY GINGER GOT CALLED IN AND OFFICIALLY SUSPENDED FROM WESTHILLS.
ON WEDNESDAY WE SAID OUR GOODBYES AT THE AIRPORT...
...PROMISING OURSELVES LOADS OF PHONE CALLS AND A REUNION WHEN PRACTICALITIES PERMITTED.
WHICH LEFT YOU FREE ON THURSDAY TO LAUNCH YOUR PERFORMANCE AS THE POOR, ABANDONED SUITOR!
I'VE NEVER SAID I DIDN'T MILK THE SITUATION FOR SYMPATHY.
I'LL ALWAYS REMEMBER SITTING AROUND THE GAS STATION WITH STONY, THE TWO OF US GOING ON AND ON ABOUT LOSS AND LONELINESS. I DON'T GUESS I'VE EVER FELT STRAIGHTER.
I KNOW HOW ROUGH IT IS, BUDDY. I'VE BEEN THERE.
I REMEMBER HOW IT WAS AFTER BECKY DROPPED ME. I WOKE UP IN THE MIDDLE OF THE NIGHT CRYIN' MORE THAN ONCE, AN' I'M NOT ASHAMED TO ADMIT IT.
SOMETIMES I WONDER WHAT THE FUCKIN' POINT IS, STONY. THE NEED TO HOLD A GIRL IN YOUR ARMS RUNS SO DEEP...BUT IS IT WORTH IT IF IT COMES WITH ALL THIS PAIN?
AND YOU CAN BET I LIKED THE MANLY WAY HE'D THROW HIS ARM AROUND MY SHOULDER WHILE WE TALKED.
BUT Y'GOTTA MOVE ON. YOU CAN'T GET STUCK IN THE PAST.
MY GIRL LINDA'S GOT A COUSIN NAMED SYBIL LOUISE. SHE'S PRETTY AN' SHE'S BEEN AT LOOSE ENDS LATELY SINCE HER BOYFRIEND JOINED THE PEACE CORPS.
IT'S TOO SOON, STONY. NOTHIN' AGAINST SYBIL LOUISE, BUT I NEED MORE TIME. Y'KNOW?
IT WASN'T JUST A POSE. I REALLY DID MISS GINGER A LOT.
THE FIRST FEW WEEKS OF THE SUMMER WE PHONED EACH OTHER OFTEN LIKE WE'D SAID WE WOULD.
...SO I GUESS I'LL HAVE TO TAKE THE JOB, BUT REALLY, TOLAND—YOU WOULDN'T BELIEVE THE GUY WHO INTERVIEWED ME!...
TELL 'ER I'M WAVIN' HELLO.
MM-HMM.
MAVIS SAYS TO TELL YA HI, BY THE WAY....

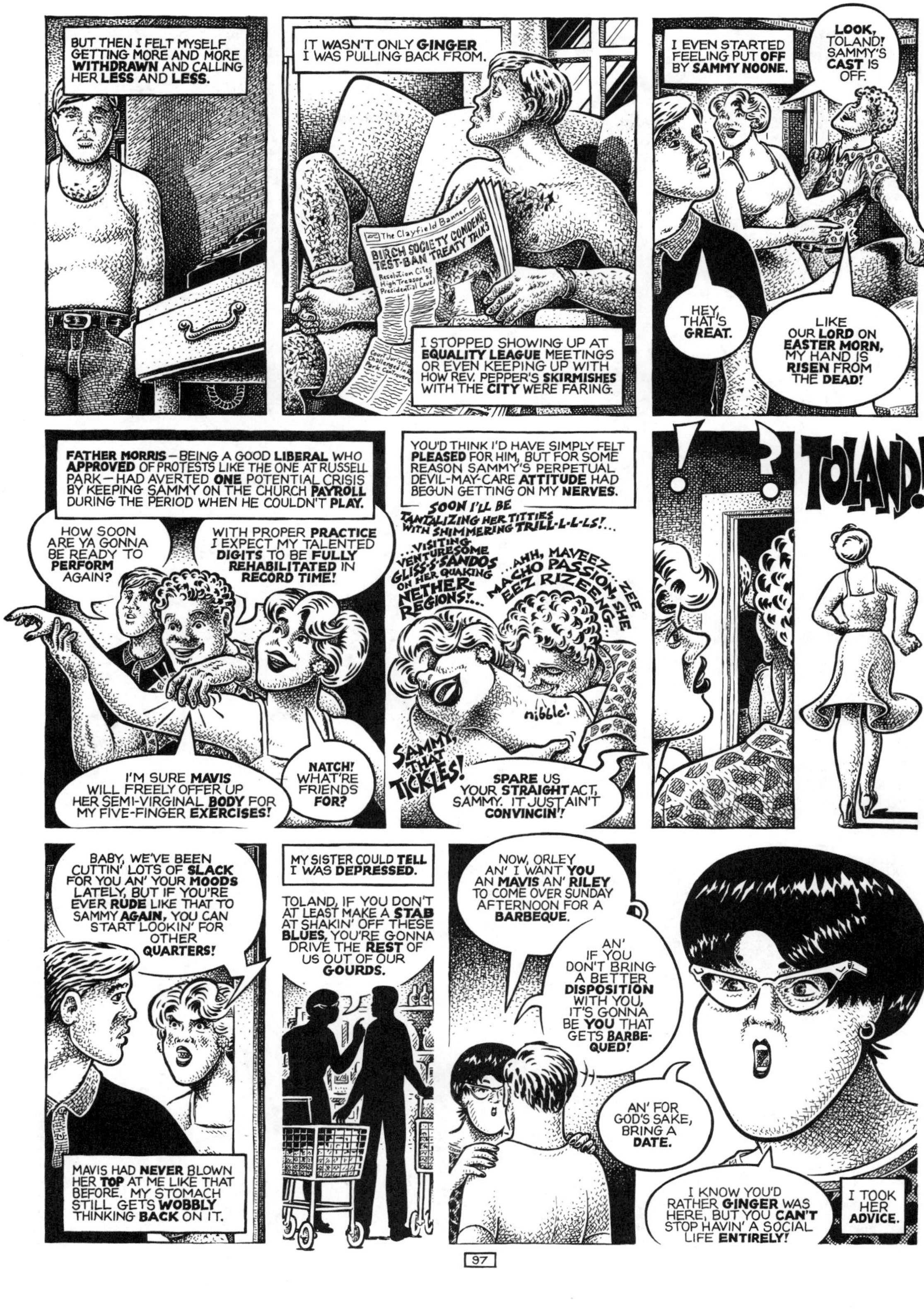

BUT THEN I FELT MYSELF GETTING MORE AND MORE WITHDRAWN AND CALLING HER LESS AND LESS.
IT WASN'T ONLY GINGER I WAS PULLING BACK FROM.
The Clayfield Banner
BIRCH SOCIETY CONDEMNS TEST-BAN TREATY TALKS
Resolution Cites High Treason of Presidential Level
I STOPPED SHOWING UP AT EQUALITY LEAGUE MEETINGS OR EVEN KEEPING UP WITH HOW REV. PEPPER'S SKIRMISHES WITH THE CITY WERE FARING.
I EVEN STARTED FEELING PUT OFF BY SAMMY NOONE.
LOOK, TOLAND! SAMMY'S CAST IS OFF.
HEY, THAT'S GREAT.
LIKE OUR LORD ON EASTER MORN, MY HAND IS RISEN FROM THE DEAD!
FATHER MORRIS—BEING A GOOD LIBERAL WHO APPROVED OF PROTESTS LIKE THE ONE AT RUSSELL PARK—HAD AVERTED ONE POTENTIAL CRISIS BY KEEPING SAMMY ON THE CHURCH PAYROLL DURING THE PERIOD WHEN HE COULDN'T PLAY.
HOW SOON ARE YA GONNA BE READY TO PERFORM AGAIN?
WITH PROPER PRACTICE I EXPECT MY TALENTED DIGITS TO BE FULLY REHABILITATED IN RECORD TIME!
I'M SURE MAVIS WILL FREELY OFFER UP HER SEMI-VIRGINAL BODY FOR MY FIVE-FINGER EXERCISES!
NATCH! WHAT'RE FRIENDS FOR?
YOU'D THINK I'D HAVE SIMPLY FELT PLEASED FOR HIM, BUT FOR SOME REASON SAMMY'S PERPETUAL DEVIL-MAY-CARE ATTITUDE HAD BEGUN GETTING ON MY NERVES.
SOON I'LL BE TANTALIZING HER TITTIES WITH SHIMMERING TRILL-L-L-LS!...
...VISITING VENTURESOME GLISS-S-SANDOS ON HER QUAKING NETHER-REGIONS!...
...AHH, MAVEEZ, ZEE MACHO PASSION, SHE EEZ RIZEENG...
nibble!
SAMMY, THAT TICKLES!
SPARE US YOUR STRAIGHT ACT, SAMMY. IT JUST AIN'T CONVINCIN'!
!
?
TOLAND!
BABY, WE'VE BEEN CUTTIN' LOTS OF SLACK FOR YOU AN' YOUR MOODS LATELY, BUT IF YOU'RE EVER RUDE LIKE THAT TO SAMMY AGAIN, YOU CAN START LOOKIN' FOR OTHER QUARTERS!
MAVIS HAD NEVER BLOWN HER TOP AT ME LIKE THAT BEFORE. MY STOMACH STILL GETS WOBBLY THINKING BACK ON IT.
MY SISTER COULD TELL I WAS DEPRESSED.
TOLAND, IF YOU DON'T AT LEAST MAKE A STAB AT SHAKIN' OFF THESE BLUES, YOU'RE GONNA DRIVE THE REST OF US OUT OF OUR GOURDS.
NOW, ORLEY AN' I WANT YOU AN MAVIS AN' RILEY TO COME OVER SUNDAY AFTERNOON FOR A BARBEQUE.
AN' IF YOU DON'T BRING A BETTER DISPOSITION WITH YOU, IT'S GONNA BE YOU THAT GETS BARBE-QUED!
AN' FOR GOD'S SAKE, BRING A DATE.
I KNOW YOU'D RATHER GINGER WAS HERE, BUT YOU CAN'T STOP HAVIN' A SOCIAL LIFE ENTIRELY!
I TOOK HER ADVICE.

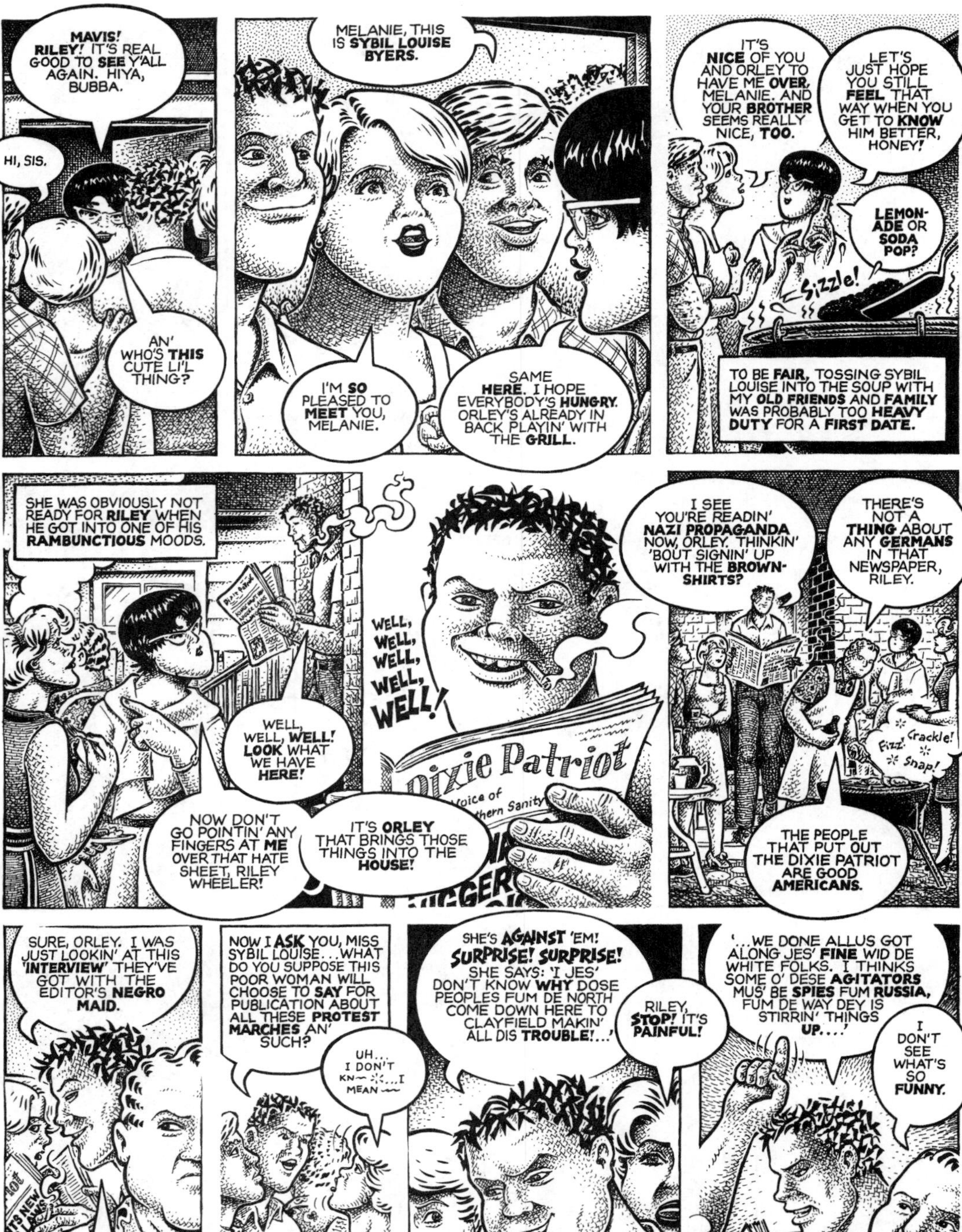

MAVIS! RILEY! IT'S REAL GOOD TO SEE Y'ALL AGAIN. HIYA, BUBBA.
HI, SIS.
AN' WHO'S THIS CUTE LI'L THING?
MELANIE, THIS IS SYBIL LOUISE BYERS.
I'M SO PLEASED TO MEET YOU, MELANIE.
SAME HERE. I HOPE EVERYBODY'S HUNGRY. ORLEY'S ALREADY IN BACK PLAYIN' WITH THE GRILL.
IT'S NICE OF YOU AND ORLEY TO HAVE ME OVER, MELANIE. AND YOUR BROTHER SEEMS REALLY NICE, TOO.
LET'S JUST HOPE YOU STILL FEEL THAT WAY WHEN YOU GET TO KNOW HIM BETTER, HONEY!
LEMON-ADE OR SODA POP?
Sizzle!
TO BE FAIR, TOSSING SYBIL LOUISE INTO THE SOUP WITH MY OLD FRIENDS AND FAMILY WAS PROBABLY TOO HEAVY DUTY FOR A FIRST DATE.
SHE WAS OBVIOUSLY NOT READY FOR RILEY WHEN HE GOT INTO ONE OF HIS RAMBUNCTIOUS MOODS.
WELL, WELL, WELL! LOOK WHAT WE HAVE HERE!
NOW DON'T GO POINTIN' ANY FINGERS AT ME OVER THAT HATE SHEET, RILEY WHEELER!
IT'S ORLEY THAT BRINGS THOSE THINGS INTO THE HOUSE!
WELL, WELL, WELL, WELL, WELL!
Dixie Patriot
I SEE YOU'RE READIN' NAZI PROPAGANDA NOW, ORLEY. THINKIN' 'BOUT SIGNIN' UP WITH THE BROWN-SHIRTS?
THERE'S NOT A THING ABOUT ANY GERMANS IN THAT NEWSPAPER, RILEY.
Fizz! Crackle! Snap!
THE PEOPLE THAT PUT OUT THE DIXIE PATRIOT ARE GOOD AMERICANS.
SURE, ORLEY. I WAS JUST LOOKIN' AT THIS 'INTERVIEW' THEY'VE GOT WITH THE EDITOR'S NEGRO MAID.
Y'GOT THAT? THE 'INTERVIEWER' IS THE GUY THAT PUTS FOOD ON THE TABLE OF THE WOMAN GETTIN' 'INTERVIEWED.'
NOW I ASK YOU, MISS SYBIL LOUISE... WHAT DO YOU SUPPOSE THIS POOR WOMAN WILL CHOOSE TO SAY FOR PUBLICATION ABOUT ALL THESE PROTEST MARCHES AN' SUCH?
UH... I DON'T KN— ...I MEAN —
SHE'S AGAINST 'EM! SURPRISE! SURPRISE! SHE SAYS: 'I JES' DON'T KNOW WHY DOSE PEOPLES FUM DE NORTH COME DOWN HERE TO CLAYFIELD MAKIN' ALL DIS TROUBLE!...'
RILEY, STOP! IT'S PAINFUL!
'...WE DONE ALLUS GOT ALONG JES' FINE WID DE WHITE FOLKS. I THINKS SOME O' DESE AGITATORS MUS' BE SPIES FUM RUSSIA, FUM DE WAY DEY IS STIRRIN' THINGS UP....'
I DON'T SEE WHAT'S SO FUNNY.
Patriot

NOW LISTEN TO WHAT THE INTERVIEWER-EDITOR —HER **BOSS,** MIND YA— HAS TO SAY AT THE **END.**

'IN MY OPINION THIS HUMBLE, UNEDUCATED COLORED WOMAN HAS MORE **BRAINS** IN HER HEAD THAN A **THOUSAND** OF THESE SIGN-WAVING, FOLKSONG-SINGING **HARVARD DROPOUTS** WHO KEEP SHOWING UP ON OUR DOORSTEPS TO TELL US HOW TO LEAD OUR **LIVES.'**

SHE'S GOT **BRAINS,** ALRIGHT!

BRAINS ENOUGH TO KNOW WHO'S GOT A **GRIP** ON THE **WHIP** AT THE OL' **PLANTATION!**

WHAT MAKES YOU SO **SURE** THE WOMAN'S NOT TELLIN' THINGS JUST THE WAY SHE **SEES** 'EM, RILEY?

AIN'T THERE SOMETHIN' A LI'L **CONDESCENDIN'** ABOUT ASSUMIN' SHE'S **NOT?**

FROM WHAT **I** HEAR, A **LOT** OF NEGROES THINK THERE'S SOMETHIN' **FISHY** ABOUT ALL THESE **RADICALS** BLOWIN' INTO TOWN TRYIN' TO —

ORLEY, THAT'S **BULL-SHIT!** THE WOMAN IS **TRAPPED!**

SHE'S GOT CRACKERS ON THE **LEFT** OF HER... CRACKERS ON THE **RIGHT** OF HER... SAME AS **US!**

WE'RE **ALL** OF US STUCK IN A **GODDAM CRACKER BOX!**

CRACKERS WRITE THE **NEWS** THAT THE CRACKERS **READ** THE NEWS THAT THE CRACKERS **WRITE.** ALL OF **US** ARE CRACKERS, **TOO!**

WE WERE **RAISED** TO BE CRACKERS! THERE'S **NO** FUCKIN' WAY **NOT** TO BE A CRACKER AROUND HERE!

IF IT MAKES ME A '**CRACKER**' TO BE **CONCERNED** ABOUT A BUNCH OF KNOW-IT-ALL **COMMUNISTS** COMIN' DOWN TO MAKE MY WORLD **OVER** FOR ME, THEN I'LL BE **HAPPY** TO FLY MY CRACKER FLAG!

YOU'VE **ALWAYS** FLOWN YOUR 'CRACKER FLAG,' HON!

YOU'VE GOT ONE ON THE **CAR!** Y'KNOW THAT **REBEL-FLAG DECAL** THAT'S STUCK ON THE **WIND-SHIELD...?**

I DON'T **BELIEVE** I JUST HEARD A **SOUTHERN-BORN WOMAN** USE THE TERM '**CRACKER FLAG**' IN REFERENCE TO THE EMBLEM OF THE **CONFEDERACY,** FOR WHICH HER **GREAT-GRANDFATHER** MAY WELL HAVE SHED HIS **BLOOD** ON THE **BATTLEFIELD!**

SYBIL LOUISE KEPT HER OPINIONS TO **HERSELF** WHILE THE REST OF US **RAVED.**

I DIDN'T REALIZE HOW **UPSET** SHE'D GOTTEN 'TIL I WAS TAKING HER **HOME** AND THE **TEARS** STARTED FLOWING.

HEY!? WHAT'S THE **MATTER?**

I DON'T THINK I CAN GO **OUT** WITH YOU **AGAIN,** TOLAND.

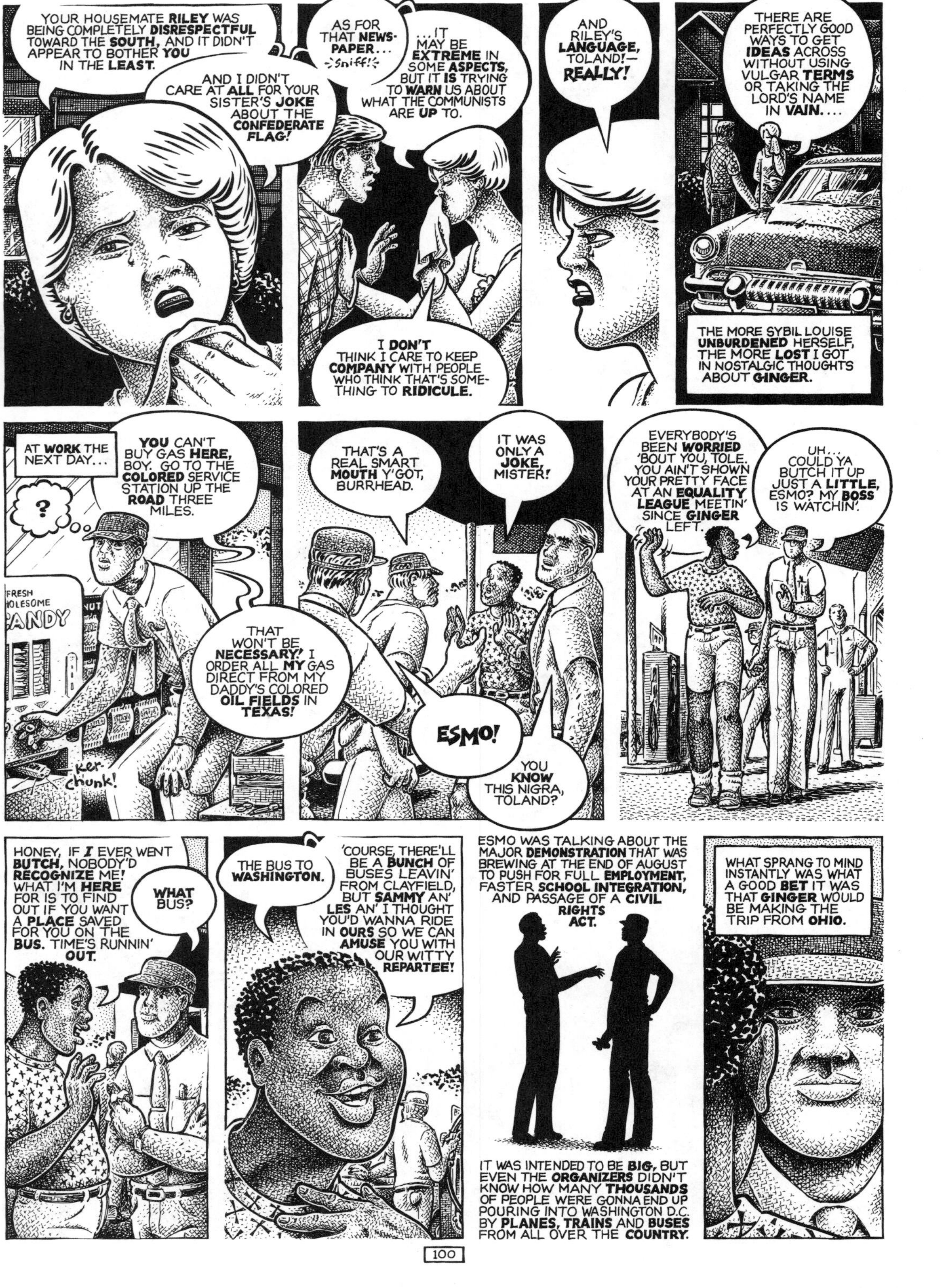

YOUR HOUSEMATE RILEY WAS BEING COMPLETELY DISRESPECTFUL TOWARD THE SOUTH, AND IT DIDN'T APPEAR TO BOTHER YOU IN THE LEAST.
AND I DIDN'T CARE AT ALL FOR YOUR SISTER'S JOKE ABOUT THE CONFEDERATE FLAG!
AS FOR THAT NEWSPAPER... -SNIFF!-
...IT MAY BE EXTREME IN SOME ASPECTS, BUT IT IS TRYING TO WARN US ABOUT WHAT THE COMMUNISTS ARE UP TO.
I DON'T THINK I CARE TO KEEP COMPANY WITH PEOPLE WHO THINK THAT'S SOMETHING TO RIDICULE.
AND RILEY'S LANGUAGE, TOLAND!— REALLY!
THERE ARE PERFECTLY GOOD WAYS TO GET IDEAS ACROSS WITHOUT USING VULGAR TERMS OR TAKING THE LORD'S NAME IN VAIN....
THE MORE SYBIL LOUISE UNBURDENED HERSELF, THE MORE LOST I GOT IN NOSTALGIC THOUGHTS ABOUT GINGER.
AT WORK THE NEXT DAY...
?
YOU CAN'T BUY GAS HERE, BOY. GO TO THE COLORED SERVICE STATION UP THE ROAD THREE MILES.
FRESH WHOLESOME CANDY
THAT WON'T BE NECESSARY! I ORDER ALL MY GAS DIRECT FROM MY DADDY'S COLORED OIL FIELDS IN TEXAS!
KER-CHUNK!
THAT'S A REAL SMART MOUTH Y'GOT, BURRHEAD.
IT WAS ONLY A JOKE, MISTER!
ESMO!
YOU KNOW THIS NIGRA, TOLAND?
EVERYBODY'S BEEN WORRIED 'BOUT YOU, TOLE. YOU AIN'T SHOWN YOUR PRETTY FACE AT AN EQUALITY LEAGUE MEETIN' SINCE GINGER LEFT.
UH... COULD YA BUTCH IT UP JUST A LITTLE, ESMO? MY BOSS IS WATCHIN'.
HONEY, IF I EVER WENT BUTCH, NOBODY'D RECOGNIZE ME! WHAT I'M HERE FOR IS TO FIND OUT IF YOU WANT A PLACE SAVED FOR YOU ON THE BUS. TIME'S RUNNIN' OUT.
WHAT BUS?
THE BUS TO WASHINGTON.
'COURSE, THERE'LL BE A BUNCH OF BUSES LEAVIN' FROM CLAYFIELD, BUT SAMMY AN' LES AN' I THOUGHT YOU'D WANNA RIDE IN OURS SO WE CAN AMUSE YOU WITH OUR WITTY REPARTEE!
ESMO WAS TALKING ABOUT THE MAJOR DEMONSTRATION THAT WAS BREWING AT THE END OF AUGUST TO PUSH FOR FULL EMPLOYMENT, FASTER SCHOOL INTEGRATION, AND PASSAGE OF A CIVIL RIGHTS ACT.
IT WAS INTENDED TO BE BIG, BUT EVEN THE ORGANIZERS DIDN'T KNOW HOW MANY THOUSANDS OF PEOPLE WERE GONNA END UP POURING INTO WASHINGTON D.C. BY PLANES, TRAINS AND BUSES FROM ALL OVER THE COUNTRY.
WHAT SPRANG TO MIND INSTANTLY WAS WHAT A GOOD BET IT WAS THAT GINGER WOULD BE MAKING THE TRIP FROM OHIO.

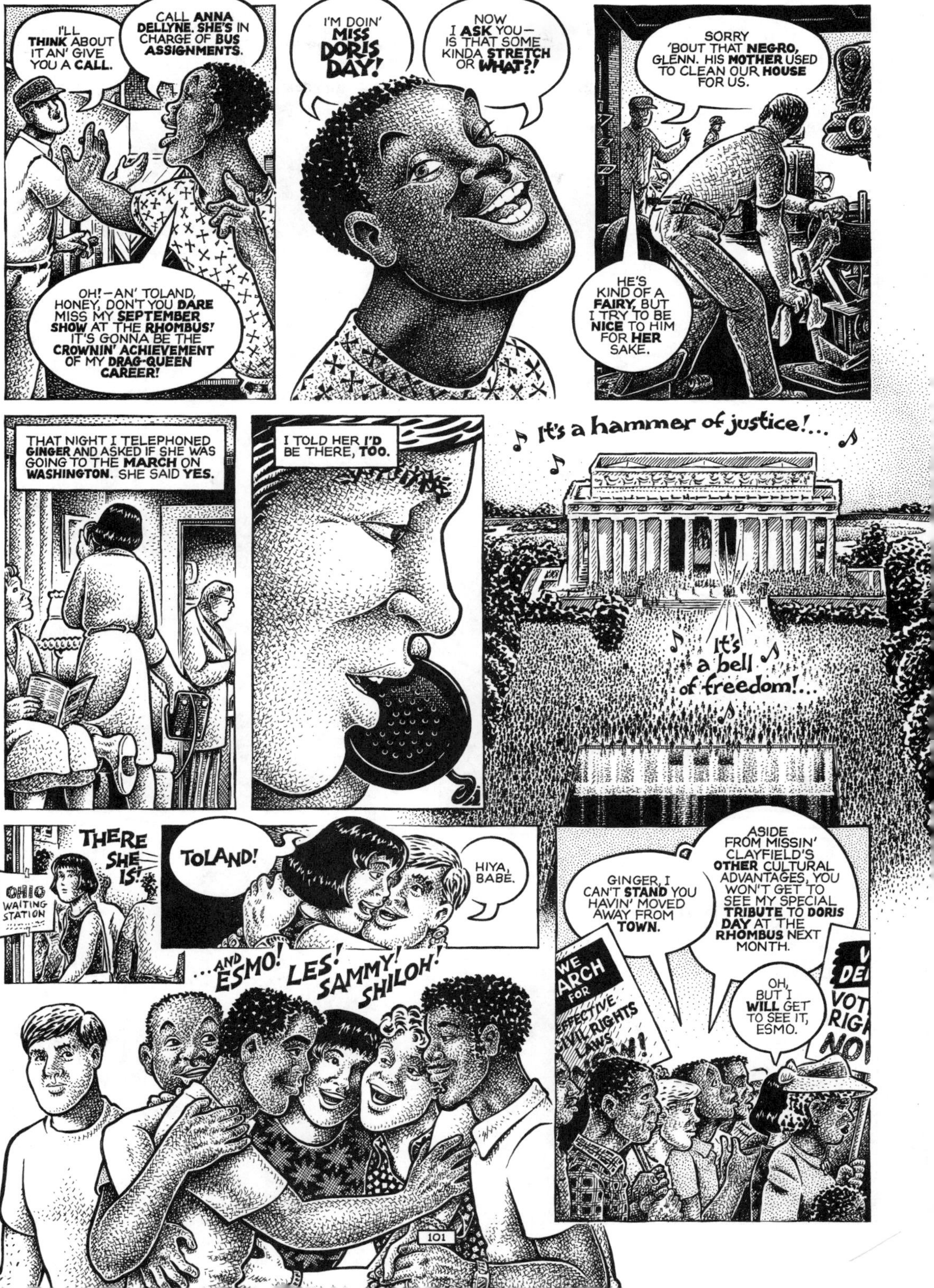
I'LL THINK ABOUT IT AN' GIVE YOU A CALL.
CALL ANNA DELLYNE. SHE'S IN CHARGE OF BUS ASSIGNMENTS.
OH!—AN' TOLAND, HONEY, DON'T YOU DARE MISS MY SEPTEMBER SHOW AT THE RHOMBUS! IT'S GONNA BE THE CROWNIN' ACHIEVEMENT OF MY DRAG-QUEEN CAREER!
I'M DOIN' MISS DORIS DAY!
NOW I ASK YOU— IS THAT SOME KINDA STRETCH OR WHAT?!
SORRY 'BOUT THAT NEGRO, GLENN. HIS MOTHER USED TO CLEAN OUR HOUSE FOR US.
HE'S KIND OF A FAIRY, BUT I TRY TO BE NICE TO HIM FOR HER SAKE.
THAT NIGHT I TELEPHONED GINGER AND ASKED IF SHE WAS GOING TO THE MARCH ON WASHINGTON. SHE SAID YES.
I TOLD HER I'D BE THERE, TOO.
It's a hammer of justice!...
It's a bell of freedom!...
OHIO WAITING STATION
THERE SHE IS!
TOLAND!
HIYA, BABE.
...AND ESMO! LES! SAMMY! SHILOH!
GINGER, I CAN'T STAND YOU HAVIN' MOVED AWAY FROM TOWN.
ASIDE FROM MISSIN' CLAYFIELD'S OTHER CULTURAL ADVANTAGES, YOU WON'T GET TO SEE MY SPECIAL TRIBUTE TO DORIS DAY AT THE RHOMBUS NEXT MONTH.
OH, BUT I WILL GET TO SEE IT, ESMO.
WE MARCH FOR EFFECTIVE CIVIL RIGHTS LAWS

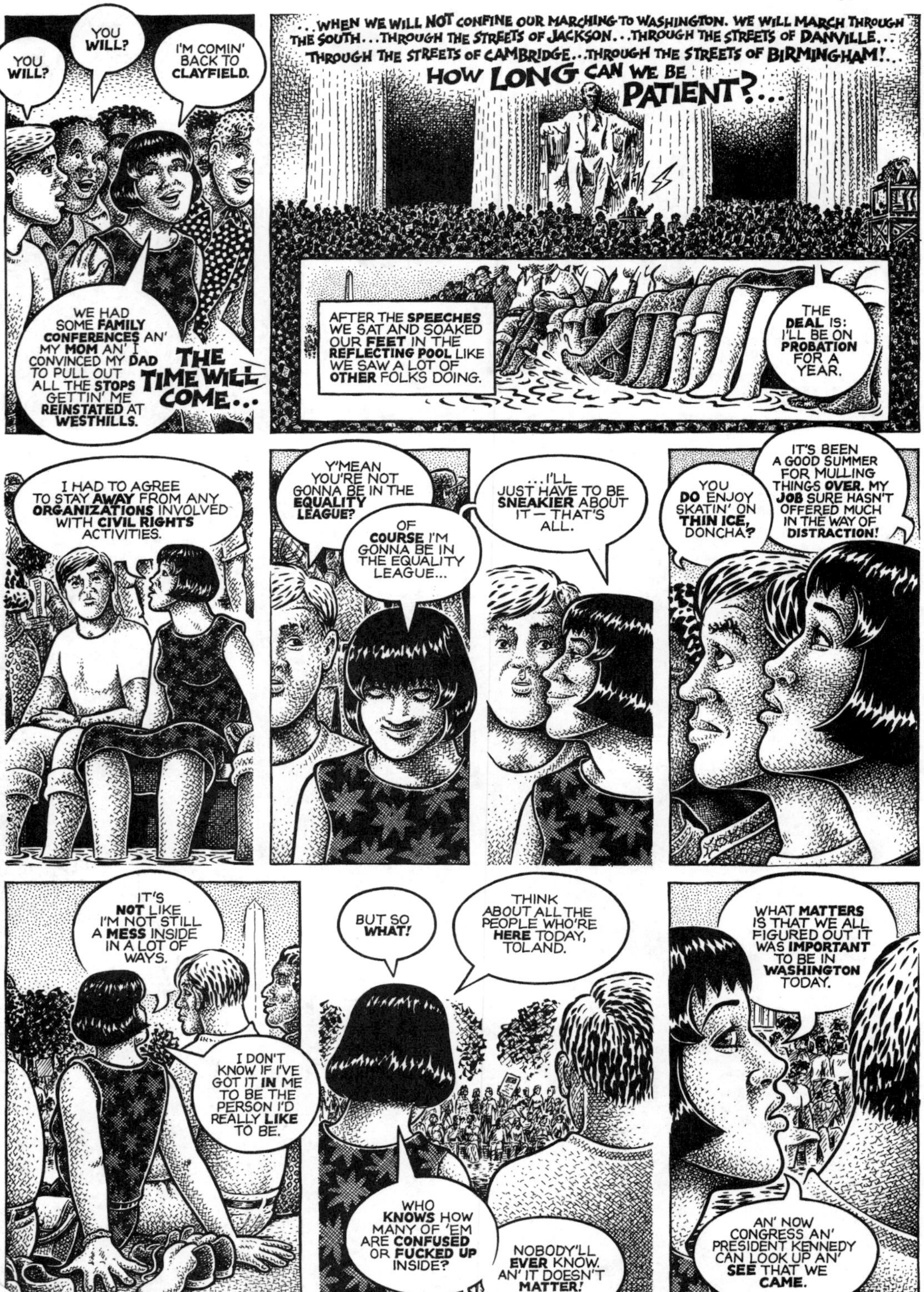
YOU WILL?
YOU WILL?
I'M COMIN' BACK TO CLAYFIELD.
WE HAD SOME FAMILY CONFERENCES AN' MY MOM AN' I CONVINCED MY DAD TO PULL OUT ALL THE STOPS GETTIN' ME REINSTATED AT WESTHILLS.
...WHEN WE WILL NOT CONFINE OUR MARCHING TO WASHINGTON. WE WILL MARCH THROUGH THE SOUTH...THROUGH THE STREETS OF JACKSON...THROUGH THE STREETS OF DANVILLE...THROUGH THE STREETS OF CAMBRIDGE...THROUGH THE STREETS OF BIRMINGHAM!...
HOW LONG CAN WE BE PATIENT?...
THE TIME WILL COME...
AFTER THE SPEECHES WE SAT AND SOAKED OUR FEET IN THE REFLECTING POOL LIKE WE SAW A LOT OF OTHER FOLKS DOING.
THE DEAL IS: I'LL BE ON PROBATION FOR A YEAR.
I HAD TO AGREE TO STAY AWAY FROM ANY ORGANIZATIONS INVOLVED WITH CIVIL RIGHTS ACTIVITIES.
Y'MEAN YOU'RE NOT GONNA BE IN THE EQUALITY LEAGUE?
OF COURSE I'M GONNA BE IN THE EQUALITY LEAGUE...
...I'LL JUST HAVE TO BE SNEAKIER ABOUT IT — THAT'S ALL.
YOU DO ENJOY SKATIN' ON THIN ICE, DONCHA?
IT'S BEEN A GOOD SUMMER FOR MULLING THINGS OVER. MY JOB SURE HASN'T OFFERED MUCH IN THE WAY OF DISTRACTION!
IT'S NOT LIKE I'M NOT STILL A MESS INSIDE IN A LOT OF WAYS.
I DON'T KNOW IF I'VE GOT IT IN ME TO BE THE PERSON I'D REALLY LIKE TO BE.
BUT SO WHAT!
THINK ABOUT ALL THE PEOPLE WHO'RE HERE TODAY, TOLAND.
WHO KNOWS HOW MANY OF 'EM ARE CONFUSED OR FUCKED UP INSIDE?
NOBODY'LL EVER KNOW. AN' IT DOESN'T MATTER!
WHAT MATTERS IS THAT WE ALL FIGURED OUT IT WAS IMPORTANT TO BE IN WASHINGTON TODAY.
AN' NOW CONGRESS AN' PRESIDENT KENNEDY CAN LOOK UP AN' SEE THAT WE CAME.

NO MATTER HOW I HASH IT **OVER** IN MY MIND, IT KEEPS SEEMIN' LIKE **CLAYFIELD'S** THE RIGHT PLACE FOR ME TO **BE** THIS YEAR.

I **CARE** ABOUT WHAT'S **HAPPENIN'** THERE.

I THOUGHT YOU SAID YOU DIDN'T 'BELONG' THERE.

D'YA **KNOW** THAT FEELIN' I'M TALKIN' ABOUT, TOLAND...

IT'S ALL **RELATIVE.** I'D FORGOTTEN HOW MUCH **LESS** I BELONG IN **AKRON.**

WHERE THE **QUESTIONS** YOU'VE GOT ABOUT YOURSELF STOP **MATTERIN'** NEXT TO THE SIMPLE FACT THAT YOU'RE WHERE IT'S **RIGHT** FOR YOU TO **BE...** DOIN' WHAT IT'S **RIGHT** FOR YOU TO **DO?**

YOU'VE FELT THAT WAY, HAVEN'T YOU?

HER QUESTION CAUGHT ME **SHORT** BECAUSE THE FACT WAS, I **HADN'T** FELT THAT WAY.

I'D PRETTY MUCH **ALWAYS** FELT LIKE AN INADEQUATE **BOZO** STUCK IN THE **WRONG** PLACE, DOING **WRONG** THINGS NINE-TENTHS OF THE TIME.

BUT MAYBE NOT **THIS** TIME, I THOUGHT, LOOKING AROUND ME.

THE FACT WAS, BEING THERE IN WASHINGTON THAT PARTICULAR DAY COULD **PASS** FOR THE FEELING OF RIGHTNESS THAT GINGER WAS **TALKING** TO ME ABOUT.

THERE WAS A GENERAL **HIGH** THAT PERSISTED FOR A COUPLE OF **WEEKS** AFTER WASHINGTON. **EVERYBODY** FELT IT.

This little light of mine, oh Lord... I'm gonna Let it shine!*...*

≥whew!≤ OUT**RAGE**OUS, FOLKS!

SHILOH SAID HE COULD **SWEAR** THE KIDS IN HIS **FREEDOM CHORUS** GAINED AN **OCTAVE'S** WORTH OF RANGE OVERNIGHT—JUST FROM BEING PART OF THAT **THRONG.**

MELODY MOTEL
NO VACANCY

THEN CAME THE **BOMBING** AT THE **MELODY.**

NOT THE **FIRST...** BUT DEFINITELY THE **WORST.**

CAN YOU GET IN?

SHILOH! CAN YOU **HEAR** US?

THERE'S SOMETHIN' BLOCKIN' THE DOOR.

Let it Shine!... Let it Shine!...
Let it Shine!...

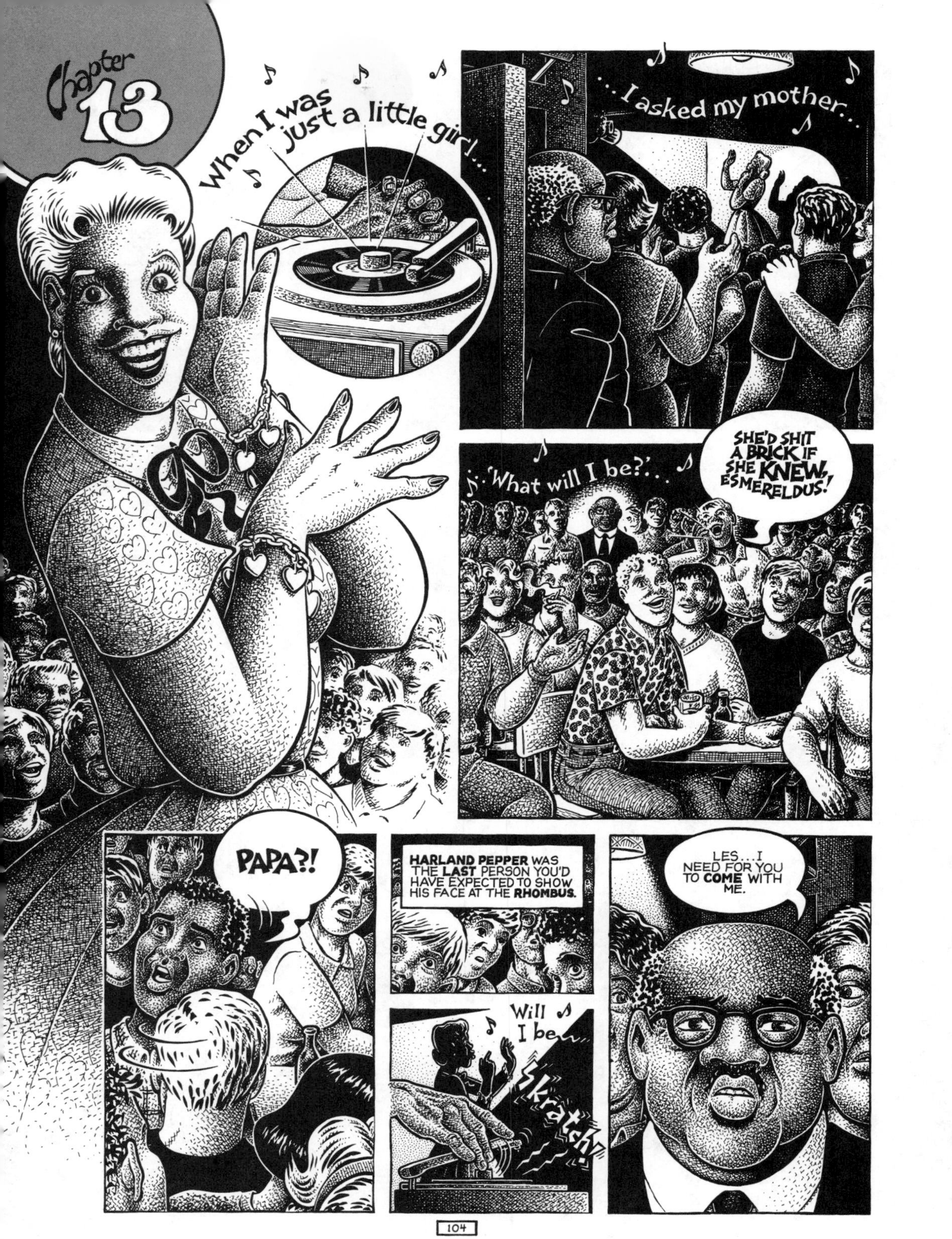
Chapter 13
When I was just a little girl...
...I asked my mother...
'What will I be?'...
SHE'D SHIT A BRICK IF SHE KNEW, ESMERELDUS!
PAPA?!
HARLAND PEPPER WAS THE LAST PERSON YOU'D HAVE EXPECTED TO SHOW HIS FACE AT THE RHOMBUS.
Will I be...
Skratch!
LES...I NEED FOR YOU TO COME WITH ME.

SURE, PAPA.

I'M **SORRY** TO HAVE **INTERRUPTED** THINGS HERE, BUT THERE'S BEEN A TERRIBLE **TRAGEDY** THIS EVENIN'.

A BOMB GOT SET OFF AT THE **MELODY MOTEL**.

MOST OF THE ROOMS THAT GOT HIT WERE **EMPTY**...

...BUT THERE'S A **CONFERENCE ROOM** THEY'VE BEEN LETTIN' SHILOH REED'S **FREEDOM CHORUS** USE FOR **REHEARSALS**, AN'...

REV. PEPPER...WAS ANYBODY—?

THERE **HAVE** BEEN SOME **DEATHS**, SAMMY. I DON'T KNOW **WHO** OR HOW **MANY**.

DAMN, ESMO! I **SWEAR** I FELT THE BAR **SHAKE** EARLIER, BUT I THOUGHT IT WAS JUST MY **IMAGINATION**....

I CAN'T **STAND** ANY **MORE** OF THIS, MABEL.

THAT WAS ONE ROOMFUL OF **STUNNED QUEERS** THE PREACHER LEFT BEHIND! FOR **SURE**, NOBODY WAS OF A MIND TO HANG AROUND FOR MORE **LAUGHS**!

RILEY WAS ADAMANT THAT WE SHOULD **HAUL ASS** BACK TO THE **WHEELERY**.

I'M **TELLIN'** YA, THERE'S GONNA BE A LOT OF **PISSED-OFF NEGROES** RUNNIN' 'ROUND TOWN.

I **CAN'T** HEAD HOME **YET**. I WANNA FIND OUT WHAT'S HAPPENED TO **SHILOH**.

SAME **HERE**.

HERE'S MY **KEYS** TO THE **MERCURY**, RILEY. **YOU** DRIVE IT ON HOME **NOW** AN' **SAMMY** CAN BRING ME BY AFTER WE'VE **SCOUTED** THINGS **OUT**.

YOU TWO ARE **NUTS**!

YOU AN' **MAVIS** WON'T MIND DROPPIN' **GINGER** OFF AT THE **CAMPUS**, WILLYA?

FORGET THAT! I'M COMIN' WITH **YOU** AN' **SAMMY**.

WE COULDN'T GET ANYWHERE **NEAR** THE **MELODY**. **STREETS** WERE BLOCKED AND ALL YOU COULD SEE WERE **COP CARS** AND **FIRE ENGINES**.

LOOK, SAMMY— THERE'S **RAEBURN**.

ROLL DOWN THE **WINDOW**.

GOTCHA.

DON'T BOTHER WITH THE **MOTEL**, SAMMY. ANY- BODY THAT'S **HURT** IS BEIN' TAKEN TO **RATTLER HILL**.

'RATTLER HILL' HAD BEEN THE DISRESPECT- FUL **NICKNAME** FOR THE BLACK FOLKS' HOSPITAL FOR SO **LONG**, IT HAD ALL BUT BECOME **OFFICIAL**.

DURING THE TENSE DRIVE THROUGH **SMITH CITY** WE WERE TREATED TO INSIGHT- FUL **COMMENTARY** BY OUR FAVORITE **PUBLIC SERVANT**.

Commissioner Chopper, given the motel's reputation as a focus of integrationist activity, is it true that your investigators suspect a political motive for tonight's bombing?

MORE **CLEVER SLEUTHING** BY OUR **BOYS IN BLUE**!

WHILE THE THREE OF US **LISTENED** AND **GLOWERED**, I GOT LOST IN CONTEMPLATION OF THE **MUSCLES** THAT WERE FLEXING IN SAMMY'S **JAW**.

That's right, Bill... And as shocked as we all are by this deplorable crime, I'm obliged to point out that those sweet children would be alive right now were it not for the inflammatory street demonstrations we've all been subjected to by local malcontents as well as Communistic outside agitators...

EVEN WITH HIS FACE **HIDDEN**, IT WAS CLEAR HIS **BLOOD** WAS **BOILING**.

JEROME RADLER HILL MEMORIAL HOSPITAL FOR NEGROES

AT RATTLER HILL WE HAD TO WEAVE PAST **NEWS CREWS** FROM THE LOCAL **TELEVISION STATIONS**.

THEY WEREN'T BEING ALLOWED **INSIDE**, BUT THAT WASN'T STOPPING THEM FROM ANGLING FOR DRAMATIC FOOTAGE IN THE **PARKING LOT**.

WE SQUEEZED INTO A LOBBY THAT WAS **PACKED** WITH **FRIENDS** AND **RELATIVES** OF THE BOMB VICTIMS.

HARLAND PEPPER WAS A **SIGHT** TO **BEHOLD** AS HE DASHED BACK AND FORTH TENDING TO **FIFTEEN** EMOTIONAL CRISES A MINUTE.

LES STAYED AT HIS DADDY'S **BECK** AND **CALL**. I WAS **IMPRESSED** AT HOW A **PARTYBOY** FROM THE **RHOMBUS** COULD TURN INTO A PERFECT **PREACHER'S KID** AT THE FLICK OF A **SWITCH**.

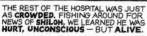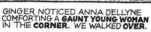

THE REST OF THE HOSPITAL WAS JUST AS **CROWDED**. FISHING AROUND FOR NEWS OF **SHILOH**, WE LEARNED HE WAS **HURT, UNCONSCIOUS** — BUT **ALIVE**.

GINGER NOTICED ANNA DELLYNE COMFORTING A **GAUNT YOUNG WOMAN** IN THE **CORNER**. WE WALKED **OVER**.

IT WAS SHILOH'S WIFE **LOTTIE**, WHOM I'D NEVER **MET**.

IT WAS PROBABLY COMMON **KNOWLEDGE** HOW FAR **GONE** SHE WAS FROM **CANCER**, BUT NOBODY HAD EVER BROUGHT UP THE SUBJECT TO **ME**.

GINGER HUGGED LOTTIE AND ANNA DELLYNE AND THE THREE FEMALES WENT INTO AN INTIMATE **WHISPERING** MODE. I FELT **EXTRANEOUS**.

SAMMY GOT **ANTSY** AND **PEELED OFF** FROM THE GROUP. AFTER EXPRESSING MY **CONCERN** TO **LOTTIE**, I DID, **TOO**.

I WANDERED AROUND, WISHING I HAD SOMEBODY TO **TALK** TO.

I SAW PLENTY OF FAMILIAR **FACES** FROM THE **EQUALITY LEAGUE**. THERE WEREN'T **MANY**, HOWEVER, THAT I'D EVER BOTHERED TO STRIKE UP A REAL **FRIENDSHIP** WITH.

AND **NOW** SEEMED AN AWKWARD TIME TO SET ABOUT **ICE-BREAKING**!

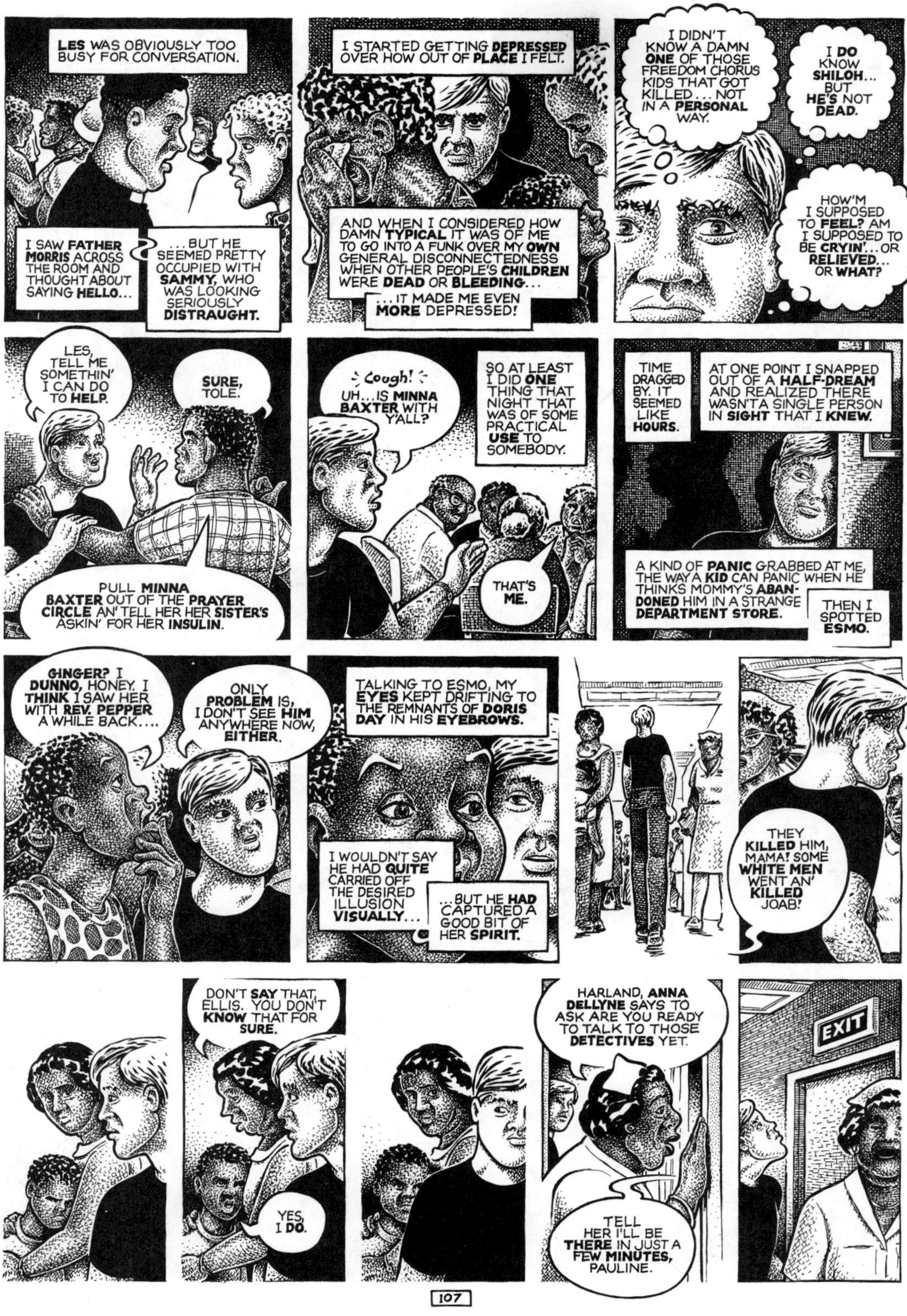

LES WAS OBVIOUSLY TOO BUSY FOR CONVERSATION.
I SAW FATHER MORRIS ACROSS THE ROOM AND THOUGHT ABOUT SAYING HELLO...
...BUT HE SEEMED PRETTY OCCUPIED WITH SAMMY, WHO WAS LOOKING SERIOUSLY DISTRAUGHT.
I STARTED GETTING DEPRESSED OVER HOW OUT OF PLACE I FELT.
AND WHEN I CONSIDERED HOW DAMN TYPICAL IT WAS OF ME TO GO INTO A FUNK OVER MY OWN GENERAL DISCONNECTEDNESS WHEN OTHER PEOPLE'S CHILDREN WERE DEAD OR BLEEDING...
...IT MADE ME EVEN MORE DEPRESSED!
I DIDN'T KNOW A DAMN ONE OF THOSE FREEDOM CHORUS KIDS THAT GOT KILLED... NOT IN A PERSONAL WAY.
I DO KNOW SHILOH... BUT HE'S NOT DEAD.
HOW'M I SUPPOSED TO FEEL? AM I SUPPOSED TO BE CRYIN'... OR RELIEVED... OR WHAT?
LES, TELL ME SOMETHIN' I CAN DO TO HELP.
SURE, TOLE.
PULL MINNA BAXTER OUT OF THE PRAYER CIRCLE AN' TELL HER HER SISTER'S ASKIN' FOR HER INSULIN.
Cough!
UH... IS MINNA BAXTER WITH Y'ALL?
SO AT LEAST I DID ONE THING THAT NIGHT THAT WAS OF SOME PRACTICAL USE TO SOMEBODY.
THAT'S ME.
TIME DRAGGED BY. IT SEEMED LIKE HOURS.
AT ONE POINT I SNAPPED OUT OF A HALF-DREAM AND REALIZED THERE WASN'T A SINGLE PERSON IN SIGHT THAT I KNEW.
A KIND OF PANIC GRABBED AT ME, THE WAY A KID CAN PANIC WHEN HE THINKS MOMMY'S ABANDONED HIM IN A STRANGE DEPARTMENT STORE.
THEN I SPOTTED ESMO.
GINGER? I DUNNO, HONEY. I THINK I SAW HER WITH REV. PEPPER A WHILE BACK....
ONLY PROBLEM IS, I DON'T SEE HIM ANYWHERE NOW, EITHER.
TALKING TO ESMO, MY EYES KEPT DRIFTING TO THE REMNANTS OF DORIS DAY IN HIS EYEBROWS.
I WOULDN'T SAY HE HAD QUITE CARRIED OFF THE DESIRED ILLUSION VISUALLY...
...BUT HE HAD CAPTURED A GOOD BIT OF HER SPIRIT.
THEY KILLED HIM, MAMA! SOME WHITE MEN WENT AN' KILLED JOAB!
DON'T SAY THAT, ELLIS. YOU DON'T KNOW THAT FOR SURE.
YES, I DO.
HARLAND, ANNA DELLYNE SAYS TO ASK ARE YOU READY TO TALK TO THOSE DETECTIVES YET.
TELL HER I'LL BE THERE IN JUST A FEW MINUTES, PAULINE.
EXIT

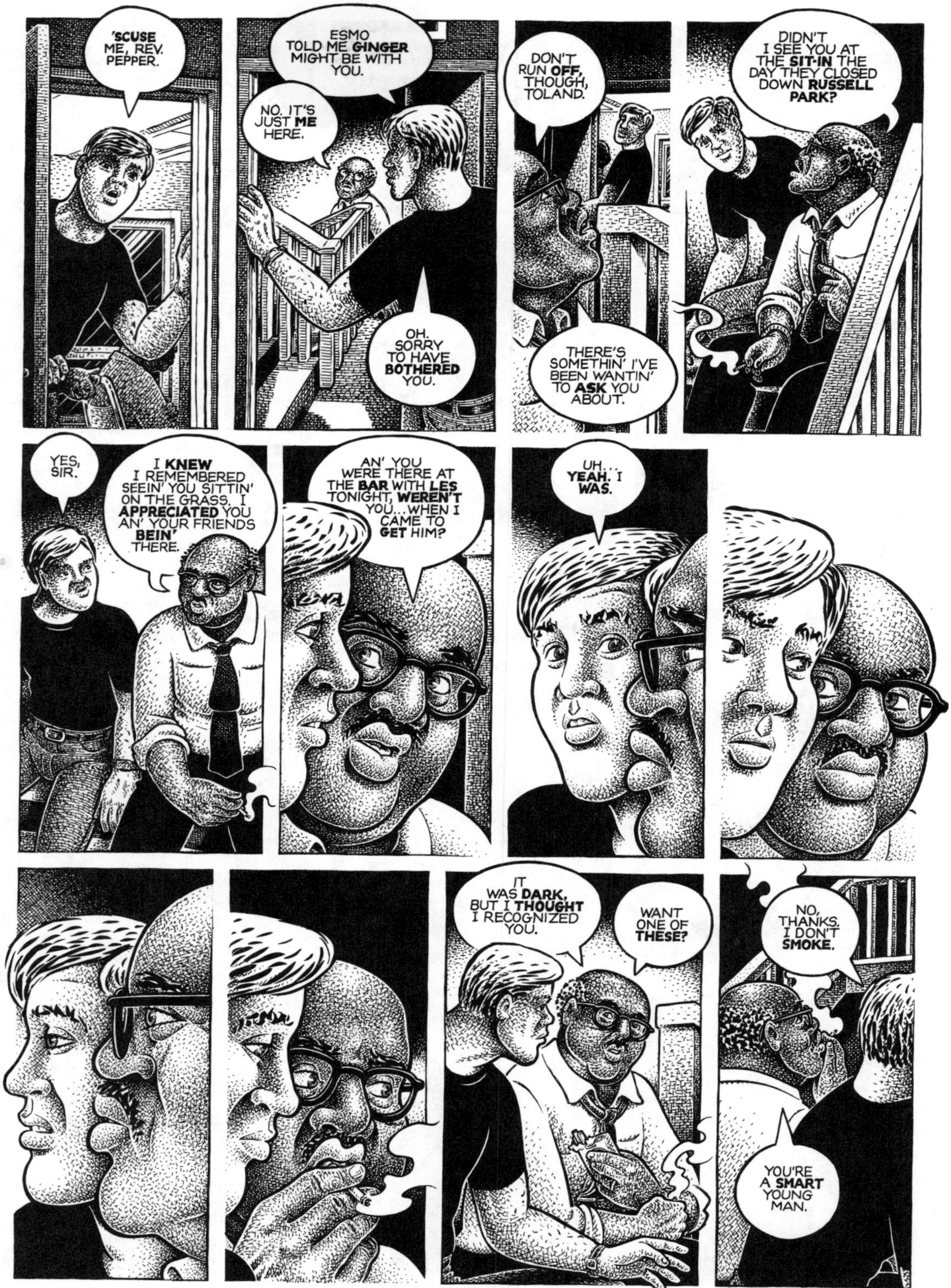

'SCUSE ME, REV. PEPPER.
ESMO TOLD ME GINGER MIGHT BE WITH YOU.
NO. IT'S JUST ME HERE.
OH. SORRY TO HAVE BOTHERED YOU.
DON'T RUN OFF, THOUGH, TOLAND.
THERE'S SOMETHIN' I'VE BEEN WANTIN' TO ASK YOU ABOUT.
DIDN'T I SEE YOU AT THE SIT-IN THE DAY THEY CLOSED DOWN RUSSELL PARK?
YES, SIR.
I KNEW I REMEMBERED SEEIN' YOU SITTIN' ON THE GRASS. I APPRECIATED YOU AN' YOUR FRIENDS BEIN' THERE.
AN' YOU WERE THERE AT THE BAR WITH LES TONIGHT, WEREN'T YOU...WHEN I CAME TO GET HIM?
UH... YEAH. I WAS.
IT WAS DARK, BUT I THOUGHT I RECOGNIZED YOU.
WANT ONE OF THESE?
NO, THANKS. I DON'T SMOKE.
YOU'RE A SMART YOUNG MAN.

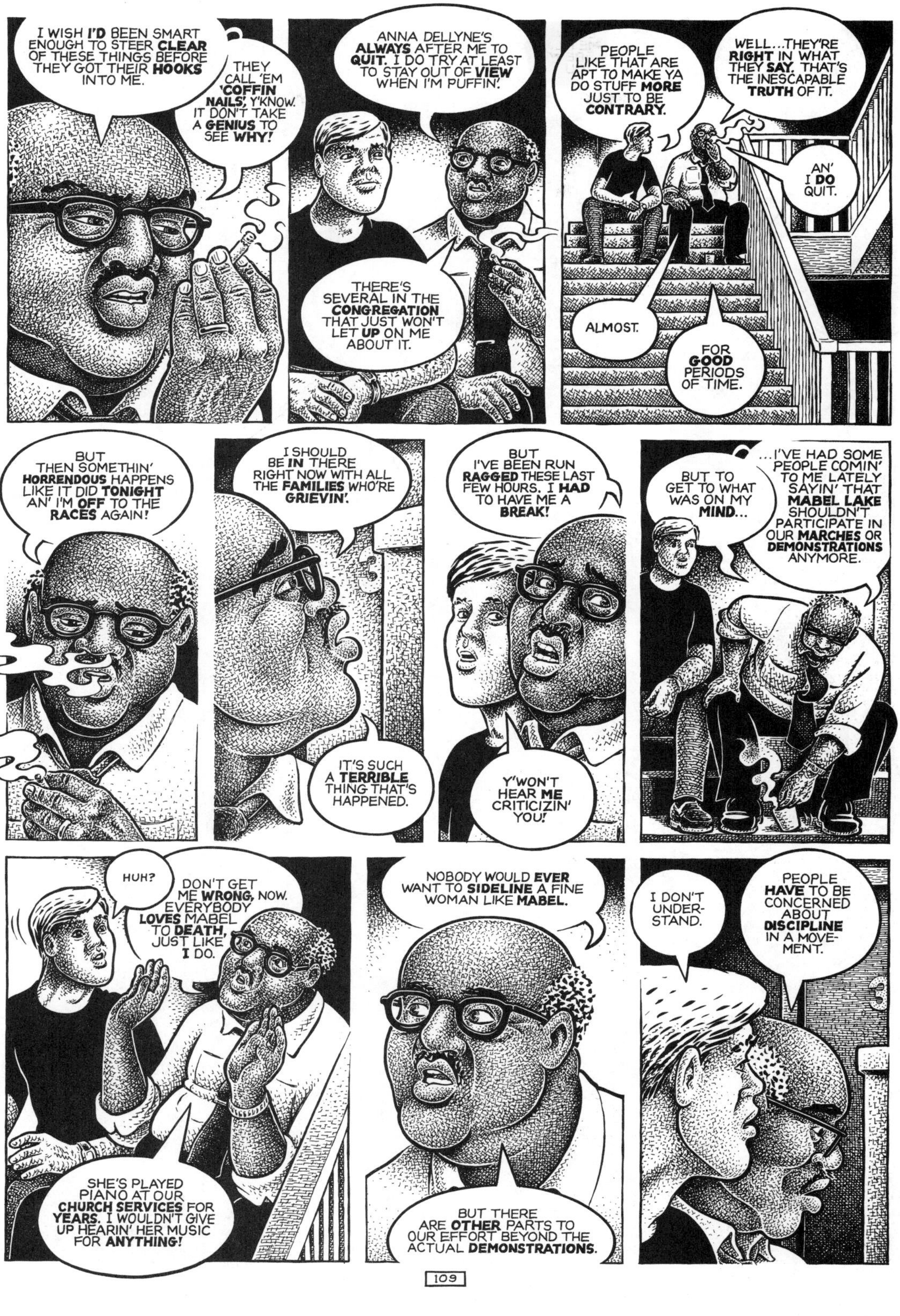

I WISH I'D BEEN SMART ENOUGH TO STEER CLEAR OF THESE THINGS BEFORE THEY GOT THEIR HOOKS INTO ME.
THEY CALL 'EM 'COFFIN NAILS,' Y'KNOW. IT DON'T TAKE A GENIUS TO SEE WHY!
ANNA DELLYNE'S ALWAYS AFTER ME TO QUIT. I DO TRY AT LEAST TO STAY OUT OF VIEW WHEN I'M PUFFIN'.
THERE'S SEVERAL IN THE CONGREGATION THAT JUST WON'T LET UP ON ME ABOUT IT.
PEOPLE LIKE THAT ARE APT TO MAKE YA DO STUFF MORE JUST TO BE CONTRARY.
WELL...THEY'RE RIGHT IN WHAT THEY SAY. THAT'S THE INESCAPABLE TRUTH OF IT.
AN' I DO QUIT.
ALMOST.
FOR GOOD PERIODS OF TIME.
BUT THEN SOMETHIN' HORRENDOUS HAPPENS LIKE IT DID TONIGHT AN' I'M OFF TO THE RACES AGAIN!
I SHOULD BE IN THERE RIGHT NOW WITH ALL THE FAMILIES WHO'RE GRIEVIN'.
IT'S SUCH A TERRIBLE THING THAT'S HAPPENED.
BUT I'VE BEEN RUN RAGGED THESE LAST FEW HOURS. I HAD TO HAVE ME A BREAK!
Y'WON'T HEAR ME CRITICIZIN' YOU!
BUT TO GET TO WHAT WAS ON MY MIND...
...I'VE HAD SOME PEOPLE COMIN' TO ME LATELY SAYIN' THAT MABEL LAKE SHOULDN'T PARTICIPATE IN OUR MARCHES OR DEMONSTRATIONS ANYMORE.
HUH?
DON'T GET ME WRONG, NOW. EVERYBODY LOVES MABEL TO DEATH, JUST LIKE I DO.
SHE'S PLAYED PIANO AT OUR CHURCH SERVICES FOR YEARS. I WOULDN'T GIVE UP HEARIN' HER MUSIC FOR ANYTHING!
NOBODY WOULD EVER WANT TO SIDELINE A FINE WOMAN LIKE MABEL.
BUT THERE ARE OTHER PARTS TO OUR EFFORT BEYOND THE ACTUAL DEMONSTRATIONS.
I DON'T UNDER-STAND.
PEOPLE HAVE TO BE CONCERNED ABOUT DISCIPLINE IN A MOVE-MENT.

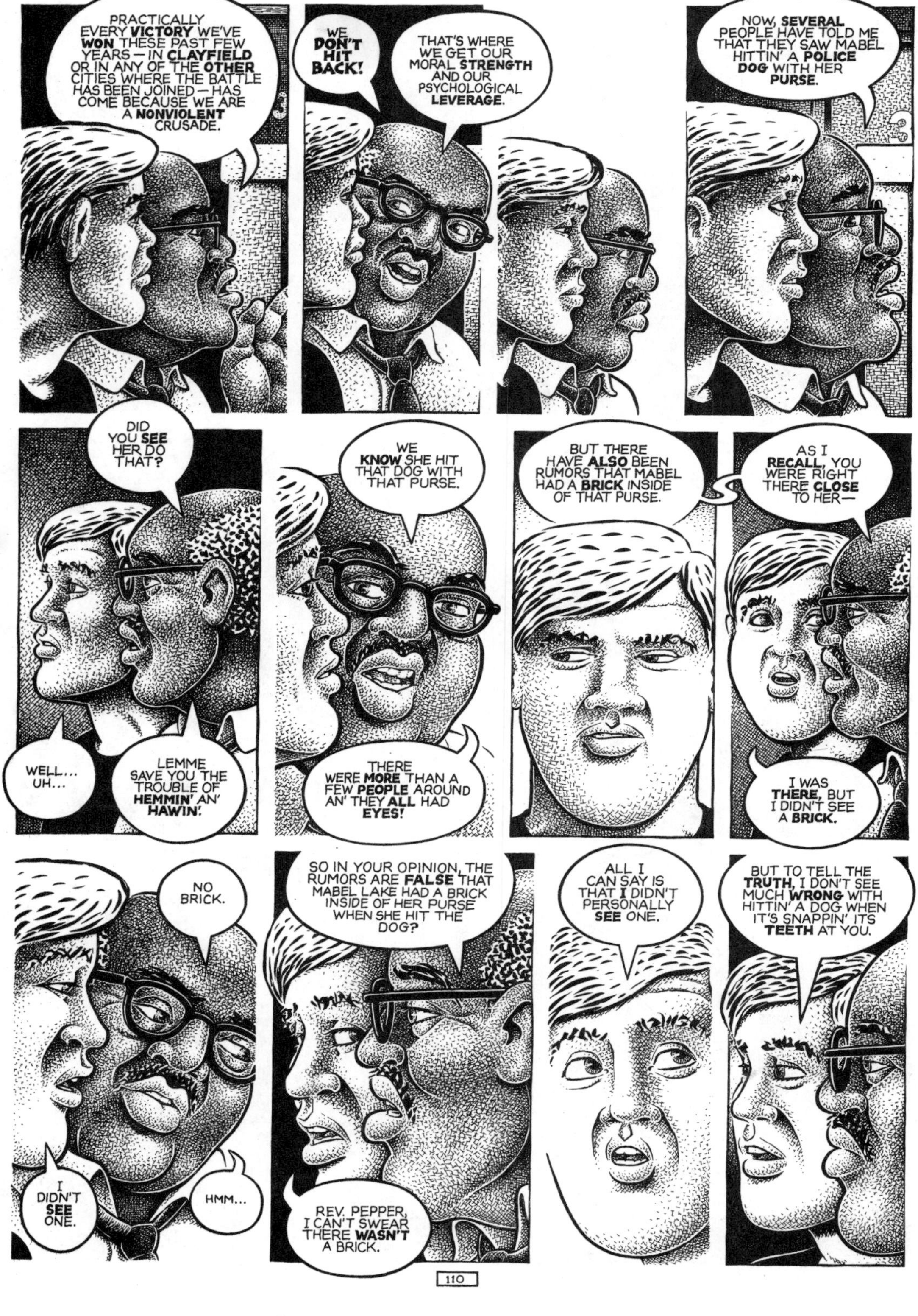
PRACTICALLY EVERY **VICTORY** WE'VE **WON** THESE PAST FEW YEARS — IN **CLAYFIELD** OR IN ANY OF THE **OTHER** CITIES WHERE THE BATTLE HAS BEEN JOINED — HAS COME BECAUSE WE ARE A **NONVIOLENT** CRUSADE.
WE **DON'T HIT BACK!**
THAT'S WHERE WE GET OUR MORAL **STRENGTH** AND OUR PSYCHOLOGICAL **LEVERAGE**.
NOW, **SEVERAL** PEOPLE HAVE TOLD ME THAT THEY SAW MABEL HITTIN' A **POLICE DOG** WITH HER **PURSE**.
DID YOU **SEE** HER DO THAT?
WELL... UH...
LEMME SAVE YOU THE TROUBLE OF **HEMMIN' AN' HAWIN'**.
WE **KNOW** SHE HIT THAT DOG WITH THAT PURSE.
THERE WERE **MORE** THAN A FEW **PEOPLE** AROUND AN' THEY **ALL** HAD **EYES!**
BUT THERE HAVE **ALSO** BEEN RUMORS THAT MABEL HAD A **BRICK** INSIDE OF THAT PURSE.
AS I **RECALL**, YOU WERE RIGHT THERE **CLOSE** TO HER—
I WAS **THERE**, BUT I DIDN'T SEE A **BRICK**.
NO BRICK.
I DIDN'T **SEE** ONE.
HMM...
SO IN YOUR OPINION, THE RUMORS ARE **FALSE** THAT MABEL LAKE HAD A BRICK INSIDE OF HER PURSE WHEN SHE HIT THE DOG?
REV. PEPPER, I CAN'T SWEAR THERE **WASN'T** A BRICK.
ALL I CAN SAY IS THAT **I** DIDN'T PERSONALLY **SEE** ONE.
BUT TO TELL THE **TRUTH**, I DON'T SEE MUCH **WRONG** WITH HITTIN' A DOG WHEN IT'S SNAPPIN' ITS **TEETH** AT YOU.

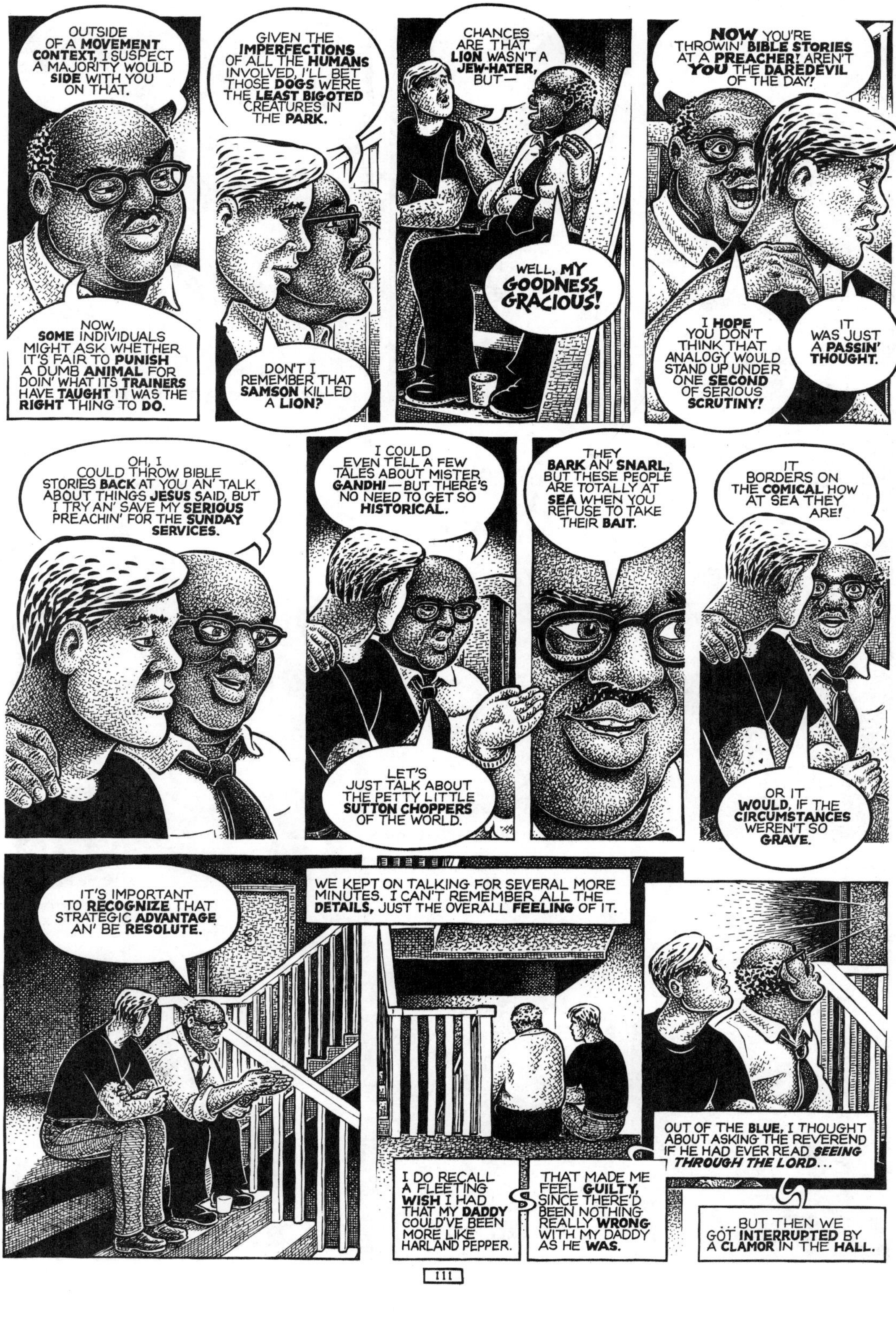

OUTSIDE OF A MOVEMENT CONTEXT, I SUSPECT A MAJORITY WOULD SIDE WITH YOU ON THAT.
NOW, SOME INDIVIDUALS MIGHT ASK WHETHER IT'S FAIR TO PUNISH A DUMB ANIMAL FOR DOIN' WHAT ITS TRAINERS HAVE TAUGHT IT WAS THE RIGHT THING TO DO.
GIVEN THE IMPERFECTIONS OF ALL THE HUMANS INVOLVED, I'LL BET THOSE DOGS WERE THE LEAST BIGOTED CREATURES IN THE PARK.
DON'T I REMEMBER THAT SAMSON KILLED A LION?
CHANCES ARE THAT LION WASN'T A JEW-HATER, BUT—
WELL, MY GOODNESS GRACIOUS!
NOW YOU'RE THROWIN' BIBLE STORIES AT A PREACHER! AREN'T YOU THE DAREDEVIL OF THE DAY!
I HOPE YOU DON'T THINK THAT ANALOGY WOULD STAND UP UNDER ONE SECOND OF SERIOUS SCRUTINY!
IT WAS JUST A PASSIN' THOUGHT.
OH, I COULD THROW BIBLE STORIES BACK AT YOU AN' TALK ABOUT THINGS JESUS SAID, BUT I TRY AN' SAVE MY SERIOUS PREACHIN' FOR THE SUNDAY SERVICES.
I COULD EVEN TELL A FEW TALES ABOUT MISTER GANDHI—BUT THERE'S NO NEED TO GET SO HISTORICAL.
LET'S JUST TALK ABOUT THE PETTY LITTLE SUTTON CHOPPERS OF THE WORLD.
THEY BARK AN' SNARL, BUT THESE PEOPLE ARE TOTALLY AT SEA WHEN YOU REFUSE TO TAKE THEIR BAIT.
IT BORDERS ON THE COMICAL HOW AT SEA THEY ARE!
OR IT WOULD, IF THE CIRCUMSTANCES WEREN'T SO GRAVE.
IT'S IMPORTANT TO RECOGNIZE THAT STRATEGIC ADVANTAGE AN' BE RESOLUTE.
WE KEPT ON TALKING FOR SEVERAL MORE MINUTES. I CAN'T REMEMBER ALL THE DETAILS, JUST THE OVERALL FEELING OF IT.
I DO RECALL A FLEETING WISH I HAD THAT MY DADDY COULD'VE BEEN MORE LIKE HARLAND PEPPER.
THAT MADE ME FEEL GUILTY, SINCE THERE'D BEEN NOTHING REALLY WRONG WITH MY DADDY AS HE WAS.
OUT OF THE BLUE, I THOUGHT ABOUT ASKING THE REVEREND IF HE HAD EVER READ SEEING THROUGH THE LORD...
...BUT THEN WE GOT INTERRUPTED BY A CLAMOR IN THE HALL.

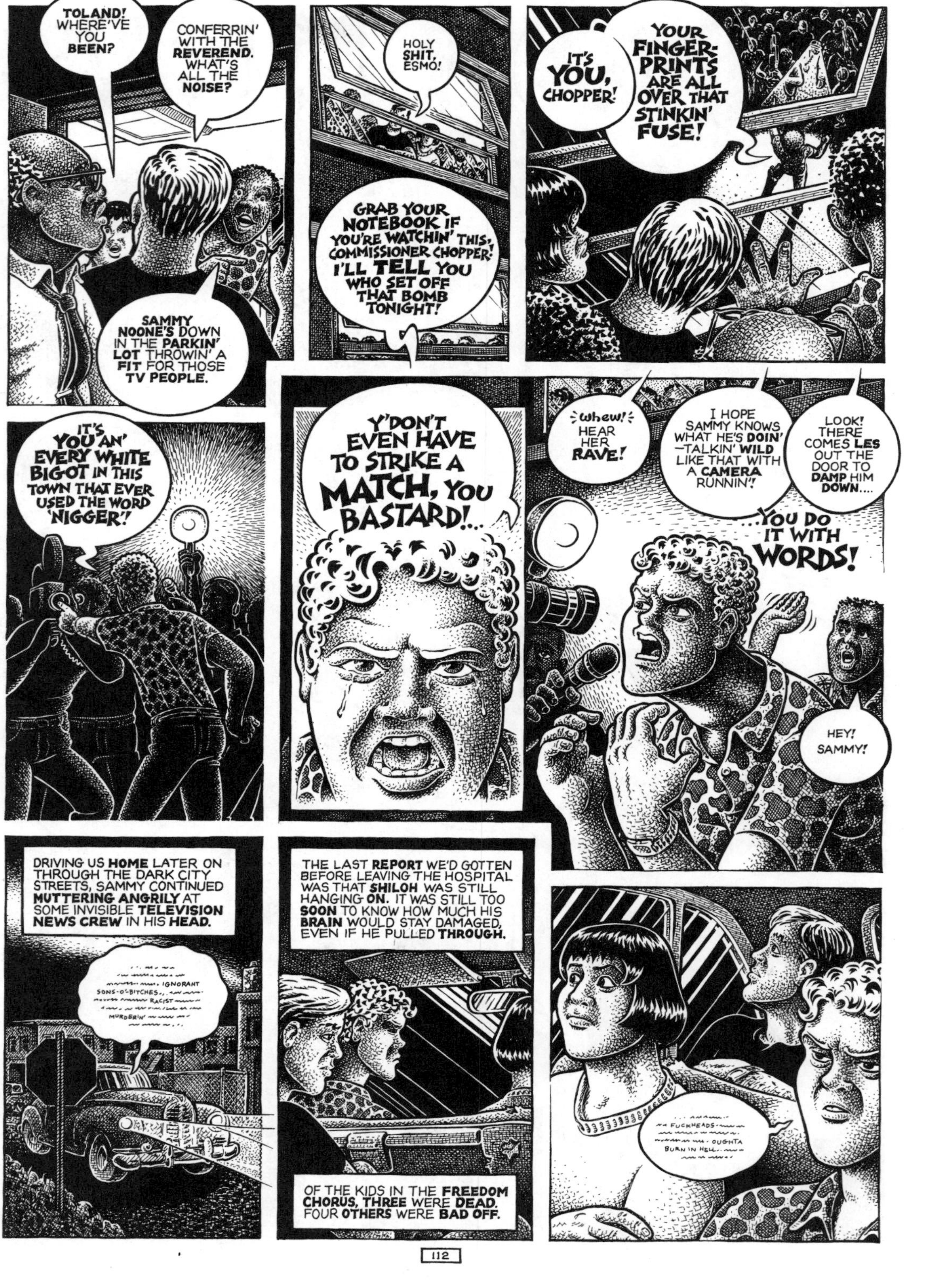
TOLAND! WHERE'VE YOU BEEN?
CONFERRIN' WITH THE REVEREND. WHAT'S ALL THE NOISE?
SAMMY NOONE'S DOWN IN THE PARKIN' LOT THROWIN' A FIT FOR THOSE TV PEOPLE.
HOLY SHIT, ESMO!
GRAB YOUR NOTEBOOK IF YOU'RE WATCHIN' THIS, COMMISSIONER CHOPPER! I'LL TELL YOU WHO SET OFF THAT BOMB TONIGHT!
IT'S YOU, CHOPPER!
YOUR FINGER-PRINTS ARE ALL OVER THAT STINKIN' FUSE!
IT'S YOU AN' EVERY WHITE BIGOT IN THIS TOWN THAT EVER USED THE WORD 'NIGGER'!
Y'DON'T EVEN HAVE TO STRIKE A MATCH, YOU BASTARD!...
...YOU DO IT WITH WORDS!
Whew! HEAR HER RAVE!
I HOPE SAMMY KNOWS WHAT HE'S DOIN' —TALKIN' WILD LIKE THAT WITH A CAMERA RUNNIN'!
LOOK! THERE COMES LES OUT THE DOOR TO DAMP HIM DOWN....
HEY! SAMMY!
DRIVING US HOME LATER ON THROUGH THE DARK CITY STREETS, SAMMY CONTINUED MUTTERING ANGRILY AT SOME INVISIBLE TELEVISION NEWS CREW IN HIS HEAD.
IGNORANT SONS-O'-BITCHES... RACIST MURDERIN'
THE LAST REPORT WE'D GOTTEN BEFORE LEAVING THE HOSPITAL WAS THAT SHILOH WAS STILL HANGING ON. IT WAS STILL TOO SOON TO KNOW HOW MUCH HIS BRAIN WOULD STAY DAMAGED, EVEN IF HE PULLED THROUGH.
OF THE KIDS IN THE FREEDOM CHORUS, THREE WERE DEAD. FOUR OTHERS WERE BAD OFF.
FUCKHEADS... OUGHTA BURN IN HELL...

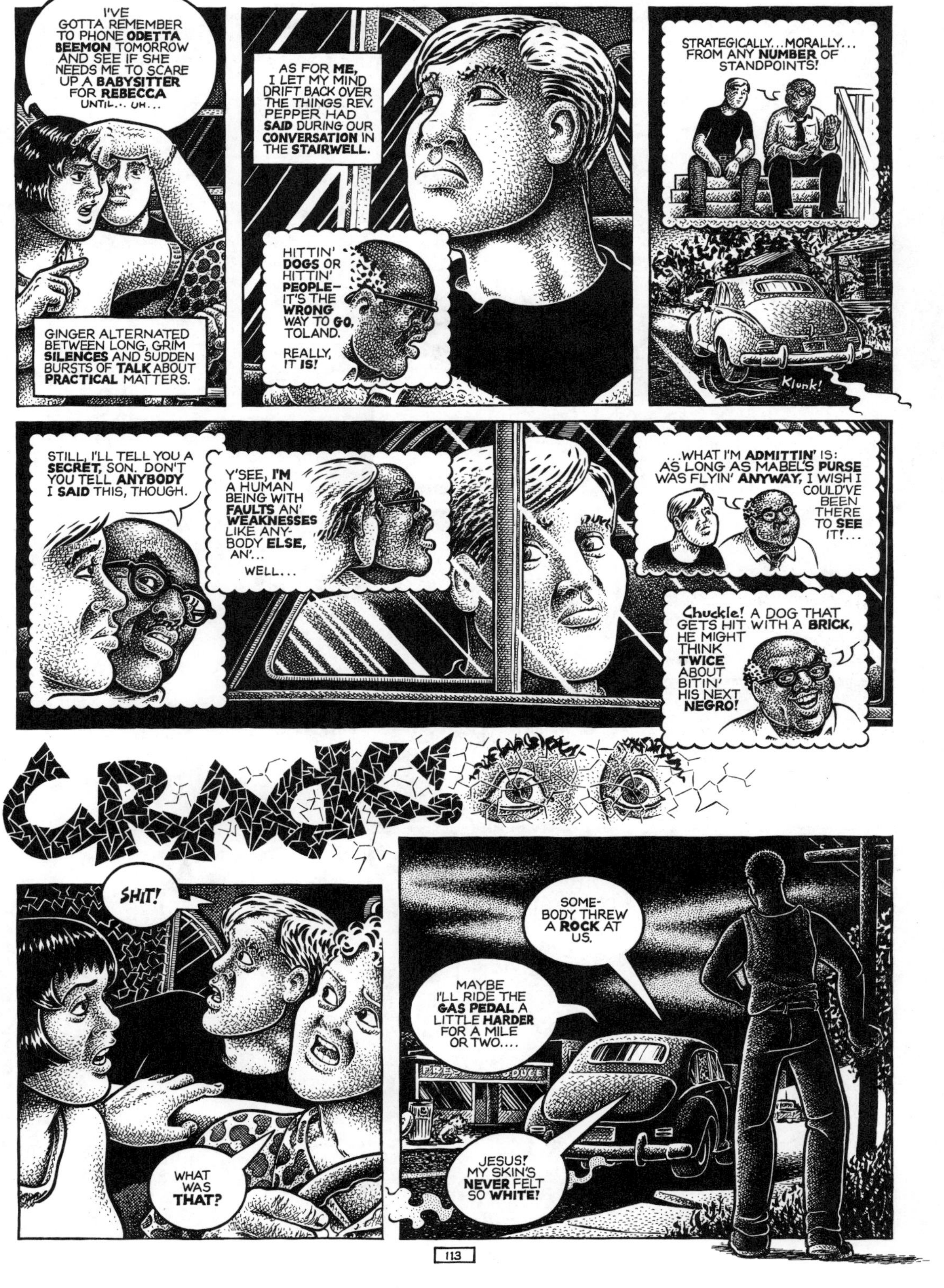
I'VE GOTTA REMEMBER TO PHONE ODETTA BEEMON TOMORROW AND SEE IF SHE NEEDS ME TO SCARE UP A BABYSITTER FOR REBECCA UNTIL... UH...
GINGER ALTERNATED BETWEEN LONG, GRIM SILENCES AND SUDDEN BURSTS OF TALK ABOUT PRACTICAL MATTERS.
AS FOR ME, I LET MY MIND DRIFT BACK OVER THE THINGS REV. PEPPER HAD SAID DURING OUR CONVERSATION IN THE STAIRWELL.
HITTIN' DOGS OR HITTIN' PEOPLE— IT'S THE WRONG WAY TO GO, TOLAND.
REALLY, IT IS!
STRATEGICALLY... MORALLY... FROM ANY NUMBER OF STANDPOINTS!
KLUNK!
STILL, I'LL TELL YOU A SECRET, SON. DON'T YOU TELL ANYBODY I SAID THIS, THOUGH.
Y'SEE, I'M A HUMAN BEING WITH FAULTS AN' WEAKNESSES LIKE ANYBODY ELSE, AN'...
WELL...
...WHAT I'M ADMITTIN' IS: AS LONG AS MABEL'S PURSE WAS FLYIN' ANYWAY, I WISH I COULD'VE BEEN THERE TO SEE IT!...
CHUCKLE! A DOG THAT GETS HIT WITH A BRICK, HE MIGHT THINK TWICE ABOUT BITIN' HIS NEXT NEGRO!
CRACK!
SHIT!
WHAT WAS THAT?
SOME-BODY THREW A ROCK AT US.
MAYBE I'LL RIDE THE GAS PEDAL A LITTLE HARDER FOR A MILE OR TWO....
JESUS! MY SKIN'S NEVER FELT SO WHITE!

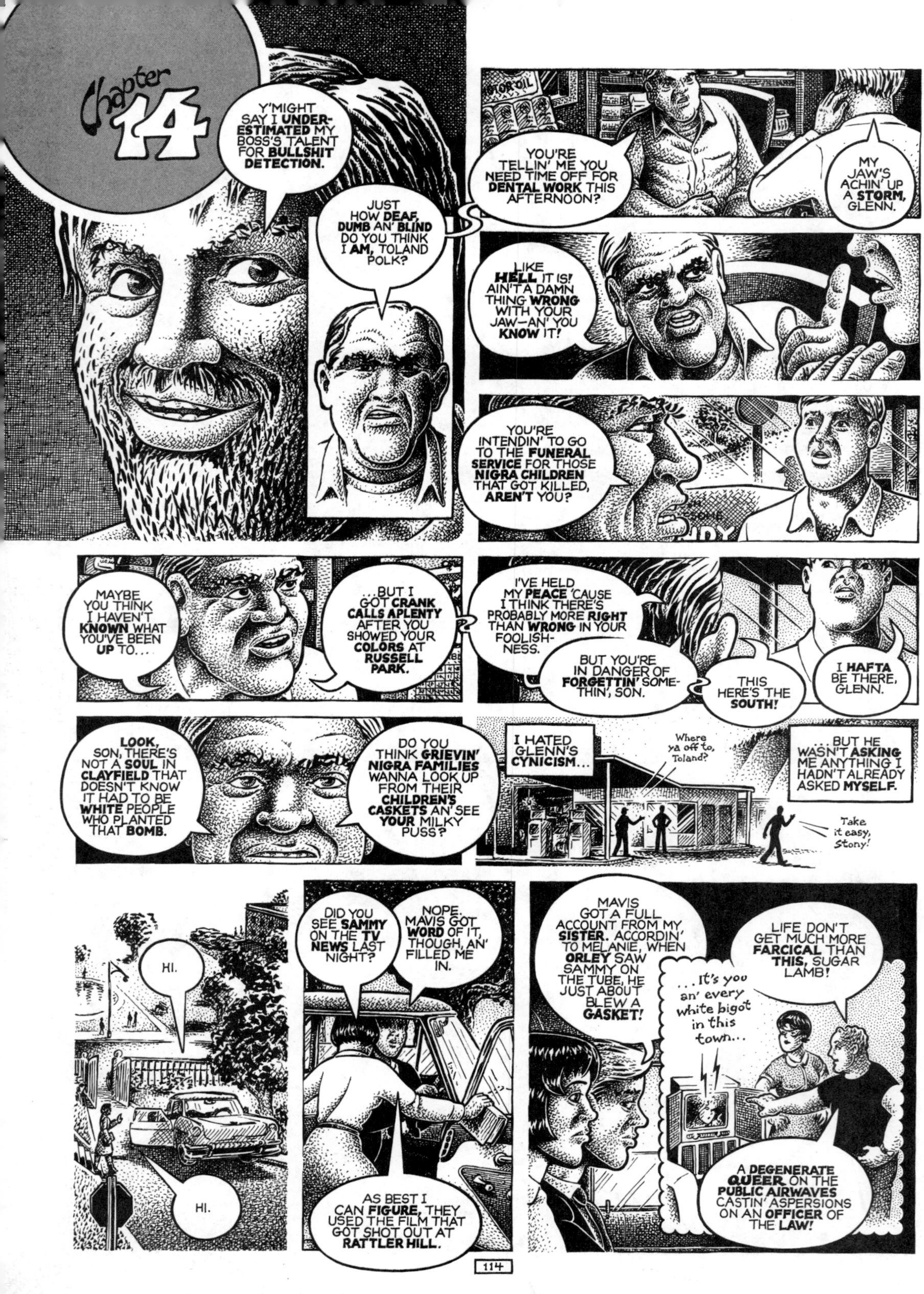

Chapter 14
Y'MIGHT SAY I UNDER-ESTIMATED MY BOSS'S TALENT FOR BULLSHIT DETECTION.
MY JAW'S ACHIN' UP A STORM, GLENN.
YOU'RE TELLIN' ME YOU NEED TIME OFF FOR DENTAL WORK THIS AFTERNOON?
JUST HOW DEAF, DUMB AN' BLIND DO YOU THINK I AM, TOLAND POLK?
LIKE HELL IT IS! AIN'T A DAMN THING WRONG WITH YOUR JAW—AN' YOU KNOW IT!
YOU'RE INTENDIN' TO GO TO THE FUNERAL SERVICE FOR THOSE NIGRA CHILDREN THAT GOT KILLED, AREN'T YOU?
MAYBE YOU THINK I HAVEN'T KNOWN WHAT YOU'VE BEEN UP TO...
...BUT I GOT CRANK CALLS APLENTY AFTER YOU SHOWED YOUR COLORS AT RUSSELL PARK.
I'VE HELD MY PEACE 'CAUSE I THINK THERE'S PROBABLY MORE RIGHT THAN WRONG IN YOUR FOOLISH-NESS.
BUT YOU'RE IN DANGER OF FORGETTIN' SOME-THIN', SON.
THIS HERE'S THE SOUTH!
I HAFTA BE THERE, GLENN.
LOOK, SON, THERE'S NOT A SOUL IN CLAYFIELD THAT DOESN'T KNOW IT HAD TO BE WHITE PEOPLE WHO PLANTED THAT BOMB.
DO YOU THINK GRIEVIN' NIGRA FAMILIES WANNA LOOK UP FROM THEIR CHILDREN'S CASKETS AN' SEE YOUR MILKY PUSS?
I HATED GLENN'S CYNICISM...
Where ya off to, Toland?
Take it easy, Stony!
...BUT HE WASN'T ASKING ME ANYTHING I HADN'T ALREADY ASKED MYSELF.
HI.
HI.
DID YOU SEE SAMMY ON THE TV NEWS LAST NIGHT?
NOPE. MAVIS GOT WORD OF IT, THOUGH, AN' FILLED ME IN.
AS BEST I CAN FIGURE, THEY USED THE FILM THAT GOT SHOT OUT AT RATTLER HILL.
MAVIS GOT A FULL ACCOUNT FROM MY SISTER. ACCORDIN' TO MELANIE, WHEN ORLEY SAW SAMMY ON THE TUBE, HE JUST ABOUT BLEW A GASKET!
LIFE DON'T GET MUCH MORE FARCICAL THAN THIS, SUGAR LAMB!
...It's you an' every white bigot in this town...
A DEGENERATE QUEER ON THE PUBLIC AIRWAVES CASTIN' ASPERSIONS ON AN OFFICER OF THE LAW!

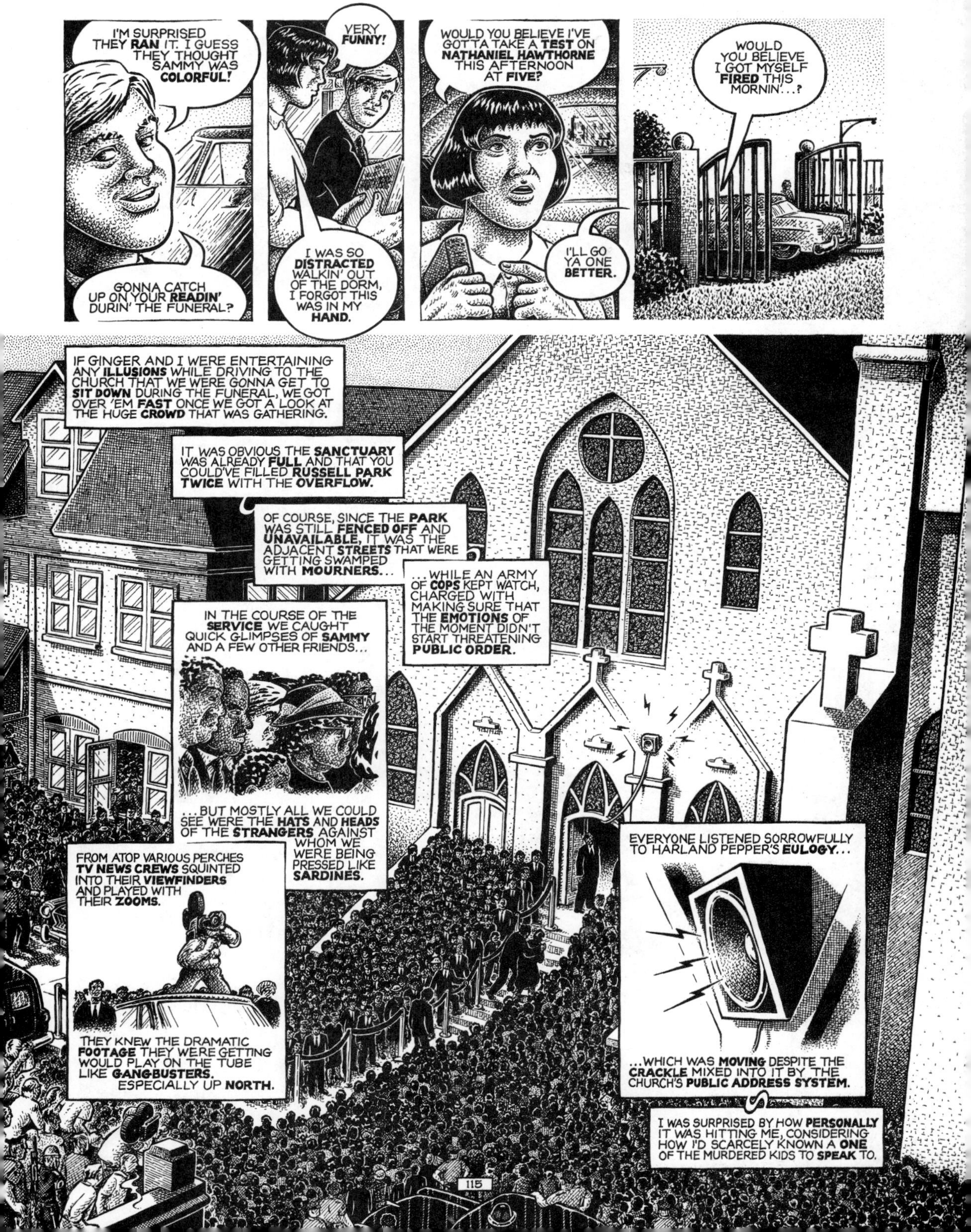

I'M SURPRISED THEY RAN IT. I GUESS THEY THOUGHT SAMMY WAS COLORFUL!
GONNA CATCH UP ON YOUR READIN' DURIN' THE FUNERAL?
VERY FUNNY!
I WAS SO DISTRACTED WALKIN' OUT OF THE DORM, I FORGOT THIS WAS IN MY HAND.
WOULD YOU BELIEVE I'VE GOTTA TAKE A TEST ON NATHANIEL HAWTHORNE THIS AFTERNOON AT FIVE?
I'LL GO YA ONE BETTER.
WOULD YOU BELIEVE I GOT MYSELF FIRED THIS MORNIN'...?
IF GINGER AND I WERE ENTERTAINING ANY ILLUSIONS WHILE DRIVING TO THE CHURCH THAT WE WERE GONNA GET TO SIT DOWN DURING THE FUNERAL, WE GOT OVER 'EM FAST ONCE WE GOT A LOOK AT THE HUGE CROWD THAT WAS GATHERING.
IT WAS OBVIOUS THE SANCTUARY WAS ALREADY FULL AND THAT YOU COULD'VE FILLED RUSSELL PARK TWICE WITH THE OVERFLOW.
OF COURSE, SINCE THE PARK WAS STILL FENCED OFF AND UNAVAILABLE, IT WAS THE ADJACENT STREETS THAT WERE GETTING SWAMPED WITH MOURNERS...
...WHILE AN ARMY OF COPS KEPT WATCH, CHARGED WITH MAKING SURE THAT THE EMOTIONS OF THE MOMENT DIDN'T START THREATENING PUBLIC ORDER.
IN THE COURSE OF THE SERVICE WE CAUGHT QUICK GLIMPSES OF SAMMY AND A FEW OTHER FRIENDS...
...BUT MOSTLY ALL WE COULD SEE WERE THE HATS AND HEADS OF THE STRANGERS AGAINST WHOM WE WERE BEING PRESSED LIKE SARDINES.
FROM ATOP VARIOUS PERCHES TV NEWS CREWS SQUINTED INTO THEIR VIEWFINDERS AND PLAYED WITH THEIR ZOOMS.
THEY KNEW THE DRAMATIC FOOTAGE THEY WERE GETTING WOULD PLAY ON THE TUBE LIKE GANGBUSTERS. ESPECIALLY UP NORTH.
EVERYONE LISTENED SORROWFULLY TO HARLAND PEPPER'S EULOGY...
...WHICH WAS MOVING DESPITE THE CRACKLE MIXED INTO IT BY THE CHURCH'S PUBLIC ADDRESS SYSTEM.
I WAS SURPRISED BY HOW PERSONALLY IT WAS HITTING ME, CONSIDERING HOW I'D SCARCELY KNOWN A ONE OF THE MURDERED KIDS TO SPEAK TO.

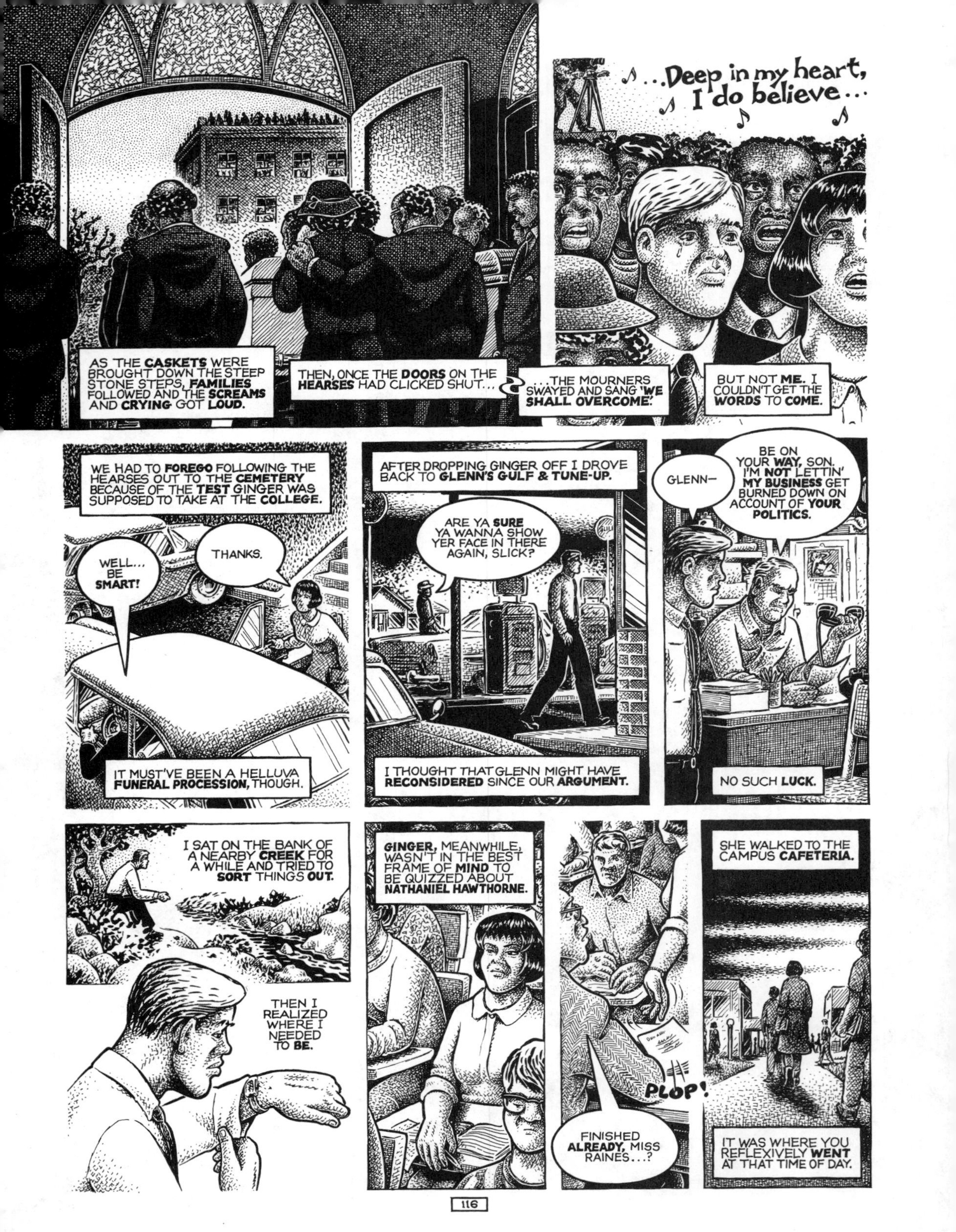
AS THE CASKETS WERE BROUGHT DOWN THE STEEP STONE STEPS, FAMILIES FOLLOWED AND THE SCREAMS AND CRYING GOT LOUD.
THEN, ONCE THE DOORS ON THE HEARSES HAD CLICKED SHUT...
...Deep in my heart, I do believe...
...THE MOURNERS SWAYED AND SANG 'WE SHALL OVERCOME'.
BUT NOT ME. I COULDN'T GET THE WORDS TO COME.
WE HAD TO FOREGO FOLLOWING THE HEARSES OUT TO THE CEMETERY BECAUSE OF THE TEST GINGER WAS SUPPOSED TO TAKE AT THE COLLEGE.
THANKS.
WELL... BE SMART!
IT MUST'VE BEEN A HELLUVA FUNERAL PROCESSION, THOUGH.
AFTER DROPPING GINGER OFF I DROVE BACK TO GLENN'S GULF & TUNE-UP.
ARE YA SURE YA WANNA SHOW YER FACE IN THERE AGAIN, SLICK?
I THOUGHT THAT GLENN MIGHT HAVE RECONSIDERED SINCE OUR ARGUMENT.
GLENN—
BE ON YOUR WAY, SON. I'M NOT LETTIN' MY BUSINESS GET BURNED DOWN ON ACCOUNT OF YOUR POLITICS.
NO SUCH LUCK.
I SAT ON THE BANK OF A NEARBY CREEK FOR A WHILE AND TRIED TO SORT THINGS OUT.
THEN I REALIZED WHERE I NEEDED TO BE.
GINGER, MEANWHILE, WASN'T IN THE BEST FRAME OF MIND TO BE QUIZZED ABOUT NATHANIEL HAWTHORNE.
PLOP!
FINISHED ALREADY, MISS RAINES...?
SHE WALKED TO THE CAMPUS CAFETERIA.
IT WAS WHERE YOU REFLEXIVELY WENT AT THAT TIME OF DAY.

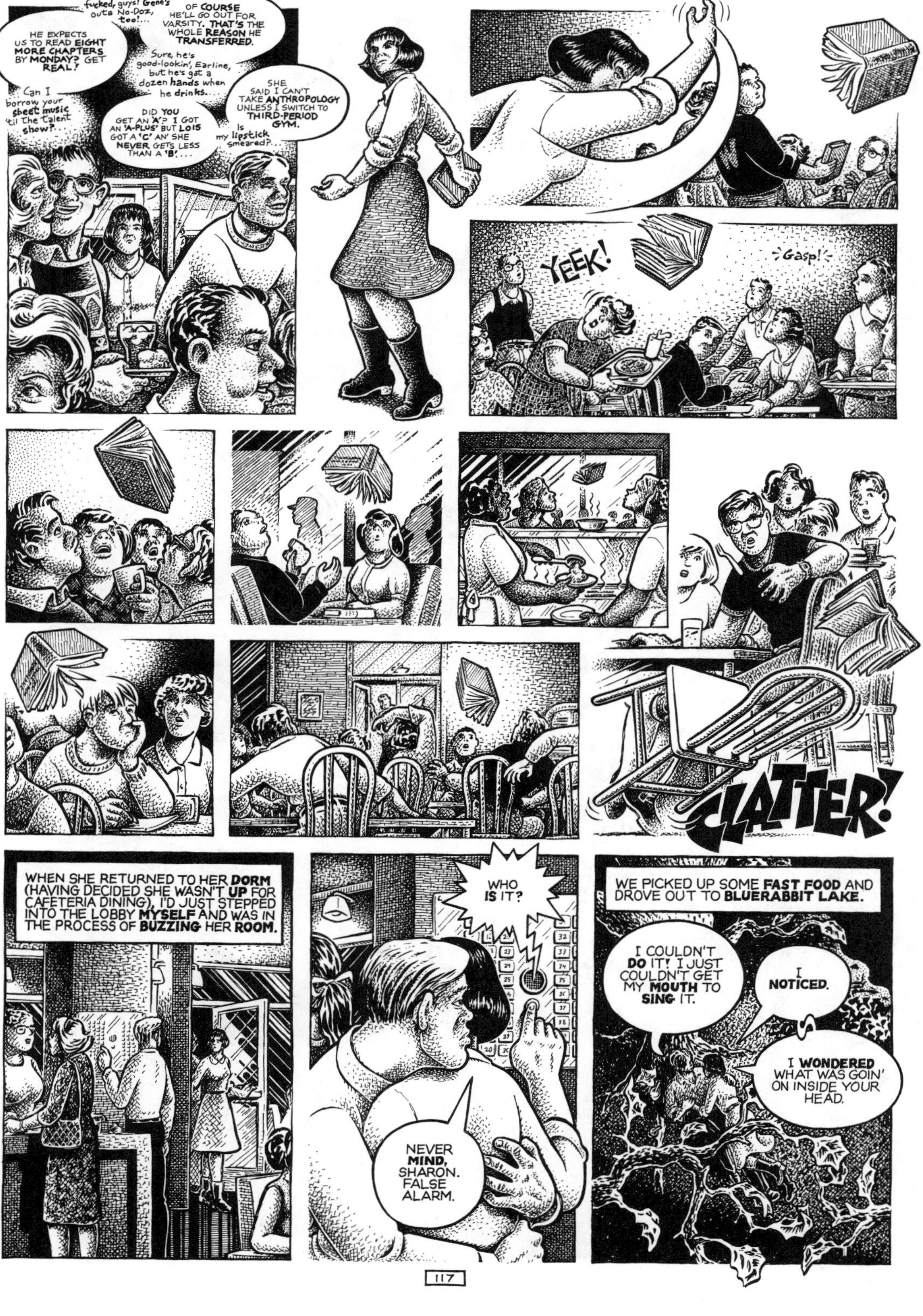
HE EXPECTS US TO READ EIGHT MORE CHAPTERS BY MONDAY? GET REAL!
We're fucked, guys! Gene's outa No-Doz, too!...
OF COURSE HE'LL GO OUT FOR VARSITY. THAT'S THE WHOLE REASON HE TRANSFERRED.
Sure, he's good-lookin', Earline, but he's got a dozen hands when he drinks...
Can I borrow your sheet music 'til the talent show?...
DID YOU GET AN 'A'? I GOT AN 'A-PLUS' BUT LOIS GOT A 'C' AN' SHE NEVER GETS LESS THAN A 'B'...
SHE SAID I CAN'T TAKE ANTHROPOLOGY UNLESS I SWITCH TO THIRD-PERIOD GYM.
Is my lipstick smeared?...
YEEK!
Gasp!
CLATTER!
WHEN SHE RETURNED TO HER DORM (HAVING DECIDED SHE WASN'T UP FOR CAFETERIA DINING), I'D JUST STEPPED INTO THE LOBBY MYSELF AND WAS IN THE PROCESS OF BUZZING HER ROOM.
WHO IS IT?
NEVER MIND, SHARON. FALSE ALARM.
WE PICKED UP SOME FAST FOOD AND DROVE OUT TO BLUERABBIT LAKE.
I COULDN'T DO IT! I JUST COULDN'T GET MY MOUTH TO SING IT.
I NOTICED.
I WONDERED WHAT WAS GOIN' ON INSIDE YOUR HEAD.

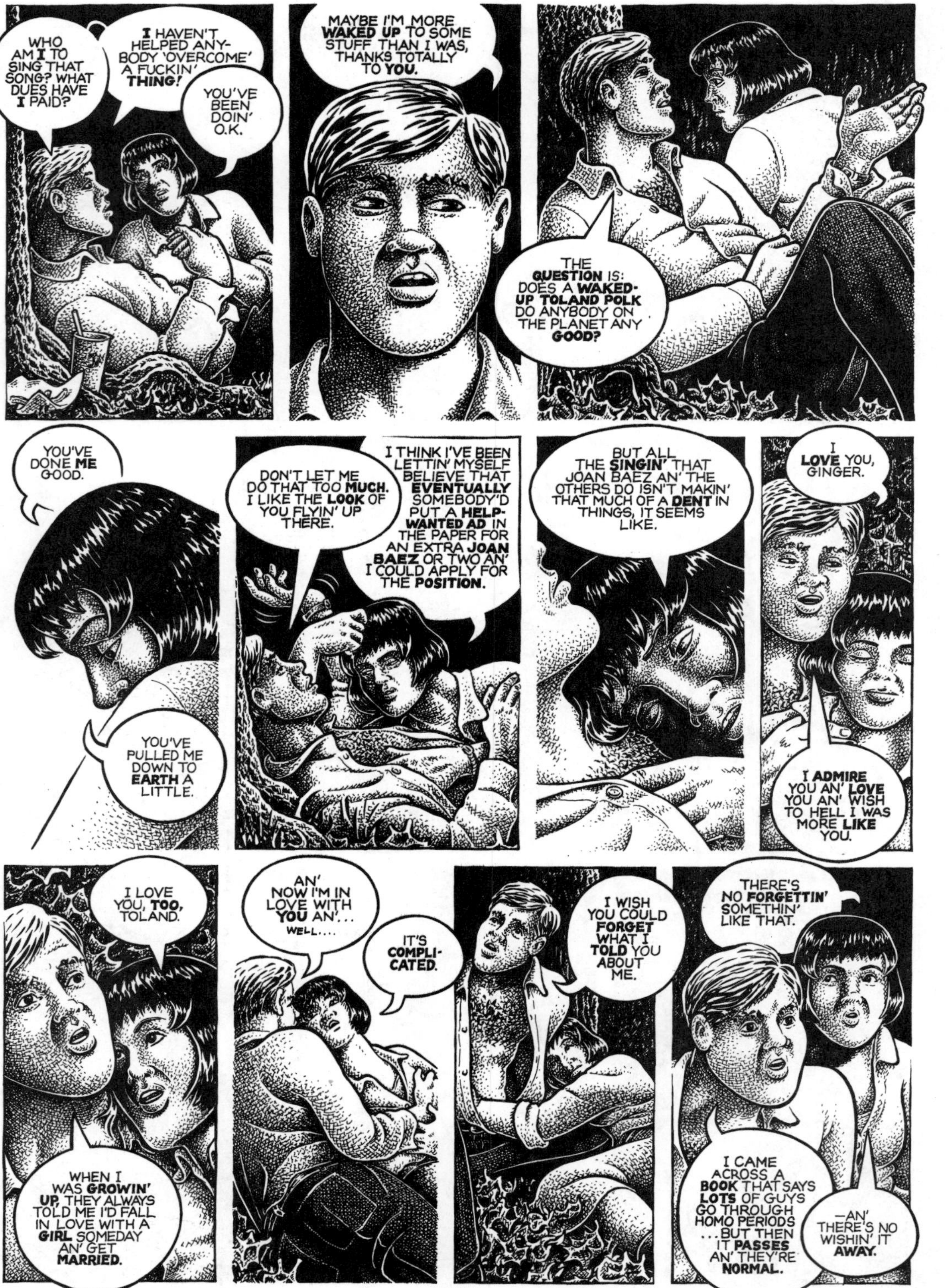

WHO AM I TO SING THAT SONG? WHAT DUES HAVE I PAID?
I HAVEN'T HELPED ANYBODY 'OVERCOME' A FUCKIN' THING!
YOU'VE BEEN DOIN' O.K.
MAYBE I'M MORE WAKED UP TO SOME STUFF THAN I WAS, THANKS TOTALLY TO YOU.
THE QUESTION IS: DOES A WAKED-UP TOLAND POLK DO ANYBODY ON THE PLANET ANY GOOD?
YOU'VE DONE ME GOOD.
YOU'VE PULLED ME DOWN TO EARTH A LITTLE.
DON'T LET ME DO THAT TOO MUCH. I LIKE THE LOOK OF YOU FLYIN' UP THERE.
I THINK I'VE BEEN LETTIN' MYSELF BELIEVE THAT EVENTUALLY SOMEBODY'D PUT A HELP-WANTED AD IN THE PAPER FOR AN EXTRA JOAN BAEZ OR TWO AN' I COULD APPLY FOR THE POSITION.
BUT ALL THE SINGIN' THAT JOAN BAEZ AN' THE OTHERS DO ISN'T MAKIN' THAT MUCH OF A DENT IN THINGS, IT SEEMS LIKE.
I LOVE YOU, GINGER.
I ADMIRE YOU AN' LOVE YOU AN' WISH TO HELL I WAS MORE LIKE YOU.
I LOVE YOU, TOO, TOLAND.
WHEN I WAS GROWIN' UP, THEY ALWAYS TOLD ME I'D FALL IN LOVE WITH A GIRL SOMEDAY AN' GET MARRIED.
AN' NOW I'M IN LOVE WITH YOU AN'... WELL....
IT'S COMPLICATED.
I WISH YOU COULD FORGET WHAT I TOLD YOU ABOUT ME.
THERE'S NO FORGETTIN' SOMETHIN' LIKE THAT.
I CAME ACROSS A BOOK THAT SAYS LOTS OF GUYS GO THROUGH HOMO PERIODS ...BUT THEN IT PASSES AN' THEY'RE NORMAL.
—AN' THERE'S NO WISHIN' IT AWAY.

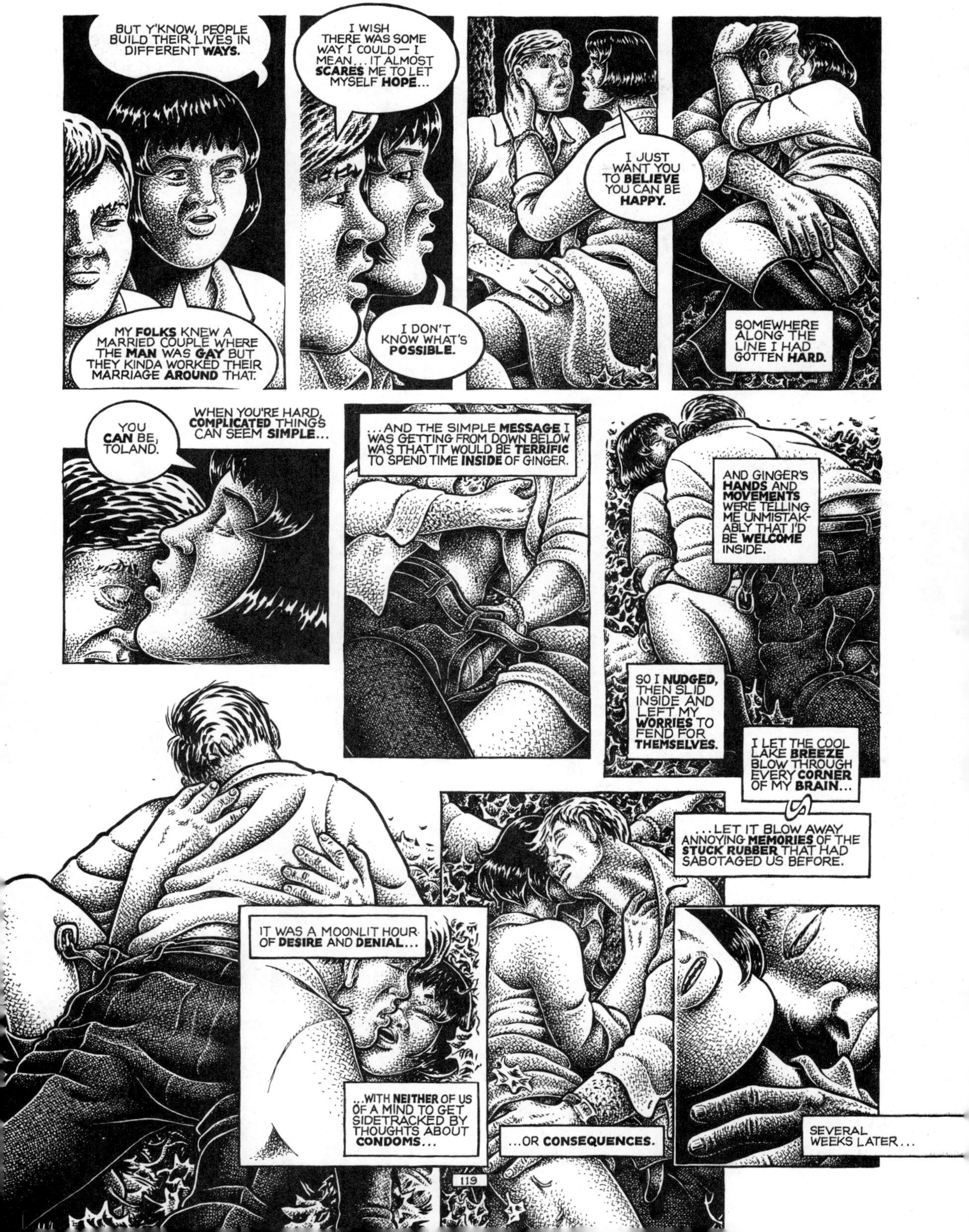

BUT Y'KNOW, PEOPLE BUILD THEIR LIVES IN DIFFERENT **WAYS.**
MY **FOLKS** KNEW A MARRIED COUPLE WHERE THE **MAN** WAS **GAY** BUT THEY KINDA WORKED THEIR MARRIAGE **AROUND** THAT.
I WISH THERE WAS SOME WAY I COULD — I MEAN... IT ALMOST **SCARES** ME TO LET MYSELF **HOPE**...
I DON'T KNOW WHAT'S **POSSIBLE.**
I JUST WANT YOU TO **BELIEVE** YOU CAN BE **HAPPY.**
SOMEWHERE ALONG THE LINE I HAD GOTTEN **HARD.**
YOU **CAN** BE, TOLAND.
WHEN YOU'RE HARD, **COMPLICATED** THINGS CAN SEEM **SIMPLE**...
...AND THE SIMPLE **MESSAGE** I WAS GETTING FROM DOWN BELOW WAS THAT IT WOULD BE **TERRIFIC** TO SPEND TIME **INSIDE** OF GINGER.
AND GINGER'S **HANDS** AND **MOVEMENTS** WERE TELLING ME UNMISTAKABLY THAT I'D BE **WELCOME** INSIDE.
SO I **NUDGED,** THEN SLID INSIDE AND LEFT MY **WORRIES** TO FEND FOR **THEMSELVES.**
I LET THE COOL LAKE **BREEZE** BLOW THROUGH EVERY **CORNER** OF MY **BRAIN**...
...LET IT BLOW AWAY ANNOYING **MEMORIES** OF THE **STUCK RUBBER** THAT HAD SABOTAGED US BEFORE.
IT WAS A MOONLIT HOUR OF **DESIRE** AND **DENIAL**...
...WITH **NEITHER** OF US OF A MIND TO GET SIDETRACKED BY THOUGHTS ABOUT **CONDOMS**...
...OR **CONSEQUENCES.**
SEVERAL WEEKS LATER...

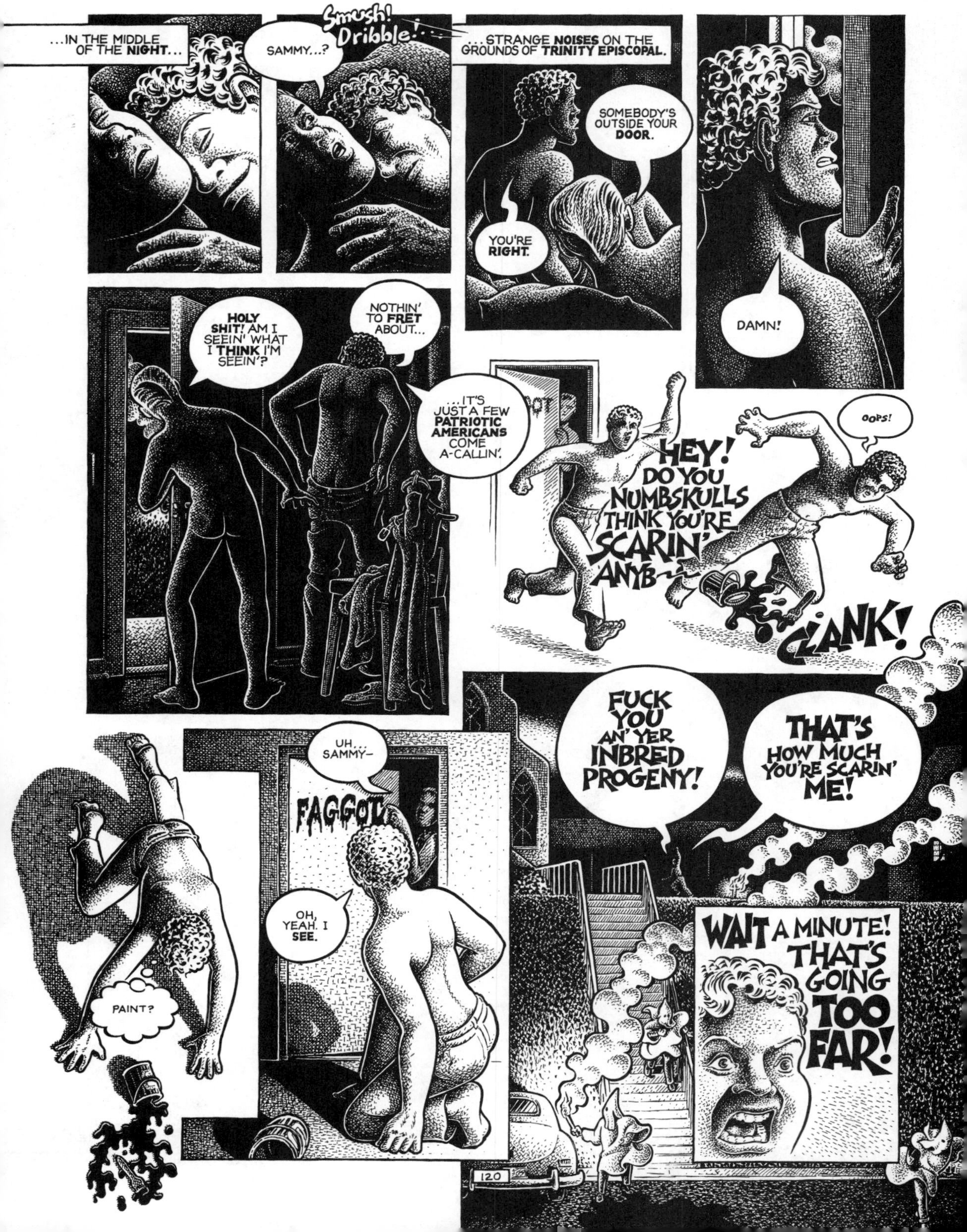
...IN THE MIDDLE OF THE NIGHT...
SAMMY...?
Smush! Dribble!
...STRANGE NOISES ON THE GROUNDS OF TRINITY EPISCOPAL.
SOMEBODY'S OUTSIDE YOUR DOOR.
YOU'RE RIGHT.
DAMN!
HOLY SHIT! AM I SEEIN' WHAT I THINK I'M SEEIN'?
NOTHIN' TO FRET ABOUT...
...IT'S JUST A FEW PATRIOTIC AMERICANS COME A-CALLIN'.
OOPS!
HEY! DO YOU NUMBSKULLS THINK YOU'RE SCARIN' ANYB
CLANK!
PAINT?
UH... SAMMY–
FAGGOT
OH, YEAH. I SEE.
FUCK YOU AN' YER INBRED PROGENY!
THAT'S HOW MUCH YOU'RE SCARIN' ME!
WAIT A MINUTE! THAT'S GOING TOO FAR!

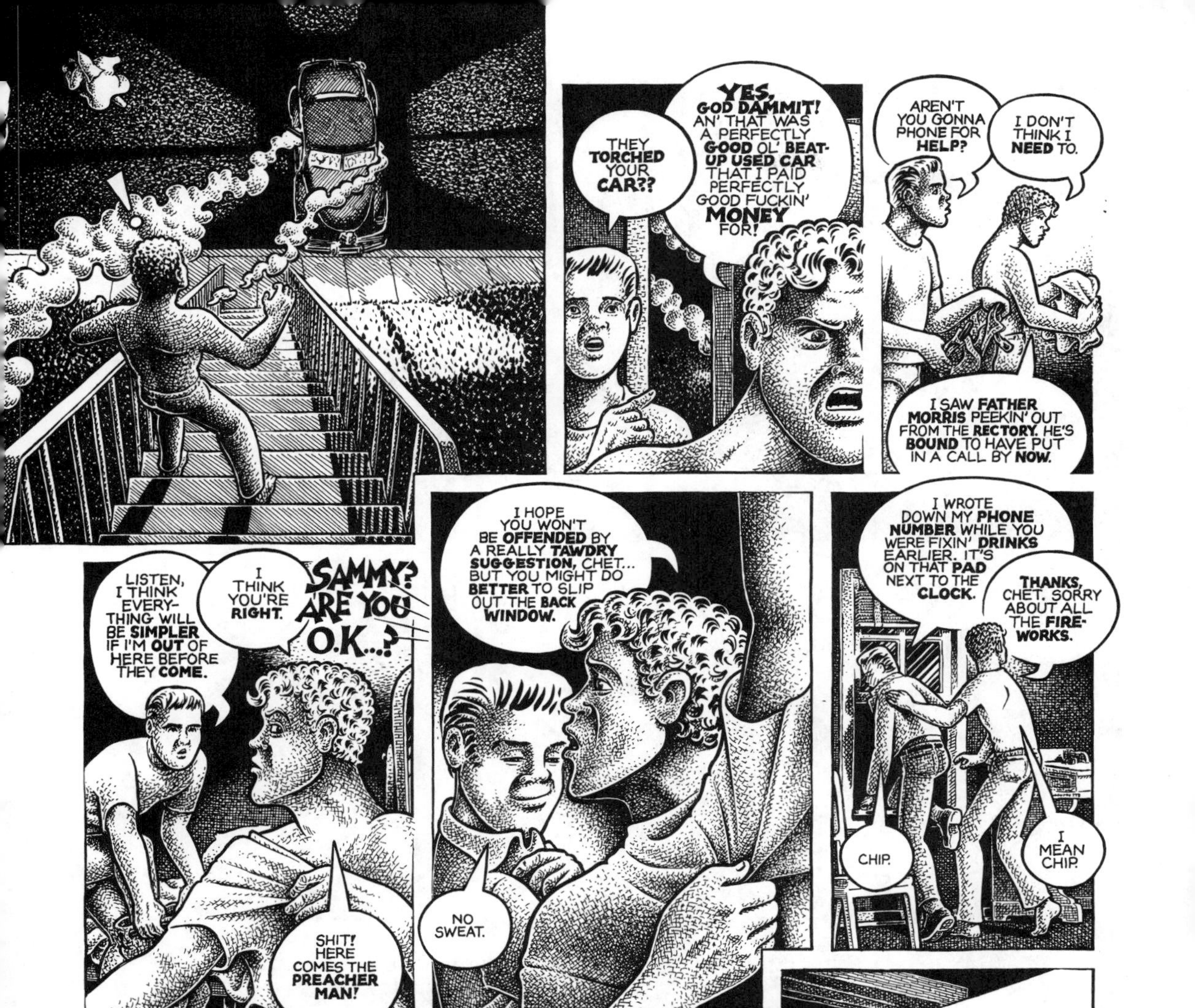

!
THEY TORCHED YOUR CAR??
YES, GOD DAMMIT! AN' THAT WAS A PERFECTLY GOOD OL' BEAT-UP USED CAR THAT I PAID PERFECTLY GOOD FUCKIN' MONEY FOR!
AREN'T YOU GONNA PHONE FOR HELP?
I DON'T THINK I NEED TO.
I SAW FATHER MORRIS PEEKIN' OUT FROM THE RECTORY. HE'S BOUND TO HAVE PUT IN A CALL BY NOW.
LISTEN, I THINK EVERY-THING WILL BE SIMPLER IF I'M OUT OF HERE BEFORE THEY COME.
I THINK YOU'RE RIGHT.
SAMMY? ARE YOU O.K...?
SHIT! HERE COMES THE PREACHER MAN!
I HOPE YOU WON'T BE OFFENDED BY A REALLY TAWDRY SUGGESTION, CHET... BUT YOU MIGHT DO BETTER TO SLIP OUT THE BACK WINDOW.
NO SWEAT.
I WROTE DOWN MY PHONE NUMBER WHILE YOU WERE FIXIN' DRINKS EARLIER. IT'S ON THAT PAD NEXT TO THE CLOCK.
THANKS, CHET. SORRY ABOUT ALL THE FIRE-WORKS.
CHIP.
I MEAN CHIP.
MMM. I'M GLAD I CAME TO THE RHOMBUS TONIGHT.
ME, TOO.
SAMMY?
THE FIRE DEPARTMENT'S ON ITS WAY... AND THE POLICE—
FAGGOT
OH.
FAGGOT

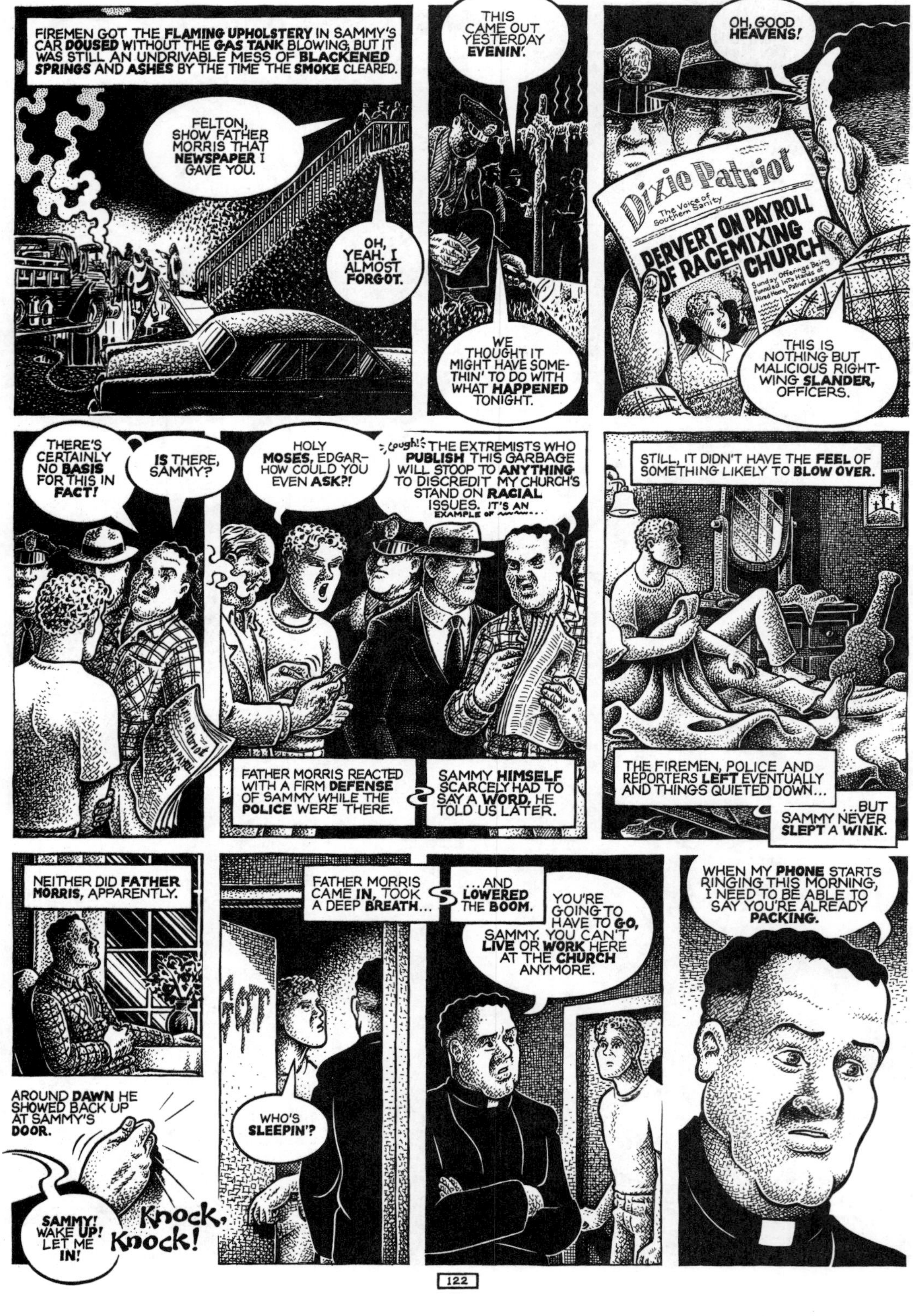
FIREMEN GOT THE **FLAMING UPHOLSTERY** IN SAMMY'S CAR **DOUSED** WITHOUT THE **GAS TANK** BLOWING, BUT IT WAS STILL AN UNDRIVABLE MESS OF **BLACKENED SPRINGS** AND **ASHES** BY THE TIME THE **SMOKE** CLEARED.
FELTON, SHOW FATHER MORRIS THAT **NEWSPAPER** I GAVE YOU.
OH, YEAH. I ALMOST **FORGOT**.
THIS CAME OUT YESTERDAY **EVENIN'**.
WE THOUGHT IT MIGHT HAVE SOMETHIN' TO DO WITH WHAT **HAPPENED** TONIGHT.
OH, GOOD **HEAVENS!**
Dixie Patriot
The Voice of Southern Sanity
PERVERT ON PAYROLL OF RACEMIXING CHURCH
Sunday Offerings Being Funneled Into Hands of Hired Homo, Patriot
THIS IS NOTHING BUT MALICIOUS RIGHT-WING **SLANDER,** OFFICERS.
THERE'S CERTAINLY NO **BASIS** FOR THIS IN **FACT!**
IS THERE, SAMMY?
HOLY **MOSES,** EDGAR-- HOW COULD YOU EVEN **ASK?!**
cough!
THE EXTREMISTS WHO **PUBLISH** THIS GARBAGE WILL STOOP TO **ANYTHING** TO DISCREDIT MY CHURCH'S STAND ON **RACIAL** ISSUES. IT'S AN EXAMPLE OF
FATHER MORRIS REACTED WITH A FIRM **DEFENSE** OF SAMMY WHILE THE **POLICE** WERE THERE.
SAMMY **HIMSELF** SCARCELY HAD TO SAY A **WORD,** HE TOLD US LATER.
STILL, IT DIDN'T HAVE THE **FEEL** OF SOMETHING LIKELY TO **BLOW OVER.**
THE FIREMEN, POLICE AND REPORTERS **LEFT** EVENTUALLY AND THINGS QUIETED DOWN...
...BUT SAMMY NEVER **SLEPT** A **WINK.**
NEITHER DID **FATHER MORRIS,** APPARENTLY.
AROUND **DAWN** HE SHOWED BACK UP AT SAMMY'S **DOOR.**
SAMMY! WAKE **UP!** LET ME **IN!**
Knock, Knock!
WHO'S **SLEEPIN'?**
FATHER MORRIS CAME **IN,** TOOK A DEEP **BREATH**...
...AND **LOWERED** THE **BOOM.**
YOU'RE GOING TO HAVE TO **GO,** SAMMY. YOU CAN'T **LIVE** OR **WORK** HERE AT THE **CHURCH** ANYMORE.
WHEN MY **PHONE** STARTS RINGING THIS MORNING, I NEED TO BE ABLE TO SAY YOU'RE ALREADY **PACKING.**

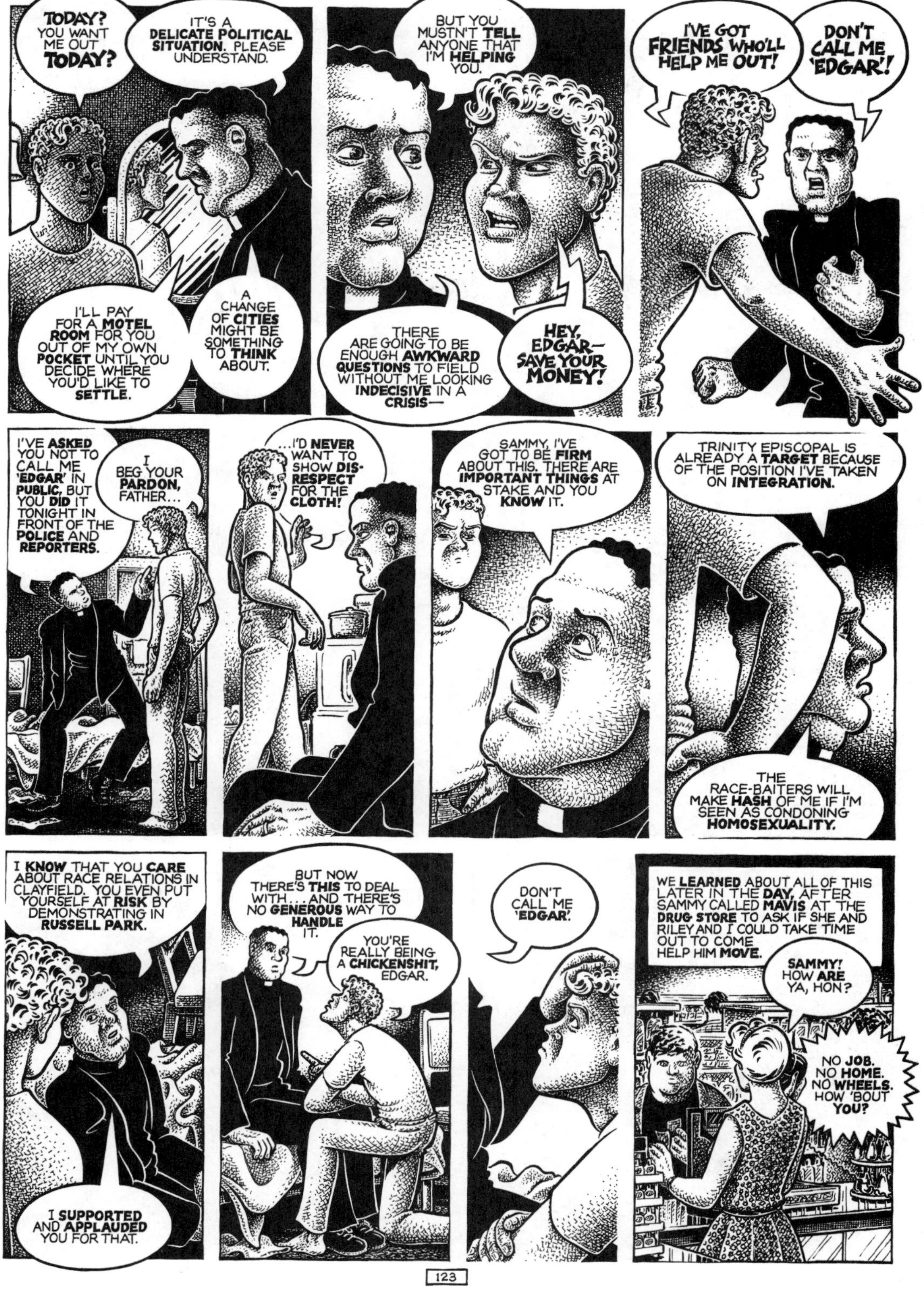
TODAY? YOU WANT ME OUT TODAY?
IT'S A DELICATE POLITICAL SITUATION. PLEASE UNDERSTAND.
I'LL PAY FOR A MOTEL ROOM FOR YOU OUT OF MY OWN POCKET UNTIL YOU DECIDE WHERE YOU'D LIKE TO SETTLE.
A CHANGE OF CITIES MIGHT BE SOMETHING TO THINK ABOUT.
BUT YOU MUSTN'T TELL ANYONE THAT I'M HELPING YOU.
THERE ARE GOING TO BE ENOUGH AWKWARD QUESTIONS TO FIELD WITHOUT ME LOOKING INDECISIVE IN A CRISIS—
HEY, EDGAR— SAVE YOUR MONEY!
I'VE GOT FRIENDS WHO'LL HELP ME OUT!
DON'T CALL ME 'EDGAR'!
I'VE ASKED YOU NOT TO CALL ME 'EDGAR' IN PUBLIC, BUT YOU DID IT TONIGHT IN FRONT OF THE POLICE AND REPORTERS.
I BEG YOUR PARDON, FATHER...
...I'D NEVER WANT TO SHOW DIS-RESPECT FOR THE CLOTH!
SAMMY, I'VE GOT TO BE FIRM ABOUT THIS. THERE ARE IMPORTANT THINGS AT STAKE AND YOU KNOW IT.
TRINITY EPISCOPAL IS ALREADY A TARGET BECAUSE OF THE POSITION I'VE TAKEN ON INTEGRATION.
THE RACE-BAITERS WILL MAKE HASH OF ME IF I'M SEEN AS CONDONING HOMOSEXUALITY.
I KNOW THAT YOU CARE ABOUT RACE RELATIONS IN CLAYFIELD. YOU EVEN PUT YOURSELF AT RISK BY DEMONSTRATING IN RUSSELL PARK.
I SUPPORTED AND APPLAUDED YOU FOR THAT.
BUT NOW THERE'S THIS TO DEAL WITH... AND THERE'S NO GENEROUS WAY TO HANDLE IT.
YOU'RE REALLY BEING A CHICKENSHIT, EDGAR.
DON'T CALL ME 'EDGAR'.
WE LEARNED ABOUT ALL OF THIS LATER IN THE DAY, AFTER SAMMY CALLED MAVIS AT THE DRUG STORE TO ASK IF SHE AND RILEY AND I COULD TAKE TIME OUT TO COME HELP HIM MOVE.
SAMMY! HOW ARE YA, HON?
NO JOB. NO HOME. NO WHEELS. HOW 'BOUT YOU?

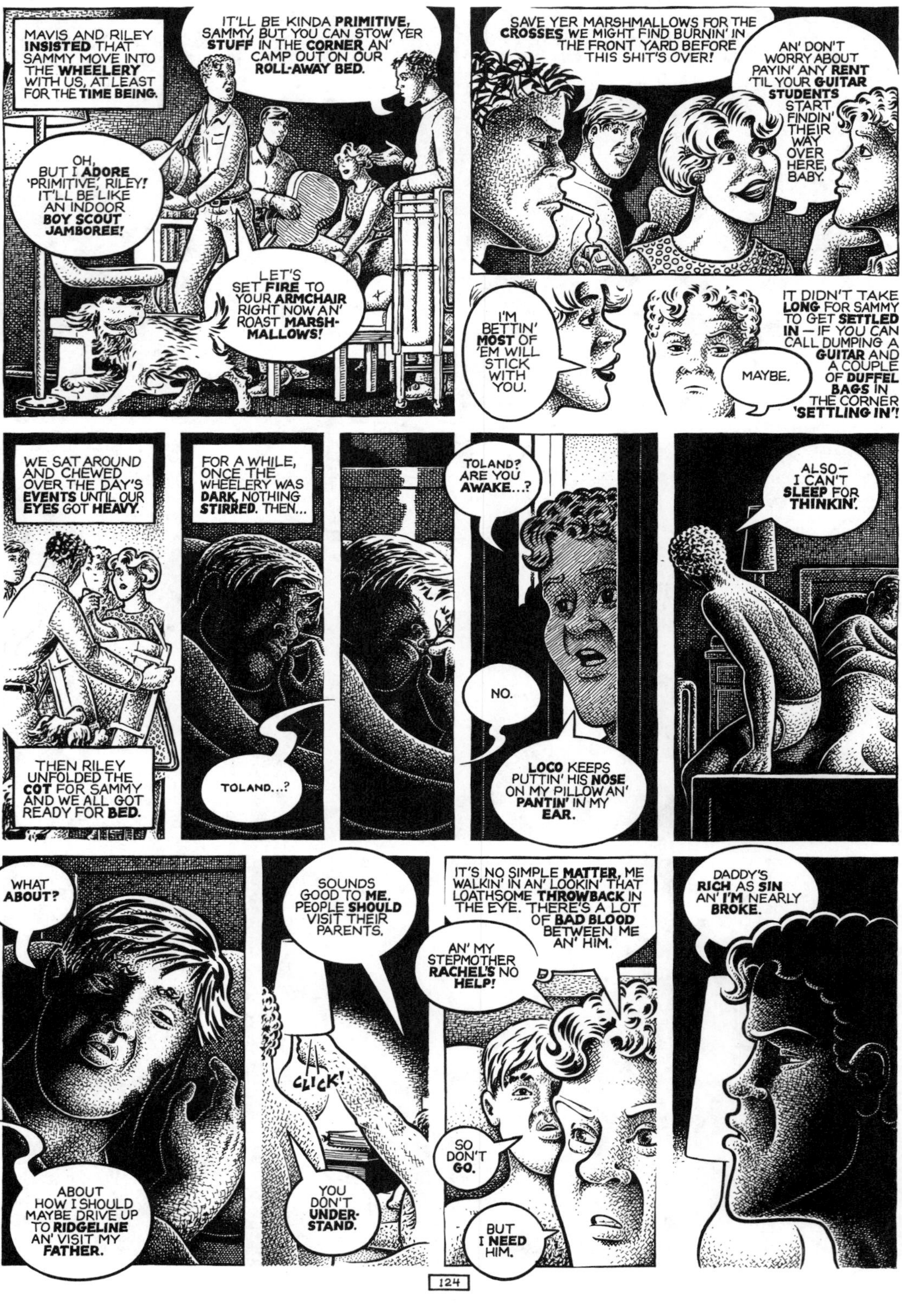

MAVIS AND RILEY INSISTED THAT SAMMY MOVE INTO THE WHEELERY WITH US, AT LEAST FOR THE TIME BEING.
IT'LL BE KINDA PRIMITIVE, SAMMY, BUT YOU CAN STOW YER STUFF IN THE CORNER AN' CAMP OUT ON OUR ROLL-AWAY BED.
OH, BUT I ADORE 'PRIMITIVE,' RILEY! IT'LL BE LIKE AN INDOOR BOY SCOUT JAMBOREE!
LET'S SET FIRE TO YOUR ARMCHAIR RIGHT NOW AN' ROAST MARSH-MALLOWS!
SAVE YER MARSHMALLOWS FOR THE CROSSES WE MIGHT FIND BURNIN' IN THE FRONT YARD BEFORE THIS SHIT'S OVER!
AN' DON'T WORRY ABOUT PAYIN' ANY RENT 'TIL YOUR GUITAR STUDENTS START FINDIN' THEIR WAY OVER HERE, BABY.
I'M BETTIN' MOST OF 'EM WILL STICK WITH YOU.
MAYBE.
IT DIDN'T TAKE LONG FOR SAMMY TO GET SETTLED IN — IF YOU CAN CALL DUMPING A GUITAR AND A COUPLE OF DUFFEL BAGS IN THE CORNER 'SETTLING IN'!
WE SAT AROUND AND CHEWED OVER THE DAY'S EVENTS UNTIL OUR EYES GOT HEAVY.
THEN RILEY UNFOLDED THE COT FOR SAMMY AND WE ALL GOT READY FOR BED.
FOR A WHILE, ONCE THE WHEELERY WAS DARK, NOTHING STIRRED. THEN...
TOLAND...?
TOLAND? ARE YOU AWAKE...?
NO.
LOCO KEEPS PUTTIN' HIS NOSE ON MY PILLOW AN' PANTIN' IN MY EAR.
ALSO— I CAN'T SLEEP FOR THINKIN'.
WHAT ABOUT?
ABOUT HOW I SHOULD MAYBE DRIVE UP TO RIDGELINE AN' VISIT MY FATHER.
SOUNDS GOOD TO ME. PEOPLE SHOULD VISIT THEIR PARENTS.
CLICK!
YOU DON'T UNDER-STAND.
IT'S NO SIMPLE MATTER, ME WALKIN' IN AN' LOOKIN' THAT LOATHSOME THROWBACK IN THE EYE. THERE'S A LOT OF BAD BLOOD BETWEEN ME AN' HIM.
AN' MY STEPMOTHER RACHEL'S NO HELP!
SO DON'T GO.
BUT I NEED HIM.
DADDY'S RICH AS SIN AN' I'M NEARLY BROKE.

I'M **SCARED**, TOLAND. I DON'T KNOW WHAT'S GONNA **HAPPEN** TO ME.

I'VE ALWAYS TAKEN **PRIDE** IN MY **CHECKERED HISTORY**, BUT I'VE NEVER GOTTEN MYSELF BRANDED A **PERVERT** ON THE FRONT PAGE OF A **NEWSPAPER** BEFORE!

WHERE'D THAT PHOTO OF YOU **COME** FROM, ANYWAY?

THE **RUSSELL PARK SIT-IN**, AS FAR AS I CAN **TELL**.

MAVIS SAYS I SHOULD POP INTO THE DIXIE PATRIOT **OFFICE** AN' ASK IF THEY'LL SELL ME SOME **EXTRA PRINTS** OF THE PHOTO FOR MY **RELATIVES**!

THE **CLAYFIELD BANNER** IS **ALWAYS** WILLIN' TO DO THAT, Y'KNOW...

...IF THEY **PRINT** YOUR **PICTURE**, YOU CAN ORDER A **COPY**.

IT'S A REGULAR **SERVICE**.

Chuckle! **THAT'D** BE A SIGHT TO SEE!

I CAN JUST **IMAGINE** THOSE DIXIE PATRIOT WEASELS **QUAKIN'** IN THEIR **BOOTS**, WATCHIN' ONE OF THE LOCAL **UNDESIRABLES** THEY'VE FINGERED COME SAUNTERIN' UP THE **DRIVEWAY**!

LOOK, PAL, I'LL DRIVE YOU TO RIDGELINE IF YOU **NEED** ME TO. IT WON'T BE MUCH **TROUBLE**.

THANKS, TOLAND. YOU'RE A REAL **FRIEND**.

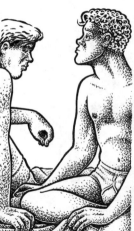

CAN I LIE DOWN **NEXT** TO YOU AN' HOLD **ON** TO YOU FOR JUST A **MINUTE**?

SAMMY... I WISH YOU WOULDN'T **ASK** THAT.

I'M NOT TALKIN' ABOUT **SEX**.

I JUST WANNA **HOLD ON** FOR **FIVE MINUTES**. I'LL GO AWAY THEN.

THAT'S O.K.— **FORGET** IT.

I JUST REMEMBERED: **LOCO** MIGHT HEAR THE **BEDSPRINGS** CREAKIN' AN' THINK I'M BEIN' **UNFAITHFUL**!

NEVER **TRIFLE** WITH THE AFFECTIONS OF A **CARNIVORE**, IS MY **MOTTO**!

G'NIGHT.

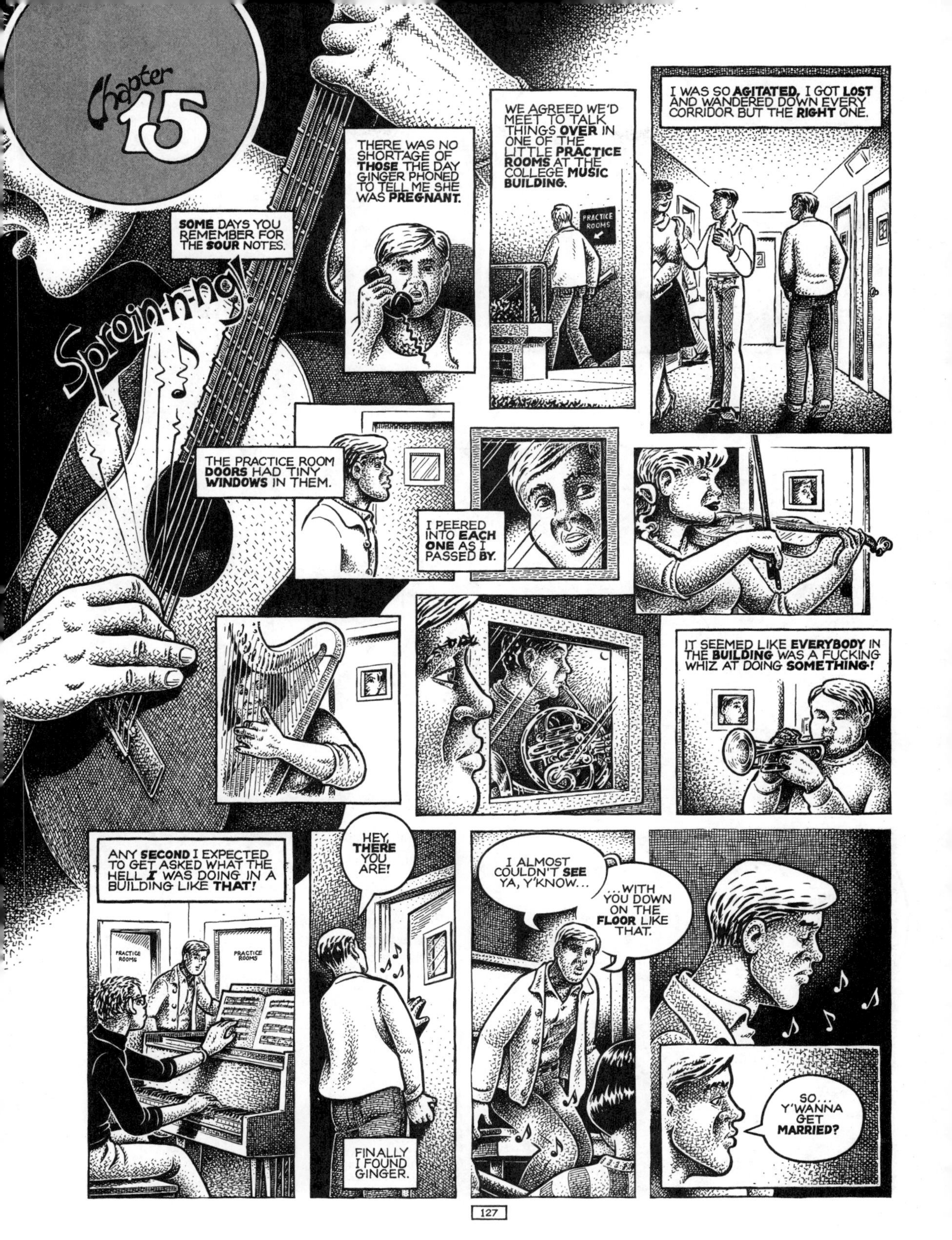
Chapter 15
SOME DAYS YOU REMEMBER FOR THE SOUR NOTES.
Sproin-n-ng!
THERE WAS NO SHORTAGE OF THOSE THE DAY GINGER PHONED TO TELL ME SHE WAS PREGNANT.
WE AGREED WE'D MEET TO TALK THINGS OVER IN ONE OF THE LITTLE PRACTICE ROOMS AT THE COLLEGE MUSIC BUILDING.
PRACTICE ROOMS
I WAS SO AGITATED, I GOT LOST AND WANDERED DOWN EVERY CORRIDOR BUT THE RIGHT ONE.
THE PRACTICE ROOM DOORS HAD TINY WINDOWS IN THEM.
I PEERED INTO EACH ONE AS I PASSED BY.
IT SEEMED LIKE EVERYBODY IN THE BUILDING WAS A FUCKING WHIZ AT DOING SOMETHING!
ANY SECOND I EXPECTED TO GET ASKED WHAT THE HELL I WAS DOING IN A BUILDING LIKE THAT!
PRACTICE ROOMS
PRACTICE ROOMS
HEY, THERE YOU ARE!
FINALLY I FOUND GINGER.
I ALMOST COULDN'T SEE YA, Y'KNOW...
...WITH YOU DOWN ON THE FLOOR LIKE THAT.
SO... Y'WANNA GET MARRIED?

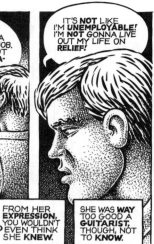

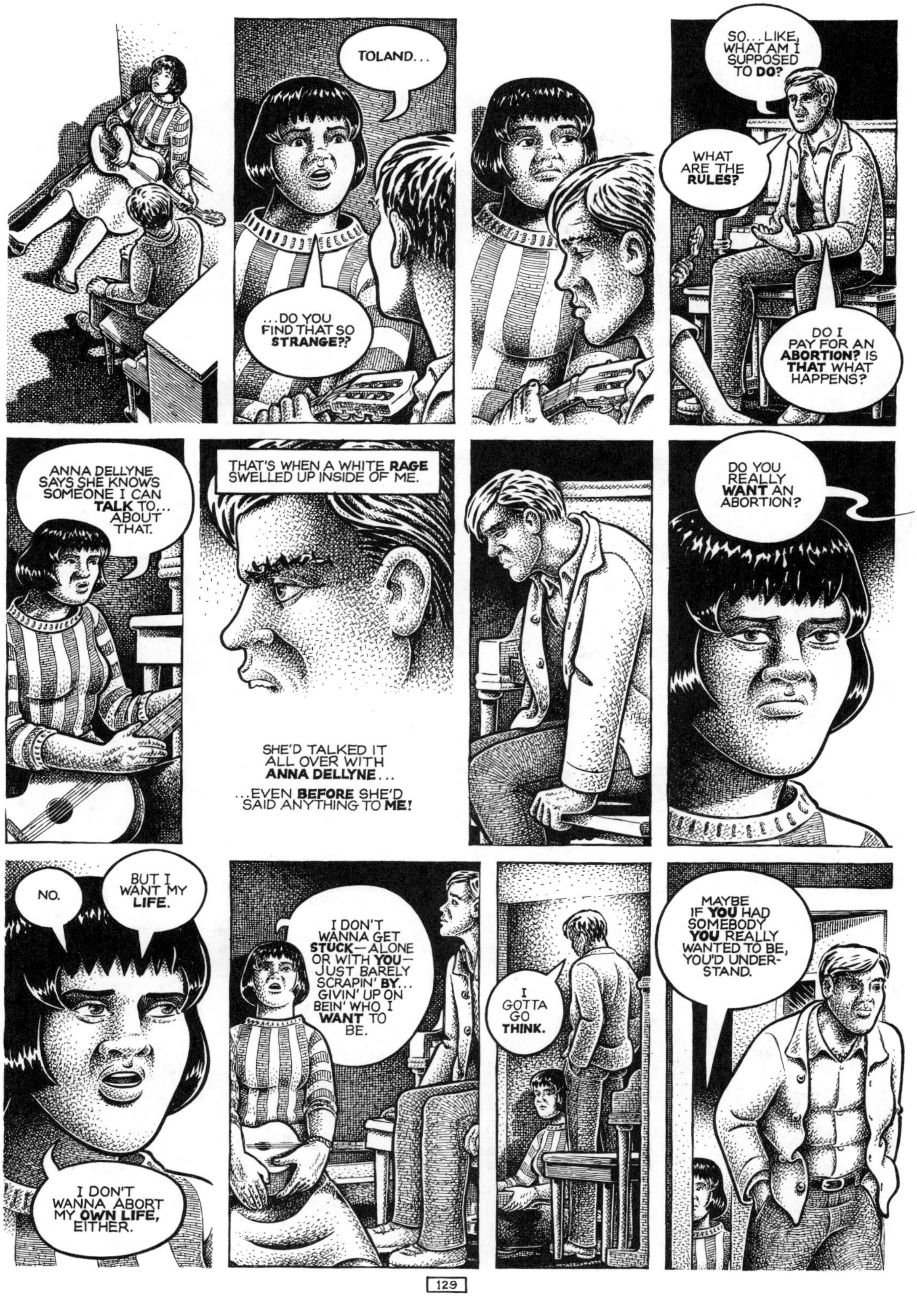
TOLAND...
...DO YOU FIND THAT SO **STRANGE?**?
SO... LIKE, WHAT AM I SUPPOSED TO **DO?**
WHAT ARE THE **RULES?**
DO I PAY FOR AN **ABORTION?** IS **THAT** WHAT HAPPENS?
ANNA DELLYNE SAYS SHE KNOWS SOMEONE I CAN **TALK** TO... ABOUT THAT.
THAT'S WHEN A WHITE **RAGE** SWELLED UP INSIDE OF ME.
SHE'D TALKED IT ALL OVER WITH **ANNA DELLYNE**...
...EVEN **BEFORE** SHE'D SAID ANYTHING TO **ME!**
DO YOU REALLY **WANT** AN ABORTION?
NO.
BUT I WANT MY **LIFE**.
I DON'T WANNA ABORT MY **OWN LIFE,** EITHER.
I DON'T WANNA GET **STUCK**—ALONE OR WITH **YOU**—JUST BARELY SCRAPIN' **BY**... GIVIN' UP ON BEIN' WHO I **WANT** TO BE.
I GOTTA GO **THINK.**
MAYBE IF **YOU** HAD SOMEBODY **YOU** REALLY WANTED TO BE, YOU'D UNDER-STAND.

REV. PEPPER!

DRIVING BACK FROM THE WESTHILLS CAMPUS, MY **THOUGHTS** WERE RACING IN EVERY **DIRECTION** AT ONCE.

THEN, AS I WAS PASSING **RUSSELL PARK**, I NOTICED **HARLAND PEPPER** STOMPING UP THE STREET TOWARD HIS **CHURCH**.

DON'T TRY TO **TALK** TO ME **NOW**, TOLAND. I'M **NAIL-SPITTIN' MAD!**

WHAT'S THE **MATTER**?

WE WON!

Y'SEE THE CHOPPER'S PRETTY **FENCE** HERE?

ITS DAYS ARE **NUMBERED**.

SO SAID THE **LAW**...AS OF **YESTER-DAY!**

THEN WHY ARE YOU—??...I MEAN, THAT'S **GOOD**, ISN'T IT?

SON, **YOU** KNOW HOW MANY **MONTHS** WE'VE HAD OUR LAWYERS TROOPIN' THROUGH EVERY ROOM OF THE **COURT-HOUSE** SUIN' TO GET THIS FARCICAL **'PARK RENOVATION'** BROUGHT TO AN END.

I'VE LISTENED TO SO MUCH TALK ABOUT **LANDSCAPIN'**, I'VE STARTED HAVIN' **DREAMS** ABOUT **BULL-DOZERS** AN' **BACKHOES!**

SO WE GO THROUGH **FIFTEEN HEARINGS** AN' DO A DANCE WITH **TWO HUNDRED CITY LAWYERS**...

...'TIL WE **FINALLY** GET THE JUDGE TO SAY: NO QUESTION **ABOUT** IT, THE FENCE HAS GOTTA **GO!**

NOW I **ASK** YOU: DO YOU SEE ANY **FENCE** COMIN' DOWN? I **DON'T!** NOR DO I SEE THE FIRST **SIGN** OF ANY **RENOVATION** UNDER WAY.

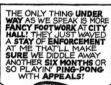

THE ONLY THING **UNDER WAY** AS WE SPEAK IS MORE **FANCY FOOTWORK** AT **CITY HALL!** THEY JUST WAVED A **STAY OF ENFORCEMENT** AT ME THAT'LL MAKE **SURE** WE DIDDLE AWAY ANOTHER **SIX MONTHS** OR SO PLAYIN' **PING-PONG** WITH **APPEALS!**

I'M TRYIN' TO DO SOMETHIN' ABOUT **RACISM** AN' THEY'VE GOT ME BALLED UP IN GLORIFIED **CHICKEN WIRE!**

IT NEVER **STOPS!** THEY JUST WEAR YOU **DOWN!**

BUT...IT'S ALL **ABSURD!** THEY'RE **STALLIN'!** YOU'LL GET YOUR PARK BACK IN THE END.

OH...I **KNOW** WE WILL. I JUST GET SO **FED UP** WITH HAVIN' TO SPEND MY **ENERGY** EVERY DAY THINKIN' ABOUT ALL THIS **CRAP!**

WHEN THE PREACHER HAD GOTTEN ENOUGH OF HIS **FUMING** DONE FOR ME TO DARE CHANGE THE **SUBJECT**, I ASKED HIM IF **ANNA DELLYNE** WAS ANYWHERE AROUND THE CHURCH THAT AFTERNOON.

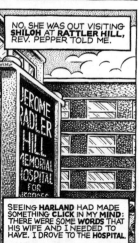

NO, SHE WAS OUT VISITING **SHILOH** AT **RATTLER HILL**, REV. PEPPER TOLD ME.

JEROME SADLER HILL MEMORIAL HOSPITAL FOR NEGROES

SEEING **HARLAND** HAD MADE SOMETHING **CLICK** IN MY **MIND**: THERE WERE SOME **WORDS** THAT HIS WIFE AND I NEEDED TO HAVE. I DROVE TO THE **HOSPITAL**.

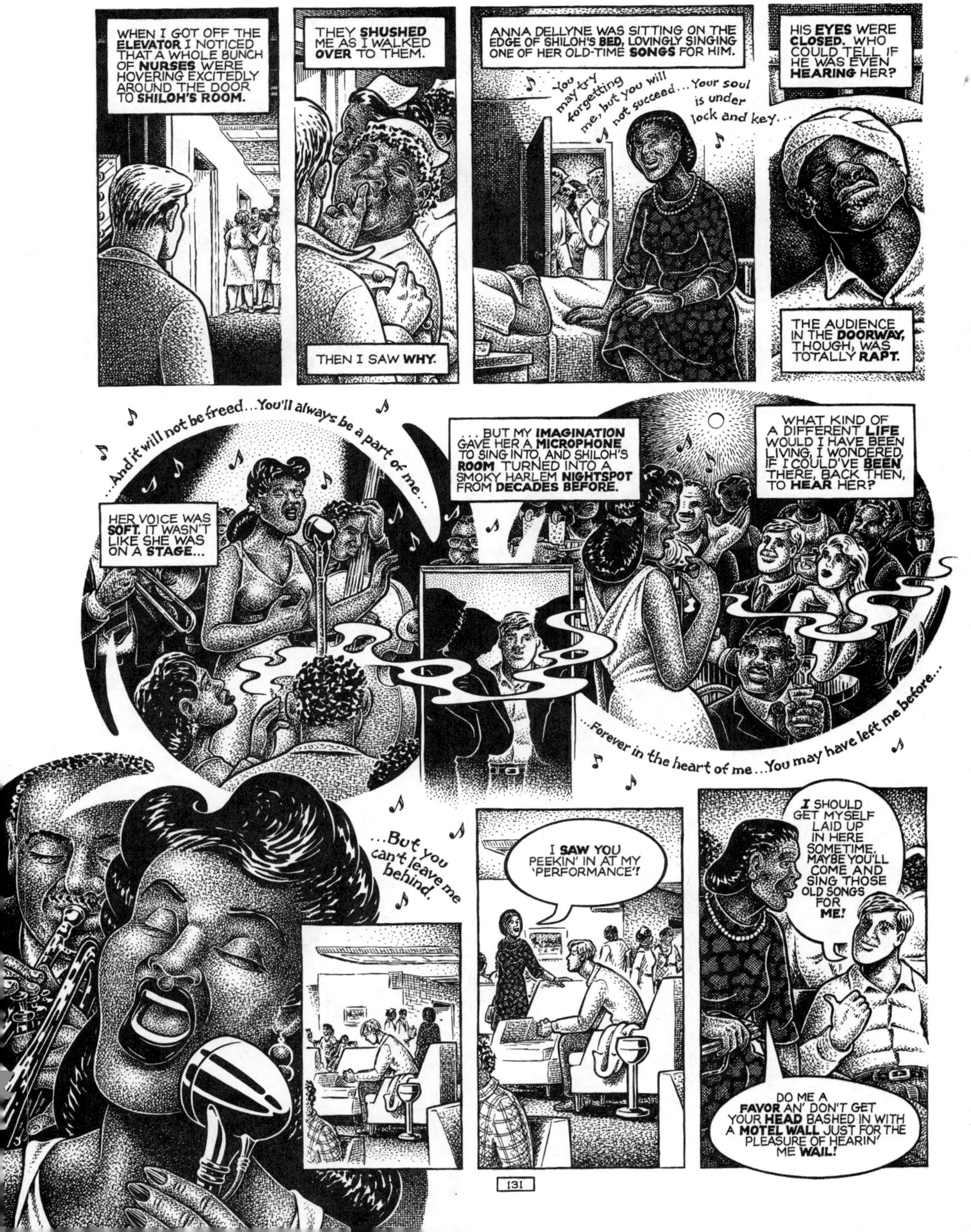
WHEN I GOT OFF THE ELEVATOR I NOTICED THAT A WHOLE BUNCH OF NURSES WERE HOVERING EXCITEDLY AROUND THE DOOR TO SHILOH'S ROOM.
THEY SHUSHED ME AS I WALKED OVER TO THEM.
THEN I SAW WHY.
ANNA DELLYNE WAS SITTING ON THE EDGE OF SHILOH'S BED, LOVINGLY SINGING ONE OF HER OLD-TIME SONGS FOR HIM.
You may try forgetting me, but you will not succeed... Your soul is under lock and key...
HIS EYES WERE CLOSED. WHO COULD TELL IF HE WAS EVEN HEARING HER?
THE AUDIENCE IN THE DOORWAY, THOUGH, WAS TOTALLY RAPT.
...And it will not be freed... You'll always be a part of me...
HER VOICE WAS SOFT. IT WASN'T LIKE SHE WAS ON A STAGE...
... BUT MY IMAGINATION GAVE HER A MICROPHONE TO SING INTO, AND SHILOH'S ROOM TURNED INTO A SMOKY HARLEM NIGHTSPOT FROM DECADES BEFORE.
WHAT KIND OF A DIFFERENT LIFE WOULD I HAVE BEEN LIVING, I WONDERED, IF I COULD'VE BEEN THERE, BACK THEN, TO HEAR HER?
...Forever in the heart of me... You may have left me before...
...But you can't leave me behind.
I SAW YOU PEEKIN' IN AT MY 'PERFORMANCE'!
I SHOULD GET MYSELF LAID UP IN HERE SOMETIME. MAYBE YOU'LL COME AND SING THOSE OLD SONGS FOR ME!
DO ME A FAVOR AN' DON'T GET YOUR HEAD BASHED IN WITH A MOTEL WALL JUST FOR THE PLEASURE OF HEARIN' ME WAIL!

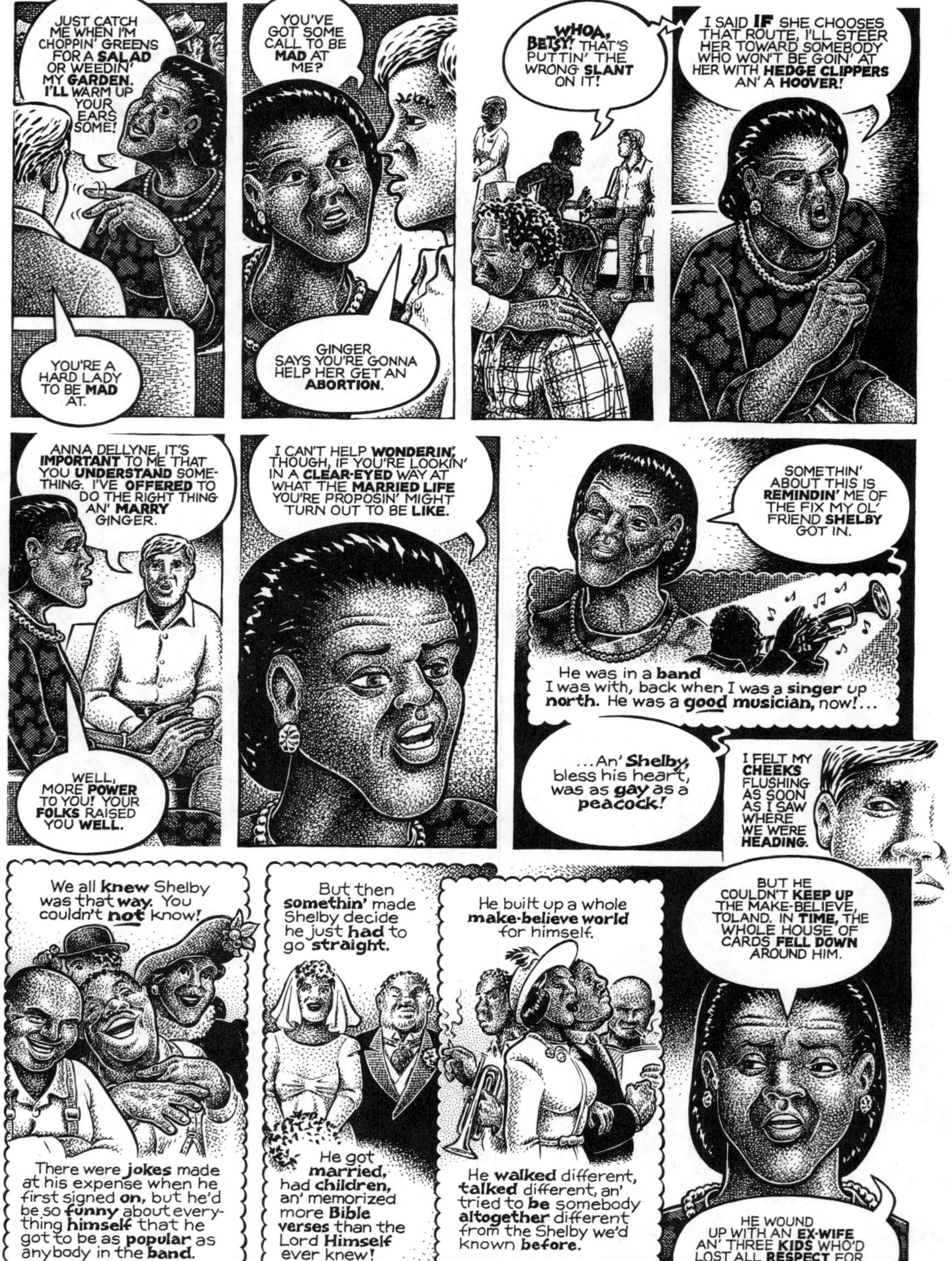

JUST CATCH ME WHEN I'M CHOPPIN' GREENS FOR A SALAD OR WEEDIN' MY GARDEN. I'LL WARM UP YOUR EARS SOME!
YOU'RE A HARD LADY TO BE MAD AT.
YOU'VE GOT SOME CALL TO BE MAD AT ME?
GINGER SAYS YOU'RE GONNA HELP HER GET AN ABORTION.
WHOA, BETSY! THAT'S PUTTIN' THE WRONG SLANT ON IT!
I SAID IF SHE CHOOSES THAT ROUTE, I'LL STEER HER TOWARD SOMEBODY WHO WON'T BE GOIN' AT HER WITH HEDGE CLIPPERS AN' A HOOVER!
ANNA DELLYNE, IT'S IMPORTANT TO ME THAT YOU UNDERSTAND SOMETHING. I'VE OFFERED TO DO THE RIGHT THING AN' MARRY GINGER.
WELL, MORE POWER TO YOU! YOUR FOLKS RAISED YOU WELL.
I CAN'T HELP WONDERIN', THOUGH, IF YOU'RE LOOKIN' IN A CLEAR-EYED WAY AT WHAT THE MARRIED LIFE YOU'RE PROPOSIN' MIGHT TURN OUT TO BE LIKE.
SOMETHIN' ABOUT THIS IS REMINDIN' ME OF THE FIX MY OL' FRIEND SHELBY GOT IN.
He was in a band I was with, back when I was a singer up north. He was a good musician, now!...
...An' Shelby, bless his heart, was as gay as a peacock!
I FELT MY CHEEKS FLUSHING AS SOON AS I SAW WHERE WE WERE HEADING.
We all knew Shelby was that way. You couldn't not know!
There were jokes made at his expense when he first signed on, but he'd be so funny about everything himself that he got to be as popular as anybody in the band.
But then somethin' made Shelby decide he just had to go straight.
He got married, had children, an' memorized more Bible verses than the Lord Himself ever knew!
He built up a whole make-believe world for himself.
He walked different, talked different, an' tried to be somebody altogether different from the Shelby we'd known before.
BUT HE COULDN'T KEEP UP THE MAKE-BELIEVE, TOLAND. IN TIME, THE WHOLE HOUSE OF CARDS FELL DOWN AROUND HIM.
HE WOUND UP WITH AN EX-WIFE AN' THREE KIDS WHO'D LOST ALL RESPECT FOR HIM BECAUSE OF HIS LIES.

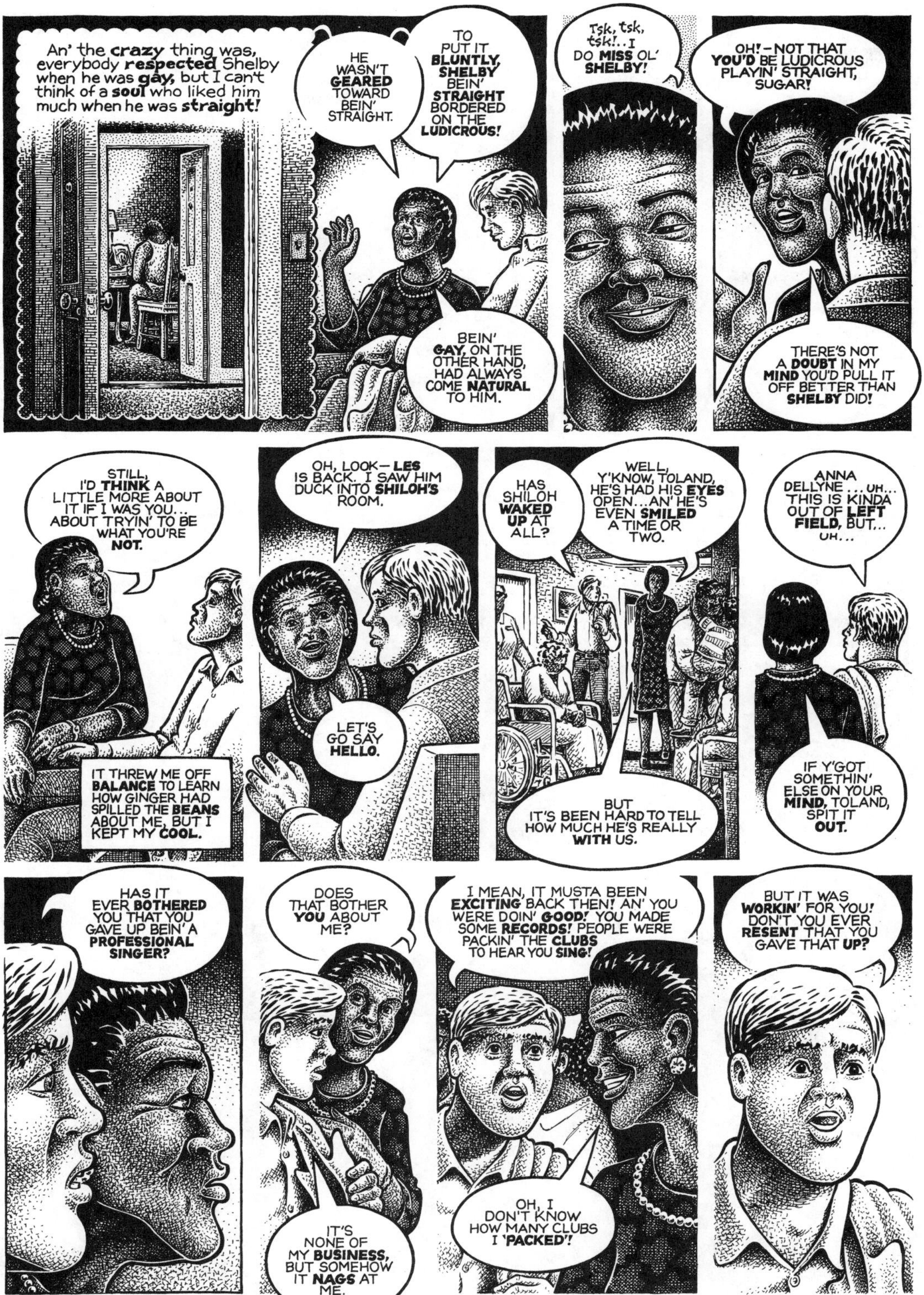

An' the crazy thing was, everybody respected Shelby when he was gay, but I can't think of a soul who liked him much when he was straight!
HE WASN'T GEARED TOWARD BEIN' STRAIGHT.
TO PUT IT BLUNTLY, SHELBY BEIN' STRAIGHT BORDERED ON THE LUDICROUS!
BEIN' GAY, ON THE OTHER HAND, HAD ALWAYS COME NATURAL TO HIM.
Tsk, tsk, tsk!..I DO MISS OL' SHELBY!
OH!—NOT THAT YOU'D BE LUDICROUS PLAYIN' STRAIGHT, SUGAR!
THERE'S NOT A DOUBT IN MY MIND YOU'D PULL IT OFF BETTER THAN SHELBY DID!
STILL, I'D THINK A LITTLE MORE ABOUT IT IF I WAS YOU... ABOUT TRYIN' TO BE WHAT YOU'RE NOT.
IT THREW ME OFF BALANCE TO LEARN HOW GINGER HAD SPILLED THE BEANS ABOUT ME, BUT I KEPT MY COOL.
OH, LOOK—LES IS BACK. I SAW HIM DUCK INTO SHILOH'S ROOM.
LET'S GO SAY HELLO.
HAS SHILOH WAKED UP AT ALL?
WELL, Y'KNOW, TOLAND, HE'S HAD HIS EYES OPEN...AN' HE'S EVEN SMILED A TIME OR TWO.
BUT IT'S BEEN HARD TO TELL HOW MUCH HE'S REALLY WITH US.
ANNA DELLYNE... UH... THIS IS KINDA OUT OF LEFT FIELD, BUT... UH...
IF Y'GOT SOMETHIN' ELSE ON YOUR MIND, TOLAND, SPIT IT OUT.
HAS IT EVER BOTHERED YOU THAT YOU GAVE UP BEIN' A PROFESSIONAL SINGER?
DOES THAT BOTHER YOU ABOUT ME?
IT'S NONE OF MY BUSINESS, BUT SOMEHOW IT NAGS AT ME.
I MEAN, IT MUSTA BEEN EXCITING BACK THEN! AN' YOU WERE DOIN' GOOD! YOU MADE SOME RECORDS! PEOPLE WERE PACKIN' THE CLUBS TO HEAR YOU SING!
OH, I DON'T KNOW HOW MANY CLUBS I 'PACKED'!
BUT IT WAS WORKIN' FOR YOU! DON'T YOU EVER RESENT THAT YOU GAVE THAT UP?

'CAUSE YOU'RE ENCOURAGIN' **GINGER** TO GO TO NEW YORK BY HERSELF LIKE **YOU** DID.

BUT WHEN ALL WAS SAID AN' DONE, **YOU** CAME BACK **HOME**.

WHAT IF NEW YORK DOESN'T WORK FOR **HER**...AN' **SHE** COMES BACK?

THEN **SHE** WON'T HAVE WHAT **SHE** WENT UP THERE LOOKIN' FOR...

...AN' MEANWHILE, THE ONLY **CHILD** I'M EVER LIKELY TO **HAVE** WILL BE **GONE FOREVER!**

I CAN'T CUT A PATH THROUGH **THAT** THICKET FOR YOU.

YOU AN' GINGER HAFTA FIND YOUR **OWN** RIGHT WAY TO GO.

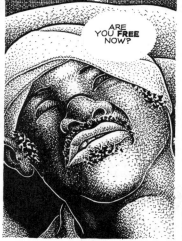
ARE YOU **FREE** NOW?

HUH?

ARE YOU **FREE** NOW?

OH. YEAH.

Y'GOT YOUR OWN **WHEELS** HERE?

YEAH.

MAMA, THE CAR'S **YOURS** TONIGHT. ME AN' TOLAND ARE GONNA GO CATCH A **BITE**.

C'MON. LET'S GET THE HELL **OUTA** HERE.

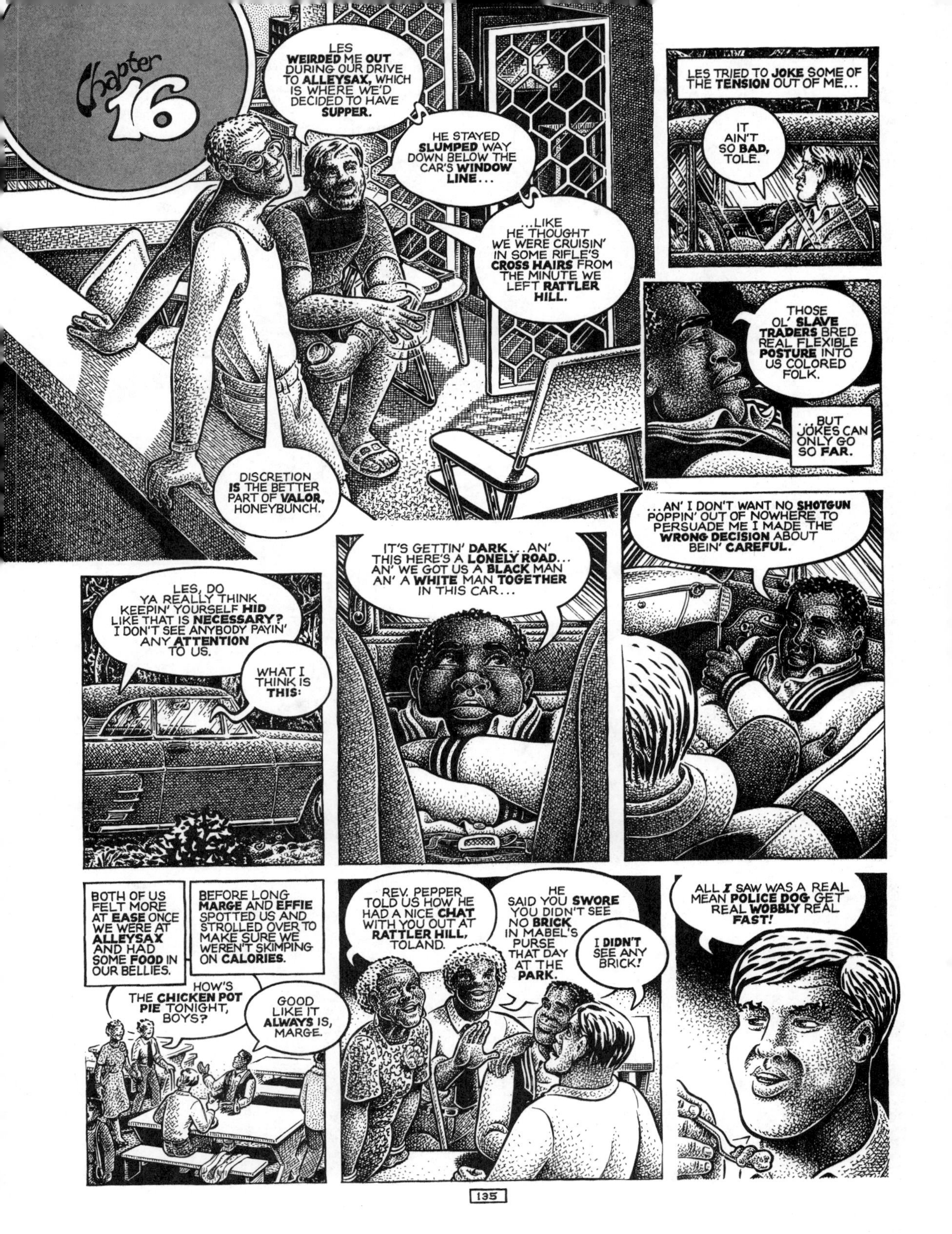
Chapter 16
LES WEIRDED ME OUT DURING OUR DRIVE TO ALLEYSAX, WHICH IS WHERE WE'D DECIDED TO HAVE SUPPER.
HE STAYED SLUMPED WAY DOWN BELOW THE CAR'S WINDOW LINE...
...LIKE HE THOUGHT WE WERE CRUISIN' IN SOME RIFLE'S CROSS HAIRS FROM THE MINUTE WE LEFT RATTLER HILL.
DISCRETION IS THE BETTER PART OF VALOR, HONEYBUNCH.
LES TRIED TO JOKE SOME OF THE TENSION OUT OF ME...
IT AIN'T SO BAD, TOLE.
THOSE OL' SLAVE TRADERS BRED REAL FLEXIBLE POSTURE INTO US COLORED FOLK.
BUT JOKES CAN ONLY GO SO FAR.
LES, DO YA REALLY THINK KEEPIN' YOURSELF HID LIKE THAT IS NECESSARY? I DON'T SEE ANYBODY PAYIN' ANY ATTENTION TO US.
WHAT I THINK IS THIS:
IT'S GETTIN' DARK...AN' THIS HERE'S A LONELY ROAD... AN' WE GOT US A BLACK MAN AN' A WHITE MAN TOGETHER IN THIS CAR...
...AN' I DON'T WANT NO SHOTGUN POPPIN' OUT OF NOWHERE TO PERSUADE ME I MADE THE WRONG DECISION ABOUT BEIN' CAREFUL.
BOTH OF US FELT MORE AT EASE ONCE WE WERE AT ALLEYSAX AND HAD SOME FOOD IN OUR BELLIES.
BEFORE LONG MARGE AND EFFIE SPOTTED US AND STROLLED OVER TO MAKE SURE WE WEREN'T SKIMPING ON CALORIES.
HOW'S THE CHICKEN POT PIE TONIGHT, BOYS?
GOOD LIKE IT ALWAYS IS, MARGE.
REV. PEPPER TOLD US HOW HE HAD A NICE CHAT WITH YOU OUT AT RATTLER HILL, TOLAND.
HE SAID YOU SWORE YOU DIDN'T SEE NO BRICK IN MABEL'S PURSE THAT DAY AT THE PARK.
I DIDN'T SEE ANY BRICK!
ALL I SAW WAS A REAL MEAN POLICE DOG GET REAL WOBBLY REAL FAST!

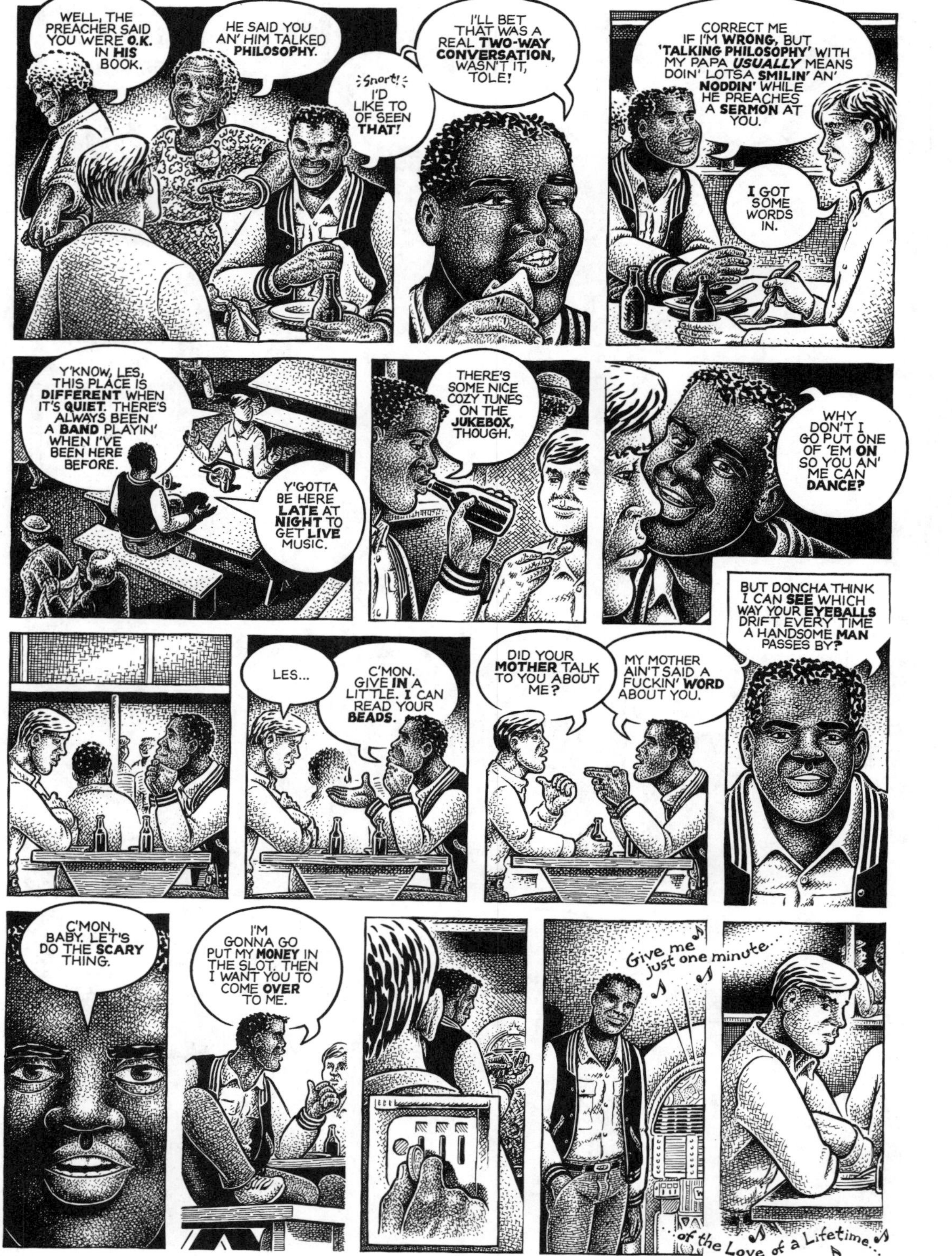
WELL, THE PREACHER SAID YOU WERE O.K. IN HIS BOOK.
HE SAID YOU AN' HIM TALKED PHILOSOPHY.
Snort!
I'D LIKE TO OF SEEN THAT!
I'LL BET THAT WAS A REAL TWO-WAY CONVERSATION, WASN'T IT, TOLE!
CORRECT ME IF I'M WRONG, BUT 'TALKING PHILOSOPHY' WITH MY PAPA USUALLY MEANS DOIN' LOTSA SMILIN' AN' NODDIN' WHILE HE PREACHES A SERMON AT YOU.
I GOT SOME WORDS IN.
Y'KNOW, LES, THIS PLACE IS DIFFERENT WHEN IT'S QUIET. THERE'S ALWAYS BEEN A BAND PLAYIN' WHEN I'VE BEEN HERE BEFORE.
Y'GOTTA BE HERE LATE AT NIGHT TO GET LIVE MUSIC.
THERE'S SOME NICE COZY TUNES ON THE JUKEBOX, THOUGH.
WHY DON'T I GO PUT ONE OF 'EM ON SO YOU AN' ME CAN DANCE?
LES...
C'MON. GIVE IN A LITTLE. I CAN READ YOUR BEADS.
DID YOUR MOTHER TALK TO YOU ABOUT ME?
MY MOTHER AIN'T SAID A FUCKIN' WORD ABOUT YOU.
BUT DONCHA THINK I CAN SEE WHICH WAY YOUR EYEBALLS DRIFT EVERY TIME A HANDSOME MAN PASSES BY?
C'MON, BABY, LET'S DO THE SCARY THING.
I'M GONNA GO PUT MY MONEY IN THE SLOT. THEN I WANT YOU TO COME OVER TO ME.
Give me just one minute...
...of the Love of a Lifetime...

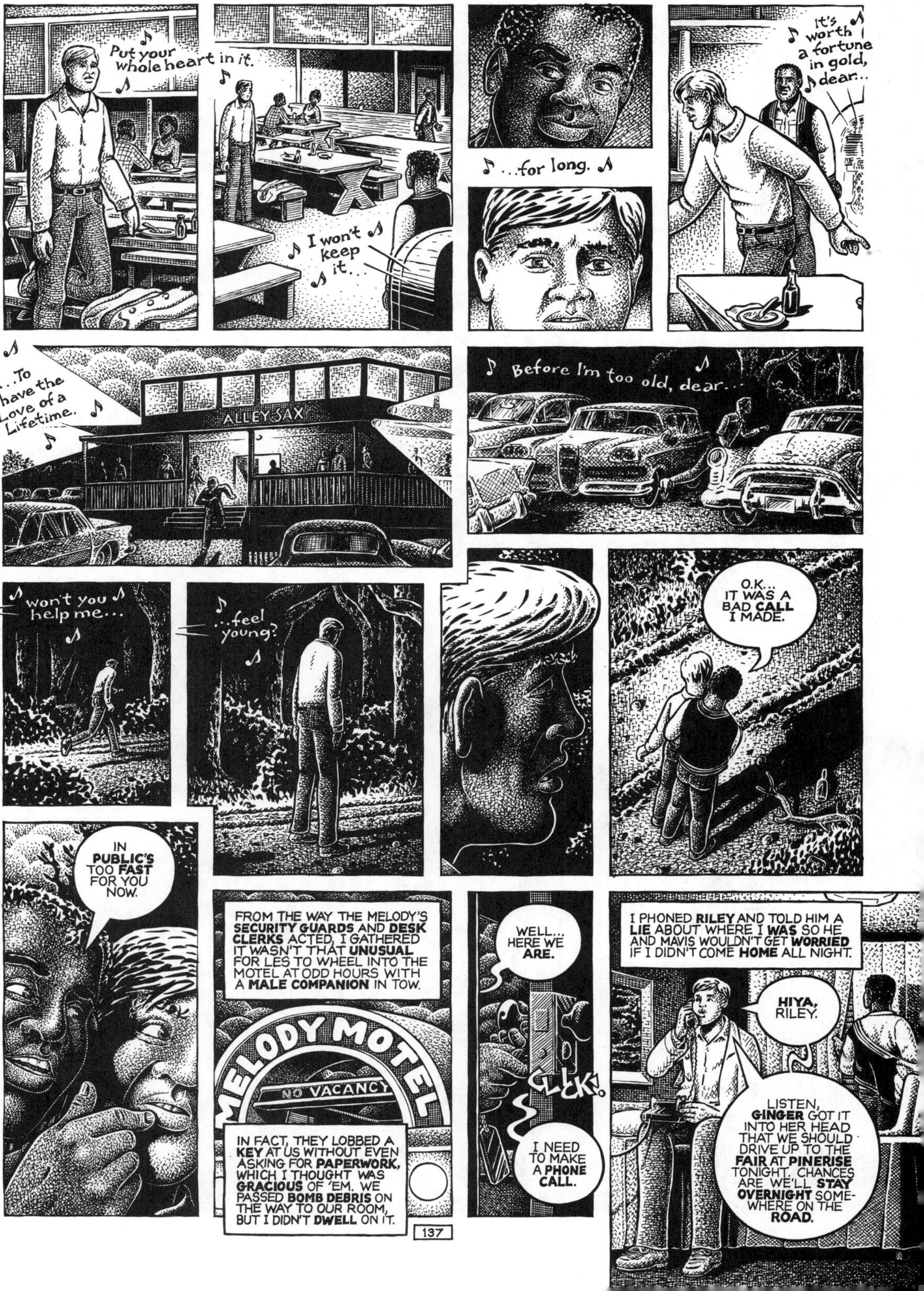
Put your whole heart in it.
I won't keep it...
...for long.
It's worth a fortune in gold, dear...
...To have the Love of a Lifetime.
ALLEY SAX
Before I'm too old, dear...
won't you help me...
...feel young?
O.K... IT WAS A BAD CALL I MADE.
IN PUBLIC'S TOO FAST FOR YOU NOW.
FROM THE WAY THE MELODY'S SECURITY GUARDS AND DESK CLERKS ACTED, I GATHERED IT WASN'T THAT UNUSUAL FOR LES TO WHEEL INTO THE MOTEL AT ODD HOURS WITH A MALE COMPANION IN TOW.
MELODY MOTEL
NO VACANCY
IN FACT, THEY LOBBED A KEY AT US WITHOUT EVEN ASKING FOR PAPERWORK, WHICH I THOUGHT WAS GRACIOUS OF 'EM. WE PASSED BOMB DEBRIS ON THE WAY TO OUR ROOM, BUT I DIDN'T DWELL ON IT.
WELL... HERE WE ARE.
CLICK!
I NEED TO MAKE A PHONE CALL.
I PHONED RILEY AND TOLD HIM A LIE ABOUT WHERE I WAS SO HE AND MAVIS WOULDN'T GET WORRIED IF I DIDN'T COME HOME ALL NIGHT.
HIYA, RILEY.
LISTEN, GINGER GOT IT INTO HER HEAD THAT WE SHOULD DRIVE UP TO THE FAIR AT PINERISE TONIGHT. CHANCES ARE WE'LL STAY OVERNIGHT SOMEWHERE ON THE ROAD.

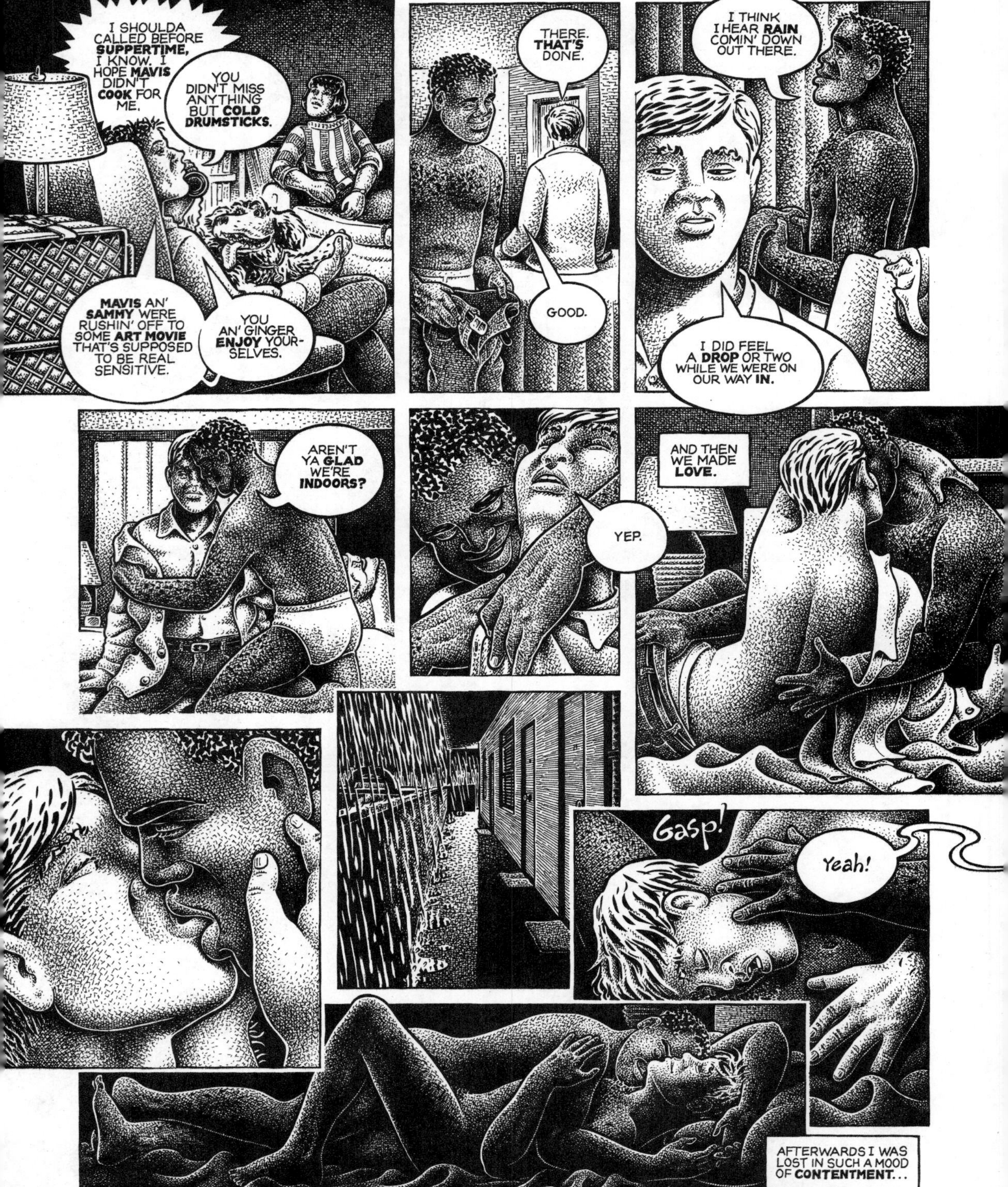

I SHOULDA CALLED BEFORE SUPPERTIME, I KNOW. I HOPE MAVIS DIDN'T COOK FOR ME.
YOU DIDN'T MISS ANYTHING BUT COLD DRUMSTICKS.
MAVIS AN' SAMMY WERE RUSHIN' OFF TO SOME ART MOVIE THAT'S SUPPOSED TO BE REAL SENSITIVE.
YOU AN' GINGER ENJOY YOURSELVES.
THERE. THAT'S DONE.
GOOD.
I THINK I HEAR RAIN COMIN' DOWN OUT THERE.
I DID FEEL A DROP OR TWO WHILE WE WERE ON OUR WAY IN.
AREN'T YA GLAD WE'RE INDOORS?
YEP.
AND THEN WE MADE LOVE.
Gasp!
Yeah!
AFTERWARDS I WAS LOST IN SUCH A MOOD OF CONTENTMENT...

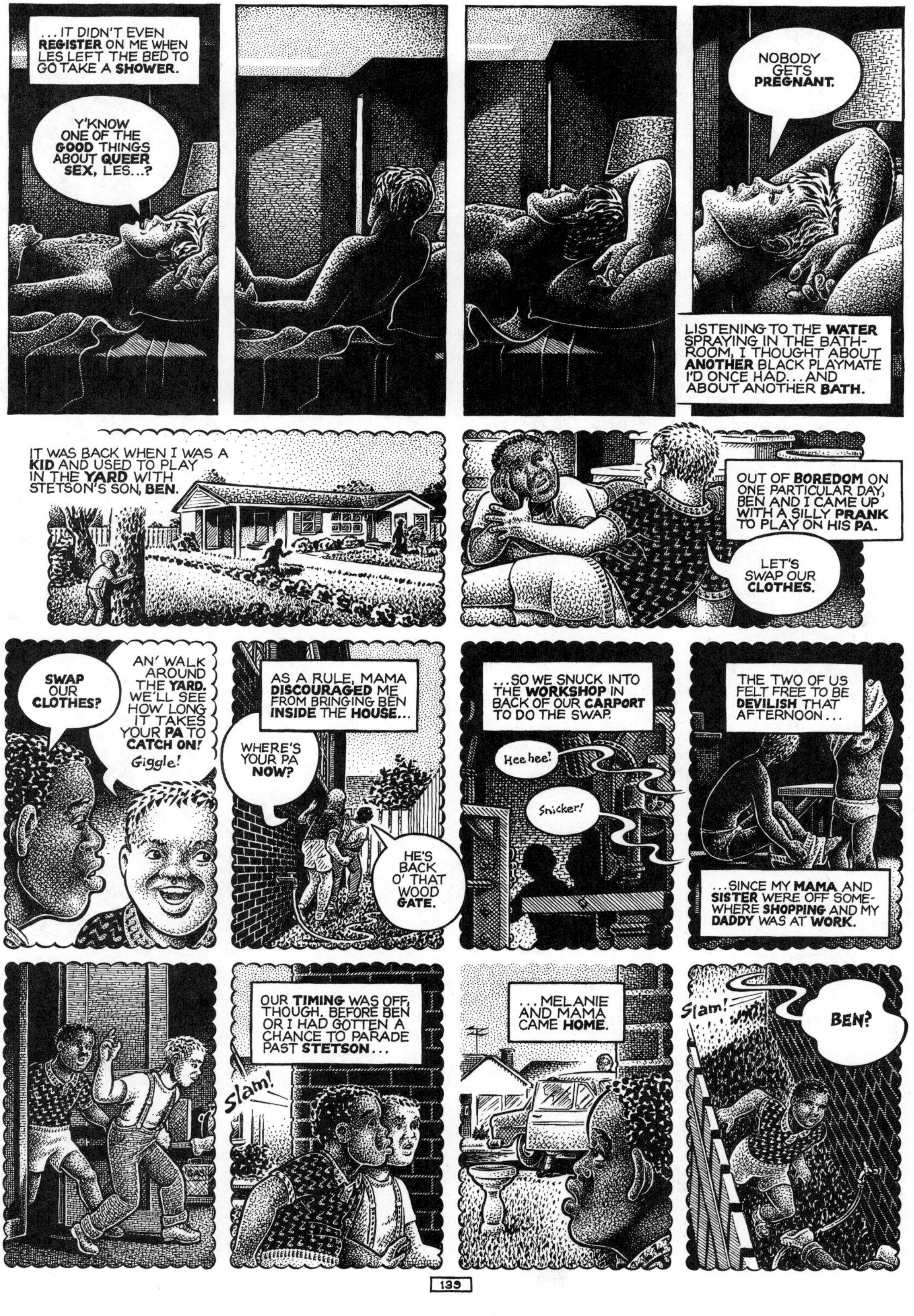

...IT DIDN'T EVEN REGISTER ON ME WHEN LES LEFT THE BED TO GO TAKE A SHOWER.
Y'KNOW ONE OF THE GOOD THINGS ABOUT QUEER SEX, LES...?
NOBODY GETS PREGNANT.
LISTENING TO THE WATER SPRAYING IN THE BATH-ROOM, I THOUGHT ABOUT ANOTHER BLACK PLAYMATE I'D ONCE HAD... AND ABOUT ANOTHER BATH.
IT WAS BACK WHEN I WAS A KID AND USED TO PLAY IN THE YARD WITH STETSON'S SON, BEN.
OUT OF BOREDOM ON ONE PARTICULAR DAY, BEN AND I CAME UP WITH A SILLY PRANK TO PLAY ON HIS PA.
LET'S SWAP OUR CLOTHES.
SWAP OUR CLOTHES?
AN' WALK AROUND THE YARD. WE'LL SEE HOW LONG IT TAKES YOUR PA TO CATCH ON!
Giggle!
AS A RULE, MAMA DISCOURAGED ME FROM BRINGING BEN INSIDE THE HOUSE...
WHERE'S YOUR PA NOW?
HE'S BACK O' THAT WOOD GATE.
...SO WE SNUCK INTO THE WORKSHOP IN BACK OF OUR CARPORT TO DO THE SWAP.
Hee hee!
Snicker!
THE TWO OF US FELT FREE TO BE DEVILISH THAT AFTERNOON...
...SINCE MY MAMA AND SISTER WERE OFF SOME-WHERE SHOPPING AND MY DADDY WAS AT WORK.
OUR TIMING WAS OFF, THOUGH. BEFORE BEN OR I HAD GOTTEN A CHANCE TO PARADE PAST STETSON...
Slam!
...MELANIE AND MAMA CAME HOME.
Slam!
BEN?

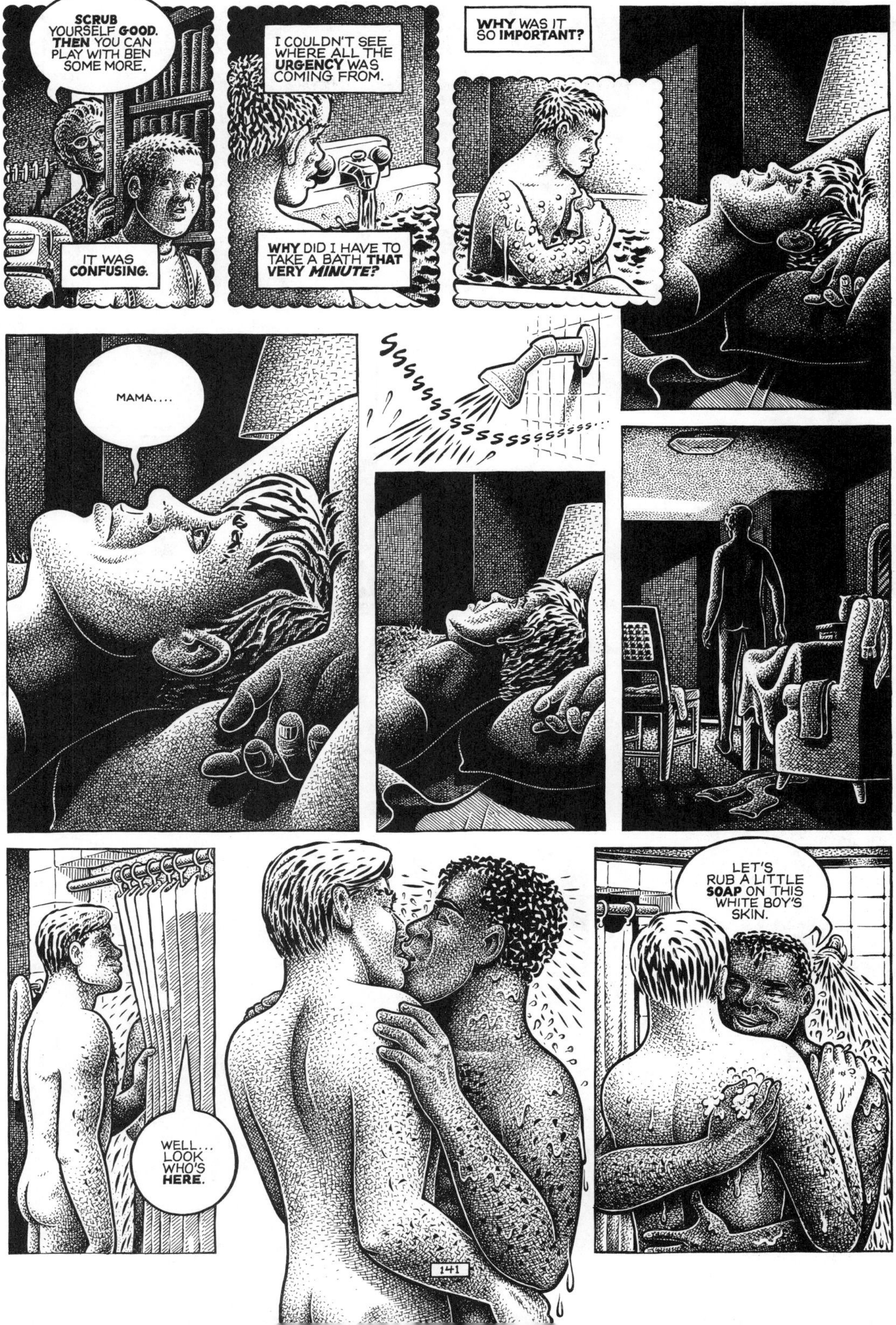
SCRUB YOURSELF GOOD. THEN YOU CAN PLAY WITH BEN SOME MORE.
IT WAS CONFUSING.
I COULDN'T SEE WHERE ALL THE URGENCY WAS COMING FROM.
WHY DID I HAVE TO TAKE A BATH THAT VERY MINUTE?
WHY WAS IT SO IMPORTANT?
MAMA....
SSSSSSSSSSSSSSSSSSSSSSSSSS...
WELL... LOOK WHO'S HERE.
LET'S RUB A LITTLE SOAP ON THIS WHITE BOY'S SKIN.

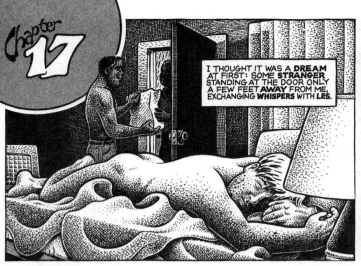

Chapter 17

I THOUGHT IT WAS A **DREAM** AT FIRST: SOME **STRANGER** STANDING AT THE DOOR ONLY A FEW FEET **AWAY** FROM ME, EXCHANGING **WHISPERS** WITH **LES**.

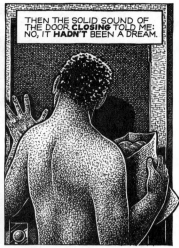

THEN THE SOLID SOUND OF THE DOOR **CLOSING** TOLD ME: NO, IT **HADN'T** BEEN A DREAM.

I WAS **EMBARRASSED**, REALIZING I'D BEEN RIGHT THERE IN FULL **VIEW** THE WHOLE **TIME**, NAKED ON A CLUMP OF TANGLED **BEDSHEETS**.

BUT IT DIDN'T SEEM TO HAVE BOTHERED **LES**, SO I FIGURED, WHAT THE **HELL!**

MORNING **LIGHT** WAS WARMING MY **EYELIDS**, BUT I KEPT THEM SHUT AND TRIED TO GO BACK TO **SLEEP**. I WANTED MORE OF THE DREAMS I'D BEEN HAVING **EARLIER**.

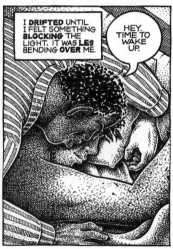

I **DRIFTED** UNTIL I FELT SOMETHING **BLOCKING** THE LIGHT. IT WAS **LES** BENDING **OVER** ME.

HEY. TIME TO WAKE UP.

Whoops!

C'MERE. BACK TO **BED**.

MAN! LOOK AT SLEEPIN' BEAUTY GET WIDE AWAKE **FAST!**

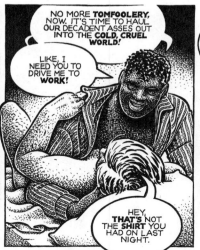

NO MORE **TOMFOOLERY**, NOW. IT'S TIME TO HAUL OUR DECADENT ASSES OUT INTO THE **COLD, CRUEL WORLD!**

LIKE, I NEED YOU TO DRIVE ME TO **WORK!**

HEY, **THAT'S** NOT THE **SHIRT** YOU HAD ON LAST NIGHT.

WHERE'D YOU GET A CHANGE OF **CLOTHES?**

MY FRIEND **RUPE** WAS JUST HERE.

HE LOOKS **OUT** FOR ME WHEN THESE '**SPECIAL OCCASIONS**' ARISE.

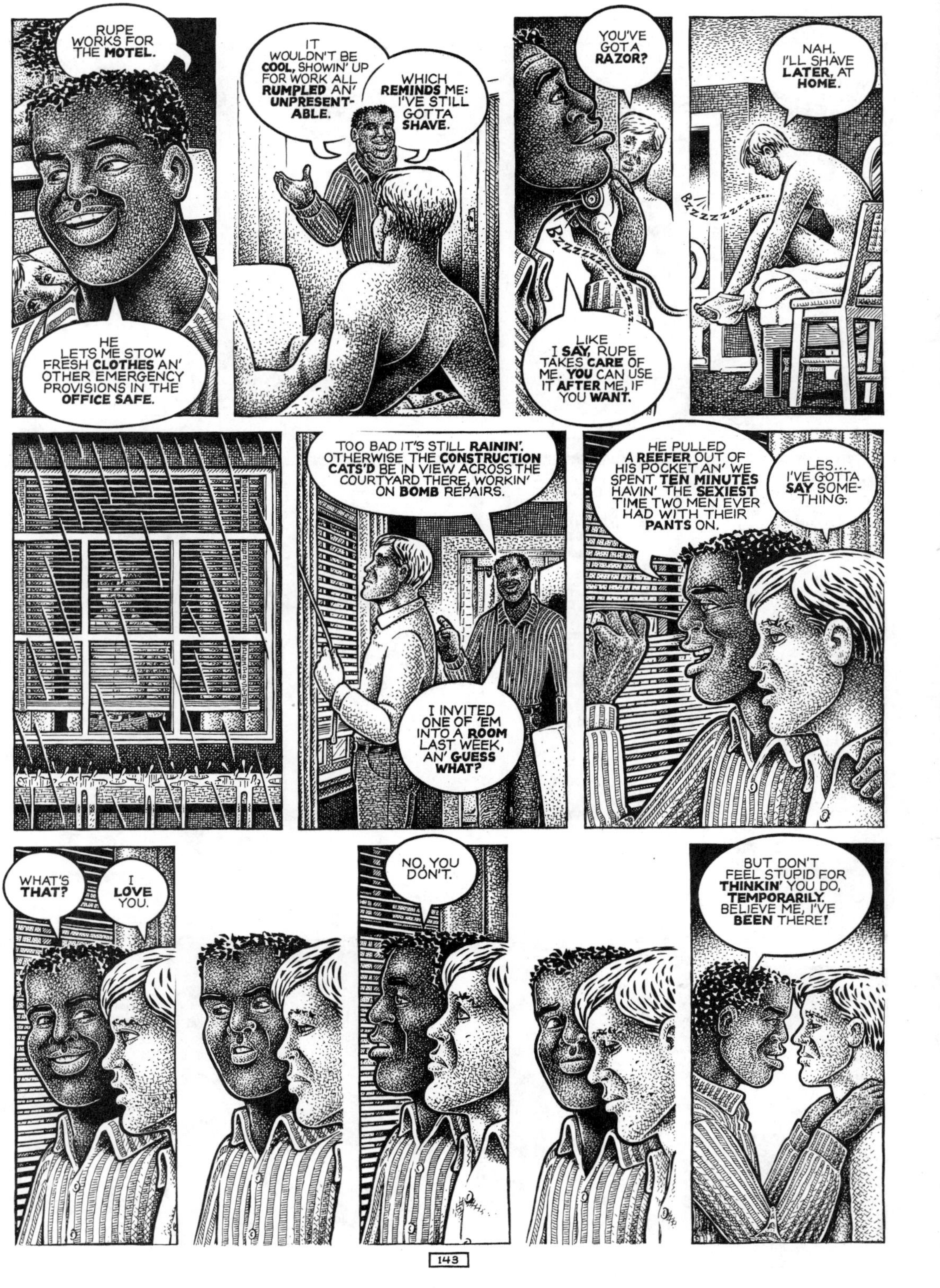
RUPE WORKS FOR THE **MOTEL**.
HE LETS ME STOW FRESH **CLOTHES** AN' OTHER EMERGENCY PROVISIONS IN THE **OFFICE SAFE**.
IT WOULDN'T BE **COOL**, SHOWIN' UP FOR WORK ALL **RUMPLED** AN' **UNPRESENT-ABLE**.
WHICH **REMINDS** ME: I'VE STILL GOTTA **SHAVE**.
YOU'VE GOT A **RAZOR?**
BZZZZZZZZZZZ
LIKE I **SAY**, RUPE TAKES **CARE** OF ME. **YOU** CAN USE IT **AFTER** ME, IF YOU **WANT**.
NAH. I'LL SHAVE **LATER**, AT **HOME**.
BZZZZZZZZZ
TOO BAD IT'S STILL **RAININ'**. OTHERWISE THE **CONSTRUCTION CATS'D** BE IN VIEW ACROSS THE COURTYARD THERE, WORKIN' ON **BOMB** REPAIRS.
I INVITED ONE OF 'EM INTO A **ROOM** LAST WEEK, AN' **GUESS WHAT?**
HE PULLED A **REEFER** OUT OF HIS POCKET AN' WE SPENT **TEN MINUTES** HAVIN' THE **SEXIEST** TIME TWO MEN EVER HAD WITH THEIR **PANTS** ON.
LES... I'VE GOTTA **SAY** SOME-THING.
WHAT'S **THAT?**
I **LOVE** YOU.
NO, YOU DON'T.
BUT DON'T FEEL STUPID FOR **THINKIN'** YOU DO, **TEMPORARILY**. BELIEVE ME, I'VE **BEEN** THERE!

IT THROWS YOU **OFF**, DOIN' IT FOR THE FIRST TIME.

MY FIRST TIME, I WAS LIKE A **BABY GOOSE** RIGHT OUT OF THE **EGG**, READY TO WADDLE AFTER THE FIRST WARM **BODY** THAT COULD **PASS** FOR A **MAMA!**

DON'T **WORRY**...YOU'LL GET YOUR **SEA LEGS.**

I **TELL** YOU, THOUGH, TOLE— I HAD A **FINE TIME** WITH YOU LAST NIGHT. I SEE A GREAT **FUTURE** FOR YOU IN THE **LAND O' LOVESVILLE!**

DON'T FORGET YOUR **JACKET.**

NOW IF I WAS **SMART,** I'D OF HAD A COUPLE OF **UMBRELLAS** SQUIRRELED AWAY IN **RUPE'S** SAFE.

BUT **NOT BEIN'** SMART, I **DON'T!** I'VE **LUCKED OUT** ON WEATHER SO MUCH UP TO NOW, I GOT **COMPLACENT!**

YOU THINK YOU'VE PLANNED FOR **EVERY CONTINGENCY,** BUT YOU ALWAYS FORGET **SOMETHIN'!**

SPEAKING OF **PLANS...**

...MY PLAN WAS TO DROP **LES** OFF AT WORK AND THEN GO FIND **GINGER** AT **WESTHILLS.**

G'BYE. DON'T GET **WET.**

VERY **FUNNY.**

THE **CONTINGENCY** I WAS FORGETTING WAS THAT SHE HAD **THREE CLASSES** IN A **ROW** THURSDAY MORNINGS, STARTING AT **EIGHT.**

DAMN!...

SNAP!

THAT WAS TOO LONG TO **WAIT.** I WAS ALL **CHARGED UP** AND IN NEED OF A **FRIEND** TO TALK TO _NOW!_

SO I CALLED UP MY **SISTER** AND ASKED HER OUT.

HEY, **MELANIE**— WANNA GO TO THE **PANCAKE HOUSE?**

ON MY WAY TO THE PANCAKE HOUSE I MUST'VE MADE A **DECISION** WITHOUT EVEN NOTICING I WAS **DOING** IT...

...BECAUSE THE **FIRST** THING I DID ONCE **COFFEE** WAS POURED WAS TELL MELANIE THAT I HAD GOTTEN GINGER **PREGNANT.**

PANCAKE HOUSE

AND **THEN** I TOLD HER ABOUT THE NIGHT I'D JUST SPENT WITH **LES.**

I COULDN'T QUITE **BELIEVE** THAT MUCH **TRUTHFULNESS** COMING OUT OF MY MOUTH IN ONE **SITTING!**

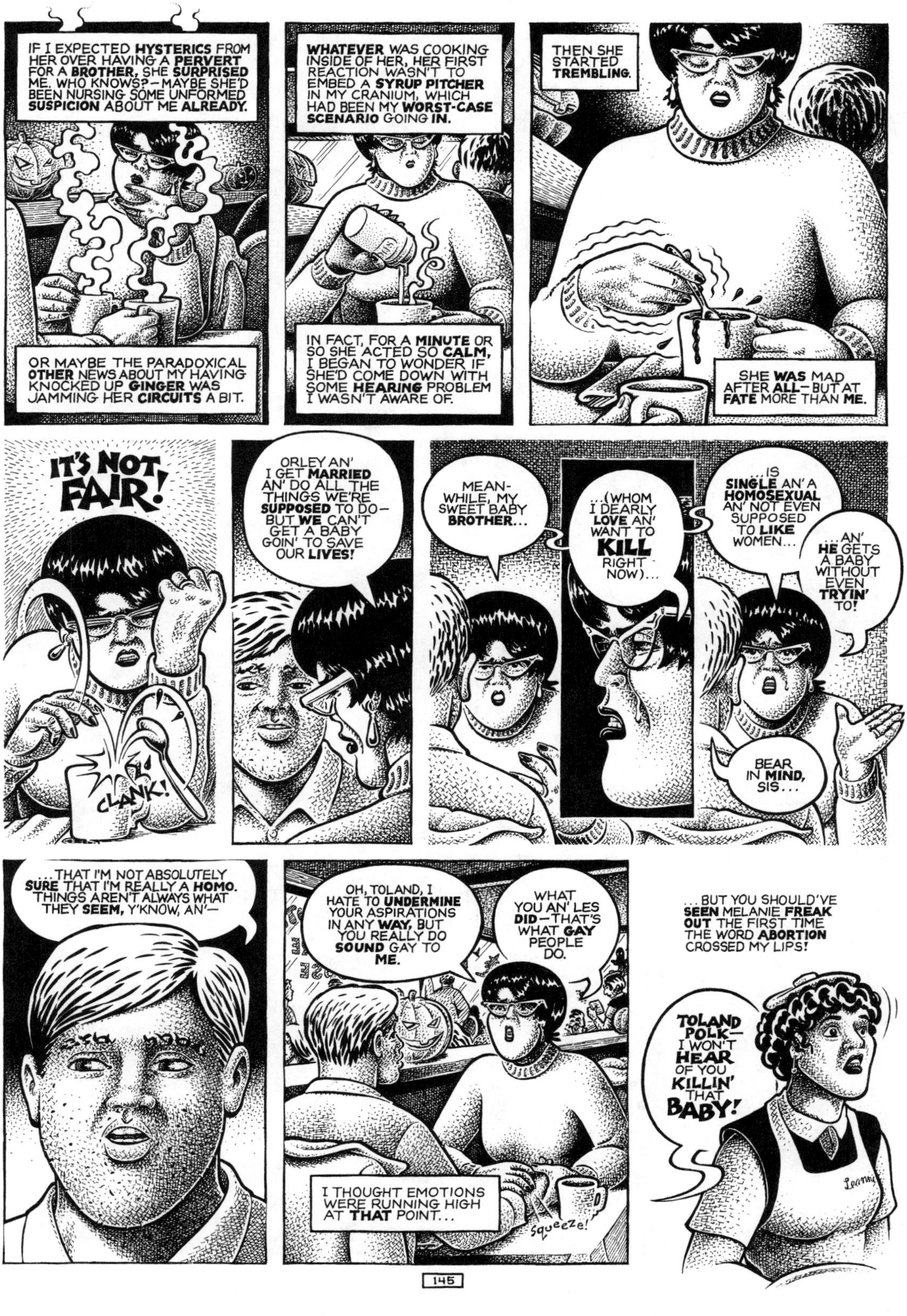
IF I EXPECTED HYSTERICS FROM HER OVER HAVING A PERVERT FOR A BROTHER, SHE SURPRISED ME. WHO KNOWS?—MAYBE SHE'D BEEN NURSING SOME UNFORMED SUSPICION ABOUT ME ALREADY.
OR MAYBE THE PARADOXICAL OTHER NEWS ABOUT MY HAVING KNOCKED UP GINGER WAS JAMMING HER CIRCUITS A BIT.
WHATEVER WAS COOKING INSIDE OF HER, HER FIRST REACTION WASN'T TO EMBED A SYRUP PITCHER IN MY CRANIUM, WHICH HAD BEEN MY WORST-CASE SCENARIO GOING IN.
IN FACT, FOR A MINUTE OR SO SHE ACTED SO CALM, I BEGAN TO WONDER IF SHE'D COME DOWN WITH SOME HEARING PROBLEM I WASN'T AWARE OF.
THEN SHE STARTED TREMBLING.
SHE WAS MAD AFTER ALL—BUT AT FATE MORE THAN ME.
IT'S NOT FAIR!
CLANK!
ORLEY AN' I GET MARRIED AN' DO ALL THE THINGS WE'RE SUPPOSED TO DO—BUT WE CAN'T GET A BABY GOIN' TO SAVE OUR LIVES!
MEAN-WHILE, MY SWEET BABY BROTHER...
...(WHOM I DEARLY LOVE AN' WANT TO KILL RIGHT NOW)...
...IS SINGLE AN' A HOMOSEXUAL AN' NOT EVEN SUPPOSED TO LIKE WOMEN...
...AN' HE GETS A BABY WITHOUT EVEN TRYIN' TO!
BEAR IN MIND, SIS...
...THAT I'M NOT ABSOLUTELY SURE THAT I'M REALLY A HOMO. THINGS AREN'T ALWAYS WHAT THEY SEEM, Y'KNOW, AN'—
OH, TOLAND, I HATE TO UNDERMINE YOUR ASPIRATIONS IN ANY WAY, BUT YOU REALLY DO SOUND GAY TO ME.
WHAT YOU AN' LES DID—THAT'S WHAT GAY PEOPLE DO.
I THOUGHT EMOTIONS WERE RUNNING HIGH AT THAT POINT...
squeeze!
...BUT YOU SHOULD'VE SEEN MELANIE FREAK OUT THE FIRST TIME THE WORD ABORTION CROSSED MY LIPS!
TOLAND POLK—I WON'T HEAR OF YOU KILLIN' THAT BABY!

C'MON, IT'S **NOT** A BABY **YET!** IT'S JUST A LITTLE GLOB OF **CELLS!**

YOU WASH MORE STRAY CELLS THAN **THAT** DOWN THE **BATHTUB DRAIN** EVERY DAY!

HONESTLY, TOLAND! IT'S JUST **LIKE YOU** TO LOOK AT THINGS IN A **NUMBSKULL WAY** LIKE **THAT!**

THAT **'GLOB** OF **CELLS'** YOU'RE PLANNIN' ON WASHIN' DOWN THE DRAIN HAS A LITTLE BIT OF **YOU** AN' A LITTLE BIT OF **GINGER** IN IT— AN' IT'S **ALIVE! THINK** ABOUT IT!

JESUS, MELANIE! DON'T GET SO **OVER-WROUGHT!**

YOU'RE GONNA FIND OUT WHAT **'OVERWROUGHT' IS** IF I HAVE TO LISTEN TO MORE **DOUBLETALK** FROM YOU ABOUT **'CELL GLOBS?'**

GINGER'S SO **SMART AN' TALENTED.** I'VE **ENVIED** HER RIGHT FROM THE **BEGINNING.**

AN' EVEN **YOU** HAVE BEEN KNOWN TO EXHIBIT A **TRAIT** OR TWO WORTH PASSIN' ON.

A **BABY** MADE OUT OF THE **TWO** OF YOU COULD GROW UP TO BE SOMEBODY REALLY **SPECIAL.** OR **INTERESTING,** AT **LEAST!**

NOW I WANT YOU TO LOOK ME **DIRECTLY** IN THE **EYE,** DEAR HEART, AND **TELL** ME THAT NONE OF THAT **MATTERS** TO YOU AT **ALL.**

I **SIDESTEPPED** HER CHALLENGE WHILE WE WERE THERE AT THE **PANCAKE HOUSE...**

...BUT IT HAD **CLAMPED** ITSELF ONTO MY **MIND** THE WAY A **DOG** CLAMPS ONTO PANTS CUFFS.

THE **RAIN** HAD STOPPED BY THE TIME MY SISTER AND I PARTED COMPANY. THERE WERE **PUDDLES** EVERYWHERE AND A GRAY OCTOBER **CHILL** HAD SETTLED IN.

NOT THE MOST **INVITING** CONDITIONS FOR A TRIP OUT TO BLUERABBIT LAKE—BUT **THAT'S** WHERE I FELT LIKE **GOING.**

IT BEING TOO **MUDDY** FOR ME TO SPRAWL ON THE **BANK** IN MY **USUAL** FASHION, I FOUND A DAMP **TREE STUMP** TO SIT ON.

PART OF ME STAYED AWARE OF THE STUMP'S **WETNESS,** WHICH CREPT THROUGH MY **JEANS** UNTIL MY **HINDSIDE** WAS **NUMB** AND **CLAMMY.**

ANOTHER PART WATCHED THE IMAGINARY **CHILDREN** WHO WERE SCAMPERING OVER THE WATER'S RIPPLING **SURFACE.**

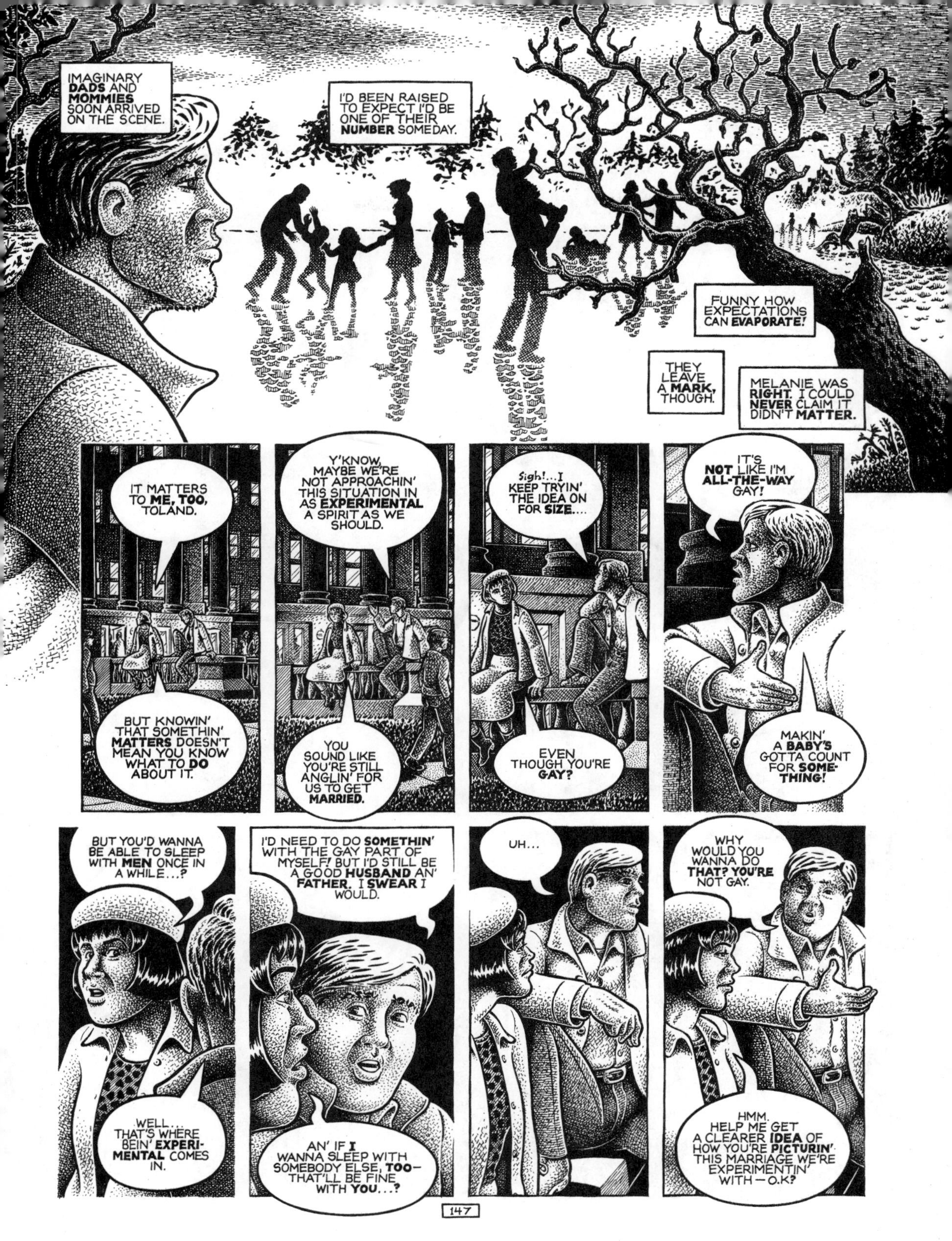

IMAGINARY DADS AND MOMMIES SOON ARRIVED ON THE SCENE.
I'D BEEN RAISED TO EXPECT I'D BE ONE OF THEIR NUMBER SOMEDAY.
FUNNY HOW EXPECTATIONS CAN EVAPORATE!
THEY LEAVE A MARK, THOUGH.
MELANIE WAS RIGHT. I COULD NEVER CLAIM IT DIDN'T MATTER.
IT MATTERS TO ME, TOO, TOLAND.
BUT KNOWIN' THAT SOMETHIN' MATTERS DOESN'T MEAN YOU KNOW WHAT TO DO ABOUT IT.
Y'KNOW, MAYBE WE'RE NOT APPROACHIN' THIS SITUATION IN AS EXPERIMENTAL A SPIRIT AS WE SHOULD.
YOU SOUND LIKE YOU'RE STILL ANGLIN' FOR US TO GET MARRIED.
Sigh!...I KEEP TRYIN' THE IDEA ON FOR SIZE....
EVEN THOUGH YOU'RE GAY?
IT'S NOT LIKE I'M ALL-THE-WAY GAY!
MAKIN' A BABY'S GOTTA COUNT FOR SOME-THING!
BUT YOU'D WANNA BE ABLE TO SLEEP WITH MEN ONCE IN A WHILE...?
WELL... THAT'S WHERE BEIN' EXPERI-MENTAL COMES IN.
I'D NEED TO DO SOMETHIN' WITH THE GAY PART OF MYSELF! BUT I'D STILL BE A GOOD HUSBAND AN' FATHER. I SWEAR I WOULD.
AN' IF I WANNA SLEEP WITH SOMEBODY ELSE, TOO— THAT'LL BE FINE WITH YOU...?
UH...
WHY WOULD YOU WANNA DO THAT? YOU'RE NOT GAY.
HMM. HELP ME GET A CLEARER IDEA OF HOW YOU'RE PICTURIN' THIS MARRIAGE WE'RE EXPERIMENTIN' WITH—O.K?

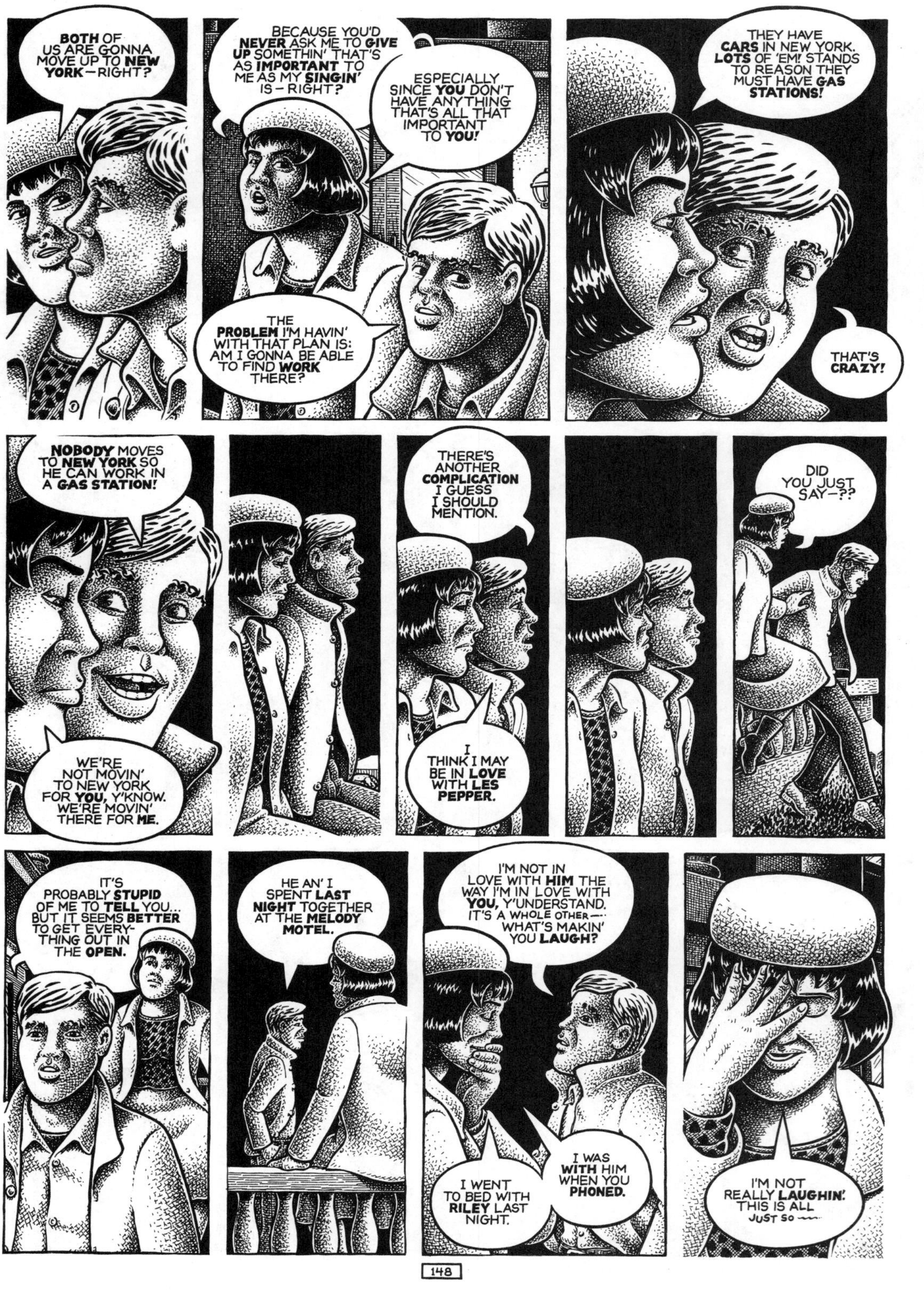
BOTH OF US ARE GONNA MOVE UP TO NEW YORK—RIGHT?
BECAUSE YOU'D NEVER ASK ME TO GIVE UP SOMETHIN' THAT'S AS IMPORTANT TO ME AS MY SINGIN' IS—RIGHT?
ESPECIALLY SINCE YOU DON'T HAVE ANYTHING THAT'S ALL THAT IMPORTANT TO YOU!
THE PROBLEM I'M HAVIN' WITH THAT PLAN IS: AM I GONNA BE ABLE TO FIND WORK THERE?
THEY HAVE CARS IN NEW YORK. LOTS OF 'EM! STANDS TO REASON THEY MUST HAVE GAS STATIONS!
THAT'S CRAZY!
NOBODY MOVES TO NEW YORK SO HE CAN WORK IN A GAS STATION!
WE'RE NOT MOVIN' TO NEW YORK FOR YOU, Y'KNOW. WE'RE MOVIN' THERE FOR ME.
THERE'S ANOTHER COMPLICATION I GUESS I SHOULD MENTION.
I THINK I MAY BE IN LOVE WITH LES PEPPER.
DID YOU JUST SAY—??
IT'S PROBABLY STUPID OF ME TO TELL YOU... BUT IT SEEMS BETTER TO GET EVERY-THING OUT IN THE OPEN.
HE AN' I SPENT LAST NIGHT TOGETHER AT THE MELODY MOTEL.
I'M NOT IN LOVE WITH HIM THE WAY I'M IN LOVE WITH YOU, Y'UNDERSTAND. IT'S A WHOLE OTHER— WHAT'S MAKIN' YOU LAUGH?
I WENT TO BED WITH RILEY LAST NIGHT.
I WAS WITH HIM WHEN YOU PHONED.
I'M NOT REALLY LAUGHIN'. THIS IS ALL JUST SO—

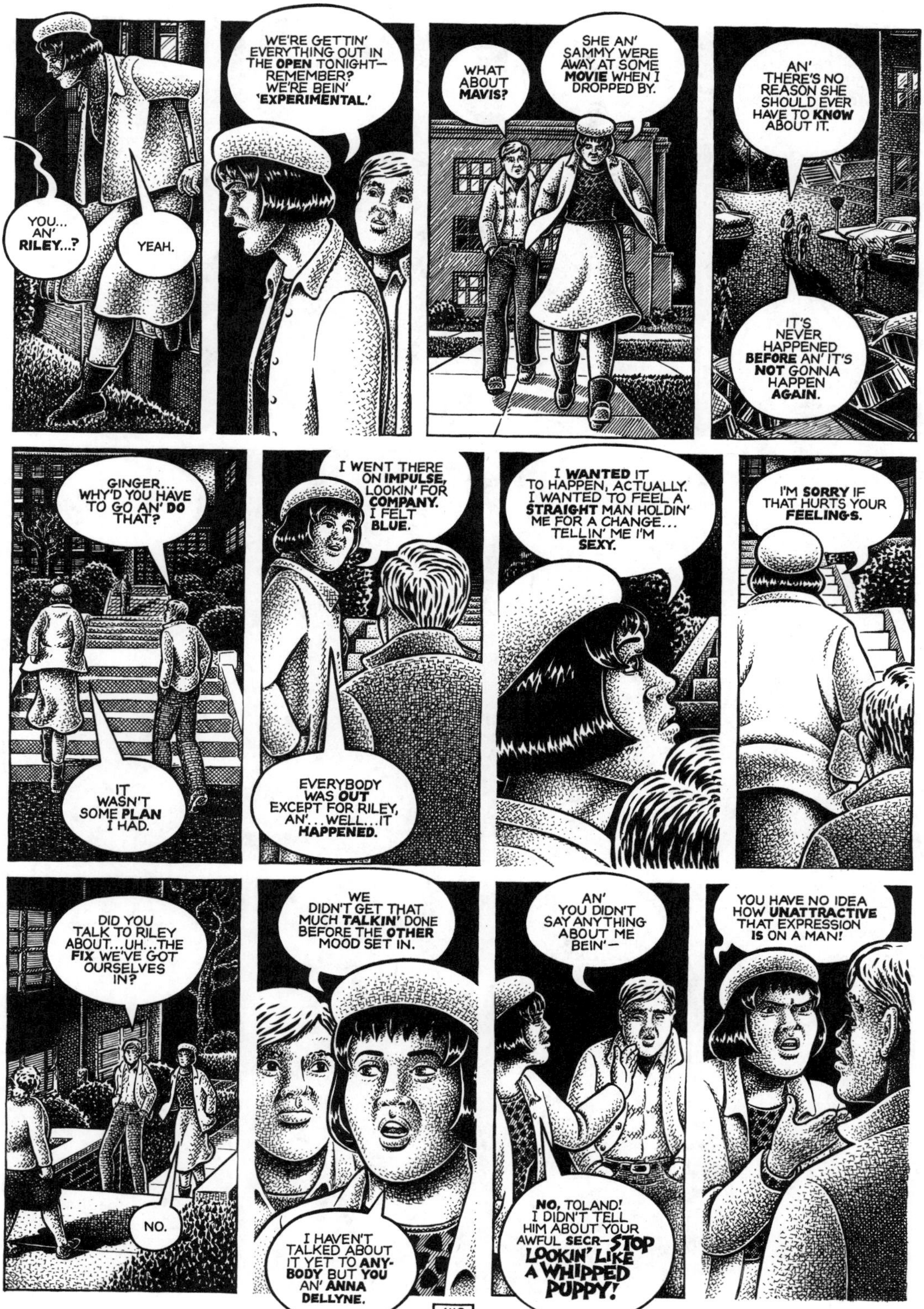

YOU... AN' RILEY...?
YEAH.
WE'RE GETTIN' EVERYTHING OUT IN THE OPEN TONIGHT— REMEMBER? WE'RE BEIN' 'EXPERIMENTAL.'
WHAT ABOUT MAVIS?
SHE AN' SAMMY WERE AWAY AT SOME MOVIE WHEN I DROPPED BY.
AN' THERE'S NO REASON SHE SHOULD EVER HAVE TO KNOW ABOUT IT.
IT'S NEVER HAPPENED BEFORE AN' IT'S NOT GONNA HAPPEN AGAIN.
GINGER... WHY'D YOU HAVE TO GO AN' DO THAT?
IT WASN'T SOME PLAN I HAD.
I WENT THERE ON IMPULSE, LOOKIN' FOR COMPANY. I FELT BLUE.
EVERYBODY WAS OUT EXCEPT FOR RILEY, AN'...WELL...IT HAPPENED.
I WANTED IT TO HAPPEN, ACTUALLY. I WANTED TO FEEL A STRAIGHT MAN HOLDIN' ME FOR A CHANGE... TELLIN' ME I'M SEXY.
I'M SORRY IF THAT HURTS YOUR FEELINGS.
DID YOU TALK TO RILEY ABOUT...UH...THE FIX WE'VE GOT OURSELVES IN?
NO.
WE DIDN'T GET THAT MUCH TALKIN' DONE BEFORE THE OTHER MOOD SET IN.
I HAVEN'T TALKED ABOUT IT YET TO ANYBODY BUT YOU AN' ANNA DELLYNE.
AN' YOU DIDN'T SAY ANYTHING ABOUT ME BEIN'—
NO, TOLAND! I DIDN'T TELL HIM ABOUT YOUR AWFUL SECR— STOP LOOKIN' LIKE A WHIPPED PUPPY!
YOU HAVE NO IDEA HOW UNATTRACTIVE THAT EXPRESSION IS ON A MAN!

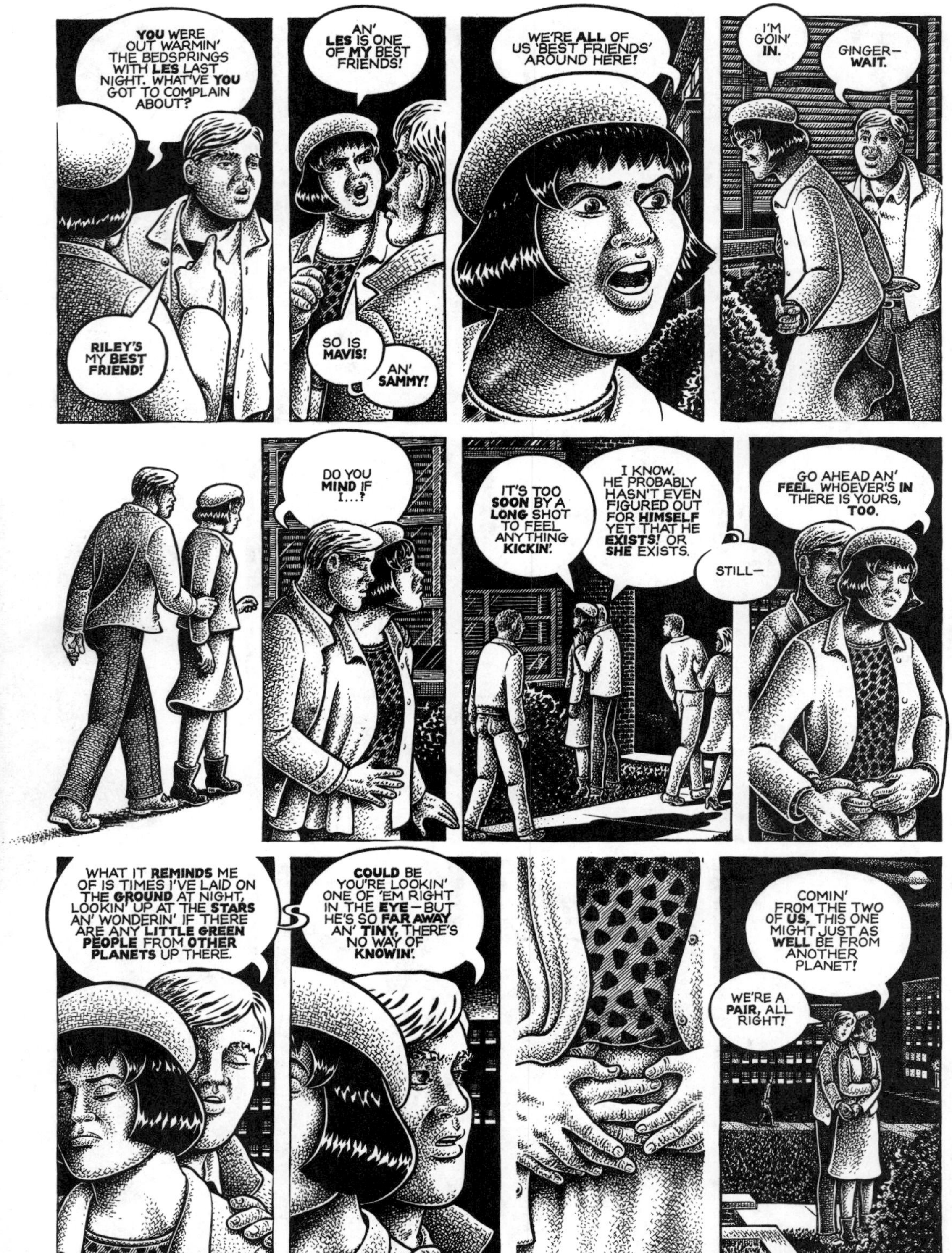
YOU WERE OUT WARMIN' THE BEDSPRINGS WITH LES LAST NIGHT. WHAT'VE YOU GOT TO COMPLAIN ABOUT?
RILEY'S MY BEST FRIEND!
AN' LES IS ONE OF MY BEST FRIENDS!
SO IS MAVIS!
AN' SAMMY!
WE'RE ALL OF US 'BEST FRIENDS' AROUND HERE!
I'M GOIN' IN.
GINGER— WAIT.
DO YOU MIND IF I...?
IT'S TOO SOON BY A LONG SHOT TO FEEL ANYTHING KICKIN'.
I KNOW. HE PROBABLY HASN'T EVEN FIGURED OUT FOR HIMSELF YET THAT HE EXISTS! OR SHE EXISTS.
STILL—
GO AHEAD AN' FEEL. WHOEVER'S IN THERE IS YOURS, TOO.
WHAT IT REMINDS ME OF IS TIMES I'VE LAID ON THE GROUND AT NIGHT, LOOKIN' UP AT THE STARS AN' WONDERIN' IF THERE ARE ANY LITTLE GREEN PEOPLE FROM OTHER PLANETS UP THERE.
COULD BE YOU'RE LOOKIN' ONE OF 'EM RIGHT IN THE EYE—BUT HE'S SO FAR AWAY AN' TINY, THERE'S NO WAY OF KNOWIN'.
COMIN' FROM THE TWO OF US, THIS ONE MIGHT JUST AS WELL BE FROM ANOTHER PLANET!
WE'RE A PAIR, ALL RIGHT!

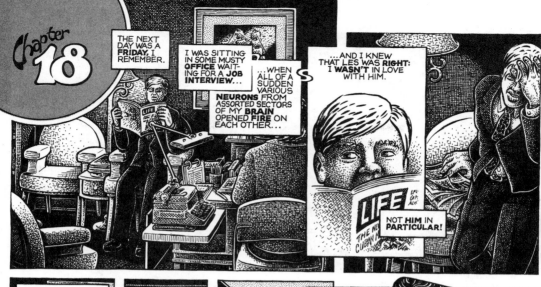

Chapter **18**

THE NEXT DAY WAS A **FRIDAY,** I REMEMBER.

I WAS SITTING IN SOME MUSTY **OFFICE** WAITING FOR A **JOB INTERVIEW...**

...WHEN ALL OF A SUDDEN VARIOUS **NEURONS** FROM ASSORTED SECTORS OF MY **BRAIN** OPENED **FIRE** ON EACH OTHER...

...AND I KNEW THAT LES WAS **RIGHT:** I **WASN'T** IN LOVE WITH HIM.

LIFE

NOT **HIM** IN **PARTICULAR!**

SOME **EMOTIONS** I DIDN'T **UNDERSTAND** TOOK HOLD OF ME...

MR. POLK...?

...AND I **BOLTED** OUT THE **DOOR.**

THE **MAGAZINE** I'D BEEN LEAFING THROUGH HAD HAD A PHOTOGRAPH OF **SAL MINEO** IN IT.

WHICH REMINDED ME OF THE NIGHT I'D GONE TO SEE **'REBEL WITHOUT A CAUSE'** A FEW YEARS BACK...

...AND COME HOME UNABLE TO THINK ABOUT **ANYTHING** EXCEPT WANTING TO HOLD JAMES DEAN'S DARK-EYED FRIEND IN MY **ARMS** AND **COMFORT** HIM.

IT COULDN'T BE **'LOVE'** I FELT, COULD IT? NOT FOR A **MOVIE ACTOR** I WAS NEVER GONNA BE WITHIN A **THOUSAND MILES** OF...AND NOT WITH **LES PEPPER,** EITHER!

'LOVE' HAD TO BE SOMETHING **ELSE!**

SOMETHING YOU COULD FIT INTO **SONG LYRICS** AND **DANCE** TO!

WHAT I WAS FEELING WAS A YEARNING **ACHE** THAT HAD TO DO WITH **MORE** THAN SOME **ONE GUY** I'D HAD MY ARMS AROUND IN A **MOTEL.**

I SAT ON MY **CAR FENDER** AND WATCHED THE RUSH HOUR **TRAFFIC** BUILD.

A PERSON COULD **HOP** RIGHT OUT INTO THE **MIDDLE** OF IT IF HE WANTED TO.

ONE WELL-TIMED **CARTWHEEL** AND IT'D BE **HELLO-O-O, OBLIVION!**

I WASN'T LOOKING **FORWARD** TO DRIVING BACK TO THE **WHEELERY.**

NOTHING THERE WAS THE WAY IT **USED** TO BE ANYMORE.

SINCE **WEDNESDAY**, RILEY AND I HAD BEEN **DODGING** EACH OTHER'S **GLANCES** WHEN WE PASSED.

AND THERE WERE **OTHER** TENSIONS BUILDING AS **WELL**...

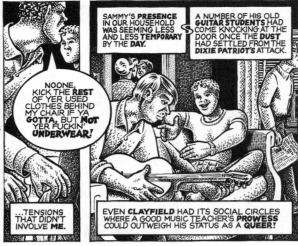

NOONE, KICK THE **REST** OF YER USED CLOTHES BEHIND MY CHAIR IF YA **GOTTA**, BUT **NOT** YER FUCKIN' **UNDERWEAR!**

...TENSIONS THAT DIDN'T INVOLVE **ME**.

SAMMY'S **PRESENCE** IN OUR HOUSEHOLD WAS SEEMING LESS AND LESS **TEMPORARY** BY THE **DAY**.

A NUMBER OF HIS OLD **GUITAR STUDENTS** HAD COME KNOCKING AT THE DOOR ONCE THE **DUST** HAD SETTLED FROM THE **DIXIE PATRIOT'S** ATTACK.

EVEN **CLAYFIELD** HAD ITS SOCIAL CIRCLES WHERE A GOOD MUSIC TEACHER'S **PROWESS** COULD OUTWEIGH HIS STATUS AS A **QUEER!**

BEFORE **LONG**, SAMMY WAS FANTASIZING ABOUT SAVING UP FOR AN **ORGAN** TO PUT IN THE CORNER.

IT'S MY AREA OF GREATEST **EXPERTISE.**

I COULD **DOUBLE** MY **STUDENT LOAD** IN A **MONTH.**

AREN'T **ORGANS EXPENSIVE**, SAMMY...?

THE **EDGE** THAT WOULD CREEP INTO RILEY'S VOICE WHEN SAMMY TALKED LIKE THAT **SCARED** ME.

I GET **MORE'N** ENOUGH **ORGAN NOISE** TO SUIT ME WALKIN' PAST THE **METHODIST CHURCH** ON SUNDAYS.

Chuckle!

OR MAYBE I WAS JUST SPOOKED BY THE WAY **EVERYTHING** THAT HAD SEEMED **STABLE** IN MY LIFE WAS COMING **UNHINGED** ALL AT **ONCE.**

SOME **VOICE** FROM A CORNER OF MY BRAIN WAS **REMINDING** ME THAT THE WHEELERY WASN'T LIKELY TO **KEEP ON** BEING **HOME** FOR ME **FOREVER.**

ON **SATURDAY** GINGER BIT THE **BULLET** AND TELEPHONED HER **PARENTS** IN **OHIO** TO TELL THEM SHE WAS **PREGNANT.**

SHE USED THE **PAY PHONE** IN A **LAUNDROMAT** SEVERAL MILES FROM THE COLLEGE, NOT WANTING ANY **DORMMATES** TO WANDER BY UNEXPECTEDLY.

SHE ASKED ME TO STAY **NEXT** TO HER FOR **MORAL SUPPORT.**

FROM WHAT I COULD TELL OF THE CONVERSATION'S **DRIFT**, THEY WEREN'T GIVING HER A TIME AS **HARD** AS YOU MIGHT HAVE **EXPECTED.**

Ker chunk!
Ker chunk!
Ker chunk!

DAD WANTS TO **SPEAK** TO YOU.

ME?! YOU **TOLD** HIM I WAS **HERE?!**

HE **GUESSED.**

H'LO, MR. RAINES. UH...

HELLO, TOLAND. IT'S GOOD TO **TALK** TO YOU AT **LAST.** GINGER'S TOLD US A LOT **ABOUT** YOU, SON, AND YOU'VE ALWAYS SOUNDED LIKE A **RESPONSIBLE** KIND OF FELLOW WHO'D WANT TO DO THE **RIGHT** THING. . . .

Ker-chunk!
Ker chunk!!

CONSIDERING THE **CIRCUMSTANCES**, I GIVE THE OL' GUY CREDIT FOR **FORBEARANCE** ABOVE AND BEYOND THE CALL OF **DUTY!**

YESSIR.

YESSIR.

THAT SOUNDS GOOD TO **ME**, SIR.

HE SAID THAT HE AND GINGER'S MOTHER WOULD MAKE A **TRIP SOUTH** VERY SHORTLY SO THAT WE COULD ALL **STRATEGIZE** TOGETHER ABOUT WHAT TO DO **NEXT.**

THEN ON MONDAY, AS IF THINGS HADN'T BEEN STIRRED UP ENOUGH YET, MY SISTER HAD HER BRAINSTORM.
MELANIE! ORLEY! WHAT A NICE SURPRISE!
WE'RE A SURPRISE?
DIDN'T MY BROTHER TELL YOU TO EXPECT US?
UH... NO.
Sigh! TYPICAL!
I TALKED TO HIM EARLIER TODAY AN' SAID WE'D BE COMIN' OVER TONIGHT WITH SOMETHIN' IMPORTANT TO DISCUSS.
I TOLD HIM TO PRY HIS GIRLFRIEND AWAY FROM HER BOOKS AN' GET HER OVER HERE, TOO. I NEED TO TALK TO BOTH OF 'EM.
WELL, COME ON INSIDE. THEY'RE NOT HERE YET, BUT CHANCES ARE THEY'RE ON THEIR WAY.
YOU CAN KEEP ME COMPANY WHILE I FINISH DRYIN' SOME DISHES.
RILEY! SAMMY! SAY HELLO TO MELANIE AN' ORLEY.
HI, ORLEY.
HI, MELANIE.
DON'T EXPECT THOSE TWO TO SHOW ANY MANNERS! THEY'RE TOO WRAPPED UP IN THEIR CHESS GAME!
WHAT'S THE CHURCH-MUSIC GUY DOIN' HERE?
SAMMY'S BEEN LIVIN' HERE AT THE WHEELERY SINCE THAT DIXIE PATRIOT STORY LOST HIM HIS JOB.
ORLEY, DON'T GET US SIDETRACKED ONTO SAMMY NOONE.
I WANNA HEAR WHAT MAVIS THINKS OF OUR PLAN.
Y'SEE, MAVIS, ORLEY AN' I HAVE BEEN WRACKIN' OUR BRAINS FOR DAYS, TRYIN' TO THINK WHAT TOLAND AN' GINGER CAN DO ABOUT THE BABY, AN'—
ABOUT THE...
THE BABY??
!
YOU DIDN'T KNOW...?

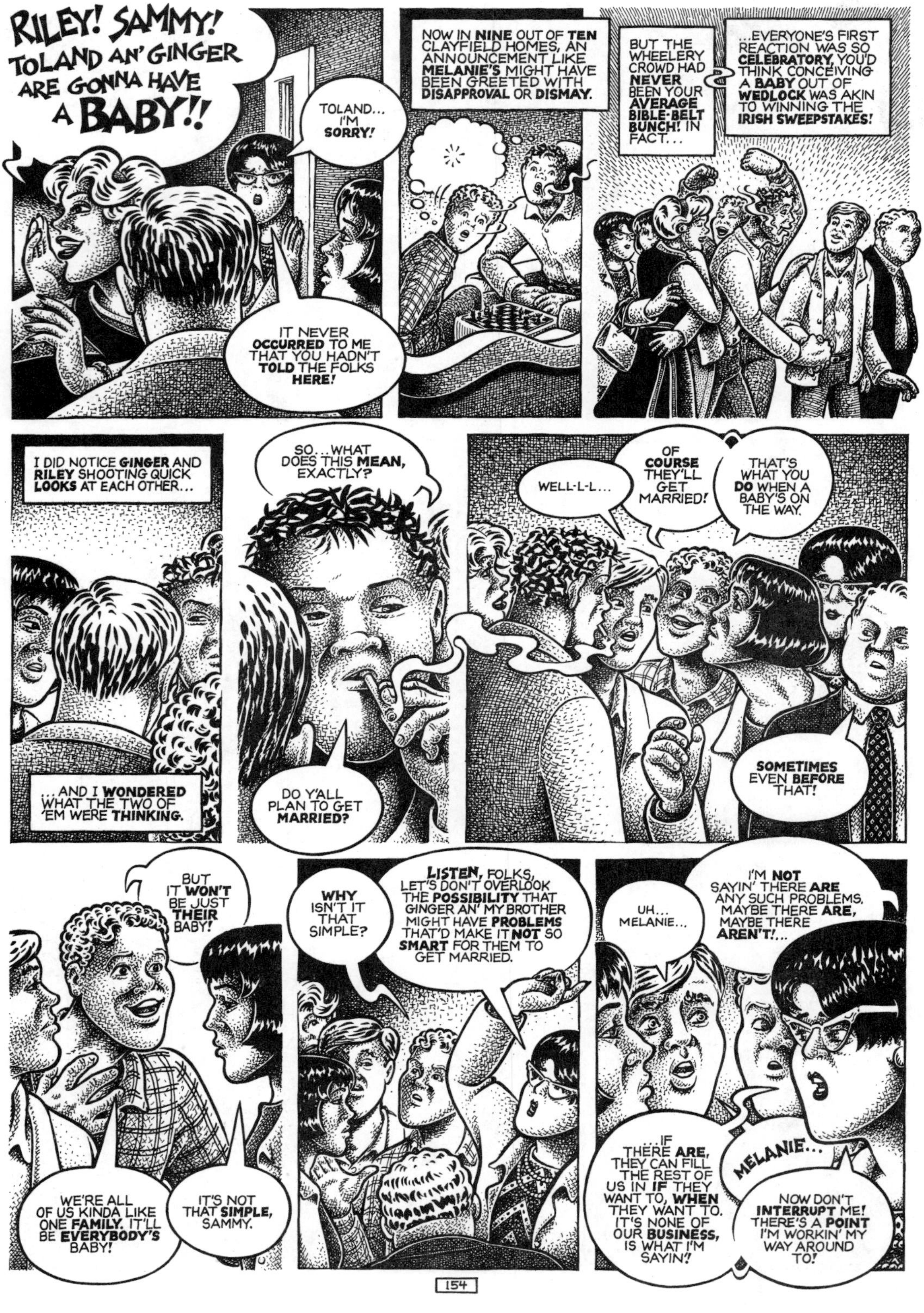
RILEY! SAMMY! TOLAND AN' GINGER ARE GONNA HAVE A BABY!!
TOLAND... I'M SORRY!
IT NEVER OCCURRED TO ME THAT YOU HADN'T TOLD THE FOLKS HERE!
NOW IN NINE OUT OF TEN CLAYFIELD HOMES, AN ANNOUNCEMENT LIKE MELANIE'S MIGHT HAVE BEEN GREETED WITH DISAPPROVAL OR DISMAY.
BUT THE WHEELERY CROWD HAD NEVER BEEN YOUR AVERAGE BIBLE-BELT BUNCH! IN FACT...
...EVERYONE'S FIRST REACTION WAS SO CELEBRATORY, YOU'D THINK CONCEIVING A BABY OUT OF WEDLOCK WAS AKIN TO WINNING THE IRISH SWEEPSTAKES!
I DID NOTICE GINGER AND RILEY SHOOTING QUICK LOOKS AT EACH OTHER...
...AND I WONDERED WHAT THE TWO OF 'EM WERE THINKING.
SO...WHAT DOES THIS MEAN, EXACTLY?
DO Y'ALL PLAN TO GET MARRIED?
WELL-L-L...
OF COURSE THEY'LL GET MARRIED!
THAT'S WHAT YOU DO WHEN A BABY'S ON THE WAY.
SOMETIMES EVEN BEFORE THAT!
BUT IT WON'T BE JUST THEIR BABY!
WE'RE ALL OF US KINDA LIKE ONE FAMILY. IT'LL BE EVERYBODY'S BABY!
IT'S NOT THAT SIMPLE, SAMMY.
WHY ISN'T IT THAT SIMPLE?
LISTEN, FOLKS, LET'S DON'T OVERLOOK THE POSSIBILITY THAT GINGER AN' MY BROTHER MIGHT HAVE PROBLEMS THAT'D MAKE IT NOT SO SMART FOR THEM TO GET MARRIED.
UH... MELANIE...
I'M NOT SAYIN' THERE ARE ANY SUCH PROBLEMS. MAYBE THERE ARE, MAYBE THERE AREN'T!...
...IF THERE ARE, THEY CAN FILL THE REST OF US IN IF THEY WANT TO, WHEN THEY WANT TO. IT'S NONE OF OUR BUSINESS, IS WHAT I'M SAYIN'!
MELANIE...
NOW DON'T INTERRUPT ME! THERE'S A POINT I'M WORKIN' MY WAY AROUND TO!

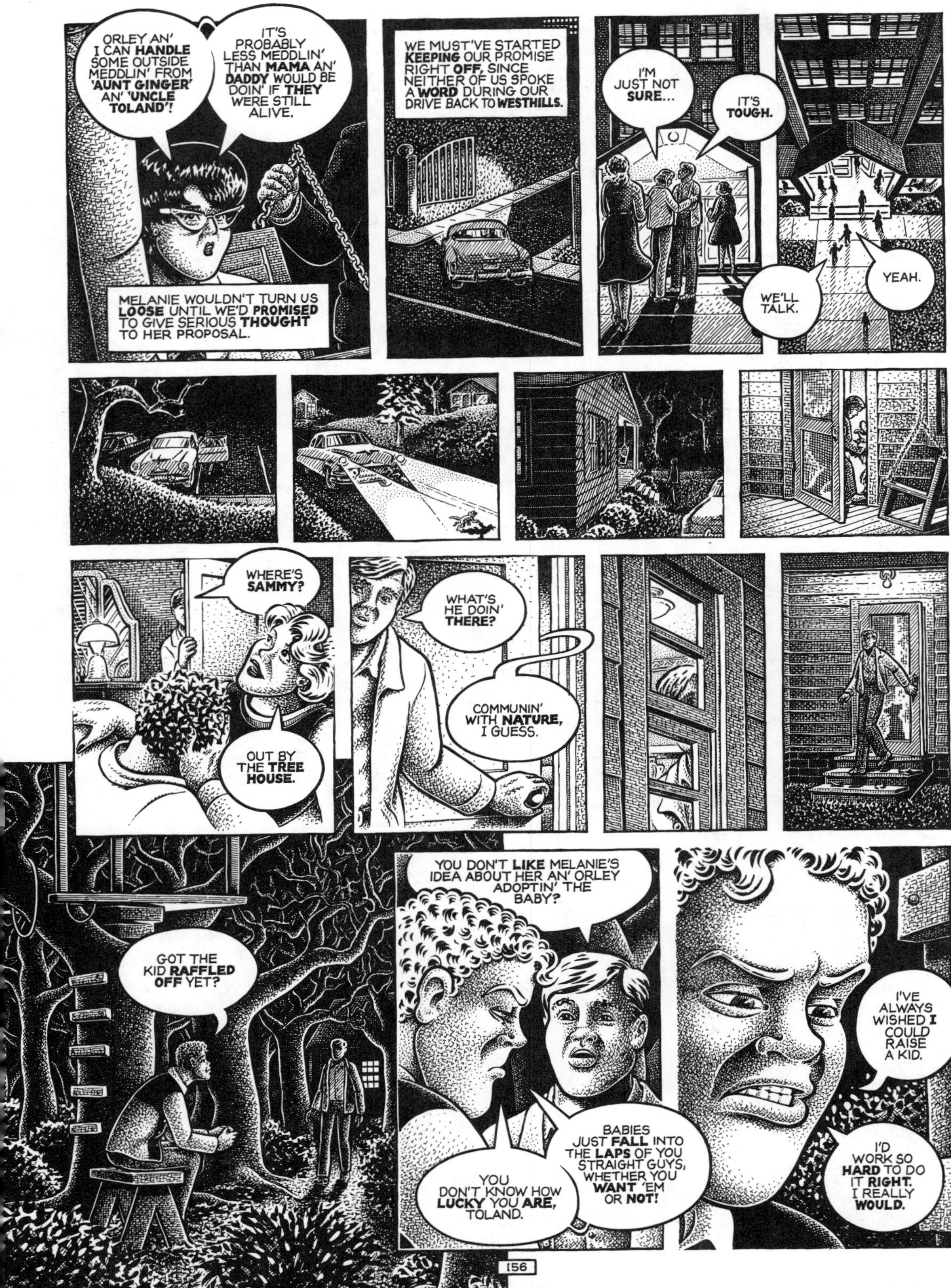
ORLEY AN' I CAN HANDLE SOME OUTSIDE MEDDLIN' FROM 'AUNT GINGER' AN' 'UNCLE TOLAND'!
IT'S PROBABLY LESS MEDDLIN' THAN MAMA AN' DADDY WOULD BE DOIN' IF THEY WERE STILL ALIVE.
MELANIE WOULDN'T TURN US LOOSE UNTIL WE'D PROMISED TO GIVE SERIOUS THOUGHT TO HER PROPOSAL.
WE MUST'VE STARTED KEEPING OUR PROMISE RIGHT OFF, SINCE NEITHER OF US SPOKE A WORD DURING OUR DRIVE BACK TO WESTHILLS.
I'M JUST NOT SURE...
IT'S TOUGH.
WE'LL TALK.
YEAH.
WHERE'S SAMMY?
OUT BY THE TREE HOUSE.
WHAT'S HE DOIN' THERE?
COMMUNIN' WITH NATURE, I GUESS.
GOT THE KID RAFFLED OFF YET?
YOU DON'T LIKE MELANIE'S IDEA ABOUT HER AN' ORLEY ADOPTIN' THE BABY?
YOU DON'T KNOW HOW LUCKY YOU ARE, TOLAND.
BABIES JUST FALL INTO THE LAPS OF YOU STRAIGHT GUYS, WHETHER YOU WANT 'EM OR NOT!
I'VE ALWAYS WISHED I COULD RAISE A KID.
I'D WORK SO HARD TO DO IT RIGHT. I REALLY WOULD.

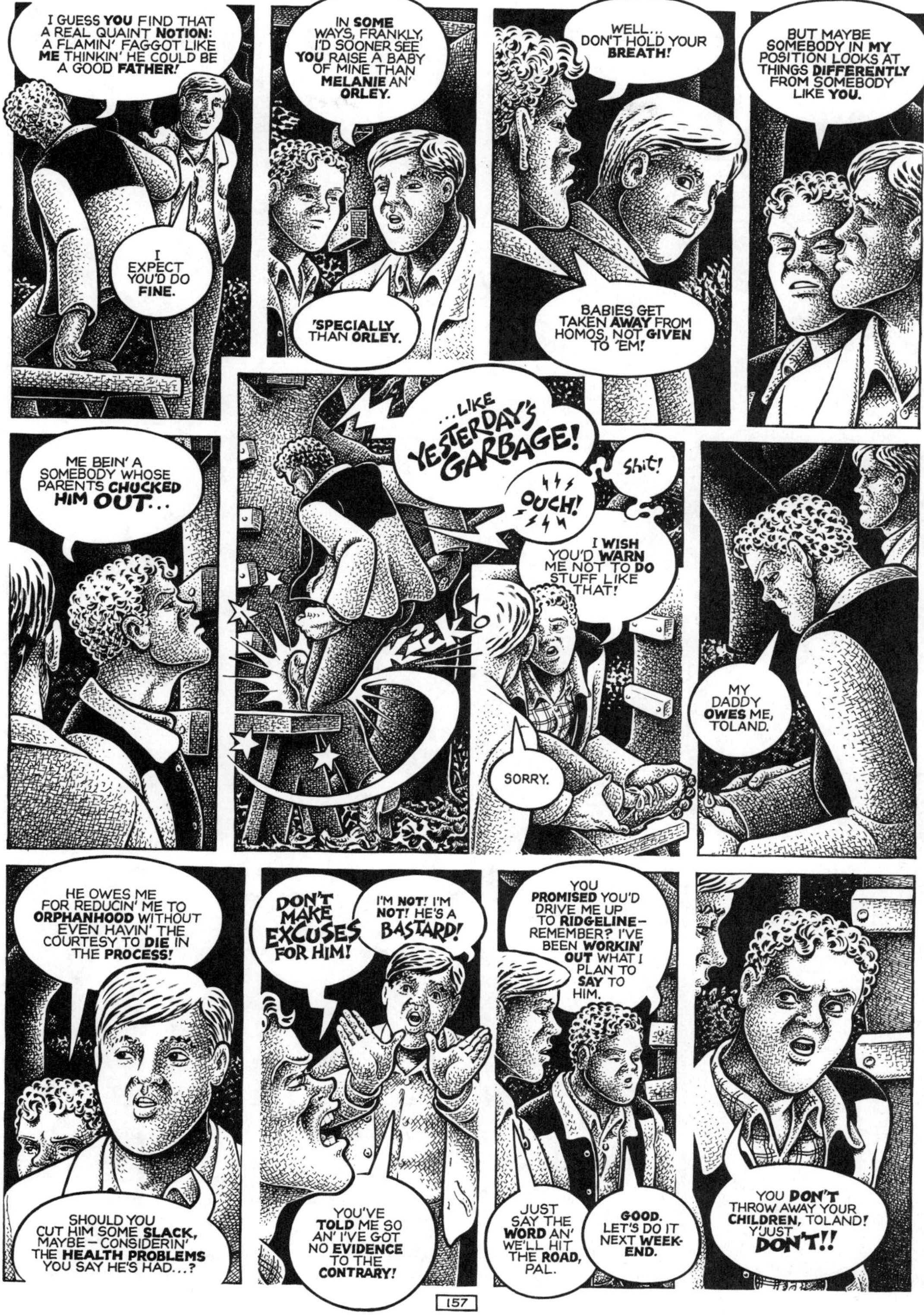
I GUESS YOU FIND THAT A REAL QUAINT NOTION: A FLAMIN' FAGGOT LIKE ME THINKIN' HE COULD BE A GOOD FATHER!
I EXPECT YOU'D DO FINE.
IN SOME WAYS, FRANKLY, I'D SOONER SEE YOU RAISE A BABY OF MINE THAN MELANIE AN' ORLEY.
'SPECIALLY THAN ORLEY.
WELL... DON'T HOLD YOUR BREATH!
BABIES GET TAKEN AWAY FROM HOMOS, NOT GIVEN TO 'EM!
BUT MAYBE SOMEBODY IN MY POSITION LOOKS AT THINGS DIFFERENTLY FROM SOMEBODY LIKE YOU.
ME BEIN' A SOMEBODY WHOSE PARENTS CHUCKED HIM OUT...
...LIKE YESTERDAY'S GARBAGE!
KICK!
OUCH!
Shit!
I WISH YOU'D WARN ME NOT TO DO STUFF LIKE THAT!
SORRY.
MY DADDY OWES ME, TOLAND.
HE OWES ME FOR REDUCIN' ME TO ORPHANHOOD WITHOUT EVEN HAVIN' THE COURTESY TO DIE IN THE PROCESS!
SHOULD YOU CUT HIM SOME SLACK, MAYBE—CONSIDERIN' THE HEALTH PROBLEMS YOU SAY HE'S HAD...?
DON'T MAKE EXCUSES FOR HIM!
I'M NOT! I'M NOT! HE'S A BASTARD!
YOU'VE TOLD ME SO AN' I'VE GOT NO EVIDENCE TO THE CONTRARY!
YOU PROMISED YOU'D DRIVE ME UP TO RIDGELINE—REMEMBER? I'VE BEEN WORKIN' OUT WHAT I PLAN TO SAY TO HIM.
JUST SAY THE WORD AN' WE'LL HIT THE ROAD, PAL.
GOOD. LET'S DO IT NEXT WEEK-END.
YOU DON'T THROW AWAY YOUR CHILDREN, TOLAND! Y'JUST DON'T!!

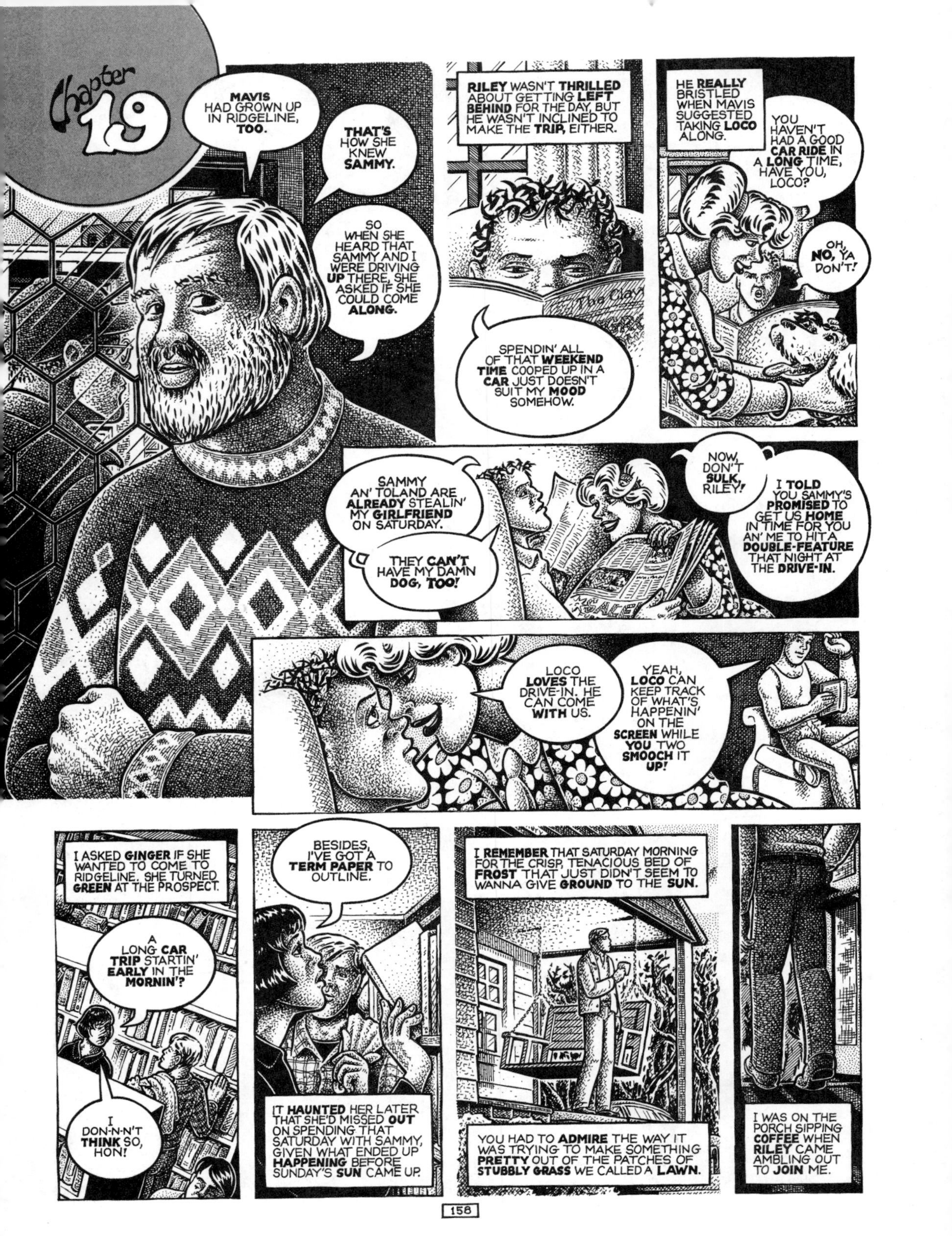
Chapter 19
MAVIS HAD GROWN UP IN RIDGELINE, TOO.
THAT'S HOW SHE KNEW SAMMY.
SO WHEN SHE HEARD THAT SAMMY AND I WERE DRIVING UP THERE, SHE ASKED IF SHE COULD COME ALONG.
RILEY WASN'T THRILLED ABOUT GETTING LEFT BEHIND FOR THE DAY, BUT HE WASN'T INCLINED TO MAKE THE TRIP, EITHER.
SPENDIN' ALL OF THAT WEEKEND TIME COOPED UP IN A CAR JUST DOESN'T SUIT MY MOOD SOMEHOW.
HE REALLY BRISTLED WHEN MAVIS SUGGESTED TAKING LOCO ALONG.
YOU HAVEN'T HAD A GOOD CAR RIDE IN A LONG TIME, HAVE YOU, LOCO?
OH, NO, YA DON'T!
SAMMY AN' TOLAND ARE ALREADY STEALIN' MY GIRLFRIEND ON SATURDAY.
THEY CAN'T HAVE MY DAMN DOG, TOO!
NOW, DON'T SULK, RILEY!
I TOLD YOU SAMMY'S PROMISED TO GET US HOME IN TIME FOR YOU AN' ME TO HIT A DOUBLE-FEATURE THAT NIGHT AT THE DRIVE-IN.
LOCO LOVES THE DRIVE-IN. HE CAN COME WITH US.
YEAH, LOCO CAN KEEP TRACK OF WHAT'S HAPPENIN' ON THE SCREEN WHILE YOU TWO SMOOCH IT UP!
I ASKED GINGER IF SHE WANTED TO COME TO RIDGELINE. SHE TURNED GREEN AT THE PROSPECT.
A LONG CAR TRIP STARTIN' EARLY IN THE MORNIN'?
I DON-N-N'T THINK SO, HON!
BESIDES, I'VE GOT A TERM PAPER TO OUTLINE.
IT HAUNTED HER LATER THAT SHE'D MISSED OUT ON SPENDING THAT SATURDAY WITH SAMMY, GIVEN WHAT ENDED UP HAPPENING BEFORE SUNDAY'S SUN CAME UP.
I REMEMBER THAT SATURDAY MORNING FOR THE CRISP, TENACIOUS BED OF FROST THAT JUST DIDN'T SEEM TO WANNA GIVE GROUND TO THE SUN.
YOU HAD TO ADMIRE THE WAY IT WAS TRYING TO MAKE SOMETHING PRETTY OUT OF THE PATCHES OF STUBBLY GRASS WE CALLED A LAWN.
I WAS ON THE PORCH SIPPING COFFEE WHEN RILEY CAME AMBLING OUT TO JOIN ME.

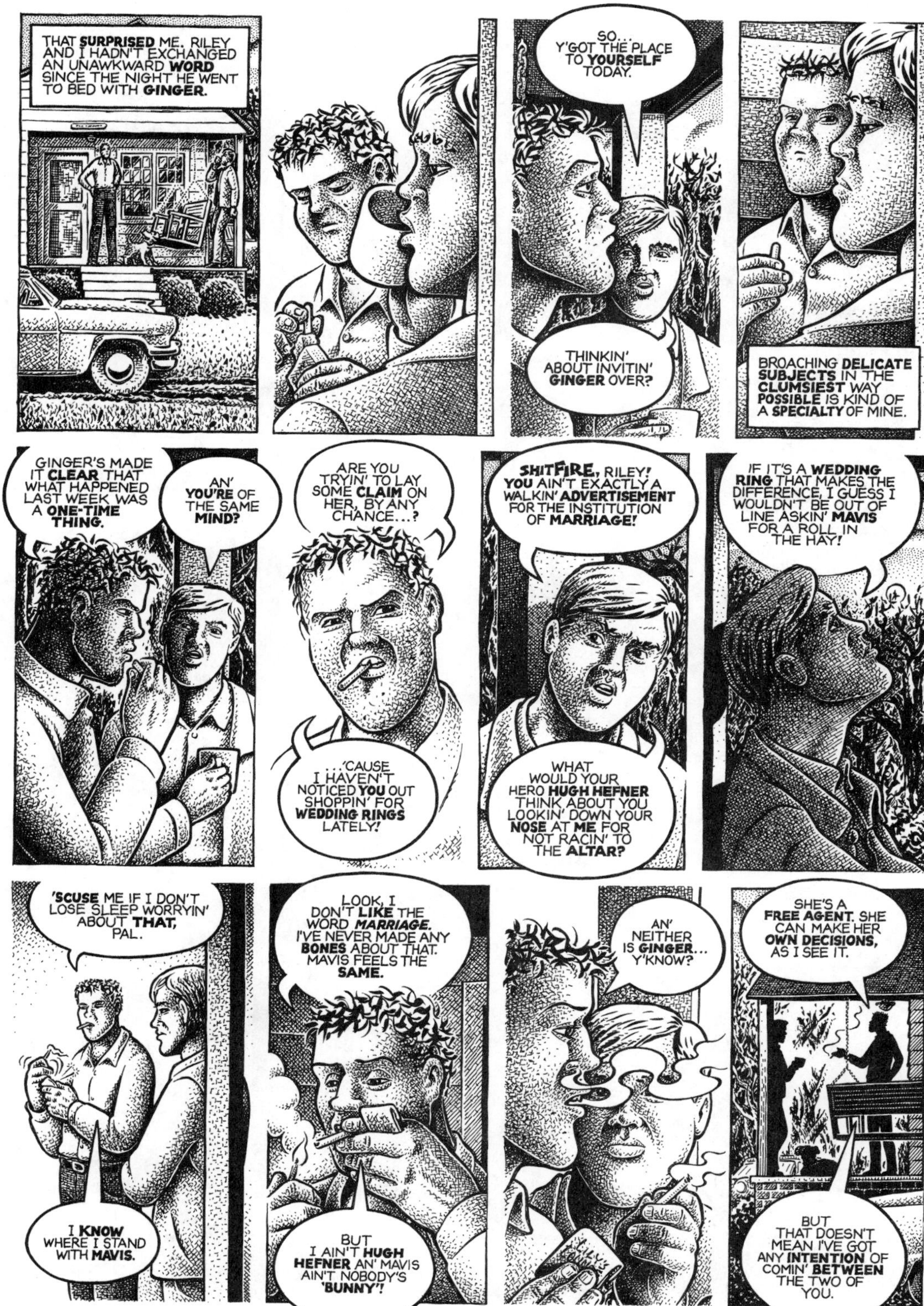
THAT SURPRISED ME. RILEY AND I HADN'T EXCHANGED AN UNAWKWARD WORD SINCE THE NIGHT HE WENT TO BED WITH GINGER.
SO... Y'GOT THE PLACE TO YOURSELF TODAY.
THINKIN' ABOUT INVITIN' GINGER OVER?
BROACHING DELICATE SUBJECTS IN THE CLUMSIEST WAY POSSIBLE IS KIND OF A SPECIALTY OF MINE.
GINGER'S MADE IT CLEAR THAT WHAT HAPPENED LAST WEEK WAS A ONE-TIME THING.
AN' YOU'RE OF THE SAME MIND?
ARE YOU TRYIN' TO LAY SOME CLAIM ON HER, BY ANY CHANCE...?
...'CAUSE I HAVEN'T NOTICED YOU OUT SHOPPIN' FOR WEDDING RINGS LATELY!
SHITFIRE, RILEY! YOU AIN'T EXACTLY A WALKIN' ADVERTISEMENT FOR THE INSTITUTION OF MARRIAGE!
WHAT WOULD YOUR HERO HUGH HEFNER THINK ABOUT YOU LOOKIN' DOWN YOUR NOSE AT ME FOR NOT RACIN' TO THE ALTAR?
IF IT'S A WEDDING RING THAT MAKES THE DIFFERENCE, I GUESS I WOULDN'T BE OUT OF LINE ASKIN' MAVIS FOR A ROLL IN THE HAY!
'SCUSE ME IF I DON'T LOSE SLEEP WORRYIN' ABOUT THAT, PAL.
I KNOW WHERE I STAND WITH MAVIS.
LOOK, I DON'T LIKE THE WORD MARRIAGE. I'VE NEVER MADE ANY BONES ABOUT THAT. MAVIS FEELS THE SAME.
BUT I AIN'T HUGH HEFNER AN' MAVIS AIN'T NOBODY'S 'BUNNY'!
AN' NEITHER IS GINGER... Y'KNOW?
SHE'S A FREE AGENT. SHE CAN MAKE HER OWN DECISIONS, AS I SEE IT.
BUT THAT DOESN'T MEAN I'VE GOT ANY INTENTION OF COMIN' BETWEEN THE TWO OF YOU.

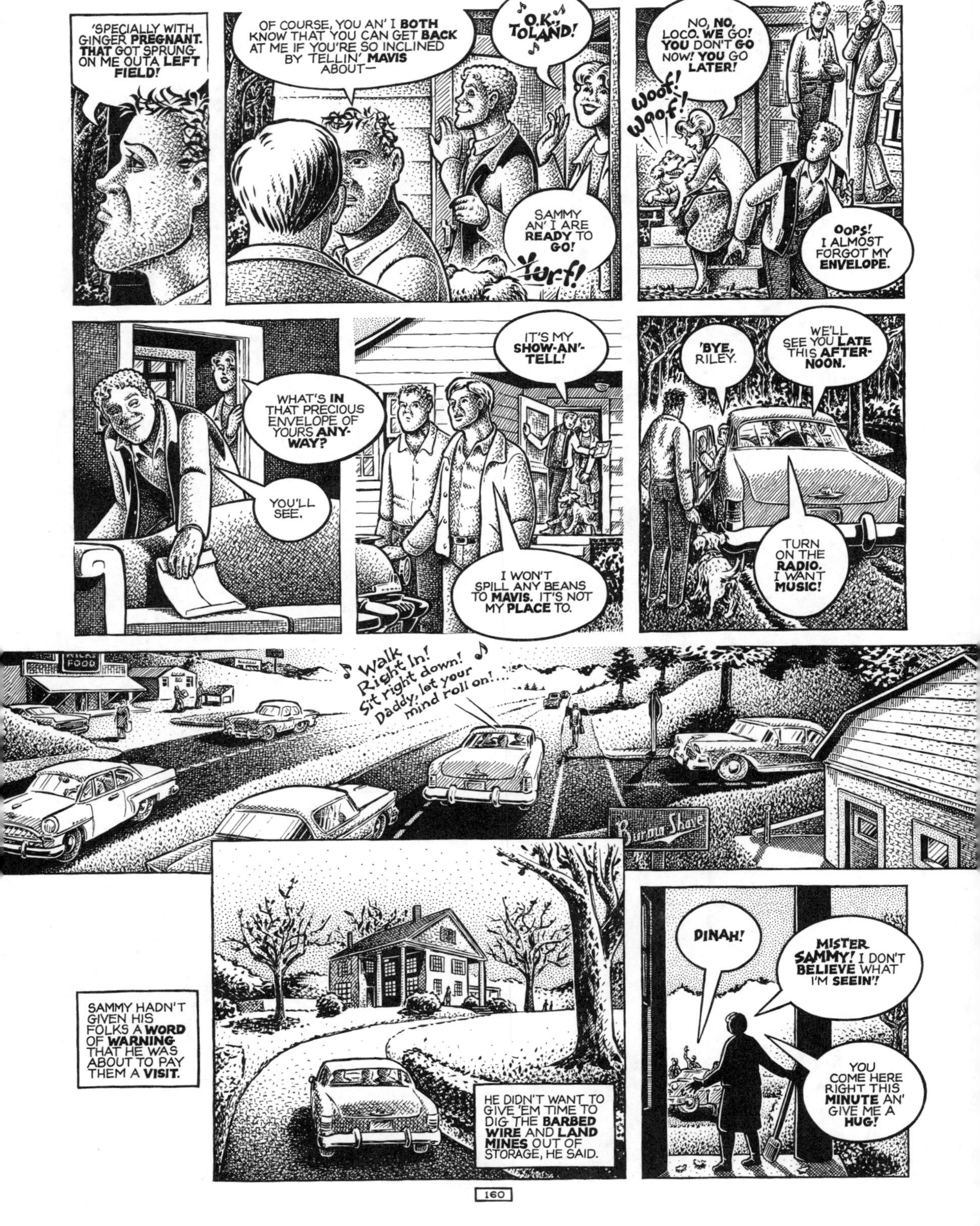

'SPECIALLY WITH GINGER PREGNANT. THAT GOT SPRUNG ON ME OUTA LEFT FIELD!
OF COURSE, YOU AN' I BOTH KNOW THAT YOU CAN GET BACK AT ME IF YOU'RE SO INCLINED BY TELLIN' MAVIS ABOUT—
O.K., TOLAND!
SAMMY AN' I ARE READY TO GO!
YURF!
NO, NO, LOCO. WE GO! YOU DON'T GO NOW! YOU GO LATER!
WOOF! WOOF!
OOPS! I ALMOST FORGOT MY ENVELOPE.
WHAT'S IN THAT PRECIOUS ENVELOPE OF YOURS ANYWAY?
YOU'LL SEE.
IT'S MY SHOW-AN'-TELL!
I WON'T SPILL ANY BEANS TO MAVIS. IT'S NOT MY PLACE TO.
'BYE, RILEY.
WE'LL SEE YOU LATE THIS AFTERNOON.
TURN ON THE RADIO. I WANT MUSIC!
FOOD
Walk Right In! Sit right down! Daddy, let your mind roll on!...
Burma Shave
SAMMY HADN'T GIVEN HIS FOLKS A WORD OF WARNING THAT HE WAS ABOUT TO PAY THEM A VISIT.
HE DIDN'T WANT TO GIVE 'EM TIME TO DIG THE BARBED WIRE AND LAND MINES OUT OF STORAGE, HE SAID.
DINAH!
MISTER SAMMY! I DON'T BELIEVE WHAT I'M SEEIN'!
YOU COME HERE RIGHT THIS MINUTE AN' GIVE ME A HUG!

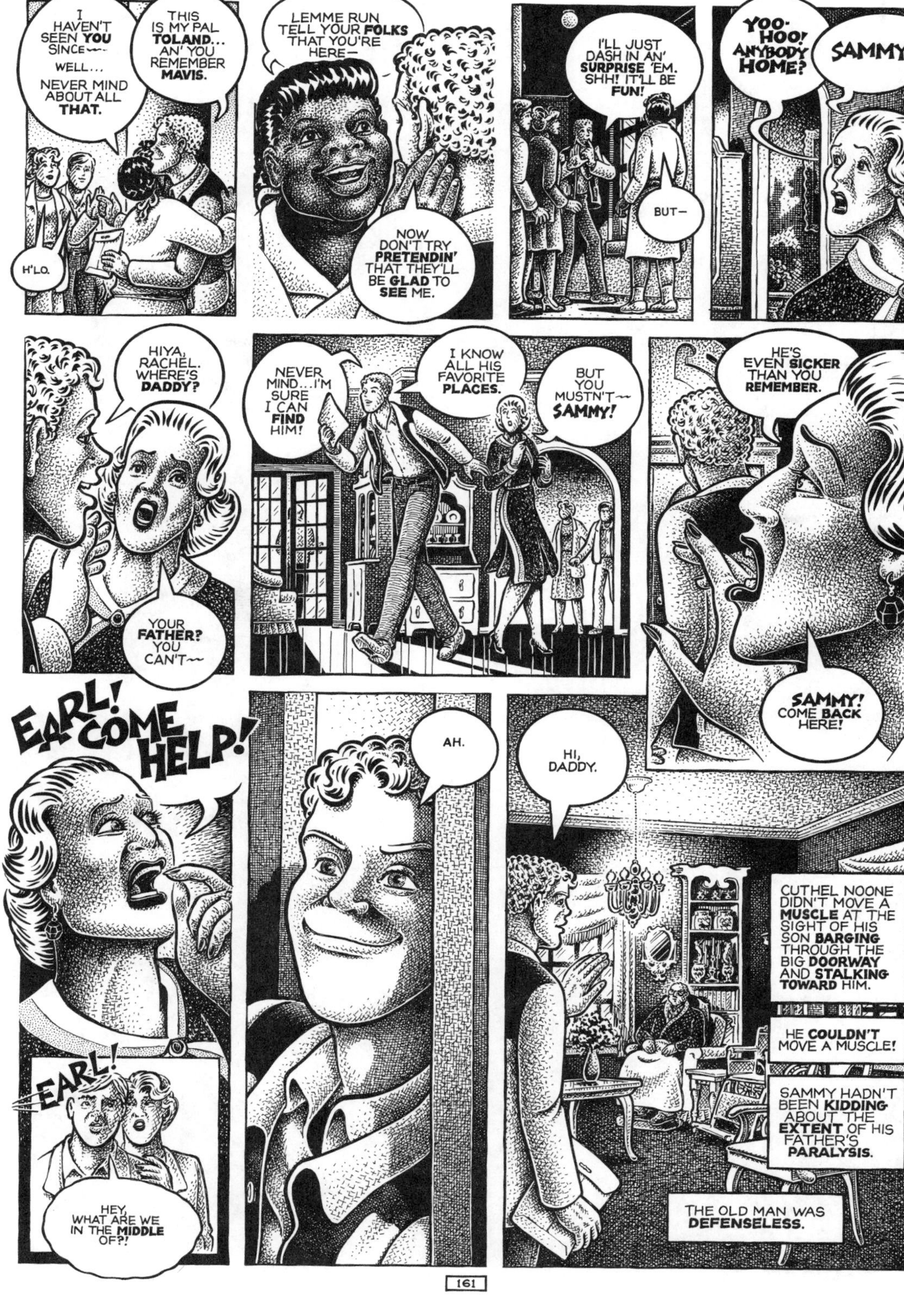

I HAVEN'T SEEN YOU SINCE~~ WELL... NEVER MIND ABOUT ALL THAT.
THIS IS MY PAL TOLAND... AN' YOU REMEMBER MAVIS.
H'LO.
LEMME RUN TELL YOUR FOLKS THAT YOU'RE HERE—
NOW DON'T TRY PRETENDIN' THAT THEY'LL BE GLAD TO SEE ME.
I'LL JUST DASH IN AN' SURPRISE 'EM. SHH! IT'LL BE FUN!
BUT—
YOO-HOO! ANYBODY HOME?
SAMMY?
HIYA, RACHEL. WHERE'S DADDY?
YOUR FATHER? YOU CAN'T~~
NEVER MIND... I'M SURE I CAN FIND HIM!
I KNOW ALL HIS FAVORITE PLACES.
BUT YOU MUSTN'T~~ SAMMY!
HE'S EVEN SICKER THAN YOU REMEMBER.
SAMMY! COME BACK HERE!
EARL! COME HELP!
EARL!
HEY, WHAT ARE WE IN THE MIDDLE OF?!
AH.
HI, DADDY.
CUTHEL NOONE DIDN'T MOVE A MUSCLE AT THE SIGHT OF HIS SON BARGING THROUGH THE BIG DOORWAY AND STALKING TOWARD HIM.
HE COULDN'T MOVE A MUSCLE!
SAMMY HADN'T BEEN KIDDING ABOUT THE EXTENT OF HIS FATHER'S PARALYSIS.
THE OLD MAN WAS DEFENSELESS.

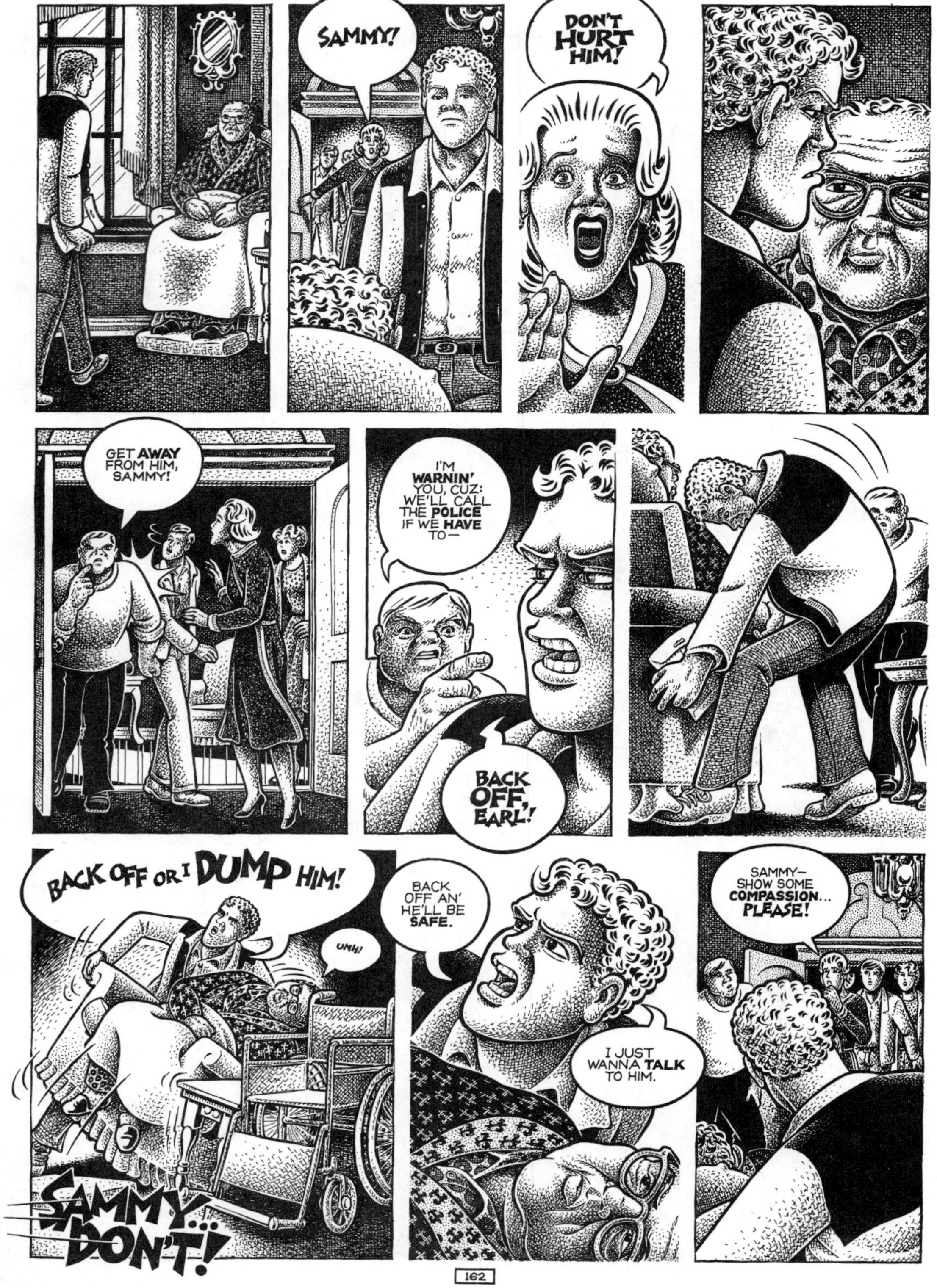
SAMMY!
DON'T HURT HIM!
GET AWAY FROM HIM, SAMMY!
I'M WARNIN' YOU, CUZ: WE'LL CALL THE POLICE IF WE HAVE TO—
BACK OFF, EARL!
BACK OFF OR I DUMP HIM!
UNH!
SAMMY... DON'T!
BACK OFF AN' HE'LL BE SAFE.
I JUST WANNA TALK TO HIM.
SAMMY— SHOW SOME COMPASSION... PLEASE!

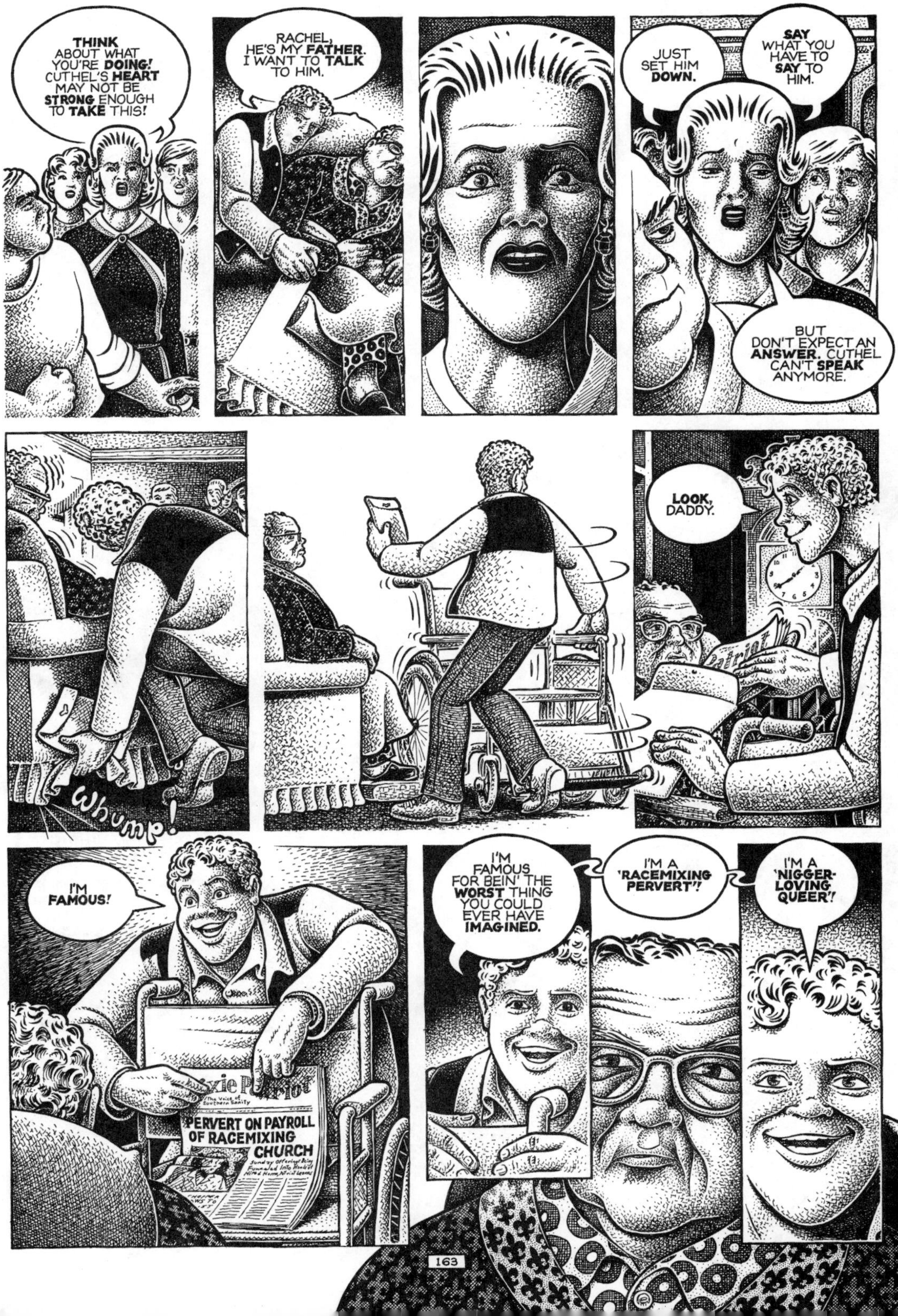
THINK ABOUT WHAT YOU'RE DOING! CUTHEL'S HEART MAY NOT BE STRONG ENOUGH TO TAKE THIS!
RACHEL, HE'S MY FATHER. I WANT TO TALK TO HIM.
JUST SET HIM DOWN.
SAY WHAT YOU HAVE TO SAY TO HIM.
BUT DON'T EXPECT AN ANSWER. CUTHEL CAN'T SPEAK ANYMORE.
Whump!
LOOK, DADDY.
Patriot
I'M FAMOUS!
The Voice of Southern Sanity
PERVERT ON PAYROLL OF RACEMIXING CHURCH
I'M FAMOUS FOR BEIN' THE WORST THING YOU COULD EVER HAVE IMAGINED.
I'M A 'RACEMIXING PERVERT'!
I'M A 'NIGGER-LOVING QUEER'!

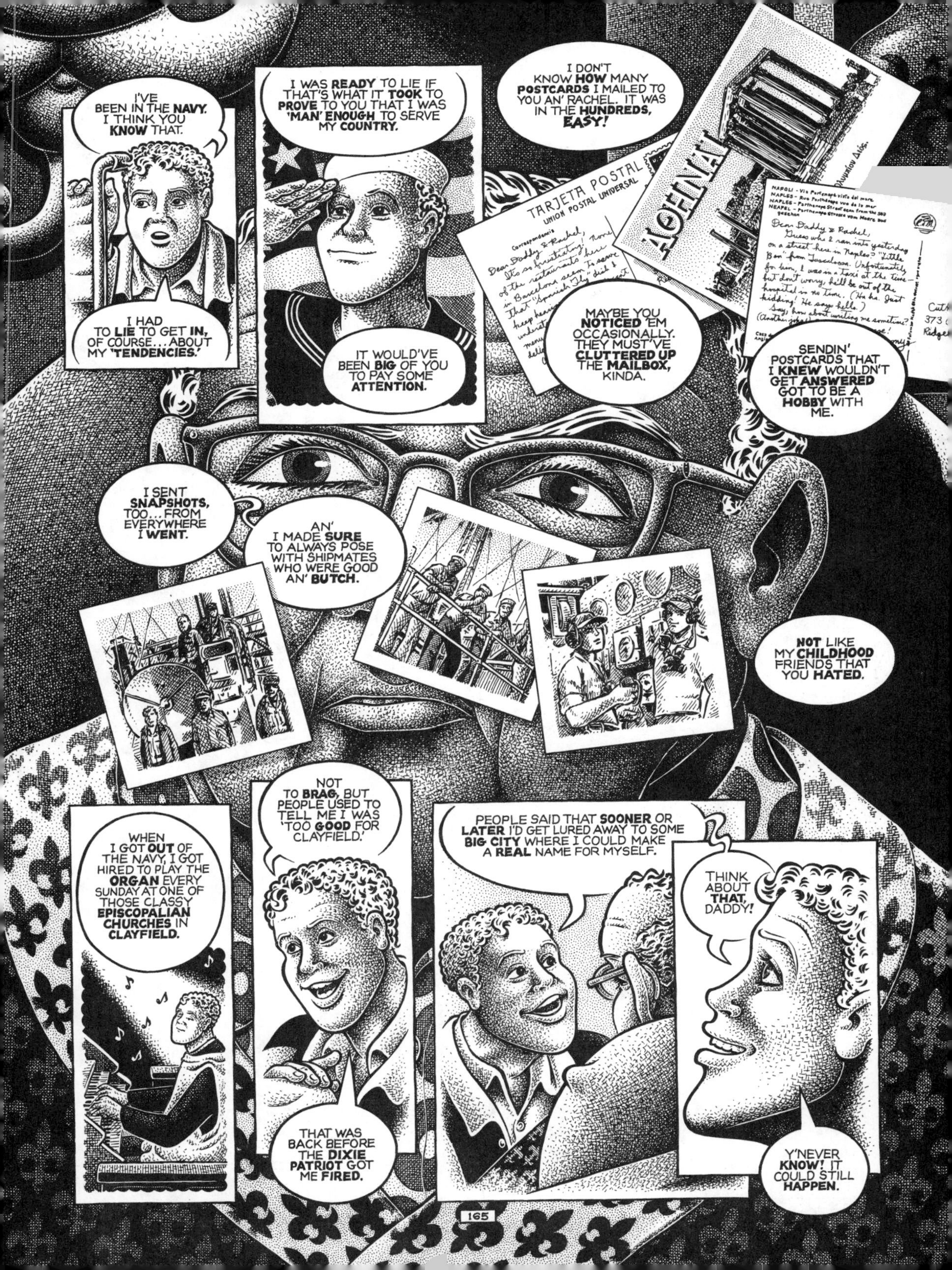
I'VE BEEN IN THE NAVY. I THINK YOU KNOW THAT.
I HAD TO LIE TO GET IN, OF COURSE... ABOUT MY 'TENDENCIES.'
I WAS READY TO LIE IF THAT'S WHAT IT TOOK TO PROVE TO YOU THAT I WAS 'MAN' ENOUGH TO SERVE MY COUNTRY.
IT WOULD'VE BEEN BIG OF YOU TO PAY SOME ATTENTION.
I DON'T KNOW HOW MANY POSTCARDS I MAILED TO YOU AN' RACHEL. IT WAS IN THE HUNDREDS, EASY!
TARJETA POSTAL
UNION POSTAL UNIVERSAL
MAYBE YOU NOTICED 'EM OCCASIONALLY. THEY MUST'VE CLUTTERED UP THE MAILBOX, KINDA.
SENDIN' POSTCARDS THAT I KNEW WOULDN'T GET ANSWERED GOT TO BE A HOBBY WITH ME.
I SENT SNAPSHOTS, TOO... FROM EVERYWHERE I WENT.
AN' I MADE SURE TO ALWAYS POSE WITH SHIPMATES WHO WERE GOOD AN' BUTCH.
NOT LIKE MY CHILDHOOD FRIENDS THAT YOU HATED.
WHEN I GOT OUT OF THE NAVY, I GOT HIRED TO PLAY THE ORGAN EVERY SUNDAY AT ONE OF THOSE CLASSY EPISCOPALIAN CHURCHES IN CLAYFIELD.
NOT TO BRAG, BUT PEOPLE USED TO TELL ME I WAS 'TOO GOOD FOR CLAYFIELD.'
THAT WAS BACK BEFORE THE DIXIE PATRIOT GOT ME FIRED.
PEOPLE SAID THAT SOONER OR LATER I'D GET LURED AWAY TO SOME BIG CITY WHERE I COULD MAKE A REAL NAME FOR MYSELF.
THINK ABOUT THAT, DADDY!
Y'NEVER KNOW! IT COULD STILL HAPPEN.

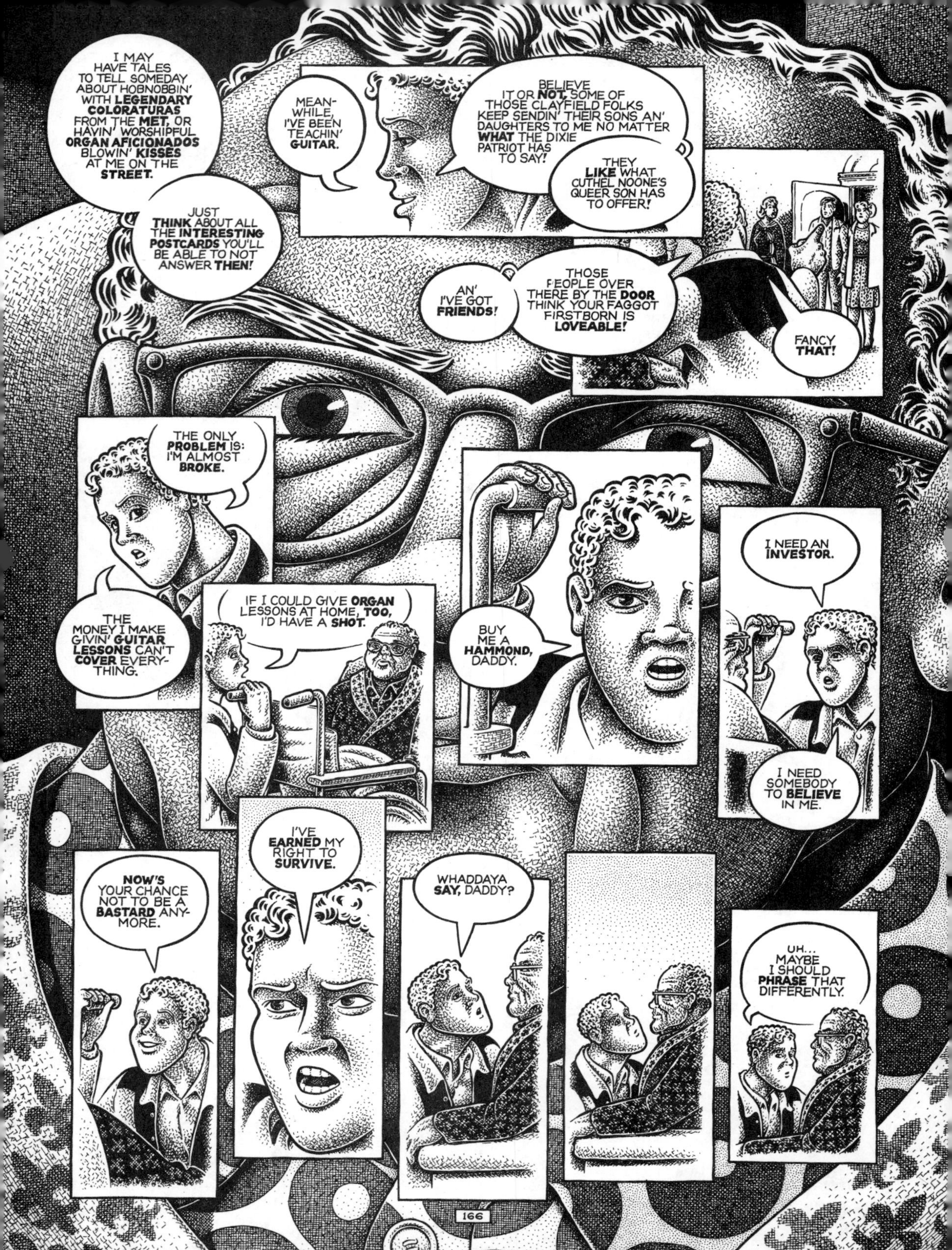

I MAY HAVE TALES TO TELL SOMEDAY ABOUT HOBNOBBIN' WITH **LEGENDARY COLORATURAS** FROM THE **MET**, OR HAVIN' WORSHIPFUL **ORGAN AFICIONADOS** BLOWIN' **KISSES** AT ME ON THE **STREET**.
JUST **THINK** ABOUT ALL THE **INTERESTING POSTCARDS** YOU'LL BE ABLE TO NOT ANSWER **THEN**!
MEAN-WHILE, I'VE BEEN TEACHIN' **GUITAR**.
BELIEVE IT OR **NOT**, SOME OF THOSE CLAYFIELD FOLKS KEEP SENDIN' THEIR SONS AN' DAUGHTERS TO ME NO MATTER **WHAT** THE DIXIE PATRIOT HAS TO SAY!
THEY **LIKE** WHAT CUTHEL NOONE'S QUEER SON HAS TO OFFER!
AN' I'VE GOT **FRIENDS**!
THOSE PEOPLE OVER THERE BY THE **DOOR** THINK YOUR FAGGOT FIRSTBORN IS **LOVEABLE**!
FANCY **THAT**!
THE ONLY **PROBLEM** IS: I'M ALMOST **BROKE**.
THE MONEY I MAKE GIVIN' **GUITAR LESSONS** CAN'T **COVER** EVERY-THING.
IF I COULD GIVE **ORGAN** LESSONS AT HOME, **TOO**, I'D HAVE A **SHOT**.
BUY ME A **HAMMOND**, DADDY.
I NEED AN **INVESTOR**.
I NEED SOMEBODY TO **BELIEVE** IN ME.
NOW'S YOUR CHANCE NOT TO BE A **BASTARD** ANY-MORE.
I'VE **EARNED** MY RIGHT TO **SURVIVE**.
WHADDAYA **SAY**, DADDY?
UH... MAYBE I SHOULD **PHRASE** THAT DIFFERENTLY.

Chapter 20

WHEN WE GOT BACK TO THE **WHEELERY**, I TELEPHONED **GINGER** AND TOLD HER ALL ABOUT OUR WEIRD TRIP TO **RIDGELINE**.

THEN WE MOVED ON TO **OTHER** SUBJECTS AND I LOST TRACK OF **TIME** ...'TIL **MAVIS** BROKE IN.

TOLAND, I'M **SORRY**... I'VE JUST **GOTTA** INTERRUPT YOU.

HOLD **ON** A SEC, GINGER. **MAVIS** WANTS SOMETHIN'.

BE A HONEY AN' GO **LOOK IN** ON **SAMMY**. I'D DO IT, BUT I'VE GOT **SUPPER** COMIN' OFF THE STOVE.

WHY? WHAT'S WITH **SAMMY?**

HE'S BEEN HITTIN' THE **BOTTLE** SO HARD SINCE WE GOT HOME, IT'S **WORRYIN'** ME.

REALLY? I THOUGHT HE WAS IN A **GREAT MOOD**.

MAYBE HE'S JUST **CELEBRATIN'!**

COULD **BE**... BUT IT DOESN'T HAVE THAT **FEEL** TO ME.

I'VE GOTTA **GO**, GINGER.

YOU'RE LOOKIN' DOWNRIGHT **STONKERED**, FELLA.

SHOULD YOU MAYBE SLOW **DOWN**...?

JUST **WINDIN' DOWN** FROM A **THRILL-PACKED DAY!**

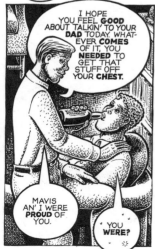

I HOPE YOU FEEL **GOOD** ABOUT TALKIN' TO YOUR **DAD** TODAY. WHATEVER **COMES** OF IT, YOU **NEEDED** TO GET THAT STUFF OFF YOUR **CHEST**.

MAVIS AN' I WERE **PROUD** OF YOU.

YOU **WERE?**

WHAT A **COINCIDENCE!** **I** WAS PROUD OF MYSELF, **TOO!**

THE **ONLY** THING THAT WOULD'VE MADE ME **PROUDER** WOULD BE IF I'D **DRIBBLED** THE OL' BASTARD AROUND THE ROOM LIKE A **BASKETBALL** AN' **DROP-KICKED** HIM OUT THE **WINDOW!**

BUT IF I'D DONE **THAT**, HE MIGHT NOT'VE GIVEN ME MY **HAMMOND!**

I **THINK** I'M GONNA PUT IT RIGHT... **OVER**... **THERE**....

LOOK, IT'S **SUPPERTIME**. THINK YOU CAN WOBBLE YOUR WAY TO THE **KITCHEN?**

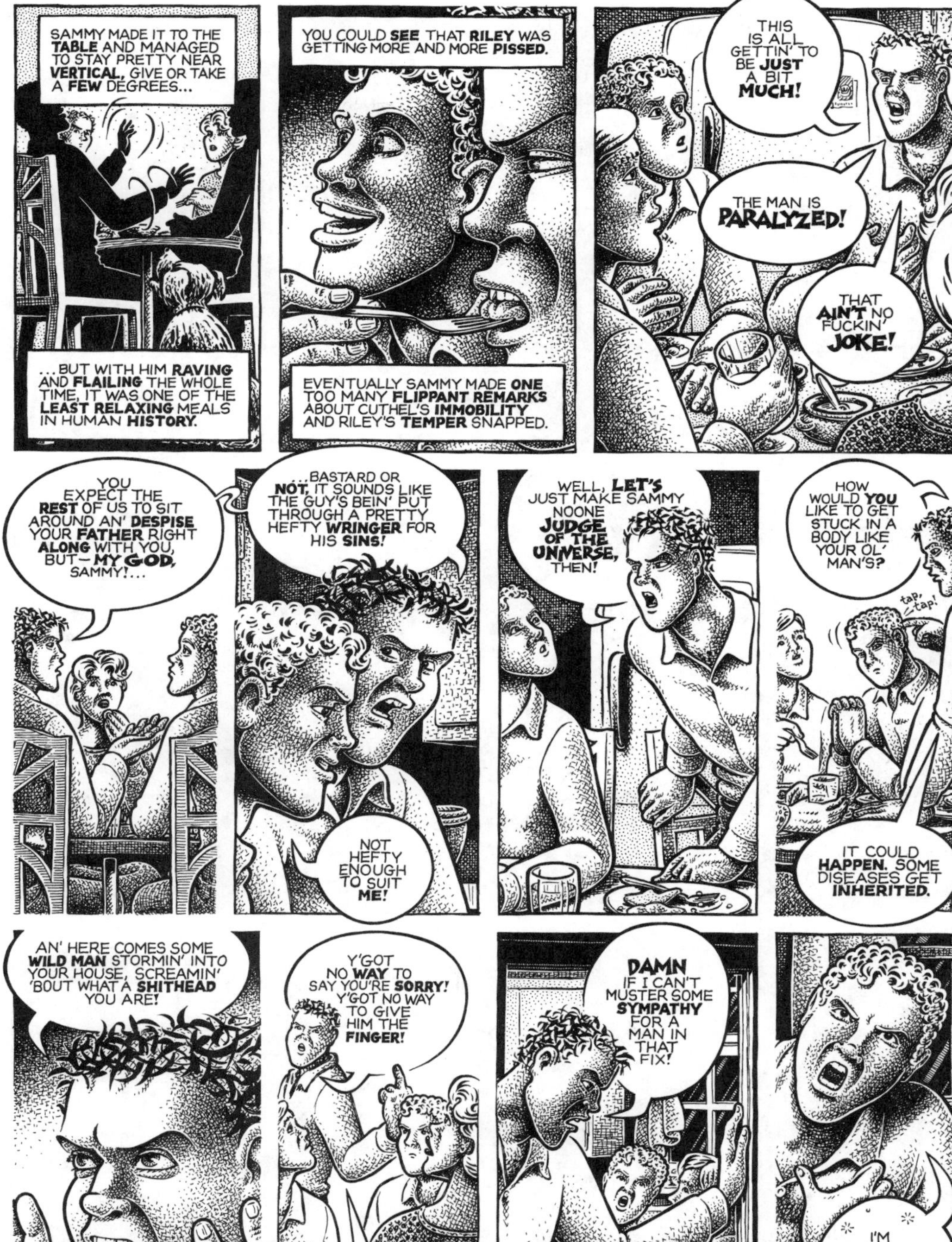

SAMMY MADE IT TO THE **TABLE** AND MANAGED TO STAY PRETTY NEAR **VERTICAL**, GIVE OR TAKE A **FEW** DEGREES...
...BUT WITH HIM **RAVING** AND **FLAILING** THE WHOLE TIME, IT WAS ONE OF THE **LEAST RELAXING** MEALS IN HUMAN **HISTORY**.
YOU COULD **SEE** THAT **RILEY** WAS GETTING MORE AND MORE **PISSED**.
EVENTUALLY SAMMY MADE **ONE** TOO MANY **FLIPPANT REMARKS** ABOUT CUTHEL'S **IMMOBILITY** AND RILEY'S **TEMPER** SNAPPED.
THIS IS ALL GETTIN' TO BE **JUST** A BIT **MUCH!**
THE MAN IS **PARALYZED!**
THAT **AIN'T** NO FUCKIN' **JOKE!**
YOU EXPECT THE **REST** OF US TO SIT AROUND AN' **DESPISE** YOUR **FATHER** RIGHT **ALONG** WITH YOU, BUT—**MY GOD,** SAMMY!...
...BASTARD OR **NOT**, IT SOUNDS LIKE THE GUY'S BEIN' PUT THROUGH A PRETTY HEFTY **WRINGER** FOR HIS **SINS**!
NOT HEFTY ENOUGH TO SUIT **ME!**
WELL, **LET'S** JUST MAKE SAMMY NOONE **JUDGE OF THE UNIVERSE,** THEN!
HOW WOULD **YOU** LIKE TO GET STUCK IN A BODY LIKE YOUR OL' MAN'S?
tap, tap!
IT COULD **HAPPEN.** SOME DISEASES GET **INHERITED.**
AN' HERE COMES SOME **WILD MAN** STORMIN' INTO YOUR HOUSE, SCREAMIN' 'BOUT WHAT A **SHITHEAD** YOU ARE!
Y'GOT NO **WAY** TO SAY YOU'RE **SORRY!** Y'GOT NO WAY TO GIVE HIM THE **FINGER!**
YOU'RE **WAY** PAST BEIN' ABLE TO MAKE **AMENDS** FOR PAST **FAILINGS!**
DAMN IF I CAN'T MUSTER SOME **SYMPATHY** FOR A MAN IN THAT FIX!
Y'KNOW, I **WASN'T** JUST SOME **STRAY PSYCHO** BARGIN' IN ON HIM TODAY!
I'M HIS **SON!** ...AN' I'VE GOT AMPLE **CAUSE** TO BE MAD AT HIM!

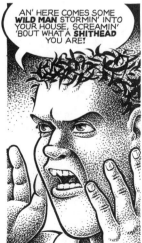

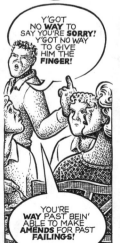

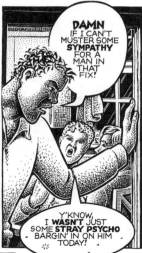

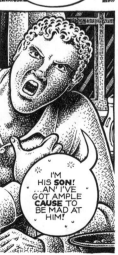

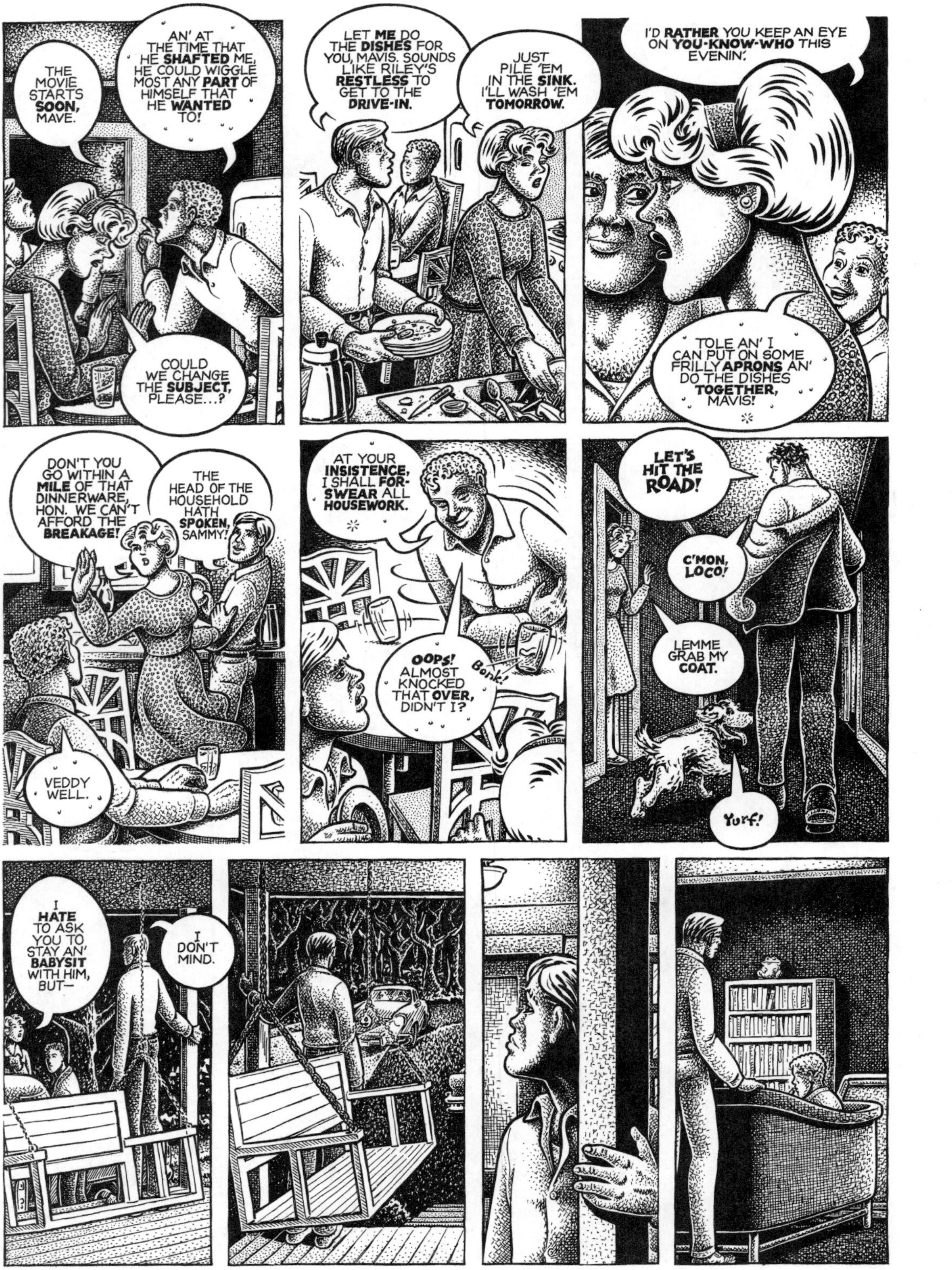
THE MOVIE STARTS SOON, MAVE.
AN' AT THE TIME THAT HE SHAFTED ME, HE COULD WIGGLE MOST ANY PART OF HIMSELF THAT HE WANTED TO!
COULD WE CHANGE THE SUBJECT, PLEASE...?
LET ME DO THE DISHES FOR YOU, MAVIS. SOUNDS LIKE RILEY'S RESTLESS TO GET TO THE DRIVE-IN.
JUST PILE 'EM IN THE SINK. I'LL WASH 'EM TOMORROW.
I'D RATHER YOU KEEP AN EYE ON YOU-KNOW-WHO THIS EVENIN'.
TOLE AN' I CAN PUT ON SOME FRILLY APRONS AN' DO THE DISHES TOGETHER, MAVIS!
DON'T YOU GO WITHIN A MILE OF THAT DINNERWARE, HON. WE CAN'T AFFORD THE BREAKAGE!
THE HEAD OF THE HOUSEHOLD HATH SPOKEN, SAMMY!
VEDDY WELL.
AT YOUR INSISTENCE, I SHALL FOR-SWEAR ALL HOUSEWORK.
OOPS! ALMOST KNOCKED THAT OVER, DIDN'T I?
Bonk!
LET'S HIT THE ROAD!
C'MON, LOCO!
LEMME GRAB MY COAT.
Yurf!
I HATE TO ASK YOU TO STAY AN' BABYSIT WITH HIM, BUT—
I DON'T MIND.

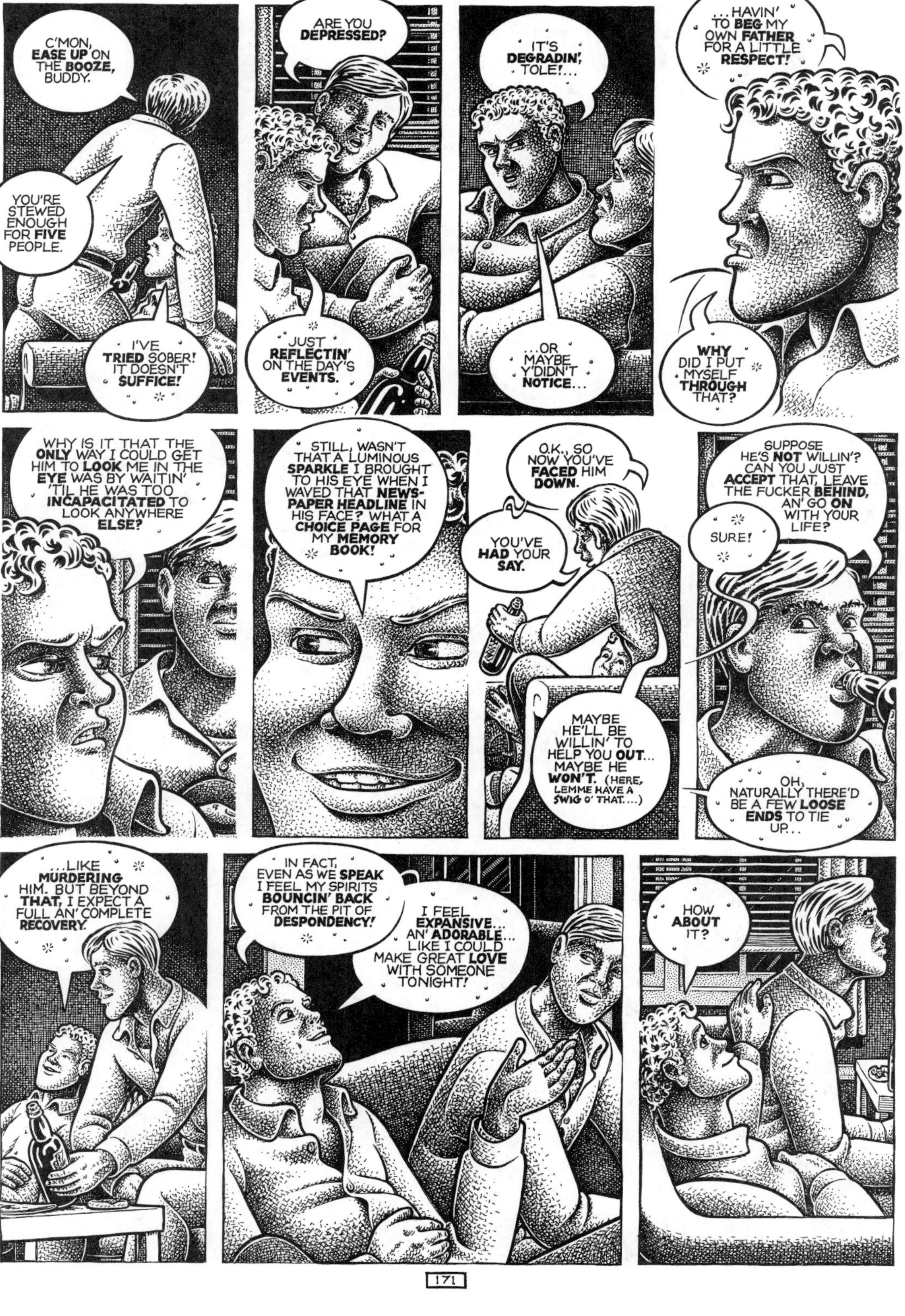
C'MON, EASE UP ON THE BOOZE, BUDDY.
YOU'RE STEWED ENOUGH FOR FIVE PEOPLE.
I'VE TRIED SOBER! IT DOESN'T SUFFICE!
ARE YOU DEPRESSED?
JUST REFLECTIN' ON THE DAY'S EVENTS.
IT'S DEGRADIN', TOLE!...
...OR MAYBE Y'DIDN'T NOTICE...
...HAVIN' TO BEG MY OWN FATHER FOR A LITTLE RESPECT!
WHY DID I PUT MYSELF THROUGH THAT?
WHY IS IT THAT THE ONLY WAY I COULD GET HIM TO LOOK ME IN THE EYE WAS BY WAITIN' 'TIL HE WAS TOO INCAPACITATED TO LOOK ANYWHERE ELSE?
STILL, WASN'T THAT A LUMINOUS SPARKLE I BROUGHT TO HIS EYE WHEN I WAVED THAT NEWSPAPER HEADLINE IN HIS FACE? WHAT A CHOICE PAGE FOR MY MEMORY BOOK!
O.K., SO NOW YOU'VE FACED HIM DOWN.
YOU'VE HAD YOUR SAY.
MAYBE HE'LL BE WILLIN' TO HELP YOU OUT... MAYBE HE WON'T. (HERE, LEMME HAVE A SWIG O' THAT....)
SUPPOSE HE'S NOT WILLIN'? CAN YOU JUST ACCEPT THAT, LEAVE THE FUCKER BEHIND, AN' GO ON WITH YOUR LIFE?
SURE!
OH, NATURALLY THERE'D BE A FEW LOOSE ENDS TO TIE UP...
...LIKE MURDERING HIM. BUT BEYOND THAT, I EXPECT A FULL AN' COMPLETE RECOVERY.
IN FACT, EVEN AS WE SPEAK I FEEL MY SPIRITS BOUNCIN' BACK FROM THE PIT OF DESPONDENCY!
I FEEL EXPANSIVE... AN' ADORABLE... LIKE I COULD MAKE GREAT LOVE WITH SOMEONE TONIGHT!
HOW ABOUT IT?

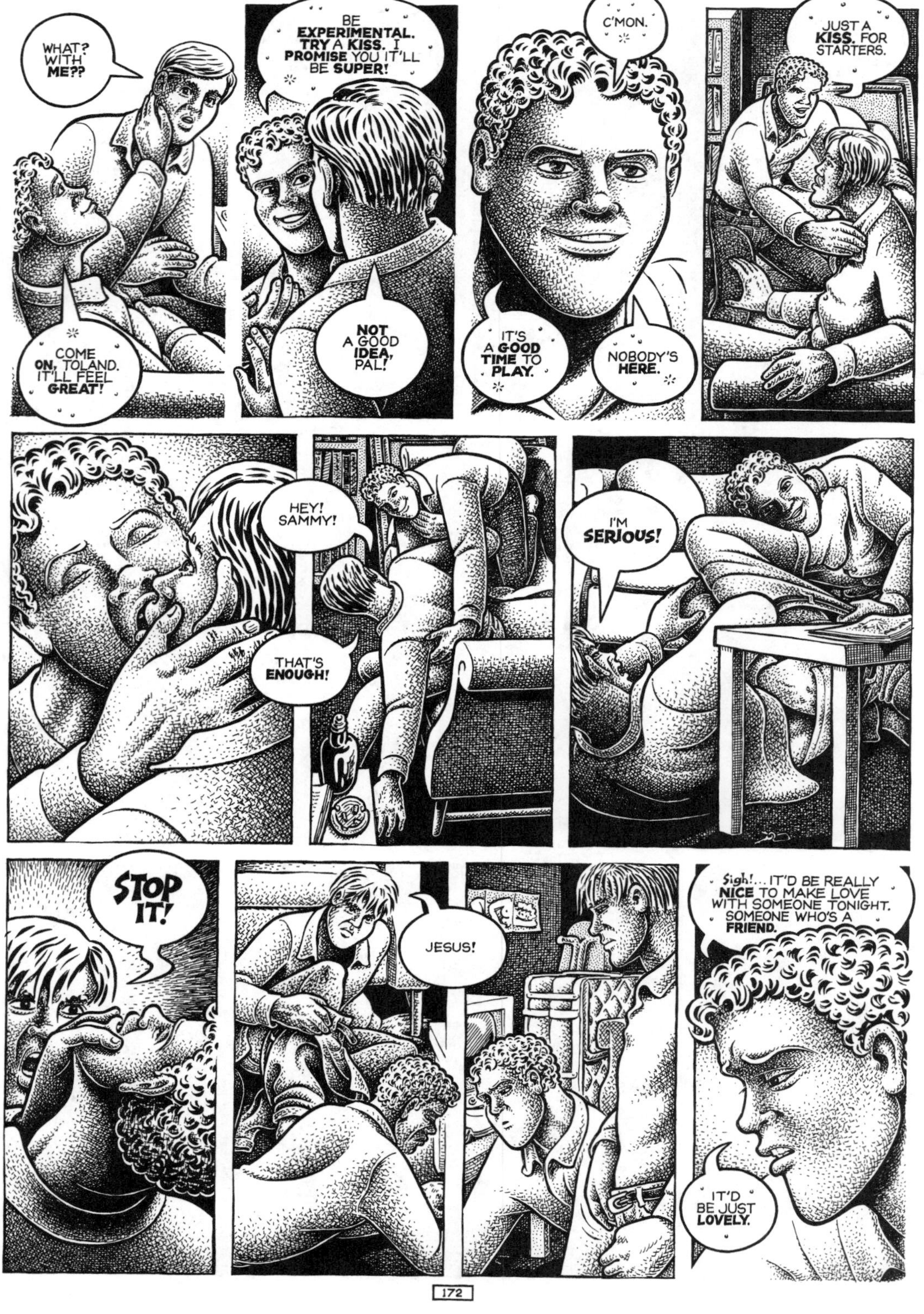
WHAT? WITH ME??
COME ON, TOLAND. IT'LL FEEL GREAT!
BE EXPERIMENTAL. TRY A KISS. I PROMISE YOU IT'LL BE SUPER!
NOT A GOOD IDEA, PAL!
C'MON.
IT'S A GOOD TIME TO PLAY.
NOBODY'S HERE.
JUST A KISS. FOR STARTERS.
THAT'S ENOUGH!
HEY! SAMMY!
I'M SERIOUS!
STOP IT!
JESUS!
Sigh!... IT'D BE REALLY NICE TO MAKE LOVE WITH SOMEONE TONIGHT. SOMEONE WHO'S A FRIEND.
IT'D BE JUST LOVELY.

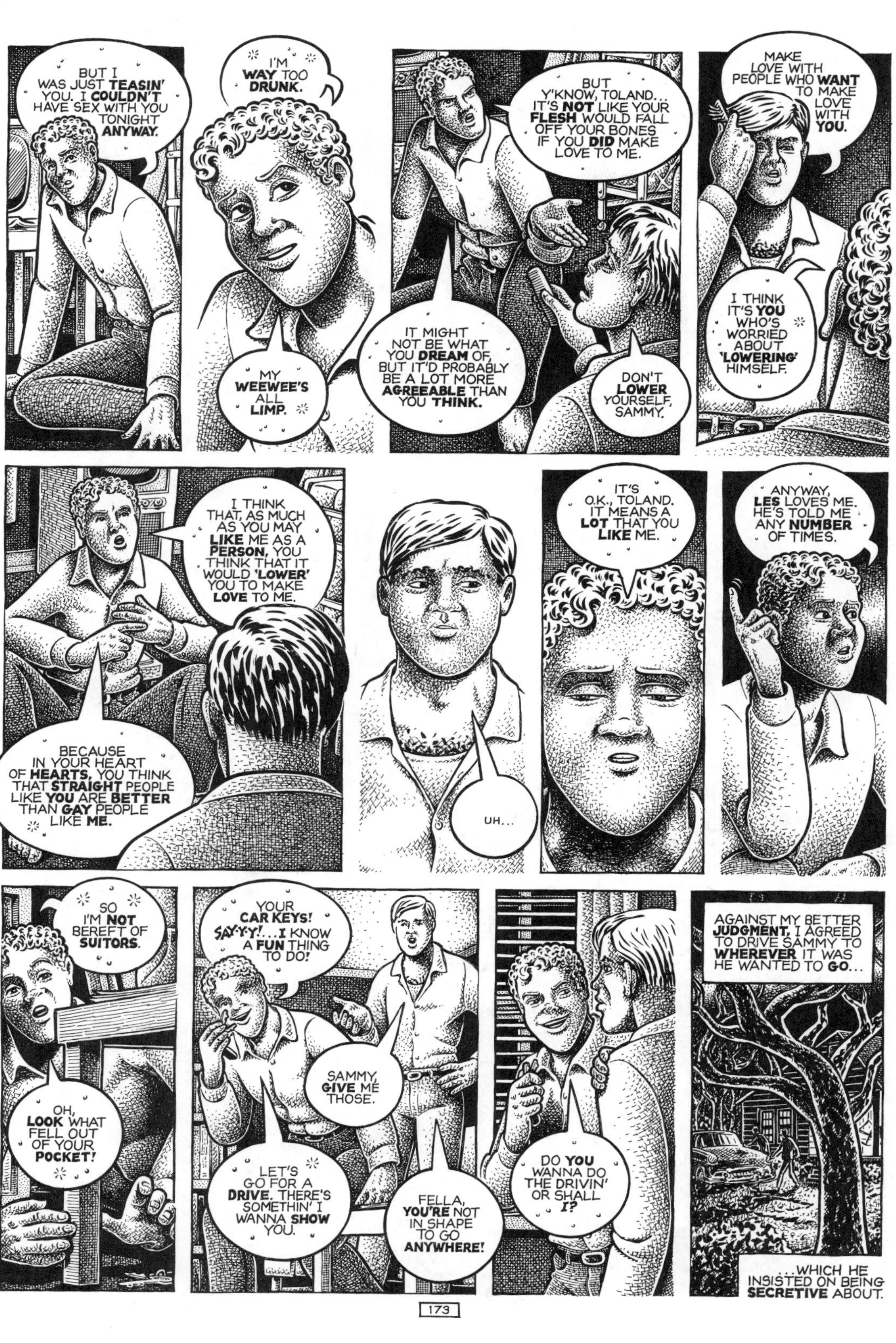
BUT I WAS JUST TEASIN' YOU. I COULDN'T HAVE SEX WITH YOU TONIGHT ANYWAY.
I'M WAY TOO DRUNK.
MY WEEWEE'S ALL LIMP.
BUT Y'KNOW, TOLAND... IT'S NOT LIKE YOUR FLESH WOULD FALL OFF YOUR BONES IF YOU DID MAKE LOVE TO ME.
IT MIGHT NOT BE WHAT YOU DREAM OF, BUT IT'D PROBABLY BE A LOT MORE AGREEABLE THAN YOU THINK.
DON'T LOWER YOURSELF, SAMMY.
MAKE LOVE WITH PEOPLE WHO WANT TO MAKE LOVE WITH YOU.
I THINK IT'S YOU WHO'S WORRIED ABOUT 'LOWERING' HIMSELF.
I THINK THAT, AS MUCH AS YOU MAY LIKE ME AS A PERSON, YOU THINK THAT IT WOULD 'LOWER' YOU TO MAKE LOVE TO ME.
BECAUSE IN YOUR HEART OF HEARTS, YOU THINK THAT STRAIGHT PEOPLE LIKE YOU ARE BETTER THAN GAY PEOPLE LIKE ME.
UH...
IT'S O.K., TOLAND. IT MEANS A LOT THAT YOU LIKE ME.
ANYWAY, LES LOVES ME. HE'S TOLD ME ANY NUMBER OF TIMES.
SO I'M NOT BEREFT OF SUITORS.
OH, LOOK WHAT FELL OUT OF YOUR POCKET!
YOUR CAR KEYS! SAY-Y-Y!... I KNOW A FUN THING TO DO!
SAMMY, GIVE ME THOSE.
LET'S GO FOR A DRIVE. THERE'S SOMETHIN' I WANNA SHOW YOU.
FELLA, YOU'RE NOT IN SHAPE TO GO ANYWHERE!
DO YOU WANNA DO THE DRIVIN' OR SHALL I?
AGAINST MY BETTER JUDGMENT, I AGREED TO DRIVE SAMMY TO WHEREVER IT WAS HE WANTED TO GO...
...WHICH HE INSISTED ON BEING SECRETIVE ABOUT.

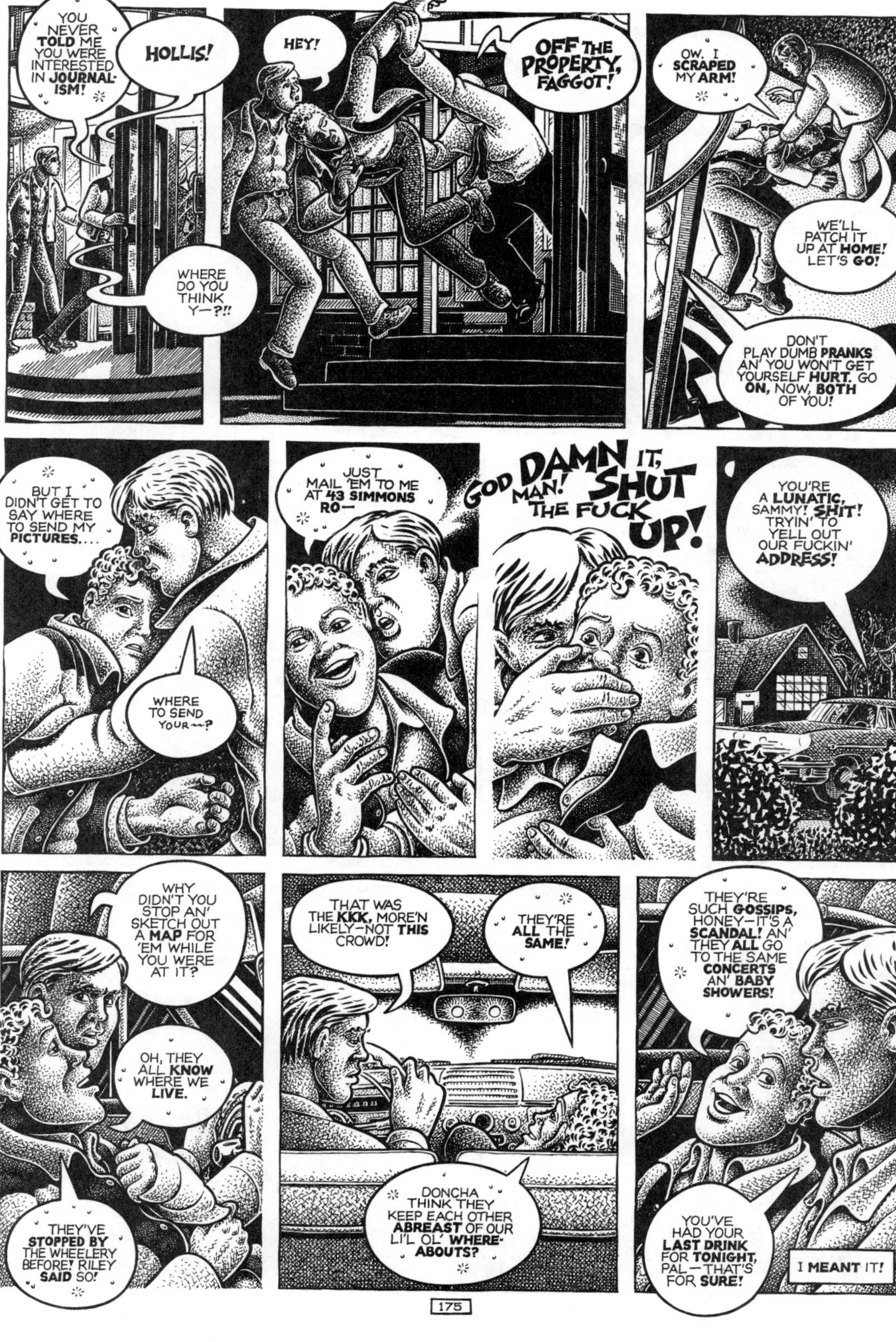

YOU NEVER TOLD ME YOU WERE INTERESTED IN JOURNALISM!
HOLLIS!
WHERE DO YOU THINK Y—?!!
HEY!
OFF THE PROPERTY, FAGGOT!
OW. I SCRAPED MY ARM!
WE'LL PATCH IT UP AT HOME! LET'S GO!
DON'T PLAY DUMB PRANKS AN' YOU WON'T GET YOURSELF HURT. GO ON, NOW, BOTH OF YOU!
BUT I DIDN'T GET TO SAY WHERE TO SEND MY PICTURES....
WHERE TO SEND YOUR—?
JUST MAIL 'EM TO ME AT 43 SIMMONS RO—
GOD DAMN IT, MAN! SHUT THE FUCK UP!
YOU'RE A LUNATIC, SAMMY! SHIT! TRYIN' TO YELL OUT OUR FUCKIN' ADDRESS!
WHY DIDN'T YOU STOP AN' SKETCH OUT A MAP FOR 'EM WHILE YOU WERE AT IT?
OH, THEY ALL KNOW WHERE WE LIVE.
THEY'VE STOPPED BY THE WHEELERY BEFORE! RILEY SAID SO!
THAT WAS THE KKK, MORE'N LIKELY—NOT THIS CROWD!
THEY'RE ALL THE SAME!
DONCHA THINK THEY KEEP ABREAST OF EACH OTHER OUR LI'L OL' WHERE-ABOUTS?
THEY'RE SUCH GOSSIPS, HONEY—IT'S A SCANDAL! AN' THEY ALL GO TO THE SAME CONCERTS AN' BABY SHOWERS!
YOU'VE HAD YOUR LAST DRINK FOR TONIGHT, PAL—THAT'S FOR SURE!
I MEANT IT!

WHEN WE GOT **HOME**, I SET ABOUT CONFISCATING EVERY DROP OF **ALCOHOL** ON THE **PREMISES**...

DON'T PUT YOURSELF **OUT** SO, TOLAND.

...EXCEPT FOR THE **'RUBBING'** KIND WE DOUSED ON SAMMY'S **SCRAPES**.

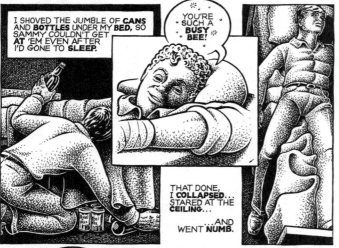

I SHOVED THE JUMBLE OF **CANS** AND **BOTTLES** UNDER MY **BED**, SO SAMMY COULDN'T GET **AT** 'EM EVEN AFTER I'D GONE TO **SLEEP**.

YOU'RE SUCH A **BUSY BEE**!

THAT DONE, I **COLLAPSED**... STARED AT THE **CEILING**...

...AND WENT **NUMB**.

MY MIND **DRIFTED** AND **SPUN**...

...'TIL I HEARD A **NOISE**...

...WHICH I TOOK TO BE SAMMY **BARFING** OUT IN THE **YARD**.

SAMMY...?

I WALKED OUT THE **BACK DOOR** TO MAKE SURE HE FELT **STEADY** ENOUGH TO GET BACK **INSIDE**.

AND THAT'S ALL I **REMEMBER**.

KRAK

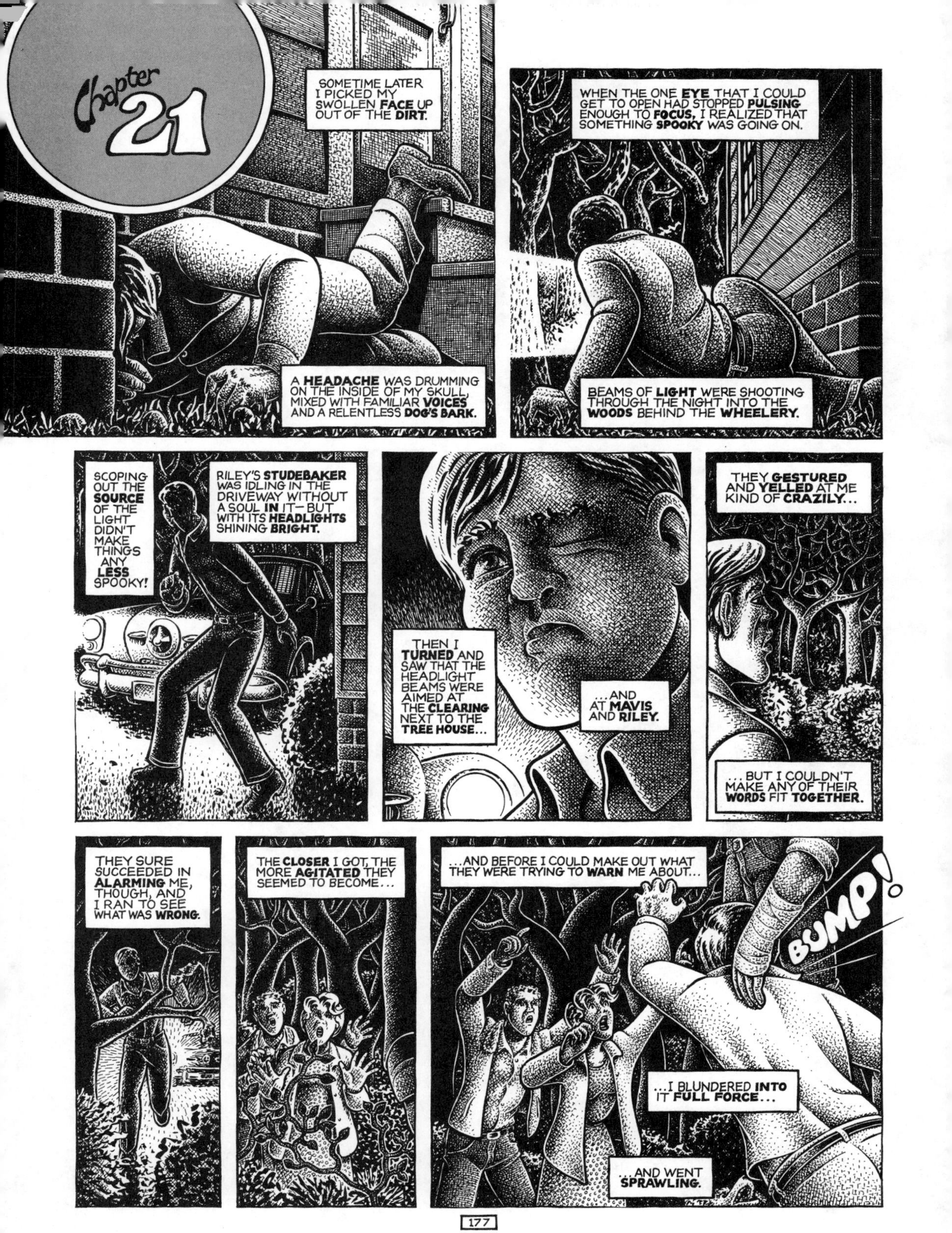
Chapter 21
SOMETIME LATER I PICKED MY SWOLLEN FACE UP OUT OF THE DIRT.
A HEADACHE WAS DRUMMING ON THE INSIDE OF MY SKULL, MIXED WITH FAMILIAR VOICES AND A RELENTLESS DOG'S BARK.
WHEN THE ONE EYE THAT I COULD GET TO OPEN HAD STOPPED PULSING ENOUGH TO FOCUS, I REALIZED THAT SOMETHING SPOOKY WAS GOING ON.
BEAMS OF LIGHT WERE SHOOTING THROUGH THE NIGHT INTO THE WOODS BEHIND THE WHEELERY.
SCOPING OUT THE SOURCE OF THE LIGHT DIDN'T MAKE THINGS ANY LESS SPOOKY!
RILEY'S STUDEBAKER WAS IDLING IN THE DRIVEWAY WITHOUT A SOUL IN IT— BUT WITH ITS HEADLIGHTS SHINING BRIGHT.
THEN I TURNED AND SAW THAT THE HEADLIGHT BEAMS WERE AIMED AT THE CLEARING NEXT TO THE TREE HOUSE...
...AND AT MAVIS AND RILEY.
THEY GESTURED AND YELLED AT ME KIND OF CRAZILY...
...BUT I COULDN'T MAKE ANY OF THEIR WORDS FIT TOGETHER.
THEY SURE SUCCEEDED IN ALARMING ME, THOUGH, AND I RAN TO SEE WHAT WAS WRONG.
THE CLOSER I GOT, THE MORE AGITATED THEY SEEMED TO BECOME...
...AND BEFORE I COULD MAKE OUT WHAT THEY WERE TRYING TO WARN ME ABOUT...
BUMP!
...I BLUNDERED INTO IT FULL FORCE...
...AND WENT SPRAWLING.

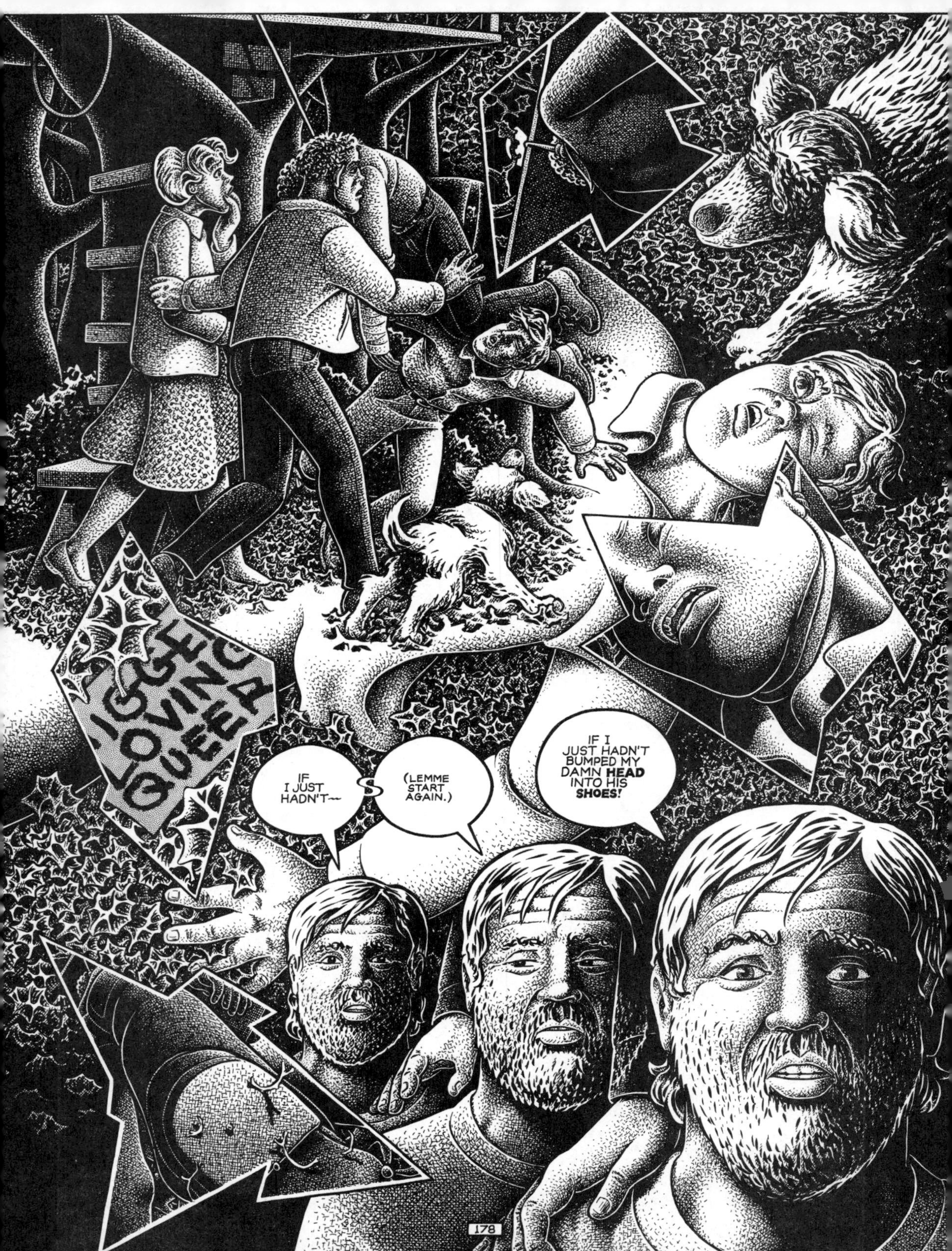
IGGE
LOVING
QUEER
IF I JUST HADN'T—
(LEMME START AGAIN.)
IF I JUST HADN'T BUMPED MY DAMN **HEAD** INTO HIS **SHOES!**

THAT'S THE MEMORY THAT STAYS WITH ME:
THE CLUMSY WEIGHT OF HIS CALVES THUDDING AGAINST MY EAR... AND THE SMELL OF THE DRIED SWEAT IN HIS DENIM.
I CAN CLOSE MY EYES AND FEEL HIS SHOES ROLLING AROUND THE BACK OF MY NECK... 'CAUSE MY STUMBLING INTO HIM HAD STARTED HIM SWINGING...
...AND THERE WERE CLUMPS OF MUD AND LEAF STEMS THAT I CAN STILL TASTE, THAT HAD PEELED OFF HIS SOLES AND LANDED ON MY LIPS.
I REMEMBER LYING FROZEN ON MY BACK, WITH LOCO BARKING ALL AROUND ME...
...AND THEN I STARTED SCRAMBLING LIKE SOME CRAZY, TRAPPED ANIMAL...
...TRYING TO GET AWAY FROM WHAT WAS DANGLING OVERHEAD.
IF I JUST HADN'T TOUCHED IT~
~IF IT HAD JUST BEEN A SCARY PICTURE OF SOMETHING AWFUL IN THE WOODS~
~I MIGHT'VE HAD A SAFE PLACE IN MY MEMORY TO STASH IT.
SOMEPLACE WHERE IT'D STAY PUT AND LEAVE ME ALONE.

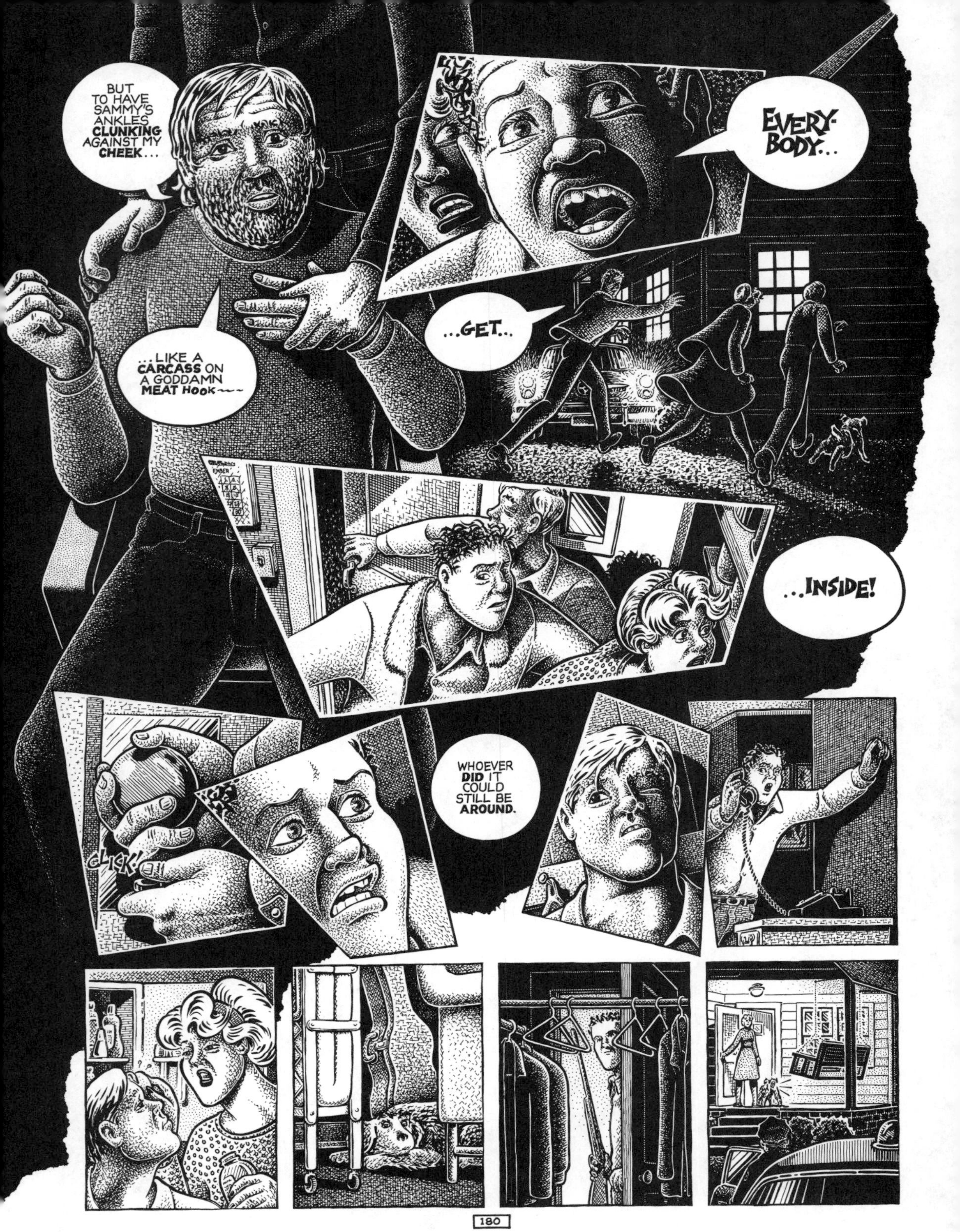
BUT TO HAVE SAMMY'S ANKLES CLUNKING AGAINST MY CHEEK...
EVERY-BODY...
...LIKE A CARCASS ON A GODDAMN MEAT HOOK~~~
...GET...
...INSIDE!
CLICK!
WHOEVER DID IT COULD STILL BE AROUND.

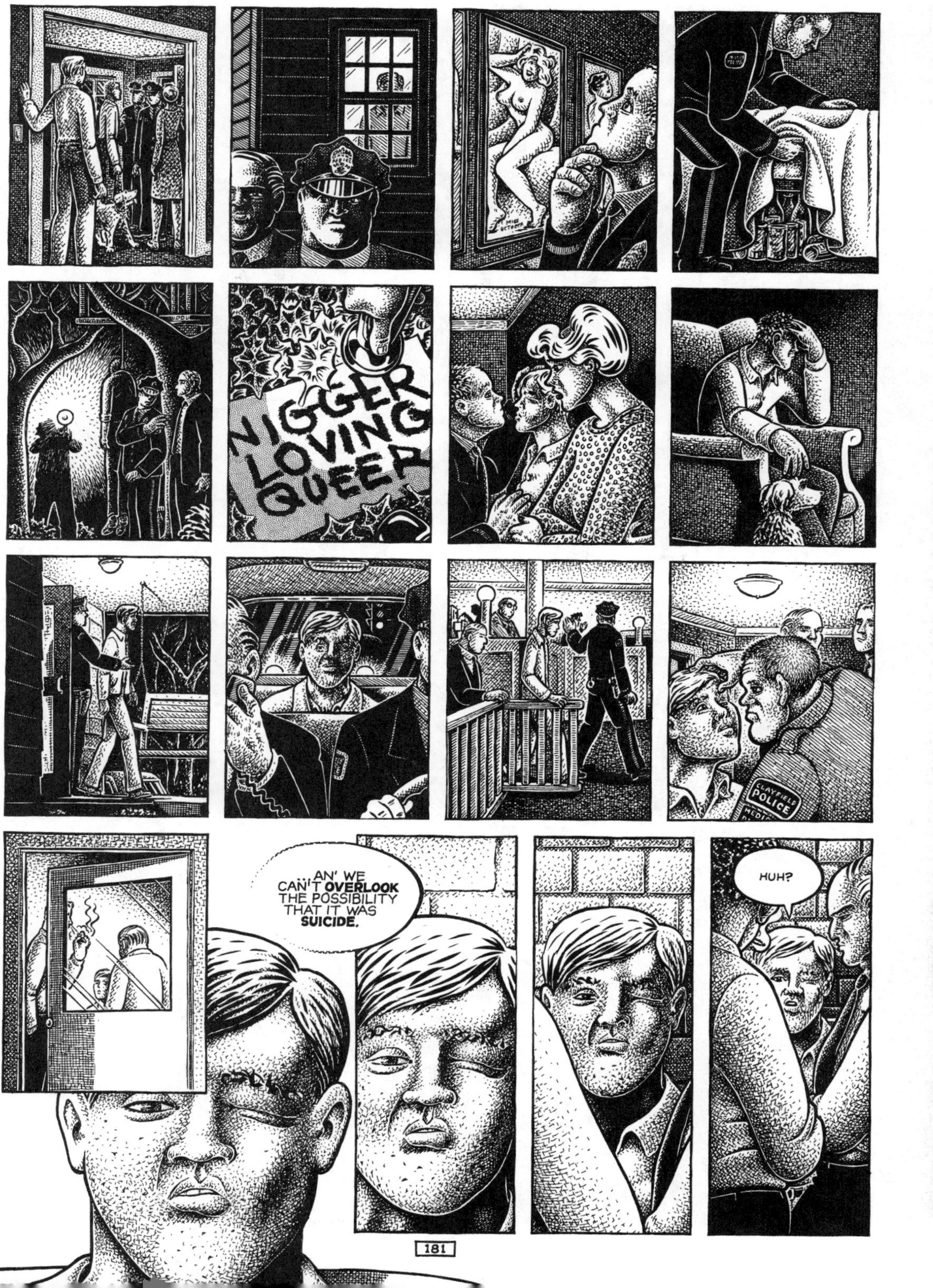
NIGGER LOVING QUEER
POLICE
...AN' WE CAN'T **OVERLOOK** THE POSSIBILITY THAT IT WAS **SUICIDE.**
HUH?

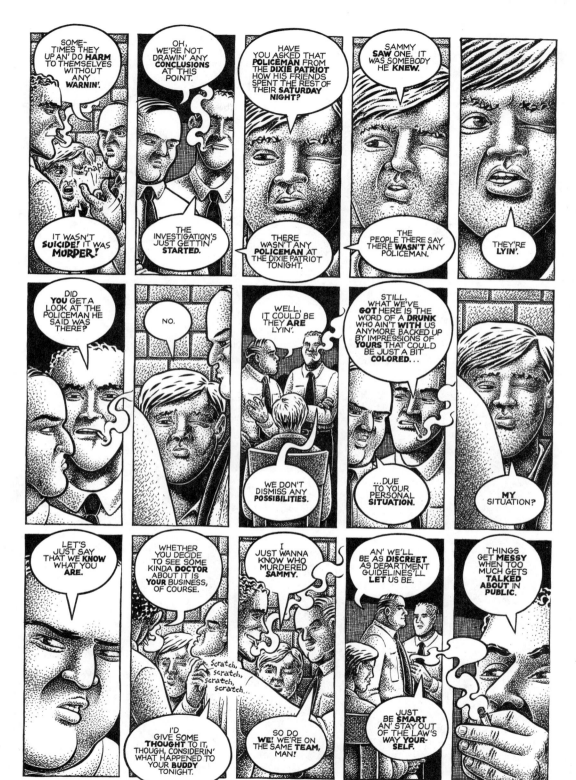

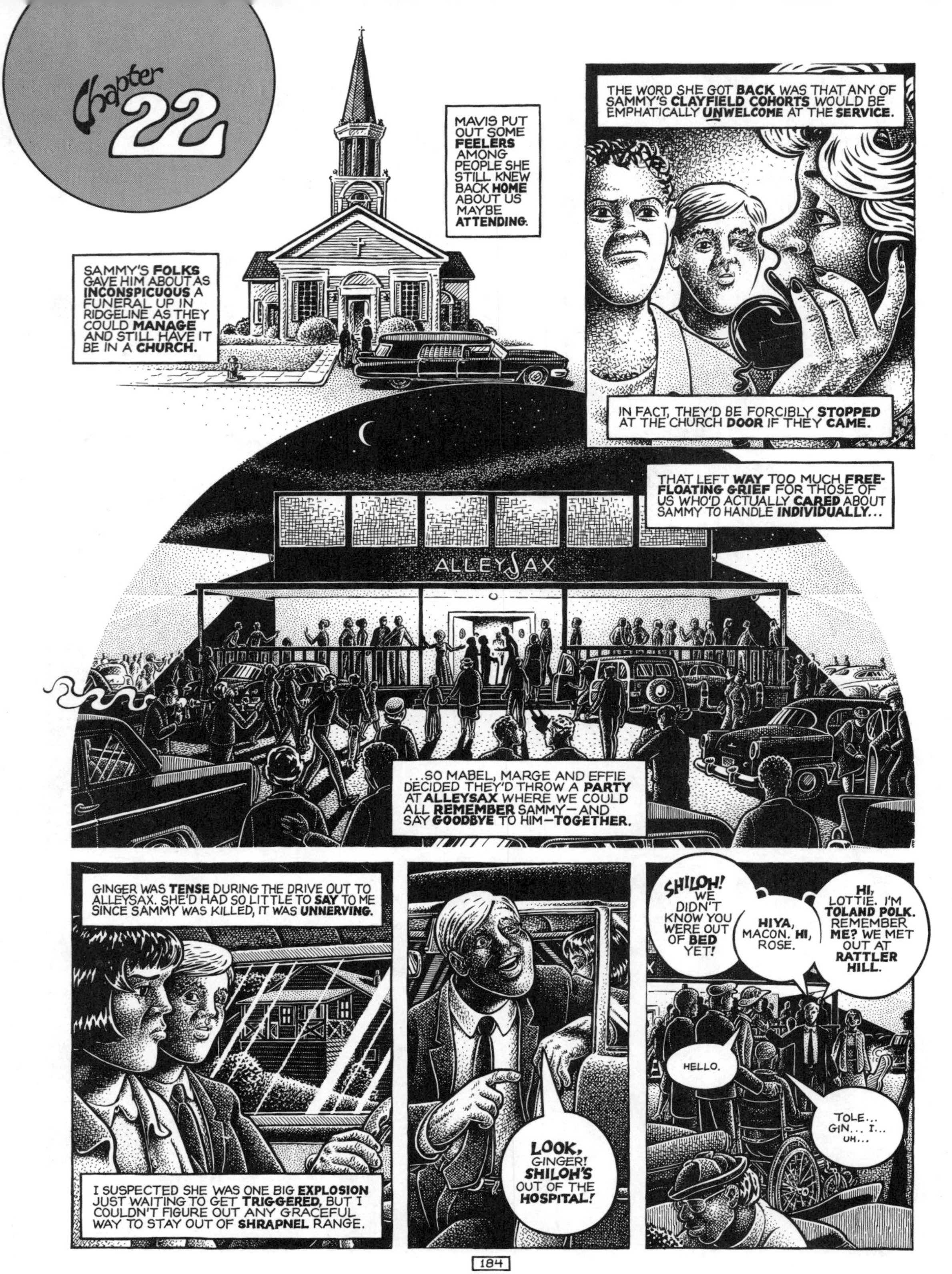
Chapter 22
SAMMY'S FOLKS GAVE HIM ABOUT AS INCONSPICUOUS A FUNERAL UP IN RIDGELINE AS THEY COULD MANAGE AND STILL HAVE IT BE IN A CHURCH.
MAVIS PUT OUT SOME FEELERS AMONG PEOPLE SHE STILL KNEW BACK HOME ABOUT US MAYBE ATTENDING.
THE WORD SHE GOT BACK WAS THAT ANY OF SAMMY'S CLAYFIELD COHORTS WOULD BE EMPHATICALLY UNWELCOME AT THE SERVICE.
IN FACT, THEY'D BE FORCIBLY STOPPED AT THE CHURCH DOOR IF THEY CAME.
THAT LEFT WAY TOO MUCH FREE-FLOATING GRIEF FOR THOSE OF US WHO'D ACTUALLY CARED ABOUT SAMMY TO HANDLE INDIVIDUALLY...
ALLEYSAX
...SO MABEL, MARGE AND EFFIE DECIDED THEY'D THROW A PARTY AT ALLEYSAX WHERE WE COULD ALL REMEMBER SAMMY—AND SAY GOODBYE TO HIM—TOGETHER.
GINGER WAS TENSE DURING THE DRIVE OUT TO ALLEYSAX. SHE'D HAD SO LITTLE TO SAY TO ME SINCE SAMMY WAS KILLED, IT WAS UNNERVING.
I SUSPECTED SHE WAS ONE BIG EXPLOSION JUST WAITING TO GET TRIGGERED, BUT I COULDN'T FIGURE OUT ANY GRACEFUL WAY TO STAY OUT OF SHRAPNEL RANGE.
LOOK, GINGER! SHILOH'S OUT OF THE HOSPITAL!
SHILOH! WE DIDN'T KNOW YOU WERE OUT OF BED YET!
HIYA, MACON. HI, ROSE.
HI, LOTTIE. I'M TOLAND POLK. REMEMBER ME? WE MET OUT AT RATTLER HILL.
HELLO.
TOLE... GIN... I... UH...

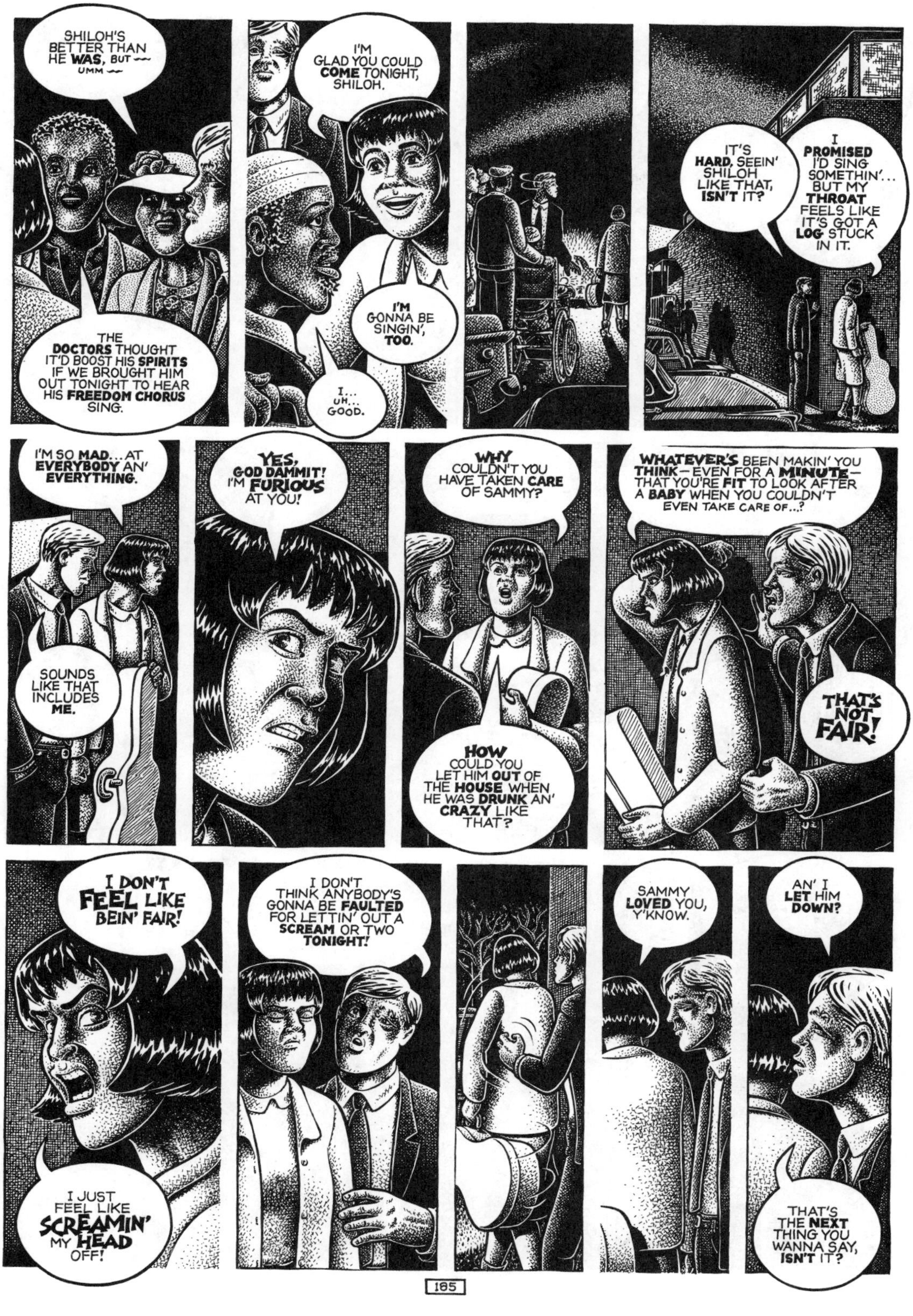

SHILOH'S BETTER THAN HE WAS, BUT ~~ UMM ~~
THE DOCTORS THOUGHT IT'D BOOST HIS SPIRITS IF WE BROUGHT HIM OUT TONIGHT TO HEAR HIS FREEDOM CHORUS SING.
I'M GLAD YOU COULD COME TONIGHT, SHILOH.
I'M GONNA BE SINGIN', TOO.
I... UH... GOOD.
IT'S HARD, SEEIN' SHILOH LIKE THAT, ISN'T IT?
I PROMISED I'D SING SOMETHIN'... BUT MY THROAT FEELS LIKE IT'S GOT A LOG STUCK IN IT.
I'M SO MAD... AT EVERYBODY AN' EVERYTHING.
SOUNDS LIKE THAT INCLUDES ME.
YES, GOD DAMMIT! I'M FURIOUS AT YOU!
WHY COULDN'T YOU HAVE TAKEN CARE OF SAMMY?
HOW COULD YOU LET HIM OUT OF THE HOUSE WHEN HE WAS DRUNK AN' CRAZY LIKE THAT?
WHATEVER'S BEEN MAKIN' YOU THINK — EVEN FOR A MINUTE — THAT YOU'RE FIT TO LOOK AFTER A BABY WHEN YOU COULDN'T EVEN TAKE CARE OF...?
THAT'S NOT FAIR!
I DON'T FEEL LIKE BEIN' FAIR!
I JUST FEEL LIKE SCREAMIN' MY HEAD OFF!
I DON'T THINK ANYBODY'S GONNA BE FAULTED FOR LETTIN' OUT A SCREAM OR TWO TONIGHT!
SAMMY LOVED YOU, Y'KNOW.
AN' I LET HIM DOWN?
THAT'S THE NEXT THING YOU WANNA SAY, ISN'T IT?

SHE'D SURE AS HELL DISLODGED THAT **LOG** FROM HER THROAT!

♪ We shall meet... But we shall miss him... ♪

I COULD ALMOST FEEL **SAMMY** STANDING BEHIND ME, BREATHING PLAYFULLY INTO MY **COLLAR** THE WAY HE HAD BACK WHEN **SHILOH** WAS **WHOLE** AND SINGING **DUETS** WITH GINGER AT THE **MELODY MOTEL**.

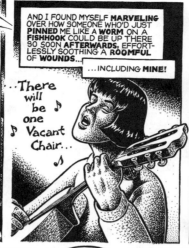

AND I FOUND MYSELF **MARVELING** OVER HOW SOMEONE WHO'D JUST **PINNED** ME LIKE A **WORM** ON A **FISHHOOK** COULD BE UP THERE SO SOON **AFTERWARDS**, EFFORTLESSLY SOOTHING A **ROOMFUL** OF **WOUNDS**...

...INCLUDING **MINE**!

♪ There will be one Vacant Chair... ♪

I STOOD IN THE ALLEY/SAX SHADOWS FEELING A KIND OF **AWE** AT MY OWN **INEPTITUDE**.

FOR ALL WE'D BEEN THROUGH, GINGER WAS STILL LIKE A TRICKY **PICTURE PUZZLE** FRESH OUT OF THE **BOX**.

♪ We shall linger to caress him... ♪

PATCHES OF **BLUE SKY** OVER **HERE**!

FRAGMENTS OF **STORM CLOUDS** OVER **THERE**!

NOT ONLY HAD I SCORED **ZERO** THUS FAR AT FITTING THE PIECES **TOGETHER**...

...BUT IT WAS **DAWNING** ON ME THAT, JUST **POSSIBLY**, I NEVER **WOULD**.

♪ while we breathe... our evening prayer... ♪

WHENEVER I TRY TO SORT IT ALL **OUT**...

...I KEEP REMEMBERING A **DIFFERENT**, MORE **RECENT** OCCASION... DURING THE EARLY **REAGAN** YEARS... WHEN I SAW GINGER SING.

I WAS ON THE **ROAD** AND, PURELY BY **CHANCE**, I SPOTTED HER **NAME** ON A **POSTER**.

Ginger Raines IN CONCERT

BENEFIT PERFORMANCE for the UNITED FARM WORKERS

WELL, WHADDAYA KNOW!

I CALLED FROM A **PAY PHONE** AND RESERVED MY **TICKET**.

HER SINGING WAS AS **IRRESISTIBLE** AS IT HAD BEEN TWENTY YEARS **BEFORE**.

♪ It's a mighty long row that these poor hands have hoed... ♪

THE AUDIENCE WAS IN **LOVE** WITH HER. **I** WAS, TOO.

WHEN THE CONCERT WAS **DONE** I BUTTONHOLED AN **USHER**, EXPLAINED THAT I WAS AN **OLD FRIEND** OF GINGER'S, AND ASKED IF I COULD SAY **HI** TO HER.

HE LED ME DOWN A BACKSTAGE **CORRIDOR** AND POINTED TO HER **DRESSING ROOM**.

I WALKED TOWARD THE HALF-OPEN **DOOR** ...THEN **HESITATED**.

HER **BACK** WAS TO ME. SHE WAS **GIGGLING** AT SOME **JOKE** THAT HAD JUST BEEN CRACKED BY ONE OF THE **STAGEHANDS**.

CONSIDERING THE **MEMORIES** WE SHARED, I WAS SURE I COULD COAX A REFLEXIVE **SMILE** AND **EMBRACE** OUT OF HER BY SIMPLY **STEPPING** INTO THE **LIGHT**.

I DIDN'T **DO** IT, THOUGH.

I SAVORED THE SOUND OF HER **BANTER** FOR A FEW SECONDS, THEN TURNED AND WALKED BACK OUT ONTO THE **SIDEWALK**.

SOMEHOW I **KNEW** THAT— **SMILE** OR **NO** SMILE — IF I STEPPED INTO THAT ROOM WITH GINGER, THERE WOULD BE A **CHASM** BETWEEN US BEYOND **IGNORING**.

AND THE **PARADOX** OF IT IS **THIS**:

IN A **SPOTLIGHT**, WITH A FEW **DOZEN** (OR A **HUNDRED** OR A **THOUSAND**) **OTHER** AUDIENCE MEMBERS **ALONG** FOR THE **RIDE**...

...How our noble brother fell...♪

...SHE'LL **ALWAYS** BE ABLE TO STRETCH OUT THOSE SOFT **ARMS** OF HERS AND **DRAW** ME RIGHT **IN**...

...AS IF **NOTHING** ABOUT OUR LOVE WAS **COMPLICATED** AND **EVERYTHING** ABOUT OUR TIME TOGETHER WAS **ETERNAL**.

ESMERELDUS IS COMIN' UP HERE NOW. SHE'S GOT **ANOTHER** SONG FOR YOU THAT WAS A FAVORITE OF **SAMMY'S**.

GINGER, YOUR **PIPES** GIVE ME PALPITATIONS!

Squeeze!

click!

LISTEN, I CAN'T GO **ON** UNTIL I **SAY** SOMETHIN' TO Y'ALL...AN' TO **SAMMY**, TOO.

IT'S ABOUT A **SACRIFICE** I'M PREPARED TO MAKE.

AN' SAMMY, DON'T THINK I CAN'T **FEEL** YOU UP THERE **FIDGETIN'** AN' **TWIDDLIN'** YOUR FLUFFY NEW **WINGS** AN' WONDERIN' WHEN THE **HELL** THIS QUEEN IS GONNA GET **ON** WITH HER **ACT**!

BUT I'M THINKIN' THAT I MAY HAFTA **DISAPPOINT** YOU.

Y'SEE, EVEN THOUGH I'VE **ALREADY** GONE TO THE TROUBLE OF PUTTIN' ON MY **WIG** AN' ALL OF THIS GORGEOUS **MAKEUP**...

...AN' EVEN THOUGH GOD **KNOWS** THAT NOBODY'S MORE INCLINED TO **HOG** A SPOT-**LIGHT** THAN **I** AM...

...WE ALL KNOW THAT THE LADY WHO'LL **OWN** THIS SONG **FOREVER** IS RIGHT HERE **WITH** US IN THIS **ROOM**.

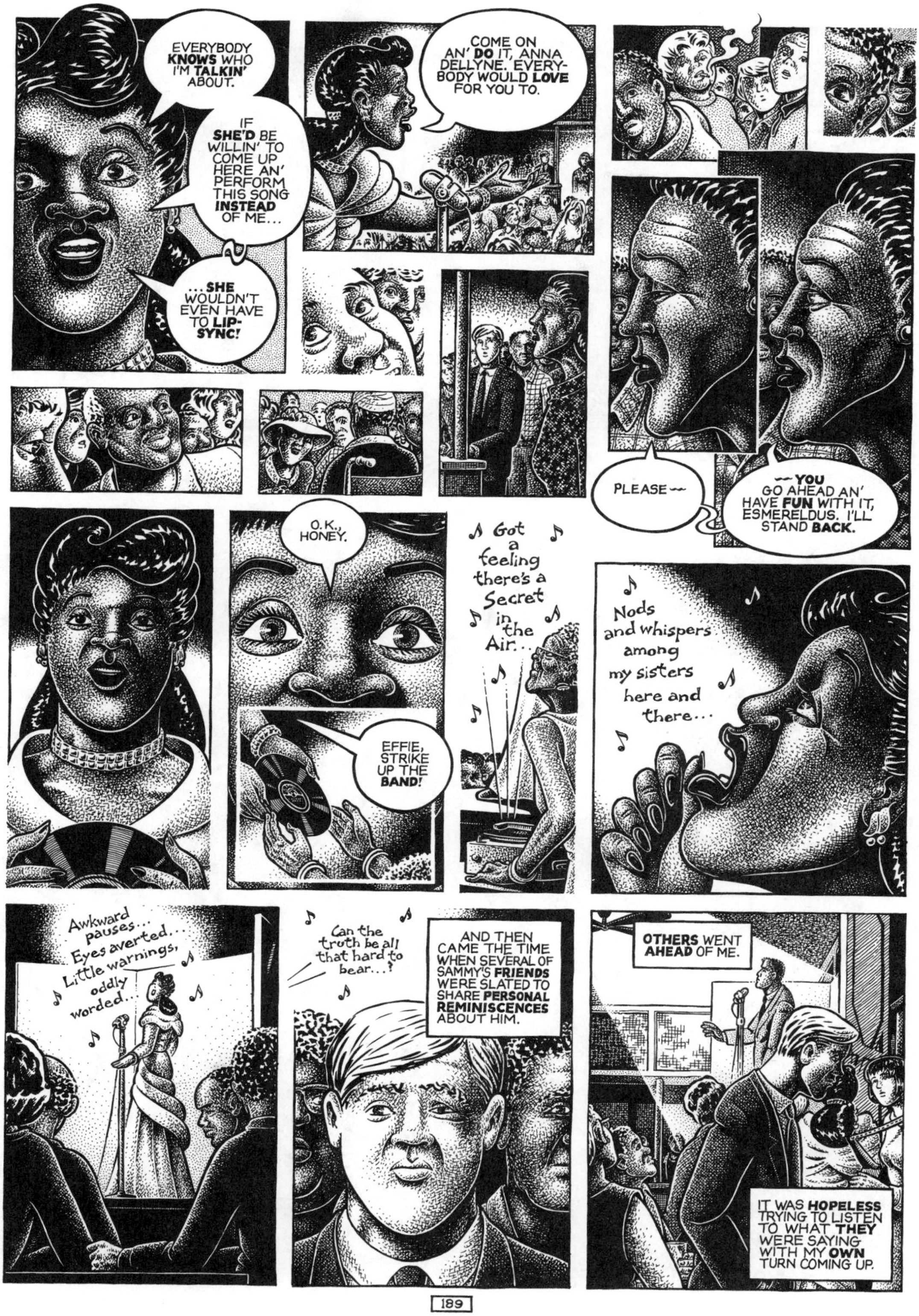
EVERYBODY KNOWS WHO I'M TALKIN' ABOUT.
IF SHE'D BE WILLIN' TO COME UP HERE AN' PERFORM THIS SONG INSTEAD OF ME...
...SHE WOULDN'T EVEN HAVE TO LIP-SYNC!
COME ON AN' DO IT, ANNA DELLYNE. EVERY-BODY WOULD LOVE FOR YOU TO.
PLEASE--
--YOU GO AHEAD AN' HAVE FUN WITH IT, ESMERELDUS. I'LL STAND BACK.
O.K., HONEY.
EFFIE, STRIKE UP THE BAND!
Got a feeling there's a Secret in the Air...
Nods and whispers among my sisters here and there...
Awkward pauses... Eyes averted... Little warnings, oddly worded...
Can the truth be all that hard to bear...?
AND THEN CAME THE TIME WHEN SEVERAL OF SAMMY'S FRIENDS WERE SLATED TO SHARE PERSONAL REMINISCENCES ABOUT HIM.
OTHERS WENT AHEAD OF ME.
IT WAS HOPELESS TRYING TO LISTEN TO WHAT THEY WERE SAYING WITH MY OWN TURN COMING UP.

WHEN MY TIME CAME TO **SPEAK,** I SURPRISED MYSELF BY WINDING MY WAY FAIRLY **ARTICULATELY** THROUGH THE **ANECDOTES** I'D MAPPED OUT IN MY HEAD **BEFOREHAND.**

I WON'T BOTHER **REPEATING** 'EM **NOW.**

MOST OF 'EM I'VE TOLD YOU ABOUT **ALREADY.**

ONCE I'D **FINISHED,** THE **CORRECT** THING TO DO, OBVIOUSLY, WOULD'VE BEEN TO TURN AND STEP **DOWN** FROM THE **PLATFORM.**

BUT TO MY **EMBARRASSMENT,** SOME **WEIRDNESS** TOOK HOLD OF ME.

I COULDN'T GET MYSELF TO STOP LOOKING AT ALL THE **FACES.**

I FELL SILENT AND JUST **STOOD** THERE – **FROZEN!**

AND WITH EVERY **SECOND** THAT TICKED BY, I BECAME MORE **AWARE** OF HOW THOROUGHLY EVERYONE **ELSE** HAD FALLEN SILENT, **TOO.**

AND I WAS AWARE THAT THE **AMPS** WERE GIVING OFF A LOW **HUM.**

AND I WAS AWARE OF THE **CHILLINESS** OF THE STEEL **MIKE STAND** MY FIST WAS CLUTCHING.

AND I WONDERED IF I WAS GOING TO PASS OUT...

'CAUSE ALL OF THE **FACES** I WAS LOOKING DOWN AT WERE BEGINNING TO DROP **AWAY...**

...LIKE THEY WERE SPIRALING HEADLONG DOWN A WEIRDLY LIT **SHAFT** THAT I WAS IN SOME **DANGER** OF TOPPLING INTO **MYSELF!**

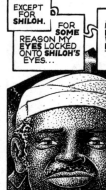

EXCEPT FOR **SHILOH.**

FOR **SOME** REASON MY EYES LOCKED ONTO **SHILOH'S** EYES...

...AND IT CAME **BACK** TO ME, WHAT HAD **PUT** HIM IN THAT **WHEEL-CHAIR...**

...AND I IMAGINED THE **EXPLOSION** AT THE **MELODY MOTEL...**

...AND WHAT IT MUST'VE BEEN LIKE TO **BE** SHILOH...

...AND SEE A **FLAMING TORNADO** OF **SHATTERED BEAMS** AND **CONCRETE** BLASTING TOWARD ME...

...AND THEN I WAS ON THE BACK STEPS OF THE **WHEELERY** AGAIN...

...WATCHING **HARD STEEL** WHIZ OUT OF **BLACKNESS.**

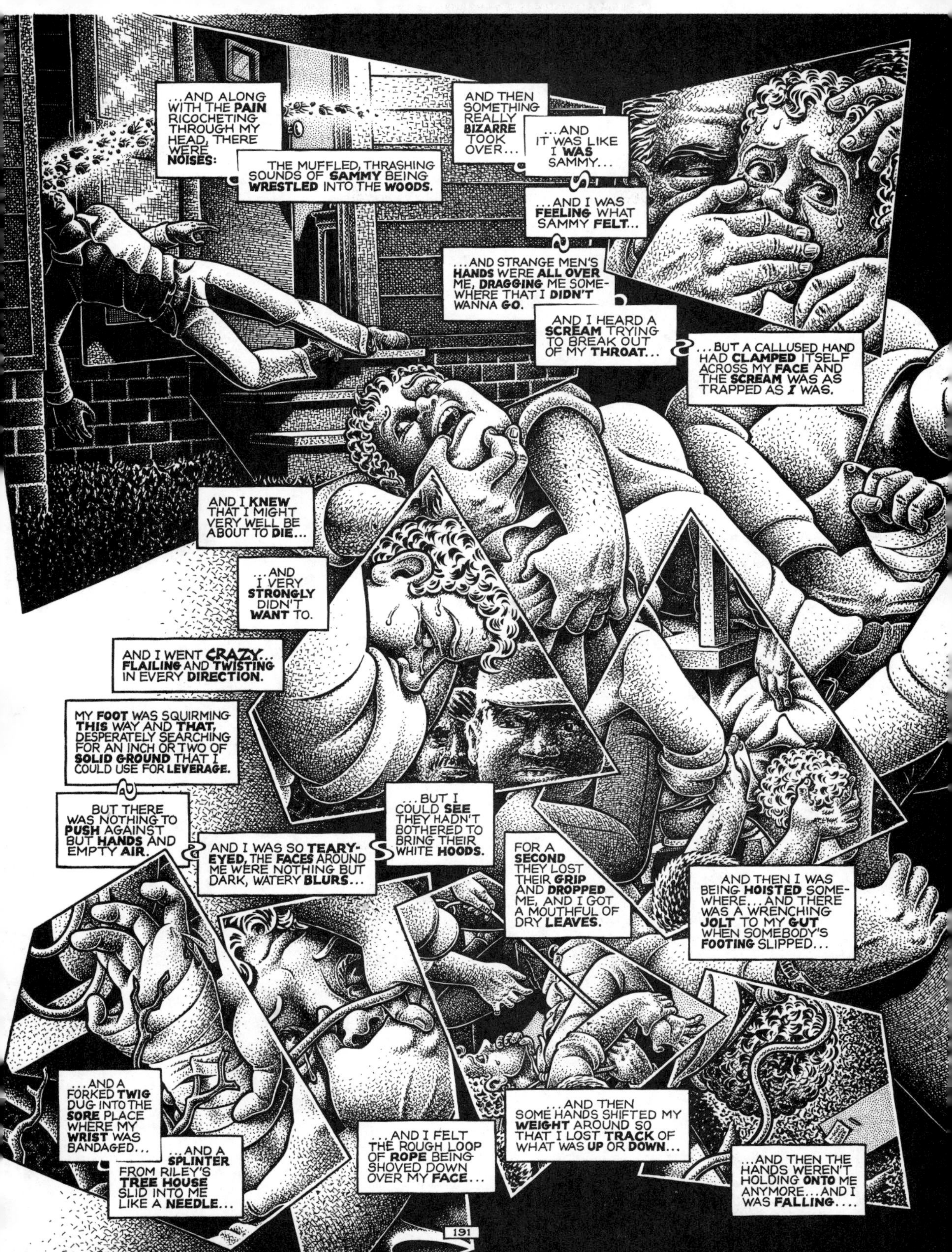

...AND ALONG WITH THE PAIN RICOCHETING THROUGH MY HEAD, THERE WERE NOISES:
THE MUFFLED, THRASHING SOUNDS OF SAMMY BEING WRESTLED INTO THE WOODS.
AND THEN SOMETHING REALLY BIZARRE TOOK OVER...
...AND IT WAS LIKE I WAS SAMMY...
...AND I WAS FEELING WHAT SAMMY FELT...
...AND STRANGE MEN'S HANDS WERE ALL OVER ME, DRAGGING ME SOMEWHERE THAT I DIDN'T WANNA GO.
AND I HEARD A SCREAM TRYING TO BREAK OUT OF MY THROAT...
...BUT A CALLUSED HAND HAD CLAMPED ITSELF ACROSS MY FACE AND THE SCREAM WAS AS TRAPPED AS I WAS.
AND I KNEW THAT I MIGHT VERY WELL BE ABOUT TO DIE...
...AND I VERY STRONGLY DIDN'T WANT TO.
AND I WENT CRAZY... FLAILING AND TWISTING IN EVERY DIRECTION.
MY FOOT WAS SQUIRMING THIS WAY AND THAT, DESPERATELY SEARCHING FOR AN INCH OR TWO OF SOLID GROUND THAT I COULD USE FOR LEVERAGE.
BUT THERE WAS NOTHING TO PUSH AGAINST BUT HANDS AND EMPTY AIR.
AND I WAS SO TEARY-EYED, THE FACES AROUND ME WERE NOTHING BUT DARK, WATERY BLURS...
...BUT I COULD SEE THEY HADN'T BOTHERED TO BRING THEIR WHITE HOODS.
FOR A SECOND THEY LOST THEIR GRIP AND DROPPED ME, AND I GOT A MOUTHFUL OF DRY LEAVES.
AND THEN I WAS BEING HOISTED SOMEWHERE... AND THERE WAS A WRENCHING JOLT TO MY GUT WHEN SOMEBODY'S FOOTING SLIPPED...
...AND A FORKED TWIG DUG INTO THE SORE PLACE WHERE MY WRIST WAS BANDAGED...
...AND A SPLINTER FROM RILEY'S TREE HOUSE SLID INTO ME LIKE A NEEDLE...
...AND I FELT THE ROUGH LOOP OF ROPE BEING SHOVED DOWN OVER MY FACE...
...AND THEN SOME HANDS SHIFTED MY WEIGHT AROUND SO THAT I LOST TRACK OF WHAT WAS UP OR DOWN...
...AND THEN THE HANDS WEREN'T HOLDING ONTO ME ANYMORE... AND I WAS FALLING...

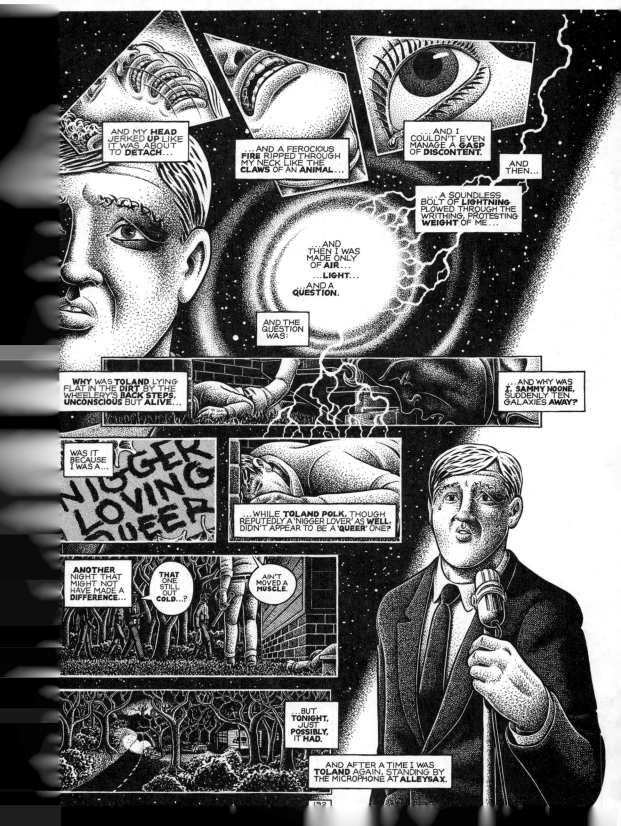

AND MY **HEAD** JERKED **UP** LIKE IT WAS ABOUT TO **DETACH**...

...AND A FEROCIOUS **FIRE** RIPPED THROUGH MY NECK LIKE THE **CLAWS OF AN ANIMAL**...

...AND I COULDN'T EVEN MANAGE A **GASP** OF **DISCONTENT**.

AND THEN...

A SOUNDLESS BOLT OF **LIGHTNING** PLOWED THROUGH THE WRITHING, PROTESTING **WEIGHT** OF ME...

...AND THEN I WAS MADE ONLY OF **AIR**...

...**LIGHT**...

...AND A **QUESTION**.

AND THE QUESTION WAS:

WHY WAS **TOLAND** LYING FLAT IN THE **DIRT** BY THE WHEELERY'S **BACK STEPS**, **UNCONSCIOUS** BUT **ALIVE**...

...AND WHY WAS **I, SAMMY NOONE**, SUDDENLY TEN GALAXIES **AWAY**?

WAS IT BECAUSE I WAS A...

NIGGER LOVING QUEER

...WHILE **TOLAND POLK**, THOUGH REPUTEDLY A 'NIGGER LOVER' AS **WELL**, DIDN'T APPEAR TO BE A 'QUEER' ONE?

ANOTHER NIGHT THAT MIGHT NOT HAVE MADE A **DIFFERENCE**...

THAT ONE STILL OUT COLD...?

AIN'T MOVED A **MUSCLE**.

...BUT **TONIGHT**, JUST POSSIBLY, IT **HAD**.

AND AFTER A TIME I WAS **TOLAND** AGAIN, STANDING BY THE MICROPHONE AT **ALLEYSAX**.

AND LIKE A **FOOL** I WAS UP THERE **SOBBING** IN FRONT OF **EVERYBODY**.

I **DOUBT** ANYBODY THOUGHT **LESS** OF ME FOR IT, OF COURSE.

IT **WAS** A NIGHT FOR **GRIEVING**, AFTER ALL.

BUT I DIDN'T **DARE** LEAVE PEOPLE THINKING THAT MY TEARS HAD BEEN FLOWING FOR A MURDERED FRIEND AND NOTHING **MORE**.

'CAUSE I **KNEW** THAT, IF I **DIDN'T** SAY THE WORDS **RIGHT THEN**—

—(AND I'M TALKING ABOUT THE REALLY **FRIGHTENING** WORDS THAT ALL THE **HABITS** OF A **LIFETIME** WERE **SCREAMING** AT ME TO HOLD **BACK** AND LEAVE **UNSAID**)—

—I MIGHT JUST **CONTINUE** ON MY **COWARD'S** WAY THE **NEXT** DAY AND THE **NEXT**... AND THE DAY AFTER **THAT**...

...AND **ALL** THE DAYS **THEREAFTER**.

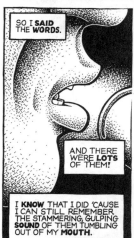

SO I **SAID** THE **WORDS**.

AND THERE WERE **LOTS** OF THEM!

I **KNOW** THAT I DID 'CAUSE I CAN STILL REMEMBER THE STAMMERING, GULPING **SOUND** OF THEM TUMBLING OUT OF MY **MOUTH**.

AND I'LL BE **DAMNED** IF I CAN RECALL WHAT ANY OF THEM **WERE** IN **PARTICULAR** —EXCEPT FOR THESE **FOUR**:

IT COULD'VE BEEN **ME**.

AND I **REALIZED** AS I **SPOKE** THOSE FOUR WORDS THAT I WAS SAYING THEM TO **SHILOH** MORE THAN TO ANYONE **ELSE**.

I KNEW I'D FIND **UNDERSTANDING** IN SHILOH'S **EYES**.

EVENTUALLY A POINT CAME WHEN I KNEW I WAS **DONE** TALKING.

I'D **SAID** WHAT NEEDED **SAYING**.

AND PART OF ME WAS **EMBARRASSED** BY THE **WETNESS** OF MY **CHEEKS** AND BY THE EMOTIONAL **EXCESSES** I KNEW I'D PROBABLY COMMITTED...

...BUT **ANOTHER** PART OF ME WAS LEFT WITH AN ALMOST **GIDDY** SERENITY.

IN THE DAYS THAT **FOLLOWED**, THE DELICATE SUBJECT OF MY ALLEY-SAX **OUTBURST** GOT **RAISED** A FEW TIMES BY FRIENDS WHO'D **WITNESSED** IT.

I DIDN'T **SAY** TOO MUCH, FIGURING THAT THE MORE I WENT **INTO** IT, THE **CRAZIER** I'D SEEM.

I'M **STILL** NOT A HUNDRED PERCENT **SURE** WHAT REALLY **HAPPENED** THAT NIGHT...

...BUT THE CLEAR **EFFECT** OF IT WAS TO PUT TO **REST** ANY **MISIMPRESSIONS** I'D FOSTERED THAT **TOLAND POLK** WAS ANY **STRAIGHTER** THAN **SAMMY NOONE** HAD BEEN!

SAY IT **ONCE** IN **PUBLIC** AND THE **GRAPEVINE'LL** TAKE IT FROM **THERE**!

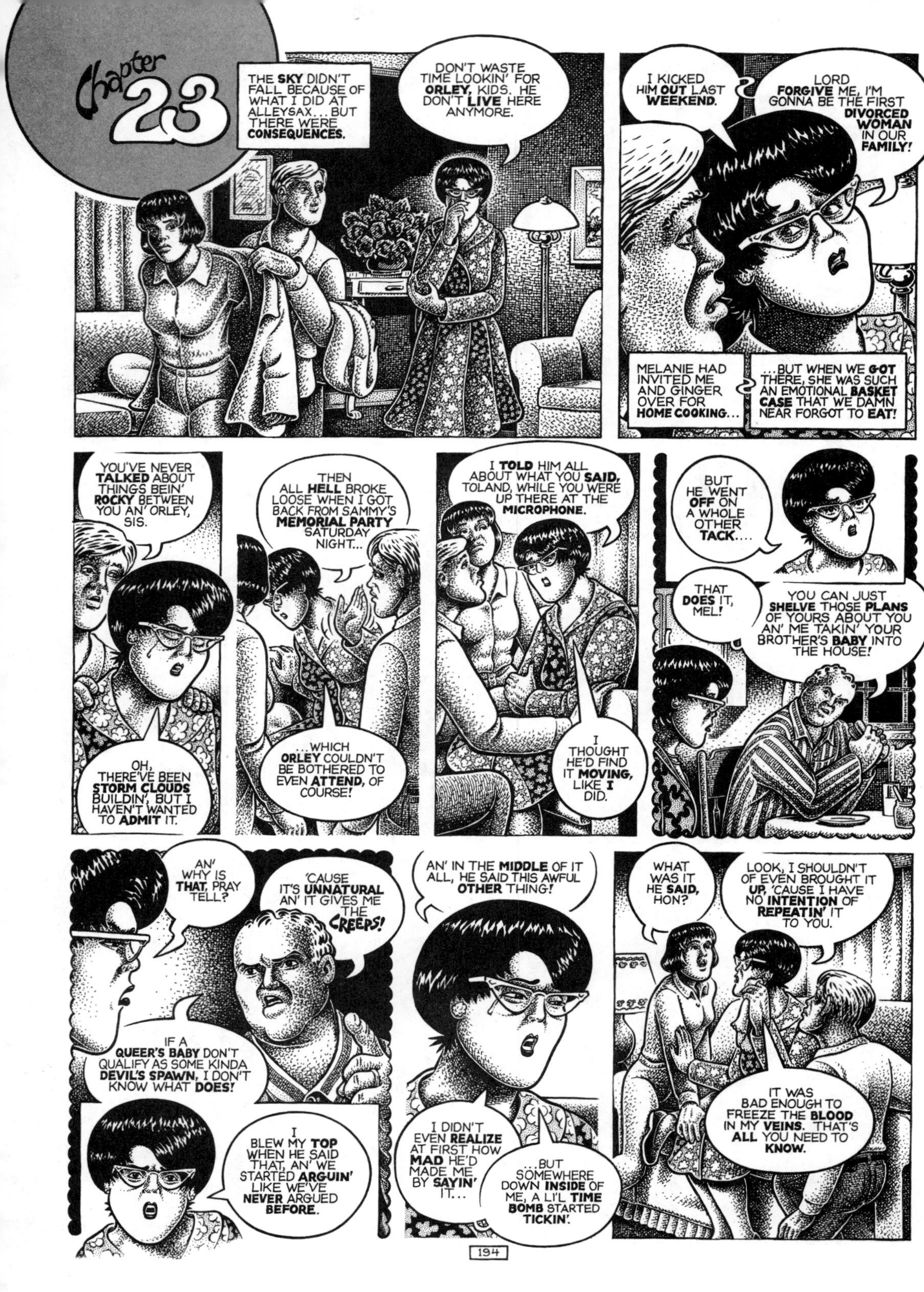
Chapter 23
THE SKY DIDN'T FALL BECAUSE OF WHAT I DID AT ALLEYSAX... BUT THERE WERE CONSEQUENCES.
DON'T WASTE TIME LOOKIN' FOR ORLEY, KIDS. HE DON'T LIVE HERE ANYMORE.
I KICKED HIM OUT LAST WEEKEND.
LORD FORGIVE ME, I'M GONNA BE THE FIRST DIVORCED WOMAN IN OUR FAMILY!
MELANIE HAD INVITED ME AND GINGER OVER FOR HOME COOKING...
...BUT WHEN WE GOT THERE, SHE WAS SUCH AN EMOTIONAL BASKET CASE THAT WE DAMN NEAR FORGOT TO EAT!
YOU'VE NEVER TALKED ABOUT THINGS BEIN' ROCKY BETWEEN YOU AN' ORLEY, SIS.
OH, THERE'VE BEEN STORM CLOUDS BUILDIN', BUT I HAVEN'T WANTED TO ADMIT IT.
THEN ALL HELL BROKE LOOSE WHEN I GOT BACK FROM SAMMY'S MEMORIAL PARTY SATURDAY NIGHT...
...WHICH ORLEY COULDN'T BE BOTHERED TO EVEN ATTEND, OF COURSE!
I TOLD HIM ALL ABOUT WHAT YOU SAID, TOLAND, WHILE YOU WERE UP THERE AT THE MICROPHONE.
I THOUGHT HE'D FIND IT MOVING, LIKE I DID.
BUT HE WENT OFF ON A WHOLE OTHER TACK....
THAT DOES IT, MEL!
YOU CAN JUST SHELVE THOSE PLANS OF YOURS ABOUT YOU AN' ME TAKIN' YOUR BROTHER'S BABY INTO THE HOUSE!
AN' WHY IS THAT, PRAY TELL?
'CAUSE IT'S UNNATURAL AN' IT GIVES ME THE CREEPS!
IF A QUEER'S BABY DON'T QUALIFY AS SOME KINDA DEVIL'S SPAWN, I DON'T KNOW WHAT DOES!
I BLEW MY TOP WHEN HE SAID THAT, AN' WE STARTED ARGUIN' LIKE WE'VE NEVER ARGUED BEFORE.
AN' IN THE MIDDLE OF IT ALL, HE SAID THIS AWFUL OTHER THING!
I DIDN'T EVEN REALIZE AT FIRST HOW MAD HE'D MADE ME BY SAYIN' IT...
...BUT SOMEWHERE DOWN INSIDE OF ME, A LI'L TIME BOMB STARTED TICKIN'.
WHAT WAS IT HE SAID, HON?
LOOK, I SHOULDN'T OF EVEN BROUGHT IT UP, 'CAUSE I HAVE NO INTENTION OF REPEATIN' IT TO YOU.
IT WAS BAD ENOUGH TO FREEZE THE BLOOD IN MY VEINS. THAT'S ALL YOU NEED TO KNOW.

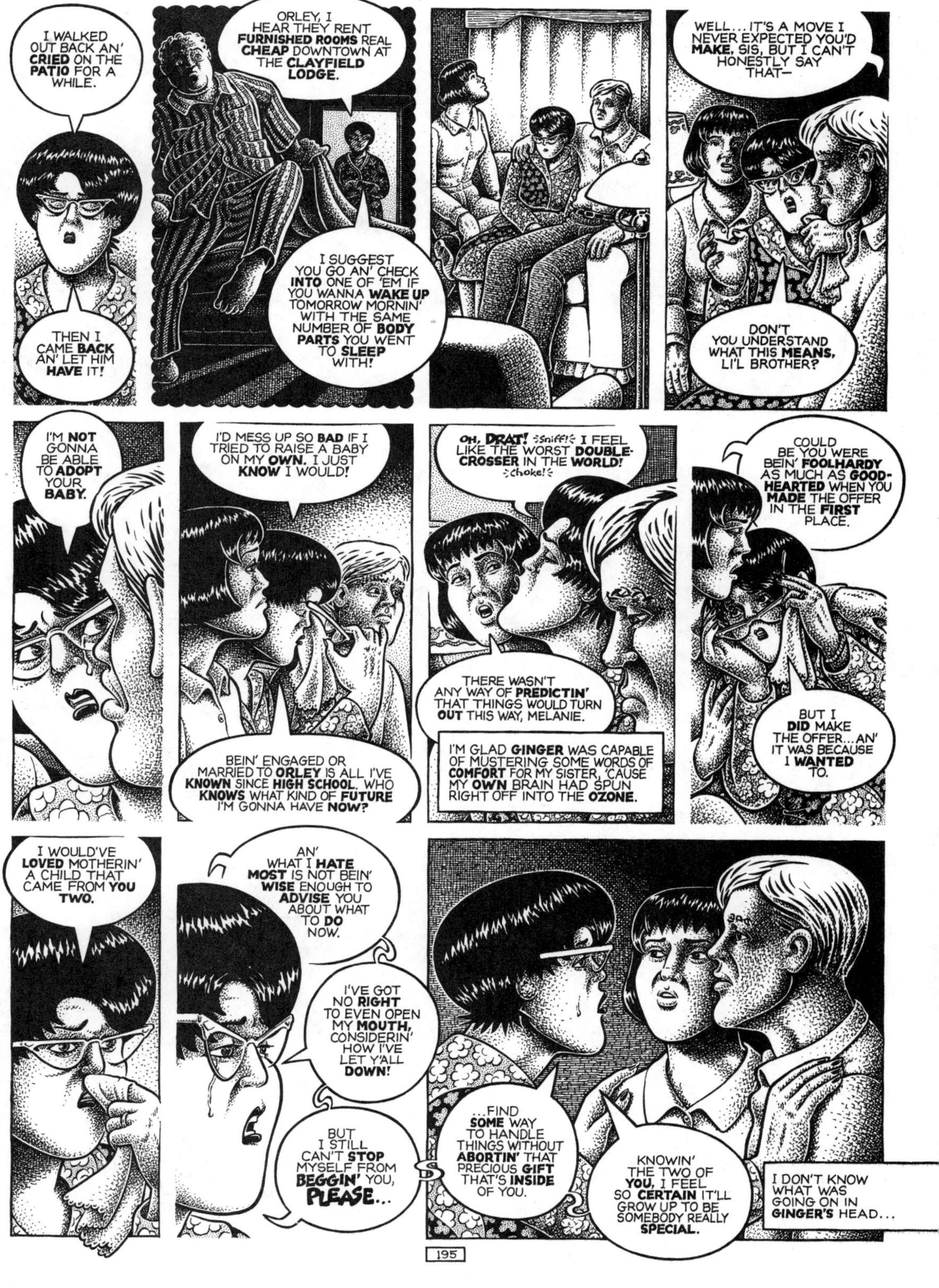
I WALKED OUT BACK AN' CRIED ON THE PATIO FOR A WHILE.
THEN I CAME BACK AN' LET HIM HAVE IT!
ORLEY, I HEAR THEY RENT FURNISHED ROOMS REAL CHEAP DOWNTOWN AT THE CLAYFIELD LODGE.
I SUGGEST YOU GO AN' CHECK INTO ONE OF 'EM IF YOU WANNA WAKE UP TOMORROW MORNIN' WITH THE SAME NUMBER OF BODY PARTS YOU WENT TO SLEEP WITH!
WELL... IT'S A MOVE I NEVER EXPECTED YOU'D MAKE, SIS, BUT I CAN'T HONESTLY SAY THAT—
DON'T YOU UNDERSTAND WHAT THIS MEANS, LI'L BROTHER?
I'M NOT GONNA BE ABLE TO ADOPT YOUR BABY.
I'D MESS UP SO BAD IF I TRIED TO RAISE A BABY ON MY OWN. I JUST KNOW I WOULD!
BEIN' ENGAGED OR MARRIED TO ORLEY IS ALL I'VE KNOWN SINCE HIGH SCHOOL. WHO KNOWS WHAT KIND OF FUTURE I'M GONNA HAVE NOW?
OH, DRAT! SNIFF! I FEEL LIKE THE WORST DOUBLE-CROSSER IN THE WORLD! CHOKE!
THERE WASN'T ANY WAY OF PREDICTIN' THAT THINGS WOULD TURN OUT THIS WAY, MELANIE.
I'M GLAD GINGER WAS CAPABLE OF MUSTERING SOME WORDS OF COMFORT FOR MY SISTER, 'CAUSE MY OWN BRAIN HAD SPUN RIGHT OFF INTO THE OZONE.
COULD BE YOU WERE BEIN' FOOLHARDY AS MUCH AS GOOD-HEARTED WHEN YOU MADE THE OFFER IN THE FIRST PLACE.
BUT I DID MAKE THE OFFER... AN' IT WAS BECAUSE I WANTED TO.
I WOULD'VE LOVED MOTHERIN' A CHILD THAT CAME FROM YOU TWO.
AN' WHAT I HATE MOST IS NOT BEIN' WISE ENOUGH TO ADVISE YOU ABOUT WHAT TO DO NOW.
I'VE GOT NO RIGHT TO EVEN OPEN MY MOUTH, CONSIDERIN' HOW I'VE LET Y'ALL DOWN!
BUT I STILL CAN'T STOP MYSELF FROM BEGGIN' YOU, PLEASE...
...FIND SOME WAY TO HANDLE THINGS WITHOUT ABORTIN' THAT PRECIOUS GIFT THAT'S INSIDE OF YOU.
KNOWIN' THE TWO OF YOU, I FEEL SO CERTAIN IT'LL GROW UP TO BE SOMEBODY REALLY SPECIAL.
I DON'T KNOW WHAT WAS GOING ON IN GINGER'S HEAD...

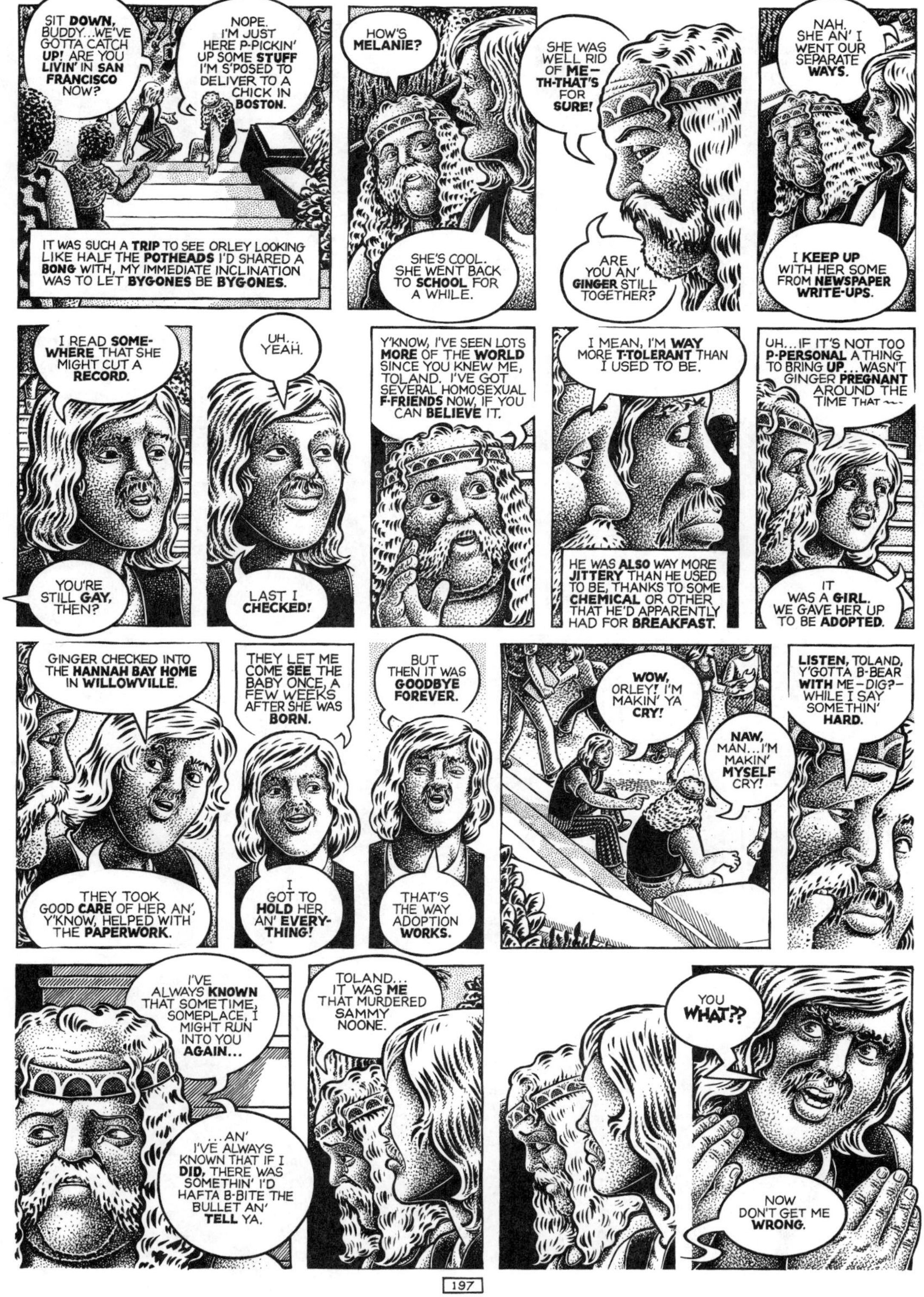

SIT DOWN, BUDDY...WE'VE GOTTA CATCH UP! ARE YOU LIVIN' IN SAN FRANCISCO NOW?
NOPE. I'M JUST HERE P-PICKIN' UP SOME STUFF I'M S'POSED TO DELIVER TO A CHICK IN BOSTON.
IT WAS SUCH A TRIP TO SEE ORLEY LOOKING LIKE HALF THE POTHEADS I'D SHARED A BONG WITH, MY IMMEDIATE INCLINATION WAS TO LET BYGONES BE BYGONES.
HOW'S MELANIE?
SHE'S COOL. SHE WENT BACK TO SCHOOL FOR A WHILE.
SHE WAS WELL RID OF ME— TH-THAT'S FOR SURE!
ARE YOU AN' GINGER STILL TOGETHER?
NAH. SHE AN' I WENT OUR SEPARATE WAYS.
I KEEP UP WITH HER SOME FROM NEWSPAPER WRITE-UPS.
I READ SOME-WHERE THAT SHE MIGHT CUT A RECORD.
YOU'RE STILL GAY, THEN?
UH... YEAH.
LAST I CHECKED!
Y'KNOW, I'VE SEEN LOTS MORE OF THE WORLD SINCE YOU KNEW ME, TOLAND. I'VE GOT SEVERAL HOMOSEXUAL F-FRIENDS NOW, IF YOU CAN BELIEVE IT.
I MEAN, I'M WAY MORE T-TOLERANT THAN I USED TO BE.
HE WAS ALSO WAY MORE JITTERY THAN HE USED TO BE, THANKS TO SOME CHEMICAL OR OTHER THAT HE'D APPARENTLY HAD FOR BREAKFAST.
UH...IF IT'S NOT TOO P-PERSONAL A THING TO BRING UP...WASN'T GINGER PREGNANT AROUND THE TIME THAT~~~
IT WAS A GIRL. WE GAVE HER UP TO BE ADOPTED.
GINGER CHECKED INTO THE HANNAH BAY HOME IN WILLOWVILLE.
THEY TOOK GOOD CARE OF HER AN', Y'KNOW, HELPED WITH THE PAPERWORK.
THEY LET ME COME SEE THE BABY ONCE, A FEW WEEKS AFTER SHE WAS BORN.
I GOT TO HOLD HER AN' EVERY-THING!
BUT THEN IT WAS GOODBYE FOREVER.
THAT'S THE WAY ADOPTION WORKS.
WOW, ORLEY! I'M MAKIN' YA CRY!
NAW, MAN...I'M MAKIN' MYSELF CRY!
LISTEN, TOLAND, Y'GOTTA B-BEAR WITH ME—DIG?— WHILE I SAY SOMETHIN' HARD.
I'VE ALWAYS KNOWN THAT SOMETIME, SOMEPLACE, I MIGHT RUN INTO YOU AGAIN...
...AN' I'VE ALWAYS KNOWN THAT IF I DID, THERE WAS SOMETHIN' I'D HAFTA B-BITE THE BULLET AN' TELL YA.
TOLAND... IT WAS ME THAT MURDERED SAMMY NOONE.
YOU WHAT??
NOW DON'T GET ME WRONG.

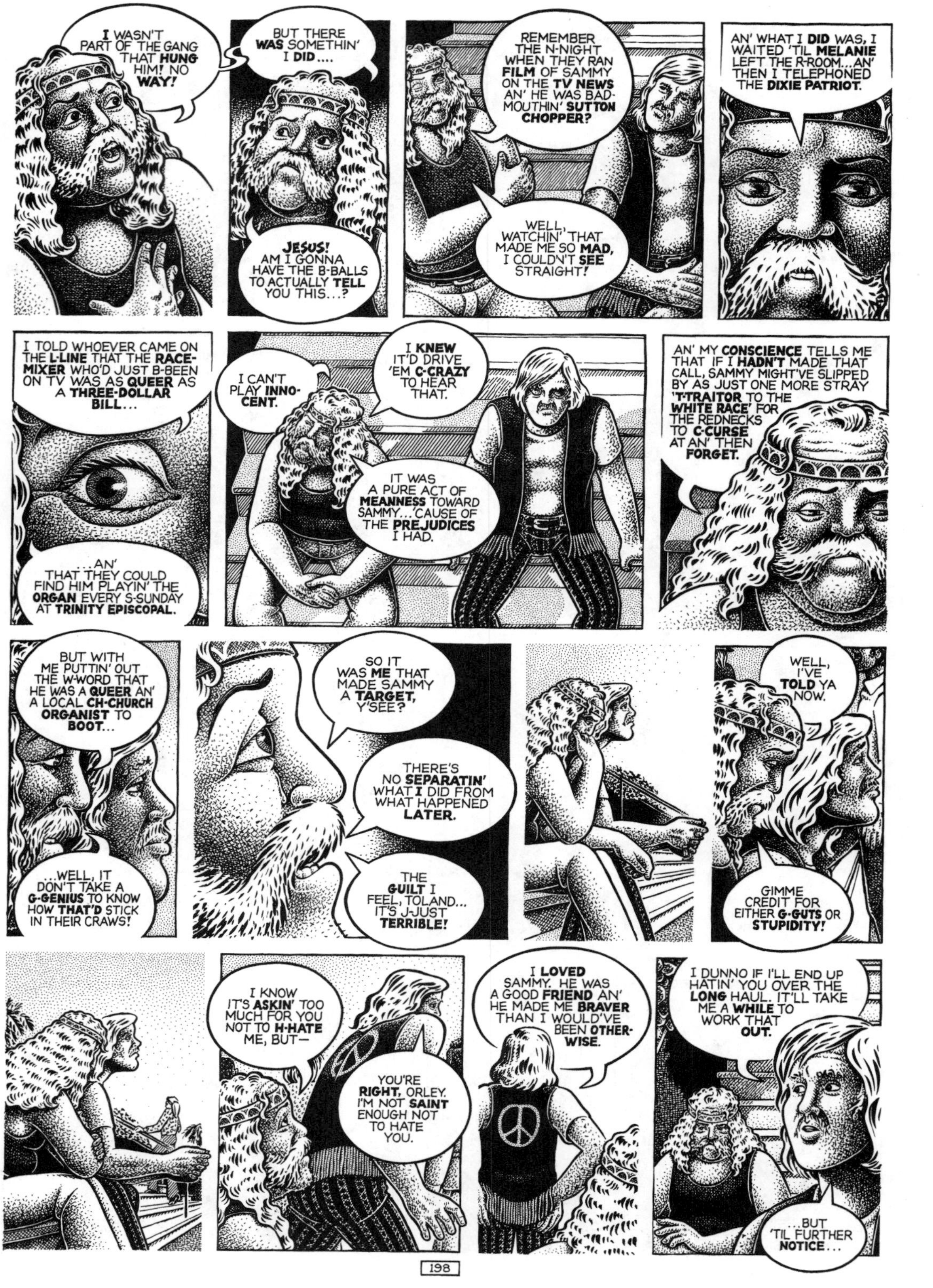
I WASN'T PART OF THE GANG THAT HUNG HIM! NO WAY!
BUT THERE WAS SOMETHIN' I DID....
JESUS! AM I GONNA HAVE THE B-BALLS TO ACTUALLY TELL YOU THIS...?
REMEMBER THE N-NIGHT WHEN THEY RAN FILM OF SAMMY ON THE TV NEWS AN' HE WAS BAD-MOUTHIN' SUTTON CHOPPER?
WELL, WATCHIN' THAT MADE ME SO MAD, I COULDN'T SEE STRAIGHT!
AN' WHAT I DID WAS, I WAITED 'TIL MELANIE LEFT THE R-ROOM...AN' THEN I TELEPHONED THE DIXIE PATRIOT.
I TOLD WHOEVER CAME ON THE L-LINE THAT THE RACE-MIXER WHO'D JUST B-BEEN ON TV WAS AS QUEER AS A THREE-DOLLAR BILL...
...AN' THAT THEY COULD FIND HIM PLAYIN' THE ORGAN EVERY S-SUNDAY AT TRINITY EPISCOPAL.
I CAN'T PLAY INNO-CENT.
I KNEW IT'D DRIVE 'EM C-CRAZY TO HEAR THAT.
IT WAS A PURE ACT OF MEANNESS TOWARD SAMMY...'CAUSE OF THE PREJUDICES I HAD.
AN' MY CONSCIENCE TELLS ME THAT IF I HADN'T MADE THAT CALL, SAMMY MIGHT'VE SLIPPED BY AS JUST ONE MORE STRAY 'T-TRAITOR TO THE WHITE RACE' FOR THE REDNECKS TO C-CURSE AT AN' THEN FORGET.
BUT WITH ME PUTTIN' OUT THE W-WORD THAT HE WAS A QUEER AN' A LOCAL CH-CHURCH ORGANIST TO BOOT...
...WELL, IT DON'T TAKE A G-GENIUS TO KNOW HOW THAT'D STICK IN THEIR CRAWS!
SO IT WAS ME THAT MADE SAMMY A TARGET, Y'SEE?
THERE'S NO SEPARATIN' WHAT I DID FROM WHAT HAPPENED LATER.
THE GUILT I FEEL, TOLAND... IT'S J-JUST TERRIBLE!
WELL, I'VE TOLD YA NOW.
GIMME CREDIT FOR EITHER G-GUTS OR STUPIDITY!
I KNOW IT'S ASKIN' TOO MUCH FOR YOU NOT TO H-HATE ME, BUT—
YOU'RE RIGHT, ORLEY. I'M NOT SAINT ENOUGH NOT TO HATE YOU.
I LOVED SAMMY. HE WAS A GOOD FRIEND AN' HE MADE ME BRAVER THAN I WOULD'VE BEEN OTHER-WISE.
I DUNNO IF I'LL END UP HATIN' YOU OVER THE LONG HAUL. IT'LL TAKE ME A WHILE TO WORK THAT OUT.
...BUT 'TIL FURTHER NOTICE...

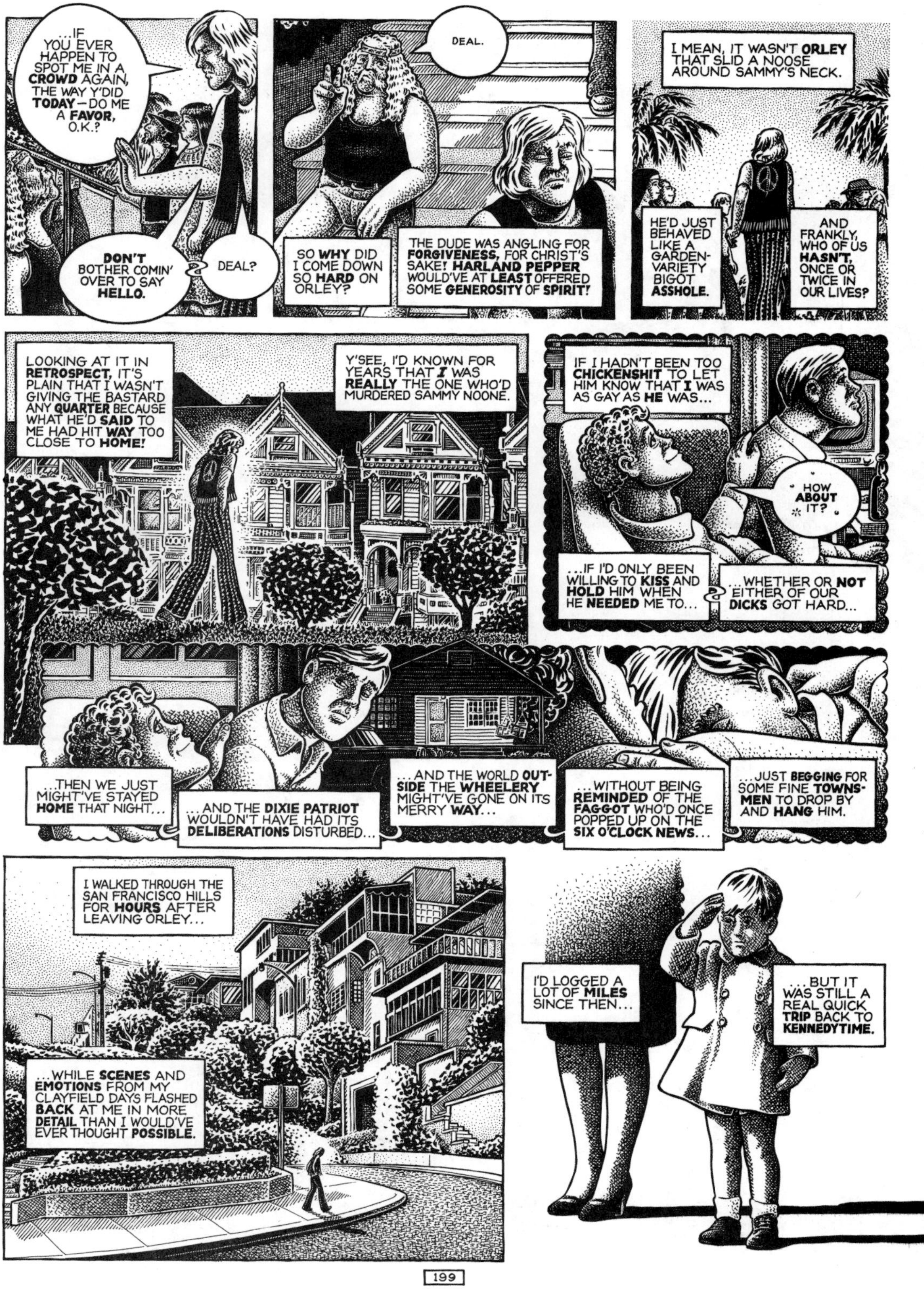
...IF YOU EVER HAPPEN TO SPOT ME IN A CROWD AGAIN, THE WAY Y'DID TODAY—DO ME A FAVOR, O.K.?
DON'T BOTHER COMIN' OVER TO SAY HELLO.
DEAL?
DEAL.
SO WHY DID I COME DOWN SO HARD ON ORLEY?
THE DUDE WAS ANGLING FOR FORGIVENESS, FOR CHRIST'S SAKE! HARLAND PEPPER WOULD'VE AT LEAST OFFERED SOME GENEROSITY OF SPIRIT!
I MEAN, IT WASN'T ORLEY THAT SLID A NOOSE AROUND SAMMY'S NECK.
HE'D JUST BEHAVED LIKE A GARDEN-VARIETY BIGOT ASSHOLE.
AND FRANKLY, WHO OF US HASN'T, ONCE OR TWICE IN OUR LIVES?
LOOKING AT IT IN RETROSPECT, IT'S PLAIN THAT I WASN'T GIVING THE BASTARD ANY QUARTER BECAUSE WHAT HE'D SAID TO ME HAD HIT WAY TOO CLOSE TO HOME!
Y'SEE, I'D KNOWN FOR YEARS THAT I WAS REALLY THE ONE WHO'D MURDERED SAMMY NOONE.
IF I HADN'T BEEN TOO CHICKENSHIT TO LET HIM KNOW THAT I WAS AS GAY AS HE WAS...
HOW ABOUT IT?
...IF I'D ONLY BEEN WILLING TO KISS AND HOLD HIM WHEN HE NEEDED ME TO...
...WHETHER OR NOT EITHER OF OUR DICKS GOT HARD...
...THEN WE JUST MIGHT'VE STAYED HOME THAT NIGHT...
...AND THE DIXIE PATRIOT WOULDN'T HAVE HAD ITS DELIBERATIONS DISTURBED...
...AND THE WORLD OUTSIDE THE WHEELERY MIGHT'VE GONE ON ITS MERRY WAY...
...WITHOUT BEING REMINDED OF THE FAGGOT WHO'D ONCE POPPED UP ON THE SIX O'CLOCK NEWS...
...JUST BEGGING FOR SOME FINE TOWNSMEN TO DROP BY AND HANG HIM.
I WALKED THROUGH THE SAN FRANCISCO HILLS FOR HOURS AFTER LEAVING ORLEY...
...WHILE SCENES AND EMOTIONS FROM MY CLAYFIELD DAYS FLASHED BACK AT ME IN MORE DETAIL THAN I WOULD'VE EVER THOUGHT POSSIBLE.
I'D LOGGED A LOT OF MILES SINCE THEN...
...BUT IT WAS STILL A REAL QUICK TRIP BACK TO KENNEDYTIME.

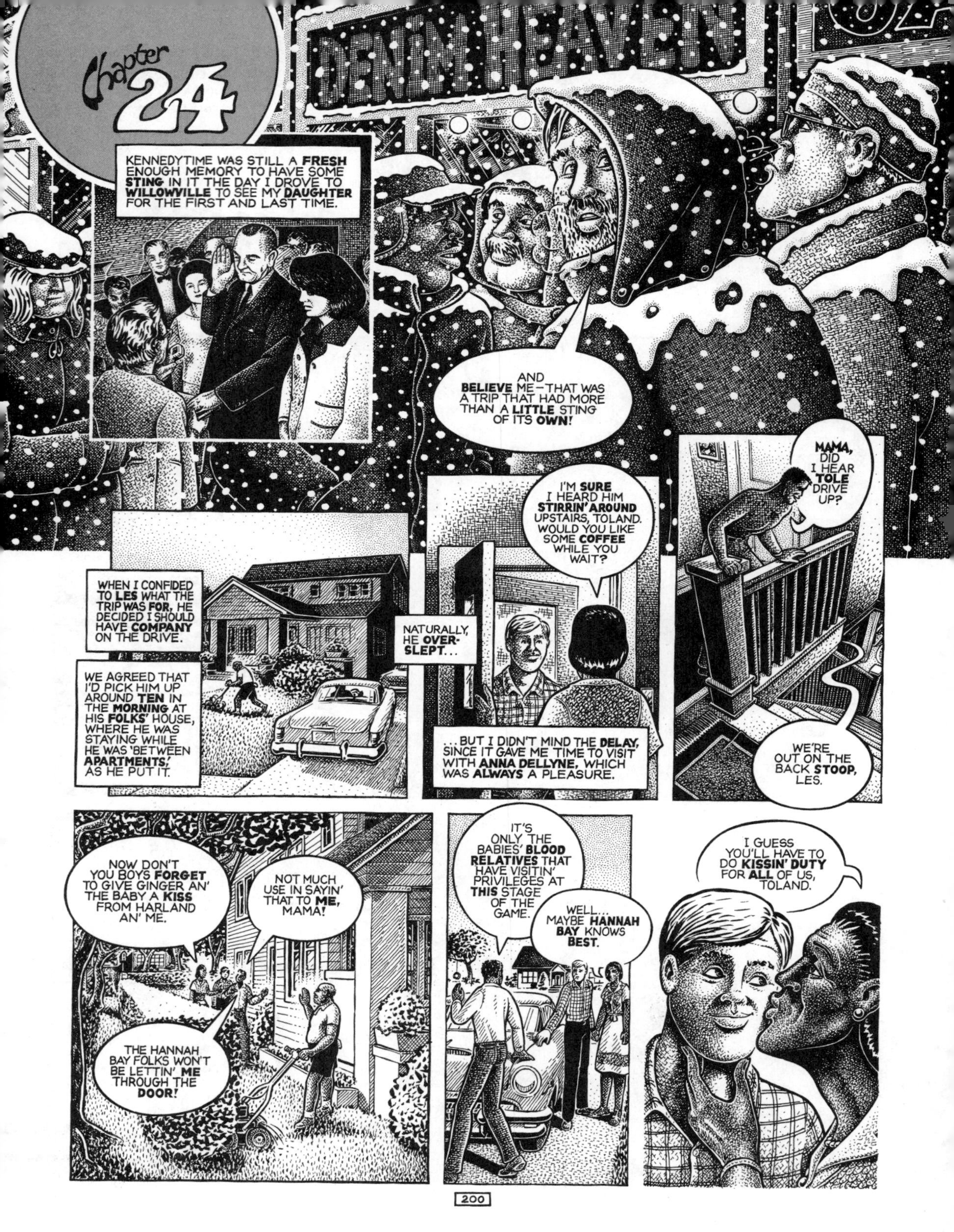
Chapter 24
DENIM HEAVEN
KENNEDYTIME WAS STILL A FRESH ENOUGH MEMORY TO HAVE SOME STING IN IT THE DAY I DROVE TO WILLOWVILLE TO SEE MY DAUGHTER FOR THE FIRST AND LAST TIME.
AND BELIEVE ME—THAT WAS A TRIP THAT HAD MORE THAN A LITTLE STING OF ITS OWN!
WHEN I CONFIDED TO LES WHAT THE TRIP WAS FOR, HE DECIDED I SHOULD HAVE COMPANY ON THE DRIVE.
WE AGREED THAT I'D PICK HIM UP AROUND TEN IN THE MORNING AT HIS FOLKS' HOUSE, WHERE HE WAS STAYING WHILE HE WAS 'BETWEEN APARTMENTS,' AS HE PUT IT.
NATURALLY, HE OVERSLEPT...
I'M SURE I HEARD HIM STIRRIN' AROUND UPSTAIRS, TOLAND. WOULD YOU LIKE SOME COFFEE WHILE YOU WAIT?
...BUT I DIDN'T MIND THE DELAY, SINCE IT GAVE ME TIME TO VISIT WITH ANNA DELLYNE, WHICH WAS ALWAYS A PLEASURE.
MAMA, DID I HEAR TOLE DRIVE UP?
WE'RE OUT ON THE BACK STOOP, LES.
NOW DON'T YOU BOYS FORGET TO GIVE GINGER AN' THE BABY A KISS FROM HARLAND AN' ME.
NOT MUCH USE IN SAYIN' THAT TO ME, MAMA!
THE HANNAH BAY FOLKS WON'T BE LETTIN' ME THROUGH THE DOOR!
IT'S ONLY THE BABIES' BLOOD RELATIVES THAT HAVE VISITIN' PRIVILEGES AT THIS STAGE OF THE GAME.
WELL... MAYBE HANNAH BAY KNOWS BEST.
I GUESS YOU'LL HAVE TO DO KISSIN' DUTY FOR ALL OF US, TOLAND.

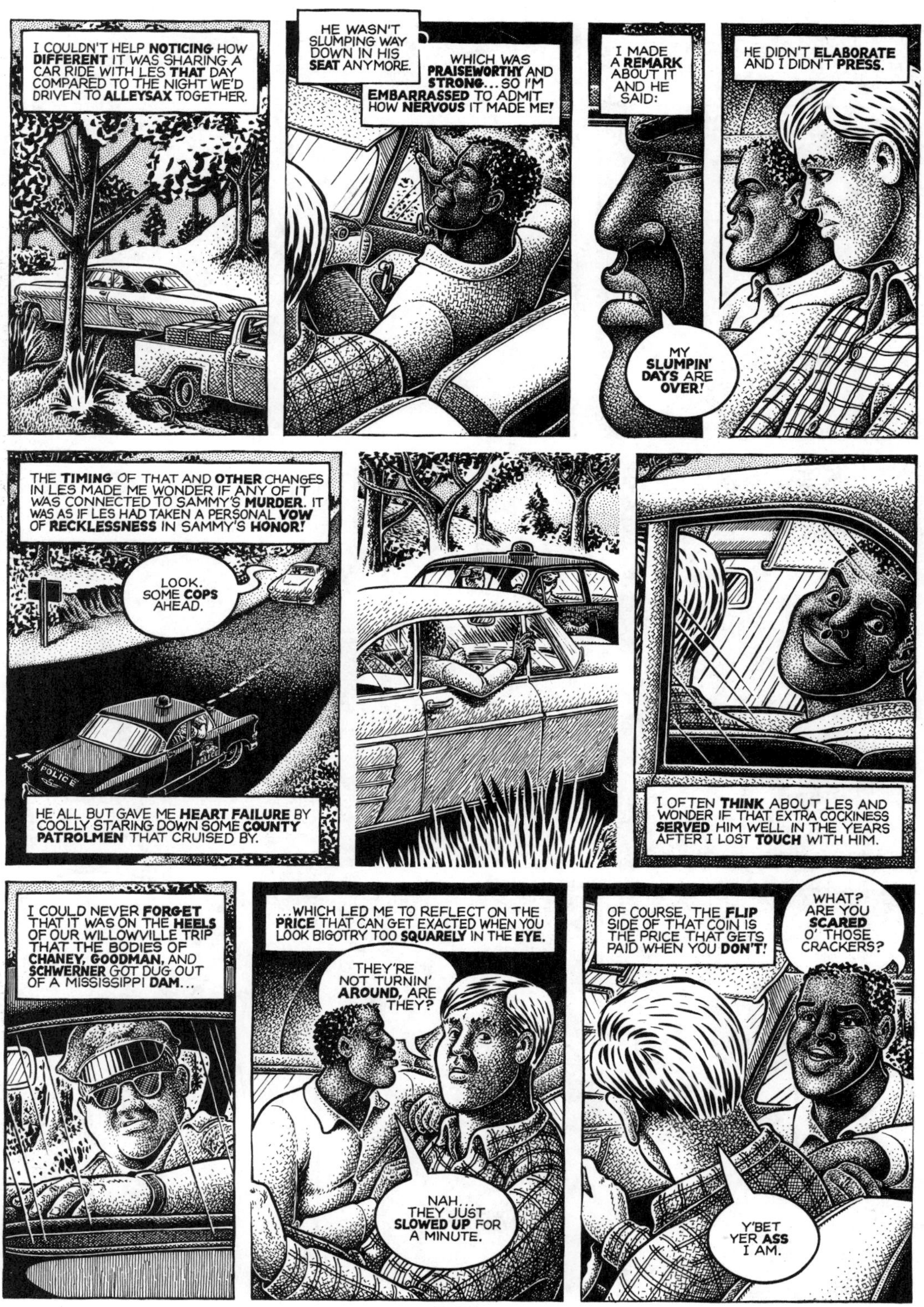

I COULDN'T HELP NOTICING HOW DIFFERENT IT WAS SHARING A CAR RIDE WITH LES THAT DAY COMPARED TO THE NIGHT WE'D DRIVEN TO ALLEYSAX TOGETHER.
HE WASN'T SLUMPING WAY DOWN IN HIS SEAT ANYMORE.
WHICH WAS PRAISEWORTHY AND STRONG... SO I'M EMBARRASSED TO ADMIT HOW NERVOUS IT MADE ME!
I MADE A REMARK ABOUT IT AND HE SAID:
MY SLUMPIN' DAYS ARE OVER!
HE DIDN'T ELABORATE AND I DIDN'T PRESS.
THE TIMING OF THAT AND OTHER CHANGES IN LES MADE ME WONDER IF ANY OF IT WAS CONNECTED TO SAMMY'S MURDER. IT WAS AS IF LES HAD TAKEN A PERSONAL VOW OF RECKLESSNESS IN SAMMY'S HONOR!
LOOK. SOME COPS AHEAD.
POLICE
HE ALL BUT GAVE ME HEART FAILURE BY COOLLY STARING DOWN SOME COUNTY PATROLMEN THAT CRUISED BY.
I OFTEN THINK ABOUT LES AND WONDER IF THAT EXTRA COCKINESS SERVED HIM WELL IN THE YEARS AFTER I LOST TOUCH WITH HIM.
I COULD NEVER FORGET THAT IT WAS ON THE HEELS OF OUR WILLOWVILLE TRIP THAT THE BODIES OF CHANEY, GOODMAN, AND SCHWERNER GOT DUG OUT OF A MISSISSIPPI DAM...
...WHICH LED ME TO REFLECT ON THE PRICE THAT CAN GET EXACTED WHEN YOU LOOK BIGOTRY TOO SQUARELY IN THE EYE.
THEY'RE NOT TURNIN' AROUND, ARE THEY?
NAH... THEY JUST SLOWED UP FOR A MINUTE.
OF COURSE, THE FLIP SIDE OF THAT COIN IS THE PRICE THAT GETS PAID WHEN YOU DON'T!
WHAT? ARE YOU SCARED O' THOSE CRACKERS?
Y'BET YER ASS I AM.

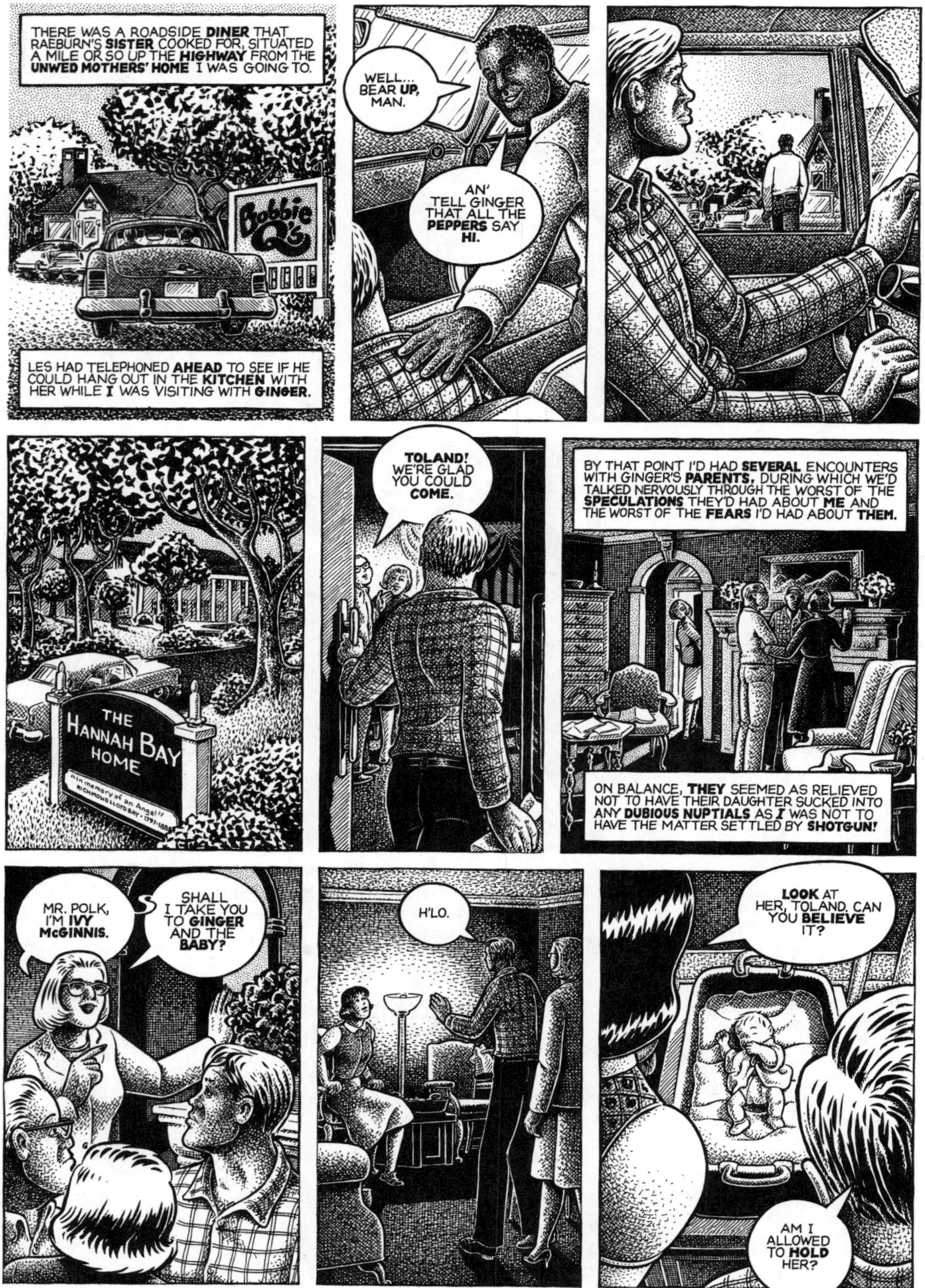

THERE WAS A ROADSIDE DINER THAT RAEBURN'S SISTER COOKED FOR, SITUATED A MILE OR SO UP THE HIGHWAY FROM THE UNWED MOTHERS' HOME I WAS GOING TO.
Bobbie Q's
LES HAD TELEPHONED AHEAD TO SEE IF HE COULD HANG OUT IN THE KITCHEN WITH HER WHILE I WAS VISITING WITH GINGER.
WELL... BEAR UP, MAN.
AN' TELL GINGER THAT ALL THE PEPPERS SAY HI.
THE HANNAH BAY HOME
TOLAND! WE'RE GLAD YOU COULD COME.
BY THAT POINT I'D HAD SEVERAL ENCOUNTERS WITH GINGER'S PARENTS, DURING WHICH WE'D TALKED NERVOUSLY THROUGH THE WORST OF THE SPECULATIONS THEY'D HAD ABOUT ME AND THE WORST OF THE FEARS I'D HAD ABOUT THEM.
ON BALANCE, THEY SEEMED AS RELIEVED NOT TO HAVE THEIR DAUGHTER SUCKED INTO ANY DUBIOUS NUPTIALS AS I WAS NOT TO HAVE THE MATTER SETTLED BY SHOTGUN!
MR. POLK, I'M IVY McGINNIS.
SHALL I TAKE YOU TO GINGER AND THE BABY?
H'LO.
LOOK AT HER, TOLAND. CAN YOU BELIEVE IT?
AM I ALLOWED TO HOLD HER?

Panel 1:
Whew! THIS IS **REALLY** SOMETHIN' **ELSE!**

ARE YOU **PLEASED** TO SEE YOUR DAUGHTER, MR. POLK?

Panel 2:
MOST **DEFINITELY,** MA'AM. I JUST WISH IT WAS UNDER DIFFERENT **CIRCUMSTANCES.**

I NAMED HER **MELANIE.**

Panel 3:
YEAH? I KNOW SOME-BODY WHO'LL LOVE **THAT!**

IT'LL GET **CHANGED** ONCE SHE'S BEEN **ADOPTED,** PROBABLY...BUT IT FELT NICE WRITIN' THAT DOWN ON THE **FORM.**

Panel 4:
I'LL SLIP INTO MY **OFFICE** SO YOU TWO CAN **VISIT.**

THANKS.

THANKS, IVY.

Panel 5:
SHE'S SO **TINY,** GINGER...I'M SCARED I'LL **BREAK** HER! WHAT IF SHE STARTS **CRYIN'?**

I'LL TAKE HER **BACK** IF SHE GETS **RESTLESS.** GO AHEAD AN' SIT **DOWN.**

SO WE HAD THE **VISIT** I'D DRIVEN TO **WILLOWVILLE** FOR. WE TALKED ABOUT WHAT OUR **FRIENDS** WERE UP TO AND WHAT MIGHT LIE IN **STORE** FOR **HER** AND FOR ME.

WHAT I REMEMBER **MOST** IS HOW **HARD** WE BOTH WORKED TO IGNORE THE SHADOW OF **FINALITY** THAT DIMMED EVERY CORNER OF THE **ROOM.**

Panel 6:
GINGER SAID SHE'D DECIDED **AGAINST** GOING BACK TO **CLAY-FIELD.** SHE FELT READY TO HEAD **NORTH** AND SEE WHAT **NEW YORK** HAD TO OFFER.

I DIDN'T **ARGUE.** IT WAS **ALL** GROUND THAT WE'D COVERED **BEFORE.**

AT **ONE** POINT I FOUND MYSELF DESCRIBING THE CONVERSATION THAT I'D HAD WITH **ANNA DELLYNE** EARLIER THAT DAY.

YOU MAKE **TOO MUCH** OF IT, HONEY.

Panel 7:
I KNOW IT'S **HARD** FOR YOU TO UNDERSTAND WHY I WON'T **SING** IN **PUBLIC.**

NOT MY OLD SONGS FROM THE **CLUBS,** I MEAN.

Panel 8:
I GUESS YOU LOOK ON SHOW BUSINESS AS BEIN' SO **GLAMOROUS,** YOU CAN'T **BELIEVE** IT'S NOT STILL IN MY **BLOOD** SOME-WHERE!

IT'S NOT **SHOW BUSINESS** I'M TALKIN' ABOUT. IT'S SINGIN' HERE IN **CLAYFIELD.**

Panel 9:
YOU COULD GIVE SO MANY PEOPLE AROUND HERE SUCH A **KICK!**

YOU **USED** TO THINK THEY WERE **GOOD** SONGS. DO YA **NOT** THINK SO NOW?

Panel 10:
NO...THEY'LL **ALWAYS** BE GOOD.

DO YA THINK THEY'RE **SINFUL?** IS IT 'CAUSE YOU'RE A **PREACHER'S WIFE** NOW?

HE **INSISTS** ON MOWIN' THAT GRASS **HIMSELF**, EVEN THOUGH **LES** IS PERFECTLY WILLIN' TO DO THE JOB **FOR** HIM.

HE SAYS HE **ENJOYS** IT. SAYS IT KEEPS HIS **SWEAT GLANDS** IRRIGATED!

I **HAVE** FELT LIKE I'VE KNOWN WHO I WAS SINCE I'VE BEEN BACK IN **CLAYFIELD**, TOLAND.

I **LIKE** BEIN' PART OF HARLAND'S **WORK**.

I'VE **KNOWN** THAT MAN SINCE HE WAS A SMART-ALECKY LITTLE **BUTTERBALL** IN **GRAMMAR SCHOOL**...

...AN' THERE'S HARDLY BEEN A **TIME** IN HIS **LIFE** WHEN HE WASN'T LOCKED ONTO SOME **GOAL** THAT I THOUGHT WAS **ADMIRABLE**.

NOW **LOOK** AT YOU! YOU'RE **DISAPPOINTED** IN ME, **AREN'T** YOU?

I JUST DON'T THINK YOU'RE **RIGHT**, CALLIN' YOURSELF A **COWARD**.

I'M A **COWARD** IN **SOME** WAYS... BUT IN **OTHER** WAYS, I'M **BRAVE**.

NOBODY'S BRAVE **ALL** THE TIME!

BUT FOR GOODNESS' **SAKE**, TOLAND—DON'T ACT SO **DEPRIVED!**

IF YOU **WANT** ME TO **SING** FOR YOU, I'LL **SING** FOR YOU.

JUST COME OVER HERE TO THE **HOUSE** NOW AN' AGAIN WHEN YOU'VE GOT **TIME** TO KILL.

WE'LL COME OUT HERE ON THE **STOOP** AN' YOU CAN WATCH ME SING FOR THOSE **BIRDS** IN THE YARD!

THEY DON'T COME TO **REVIEW** ME FOR THE **NEWSPAPERS!**

THEY DON'T **CLUSTER** UP IN CHAIRS TO **STARE** AT ME!

AN' THEY DON'T EXPECT ME TO BE **ANYBODY** BESIDES WHO I NATURALLY **AM!**

BE LIKE **THEM**, HONEY, AN' I'LL SING FOR YOU WHENEVER YOU **LIKE**.

I WONDER IF **I'LL** LIKE NEW YORK ANY BETTER THAN **SHE** DID.

YOU'LL **ALWAYS** BE WELCOME TO MAKE YOUR HOME BACK IN **CLAYFIELD**.

YEAH... I'M **SURE** SUTTON CHOPPER'LL ROLL THAT OL' **RED CARPET** RIGHT **OUT** FOR ME!

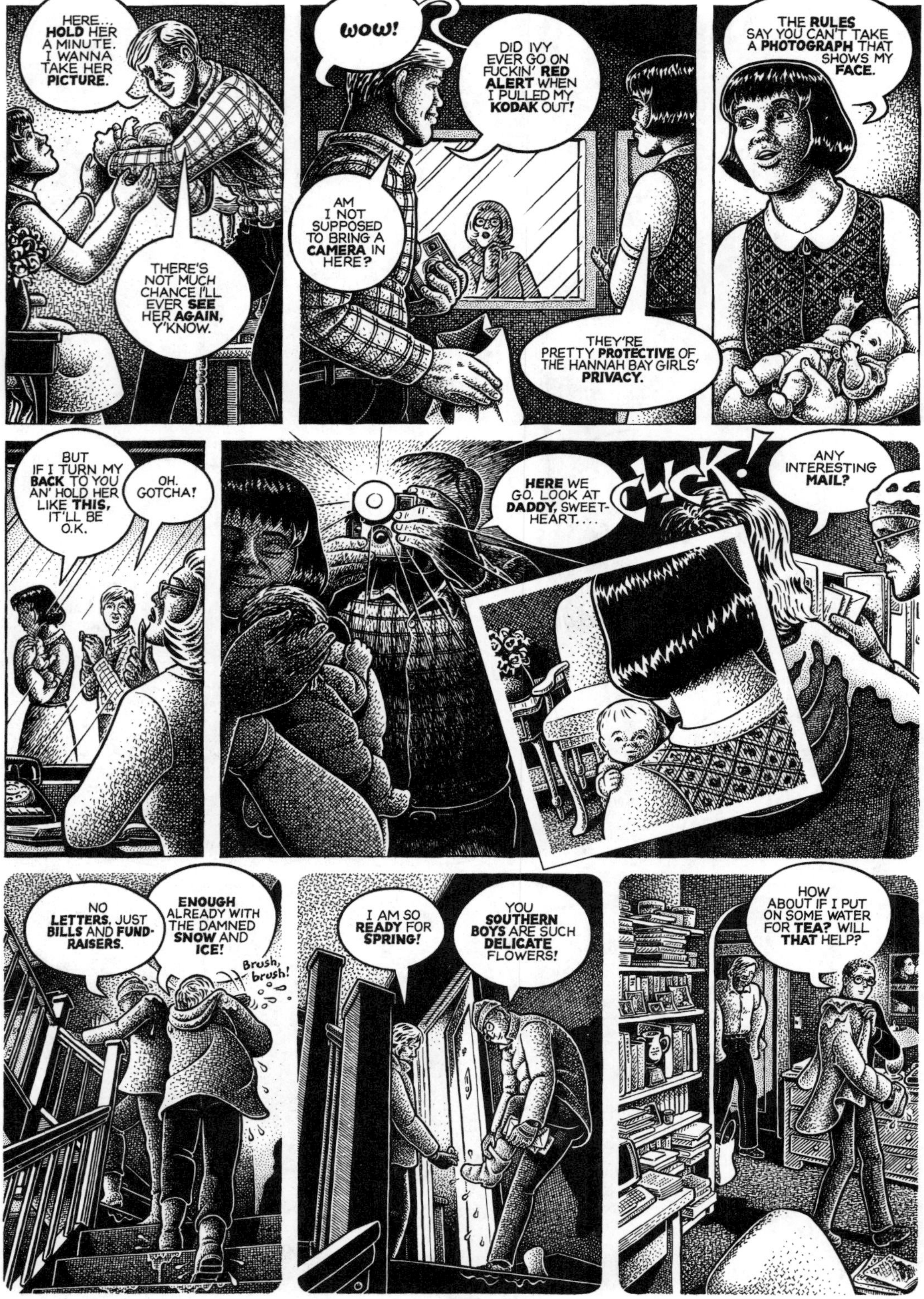
HERE... HOLD HER A MINUTE. I WANNA TAKE HER PICTURE.
THERE'S NOT MUCH CHANCE I'LL EVER SEE HER AGAIN, Y'KNOW.
WOW!
DID IVY EVER GO ON FUCKIN' RED ALERT WHEN I PULLED MY KODAK OUT!
AM I NOT SUPPOSED TO BRING A CAMERA IN HERE?
THEY'RE PRETTY PROTECTIVE OF THE HANNAH BAY GIRLS' PRIVACY.
THE RULES SAY YOU CAN'T TAKE A PHOTOGRAPH THAT SHOWS MY FACE.
BUT IF I TURN MY BACK TO YOU AN' HOLD HER LIKE THIS, IT'LL BE O.K.
OH. GOTCHA!
HERE WE GO. LOOK AT DADDY, SWEET-HEART....
CLICK!
ANY INTERESTING MAIL?
NO LETTERS, JUST BILLS AND FUND-RAISERS.
ENOUGH ALREADY WITH THE DAMNED SNOW AND ICE!
Brush, brush!
I AM SO READY FOR SPRING!
YOU SOUTHERN BOYS ARE SUCH DELICATE FLOWERS!
HOW ABOUT IF I PUT ON SOME WATER FOR TEA? WILL THAT HELP?

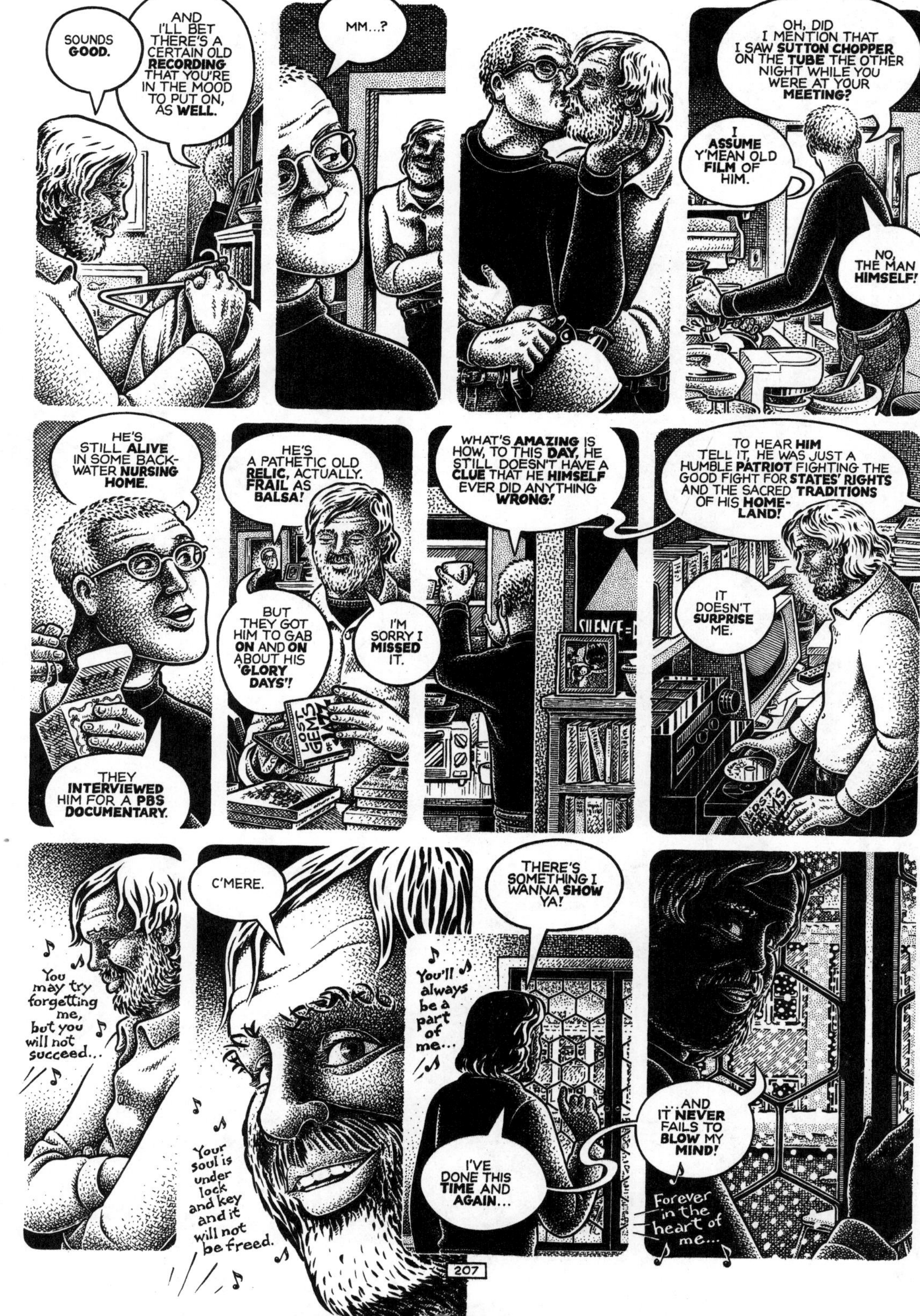
SOUNDS GOOD.
AND I'LL BET THERE'S A CERTAIN OLD RECORDING THAT YOU'RE IN THE MOOD TO PUT ON, AS WELL.
MM...?
OH, DID I MENTION THAT I SAW SUTTON CHOPPER ON THE TUBE THE OTHER NIGHT WHILE YOU WERE AT YOUR MEETING?
I ASSUME Y'MEAN OLD FILM OF HIM.
NO, THE MAN HIMSELF!
HE'S STILL ALIVE IN SOME BACK-WATER NURSING HOME.
THEY INTERVIEWED HIM FOR A PBS DOCUMENTARY.
HE'S A PATHETIC OLD RELIC, ACTUALLY. FRAIL AS BALSA!
BUT THEY GOT HIM TO GAB ON AND ON ABOUT HIS 'GLORY DAYS'!
I'M SORRY I MISSED IT.
LOST GEMS
WHAT'S AMAZING IS HOW, TO THIS DAY, HE STILL DOESN'T HAVE A CLUE THAT HE HIMSELF EVER DID ANYTHING WRONG!
SILENCE=
TO HEAR HIM TELL IT, HE WAS JUST A HUMBLE PATRIOT FIGHTING THE GOOD FIGHT FOR STATES' RIGHTS AND THE SACRED TRADITIONS OF HIS HOME-LAND!
IT DOESN'T SURPRISE ME.
LOST GEMS
You may try forgetting me, but you will not succeed...
C'MERE.
Your soul is under lock and key and it will not be freed.
THERE'S SOMETHING I WANNA SHOW YA!
You'll always be a part of me...
I'VE DONE THIS TIME AND AGAIN...
...AND IT NEVER FAILS TO BLOW MY MIND!
Forever in the heart of me...

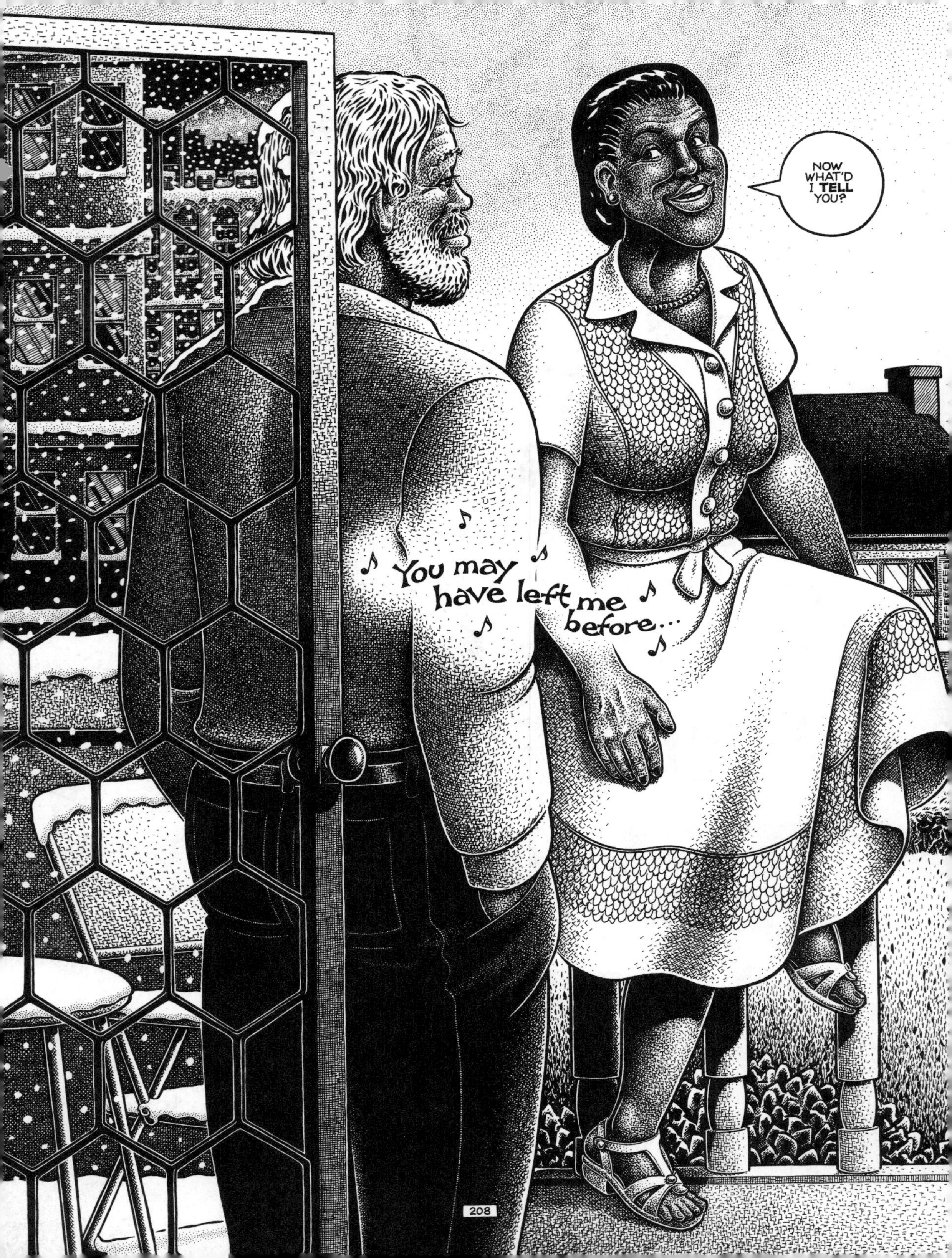
NOW WHAT'D I **TELL** YOU?
♪ You may have left me before... ♪

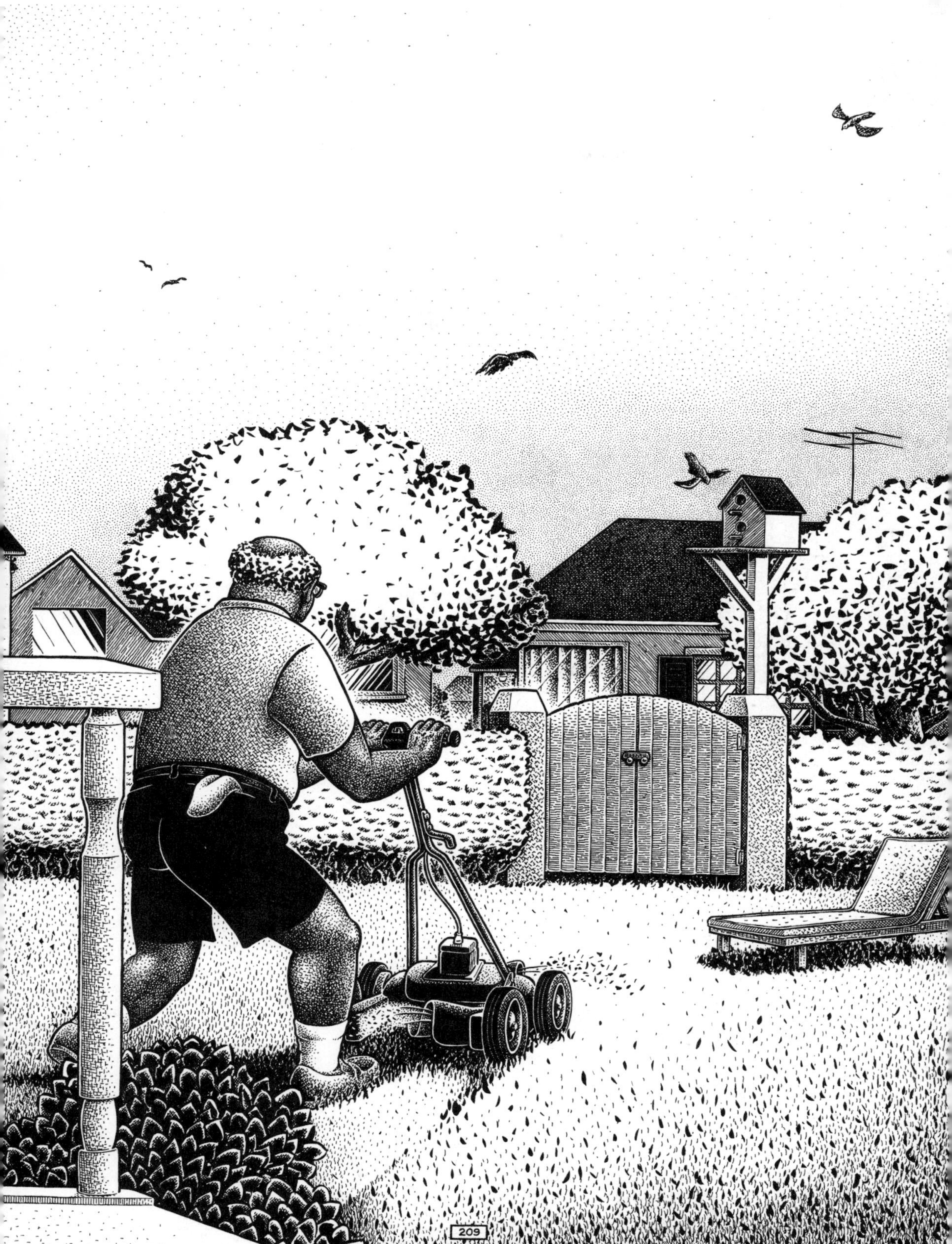

♪ ♪
♪
. . . But you can't leave me behind. ♪
♪

♪

ACKNOWLEDGMENTS

S*tuck Rubber Baby* is a work of fiction, not autobiography. Its characters are inventions of mine, and Clayfield is a make-believe city.

That said, it's doubtful I'd have been moved to write and draw this graphic novel if I hadn't come of age in Birmingham, Alabama, during the early '60s. My own experiences as well as those of old friends and new acquaintances who were kind enough to share their memories with me have served as springboards for various incidents in my narrative, as have the news accounts that I and a nation watched together. I'm grateful to the following individuals for setting aside time to tell me tales: Bob Bailey; Irene Beavers; Clyde and Linda Buzzard; Nina Cain; Dr. Dodson Curry; William A. Dry; John Fuller; Harry Garwood; Mary Larsen; Bill Miller; Bertram N. Perry; Cora Pitt; Perry Schwartz; Jim and Eileen Walbert; Jack Williamson; and Thomas E. Wrenn.

Let me emphasize that none of the individuals cited above had any hand in the actual development of my storyline nor any opportunity to evaluate the liberties I've taken in bringing my own point of view to the fictional incidents loosely inspired by their accounts. Any errors of history or perceived wrong-headedness of interpretation should be laid at my door, not theirs.

Others have aided me, too, in varying ways. Much help was provided at the outset by Marvin Whiting, the Birmingham Public Library's distinguished archivist. I have turned for enlightenment on technical points of law to David Fleischer and to David Hansell. Ed Still provided background on the history of Jim Crow laws. John Gillick helped me with guns; Diana Arecco provided architectural reference; and Murdoch Matthew and Gary Gilbert instructed me on Episcopalian matters. Mary McClain, Stephen Solomita, Dennis O'Neil and John Townsend also provided important nuggets of information.

I'm grateful to Harvey Pekar for answering my questions about jazz lore and to Wade Black of Bozart Mountain/Jade Films for letting me photograph his old movie cameras for reference. And it's by the good graces of Morton J. Savada of Records Revisited in Manhattan that Anna Dellyne's record labels and sleeves have a touch of authenticity.

I'm especially indebted to Leonard Shiller of the Antique Auto Association of Brooklyn, Inc., for cheerfully escorting me from garage to garage in his borough as I photographed not only classic cars but also his fascinating cache of gas pumps, washing machines, vacuum cleaners, scooters, bicycles, beverage trucks, fire engines and other collectibles from a bygone era.

I owe thanks to those who admitted me into their private domains so I could snap reference photos of old furniture, appliances, and representative bits of architecture: Arthur Davis and Ellen Elliott; David Nimmons and David Fleischer; Howie Katz; Elyse Taylor and Leonard Shiller; and Tony Ward and Richard Goldstein. And I'm grateful as well for the special contributions of Grady Clarkson, Tim J. Luddy, and David Hutchison.

I want to thank Andrew Helfer and Bronwyn Taggart, respectively the group editor and editor of Paradox Press, for supporting *Stuck Rubber Baby* unwaveringly during its extended incubation and for allowing me great artistic autonomy in its execution. I'm indebted to Mark Nevelow, the founding editor-in-chief of Piranha Press (Paradox's predecessor), who said yes in 1990 to my proposal for a graphic novel embodying themes that might have tempted a less adventurous editor to stand back, and whose subsequent feedback contributed to a sturdier narrative; and to Margaret Clark, Ms. Taggart's predecessor as editor, for her helpfulness while in that position. My agent, Mike Friedrich of Star∗Reach Productions, Inc., has been an effective problem solver and a valued advisor with regard to both pictures and text. And I'm especially grateful to my longtime friend Martha Thomases, publicity manager of DC Comics, for the help she has provided on too many fronts to mention here, as well as for her seminal insistence, in the face of my initial skepticism, that space might exist at the House of Superman for an underground cartoonist's pursuit of a labor of love.

When I started *Stuck Rubber Baby*, I thought I could do it in two years. It took four. Thus was precipitated a personal budgetary crisis of unnerving proportions, one that forced an unwelcome diversion of energy into the search for enough supplemental funds to cover two unanticipated years of full-time drawing.

Accustomed as I am to creating art in relative solitude, it's been disorienting to find myself so dependent on assistance from others. But dependent I've been, and it's with deep gratitude that I catalog here the varied ways that friends and creative colleagues have gone to bat for me during difficult times.

Most of the forms I filled out in applying for foundation grants asked for letters of endorsement from individuals of creative accomplishment. The following people wrote such letters in my behalf: Stephen R. Bissette; Martin Duberman; Will Eisner; Harvey Fierstein; Richard Goldstein; Maurice Horn; Scott McCloud; Ida Panicelli; and Harvey Pekar.

When things seemed most precarious, a fundraising tactic was devised by which individuals could become "sponsors" of this book through the purchase of original artwork from it — at higher than market value and in advance of its even being drawn. In support of this tactic, a letter of endorsement for *Stuck Rubber Baby* was drafted and signed by fifteen writers, artists, film and TV producers, and other cultural leaders. Those who signed that letter were: Michael Feingold; Matt Foreman; David Frankel; Richard Goldstein; Arnie Kantrowitz; Tony Kushner; Harvey Marks; Lawrence D. Mass; Jed Mattes; Armistead Maupin; Michael Musto; Robert Newman; John Scagliotti; Randy Shilts; and John Wessel. Crucial technical tasks related to fundraising were performed by Tony Ward, Jennifer Camper, Robert Hanna, and Suk Choi of Box Graphics, Inc. I appreciate the willingness of Paul Levitz, the executive vice-president and publisher of DC Comics, to sanction the bending of some normal company practices in the assembly of our fundraising prospectus.

I am deeply grateful to the individual sponsors themselves, whose advance purchases of original art from this graphic novel made the completion of *Stuck Rubber Baby* possible. They are:

Fred Adams
Allan Cruse
Kevin Eastman
Richard Goldstein
Tony Kushner
Stanley Reed
Martha Thomases and John R. Tebbel
Bob Wingate

Additional support for this project was provided by:

Joan Cullman
Glenn Izutsu
Chopeta Lyons
The Anderson Prize Foundation

Let me finish by thanking Ed Sedarbaum, my companion of sixteen years, for his unshakable belief in me and in the merits of this graphic novel; for the concrete help he offered when practical problems loomed; and for the encouragement and thoughtful feedback he has provided as successive chapters have been offered for his assessment.

Howard Cruse
July 1995

ABOUT THE AUTHOR

Howard Cruse, creator of *Barefootz* and *Wendel* and the founding editor of *Gay Comix*, is an Alabama preacher's kid who counted *The Baptist Student* among his cartoon markets while still in high school. Since then his comic strips and cartoon illustrations have appeared in dozens of national magazines, underground comic books, and anthologies as well as in four book collections of his own. Since 1979 he has shared his life in New York City with book editor and political activist Ed Sedarbaum.